I0831831

This book is dedicated to the memory of James Huntington Turner, who taught me anything is possible if you try.

Look for other books by C.A. King, including:

The Portal Prophecies:

Book I - A Keeper's Destiny
Book II - A Halloween's Curse
Book III - Frost Bitten
Book IV - Sleeping Sands
Book V - Deadly Perceptions
Book VI - Finding Balance

Tomoiya's Story:

Book I: Escape to Darkness
Book II: Collecting Tears

Surviving the Sins:

Book I: Answering the Call
Book II: Pride
Book III: Lust

When Leaves Fall: A Different Point of View Story

Peach Coloured Daisies: A Cursed by the Gods Story

Flower Shields: A Four Horsemen Novel

Drawing Strength From Words: A Four Horsemen Novel

Miracles Not Included

Twisted Tales of A Dead End Street
Shot Through The Heart: A Faerie Tale

The Portal Prophecies

Volume II

By

C. A. King

*Cover Design by **Eyes of a Crow***

Editor: J.D. Cunegan

Cover Art by Eyes of a Crow

First Printing: 2018

ISBN 978-1-988301-48-8

Kings Toe Publishing
kingstoepublishing@gmail.com
Burlington, Ontario. Canada

Chapter One

Willow sat quietly, watching her two best friends chatting with excitement. For them, heading to a school was something to look forward to, an adventure waiting to happen. For Willow, it was a disaster.

Fighting back her tears, she slouched down, pulling her blankets up so they almost covered her nose - already feeling how alone she would be in the months to come. Occasionally, Clairity and Ashlyn glanced over at her, changing their cheery expressions to those of pity before faking smiles and returning to their conversation. Soon, chatter changed to sleep for the two girls.

Willow's mind faded to memories from a few weeks ago. The three girls should have been enthusiastically chatting about her first kiss, the first real kiss any of them had experienced. With the pain and heaviness surrounding her now, even Willow couldn't manage to think about how either William or Lance's embrace made her feel.

That fateful night in Pewterclaw, when the assassin attack left William fighting for his life, changed everything. No one said anything to her, but she saw it in their faces, heard it in their voices, and felt it from their actions.

Giving up on the idea of sleeping, Willow headed to the cabin that was built to be the camp's new command centre. The events of the past few weeks were still shifting around, making circles in her mind, jumping from one detail to another. As she approached her destination, she caught a glimpse out of the corner of her eye of Aslo and Kiera walking in the distance. The guardians were all on high alert at the moment, afraid of another possible assassin attack. Even their roles were affected.

She swung the door of the cabin open, revealing a cold, dark room. There was nothing familiar about the atmosphere to her. This new location wasn't home somehow. Memories of middle-of-the-night meetings haunted her... William walking in tired and yawning... a fire blazing bright... Zsiga brewing coffee in the corner... maps and notes scattered everywhere. There was no hint of that here.

Letting out a sigh, she stepped inside and flipped on the lights - the door slamming closed behind her. This room was void of character. Her eyes drifted towards a large rectangular table sitting directly in the centre. It was at least three times the size of the one she was accustomed to. She closed her eyes, trying to create a vision of everyone, but a picture wouldn't form.

Sitting on the table were the two *Portal Prophecies* books, the files Jade provided from Pewterclaw's records, and a stack of *The Empowered* newspapers. There were so many questions about each pile - questions she needed some answers to before she left for school. She had put everything aside to worry about William and now time was short. It was evident from the state of the resources in front of her that no one else had made any progress deciphering what was happening either. Not even a prophecy had been found.

Willow let out a lengthy sigh as she picked up the newspapers in front of her. They were riddled with articles about the camp, each one trying to answer who they were and what they were trying to accomplish - all with the ability to leave negative impressions after reading them. There was no denying the power of the writing. This reporter, Keith Quidnunk, was talented. His stories flowed with visions of daily news, capturing the attention of readers throughout the magical world. He had only one flaw. The stories weren't completely true. Of course, there was a base truth to every article he wrote, but the details in between tended to be stretched or fabricated. The end result was a story that led readers to make the wrong conclusions. It was sensationalism at its best.

She let the first newspaper fall back down to the table and picked up a second one. The headline read *Heroine Runs from Fight, Leaves Friends in Peril.* Tears swelled in her eyes as she glanced over the words of the article describing the events that led to William's current condition. The undertone suggested blame for the whole situation was on Willow for running away from the assassins.

The paper slammed down on the table. Willow closed her eyes, her arms shaking all the way down to the palms of her hands, which were spread out flat, pressing hard on the wood in front of her. She clenched her fists and took in a deep breath. Letting it out, she sat down again.

After a few minutes, her pulse and breathing returned to normal. She reached for another newspaper. The contents weren't much better. It outlined the plan for the members of their camp to be enrolled in schools - highlighting the dangers from the probability of assassins posing as students. Willow's eyes widened as she read the words emphasizing the possibility of anyone close to her being hurt in crossfire. Her thoughts drifted back to William lying unconscious in the medical facility.

The paper before her blurred. She drifted into a haze. It was true... all true. Anyone who was close to her could become injured by accident. If that happened to someone else, would she be able to handle it?

The cabin door burst open, a gust of wind blowing directly at the table. Willow bent over, her arms protecting the newspapers before her. Looking up, as the air settled around her, she realized the only thing affected was the *Portal Prophecies* book - lying open. She jumped at the sound of the door closing. Sitting back down, she pulled the book within reading distance and recited the prophecy it opened to out loud:

Time is fleeting, things now change.

Alone in sadness all seems strange.

Protection comes look in the sand.

Help is offered by outstretched hand.

The key to knowledge was taken away.

Hidden and lost, you must not sway.

Another foe not yet discovered.

Misplaced distrust, faith recovered.

Far away one must travel.

She spins a web of lies to unravel.

To stay safe from threats unknown.

A queen hopes to sit on a new throne.

A prophecy that fits, she thought to herself. Could this be the one she was looking for? How odd that the wind should blow it open to that exact spot. Willow let out a sigh, pushing the book away from her, but leaving it open at the page of the prophecy. She pulled the file folders in front of her - glancing through each one.

More questions. Where were the missing children? What were the school records about for the reporter... his sister... Jessica? What was going on in that city? There wasn't enough in the files for her to draw any conclusions. Willow drifted so deep in her own thoughts, she didn't notice the guardians enter the cabin.

"Hm? Is something on your mind? You look lost. If you share your problems, we might be able to help solve them," Aslo said.

"There is so much information here and yet no definite answers. I can't wrap my mind around it all. I guess I am feeling a little overwhelmed." Willow put her hands on her head, covering her eyes.

"If you keep it all safe in your mind, it might just come to make sense in the end," Aslo suggested. "Don't dwell on finding all the answers all at once. That is unlikely to happen. Instead, celebrate when one new piece of the puzzle fits." Aslo jumped up on the table in cat form. "I thought we should discuss something important with you. We have decided to go with you to the school."

"To the school?! But once I enter the grounds, all magic ceases to work. Don't we run the chance that we will separate at the gate?" she asked.

Aslo's tail flicked back and forth. "If we consider that the only magic we will be using is in our joining and separating, I don't think there will be any consequences for passing through the gate with you as our host. No one should know."

"But wouldn't that mean that you would be stuck? If something happened to me, it could wipe out all of you as well." Willow shook her head. "I can't take that chance!" she yelled.

"The choice isn't yours," Tika said. "Things are changing. Our place is with you for now. Trust in yourself, child. This decision is one we need you to accept. We haven't decided this lightly. Each of us has put great thought into it."

"When you look around, we know you see it... you feel it," Shelby said, flying over to the table. "This camp isn't the same... it isn't the same home we had before the move. Things may never be the same again."

"I do," Willow answered without looking up from the table. "But I thought it was just me." The shape of her mouth curved downward - a slight quiver forming on her bottom lip.

"We don't know what the future will bring," Kiera said. "It could be that things will work out in the end and we will all live happily ever after. But we can't take that chance. For the moment, we should stay together. We belong together."

"What about William, Clairity, and Ashlyn? Shouldn't you stay with them? They are keepers as well now," Willow argued.

"That is not the feeling we have. We discussed this in-depth and have all agreed: for now, our place is with you. When the school year is over, we can return. The strongest power any of us have is our instincts. Let us follow ours," Aslo requested. "Besides, you may need some friends with you at school. We want to be there for you."

Willow let out a sigh. "To be honest, I have been nervous about being alone. But... is it really worth it to risk all of you? We don't even know if we will be able to communicate within the grounds."

"One thing we have always told you is that there are many different forms of magic. The most basic of which: no one can restrict." Kiera moved directly in front of Willow. "Trust in your heart that our connection with you is a basic instinct rather than a rare magic and everything will be fine."

Willow nodded her head, doubt still lingering in her mind. This was something she needed to sort out herself, not something anyone could tell her. She understood the basics. Emotions held magic within them. Love - hate - jealousy - she had seen them all make powerful things happen over the past few months. Those feelings, no one could control. But was that where her magic came from? Was her magic there first, or did it stem from her emotions?

Willow stood and walked outside. Stopping, she turned her attention to the sky and shivered as if she was a prophet foretelling a future of despair. Wisps of dark clouds swirled around a full moon, exposing only the slightest glimmers of light shining down on the surrounding trees - creating the perfect ambience for a horror movie. She found herself unable to move, mesmerized by her surroundings and trapped by her thoughts. A tear fell down her cheek, the salty taste reaching her lips. At first, she wasn't sure what she was crying about. Her mind wandered back to the conversation with the guardians. She admitted to herself for the first time it was true, things were changing. There was no going back now. Her future was about to unfold in a new direction.

Chapter Two

Opening her eyes, Willow was sitting in the medical centre beside William. She wasn't sure how or when she arrived there. If the light shining in through the window was any indication, it was morning.

Willow glanced down at William. His condition hadn't changed. She sighed. One hand reached out to brush his sandy coloured hair from his face as he lay perfectly still without even the slightest sign of activity. She rested her head on the bed beside him and closed her eyes - the weariness of the past few weeks catching up to her.

She needed to come to terms with her feelings. The problem was, deep down, she still believed it was her fault. Maybe there was something more she could have done. What if she had never come through the portal from her home world? Would William have been hurt? Maybe in some way she had caused this.

In reality, what had she accomplished by being there? Everything that had happened was simply a domino effect, derived from arrival. She was no closer to defeating Cornelius than she was before she heard his name. The only difference was, the people close to her - the ones she cared about - were getting hurt. Was any of it worth it?

“Hey,” Mike said, poking her shoulder. “Wake up, sleepyhead. We are about to have one final meeting before everyone goes.”

Everyone goes, she thought, lifting her head. “Yeah, I'll be right there. Is everyone already gathered?”

“Yup,” Mike answered, smiling. “Just waiting for you.”

Willow stood and followed Mike out the door. He shoved his hands in his pockets and stopped for a moment, glancing back at her. After letting out a sigh, he started walking again, this time a little faster. A silent awkwardness flowed between them, keeping them separated. His desire to talk to her was trumped by a loss for words. It was probably better that way. Her emotions rested on egg shells, waiting to crack at any wrong word. If that same feeling put a rift between her and everyone else from the camp, she would be devastated. This was the last time she was going to see them all together for a very long time... if ever again.

Opening the door, her worst fears were confirmed. The tension in the air was thicker than smog and more lethal. An aura of deep purple swirled, flowing in her direction from the people she considered her closest friends. It was worry... fear... despair. That's what they felt towards her. She could see it - feel it - taste it and hear it in their whispers. A sour taste filled her mouth. Butterflies raced up from her stomach to her throat, transforming nervousness into nausea instantly.

The smell of fresh coffee drifted past her nostrils, breaking her train of thought - a momentary distraction from the uncomfortable surroundings. It was the same coffee that Zsiga brewed at every meeting - the bold scent she had come to adore of a drink she had never tried. She inhaled deeply, savouring the smell and walked over to where the coffee was brewing.

“I'd like to try a cup,” she said with a smile.

“You would?” Zsiga asked. “You don't drink coffee.”

“Things change,” she answered. She added some cream and sugar to the black liquid as she had watched people do when they prepared a mug for William so many times before. Pulling the cup to her lips, she blew slightly on the steaming fluid and took her first sip. The warmth of the liquid awakened her taste buds. A smile crossed her face. It was bitter and sweet at the same time, perhaps even a little nutty. The flavour was unusual, but not bad.

After a few sips, a wave of refreshment flowed through her body. Even the smallest of her nerves were being tickled to life - each rejuvenated with excitement. All in all, she was glad she took the time to try Zsiga's brew. There would be no regrets now if she never had the chance again.

Taking a seat at the table, she looked up, realizing everyone was staring at her. “We have to keep moving forward,” she said.

“That's true,” Malarchy agreed from the doorway. “Sorry to disturb, but the Director of Knowledge wanted to address everyone this morning.”

Standing beside him was the Director of Knowledge, Cassandrhea Tibbins - wearing mesmerizing clothing, namely a black dress. The top part of the dress was a refined Victorian style with a high neckline - fastened tight enough that it most likely would have choked the life out of anyone else. That, however, wasn't the attention grabber. Her full-length skirt was. It spiralled out, swirling around in a hypnotic manner as she walked.

“Things have changed,” Cassandrhea said, moving to the table. “In light of the recent newspaper articles, I have had to make a few last-minute adjustments to ensure the safety of all of our students.” She handed a backpack to Nathan.

“What's this?” he asked.

“That,” the Director answered, her face void of emotion, “is a set of instructions for the new school chosen for you.”

Diana closed her eyes and whispered, “Thank goodness.”

Willow's gaze fell upon the storyteller's face. A look of relief was on display, front and centre - as if the weight of the world had been lifted from her in that one moment. For the first time, Willow realized the people around her were scared.

Fighting back tears, Willow glanced away. “Is there a change of plans for myself as well?” she asked.

"Yes," Cassandrhea answered. "But those plans, only I know. We will be leaving ahead of the others and I will fill you in on important details then. As soon as you finish your meeting here today, we will depart." She gracefully turned, giving off an air of royalty as she strolled outside to wait.

"No pressure on time there," Mike said, rubbing the back of his neck. "Guess we should start."

Silence followed. It was a disease that spread, stealing their words. Willow stood. "I will be taking the books with me," she blurted out.

Nathan shot a glare in her direction. "Why?"

"Anything related to the prophecies will be coming with me. It will take pressure off everyone else," Willow explained. In a low voice, she continued, "The guardians will all be leaving with me as well. They made the decision last night. There will be nothing that can connect any of you to me. You will all be safer that way."

"What about you?" Mike asked.

Willow chuckled a little. Even in this situation... even though he had Sissy now... Mike was still worried about her in some small way. He cared about her. It wasn't a romantic feeling, but still it made her feel warm inside. It was the same feeling he gave her before - one she enjoyed - one she hoped she would feel again someday.

"I'll be fine. This is what I am meant to do." She turned to Malarchy. "The files need to be returned, so no one misses them. I don't want you or Jade in any more danger than you already are in living in that city. There is something else going on there - something other than Cornelius. I suggest diligence on your part until all the facts have been revealed."

Malarchy nodded but remained silent. The only noise in the room remained Willow's voice.

"The newspapers... I would like to take them for reference. I haven't read them all yet and they may have some information I will need." She pulled the papers to her and pushed them into an empty backpack. Reaching for the prophecy book, she passed it to

Nathan and asked him to read the prophecy it was still open at from the night before.

"Please share this with everyone else before leaving. I believe this is the prophecy we are facing. Although I think that I will be the only one directly involved, if any controversy arises while each of you are away..." Her words faded. "Let's just say I would feel better if all of you were careful and aware as well - better safe than sorry." She turned her attention to Micca. "I will be taking the antidotes with me as well. Please take a few syringes of each for camp use, if necessary."

Micca nodded in agreement.

"If there is nothing else," Willow said, "be safe and enjoy school."

Malarchy stepped forward. "If I may, before we adjourn for the school year, I would like to ask Diana to explain something to our young adventurers. I had hoped Jade would be present for this discussion as well, but as things stand, she was unable to attend."

Diana's face crinkled up in a question mark. "What would you like me to explain?" she asked.

"The Pledge," he answered. "They are all at that age and I think it best they understand our ways in detail before they go off and have no one to explain it to them."

"I see what you mean," she answered. A look of thoughtfulness crossed her face. "This is a delicate topic, so I hope everyone here is able to take it seriously." Her eyes glanced over at the Shinning brothers, each of whom were already smirking and hiding sly smiles.

The Pledge, Willow thought to herself. She knew the basics, barely. It was the way in which those from her world chose life-mates. Usually, shortly after attaining their sixteenth cycle, their kind became more aware of those around them, noticing things that would make for an ideal pairing. It was a magical event. Normally, parents explained such things in detail. A simple glance around the room, confirmed that theory. The others had more information on the topic than she did. Of course, that was to be expected. She, after all, had grown up alone.

"The Pledge is a sacred ritual to our world. It has many of the qualities that marriage of this realm has. When two people decide they are meant to live together, the woman initiates the process by saying *I pledge myself to you*. The man responds with *I accept your pledge for eternity.* A ring of gold emerges and encircles the two and if a match has been made, the ring divides into two and binds to a finger of each person, symbolizing their eternal promise." Tears filled Diana's eyes as she looked down at the ring on her finger. Her husband, as well as Nathan's mother and father, were still missing, held captive by her brother, Cornelius.

"What if both parties do not feel the same?" Clairity asked. "I have a feeling there is more to the process than we currently understand."

"The magical ring will simply not bind the two together; in fact, it will disperse." Diana's eyes never left her ring as she spoke. "There are a few things you all should understand. First, this isn't something to take lightly. It is a promise that spans your whole lifetime. Only upon death will the promise ring disappear from your finger."

So, Willow thought to herself. *Her husband is still alive somewhere. She has known all this time.* Her head turned away, hiding expressions of disappointment. She had considered herself close to the storyteller. Why hadn't Diana mentioned before now that her husband had to be alive somewhere?

"Also, the binding process is of a magical nature. The ring knows what is in your heart and soul. Only those who are destined to be together can be bound. You cannot fool or trick the ring. Likewise, no one under the effects of a love potion or similar magical spell can be bound by this process. If there is doubt, the binding will fail."

"Is there any reason not to marry in the traditional sense of this realm?" Mike asked. "After all, everyone here is a part of this world now."

"I suppose not," Malarchy answered, raising an eyebrow at the suggestion. "Of course, this world offers a way to demolish a marriage that fails and that is against the fundamental principles of our people. But if anyone should wish to engage in this form of matching, I am sure we would all support them. I suggest careful thought on the topic before formulating any decision."

"I think everyone here has a lot to think about over the next few months." Diana stood without making eye contact with anyone. "Good luck to each of you and be safe." She took the hand of her grandson Nathan and exited the building.

A shiver ran down Willow's back. Diana seemed so cold and distant. They all did. Was she truly alone?

Chapter Three

Opening the door to the medical centre, Willow was greeted with a surprise she never anticipated. Not only were all the guardians gathered around William, but some other friends were present as well.

"Willow," Nick said in his usual cheerful manner. "You look pale, my dear. Is everything okay? Are you eating?"

The edges of Willow's lips turned upwards. "What are you doing here? It's wonderful to see you."

"Well," Nick answered. "I can't take the credit, I am afraid. Although I am glad I get to say goodbye before you head off to school. This is their doing." He pointed towards the two Olcsanka sitting beside him.

"Jawfree! Deacon!" Willow exclaimed.

"They insisted they needed to be here today. They want to go with you." Nick smiled with a warmth that made the uneasiness inside her dissipate.

"Go with me? But ..."

Jawfree cut off her words with his own. "We need to be with you for now. There is no sense arguing. It has already been decided." The two disappeared, reappearing as pictures on her leg.

"It's time," Aslo said, as he, Kiera and their children performed the same process.

One by one, the others followed suit, starting with Shelby and the two guardian birds from the Frostica world, Souey and Xako - followed by Nero and Tika. The pictures they all formed on her skin moved around until they were completely hidden by her clothing. Taking in a deep breath, she closed her eyes, letting the words of the guardians cycle through her mind. She could hear them - feel them. She felt whole again.

"Sorry to interrupt," Micca said, handing her the box containing the antidote bottles and the key to the lock. "I took enough for several doses of each. I don't anticipate a need for even that much."

"Thank you," Willow answered, placing the items in her backpack with the books and newspapers. "Please take care of him for me." She gestured towards William's motionless body.

"Of course. I know it doesn't feel like it at the moment, but we will be here when you get back. Don't lose too much faith in those around you. Things are tough right now, but we still care." Micca smiled and gave Willow a pat on the head before turning and leaving the building.

"He's right, you know," Nick said. "Never give up, Willow. Sometimes all you need is a little luck." He took the pendant around her neck between his fingers and smiled. "Remember that when times are hard." Releasing the charm Meredith gave Willow, he turned heading for the door. "Well, I best be getting back to work. Lots to do. You keep safe and trust your intuition. I hope to see you come Christmas time."

Willow let out a sigh as she watched him go. Once alone, she moved over to William's bedside and sat in the chair beside him. Her hands trembling, she reached out and interlocked her fingers with his. Tears flowed from her eyes again as she said goodbye, wondering if the future would bring them back together one day.

Stepping outside the building, a gust of wind blew the remnants of her tears from her face as if they never existed - a sign it was time for her to move forward. Ahead, in the distance, Faramund stood with Cassandrhea - her luggage surrounding them. As if on impulse, her legs began moving, carrying her swiftly towards them.

"Are you ready?" The Director of Knowledge asked.

"Um." Willow glanced around, expecting at least one or two people to come say goodbye. No one had. "I guess."

"Very well. I trust you have said your goodbyes?" Cassandrhea tilted her head towards Willow as if trying to peek inside her mind.

"Yeah," Willow answered. "I guess I have."

A familiar green gas surrounded them. Within seconds, she was standing in the middle of a forest she didn't recognize.

"Thank you for the teleport, Faramund. You may go now. I am afraid there are things we cannot share with even you from this point on. Someone will contact you when the time comes to bring Willow home." Cassandrhea walked away from the guard.

"Thanks," Willow said, forcing a half-smile on her face.

"You take care of yourself," Faramund answered. "It won't be long until we are back together again. You can count on that." His eyes watered and voice cracked. "We'll be just like a family again one day. I promise."

Lunging forward, Willow threw her arms around the neck of the guard, squeezing tightly as if they were parting forever. He had protected her since the day they met. A thought ran through her mind - she loved him. Not like she felt for Lance or William. It was a different kind of love, but love nonetheless. "I will definitely miss you," she sobbed, her face still buried in his chest.

"As I will you," he answered. "Be strong and know, even though we may have to part right now, we are all destined to be together in the end."

Willow watched as the guard teleported away, losing herself in a black hole of thought. The sound of her own name dragged her back to reality.

"Willow!" Cassandrhea's voice sounded loudly. "Willow, are you listening to me? We need to move on before we are found. There is no time for thoughtful reminiscing now. When you are safely concealed, you will have time for soul searching."

Safely concealed, she thought.

Who would have thought? Aslo's thoughts came through loud and clear in her mind. *The Director might actually have a plan to help you.*

Willow picked up her bags, moving as quickly as possible while carrying all the luggage herself. At one point, she almost toppled over from the weight. When she arrived at Cassandrhea's side, she saw a swirling purple mist forming a doorway.

"We are going through there," the Director said, walking directly into the violet haze without even an inkling of hesitation.

Willow took in a deep breath and followed. On the other side was Malarchy's apartment. "Why are we here?" she asked. "What was that doorway we came through? Did you make it?"

"Well," Cassandrhea answered, "it's too dangerous for us to let you attend school as you are. I am afraid you are a target of far too many assassins now. I understand there are several hefty bounties on your life. I have a job to do and it involves keeping you, as well as all the other students, safe. So you are here to become disguised. As for the manner in which we arrived, let's just say we both have secrets we need to keep if we are to survive the school year."

"Disguise?" Willow's eyes grew two sizes bigger than usual. "I thought transformation magic couldn't be used within the school grounds."

"Yes, that is correct. No unauthorized magic can be used within the school grounds. It is for that reason you will be wearing a good old-fashioned physical costume." The Director pointed to a pile of clothes on a chair. "You will find everything you need right there, including a wig."

Walking over to the chair cautiously, Willow picked up a wig made of short black hair between two fingers, examining it for a moment. Placing it back down, she scratched her head. “Excuse me, Director, but aren't these clothes a boy's uniform?”

“Yes, my dear,” Cassandrhea said in a monotone voice. She pulled out a wand and pointed it at Willow's bags. They disappeared. “Your belongings will be waiting for you in your room... not that much of it will be of any use to you. I have arranged for uniforms and everyday clothes, all baggy to disguise your feminine figure, as well as any other needs you may have.” She turned to face Willow directly. “This is important, so listen carefully. You cannot let anyone know your identity. No one!” The pupils of her eyes enlarged. Her gaze burned into Willow's mind, leaving a permanent scar.

“What about the other Directors? Won't they want proof I am attending?”

“I have told them I disguised you, and you are attending. For now, that seems good enough.” She motioned for Willow to change clothes, turning to face away from her. “I will protect your secret. As of now, I am your only ally. You cannot trust anyone... not old friends... not new friends... not other teachers.”

“What about the person who was the test?” Willow asked, struggling with the tie.

Cassandrhea let out a giggle. “The test,” she said. “Yes, you had some unusual results.” She let out a sigh before continuing. “I will let you in on a secret. I was bringing you to my school no matter what the test results were. Your answers were an added bonus.”

“I'm not sure I understand,” Willow said, fiddling with her hair to make it fit under the wig.

“There is something changing in the world. Those of us who are in tune with nature can feel it. Something is going to happen very soon and you, my dear, are smack dab in the middle of it. That's why your life is in danger. We may not believe in your guardians, but you have a special power and it's scaring a lot of people.”

“What about magic trees?” Willow blurted out the question before she realized what she was saying.

“What do you mean?” the Director asked back.

Scrunching her eyes and making a sour face she answered, "Do you believe in them?"

"Magic trees?" Cassandrhea's lips pressed together tightly, as if she was trying to keep something from escaping. She sighed. "There is, I believe, an old elf folk lore about seven magical trees. Each one represented some different aspect of the world, like hope and love."

"Or justice?" Willow blurted out again.

"Yes," the Director answered. "But there is little known about the elves, their lore, history, or traditions. They tend to keep to their own circles. It's rare they concern themselves with the everyday lives of any race outside their own and even more rare that they bring an outsider into their world. There are no books or resources. I would suggest you forget about magical trees."

Willow looked at herself in the mirror and chuckled. "I make a rather cute boy!" she exclaimed with a smile spanning the entire width of her face.

"You'll need to practice lowering your voice, but I think you can pull it off nicely." The Director handed Willow a placement card. "Your name will be *Will* now and you will need to learn your background. I have put my faith in your abilities. You will spend this year grouped with four elves. Each of them are top students. I hope you can keep up. If not, you will bring their marks down as well. They won't be thanking you much for that. It'll be hard enough to get along with them as it is."

"Great," Willow said, rubbing her forehead. "Is the one from the test paper part of the group?"

Cassandrhea's eyes slanted, her lips all but disappearing. "Are you listening to anything I am saying?" she asked. "You are not to look for the assistant who helped with the tests. You are not to do anything that could give away your identity. Staying safe and alive throughout this school year is the important thing. That means for you and all the other students as well."

The Director moved towards Willow and placed her hands on her shoulders. "Let me worry about sorting out what is happening in the outside world for a bit. I'm on your side. It's time to go now. Wait five minutes after I leave and then follow the doorway that opens." A portal opened in front of the woman. She turned back before entering. "Oh and Willow, if anything happens out of the usual, I trust you will come and tell me as soon as possible."

Willow watched the woman vanish. The door shut, disappearing immediately after. As if on cue, exactly five minutes later, another door opened. Willow took a deep breath and closed her eyes, stepping through to what would be her new life for the next several months.

Opening her eyes, Willow glanced behind her. The doorway was gone. *How are portals like this being used?* she thought to herself, hoping her guardian friends could still hear her.

An excellent question. As far as we knew, only guardian portals existed for such travel. Perhaps it's a disguised teleportation spell of some sort. Aslo answered.

Hearing his thoughts calmed her nerves. The worry of not hearing anything from them for the whole school year was taking its toll on her psyche.

Of course, they weren't out of the woods yet. Fog covered the ground, blocking sight as to what lay beneath her feet. Directly in front of her were two of the largest brown doors she had ever seen, both made from an aged wood. Door knobs sat untouched, well above her height, the tops of the doors themselves extended beyond the limits of her vision. To the right and left, a dense mist stood as still as a brick wall, daring her to try to disturb its smooth surface.

Well, she thought, *guess we go forward. Those doors must be the magic barrier we heard about. Let's hope this works.*

Don't worry, Kiera answered back. *I think the odds are in our favour that the magic barrier will have no effect on us at all. I still believe the worst that might happen is that we lose the ability to communicate with each other.*

This year was going to be hard enough as it was without losing her guardian friends to talk to. Dressing like a boy, and even worse, being called Will would take some getting used to. Her mind wandered back to William lying in the medical bed back at the camp.

She clenched her fists, sucking in a deep breath as she moved towards the doors. One hand lifted her hand to knock, but before her knuckles could make contact, the two doors creaked opened.

Willow put one foot carefully over the threshold followed by the other. She spun around, letting out a sigh of relief. The guardians made it through without being detected. After taking a few steps forward, an alarm sounded. Willow jumped, her body trembling. Had her secret been discovered?

Chapter Four

Turning quickly towards the doors she had just passed through, Willow caught sight of two young girls running towards the school dormitories wearing nothing except their underwear. Quivering lips steadied, a chuckle making its way passed. The pair obviously hadn't believed the barrier could break their illusion spells. Why would anyone not heed the Director's warnings?

She stayed put, allowing her heart rate to return to normal before continuing her exploration. That provided her a chance to glance around, taking in all of the campus scenery.

There was one main paved walkway, bordered by a brick retaining wall - no bigger than two feet tall. The ground on the opposite side of the wall was even to the bricks and grass covered. Trees of all varieties were scattered across the lawn. Students stood on the bricks and under trees in clusters, discussing their courses and the groups they were in for the year. The whole campus was buzzing with excitement.

A group of students to her left attempted to perform magic without permission. For a moment, Willow thought of Nathan. If he had been there, he, no doubt, would have been able to identify where they were from. It wasn't from anywhere she recognized.

They all had pale blue skin and dark blue hair. The dark crimson colour of their eyes matched the colour of their fingernails, which were more claw-like than anything else. A burst of light exploded over their heads.

"Stop right there! Magic is strictly prohibited except as authorized by teachers!"

Willow's head turned towards the school in time to see a funny-looking creature running towards the blue coloured students. She bit her bottom lip, stifling a laugh. In all honesty, it looked like an oversized rabbit wearing jean overalls was out for a jog.

"He's the head groundskeeper and a teacher here."

Turning back around, a young man stood in front of her. There didn't seem to be anything unusual about him at all. His sandy coloured hair reminded her of William, albeit a bit too long and way too messy. Other than that, his appearance was immaculate. His uniform was freshly pressed with a crisp white linen shirt tucked in properly and a tie in perfect order. Even his shoes were shiny enough to see her reflection in.

"Is it that obvious what I was thinking?" Willow asked in as low a voice as she could without sounding silly.

"Pretty much," he said, smiling. "I'm Sebastian." He outstretched his hand to shake hello.

Willow's hand met his, instantly feeling the difference in their grips. His was tight, applying pressure as if he was trying to make a statement. She had a lot to learn about boys, especially if she was going to be one for the whole school year. Sebastian's brow crinkled up slightly at the lack of strength in her grip.

"I'm Will," she said, pulling back her hand.

"Yeah," he said, with an even more perplexed look on his face. "We're grouped together for the year. I have to admit I am a bit curious about a regular Joe keeping up with elves. You must be something extraordinary."

"You're an elf?" she blurted out, pressing her lips together immediately after, realizing she sounded a bit too much like a girl.

Sebastian let out a laugh and flashed a smile, a full set of polished white teeth gleaming. “Yeah,” he said. “I'm what is known as a river elf. Our appearances are the most similar to terunji of all the elves.”

“My apologies for being a bit stunned,” she said, trying to cover up anything she might have let out about her real identity. “I don't know much about elves in general. Actually, I don't think many people do.” She paused and pressed her lips together again. “I was told that elves don't generally talk to outsiders, though. So I can't help but wonder...”

“Why I am talking to you now?” Sebastian said, his mouth forming a sly grin. “So that's it. I wondered for a moment why you seemed a bit different.” He sighed heavily then whispered in her ear, “It's true.” Pulling back from her, he moved to a tree and leaned against it.

“What is?” she asked, following him.

“We don't speak to outsiders, or generally acknowledge their existence... much,” he answered. Sebastian spiralled around the tree and came face-to-face with Willow again, his light green eyes matching her stare.

“So why are you talking to me?”

“Why indeed,” he said, with an almost playful tone to his voice. “You don't know?”

“If I knew, I wouldn't be asking,” she replied with the beginnings of a pout forming on her face.

“What an interesting expression,” Sebastian said, tilting his head to the left. “Your kind do have a way with expressing emotions, although, I usually don't notice them quite as much on a male as I would a female.”

Willow took a deep breath in. Her eyes widened. She turned to walk away and felt a hand stern on her shoulder pulling her back.

“It wasn't an insult, Will,” Sebastian said. “Just an observation. Sometimes I forget how sensitive your kind can be. I'll answer your question if you forgive me.”

Willow turned and faced the elf. “Okay.”

“Good!” Sebastian smiled playfully. “As I already said, you are grouped with me for the year, along with three other elves... a mountain elf... a light elf... and a dark elf.”

“How many types of elves are there?” Willow interrupted.

“Five, but you only need concern yourself with the four,” he answered. “The problem is, the other three have less friendly personalities. In fact, they probably won't speak to you for the entire school year - except to insult you.”

“Brilliant,” Willow said, turning to walk away again.

This time Sebastian followed. “Unfortunately, we have been assigned to be a team and that means my marks depend on all the other team members, including you. So in the interest of a good school year, I took it upon myself to be a liaison of sorts.”

Willow stopped. “So this is a temporary gentleman's agreement and at the end of the year you go back to hating me?”

Sebastian rolled his eyes upwards. “Pretty much,” he answered.

“Your lack of emotion is frightening,” Willow said, starting to walk again.

“Elves generally don't display emotions of any sort. They are pointless to us,” Sebastian said.

Willow's face crinkled. She stopped walking. “No emotions?” she asked. “Not even love? How do you stop them?”

“It's rather complicated,” Sebastian answered, starting to walk again. “It's not that we don't have them, because we do, we just see no need for displaying them, so we suppress them.”

“That must be horrible,” Willow said.

“Not really, it eliminates much of the pettiness in life and allows us to focus on more important things. Anyways, that's about all you need to know on that topic.”

“Right,” Willow answered, trying to keep up to the fast pace he set. “So what is the difference between the types of elves?”

“Other than appearance, which you will figure out for yourself later,” he said, “mountain elves live in... the mountains. Their natural magical affinity is earth, more so rocks and metals, with a touch of fire thrown in. You could say alchemy is one of their strong suits.”

“Rocks?” Willow asked. “I have never heard of rock magic before.”

Sebastian laughed. “I am sure you will find many types of magic during this year you have not seen or heard of before.” He dismissed her request for information altogether and continued. “Light elves are named after their appearance. They tend to live in the most dense forest areas of our world and have a magical affinity to botany and nature. Dark elves are also named for their appearance. They, however, live in cave regions and are the most scientific of the elves, specializing in potions and healing.”

“And you? Why are you called a river elf?” she asked.

“Well, other than the fact we tend to live on river banks, we have an affinity to water magic.” Sebastian turned to her and stopped walking again. “All elves have other extraordinary abilities as well, including strength, speed, agility, and a few you don't need to know about.”

“When you speak of abilities and affinities, what do you mean?” Willow asked.

Sebastian smiled again. “If you have an affinity to a certain magic... well, let's just say it's more a part of you rather than a thing you do.”

“So you mean the magic barrier of the school grounds would have no effect on you using your skills. No one would know.” Willow wondered if she crossed the line asking.

Sebastian let out another laugh. “I am starting to see why you were allowed to be in our group. You seem to have a deeper understanding of magic than I first gave you credit for. I have told you all I can about us for now. We generally don't let outsiders know elf business and you, my friend, already know more than should have been disclosed.”

"That's fine," she answered with a half-grin. "We all have our secrets."

Sebastian tilted his head towards her and smiled back. "Indeed."

The two walked in silence until they reached an unusual building, the likes of which, Willow had never seen before. The outside was constructed entirely of a reddish colour brick, except for the windows which were a white wood with shutters. Trellises covered with a climbing ivy, which appeared to move when anyone approached it, lined the sides of the building, reaching all the way to the flat rooftop. The entire building was constructed from rectangles and squares, all using precise angles. The entrance way was two large white doors which were in such pristine condition they might have just been painted. She reached for the handle and realized they too were rectangular in shape.

The inside of the building wasn't much different. Willow paused for a moment and studied some of the art that lined the walls. They were beautiful pictures, but whoever created them used only squares and rectangles. In the corner, she read the name of the artist. "Kasper Deogole," she said, "the Director of Secrecy?"

Sebastian let out a puff of air. "Hmm, never noticed before... interesting. Our quarters are on the top floor," he said, climbing the stairs.

A burning sensation ran through Willow's chest. *Our quarters,* she thought. Surely Cassandrhea Tibbins didn't expect her to sleep in the same room with four boys. She felt a drop of sweat trickling down her face from her forehead. Her heart raced. Reaching the top of the stairs, she found Sebastian leaning against the wall waiting for her.

"I know elves are fast, but you might be a bit slow," he said, opening a door and motioning for her to go inside.

She peeked her head around the door and slowly stepped inside. The room was a living and study area, boasting a similar set up to the cabin she became accustomed to using as a command centre back when she first arrived in this world. There were whiteboards to write on and large maps in one corner. Desks, stacked with books for the year, lined the back wall against a series of windows. The middle of the room was divided into two sections. The first contained a table which sat six and the second was a sitting area with a couch and chairs. There were five doors other than the one she came through.

"Your room is the far one on the left," Sebastian said, pushing past her. "I believe all your things arrived earlier. You should check it out to make sure you got the right luggage. Occasionally, they make mistakes."

"Where are the others?" she asked.

"In their rooms," he answered, planting himself on the couch and his feet on the coffee table as if it were an ottoman. "After you get settled, we can handle introductions. The opening ceremony is in two hours, so you should probably unpack now."

Taking his advice, Willow went straight to her new room. Slamming the door behind her, she threw herself on the gigantic bed in the centre and rolled around for a moment.

"Having fun?" Aslo asked.

Willow spun around quickly to face the black cat sitting beside her. "Are you sure it's safe for you to appear like this? What if you can't return?"

"It's a chance we needed to take. Besides, when we made it through the barrier without separating, it was a good sign that our connection is not affected by the magic ban. It is, however, affecting our communication. Which means one of us will have to separate to stay in the loop."

"Can you communicate with each other, then?" Willow asked.

"Oddly enough, yes," Aslo answered.

While filling in the guardian with everything that happened since she arrived, Willow went through her closet and belongings. Just as the Director promised, there were all the boys clothes she would need... in baggy sizes - even socks were provided. The only thing of her own she needed to unpack was underwear.

Picking up her backpack, she examined the contents, making sure both *Portal Prophecies* books were still there, along with the wooden chest containing the antidotes to ancient poisons and newspaper articles. Everything appearing in order, she hid the bag at the back of the closet behind her other luggage containing her girl clothes.

"Elves," Aslo said. "They can be difficult to deal with. You will have to find some way to outwit them to make them accept you."

"Don't guardians know anything about elves?" Willow asked.

"Yes," the cat replied. "But we can only divulge so much. It's a type of agreement we have with them."

"Even to me?" Willow shrieked, quickly covering her mouth with her hands.

"I am afraid so," Aslo answered. "To be honest, what we do know is from long ago and might very well be outdated. I think you will pick up much of the basic information on their race as the school year progresses yourself. Trust your instincts and remember, although elves are powerful allies, they rarely can be bothered to get involved in the affairs of others or come to their aid."

"Funny enough," Willow said, "that I already figured out."

Aslo jumped to the window ledge and looked out. "It's getting dark. Shouldn't you be at the opening ceremony?"

Willow picked up a clock from the nightstand beside her bed and jumped up. "Hurry, I have ten minutes before I am late. I thought for sure Sebastian would have knocked to tell me we were leaving by now. Maybe he lost track of time too."

Aslo quickly brushed up against her hand, taking his place as a picture again. There was no time to celebrate the success of his return. She was more concerned about the impression she would make by starting off late. Running into the main room of her new quarters, it was empty with all the lights turned off.

"Sebastian?" she called. "Hello, is anyone here? We are going to be late."

No one answered. Willow let out a sigh. Time was too short to stand around. She needed to be in the main hall and had absolutely no idea where that was. Sifting through the maps stacked against a wall she came across the one showing the grounds. After letting out an under-her-breath *Yes*, she took a few moments to memorize the quickest path to where the ceremony was being held. Unfortunately, it was a fair distance away from the dormitory.

The most direct path led through a wooded area. Without a thought, she said out loud, “Please hear me. I need to cross to the other side of the forest quickly. Will you help me?”

In front of her, the trees swayed and bowed, creating a staircase for her to climb. She sped across the top the branches that crowded together beneath her - keeping her steady in the correct direction. As the wind blew passed her ears she heard the voice of the forest. “We will always be here for you, no matter which world you travel to.”

A smile crossed her face. It had been too long since she climbed to the top of a forest and ran freely, the leaves underneath her feet forming a cushion of softness. She thanked them for their kindness, but there was no time to linger. Once at the end of the trees she grabbed a branch, which understanding her intentions, swung her down to the ground. Without looking back, Willow bolted towards the hall. It was in her sight now with only a few minutes left. If she hadn't possessed certain latent abilities she never would have made it in time.

Throwing open the doors and stepping through, she heard a loud chime indicating the time. She had made it, but with only a few seconds to spare and was clearly the last to arrive. The other occupants of the hall turned to offer their stares, accompanying a chorus of whispers and rumbles.

So much for not drawing attention, she thought to herself, taking a seat at the back of the hall. She bowed her head down, attempting to control her breathing and heart rate. Glancing up, she met a glare from Cassandrhea Tibbins head-on.

“Well,” the Director said, pulling attention away from Willow as quickly as she could. “If we are all here, shall we begin?” She walked to the middle of a stage-like platform at the front of the hall.

“Welcome to a new year here at Sleeping Sands. We hope to see the best performances from each of you this year. Our itinerary is based on pushing each of you in a direction that you lack. In that sense, you will find you have been matched with four other individuals to work as a team. Each member of your team has something unique to add to your learning this year. It may not be evident at first, but believe me, your teams were matched for a reason.”

The Director paused for a moment, taking stock of the room. “Cooperation is key to your success here. In that light, your marks will be an average between the best mark in your group and the worst mark in your group.”

A rumble of dissatisfaction echoed through the hall.

“Silence!” Cassandrhea bellowed. “If you are to succeed, you will need to not only study hard on your own, but also help your group along as well. Ensure the success of your peers to ensure your own success.”

Low grumbles and mumbles came from every direction, although Willow was unable to ascertain exactly who was doing the complaining. She scanned the room looking for Sebastian, but he was nowhere to be seen.

“Before anyone asks,” the Director continued, “there will be no switching of groups, under any circumstances. If anyone is injured, your group will be at a disadvantage, especially for competitions. I would advise you to keep each other safe and healthy.” Cassandrhea paced the platform she stood on. “Your first-term itinerary will be on your table when you return to your dormitories. It has been specially selected for your group for a reason. These are the courses you will be taking and they are non-negotiable. Your second-term courses will depend on your success in the first term. If you wish to work with harder forms of magic next term, I suggest you do well now.” She bowed her head and paused again. “Now for a few notes on rules and safety. Kasper Deogole has taken the time from his busy schedule to join us today, so please listen closely.”

“Thank you, Ms. Tibbins,” Kasper said. “Most of you should know I am the Director of Secrecy. As such, I wanted to dispel a few rumours that are going around. Firstly, the Directors deny the existence of guardians. There is no basis to believe they exist in current day or, for that matter, ever did. There is to be no mention of such creatures here at the school. Anyone caught spreading further lies will be severely punished and their group will lose twenty-five percent of its mark."

A loud uproar exploded through the building.

"Silence," Kasper bellowed. "Next, because of safety issues within the school grounds, we have changed plans for a certain redheaded girl. Anyone attending here solely for the purpose of fulfilling a bounty can see me after this assembly for immediate removal from the school. There will be no punishments for such individuals. There is no need to waste your time or endanger any of our students further. If you choose not to believe me and remain, you will be forced to comply with the same rules and regulations as the rest of the school. Bullying and violence are not allowed on school grounds. Know this, once the property is sealed after I leave, I may not be able to remove you immediately, but the school is equipped with a fully functional detainment unit in the dungeon. I trust we understand each other."

He scanned the room as if trying to identify someone before taking a seat again.

"Thank you," Cassandrhea said, taking her place in the middle of the stage. "We take the safety of our students very seriously here. In that spirit, I would ask each of you to take some time and learn the locations of the medical facilities in case of accidents."

The expression on her face changed as a soft smile crossed her lips. "Here at Sleeping Sands, we pride ourselves on teaching the most skilled of all of the races. Each of you has proven that you belong here. Now is your time to shine. Don't worry about where your group comes from, or what race, but instead learn what you can from each other. This is not a place for prejudice. No one here is better than the other. You are all here for the same reason. Let's make this year spectacular. Please file out in an orderly fashion. You are dismissed."

One line at a time stood and exited the building. The crowd outside proved too large for Willow to locate Sebastian, no matter how hard she tried. Giving up, she slowly followed the longer route back to the dormitory, determined to find out why the others hadn't told her they were leaving.

Chapter Five

She was one of the first to leave the assembly, but to her surprise she was the last to return to their quarters.

"Did you all miss the ceremony?" she asked.

Sebastian laughed. "Of course not, although you cut it a little close."

"You could have told me you were leaving," she snarled back.

"Are we to be your clock for the whole year?"

Willow turned her attention to the others in the room, realizing this was the first time seeing any of them and they were all extremely good-looking. The boy speaking was, no doubt, the light elf she saw writing the entrance test. His long straight golden hair shimmered like the sun was shining on it, even inside. Standing this close to him, she now noticed his pale skin had a sparkle of golden dust, illuminating him like a child born of the sun and moon. An urge surged through her body to turn the lights off to see if he would be bright enough to light the room.

“No, but I didn't have a clue where I was going,” she answered, still absorbing the warmth of his glow. Her attention snapped back to reality at the sound of another voice.

“Perhaps we should be your map, then?”

The elf speaking this time, Willow deduced, must have been a mountain elf. His long, straight, greyish hair was tied back neatly. Gleaming red eyes locked on her gaze. Heat raced through her veins as if her body had been set ablaze.

Taking a deep breath in and letting it out with a sigh, she reached deep inside herself, controlling the burning sensation. “No, but that whole cooperation thing the Director was speaking about, and maybe a little courtesy, would have been nice. You know, to get off on the right foot,” she replied, allowing no emotions to show in the tone of her voice.

She expected the final elf to speak, but he remained silent. Again, she recognized him from the test. His short, black, spiky hair accentuated his piercing, baby-blue eyes, making them stand out like crystals.

“I guess I should introduce you all. The blinding light is Gabriel, the silent one is Seth, and the real charmer over there is Kayleb,” Sebastian said. He made a motion with his right hand towards Willow. “This is our final group member, Will.” The three remained motionless.

“Well, at least they said something. That was better than I hoped for.” Turning her attention to the papers lying on the table, she quickly glanced over the list of courses. “Have you looked at these?” she asked.

Sebastian moved beside her and picked up one of the schedules. “Not too many surprises,” he said. His forehead crinkled and the curve of his mouth tilted downwards.

Willow's curiosity piqued. “Something wrong?”

He ignored her at first, then shook his head, the smile returning to his perfect face. “Not at all. I just anticipated one of the courses on our list to be a second-semester level.”

Willow took a seat with the other elves, ignoring their glares. All of her attention focused on the classes they were about to enter. "Alchemy and potions," she said out loud, not speaking to anyone in particular. She rubbed her chin between her thumb and forefinger completely absorbed in her own thoughts. "Not my strong suit. I may need some help there. Hmm."

"No!" a loud voice rang out, breaking her concentration.

Looking up, she saw the dark elf standing, facing her direction, his fists clenched and arms slightly shaking. "Excuse me?" she said, tilting her head. Her lips parted slightly to continue, but froze before any words formed. The cold of his stare sent shivers down her spine - the tiny hairs on her arms sticking up. It was a completely opposite feeling from what she experienced with the other three elves. Goosebumps covered her skin. His gaze held her frozen where she sat, unable to speak or move. This elf was cold and dark - yet somehow beautiful at the same time.

Kayleb broke her trance. "There is a library with books. I suggest you make use and study. If you are looking for a free ride, it won't happen here. The four of us anticipate top score in this course. We are all proficient. If your inadequacies bring us down, we will take issue."

"Brilliant. I can see that teamwork is off to a great start," Willow said, forcing a smile. She turned her attention back to the paper clenched tightly in her hand. "So you are all completely proficient in all of these subjects?" she asked.

Kayleb stood and strolled to the table. Picking up the first term schedule, he glanced over it slowly. The same frown appeared on his face as Sebastian displayed earlier.

"Something wrong?" Willow asked, fishing for some possible flaw in his apparent perfectness.

"Humph," the mountain elf said, returning to his seat and handing the other two their copies of the list of classes.

"As Kayleb said, we four are expected to be the best in Alchemy and Potions. It's a strong suit for us," Sebastian answered.

"Elemental magic?" Willow asked

“Seth is accomplished in all forms. Kayleb is strong suited to fire and I specialize in water. That leaves air magic.” Sebastian took a seat on the arm of the chair beside Willow.

“Air magic? As in moving things around with wind?” she asked.

“Rather a crude definition, but in essence, yes,” the mountain elf answered.

“That I can do.” She could feel the eyes of each elf locked on her. There was no desire to meet any of their stares again. “Botany,” she continued.

“The study and understanding of plants and their growth,” Gabriel said. “My area of expertise.”

“Well,” Willow said with a smile, “guess we have something in common. It is one of my strong suits too.”

Gabriel threw his head to the side, refusing to acknowledge her statement.

Sebastian laughed. “Gabriel has a connection with nature that can't be compared to. You may want to rethink considering yourself at the same level as him.”

Willow placed both hands on her face, hiding a devious grin. Beating Gabriel might be her way into the circle of this bizarre group she was matched with. She returned her attention to the courses listed on the paper in front of her. Her eyebrows raised and the corners of her lips turned downwards. “Combat?” she said as a question.

“Yeah,” Sebastian answered. “Hand-to-hand, with magical weapons allowed.” He let out a low chuckle. “Surely you know how to fight.”

Willow nodded her head up and down slowly as she gazed off into space. Her thoughts travelled back to the few lessons held back at the camp. Most of her defences were instinctual - rated above average by both the guardians and the camp members. She wondered if that would be enough here.

“You still with us?” Sebastian asked, tilting his head so it faced sideways in front of hers.

“Yeah,” she answered. “I have some defensive training under my belt,” she muttered, immediately looking at the paper in her hands and blurting out, “Wand Magic.” After a moment of intense silence, Willow looked up to four sets of dead eyes staring at her. There were no intense feelings as she felt earlier from their glares. “Is there a problem with using wands?” she asked.

The silence continued, each elf turning their gaze away from her, staring off into space. Willow shifted her eyes from one to the other trying to make sense of their reactions.

“No way,” she said, covering her mouth with the fingers of one hand in an attempt to contain a giggle that was forming. She faked a cough.

After a few moments, she could no longer hold back. A full laughter erupted from deep inside her, intensifying to the point of tears streaming down her face. A stitch formed in her side causing her to wrap her arms around her waistline, griping tightly.

“I'm... sorry,” she blurted out amid the laughter. Her upper body hunched over to her knees. Raising one hand in front of her, she lifted a finger to indicate she needed a moment. After catching her breath she looked up at the four elves, all staring at her with curiosity.

“Are you okay?” Sebastian asked in a serious tone.

“Yeah, fine,” she said, mixed in with a few dying chuckles. “It's just hard to believe elves would have difficulty using wands.”

“I am not sure how that is funny,” Kayleb said.

“Well,” she answered, “it's funny to me, since I can use a wand rather efficiently.”

“You can?” Sebastian asked, his green eyes gleaming with curiosity.

“Yes,” Willow answered. “Now that I think about it, I can understand why you would have difficulty. Not sure if there are many books on how to use a wand, but I hear there is a good library you can spend time in here. I think it's past my bedtime. Have a good night. Tomorrow should be fun.”

"Will, wait," Sebastian called out to her. "You aren't going to help? This will affect your mark as well."

Without turning around, Willow answered, "I might be too busy studying alchemy and potions to have any spare time. I am sure you all understand how it is. Good night." She opened her bedroom door and entered, making sure to close it tightly behind her.

No sooner than she sat down, Aslo appeared beside her. "We were wondering when you would finally be alone for the night," he said. "It can be a little frustrating having to wait for you to be alone to be filled in on all the details."

"Sorry," she said. "I was dealing with some unfriendly elves." She filled her guardian friend in on everything that happened while getting ready for bed.

"Sounds like Wand Magic will be your way into the group," Aslo commented. "I still worry about you getting too close to this lot. I have never known elves to respect anyone else other than perhaps..." His words faded off.

"Perhaps the seven ancient trees? There are seven, aren't there?" Willow asked.

Aslo's head spun around to lock gazes with her. "Yes, there are, or were, seven originally. Not all are accounted for."

"What do you mean, not accounted for?" Willow asked, her curiosity piqued.

"Exactly what I said. We don't know what happened to them. There is some speculation that they gave up and went to sleep somewhere." Aslo moved back to the window ledge and gazed out.

"Sleep?" Willow said. "I don't think I understand."

"They just stopped appearing," Aslo answered. "We don't know why or how or where."

"What does this have to do with the elves?" she asked.

"Nothing, really," he answered. "At least that we are aware of." The black cat meowed once as he jumped back to the bed to sit in front of her. "The trees were once tended to by elves. It's folklore to them now, but still an important part of elven history. It's doubtful they have anything to do with whatever happened. It's late. You should get some sleep. Tomorrow won't be easy."

Willow glanced over at the clock on the night table beside her bed. The small round bell perched on top of it was the first line of defence against disaster. If there was one thing she didn't need, it was to draw more attention to herself. "Just in case," she mumbled, carefully setting the alarm for the morning. "Please make sure I wake up early, so I am not late for my first class."

Aslo nodded and curled up under the blanket beside her for the night.

Chapter Six

Willow opened her eyes to a close-up of a cat's face, its whiskers twitching. Her body jolted up, throwing Aslo off the bed. He spun in the air, doing several somersaults before landing on his feet on the floor, tail stuck straight up, fur puffing out.

"Sorry," she murmured. "What time is it?" She picked up the clock beside her and rubbed her eyes before focusing on it. "Did the alarm go off?" she asked.

"No," Aslo said. "Don't expect me to wake you up like that again. I may be immortal, but flying isn't in my skillset."

"Sorry," she repeated. "Seeing a cat's face up close and personal when you first open your eyes can be a bit of a shock. I'll try not to do it again." She looked back at the clock. "Why would they give us an alarm clock that doesn't work?"

"Not sure," Aslo answered. "You better get ready now." The guardian brushed against her arm, disappearing into a picture on her skin once again.

After showering and dressing in her disguise, it was time to figure out exactly where the day's classes were being held. Pulling out a pen and notebook, she drew a small map. If she got lost, there wasn't going to be anyone to ask. Knowing where everything was located before heading out was half the battle.

The sound of her own shoes on the pavement grew louder with every step. She shivered, the word *alone* ringing in her ears. There were no signs of the elves. Actually, there were very few students walking around at all. Even if it was a bit early, she expected a few others would be equally as conscientious about arriving on time for their first day.

The classroom for potions and alchemy was in a building located directly beside where the opening ceremony had been held the night before. The room itself was divided into two sections. The first section reminded Willow of the terunji church she visited on the witch's tour. There hadn't been much time in the church to soak in everything, but it definitely held some similarities with the room she was now standing in. The seating was arranged in a similar fashion to pews, with only the front row having proper desks - the other rows all having pull-out desks built into the back of the seats in front of them. High ceilings formed peaks in unique triangle designs illuminated only by light let in through windows fashioned in flamboyant stained glass. The main difference between the church's windows and these were the pictures being portrayed. The second part of the room resembled a scientific laboratory fully equipped with the finest technology.

Clasping her school books tight in her arms, she moved closer to the windows. Each scene appeared to be a landscape. On the first stained glass window, in the distance an island caught her attention. She blinked, wondering if her eyes had deceived her. It almost seemed as if the land moved and wasn't part of the glass picture at all, but rather something outside. That was impossible.

"Fascinating, isn't it?" a man's voice said from behind her.

Willow spun around to see an unusually normal-looking man standing behind her. He was medium height with short brown hair and matching eye colour. The suit he wore was a bit old-fashioned, being navy blue in colour with thin white pinstripes, over a crisp white shirt and solid blue vest. A gold chain hung noticeably from one vest pocket. The man reached in and pulled out a pocket watch attached to the chain.

"You are early," he said, waggling his eyebrows. "I'm Finkle... Professor Finkle... your teacher for this class." The man moved closer to the window. "Depiction of events in art is such an interesting topic, isn't it?"

"Depiction?" she asked, tilting her head at the picture to see if she could understand what her teacher was trying to say. "I noticed the similarity of these windows to those of a terunji church I once visited."

"Yes," he said, his eyes widening. "Yes, very good, my boy. There is a definite connection between the design of this room and a church of sorts, but more so, each of these windows has a symbol placed in them reflecting something from the terunji world... and there are quite a few. But what do they mean?" His voice radiated excitement. "I enjoy studying them in my spare time. The design of this room is an inspiration to me." He looked back at his watch. "Feel free to come back in your spare time. If the room isn't busy, you can study the art anytime. For now, best get a good seat. I expect the others will be filling up the room shortly."

Willow looked closer at the window in front of her for a moment, trying to identify any symbols she might have overlooked, but with the limited time available, she noticed none. Not wanting to upset her teacher, she gave in to his request.

Taking a seat in the front row, directly in front of where Professor Finkle's desk was located, she arranged her books on the desk. The next few minutes were spent fidgeting with her books and pens, moving them from one location on her desk to another and then looking up at the teacher - who sat with one hand propping up his face, staring at the door. His attention alternated between pulling out his watch to check the time and watching the entrance.

Willow glanced over at the windows again. There was something drawing her to them; calling her by name to join in a game of truth or dare. When the chance arose, she'd be back to examine them closer.

After several minutes passed, Finkle sighed. "Seems you are the only one who would like to attend my class this semester, my boy," he said. "No worries, no worries. A class you shall have." He stood, motioning with outstretched arms towards the ceiling. A large blackboard came down with a crash behind him. He sat down again unaffected and began writing in a book on his desk. As he wrote, white words appeared on the blackboard, *Professor Finkle ~ Alchemy & Potions*. He looked up at Willow. "I'll need to learn names. Yours is?"

"Will," she answered.

"Well, Will... bonus marks to you this semester for showing up, not just on time, but early. Shall we begin?"

"Sir," she said, grabbing his attention. "Shouldn't we wait for the others? There must be a lot of students missing. I can think of at least four. Isn't it odd that I am the only one here?"

A smile crept up half his face. "Not at all, my boy. What's odd is that you are here." Seeing the look of confusion on his student's face he continued. "Today is the first day of classes. The faculty puts a few obstacles in the way of students. It's more a test of character... a way of getting to know the personality of each of their students."

"You mean like the alarm clock not working?" she asked.

The professor's eyebrows moved up, then fell down quickly. "You caught that, did you? Well done. There are other obstacles as well, of course. But no worries about that now, because you are here."

"I suppose I should worry about the rest of my group, though," she said, looking at the book on her desk. "They seemed so self-sufficient. I had no idea they wouldn't be here."

"Yes," the professor agreed, looking in a black book on his desk. "Elves, aren't they?" After seeing Willow nod, he groaned. "I can understand why you would have thought that. Never mind though, since you are here, let's begin. First, tell me about your background experience with our subject."

"Well," Willow said, biting her bottom lip, "I knew a couple of girls who made a forbidden love potion once and almost killed three friends of mine. It was really traumatic watching their bodies twitching around on the floor." With no threats of plague or tempest, she felt safe enough to continue. "I did help collect ingredients for a few potions and visited an interesting potion supply store. The owner was quite helpful and offered some advice that I think I will always remember. He said it was the harder ingredients... the ones less common that are the most important to figure out what they could be used for. He was extremely adamant there were no shortcuts in magic as it leads to unnatural things. There were a few examples he used... wood struck by lightning sticks out in my mind. Also, he mentioned the fact there was no book to tell what these items were used for. He was very particular about that, saying anyone could memorize a book, but a true potion master could see the possibilities around him and make use of them."

"Impressive," Finkle said, clapping his hands together. "My boy, what you just said is far beyond what many of this class will ever grasp. You may not have hands-on experience with making potions, but if you can grasp what this man told you, you will do far better than a skilled scientist could." A loud noise echoed from outside. "Ah, seems the rest of the class may be finally catching up." He smiled and winked playfully.

The door at the back of the room flew open and students began filtering in. Sebastian and the three other elves were among the first to enter. They took a seat beside Willow without saying a word to her, in fact without acknowledging her existence in the room at all.

The professor stood directly in front of them and bent over at the waist to come close to their faces. "Nice of you four to join us," he whispered. "You should thank Will for keeping your group at the top of the class. Since one of you made it on time, I won't be deducting anything from your grades today." He chuckled as he walked back to his desk to write in his book. As he did, the words appeared on the blackboard behind him. *Any group who did not have at least one member present on time for class today will have five percent deducted from their total mark for the semester.*

A rumble of dissatisfaction echoed through the room as students scrambled to find out if anyone from their group arrived on time. The final moments of the class were spent in silence watching stragglers continue to arrive, only to be scolded by their peers. A clock chiming sounded loudly through the building.

The professor stood. “Best hurry to your next class and try not to be late.”

Willow stood and collected her things, then glanced at her map. The next class, Botany, was to be located in a classroom in a basement under the cafeteria. “That's odd,” she said.

Sebastian turned and looked at her. “What?” he asked in a less than friendly voice. The other elves stopped to wait for her answer. “We are going to be late if we don't go now.”

“Well,” she said. “It's just shouldn't a class on plants be held in a greenhouse or outside? It seems odd we would be scheduled to go to a classroom located in a basement.”

Finkle looked up at her and winked. “Best be off, you five. One of you needs to make it to the right place on time.” He collected his things and exited.

“Why would they tell us to go to the wrong place?” Sebastian asked, heading for the door.

“Because,” Willow yelled after him, “we are supposed to be smart enough to figure out where to be. It's the same as the alarm clocks not working and whatever else happened to you four that made you late. They are testing us. There were greenhouses on the map. Where were they?” she asked.

“They are on the other side of the sports field, but do you really think they would trick us?” Gabriel questioned without turning to face her.

“Better safe than sorry,” Willow answered. “I am going to head over there just in case. You guys can go to the basement if you want.”

“First off,” Kayleb said. “Elves are not *guys*. Second, I will go with you.” He paused. “Just in case you might be right.”

Willow smiled. “You had me completely fooled,” she replied. “I never would have guessed you were all girls.” She chuckled and pushed by him out the door.

Kayleb rolled his eyes and followed her. “We are not girls,” he grumbled, moving into a position to walk beside her.

“I know,” she said. “I was joking. It's supposed to make you laugh and loosen up a bit.”

“Such a display of emotion in public is a direct reflection of weakness,” he said.

“Sebastian laughs,” she snapped back.

“Exactly,” he replied, with no further explanation.

Willow quickened her pace when the greenhouse came into sight, the walk having been too silent and awkward for her liking. There was more to the story of the elves than she anticipated.

For now, she focused all her attention on finding out if her theory about the location of their next class was the correct option. Opening the door, she came face-to-face with the rabbit-like man from the day before. She froze in the doorway.

“Well,” the rabbit man said. “Don't stand there. Come in... come in! I am Mr. Greenfoot, your instructor for Beginner's Botany. Welcome to my class and well done catching that misprint in the locations. Well done, indeed.”

Willow flashed a smile at Kayleb before following their teacher to the other end of the greenhouse. “Are there many misprints in the schedule?” she asked. “Or is this the only one?”

“Let me see,” the instructor offered, outstretching his hand to receive her schedule and tapping one foot as if he was in a hurry.

“Thank you,” Willow said, placing the paper in the rabbit like hand before her.

“Yes, yes,” he said. “What's your name, boy?”

“Will,” she answered.

“Well, Will,” Greenfoot said. “Your places are correct, but you may want to double-check the times.” He handed the schedule back to her. “And you? What is your name?”

“Kayleb,” the elf answered.

“Very good,” the instructor muttered, looking at an attendance book. “Where are the rest of your group?”

“We split up,” Kayleb said. “We wanted to make sure someone was present at the beginning of the class. This way, if we were wrong about the location mix-up, the rest of our group would be in the right place.”

“I see,” the rabbit man said. “Wonderful teamwork and on the first day. Very impressive, especially considering the makeup of your group.”

“The makeup of our group?” Willow asked.

“Yes, well,” Greenfoot replied. “It has always been my impression elves didn't work well in a group that contained... well... individuals who were not elves.”

“Right.” Willow nodded her head. “I almost forgot about that.”

“Since you are here, let's see what you can do.” He moved to a table of plants that were doing less than well. “Tell me what is wrong with each of these plants.”

Willow looked at Kayleb. He wasn't moving. The expression on his face told her he was out of his league in this department - Gabriel was their plant expert. She moved forward and touched a leaf of the first plant on the table. Closing her eyes, she listened intently to what the suffering plant said, then picked up some of the soil it was planted in and smelt it, instantly making a face.

“The fertilizer is far too strong for it. The poor thing's roots are burning as we speak,” she said, reaching for an empty pot and some soil. Within minutes, she transplanted the plant and it thanked her by instantly blossoming a pale pink flower.

“Extraordinary!” Greenfoot exclaimed. “She has really taken to you, blooming like that. She normally only produces flowers for me. Seems you won't have a problem doing well in this class. Please continue.” He motioned to the other plants.

Willow continued solving each of the other plants' problems, from lack of water to a pot that was too small. After each was happily saved, other students began arriving, including the missing members of their group.

“Settle down now,” Greenfoot ordered, appearing irritated by the noise of the incoming students. “Students who are late will have a choice of additional work or a deduction from their final mark, with exception of Will and Kayleb's group, of course. This bunch have already learnt how to work as a team towards a good end result. The rest of you best learn the same.”

After standing doing nothing for several minutes, Willow moved closer to Mr. Greenfoot. “Excuse me, sir,” she said. “Are we going to be doing anything else today?”

“Well, you have already done it all,” he replied. “Normally, my class doesn't finish saving all the plants. Quite an accomplishment... you finished helping all these darlings in such a short amount of time. It's going to be a most interesting year to see who ends up top of this class.” His gaze moved to meet Gabriel's. Willow followed, finding Gabriel staring back at her.

“He is going to give you a run for top of the class, Gabriel,” Kayleb said. “It was impressive to watch him work.”

Sebastian laughed. “Things are going to be interesting this year. I can't wait to see where this all goes. Who knows? Maybe we will have to make Will an official elf.”

“Your overflowing emotions are making me ill,” Seth said, heading to exit the greenhouse.

“Where are you going?” Kayleb asked.

“If there is no lesson left for us today, we might as well make our way to our next class, in case we are tricked in some way into being late again,” Seth answered, leaving the building.

“He is right,” Kayleb agreed, following with the other two elves right behind him.

Willow picked up her belongings and ran after them. Catching up, she said, “Shouldn't we figure out what he meant by check the times?”

“Times?” Sebastian asked. “Did we miss something?”

"Yes," Kayleb answered. "Greenfoot looked at our schedule to see if any other locations were mixed up for us. He said we should check the times of our remaining classes."

Seth snatched the paper from Willow's hand as if it belonged to him. "The classes are all scheduled to start at proper times. I see no problem," he said, throwing the list back at her.

Willow jolted forward slightly, trying to catch the falling class schedule, but missed. It fell to the ground. Bending over to pick it up, she flashed him the nastiest expression she could, squinting her eyes and pressing her lips tightly together. "That wasn't necessary. You could have been civil enough to hand it back."

Seth grunted. "If you were a little more nimble, perhaps you might have caught it."

She sighed, turning her attention back to the schedule. "If it isn't the time we start a class, maybe a couple of classes have been mixed up," she suggested.

Gabriel sighed. "How would we know that?"

"I don't know," Willow answered. "Is there a specific class that should be taught earlier than others? Would it make sense to have a certain course before lunch?"

"Of course," Sebastian said, peering over her shoulder at the paper. "I see it now. The times don't add up right in this order if you factor in lunch."

"What do you mean? Please try to articulate in a more proficient manner," Gabriel said, his expression stern.

"It's not the start times. It's the length of the classes that isn't right," Sebastian explained. "Since all classes begin on the hour, if we were to leave Greenfoot's class on time, we would have exactly fifteen minutes to arrive at our next course. The next class on this schedule is elemental magic, which runs one hour and forty-five minutes. Lunch starts an hour after our next course does."

"Genius!" Willow said, smiling. "Our next class has to be Wand Magic, since it runs for exactly one hour."

“Although I agree with the deductions, I fail to see the point to struggling to find our classes on the first day,” Gabriel said, walking towards their new destination. “What purpose could it possibly serve?”

“Finkle mentioned it was to give the teachers a perspective on the character of their new students,” Willow answered.

The Wand Magic course was held in the same auditorium as the opening ceremony - its size more apparent now that it was empty. At one end of the room stood a pale-white woman, dressed in a soft pastel pink dress cut in petals shapes. Short hair in the same tint as her outfit, framed her pure white face. Large, round, cartoon-like eyes hosted a deeper pink shade while a rose colour softly illuminated her cheeks and lips.

“I am Tara, your instructor for Wand Magic,” she said in a soft voice that sang rather than spoke. “Welcome.”

Her greeting was cut short by the entrance of another group of students who, apparently, also figured out the correct place to be.

“Excellent,” Tara said. “It's good to see so many of you found your way here on the first day. We may actually have a class. Can we have a few introductions? As I was saying, I am Tara, the Wand Magic instructor.” She motioned to Willow's group to continue.

Before anyone could say a word, Kayleb stepped forward, handling all the introductions for them - his gaze never leaving the other five students who arrived. When he was done, he stepped back into the group and awaited their response.

In a similar fashion, the largest of the other team stepped forward. It was easy to understand why he was the leader. His sheer size alone commanded attention, standing well over seven feet with a physique to match. Black hair molded his face, stuck in place with grease and sweat. On top of his head, two horns were sticking up just enough to make them noticeable.

Looking at his skin, Willow wondered if he had spent a bit too much time in the sun, leaving him red and blistered. A burn would at least explain the look of pain that was plastered to his face. A large gold ring hung from his nose like a door knocker. All in all, his appearance was rather frightening, resembling an angered bull. He exhaled through his nose, nostrils flaring with smoke.

"I am Klurr," he announced, veins bulging in his neck and forehead as he spoke. "My team consists of Matia, Flamboya, Jin, and Tuma." He stepped back to his group again.

Jin and Tuma shared a similar appearance with their leader. The two females, however, were a blue colour with an average height. The horns on their heads were larger, curling around in the front in the same fashion as a ram's horns would.

"Wonderful," Tara said. "Who would like to begin? We will need a volunteer from each side for a simple test of wand strength."

Klurr let out a primal sounding laugh as he stepped forward to volunteer. Willow glanced at each of the faces of the elves around her and sighed, suddenly remembering they didn't know anything about wands.

"Guess that's me," she said, taking a deep breath as she moved one foot forward.

Sebastian reached out, grabbing her arm before she had a chance to fully move. She fell backwards against him. "Careful, Will," he said. "He has a reputation for being brutal with his wand, among other things."

"Brilliant," Willow replied, forcing a smile.

Sebastian gave her a little push. Willow jolted forward towards her opponent. The closer she came to him, the more frightened she became. Her hand shook, reaching in her back pocket for her wand.

The beast waited, steam coming out of his nose from a snort of disapproval.

"I thought I was having an elf for lunch," he snarled. "Instead, I get a puny terunji boy. This won't take long at all." He lifted his wand, aiming it at her.

Willow matched his movement with her own wand. Her mind focused on the fear travelling through her body. It was an emotion that was strong within her at the moment, one easily channelled into the wand. Clearing her mind, nothing else mattered. Her gaze locked on the wand of her opponent. It was all she could see. She controlled her breathing to a slow rhythm. It was all she could hear. An aroma filled her nose - the faint scent of Acacia's blossoms. It was all she could smell.

A blast of red exploded from the tip of Klurr's wand, appearing in slow motion before her. She responded with a blast of magic fuelled by the fear her opponent had himself created. A white and gold stream cut through the red one heading towards her, hitting her opponent directly in the chest. He flew backwards, his body slamming against the wall, leaving a dent.

Willow snapped back to reality, letting the air out of her lungs. For a moment, she wondered if she lost her hearing, everything was quiet - too quiet. She glanced at the others in the room, staring - their mouths wide open. Then she noticed Klurr on the floor by the wall.

"Oops," she said. "I may have let out a bit too much energy." She stepped back to her group.

"Maybe a little," Sebastian said, showing a small space between his thumb and forefinger. "I probably should have mentioned he is most likely in our combat class later today." He slapped her on the back. "No worries though, Will," he said, smiling. "I am sure he won't hold a grudge."

Willow's eyes widened as she alternated looks between Sebastian and Klurr, who was standing and heading straight for them.

"Somehow he looks like he might be holding a grudge," she said.

"You little pipsqueak!" he yelled. "Did you really think you could make a fool of Klurr?" He raised his wand - another blast flew out.

"Get down!" Willow screamed. She held out her wand and closed her eyes. Realizing nothing happened to her, she opened one eye and peered out. She was crunched down on the ground in front of the elves, who were in a similar position. A white and gold light poured out of her wand, forming an umbrella-shaped shield around them. The red energy of Klurr's attack was absorbed by the shield on contact, making it stronger.

Over and over, Klurr threw attacks at them - each one failing. His breathing became more erratic as the attacks went on, his strength faltering. The stress of constantly using power caused him to tire. He had set a pace that was impossible to continue. A ring indicated the end of the class. Klurr fell to his knees, out of breath.

"Very good. Enough now," Tara said. "Klurr, please put away your wand. Your group may go for lunch. Kayleb, if I could see your group for a moment before you go, please."

Kayleb nodded and moved closer to the small-framed lady. Willow and the rest of the elves followed. Tara waited until Klurr and his group exited the building.

"That was impressive, Will," she said when she was sure they were alone. "Your skill in wand use is far more advanced than I have seen before in a student. Simple power is one thing, as Klurr has shown, but do you have an understanding of how to manipulate wand magic? That's what I would like to know."

"Yes," Willow answered.

"Hm," the teacher said, circling her student. "Tell me how you made such a powerful blast to obliterate your opponent's magic and then to shield not just you, but your entire group as well, without using up every ounce of energy you possess." She crossed her hands over her chest, waiting for an answer.

"Fear," Willow answered, without making eye contact with her new instructor.

"Fear?" Tara repeated as a question.

"Yes," she replied back. "I was petrified of Klurr. A friend of mine showed me a technique when I first found my wand. He taught me that emotions are a powerful magic on their own. Love... hate... jealousy... rage... happiness... and fear, if you harness them, you can channel them into your wand. I learnt breathing control, focus and energy conservation on my own through practice. I still tire, but not as quickly when I combine it all together."

"Child," Tara said. "I have no idea why you are in my class. There is nothing I can teach you. The strength of your wand rests within yourself now." She exhaled loudly. "Perhaps you can help your group along. If they can master as you have, you can pass this course with top marks without finishing out the year. It is up to all of you." She turned and headed for the door. "Enjoy your lunch."

"Looks like you are our new teacher," Sebastian said.

"Does that mean I can have some help with potions?" she asked.

Sebastian snorted a laugh. "I suppose things are working out that way," he said. "Guess we should head to lunch."

"I'm going to skip the cafeteria," Willow said. "I hope you aren't offended, but the sight and smell of meat tends to make me sick."

"You're a vegetarian?" Gabriel said.

"Yeah," she answered.

"We are, too," Kayleb said, walking past her to open the door. "Greenfoot keeps an extraordinary grove of fruit trees for the elf students here at Sleeping Sands. I suppose you can join us."

Greenfoot's gardens were located to the back of the building that Willow's group was living in. Various elves were already standing under trees, selecting their fruit for lunch.

"Hello again," Greenfoot said, approaching them. "Good to see you all. I am sure you will find my trees produce some of the finest fruits you have ever tried," he said. "Come. Come." He took Willow's arm and led her to the middle of the garden. "Pick whichever you like. I grew these myself to make sure fruit would be in-season for you during the school year. This section is currently ripe. I will open the other parts as the year goes on."

Willow stepped forward and touched the trunk of a tree. "Would you mind if I ate one of your apples?" she asked. A branch dropped down in front of her. She held out her hands, forming a cup shape. A red apple dropped inside. "Thank you," she said, taking a bite out of the fruit she was given. Pivoting, she came face-to-face with Greenfoot and her roommates, all watching her with curiosity.

“Did you just speak to that tree?” Gabriel asked. For the first time, his face changed. His eyes moved closer together and his lips curled downwards.

“I... suppose,” she answered. “It's a bit rude to take fruit from a tree without asking first. Don't you think?”

“Perhaps,” Gabriel answered, moving closer to her. “But it's also rare that a tree gives fruit when asked to, don't you think?”

Willow pressed her lips together and took a deep breath. “You must not be hanging out with the right trees,” she said, forcing a smile. “Think I am going to head over and check out the next class. Elemental, isn't it?”

Sebastian laughed and picked a peach from the tree he was standing under. “I'll join you,” he said, shaking his head.

Their next class was located just over a large grass-covered hill to the south of the gardens. As Willow reached the top of the steep climb, her eyes lit up at the sight of what was waiting on the other side. They were standing at the top of a giant rock pit. Seats were carved as benches in a half-circular pattern into the hill, creating a practice stadium - one which resembled an ancient stone amphitheatre. At the bottom was a wide open space which formed more of an oval shape than a circular one - covered with loose gravel. After recovering from the initial shock, the two began their descent down one of the evenly spaced stone stairways located between rows of seating.

Directly in the centre of the arena stood a lady dressed in a black robe covered in tiny specks of red - tied with a plain thick rope. In her left hand she held a tall wooden staff, boasting elaborate carvings of the elements along with numerous different symbols. Her eyes were a crystallized grey and never seemed to move, leaving Willow to question whether or not she had the ability to see.

As they moved closer to the woman, a gust of wind picked up her long white hair and blew it around messily, accentuating a solid black streak running through it down the left side of her face.

The breeze left an unnatural shiver running down Willow's back. The blowing air was fake, as if manufactured from a giant fan, rather than a naturally occurring part of the weather.

"Which interests you more, the fact that I am blind or that I have no shoes on?" the woman asked.

Willow glanced at Sebastian and noticed his attention was locked on the woman's bare feet, standing on the gravel-covered floor.

"Personally, I was wondering if it was you who created the gust of air," Willow said, now wondering if the stones the teacher was standing on were cutting the bottoms of her feet. In the very least, it must have been uncomfortable.

The woman smiled, showing off a silver tooth. "Interesting," she said. "Come forward and announce yourselves, then."

Willow moved in front of her. "I am Will," she answered.

"Sebastian," her companion blurted out.

"An elf and a boy together. How interesting," the woman said. "I am your teacher. You can call me Miss Kelly." She lifted her foot to show them there was in fact no damage to her soles. "Everything connects in some way. The elements, nature, the sky, the ground... it is all one. Once you figure out how and learn to bend one into the other, you will become a master of your magic. When that happens, things such as rocks, thistles, or even fire will not be able to hurt you. That is what you are striving for."

"Can you see?" Sebastian asked out of the blue.

Miss Kelly laughed. "My third eye is strong enough to see what I need to know, Mr. Sebastian. If you think you can fool me, you better be able to, because if you fail, you will also fail my class. Since you are early, please pick up the buckets of water over there and bring them back for today's lessons. Will, there is some wood over there as well that needs to be retrieved."

The items were on the far side of the arena they were standing in. The water was on the right and the wood to the left. Sebastian set out to fetch the buckets.

"Excuse me," Willow said. "Is magic allowed here?"

The woman cackled. "Elemental magic is always allowed in the pit. You may call fire, water, or air to your aid."

"Thank you," Willow said. She lifted her arms to the skies and brought forth a gust of wind which swirled, forming a mini tornado. Directing it over top of the wood pile, the whirlwind picked up all of the pieces and moved them close to where she stood. They dropped into a neat pile, the air flow disbursing before Sebastian returned from his first trip carrying water. He placed the buckets down by Willow's feet. Daggers shot from his eyes at the realization he'd been bested.

Miss Kelly let out a loud cackle again. "Been beat, elf?" she asked.

"Not even close," Sebastian said, adding a demonic grin.

He raised his hands and the water from the buckets that remained flew into the air, swirling in a similar round motion as the air funnel had. The force of the spiral picked up the buckets, moving them to beside the wood pile. Each bucket dropped open side up, forming a neat row. The water then separated, falling into each container evenly without so much as a drop spilling. He stepped back and folded his arms over his chest.

"Would have been nice to know we could use our abilities."

"I asked," Willow retorted.

"Having fun?" Kayleb asked as he and the others finished descending the final steps into the arena. "Looks like you are showing off a bit, Sebastian."

"Oh, so you have some fire in your group as well," Miss Kelly said. "Tell me, when you combine all the elements together, what do you get?"

"Plasma, in other words, pure energy," Seth said, moving in front of the instructor. "Depending on the form you choose, it can be molded into a ball or used to create a moving stream." He lifted his hands in front of him. A flow of intertwining red, white and blue threads moved quickly between them. The faster the threads of colour shifted, the more purple the stream became. Flashes of miniature bolts of lightning formed within the stream. He clasped his hands together and the plasma dispersed.

"Very good," Miss Kelly said. "Seems at least one of you has an understanding of all of the elements. If your group books the arena for practice time enough, I know you will do well." She turned her attention to the rock staircase leading back towards the school grounds. "The rest of the class is coming now. Everyone will be on time today. How exciting. One might say it's... electrifying." Miss Kelly let out a cackle.

Willow couldn't help but giggle. Sebastian simply shook his head and smiled. As usual, the other three elves stood fast where they were without any interest in humour or their instructor's poor attempts at it.

Willow turned her attention to the stone stairs and the other students climbing down in their packs of five. At least Klurr wasn't one of them. For the next two hours, she was safe from retaliation. Unfortunately, she was in a whole other world of trouble. She knew one of the girls. It was Jessica.

Chapter Seven

The students formed a circular pattern around Miss Kelly while still maintaining their groups. From the centre, the instructor began a lecture on the different elemental magics. The teacher's words faded out of Willow's mind. Her energy was focused on remaining as hidden as possible from Jessica's view. If they met face-to-face, her cover could end up compromised.

The group Jessica was with were all witches of some sort. She recognized a second member of the team, a tall slender girl with glasses, from one of the files Jade and Malarchy provided. She was Krissy Quidnunk, the twin sister of the reporter for *The Empowered* newspaper.

A nagging feeling in the pit of her stomach screamed foul. The two of them being students this school term was a red flag. Both, according to the files, had applied to the school before and passed the tests, but failed to attend. So why were they there? On top of that, Jessica lied to Clairity about apprenticing until she could pass the entrance exam for Sleeping Sands. For now, Willow planned to avoid them like the plague.

“Are you okay?” Sebastian whispered in her ear, instantly shocking her back to the lesson.

Miss Kelly was still speaking about different environmental things that could affect elemental magic. She used some magnets as an example, showing how the polar opposites on each side moved the path of a wind storm or completely stopped it altogether.

"Yeah," she answered. "I am fine."

"Not in love, are you?" he asked, glancing over at Krissy. "I could help you out if you want. We happen to know that girl." His left eye winked in a suggestive manner.

"You know her? How?" Willow asked.

"So," he said with a grin, "you are interested."

"No, not at all," Willow whispered back. "I just was trying to place where I've seen her before. It's like when you know something and it's stuck somewhere in your brain... you know it's there, but you just can't find it."

"Hm?" he said. "Not quite believable. I think you aren't telling me something." He paused and looked back over at the girl. "She writes for a newspaper... her brother does, too. We were actually surprised to see her here."

"Of course! Her brother's name is Keith," Willow said. "I remember now. It was in Pewterclaw. Her brother writes some questionable articles."

"Separate your groups from each other and begin your practical work. This class will always be split into two, a theoretical lesson as you just experienced and the remainder, hands on magic. Please also send one member of your group to see me to book the arena for your homework," their new teacher directed.

Kayleb headed to the front to take care of the practice times. Seth and Gabriel chose a spot for their practical work at the far end of the arena. Luckily, it was the furthest point away from Jessica.

"Do you think we could meet with her alone sometime?" Willow asked. "I have a few questions about her brother and the articles he has been writing lately."

"Articles?" Sebastian raised one eyebrow at her. "Which articles?"

“Yes,” Willow answered. She paused for a moment, trying to find the right words. “He wrote an article about something that happened that wasn't entirely true. Parts were true, of course, but details were fabricated in between. It changed what really happened that day into something else... something horrible.”

“How do you know all this?” Sebastian asked.

“I was there... in Pewterclaw when it happened. I saw everything, start to finish.” She walked away, joining the others already practising. Sebastian glanced over at Krissy once more before shoving his hands in his pockets and following.

Willow stood back and watched how the elves called and controlled different elements. Seth was the only one proficient with multiple types. Many a practice evening was needed for each of them to become fluent in all of the elements. It didn't help that her attention was completely obsessed with the presence of the two girls in the other group, making it impossible for her to concentrate on anything else, especially a new form of magic. With a blank stare on her face, she pretended to be studying the actions of the others. Time passed without her noticing. A loud chime rang out, signalling it was time to change locations for the last time of the day.

The final course was combat. It was held in what might have been a sports field at a normal school and situated at the edge of the forest. For the first time, their group was not one of the first to arrive.

Willow made a gulping noise and froze in her tracks. Up ahead she saw their final instructor, speaking with Klurr and his group. She completely forgot about the encounter with him in wands class. What was even worse, the instructor looked as if he could have been related to Klurr.

“Did I mention the instructor for combat was Klurr's father?” Sebastian asked.

“No,” she answered. “You may have left that out.” Her face drooped as if it was suddenly fifty pounds heavier. “I am going to die, aren't I?”

“I hope not. I think I am becoming rather fond of having you around.” Sebastian smiled, quickening his pace to join with the other three elves.

Willow caught up to them and stayed at the back, allowing Kayleb to take leadership of the group. She had no desire to do any speaking or make any noises at all to draw attention to herself. The other students for the class arrived immediately after them.

Willow sighed. “Well, at least there wasn't any time for him to decapitate me before class started.”

“No worries,” Kayleb said. “We have two hours of class time for him to find you.” The corners of his lips turned upward slightly.

“Are you... smiling?” Willow asked.

“If I am not, I think it is very possible I may during this class,” the mountain elf said, leaning back towards her before heading to retrieve instructions from their teacher.

Willow watched as Kayleb argued with the instructor. After a few minutes, he shook his head as if dissatisfied and headed back towards them.

“Sorry, Will,” Kayleb said. “I tried, but Instructor Klurg has decided you will be demonstrating against Klurr. He demands another member of our group hold your wand.” He held out his hand.

“Really?” she asked.

The expression on his face didn't change. Reaching in her pocket, she removed her wand and placed it in the mountain elf's hand.

Kayleb handed the wand to Gabriel. “Take care of it, please,” he said. “Don't worry. It isn't in our best interest to let you die,” he whispered in her ear, leaving a tingling sensation long after his words faded.

The rest of the students moved into a position either behind Willow's group or behind her opponent's group. She took in a deep breath and let it out again. Her mind tried to shuffle through visions of the few hand-to-hand combat lessons William gave her. It was no use. Everything she did back then was based completely on instinct. She would have to rely on the same now and hope her latent abilities included some useful combat moves. She took a step forward towards Klurr.

Instructor Klurg came between them. “I want a clean fight. You can use natural abilities, hand-to-hand combat and magical weapons. Death is frowned upon by the Director, but I don't mind a bit of blood. On the count of three,” he said. “THREE.”

Klurr lunged forward at her, his fist connecting with her face. She went flying to the ground. Klurg put one hand on his son's chest, waiting to see if it was a knockout punch. Willow staggered slowly to her feet, holding the side of her face. She hadn't been ready for such speed. She turned and faced Klurr again, this time concentrating on him fully. She blocked out everything else, until all that existed was Klurr and the sound of her breathing, slowing to a crawl.

The instructor removed his hand from Klurr's chest. He moved forward again; this time, Willow watched his movements in slow motion. She dodged his hits left and right, then used a foot to trip her opponent, sending him falling face-first into the grass.

Klurr looked up while spitting a mouthful of dirt back to where it had come from. His upper lip lifted, releasing a loud snarl. Within seconds, he was on his feet again charging at her. She jumped in the air, somersaulting over top of him. His feet dug in the ground, leaving skid marks in the grass as he forced a stop and turned around. The charge began again. This time, Willow used a leg to kick him in the chest before leaping over him to safety.

“Enough fooling around. Let's see some combat!” Klurg yelled. At the sound of his father's orders, shiny silver swords appeared in Klurr's hands. He began his attack approach this time with malicious intent.

Willow stood fast, eyes closed - her chest slowly moving up and down. She could hear her opponent closing in and then a clang of steel on steel. She opened her eyes. Her arms were twirling around, each holding a blue glowing sword and easily matching his movements in defence.

"STOP!" Klurg bellowed.

Klurr did as commanded, moving backwards towards his group. His weapons vanished. Looking down, Willow realized her weapons had also disappeared.

"Will," Klurg said, moving closer. "This class is not defence! It is *combat*. That means you are supposed to try to attack. Your sissy moves are not impressing me. I want to see what you can do to defeat Klurr. Do you understand?" He stood right in her face, his finger poking her in the chest with each word.

"Yes," she answered, taking a step backwards from vile breath that had a stench of half-digested meat. "I prefer not to attack people. Honestly, I can't think of any reasons why I would need to."

Klurg's eyes bulged, threatening to explode out of his head. Smoke escaped from his nostrils and blew directly in her face. Willow coughed, choking on the cloud surrounding her.

"You can't," he said, backing up. He turned, glancing at the other students then back at Willow. A smile crossed his face, then vanished in one swift motion as his face moved within an inch of hers and he yelled, "How about because I am telling you to?!"

Willow fell backwards onto the ground.

The instructor walked back to a spot between his son and Willow. "Let's try this again. This time, Will, you will start the attack."

Willow glanced back at her group, hoping for anything that could help. Having only ever thought about defending herself, she didn't know how to attack. None of her roommates showed any signs of aid. She stood, brushing off her backside. Taking a deep breath, she charged at Klurr, running straight into his fist, which landed directly in the midsection of her body. Flying backwards, she landed hard on the ground, but this time her opponent was already upon her. She clenched her eyes tight, fearing the worse. Nothing happened.

Opening one eye, she peered out. Kayleb had come to her defence and was fully engaging Klurr in combat. Holding her stomach with both her arms, she watched the elf fight in her place.

He saved her, but why? Was it really because they needed her to do well in their grades for the year?

"Can you stand?" Sebastian asked, trying to lift her to an upright position.

Once on her feet, she fell forward, catching hold of him to steady herself. Their eyes met. She could see the questions filling his head. Pushing away from his grasp, she turned her attention back to Kayleb still fighting Klurr. Their movements were swift and strong. It was like watching a form of art - beautiful yet deadly. The match was captivating and for a few moments she forgot about the other students, the pain, that this was only the first day of many she would spend enduring this class and that her disguise as a boy might have been compromised.

The two continued the battle without slowing until a chime rang out ending the classes for the day. Klurg separated Kayleb and Klurr, sending them back to their groups.

"Well," he said, "although that was a fine battle, I don't remember asking for you to attack, Kayleb. I am deducting one percent from your mark for the year from your group for that. Every time you help that worthless sack of potatoes, you will lose additional marks. To have any hope of passing you will need to stand back and watch. That shouldn't be too hard for you. It is the way of the elves, isn't it... to not bother yourself with the fates of other races."

Laughter erupted from Klurr's group as they walked away.

Willow turned to talk to Kayleb, but found he and the other elves in her group had already left. She was standing alone. The pain where she had been hit was foremost in her mind now. Her knees trembled, then began to shake harder as she lost control of them. They buckled beneath her and she keeled over, her arms outstretched to stop her head from smacking against the ground. She braced herself on her knees and arms before taking a few deep breaths in an attempt to negate the agony her body was feeling. It was useless. The blows she took were too strong for her body and she collapsed, wincing in pain as her bruised torso met the solid ground.

Managing to flip over, she lay, watching the clouds swirl above her in different patterns. The distraction was just enough to allow her to regain her composure and will to move again. Carefully standing, she slowly made her way back to the dormitories.

The elves were all sitting in the main room when she returned. She could feel energy draining away. Her face was as pale white as her wand instructor's had been.

Stopping for a moment, she looked up at Kayleb. “Thanks,” she said, before falling over in a limp pile on the floor. The world spun before her eyes. “Cassandrhea Tibbins” was the last thing she mumbled before everything went dark.

King Cornelius

The breakfast table contained all of the typical sweets and pastries his father adored. Taking his usual seat, Lance reached for a carafe of coffee and poured a cup. Sweet tasting delicacies had never tickled his taste buds. This morning the smell of custards, chocolates, and jams was overwhelming to his senses. He raised his cup of coffee and inhaled the robust aroma, trying to mask the sickly sweet scents.

"Good morning," Cornelius said, barely looking up from his overflowing plate of desserts. "You appear to be in a most foul mood today."

Lance glanced over at his father, scarfing down pastries and cakes as if he were an animal. He wasn't sure which nauseated him more, the food or the manner in which it was being ingested. He moaned. "Good morning." A lack of enthusiasm portrayed in his voice.

"Is that the best you can do for your king?" Cornelius asked, looking up from his plate.

Lance glanced over at his father again. His royal face was covered in the remains of the food he was eating, and had been for presumably for some time now. The prince coughed after forcing a bit of vomit back down his throat.

For the first time, he noticed how this lifestyle was affecting the king. Over the past few months, his royal weight had increased steadily. Their meals sometimes overlapped each other, with breakfast blending into lunch more often than not. His once active and charismatic father, passionate about righting wrongs, no longer existed. The man before him was almost a stranger... a madman more interested in indulging his desires than anything else. His body and mind were decaying with every ounce of sugar he ingested.

"My apologies," Lance said. "The boredom of late is affecting my emotions."

"It's affecting all of our emotions," Zoe said. "Can we not find a new world to conquer for you, my lord? There must be something you would like your children to do for you."

"We cannot continue our plan until we deal with that girl!" Cornelius yelled. "What is the status on her activities? Has she been killed yet?"

"Unfortunately, no," Joseph answered. "Our reports indicate she disappeared. We have assassins planted in every school and they all confirm the girl is not at any of them. Every group sent at least one person back to explain the situation. Apparently, the Director of Secrecy called them out and offered a way to leave the schools before classes began, without any consequence. He cited the girl's removal from the education system as a reason for them to comply with such a departure. Pewterclaw newspapers confirm that the girl was removed from enrolment in any school, fearing harm befalling other students. It isn't clear if the Directors have hidden her somewhere or not."

"How hard can it be to kill one girl?" Cornelius asked, shaking his head. Crumbs flew off his face, landing on the floor on either side of him.

"Maybe she returned to their camp." Zoe suggested.

"Not likely," Joseph answered. "There has been little activity from camp members since the school year started. Also, our allies have planted a spy in their ranks. If she was to return, we would know immediately."

"A spy?" Lance asked, still inhaling the rich smell of his coffee.

"Yes." A sly smile crept across Joseph's face. "It was easy, from what I heard. They created a fake vampire attack and made sure the news made the story larger than life, with only a couple of survivors in an entire town. It was too good for the do-gooders to pass up. They brought the spies to their camp and offered them refuge. When the girl returns, we will be in a position to dispose of her."

"You mean if she goes back," Lance said. He looked up from his cup to find all eyes of his family locked on him. "She has escaped all of our plans before. What makes you think she won't figure this one out?"

"Quite true, my boy," Cornelius said, laughing. "I think it's time for a *Plan B*, don't you?"

"Plan B?" Zoe said, slouching back in her chair.

"Yes," the king said. He reached into his pocket pulling out a vial of liquid and placing it on the table. "This is *Plan B*."

"What is it?" Zoe asked.

"The greatest minds we have collected over the years have been working non-stop to create this potion and now it looks like it is finally ready to test. It's a memory-changing potion. It allows the person administering it to control the memories of his victim."

"What do you mean, control?" Lance asked.

"I mean exactly what I said... control," Cornelius answered. "We can change how a person remembers events from the past. We can rewrite what they believe happened to them. With this potion, we will one day be in control of every living thing in every world and they will believe wholeheartedly that I... we are meant to lead them. But for now, we need to test it out. I wouldn't want to mass murder the very people we plan to rule one day."

"I am not sure I am following the plan," Ophelia said, speaking for the first time that morning.

“Of course, dear, it is a little complex for your grasp,” the king said. “It's simple, really... when explained correctly. I plan to alienate the girl from everything and everyone she holds dear. If we can't kill her, we will break her emotionally, so she won't have the will to oppose us.”

“You plan on rewriting the memories of everyone she knows?” Simon asked.

“Exactly.” Cornelius stood and snapped his fingers. “I plan to have Lance and Joseph take a large supply to our allies in Pewterclaw. They are to send enough to the spy in the guard camp to ensure the memories of every person have been altered. Her friends are to believe that the girl used magic on them to control them into believing in guardians. I want them to believe that girl to be a villain. I want them to loathe her as much as I do.” The king sat down again. “The rest of the potions are a reward to our allies for helping us. They can do with it what they choose.”

“I'm not sure exactly how this helps us,” Ophelia said in a soft voice. Her head remained in a bowed position, so that she would not have to make eye contact with the others at the table.

“Not sure?” Cornelius laughed. “Not sure. It's simple, my child. She won't be able to go to the camp anymore, since they will despise her. The news will spread that she is a fraud and of her dastardly deeds. She will fall out of grace with those currently harbouring her. They will doubt her and wonder if the girl is casting magic on them. The masses will hate her. She won't be able to show her face in any magical city.” Cornelius let out another loud laugh. His eyes sparkled with delight. “No friends... no allies... no home... no money... no prospects... nowhere safe to go... equals no problems for us. She will be broken and useless.”

“I have to admit,” Joseph said, rubbing the stubble of a beard on his face, “this plan has promise. It could work... that is, if the potion is as effective as you boast.”

“Regardless,” the king said, shrugging his shoulders. “The worst that can happen is anyone who takes it dies. That would eliminate her friends and allies quickly. Other people would think twice before helping her in the future as well. It's a win-win scenario for us.”

“When will we be delivering the potions?” Lance asked.

“The last of them are being packed as we speak. I would like to see you boys gone at the next available opening to the main world,” Cornelius said, shoving a turnover into his mouth.

“I suppose I should dress then. If you will excuse me,” Lance said, standing.

“Yes,” Joseph said. “I need to shave if we are going into public. I was so looking forward to seeing what a full beard would look like on me, too.” He sighed. “I will check the schedule for a main world opening and let you know, brother.”

“Very good, boys,” Cornelius said, waving his hand in the air. “Oh, and try not to mess this up.”

Lance headed to his room and picked out a perfect black suit with a navy blue shirt to wear. He paused for a moment, looking in the mirror. “Where are you, Willow?” he whispered. He washed his face with cold water. There was no time to try to contact her now. He would have to wait until later, when he fell asleep. Even then, he wasn't sure he could reach her. He changed into his suit.

“We need to hurry,” Joseph said, pounding on the other side of the bedroom door. “The next opening is in about thirty minutes. I don't want to miss it.”

Lance grabbed a pair of dark sunglasses and opened the bedroom door. “I'm ready,” he said. “I'll go arrange for the potions to become mobile. You still need that shave.” He smiled with his usual charm and pushed past his brother. “See you in thirty.”

Lance descended the castle stairs until he reached the laboratories. The door to the castle's clean room was open. Inside stood stacks of boxes. Opening one, he pulled out a vial of the potion from a neatly packed container. Each carried several hundred individual doses.

“Be careful there,” a voice rang out behind him.

Lance spun around. “Is something wrong?” he asked. “I was sent to arrange for the test potions that my father wants delivered to the main world. Are these them?" He pointed to the stacks of boxes.

"Sorry, my lord, I didn't recognize you from behind," a small man wearing a white lab coat said, bowing his head. "Yes, those are the test potions."

"Are we taking all of this?" the prince asked.

"Yes, that is what I was told."

"Oh dear," Lance said. "I doubt my brother and I can manage this many boxes. Would you please fetch some soldiers to carry them?"

"Of course," the man replied. "Please wait here. I will be right back." He disappeared out the door.

Lance reached in the box he had opened and removed several vials, placing them in the inside pocket of his suit jacket. After sealing the box, he leaned back against a wall, sunglasses covering his eyes. He folded his arms on his chest and waited.

"This way," the man said, returning.

"Ah good," Lance said to the soldiers that were summoned. "I need all of these boxes moved to the next main world opening. We will need you to accompany us through the gap as well."

Lance kept his position until all of the supply was taken. He then thanked the worker and followed the soldiers to their place of departure where his brother awaited him.

"I hadn't expected quite so many boxes," Joseph said.

"Neither did I," Lance replied. "We will have to take a few men with us to carry them. We can go to the usual drop spot in Pewterclaw. I will wait with the men and cargo, while you arrange for the pickup. If that is acceptable to you, that is."

"Let's all go together this time," his brother answered. "We both could use a good leg stretch. It feels as if we have been caged far too long. We will have a bit before we can return home. I was thinking I could use a new young lady in my life." He chuckled and slapped Lance on the back.

The space in front of the two princes began to move as if they were watching the heat come off a fire. It warped and twisted in different directions until a small hole appeared. A bright light shone through the opening, teasing them as it sent a glistening beam of brightness into their world. The stream danced around happily as it twisted and turned from the distorted space surrounding it. Gradually, the hole itself became larger, allowing an extended view of the main world. The fabric between the worlds surrounding the gap became stable again and movement stopped.

"Shall we, then?" Joseph asked, putting on his glasses. He lifted one leg and stepped through into a back street alley.

Lance followed his brother, arriving in time to see him throw a dagger at a homeless man lying under a few cardboard boxes beside a dumpster. The weapon landed directly in the centre of the man's forehead. Blood trickled down his face, colouring his grey beard red.

"Was he really that much of a threat?" Lance asked.

"Better safe than sorry," Joseph replied. "He could have been a spy watching for illegal entry into the city. We can't take any chances."

Lance glanced at the soldiers behind him. "This way," he said, using his hand to make a waving motion, signalling for them to follow. He stopped beside Joseph at the main road, which was bustling with people. "Well, you can't kill all of them."

His brother laughed. "I suppose not. But..." he said, pulling out his wand and waiving it around. "I can make them blind to our existence for a short while. Unless we interact with them, they will be oblivious to our presence."

It was a two-block walk from the alley to their first destination. The two princes walked side by side, their men in tow doing all of the heavy lifting. The citizens of Pewterclaw lining the streets paid no attention to their caravan, but still managed to move aside, so they could easily manoeuvre through the crowd. It was as if the princes had a negative magnetic force pushing people and animals away from them. They stopped at a news stand. Joseph picked up a copy of the day's newspaper.

"That one is a bit raggedy, sir," the stand keeper said with a bit of a lisp, caused by an extreme overbite.

The princes took turns examining the man. He was short and out of shape. The few hairs left on his head were combed over from one side, being held in place by grease. His shirt, which once might have been white, was now grey and stained, tan coloured overalls covering it in places.

"Might I suggest this one instead? I've kept it especially pristine for purchase by a gentleman like yourself." The shop keeper handed the copy to Joseph.

Lance offered the man a red gem as payment; happily, he moved away, giving them privacy. Joseph opened the paper to the middle section. Instead of the regular news, this edition had two white pages blemished only by a sole address.

"Right then," Joseph said. "Shall we continue?"

A fairly uneventful walk led them to a doorway in another alley. The door was unlocked, and once opened, revealed a staircase leading beneath the city. At the bottom was a dark tunnel. Lance lit blue flames in the palm of his hand, taking the lead.

The smell of rot and filth burnt his nostrils, making him long for the sweet smells he had found so disgusting earlier. He pulled a crisp handkerchief from his pocket, covering his nose and mouth. The tunnel only led in one direction, with all manner of insects and rodents lining the floor and walls.

After walking for some time, they came to a few steps up and a platform blocked by iron bars.

"Drop them here, boys," Joseph said. "Then head back out."

After the soldiers had left, Joseph opened one of the boxes. He pulled out a vial of liquid and held it up. "Strange to think how dangerous this little bottle could be, isn't it?"

Lance reached in and pulled out a couple of vials. "I have been considering keeping a couple of these as well," he said, smiling.

"Do you think he'd actually do it?" his brother asked.

"For the devoted attention from his children, I believe he would sell our souls," Lance replied, still staring at the fluid within the tiny bottles. "I have no doubt, once the tests results are successful, there will be a vial with both our names on it."

"Your plan?" Joseph asked.

"Same as you, I would imagine. I will have my contacts try to come up with an antidote before that day arrives." Lance smiled at his brother as he put the vials in his pocket. "If they are successful, I will make sure there is extra for my siblings. I trust you will afford me the same courtesy."

Joseph reached in and took a few extra bottles. "Agreed, brother. Shall we find our way out of this awful place?"

"You read my mind," Lance replied, laughing. "There should be enough time left to share a bottle of wine with a pretty young lady before we head home... as well as whatever else you might like to share with her."

"Now you are reading mine, brother. I'll take the suite on Sixth Avenue if you don't mind. I am partial to the view." Joseph stepped off the platform and began the walk back through the tunnel without the aid of any light.

"I am fine with the room on Lowrey. I have a few connections to try to contact while I am here as well. I don't want to put off our project any longer than necessary." Lance flicked sparks of necrid flames at a few large bugs along the way back, smiling at each as they withered in pain before their lives were exhausted.

"True," Joseph called back. "I don't suppose we will be given many chances to escape to another world. It would be easier if there was a way other than physical to send these little bottles to someone outside our world for analysis. Perhaps in a dream."

Lance freeze on the spot. That comment hit home. Did his brother know about Willow and her unusual dreamwalking talents? He laughed as if he had just heard a joke. "If you know of a way, fill me in, would you?" he said as they emerged from the tunnel back into the alley again.

"Four hours, then?" Joseph asked.

“Back at the alley,” Lance replied. “You men,” he yelled to the soldiers. “Take this as an informal leave and have some fun in town. Stay out of controversy and trouble, but have a good time.” He turned to see his brother walking away already, waving his hand in the air to motion goodbye.

Lance chuckled, heading in the opposite direction. Rather than looking for company, he headed to the room and flopped down on the bed. He closed his eyes and drifted into a dreamworld. He searched dream after dream for any trace of Willow, but found none.

He opened his eyes and sat up. “Willow, where are you?” he asked. Standing, he pulled a vial from his pocket to examine the liquid again. “Find a way to dreamwalk soon. More is riding on your shoulders now than ever before.”

Chapter Nine

Willow opened her eyes and glanced around. She was lying on a bed in a room she didn't recognize. From past experiences, she knew better than to try to move quickly. Closing her eyes again, she remembered the combat class. Instinctively, she grabbed her stomach. The pain was gone.

"You have been here for... a while," Cassandrhea said, moving close to the bed. "It was good that you asked for me just before you passed out. I wouldn't try to move too fast, you took quite a nasty hit. I have spoken to Instructor Klurg and it shouldn't be a problem in the future."

"Did anyone notice?" Willow asked. "I mean, does anyone know I'm not a boy?"

"I don't think so," the Director answered. "You will need to exercise extreme caution from now on, though, as it is possible some from your group may suspect something isn't quite right."

"I don't know how much more cautious I can be," Willow said, slowly sitting up.

"Much more cautious. We have a spy in our midst." Cassandrhea pulled a chair beside the bed and sat down. "You'll want to read these," she said, placing a few newspapers on the bed. "When you feel better, I suggest you read the whole paper. For now, I will summarize. The first paper has a picture taken of the Director of Secrecy within the school grounds. The story goes on to say that he declared you were not on the grounds, but are rather on the loose and dangerous."

"Dangerous," Willow repeated, grabbing the paper.

"Yes," Cassandrhea said. "I think you may be missing the bigger issue. Whoever took the picture is here at Sleeping Sands and they are not your friend. We don't know how they smuggled the picture and story out of the school. It should be impossible. If this person gets wind of your true identity and prints it, you will be in a world of danger."

"You make it sound like people hate me more than before," Willow said, looking up from the paper. "Do they hate me more than before?"

Cassandrhea sighed. "The next paper is a complete issue on you. It seems your friends who remained at the camp have turned against you."

Willow grabbed the second paper and read the headline *Guardians Do Not Exist: We Were Under a Spell.* "I don't understand," she said.

"There are interviews with each of your peers. Each one says that since you left the camp, they have been released from your magic grasp. They denounce the existence of any guardians and say you were behind each of the incidents you claimed to be stopping. You used them and others to make yourself look the part of the heroine with an agenda to take over Pewterclaw. They make a strong case right down to the reason for you not returning to the camp after being withdrawn from the education system being the loss of your hold over them."

"These have to be lies. They never would have said such things," Willow said, holding back tears threatening to fall.

"I am afraid not. Kasper confirmed the stories himself. The worst being the camp leader's testimony that you led the attack on him that left him for dead."

"William?!" Willow screamed. "He's awake?" She covered her mouth with her hand. "Thank goodness." She didn't know whether to jump for joy or cry.

"Did you hear me?" Cassandrhea asked. "He is saying horrible things about you. Horrible and believable."

"Do you believe them?" she asked.

The Director glanced in her direction and took a big breath in, then let it out. "No," she said. "But if you weren't here right now... if I hadn't been to the camp myself... if I hadn't spent time with you... I would believe every written word."

"But you don't," Willow said.

"I am only one person, Willow. It won't make a difference what I think. Everyone is against you now, even Kasper and the other Directors," Cassandrhea said.

"It makes a difference to me," Willow said, the tears flowing freely down her face, dripping off her chin. "To know there is at least one person who knows the truth and believes in me gives me hope that maybe others can see and learn to trust me as well."

"My child," Cassandrhea said, "you will need to keep your disguise for longer than we anticipated under the circumstances. Outside these walls, I cannot protect you."

"Can I keep these?" Willow asked, pointing to the newspapers. "I don't think I can go through them all at once. It might be a bit emotional for me."

"Of course," the Director answered. "You should get ready to return to your room now. You have missed far too many classes that you will need to make up." She headed to the door and paused as she put one hand on the doorknob. "Oh, I should mention one thing. Your friend William, I know you were close to him. It seems he has taken a wife. You'll find the information in the third paper."

Willow didn't even notice the woman leave. She sat stunned, staring at the wall, the words *taken a wife* running through her mind over and over. How was that possible? Who would he have married? She flipped the third newspaper open to a picture of

William and someone she had never seen before. The story told of how the woman, named Lara, had been a victim of a vampire attack and came to live in William's camp. Once there, she felt the need to give back to her new family, taking up nurse's duty in the medical centre. It was there she saw William for the first time. Falling in love with him instantly, she tended to his every need while he remained unconscious. When he first opened his eyes, it was clear the feeling was mutual. She continued looking after him until he was strong enough to move around on his own again. Only a day after leaving the hospital, she learnt the customs of his world and recited the Pledge to him. He accepted. The article went on to state their love was a gift amongst the chaos *that girl* created.

Willow rubbed her temples. Besides being upset and confused, there was something else that bothered her about the articles. Something she just couldn't put her finger on. Until she regained control of her emotions, nothing was going to make sense. The shock of all this news overwhelmed her senses, rending them useless. She needed to head back to her room - to Aslo and Kiera. Maybe they could help her to understand what was going on.

The whole way back to her dormitory, Willow never once looked up. Dressed in costume again, she strolled across the campus, the newspapers tucked neatly under her arm. Her mind filled with questions and her heart ached a little more with every one she thought of.

Walking into the living quarters was no different. With her head down, she crossed the room without noticing anything or anyone.

"Will," Sebastian said. "Are you okay?"

All four elves watched her head straight towards her room in silence.

"Will!" Sebastian yelled.

Willow stopped at her door. "Sorry, did someone say something?" she asked.

"We just wondered if everything was okay," Sebastian answered. The four elves exchanged glances with each other.

“Fine,” she lied. “Everything is fine. I need to prepare to return to classes tomorrow.” Willow opened her door, slamming it behind her.

She dropped the newspapers on her bed flopping down beside them. Lying on her back. Her gaze fixed on the ceiling.

“Are you going to lie there forever?” Aslo asked.

Willow sat up and hugged him tightly, tears forming in her eyes. “I am so glad to see you. You have no idea. Aslo, I am so lost,” she said.

“Oh dear, perhaps this is a situation for a few more of us to handle,” Aslo said. Kiera, Shelby, Nero, Tika, Decon and Jawfree joined Aslo on the bed with her.

Willow's green-blue eyes lacked their usual luster, with only the red speckles in them standing out. Tiny pools of liquid formed in their corners. Suddenly, as if a dam opened, tears rushed to escape, forming a waterfall of sorrow cascading down her face.

“Now, now, dear,” Shelby said, dropping a box of tissues in her lap. “Tell us what has happened.” She glanced at the window watching storm clouds rolling in.

Willow blurted it all out, from the boy who beat her up and her inability to attack, to the newspaper articles about all of the camp hating her and ended with William waking up and taking a wife. The guardians sat and listened.

“It must be a mistake,” Tika said. “William would not have done that. He couldn't have pledged to a woman he just met. These are lies.”

“They aren't.” Willow used a tissue from the box and blew her nose. “The testimonies were all verified before this issue went into print.” She picked up the newspaper again and looked at it. “The articles were written by Jax Quidnunk, owner and senior reporter for T*he Empowered*. It was published on...” Willow's words faded. “Have I been out of it for over three weeks?” she asked.

“It has been a while, dear. We were worried, but that woman seemed to be taking good care of you,” Kiera said.

Willow flopped back on the bed again and let out a loud groan. "What am I going to do?"

"I do hate to be the bearer of more bad news, but," Nero said, "if the camp has turned against you, as it appears it has, you need to revoke some of their abilities."

"You have to be kidding," Willow said, sitting back up. "Can I even do that from here?"

"We don't know, but it might be best if you tried," Aslo said. "I know it seems cold, but if things work out, you can always make them portal guards again."

"All of them?" Willow asked, tears falling from the corners of her eyes again. "Faramund, Zsiga, Mike, William, Sarah... everyone?"

"Yes, everyone at the camp," Aslo answered. "We can't take any chances. Things are going to be hard enough as it is without dealing with that lot having extra abilities."

Willow closed her eyes and took a deep breath in, letting it out again. She counted out loud backwards from ten, controlling her emotions and breathing with each number. When she reached the number one, her body glowed a golden aura. Her hands folded together as if praying. A moment later, the aura disappeared and she opened her eyes.

"It's done," she said, followed by a sniffle. Willow picked up another tissue and blew her nose again. "How did this happen? Is it magic? Do they really hate me?"

"We don't know what happened yet," Kiera said, rubbing against her. "But I have a feeling we will find out before everything is over."

"You should put these newspapers away for now and concentrate on catching up what you have missed." Aslo nudged her hand towards the copies of *The Empowered* sprawled out across the bed. "Once you are stronger, we can take the time to go over the articles in detail and look for clues as to what affected our friends."

Willow grabbed the papers and added them to the others she had hidden at the back of her closet in a backpack. Then she crawled into bed without even changing. Her guardian friends cuddled around her for comfort until she fell asleep.

Chapter Ten

Potions class was as difficult as Willow expected after missing more than three weeks of classes. The other students had finished with the theory part of the course and were already working with hands-on potion making.

"Today," Professor Finkle said. "we are going to work on our first complex potion. I want each of your groups to create a potion of remembrance. A completed potion is one which will boost the memory of the person drinking it to the point of remembering scenes from when they were first born. Keep in mind, a member of your group will have to test your finished product and we do not want any unnecessary deaths or long absences." He looked directly at Willow. "You have the next three classes to produce your best concoction. This will count as twenty percent of your mark."

"Think I'll pass on being the guinea pig, if you guys don't mind," Willow said.

"I may have mentioned it before," Kayleb said, "we aren't guys."

"Sorry," she responded. "If you *elves* don't mind."

"We had no intention of making you the taste tester, so relax," Seth said while mixing liquids in test tubes.

“What are those?” Willow asked.

“These are different types of waters,” Seth answered. “We have a tap water, rain water, spring water, lake water, sea water, pond water and swamp water. It is believed that a balanced mix of each type is the best base to begin any potion in.”

“In other words, a potion that relies on just one form of water theoretically is less effective than one that combines all,” Kayleb added.

“Is there proof of that?” Willow asked.

“Not definitive proof, but it can't hurt to mix them.” Sebastian smiled at her. “Just in case.”

“So once we have... water,” Willow said with a sarcastic tone, “what else do we add?”

“That,” Finkle said from behind her, “is the purpose of this class. You need to figure out what to use. Let's do an exercise.” He put his hands on Willow's shoulders. “Close your eyes and take a deep breath in. Now, let it out while clearing your mind of everything but my voice. I want you to think of the word *memory*... not anything but the word. Once you have the word spelt out in your mind in big letters, I want you to imagine everyday things flowing into the word. It can be a smell, a flower, a part of an animal, anything. I want you to blurt out the items as you see them, no matter how strange they may appear.”

“Two drops of the wax of a yellow candle, green tea extract, blueberries, periwinkle seeds, penny-wort, rhodiola and the contents of four pixie sticks,” Willow said.

“Pixie sticks?” Seth asked.

“A sugary delight created by the terunji. They are quite nice. Each stick appears as a tube which contains different flavoured sugar powders,” Finkle said. “I believe you can buy some in the school store if you hurry.”

“As ridiculous as it sounds,” Sebastian said, “I will go buy the candy.” He smiled at Willow again. “Just in case.”

“Excellent,” the professor exclaimed. “I knew you were a natural from the moment we met. Now that you are better, you should spend some time with those windows. I find answers become clearer when we concentrate on what is directly before us.”

She looked over at the stained glass pictures and then back to Finkle. “Professor,” she said, “if we can make a potion to enhance memories, is it possible to make one that allows another person to change or control our memories?”

The three elves remaining at the table looked up from their work to hear the answer.

“Possible?” Finkle said. “Yes, I suppose it could be. It would be an extremely difficult potion to create and very dangerous, not to mention most definitely illegal. Why do you ask?”

“No reason, really,” she said. Seeing the looks her group and teacher were giving her she decided to make up a story very quickly. “It's silly,” she continued. “My aunt used to babysit me when I was little. She sometimes wasn't very nice and threatened me, so I wouldn't tell my parents. She always carried this little vial of liquid with her that she claimed would make me forget everyone I knew. She said she could then recreate my background as an orphan. I would never know the difference. It had me petrified for years. I was just wondering if that little vial could have actually been what she claimed it was.”

“My boy,” Finkle said, “your aunt sounds horrible. Although it is possible, I highly doubt there was anything more than a little bit of moonshine in that vial. In my opinion, it would take a team of the brightest minds in this field to develop such a potion. I highly doubt that many smart people would be breaking the law for your aunt. Think of the horrible implications if such a potion existed. You best not worry about such things now and concentrate on your work. Twenty percent of your mark!” He walked away to another group.

Sebastian returned with a lunch-sized paper bag filled with powdered sugar sticks. “Does it matter what flavour?” he asked.

“I think any four will do,” Seth said, reaching into the bag to take four. “Why did you buy so many?”

"I tried one before I came back. They are good." Sebastian took one from the bag, ripped open the bottom, and after tilting his head back, poured the powder into his mouth.

Willow laughed. "I can't believe I just saw that."

"What?" Sebastian asked. "Just because I am an elf doesn't mean I can't enjoy tasty treats. I have a sweet tooth." He smiled and held out the bag. "Want one?"

Kayleb took one from the bag. He placed a little bit of the powder on his finger and licked it cautiously. "Not bad," he said. He poured small amounts into his mouth until the tube was empty.

Willow watched with fascination. "Do you have things like this in your world?" she asked.

"No," Seth answered without looking up from the potion he was working on. "Hand me a lid that will fit this beaker. This needs to sit until tomorrow."

Gabriel handed him a lid marked with their group number and helped him pack up their work to be stored by Professor Finkle. They had just placed it safely in storage when the end of class chime rang out.

"Everyone bring your potions over, please," Finkle bellowed out. "Quickly now, you don't want to be late for your next class."

"So... Botany," Willow said as they left the potions class. "Anything I need to be filled in on?"

"No need to worry about that class," Gabriel said. "You had already completed the year's work before it even started. Elves have a certain connection with nature... an empathy towards plants and animals that others don't have. We have caught up to you."

"Greenfoot gave us all a perfect mark and we don't have to attend class anymore," Sebastian added. "That means we have spare time to work on something else."

"Well," Willow said, "next would be Wand Magic. How is that going?" She looked at each of their faces. "That good, huh?"

“We haven't quite mastered the techniques behind wand use yet,” Kayleb answered. “There is something lacking in the strength of our magic after it filters into the wand. We have read all the books and we are correctly duplicating the procedures suggested.”

“Let's start there,” Willow said. “We will need an empty field and several iron pipes. Perhaps Tara might have a few for practice.”

At first, Willow thought that the hall where their wand classes were held was empty. The lights were off and from what she could see the room was deserted. “Hello,” she called, almost jumping three feet backwards when she received a reply.

“Hello,” Tara answered. “You seem surprised I greeted you back. I do believe it is the normal response in most cultures.”

“Yes,” Willow said. “I hadn't thought anyone was in here.”

Tara frowned. “So why did you say hello?”

Willow was completely thrown off by the question. “I'm not sure. Habit, maybe? Perhaps a combination of things. I didn't want to be rude and surprise someone if they were in here.”

“Interesting,” Tara said. “You five are early.”

“We were hoping you might have iron or lead pipes that we could practice on,” Kayleb said.

“Of course,” Tara said. “I was just heading off to run a few errands before our class, so feel free to practice in here as well. No one will disturb you.” She turned on the lights and pointed to a wooden box filled with pipes sitting in the middle of the room. “What you need is in there. Good luck.”

Willow smiled. “Luck,” she said, reaching to feel the charm on her necklace through her the shirt. Bringing it, wasn't the best idea. There weren't many boys willing to wear a pink heart-shaped locket no matter who gave it to them or how lucky it was.

“Do you think she knew we were coming?” Sebastian asked, picking up a lead pipe from the box.

“I think she presumed that we would need Will's help and now that he is better, we would be by to practice,” Kayleb replied. “Still, I have no idea how she knew we were going to ask for those pipes to practice on."

"Short of asking her, we aren't going to ever find out," Willow said. "Let's get started. I want you to cut a pipe in half using only your wand." She set a pipe down on the ground in front of each of them.

The elves exchanged glances before pulling out their wands and aiming them at the pipes. A stream of light exploded from the tip of each wand.

After several minutes, Willow yelled, "Stop!" She examined each of the pipes and let out a disgruntled moan. "They are barely scratched," she said. "The thing you are missing is emotion. Before you protest, I already know elves do, in fact, have emotions. You just don't show them. Correct?"

Kayleb nodded in agreement.

"The good thing is, you don't have to show your emotions to anyone to master the wand. Mix emotions into the magic and then direct your wand as to what to do with it." She looked at each of their faces. "Sebastian," she said. "Give it a try."

Sebastian aimed his wand at the pipe. This time, the pipe dented and scratched.

"Good," Willow said. "Now, remember the stronger and more complicated the emotion, the more effective the magic."

"More complicated?" Gabriel asked.

"Yes," Willow answered. "For instance, you have a friend who is dating a girl and he really likes her. You fall in love with her. That emotion is complicated. It isn't just love. It's guilt for wanting your friend's girlfriend. It's jealousy because your friend has the girl you want. It's desire for the girl you want. It's envy. It's hate. It's love. It's fear. There are many emotions that connect to that one event. If you take something like that and direct it into your magic, the effect will be enormous."

"I think I understand," Sebastian said. He aimed his wand at the pipe and this time, it snapped in two. "Amazing," he said. "It's actually quite simple once you grasp the concept."

It took Kayleb and Gabriel several tries, but each managed to find an emotion strong enough to cut through the pipe.

"Seth," Willow said. "You need something stronger." She stood behind him and placed her hands on his shoulders. "I know this is uncomfortable for you, but close your eyes and think of something that made you angry or terrified you. If it combines both of those feelings, even better. Once you find it, hold on to that feeling. Do you have something in mind?"

Seth nodded.

"Good, now open your eyes, point your wand, and send all that you are feeling into your wand." Willow took two steps back.

Seth pointed his wand and a brilliant white force escaped from the tip. The pipe before him glowed an orange-red colour for a moment and then it exploded. All that was left was a few ash remains, floating down from the ceiling over the spot where the pipe once was.

"Maybe a little less emotion," Willow said, looking at the small pile of ashes that formed on the floor in front of the elf. "Looks like you all have the right idea. A few practices and this class will be a breeze."

They continued practising, using the pipes in the wooden box, until it was empty. The floor was littered with small pieces.

"You will have to clean that up," Tara ordered.

"Sorry," Willow said. "We didn't see you come in. Have you been there long?"

"Long enough to be impressed by the progress you have made in such a short time," Tara said. "Have you considered a career in teaching?"

"I haven't thought that far ahead yet," Willow answered.

“Well, you should.” Tara turned her attention to the elves. “A little more practice and you won't need any further instruction from myself.”

The end-of-class chime rang and moments later, students began filing into the room. Klurr led his group to the teacher's side. His eyes bulged out of their sockets at the sight of Willow. “Back from the dead, are you? You just remember who put you there. I did it once and I can do it again.”

Willow stepped back behind the rest of her group, her legs trembling. In reality, there was nothing for her to fear. Her injuries were a result of attempting to attack. She was more than capable of defending herself.

Sebastian stepped forward. “I believe it's my turn today, Klurr.”

Laughter roared from deep inside Klurr's body, making a noise loud and hideous enough to cause the other students in the room to move as far away from him as possible. “If you choose to protect the pretty boy, know this, I won't have pity on the likes of an elf who wants to play hero.”

“I didn't ask you to,” Sebastian said, his wand clenched tight in the grasp of his left hand. “Shall we get on with it?”

“If you are in that much of a hurry to spend time in a medical centre, I won't make you wait,” Klurr said, raising his hand to an attack position.

A wave of magic exploded from the tip of both wands. The silver stream of energy and magic Sebastian created tore easily through Klurr's red wave of power and knocked him to the ground. His face turned five shades of red darker as he emitted smoke from his flaring nostrils. He jumped to his feet and attacked again. This time, his friends joined in. Magical power flew through the air in every direction. Kayleb moved to Sebastian's side aiding in the raging battle, with Gabriel and Seth taking flanking positions.

Willow glanced around the room. This fight between their two groups was beyond out of control. She looked to their instructor, Tara, for help, but she was preoccupied with dodging magic that had been deflected in her direction. The situation became more dangerous. A young girl trying to run for the exit was hit and thrown up against a wall. Her body came crashing back down to the floor and lay motionless in a pile.

Willow had seen enough. Raising her wand in the air, she yelled, "Stop!" A bright white light flowed from the tip of her wand, creating an umbrella shape dome over the room. Streams of magic froze where they were.

"Thank you, Will," Tara said, weaving her way carefully under, over and around beams of different coloured magics that blocked her way to the centre of the room. "Wands," she said. "Quickly now, I want everyone's wands in my hand, except Will."

The students took turns handing over their wands to their teacher and returning to their groups, Klurr and Sebastian being the last to comply.

"After I have your wand, please step outside until I come for you," Tara instructed, waiting for all the students to exit before speaking again. "This is impressive. I am not sure what it is exactly, but very effective. Question is now, what are we going to do with all of this power?"

Willow closed her eyes and concentrated on the energy of the room. Particles began breaking off from the frozen streams of magic. A rainbow of colours in tiny specks began flying through the air and joining in with the umbrella like shield that was holding them in place.

"Amazing," Tara exclaimed, watching the light show. "You're absorbing the power into your own. A student of your level should never be able to achieve such a feat. Who are you?"

The umbrella disappeared. Willow and Tara were now the only two left in the room. "I'm afraid I don't know what you mean. I'm Will," she said, shrugging her shoulders.

"Well, Will, your group has no need to be in this class for the rest of the year. I am giving you a perfect score," the small-framed teacher said. "However, I am deducting five percent for the lack of control exercised by your elf companions." She let out a high-pitched laugh. "I never thought I would have to say that in my lifetime."

The expression on her face mutated quickly to one which appeared more robotic, lacking all emotion. “There is something different about you, Will. The teachers all sense it. I don't know what you came here for, but you better find it and leave. People are watching. Not everyone wants to save the world in the same way.”

It took only a moment for the students to file back into the room once fetched by their teacher. They all stood silently, every eye locked on Willow.

“I think we owe Will a bit of thanks for stopping that mess. Don't you?” Tara asked, her usual smile illuminating her soft delicate features. Willow couldn't help but notice the upward curve of her lips slightly recede when their eyes met. “You can share the good news with your group,” the teacher said. “Congratulations on finishing this class with honours. Good luck with your other subjects.”

Kayleb led the group outside. “What happened?” he asked.

“She gave us a perfect score and deducted five percent for the mess today. That's it. She claims there is nothing more she can teach us.” Willow said.

“That's it?” Kayleb demanded. “Why does it always feel like there is something you aren't telling us? We are a team. Maybe it's time you let us in on the secret you are hiding.”

Willow sighed. “I suppose you have told me everything?” she asked. “Perhaps you could share a lesson or two on elf history or culture?”

“That is different,” Seth replied.

“Different how?” she asked.

“Because our secrets won't get anyone hurt,” Sebastian said.

“I am not sure I agree with you. What if, locked deep inside your history, was the answer to saving the world?” Willow said. “Besides, believe it or not, Klurr's hate for me has nothing to do with any secret I might have. He really just hates me.” She pushed through the four elves, walking ahead of them to Greenfoot's garden to pick some fruit for lunch.

Sitting under a tree, Willow closed her eyes and thought back to her home world. Things had been hard then, but there was still a certain happiness she missed. Spending time with her best friends, Clairity and Ashlyn... Diana's storytelling... Dezi's silly jokes... it was all so much simpler and all gone. A tear slowly cascaded down her face as she realized she would never experience those things again. Her thoughts were broken by a tissue in front of her face.

"Is it that bad?" Sebastian asked.

Willow took the tissue he was offering. "You have no idea," she answered. "Thanks." She lifted the tissue to wipe her eyes, shook her head and took a few deep breaths in and out. "I'm good now," she said.

"Seems you have more in common with the elves than you care to admit," Sebastian said, taking a bite out of a shiny red apple. Before she could ask, he explained. "You hide your emotions well, your magic is at the level elves are believed to be at and you have secrets you aren't willing to trust anyone with. Then there is that whole not asking for help thing."

Willow laughed. "You make things sound so simple."

"No," Sebastian said, examining the apple in his hand. "It's not simple. Not for you... not for me... for Kayleb... not for Seth... not for Gabriel. But maybe we could learn to trust each other."

"What happened to the stop being friends after the school year talk?" Willow asked.

"It's not that we want that," Sebastian said. "We accepted long ago that making friends with people from other places was not feasible. We don't leave our world often and outsiders aren't welcome by our elders to visit us. Then there is the age factor. Elves age slowly... very slowly. Most people we meet have passed on before we have a chance to return to see them."

"I understand," Willow said. "For me, it's the opposite. I want friends and loved ones in my life and they always leave. I think maybe I am not destined to have anyone in my life I care about. Fate can be cruel."

“I wish I could say things would be different, but at the end of school, all four of us will be returning home. The odds of us ever meeting again are none. That's why we have kept our distance,” Sebastian explained. He stood up and looked at the three other elves. “You should know, regardless of what happens, we do think of you as our friend. When you are ready, we need to head over to practice elementals. You have some catching up to do. We'll be waiting in the arena.”

Willow took a few moments to collect her thoughts and calm her emotions. At least the skies hadn't opened up, raining down on them. Still, her head was spinning with the events of the day. As grateful as she was for Sebastian's words, they meant little to her, other than that more people would be exiting her life in the near future. There was no way she would involve any of them in her mess. Anyone who helped her always ended up hurt themselves. That was something she was determined to never let happen again.

As she stepped down the final stair into the stone arena, her attention radiated to the auras of magic coming from each of the elves.

“You need to get started if you are going to catch up,” Kayleb said as if nothing had happened earlier. “Can you try water magic?”

“I don't know how,” Willow said.

“Same as your air magic, just concentrate on water,” Sebastian said, moving out of the way.

Willow stared intensely at the water sitting in the bucket before her. Nothing happened. She moved closer. Clearing her mind, she closed her eyes and directed her entire focus on water. The clouds she had just finished silencing began to swirl. This time, drops of rain began to fall.

“Did you just make it rain?” Sebastian enquired. “We are all going to be soaked.”

Willow laughed. “You call yourselves elemental masters. What is rain?” she asked. “It's water! So use your abilities and make the rain move so that it doesn't hit you.” She raised her arms and the rain fell harder, without a single drop hitting her.

Sebastian held out a hand and smiled. He began moving raindrops around and connecting them together to make a larger stream of liquid in the air. "As fun as this is," he said, "I am not sure this is helping you any. You need to be able to make a plasma ball for us to graduate from this class."

The rain stopped instantly. "Show me one," Willow said.

Seth held out a hand, perfectly balancing a ball of energy filled with swirling elemental magic. "I don't see how this is going to help you. You need to know how to make the parts before you can put together a finished product," he said.

"Can elves see auras?" she asked, walking around Seth while examining the energy mass he was holding.

"Of course," Gabriel answered.

"What kinds?" Willow asked.

"What do you mean?" Gabriel asked back. "Everything living has an energy signature that can be seen as an aura."

"I don't see those," she said. "I can only see the auras of magic. Every different type has a unique signature that I can see." She ran her hand through the aura surrounding the plasma ball, "and feel. That is what is different about me. Now you know one of my secrets."

"How does that help you?" Seth asked.

"This particular energy I have felt and seen before." She lifted her hands up to the sky again and clouds swirled a single bolt of lightning came flying down. Rather than creating damage, the energy from the lightning bolt swirled into a circle in Willow's hands. She walked over to Seth and held the two balls next to each other. "Pure energy," she said. "They are identical."

"What does that mean?" Seth asked.

"It means," Miss Kelly said, "that the elements and nature are one and by extension, magic and nature are one... interchangeable, even. Quite the lesson to learn for your group at such a young age." She walked forward and swirled her staff in the air, creating a gust of wind. "I knew when I first met you, Will, that your magic was different. You were already using nature to fuel your air magic. But this is far beyond even my expectation. I believe your understanding of magic reaches further than anyone I have taught before. So that leaves the question, why are you here?"

"I have learnt more here than I have in the rest of my life combined," Willow said. "I may have come here with ability, but I hope to leave with a complete understanding of that ability. That is what I am here for."

"An excellent answer. I expected no less," Miss Kelly said. "Everything happens for a reason. The same aura that you see connecting magic also binds our lives together. You should be careful, child, for there are some who are cutting those ties as we speak. Learn what you can... find your answers... but do it quickly. Time is passing." She looked up at the sky. "The moon shines in your favour this evening. Your classes with me have come to an end. Even as an elemental master, I can teach you nothing more. I will submit your final marks to the Director this evening." She turned and smiled in Willow's direction. "Good luck, my dear, and remember, there are those who can help you if you need it."

The last course of the day was also the most frightening. Willow found her legs trembling to the point of almost falling several times during the walk to combat class. For some reason, Willow believed Cassandrhea's sanctioning of Klurg's behaviour would end up in a further attempt to inflict pain on her body. Even if it wasn't the actions of the teacher himself, his son Klurr most definitely could be expected to toss a few punches her way.

"Well, look who's back," Klurg scoffed. "I hope you enjoyed your vacation."

Klurr laughed. "You might end up right back there again."

"I believe I am allowed to practice defence in this class. The requirement for me to attack has been lifted by the Director herself," Willow replied, masking the shakiness of her voice.

"The Director," Klurg laughed. "The Director of Knowledge isn't here now, is she? I don't plan on letting a little runt like you get away with making me or any member of my family look bad," Klurg said. "If any student here reports I have been anything but lenient on you or that the injuries that you will sustain here today were anything but an accident, I will fail them. That goes for you and your group as well, boy."

"KLURG!" Cassandrhea yelled. "I believe you are in direct conflict with your contract here at Sleeping Sands. I am forced to immediately relieve you of your teaching duties." She waved her hand and Professor Finkle and Mr. Greenfoot appeared to escort Klurg away. "Take him to my office please, where I will further deal with this issue." She looked around at the students. "What to do with the lot of you now," she said, "so close to the end of the term. It's a shame." A smile crept up over her face as she opened the teacher's notes and read them. "It seems everyone was doing well in this class. Therefore it only seems fitting that you all graduate with honours in combat. This course is complete for all of you. Enjoy your spare time while you can. A new term is only around the corner."

Chapter Eleven

Willow opened her eyes and sat up. It was still early, but she couldn't sleep. Every day that passed meant new questions that remained unanswered in her mind. There were so many different paths to explore, but none of them seemed to connect. She flopped back, tossing a pillow over her head.

"That bad?" Aslo asked.

Willow peeked out from behind the pillow. "Everything keeps getting more confusing. There are so many odd things all around me and I know they fit together in some way," she whined. "I just don't know how." She tossed the pillow across the room, sitting up again.

"You need to sit somewhere that relaxes you and concentrate on finding the answers," Aslo said. "I always liked to watch butterflies fluttering in a field. Watching them would always bring me solace and help me find what I was looking for."

"I have heard that before somewhere," Willow said.

"Butterflies, really?" Aslo asked.

"No, not the butterflies," she answered. "The staring at something to find answers." She paused for a moment, chewing on the nail of her thumb. “Professor Finkle!” she exclaimed. “He said the stained glass had that power.”

“Stained glass?” Aslo asked.

“Yes, in the potions class the windows are all stained glass pictures. I think I should go take a closer look at them.” She jumped out of bed and put on her look-like-a-boy disguise, barely giving Aslo enough time to rejoin with her before rushing out the door.

The campus was empty and the potions room was no different. She would have about an hour before students and teachers began roaming about getting ready for the day. The sun was rising and shone dim light through the windows making the stained glass scenes stand out in the dark room. Willow stood and examined each carefully. There were several symbols from not just the terunji world, but all different worlds. Each one appeared to be in a certain position. She closed her eyes and rubbed her temples.

“Pretty, aren't they?” Sebastian asked.

Willow jumped. “Sebastian, you frightened me. What are you doing here so early?” she asked.

“Early?” he asked back. “Class is in fifteen minutes. I came to set up.”

“I guess I lost track of time,” she said, turning her attention back to the windows. “I wish there was a way I could keep their images, so I could look at them later.”

Sebastian looked at her out of the corner of his eye. “Really,” he said, laughing. “You mean like a picture?”

“Yes,” she answered. “Exactly. Do you know how to do that?”

“Yeah,” he said, taking out a cell phone. “What do you want?”

“You have a cell phone?” she asked.

“I think the question should be *you don't?*” he replied. “All elves are required to keep a cellular device on them while outside our realm... for emergencies. Although I admit it is rather useless here, it can have benefits in the main world.”

She sighed. “I need a picture of the whole window for each, in a way that I can make it bigger without distorting the original image.” Willow chomped on her thumbnail again.

“I will try my best,” he said. “What's this for, anyways?”

“I'm actually not sure. I think there is a hidden message in the pictures. It's as if they link together somehow... a mystery of sorts. Since I have extra time, I thought I would look into it,” Willow answered.

“Sounds interesting,” Sebastian said. “I'll print these off as large as possible after class.” He tossed his phone in the air, catching it on the way back down. “Perhaps I can help you solve your little mystery.”

Willow snapped her head sideways to meet his stare. “A nice offer,” she said. “But when I start sleuthing, people around me tend to get hurt. You are better off staying out of it.”

“Even more intriguing,” he said with a glimmer of mischief in his eyes. “Besides, I am already involved. I took the pictures.” He laughed and headed to the laboratory section of the room to set up.

“Have you solved the secret?” Finkle enquired from behind her.

Willow jumped. “Why do people keep sneaking up on me like that?” she asked.

“Why on earth are you so jumpy?” the professor asked. “I was just curious if you had found anything in the glass that maybe I had missed.”

“I guess I just don't want to end up in the medical centre again. The thought makes me a bit paranoid,” she admitted. “I haven't found anything new. Strange, it leaves me with the feeling that I am missing something, but I can't figure out what.”

“Yes,” Professor Finkle said, frowning. There was a flash of anger in his gaze that Willow had never seen before. “I have the same problem. I was hoping fresh insight might find what I lacked in the interpretation.”

“Sorry,” she said. “I better get ready for class now.”

Through the rest of the class, Willow found herself drifting in and out of the lesson. More often than not, she glanced over at the windows. Something drew her towards them. There was a desperation inside her begging for the puzzle to be solved and to find out where she fit into it.

Chapter Twelve

The first semester came to an end quickly. Willow and her group passed with top marks in every subject. She lay stretched out on the couch relaxing as her roommates packed to head home for the break. She was remaining at the school for the week as was agreed with the Directors when she entered the education system. All students from her camp would remain for the entire school year without any contact with each other or anyone in the outside world.

It was for the best anyways, since she couldn't return home at the moment. This week would give her time to go over the newspapers and other clues she had stashed in her bedroom closet and the guardians would be free to help her.

"Here," Sebastian said.

Willow sat upon the couch and took a stack of papers from him. "What's this?" she asked.

"You could look," he answered. "It's the pictures of the windows you wanted. Sorry it took so long. I figured you could work on your little mystery this week while no one was around to bother you." Sebastian smiled and headed for the door. "Have a good time and I expect to hear what you figured out when I return."

Kayleb followed him to the door. "Klurr is staying here for the week as well. You may want to stay inside as much as possible."

"Brilliant," she answered. "Thanks, I'll try to stay clear of him."

"It's more a matter of him staying away from you," Gabriel said. "I am sure he knows you are remaining on campus this week as well."

"He must be mad about his father being fired," Seth added. "That might actually be driving him crazy right now."

"Perfect," Willow said. "You all have a good week. Don't worry about me."

"We won't." Sebastian laughed as he closed the door behind him.

No sooner than the door shut, Willow jumped up and rushed to the table. She spread all the pictures out and began looking at the designs. Staring at the photographs, her vision began to blur.

"Ahh!" she yelled.

"Take a break and look at something else," Kiera said, appearing on the table. "Now we are alone, let us help you. Aslo and I will look at the windows for clues and you try another piece of the puzzle."

Willow agreed. After retrieving her backpack from the bedroom, she pulled out the sack of newspapers she needed to go through and the *Portal Prophecies* books.

"The prophecy," she said, holding the book in her hand. "I haven't even thought about it since I came here." She dropped the book on the table and it opened to the exact page she had been reading back in the camp.

Time is fleeting, things now change.

Alone in sadness all seems strange.

Protection comes look in the sand.

Help is offered by outstretched hand.

The key to knowledge was taken away.

Hidden and lost, you must not sway.

Another foe not yet discovered.

Misplaced distrust, faith recovered.

Far away one must travel.

She spins a web of lies to unravel.

To stay safe from threats unknown.

A queen hopes to sit on a new throne.

"I don't understand much of it. I mean, obviously things have changed and I am alone and sad. I am here with no allies and no home to go to. Protection in the sand... that could be Sleeping Sands and the Director sheltering me from the mess that is going on outside the school grounds. The key to knowledge taken away... maybe the end of the classes so early?" She stood and paced around the table while chewing on the end of a pencil. "Hidden and lost... that could be referring to the message in the windows. Finkle said he has been trying to solve it for some time. Another foe... could be Klurr or Klurg... no... it would be bigger than that. Argh! This is absolutely not working. Nothing is pulling together as it did in the past."

"Relax," Kiera said. "You are trying too hard. Let your intuition guide you."

"I've never had to do this alone before," she said. "I mean, the rest of it sounds like a spider is trying to take over the world." She stopped walking. "Is it possible an ancient might have slipped into the main world somehow?"

"Yes," Aslo answered. "Theoretically, an ancient of any of the races could pass through one of the rips in the fabric of space Cornelius has caused. That would be a completely different enemy. It's doubtful that ancient serpents would work together with spiders."

"It would explain why you are so confused as well. The answers wouldn't line up properly if there are two different problems. We need to separate what belongs to Cornelius and what does not before we can solve anything," Kiera said.

"I was so sure there was some connection between everything, though." Willow exhaled sharply as she sat down. She picked up a newspaper and started reading it. Pulling the paper close to her face, her lips curled down, her eyes squinting. She turned the page, scanning several articles quickly.

"What is it?" Shelby asked, joining the other guardians on the table. She stretched her wings out and sighed in relief. "I was getting a bit stiff."

"The articles in this paper. They are all direct interviews with people from the camp," Willow said. "But everyone refers to me as *that girl* or *the redheaded girl*. Why wouldn't they call me by my name? Unless..." She stood and paced again.

"Unless they didn't know it," Nero said, pacing beside her.

"Exactly," Willow agreed. "Someone is messing with their memories. But who?"

"I think we know who," Aslo said. "That has Cornelius' signature all over it."

"Okay," she said. "Then why?"

"To isolate you, most likely," Nero said. "Although it is good to know, I am not sure that these are the answers we need at the moment."

"I need to know what happened to them, so I can fix it," Willow cried. She sat down at the table and buried her head in her arms. "I know what you are thinking. A lot of the camp wasn't going to remain with me anyways. I saw the way they looked at me the day I left. I felt the changes. But it wasn't everyone, was it?" She looked up at the guardians sitting on the table.

"No," Kiera said, nudging Willow's nose with her head. "It wasn't everyone. But for now, we need to solve other issues. The ones happening right here at the school."

Willow looked down at the paper beneath her arms. "I wonder why there are so many different Quidnunk signatures on the articles written for *The Empowered.* I understand the father writing all the interviews as Jax, but the other ones, some were written by Keith Quidnunk and others by K. Quidnunk. Why would they be different?"

"That is odd," Shelby said. "Authors usually use the same name to signify their work, so that their followers can send letters to them easily. It would seem that whoever wrote the articles using the initial *K* is a different person from Keith."

"I wonder if Krissy writes articles as well. She could be the leak the Director was speaking about. She would have access to the information and ability to take pictures if she owns a cell phone. The only thing we don't know is how she sends the articles and pictures to the paper... and why she would be lying." Willow began chewing the end of her pencil again while frowning.

"That may be a bit difficult to figure out. It's not like you, dressed as Will, can just go ask her," Aslo said.

"Not to mention, she shares a room with Jessica," Willow added. "That's another question. Why is Jessica here? She plays some role in all this too."

"I am afraid you need more information on her connection with Pewterclaw and her position with the Directors," Shelby said. "Those details won't be found here."

"Shelby is right," Kiera said. "You are best staying away from her, at least for now."

Willow banged her head on the table several times.

"What other questions do you have?" Nero asked.

"The seven trees," Willow said, looking up slightly.

Aslo sighed. "We have told you all we can about them. Only the elves can fill in those details. Next question?"

"What am I missing in these pictures?"

"We haven't figured that out yet," Kiera said. "Anything else?"

“How am I getting something to eat without being killed by Klurr?” Willow's stomach rumbled from hunger.

“Take your wand,” Aslo replied. “We'll stay here and keep working on the stained glass puzzle. Make sure you keep alert from all angles.”

“Brilliant,” Willow said, standing and heading for the door.

Chapter Thirteen

Willow woke up realizing she had fallen asleep at the table trying to make out a pattern or connection in the pictures of the windows. It was the last day of vacation and she had accomplished nothing other than figuring out most of her questions had answers outside of Sleeping Sands. She yawned and stretched her arms. There was no choice this close to the new semester start but to have the guardians hide away again and wear her disguise at all times. Leaving the table, she went to her room to wash and change for another exciting day of staring at pictures and words.

"Ahh!" Willow said, startled.

"Hello to you, too," Sebastian said. "What's all this?" He lifted a few newspapers from the table.

"It's nothing," Willow said, hurrying over to take the papers from his hands.

"I suppose this is nothing as well?" Kayleb asked, flipping through the pages of the *Portal Prophecies* book.

"That," she said, trying to take the book from the elf's grasp, "is just a book I am reading."

Kayleb held the book high above Willow's reach. “I've never seen this book before,” he said. “Have you, Sebastian?” He passed the book to the river elf.

“Can't say I have,” Sebastian answered, looking at different pages. “Are these all real prophecies? Have they happened? What do you think, Gabriel?”

Willow tried jumping to reach the book from the elf, but she came up short with each attempt. “Can I please have my book back? It really doesn't help you in any way.”

“So you admit it is a book of prophecies?” Gabriel enquired. “Fascinating! Have any come true? Where is it from?” He handed the book to Seth, who sat down and began examining it.

“It's not from the terunji world,” Seth answered. “Come to think of it, we never asked you where you were from.”

All four sets of eyes glanced at Willow. “It doesn't matter,” she answered, sitting beside the dark elf and attempting to snatch the book away from him. “My world doesn't exist anymore. It was destroyed.”

“Sorry,” Seth said, securing his grip on the book. “Were there many survivors?”

“No,” Willow said. “A handful of us escaped.” Her attempts to pry his fingers off of the book became almost humorous.

“Escaped how?” Seth asked, flipping the page of the book and paying no attention to her clawing at one of his hands.

“It's a long story,” Willow answered, her eyes shifting between the elves. She flopped into a chair.

“We have all day,” Kayleb said, sitting at the table across from her. “Nothing like a good story to pass the time.”

Normally, Willow would have agreed with him, but this subject had so much she couldn't explain. “I have plans today,” she said, attempting to stand up.

Sebastian placed his hands on her shoulders and gently pushed her back into the seat. "I think your plans can wait," he said, taking the empty chair beside her. "How did you leave your world?"

Willow's head swirled in confusion. Should she lie to them? Could she trust them enough to tell them the truth? Maybe a part truth? "The book showed us how, kind of," she said.

The elves glanced at each other. "The book showed you how?" Seth asked. "Care to elaborate?"

"A passage in it told us how to open a portal of sorts," she answered.

Seth looked at the front cover of the book. "Hence the title *Portal Prophecies*," he said. "So you can open doors to other worlds, then?"

"No, not exactly," Willow answered. "It showed us how to activate an ancient door from our world to the main world. A portal that already existed but needed to be made active to use."

"So," Kayleb said, "it doesn't tell you how to open a portal from here to Pewterclaw or somewhere else on command?"

"No," Willow answered. "That would be convenient."

"But who created the portal you activated?" Gabriel asked.

"It's hard to say," Willow said. That was something she couldn't discuss with them. Not only was conversation about guardians forbidden, but it would also blow her cover for sure.

"Who wrote the book?" Sebastian asked.

"A prophet from my world that I never met," Willow answered. "I found the book near the place where the portal was. I never met the writer, but I know she passed away. It was created either just before I was born or right after. That's all I know."

"And this copy?" Gabriel said, pulling the gypsy copy of the book from her backpack.

Willow closed her eyes and rubbed her temples. "It's written by a gypsy witch. Her talent is to write prophecy books about prophecies. If you can match the correct two prophecies together, by alternating the lines from each book, they make a clearer version of the original. It makes the predictions less like deciphering riddles."

Seth took the second copy of the book. "Fascinating," he said. "So what exactly do you use the books for now?"

Willow glanced between each of the elves. "Honestly," she said, "to stay alive."

Seth looked up from the book. "Why would you need to use a book to do that?" he asked, tilting his head to the right slightly.

"Because someone is always trying to kill me," she said, twiddling her thumbs.

"Why is that?" Kayleb asked.

Willow leaned across the table and whispered in a voice loud enough for them all to hear. "You'll really have to ask the ones trying to kill me that. You could start with Klurr."

"Did he give you problems while we were gone?" Sebastian asked.

"No," she answered. "I spent most of my time sitting here. The one time I did see him, oddly enough, he didn't even notice me. He was too preoccupied talking to Krissy."

Sebastian moved the pictures of the stained glass windows around in circles on the table in front of his. "And these?" he asked.

"First, Finkle said that he stared at them when he needed to find answers. Then when I gave it a try, the day you took the pictures, he asked me if I solved them yet... if I was able to find a hidden meaning that eluded him. I hoped the pictures would answer some questions a prophecy raised, but then, curiosity took over and I wanted to know what Finkle was so interested to learn."

"Why didn't you tell us any of this?" Kayleb asked.

"First off," she answered. "I didn't think any of you would be interested. Second, it really doesn't affect any of you." She paused for a moment. "Finally, anyone who gets involved with the prophecies usually ends up hurt in some way."

Kayleb tapped a fingernail on the table. “The newspapers?” he asked.

“I already told Sebastian a little about that,” she said. “The reporters on some of the stories are lying. I have been trying to figure out why.”

“How do you know they are lying?” Kayleb asked, picking up the paper headlining William's fate on the bridge.

“I was there for that event,” she answered. “I saw what happened to him and it didn't happen the way it was reported. It bothered me. The names of the two junior writers bothers me too. One signed Keith and the other signed *K.* seems to indicate two different writers.”

“That's why you were interested in Krissy. You think she might be the *K.* reporter.” Sebastian chuckled. “Things are making a bit more sense now.”

“A bit,” Seth said, taking a newspaper from the table. “It doesn't explain how you received copies of the newspapers that were printed during last term. No outside influence is possible within the grounds.”

Willow sighed. “They were given to me,” she said. “I am not allowed to say by who, but by someone who is interested in the answer as well. There are some secrets I cannot share with you and some you wouldn't want me to share.”

Kayleb pulled the wooden chest out of her backpack. “What's this?”

Willow slouched down in her chair. “Do you really have to go through all of my things? I am not searching your private items.”

“I think I see something in these pictures,” Sebastian said.

“What?!” Willow exclaimed, happy to change the topic.

“They seem to fit together,” he said. “Hand me some scissors.” He cut the plain edges off of each photograph, leaving only the window then carefully began matching them together like a puzzle. “There,” he said.

Willow stood and looked over his shoulder. In the centre of the combined picture was the outline of a girl in a star of white light. Red, blue, and yellow coloured glass lines flowed from her hands to various trees, one single and two groups of three. From there, other colours exploded into various symbols and in some cases what appeared to be deities or gods of some sort. One side of the picture was brighter than the other, boasting a depiction of the sun. The other side had a soft glow reflected from the moon.

"Is this... the beginning of life?" Willow asked with one hand covering her mouth. "Are those the seven trees from elf history?"

"It's the beginning of something," Seth said, looking over Sebastian's other shoulder. "If it is in fact the seven trees you need to find, it is an impossibility. If they existed, they disappeared long ago."

"Could you tell me the story?" she asked. "There might be something in the tales that could help figure out what this means."

The elves took turns looking at each other. Kayleb took a deep breath in. "There is little to tell. When the elf race began, they were entrusted to take care of the trees. A war broke out between the four royal elf races and one which declared itself sovereign from the elf world. Some say disappointment with the fighting between the elves caused the trees to hibernate, others say they died, others think they left and the elves fell out of their favour. Regardless of what happened to them, the elves as a race experienced a decline in their abilities."

"Is that why you are here?" Willow asked.

"Yes," Kayleb answered. "We are searching for what our magic lacks. You have helped us enormously this year, but we haven't even scratched the surface for what we are looking for. There is something missing."

"Could it be the seven trees are what's missing?" Willow asked.

Sebastian laughed. "Then we are in trouble indeed," he said. "No one has seen an ancient tree in tens of thousands of years."

"I have," Willow said.

"You have?" Gabriel asked. "Why would you have seen an ancient elf tree?"

"They aren't elf trees," Willow answered. "There was one that visited my home world when needed."

"Really?" Gabriel said as a question. "Which one?"

"Acacia, the tree of justice," Willow answered.

Gabriel gasped. "How do you know that name?" he asked. "Only elves know the names of the trees. Who told you this? What game are you playing?"

"I am not playing any games. I only mentioned it because I thought the news would give you hope that whatever happened in your past could be set right again," Willow said. "Now, if you don't mind, I am taking my things and going to my room."

Willow stood and shoved all the items on the table into the backpack. She was just about to walk away when a new set of papers appeared before them.

"Class schedules," Sebastian said. "Care to go over them before you storm off?"

Willow sat down again and picked up one of the pages. "Potions and Alchemy level two, Illusion Magic, Prophecies and Predictions, Auras and Energy and Dreamwalking."

"That is a difficult lineup," Kayleb said.

"Difficult?" Willow asked. "I never expected to hear you say that about school classes. Which ones are difficult?"

"Let's just say I highly doubt we will be at the top of our class this semester. In Potions and Auras, perhaps, we will end up with high marks, but the others..." His words faded off.

"Prophecies and Predictions, I have had some experience in, at least in deciphering. I haven't actually made my own predictions yet, though. I wonder if we will have to." She paused for a moment. "Illusion magic I have seen done, but never actually attempted myself, and then dreamwalking," Willow said, smiling. "I have experience with that. I think we will do fine. We might have to work hard at illusions, but I have confidence in our group." She stood and picked up her backpack again.

"We need to visit the school store to pick up the textbooks and supplies we will need," Sebastian said. "Care to join us? I want to pick up some more candy sticks as well."

"I think I'll pass and go a little later. I'm going to my room for a bit. Welcome back."

Chapter Fourteen

Dark bags sagged under Willow's eyes. The whole night was spent being scolded by her guardian friends. She had anticipated they might be a little upset. That, however, was an understatement for the level at which they actually were infuriated. Even when she mentioned that she left out all details about guardians, they still lectured her. For hours, Aslo drilled the finer points of safety into her skull followed by a lesson on trusting strangers. Now she was experiencing the silent treatment. None of them were willing to even listen to her rants.

Willow yawned and sat up in her bed. The truth was, she had been sloppy. It was known the elves were returning. The papers and books should have been put away before they did. Maybe somewhere deep in her mind she wanted them to find it... she wanted them to help her decipher the riddles like everyone at the camp had... she wanted to feel she had friends again.

The sun was already rising, the beginnings of its radiance gently gleaming through her window. She stood and ran her hand through a single ray shining in. Turning her hand in the sunlight, she saw the similarities the beam of pure light shared to the auras of magic that had become increasingly important in her own abilities. Her thoughts drifted to the stained glass windows. The way the lines formed similar colours. Perhaps the pictures were capturing the auras of magic coming from the woman in the centre.

An urge to visit the classroom and take another look at the physical stained glass windows surged through her. A newfound energy propelled her body. Leaping out of bed, she washed and dressed within minutes.

Potions class was going to be held in the same building and at the same time as last semester. Arriving early was never an issue for her. Besides, she reasoned with herself, there might be another test of character on the first day of the second term.

Tiptoeing across the still-dark living space, she opened the front door. A large creaking sound broke the silence. “Shh,” she said.

“Talking to the door?” Sebastian asked from the couch.

Willow jumped. “I didn't see you sitting there,” she said.

“Obviously,” he answered. “Where are you off to this early?”

“I couldn't sleep. I thought I would take a look at the windows again,” she replied.

“I think I'll join you,” he said. “You don't mind, do you?”

“It's not like you would give me a choice either way,” Willow said in a low whisper.

“I heard that.” He chuckled, following her out the door.

The walk across the campus was abnormally quiet. Even for leaving so early, to not even see a single person along the way seemed odd.

“What do you think you'll find in the windows? We found the pattern yesterday,” Sebastian asked, breaking the awkward silence.

Willow glanced at him for a split second. This was the first time she had felt a tension between them. “I don't know. I still feel like there is something more to learn from them or maybe from Professor Finkle. He has a certain desperation to discover the secrets of the stained glass. It changes how he looks and I can feel it when he talks. It bothers me.”

The two continued on in silence for the rest of the walk, occasionally glancing at each other as if they had something to say, but then deciding against speaking.

The classroom was as deserted as the walk had been. Sebastian moved to turn on the lights, but Willow stopped him.

"The natural light shining through is how these windows were meant to be seen. I think it changes the picture in some way or adds to it," she said. "Of course, I could be completely insane and the light of the sun might not make a difference at all." She looked at the windows again. The rays of sunlight coming through the different colours made them come to life and dance before her eyes. It was as if she was seeing all the different auras, representing every single type of magic in existence. "It would be so much clearer if they were all together," she said.

"Together?" Finkle asked from behind them. "How do you mean? Have you figured out something?"

Willow scrambled to recover without giving away any of the information they actually had uncovered about the windows. "Not exactly," she answered. "It would just make things easier if they were closer together."

"Right," Finkle said, his voice echoing his disappointment. "I have thought that before myself." He flashed a smile. "Oh well, keep trying. I see you have brought someone to help. Bravo." The professor's voice changed back to his normal perky tone.

"Professor," Willow said. "Couldn't you ask the designer what the meaning is in these pictures?" She moved closer and examined the very bottom edges of the windows.

"There is no signature, if that's what you are looking for," the professor said, crossing his arms. "These windows were made hundreds of years ago. The artist passed before I laid eyes on them for the first time. He is quite famous, although we don't associate his name with these works. If certain... organizations were to find out we had them... well, let's just say we'd be in for a fight."

"Why would our kind be afraid of a terunji organization?" Sebastian asked.

"Don't be so naive. I swear, the elves have hidden themselves away from the other worlds so much they don't understand a thing," Finkle said. "Just because the majority of magic wielders prefer to live away from everyday life of the terunji, doesn't mean that all of them do. There are many who have etched a comfortable position for themselves separate from the rest of us... and they would very much like to keep things the way they are. That includes hiding magic and secrets that could unlock power."

"Is that what you hope to find?" Willow asked. "Secrets that unravel powers?"

"I won't lie. It is a possibility I have considered," Finkle answered. "You see, throughout the ages the terunji have depicted stories of what they couldn't explain. Pictographs... art... writing... myths handed down from one generation to another, are all examples. All of them have some basis of truth and an element of fabrication that the terunji add to make the story more believable." The professor stopped for a moment and smiled. "These windows are no different. The artist was trying to portray something that happened, or will happen."

"A prophecy?" Willow asked.

"Perhaps," Finkle answered. "It could be anything or nothing."

"Is it possible there are more windows?" she asked. "Ones that are missing?"

"It is possible," the professor said. "The organizations I mentioned earlier do their best to keep these types of works out of the hands of the masses. They want to keep the secrets for themselves and everyone else in the dark." He chuckled. "In that way, many of the terunji conspiracy theories are correct."

"If you know about these organizations," Sebastian interrupted, "why don't you simply go take back the artifacts in question?"

Finkle laughed. "Not even the most insane amongst us wishes to set in motion a magical battle. The two sides keep each other in check. If the terunji ever actually learnt the truth about everything it would mean panic... riots... destruction... war. Whether we want to admit it or not, prejudice exists on both sides of the coin." He sighed. “Food for thought,” he added. “Time to get ready for class, although I don't know how many students we will have.”

“More obstacles to test our character?” Willow asked.

“No, my boy,” he answered. “Not at all. I think all the staff has a good grasp of each of you and your abilities. I'm afraid it was a horrible article published by *The Empowered* over the holiday break. It accused our education system of being corrupt from within. Nasty stuff. Parents have been pulling out their children ever since.”

“Do you have a copy of the paper?” Willow asked.

“I believe I still do on my desk,” he answered. “I expect the Director will be calling a staff meeting at some point to discuss this semester. That won't be a fun meeting.”

“Could we borrow the paper?” Willow asked. “I would like to read the article.”

“It's against school rules,” Finkle said. “No communication from the outside world is supposed to find its way to our students.” He walked to his desk. “I suppose under the circumstances, we can make an exception. Almost everybody already knows about the article anyways.” The professor opened the drawer of his desk and handed the newspaper to Willow.

“I'll get it back to you as soon as possible,” Willow said, her eyes glistening.

“No need,” Finkle said. “You keep it and if anyone asks, it didn't come from me.” He slammed his drawer shut. “Time to take your seats now. You should put that away until later. Don't let other students see you with it. That would just add fuel to the fire, if you know what I mean.”

The potions class proved to be as dull as usual. The opening lecture of the course was meant to inspire the minds of the students to open themselves further during this semester to the possibilities around them and incorporate their ideas into their potion making. Only about half the students that had attended last semester's potions course were present, making Willow wonder if all of those missing had been pulled out of the school because of the article.

The written word, she was learning, was as deadly as any weapon in battle. Without thought, her fingers began fidgeting with the edges of the newspaper hidden away between two of her text books.

Sebastian, after noticing, kicked her leg. “We'll look at it at lunch,” he said in a whisper.

“Did we miss something?” Kayleb asked.

“Yes,” Sebastian answered. “We can't talk about it here. We'll fill you in at break.”

Chapter Fifteen

The Illusion magic room was completely empty, except for a tall woman dressed in a black full-length sundress which showed off various tattoos on her skin. The most dominant was a giant three-dimensional hairy spider. It appeared to be lunging forward from above her chest on the left side of her body.

Her hair was short curly black, but spiked up at the front as if she had applied glue before walking headfirst into a hurricane-strength wind. Every curl stood at attention along her hairline and never once moved even when the woman's head did. Her eyes were completely black, reminding Willow of two hot pits of tar, bubbling as steam escaped from within. There was absolutely no sign of any white in them at all - or any eyelashes, for that matter. Her skin had a jaundiced appearance. Most sane individuals would have rushed to a medical facility if they woke up to find themselves tinted in a similar off-yellow colour. Other than that, at first glance, the woman was completely normal.

“Welcome to the world of illusions,” she said. When she spoke, she revealed four pointed teeth in the front of her mouth and a thin forked tongue that popped out every time she pronounced an *s* sound. “I am Drakondia, your tour guide through a world of mystery and intrigue. We will learn how to fool the masses and hide the truth from even the strongest of witches." She walked behind her desk. "Please find a seat and we will begin."

"Shouldn't we wait for the other students?" Kayleb asked.

Drakondia let out a bloodcurdling shriek of a laugh. "You, my friends, are the whole class," she said. "At least you know you'll graduate with the top marks. It's impossible for you not to." She faced the blackboard and began writing. "Right then, who can tell me where illusion magic is believed to stem from? Anyone?"

"Spiders?" Willow asked, guessing from her teacher's appearance.

"Correct you are! Wonderful way for us to begin our relationship for the year. You must be Will. I have heard good things about you... scary things, but good." The instructor wrote the word *spiders* across the board in chalk, then brushed her hands together to remove any residue of the white substance from them. "Why do you think spiders would use illusions?"

"To capture prey," Seth said. "To escape being prey as well, I would imagine."

"Good answers," the teacher said, writing them down. "How did they accomplish those things?"

"By changing their appearance to blend into their surroundings," Kayleb answered. "By hiding their webs, so that potential victims would fall into their traps."

"Correct!" The woman exclaimed. "That's where we are going to begin our journey. We'll start by learning how to change our own physical appearance and the physical appearance of small items in our surroundings. As the course progresses, I hope you will all be able to mutate the appearance of large groups of people and change complete rooms into whatever you desire." She walked back around to the front of her desk and rested on it slightly. "Be forewarned. The adrenaline rush that comes from being able to fool people is addictive. You may acquire an unquenchable thirst for making others believe you are someone you are not. Be careful not to lose yourself in a world you have created with magic, for it is in our own imagination that reality can sometimes become the illusion."

A chill ran through the air, causing Willow to shiver and wonder if the cold sensation running up and down her spine was an illusion created by their teacher.

"I need to know what level the five of you are starting at. Behind that door I have a practical room." She pointed to her left. "Please open it and look around. Each of you should see it is an ordinary empty room."

Kayleb opened the door and walked around inside. "It is an empty room," he said, returning.

"Good," Drakondia said. "Who will be our first victim?"

"What do we have to do?" Willow asked.

"Will, thank you for volunteering," the teacher said, smirking. "You simply go inside, close the door and come back out again."

"Somehow, that sounds far too easy," Willow replied, walking to the door. Entering the room, she glanced back at the elves before closing it behind her.

As soon as she heard the click behind her, the room changed. In front of her mirrors appeared, forming a maze. Her mind wandered back to a fun house she visited with Mike. That day, she had thought, was the best day of her life. The amusement park held so many fond memories. A smile crossed her face for a moment then vanished again. Those days were gone. She was more alone now than ever before. She turned around to head for the door she entered through, but it was gone. All she could see around her were parts of the mirror maze.

"I'm still not entirely clear what I am supposed to be doing," she said, looking up at the ceiling. There was no answer. "Alright, then. Guess I will walk through the fun house." She shrugged her shoulders and headed to her right.

Walking through the openings that appeared in front of her, Willow found her path twisting and turning in all different directions, still everywhere she looked was a reflection of herself. Her heart rate began to speed up and a trickle of sweat ran down her brow. Frustration set in. On the verge of panic, she spun around in a complete circle with her eyes closed. When she opened them, she noticed the reflection in the mirror in front of her was different. She smiled at her distorted figure. It made her look as if someone pushed down on her head and compacted her body into an accordion form. Moving to the next panel, her body was stretched lengthwise like taffy. She let out a chuckle. Moving sideways again, the next image showed her what she would look like if her arms and legs were stretched out and her torso remained the same. She waved her arms up and down, giggling at how they moved in waves in the reflection. The next mirror showed only her head as elongated and her eyes bulging out of their sockets.

"This is fun," she said out loud. "But I am not sure I understand the object of this exercise. Am I supposed to make my reflections look normal?"

Again there was no answer. She sighed and moved to the next panel. Her reflection was normal. All of a sudden, it began bleeding from cuts that appeared all over her body. The blood soaked through her clothing and ran down her face. Willow moved her hands over her body to check for blood. There was none. She let out the air she had been holding in, her body relaxing in a slouch.

The mirror in front of her began to crack. Moving forward to examine the damage, she ran one of her fingers along the jagged line that was forming. The cracking noises intensified, coming from all directions. She twirled around, trying to figure out what was happening. All of a sudden, the mirrors exploded sending sharp shards of glass hurling through the air at her. She fell to the ground in a ball, covering her head and face from the flying daggers.

This isn't real, she thought. *You can control this. It's in your mind.* The scratches on her hands began closing up. She closed her eyes, imagining an empty room while controlling her breathing and listening to the rhythm of air as it filled her lungs then left her body. Her heart rate decreased to a slow even pattern. She counted backwards from ten slowly. Reaching for her neckline, she pulled out her necklace and held the lucky charm, then opened her eyes. The house of mirrors was gone. Willow smiled, tucking the necklace back into her shirt. She reached for the door and opened it.

"An impressive time," the teacher said. "Is something wrong?"

“The mind is a delicate thing,” Willow said, frowning. “If I hadn't realized that was an illusion, I would have believed I was seriously injured. People could die from such an illusion.”

“Yes, they could,” Drakondia said. “Now you understand the seriousness of this class. A fireball thrown straight at you, you can deal with. In combat, you see your opponent's every move. Potions have anti-potions to cure them. Duelling with wands, you see the wand motions of your enemy. But with illusion magic, if you aren't trained to detect it, you might never know you were being physically attacked or fooled.” She paused for a moment. “Take, for instance, if you go to the medical centre and I create an entire illusion that you have a deadly disease and are dying. The doctor tells you two weeks is all you have left. If you don't know you are being tricked, your mind will cause your body to shut down in that two weeks. That's why you need to learn detection of illusions first and foremost.”

The chime signalling change of classes sounded through the building. “Looks like we are out of time for today. We'll see you tomorrow.”

“What happened in there?” Sebastian asked as the group walked to their next class.

Willow explained the details of the fun house to them as they walked. “I wonder if she will still have all of you go through it tomorrow. She must realize I am telling you what happens.”

“Probably not. I think she was trying to get the point across that illusions can be dangerous and, in some cases, deadly,” Kayleb said.

“Predictions and Prophecies,” Seth said. “I hope this class has more textbook applications than illusions.” Opening the door, he peered inside. “A few more students, at least.”

The room was set up to accommodate groups of five. Round tables were placed all around the borders of the room in a *U* formation. Situated in a similar formation at each table, were five chairs, each positioned to face centre. In the middle of every table were various sized black velvet bags and a large crystal ball sitting on a brass stand shaped like a hand. In the empty centre area, but closer to the top of the room, was a throne-like chair supported by a single-step platform, made from a dark wood which was intricately carved in patterns of eyes. The seat area and back of the chair was covered by a cushion made from a red velvet material. Pillars topped each arm, perched on which were a pair of carved wooden birds, watching over whoever sat between them.

"Over there," Kayleb said, pointing to a table which had no neighbours in close proximity. "Unless more students come in, it will be easier to concentrate there."

"I guess we can start," said a woman, stepping out of the shadows. "I am Gitanna, your guide through the realm of prophecy."

She was neither tall nor short, with long curly brown hair and an olive complexion. From her clothing, it appeared she was of gypsy descent or at least wanted to appear as if she were. She wore a long white flowing skirt and a colourful blouse mixing reds, yellows, oranges, and blues in a swirling motion. The front of the shirt had a section which laced up and was meant to tie at the top. Gitanna wore hers open. A red bandana circled her head, tied to one side loosely. Gold adorned her body anywhere it could find a place. Large hoops hung from her ears. Her neck was home to multiple chains of all different sizes. When she moved her arms, they made a jingling noise from bangles and charm bracelets clanging together. Every finger on her small hands boasted oversized flashy rings. Even her ankles had chains of the precious metal wrapped around them in a prominently displayed fashion.

"What is a prophecy or prediction?" Gitanna asked, not wanting an answer. "It's a peek into the past, present, or future." She moved to the throne and took a seat, her legs open in a not so ladylike position. "That's right, it can be about the past as well," she said. "On your table are various tools which are commonly used to make predictions. Only choose the one which you plan to use. Once you open a bag, you have chosen it. Please do so now."

"How do we choose if we don't know the contents of each bag?" Seth whispered.

"I think you are meant to be drawn to a certain bag. Try holding your hand over each and see if you get a vibe from any of them."

"A vibe?" Seth asked, arching one eyebrow. "Fine." He muttered and held his hand over each bag. "Nothing."

"Maybe give it a bit extra time over each one?" Willow suggested. She closed her eyes and held her hand over top of the first bag. She concentrated on its contents.

NO rang through her mind.

Each of the elves followed her actions and, after receiving a *yes* answer, chose a bag. Kayleb received a deck of cards... Gabriel found tea leaves and cups... Sebastian's choice was dice, which had letters on every side instead of numbers and Seth chose runes.

Willow tried the final bag, receiving yet another negative answer. She sighed and looked up, her eyes locking onto the crystal sphere sitting in the middle of their table. The clear surface began to cloud and swirl before her eyes. "Excuse me," she called out. "Can I choose the ball?"

Gitanna walked over and picked up the crystal ball from their table. "This is an advanced way to start. That bag may contain something easier," she said. "No?" She glanced into it and tilted her head back and forwards. "Very well, handle it with care." Handing it to Willow, she walked away.

"By now, everyone should have their own tools for making predictions. Before you can learn to read them properly, you must learn how to decipher a prophecy. That is where we will start. I would like everyone to write a prophecy tonight. You can make one yourself... use a dream you have had... write a poem... take one from a book... anything. It doesn't have to be a real prophecy, but something we can practice interpreting tomorrow."

"Take one from a book," Sebastian said, glancing sideways at Willow.

"Absolutely not," Willow said. "That book is a secret. I don't want someone thinking it has valuable information and stealing it from me."

The end-of-class chime rang and the students began to pack up their things. "All tools back in their bags and where you found them, please," Gitanna yelled.

Finally it was lunch and time to read the newspaper article that had caused enough uproar in the magic world that students had been pulled from the school.

Chapter Sixteen

The vegetarian garden was almost as busy as usual. It seemed that the article had not affected the elf lands in the same manner as the main world. Either that or the elves didn't bother with news from outside their realm.

Willow sat under her favourite apple tree and immediately pulled out the copy of *The Empowered* newspaper to read:

Favouritism, Corruption, Secrets: When the Education System Fails

An article by K. Quidnunk

The future of our children is at risk. Evidence of favouritism in the ranks of the higher-up positions at Sleeping Sands has been exposed. In the past semester, at least one student was given preferential treatment in both leniency and marks. The cost of this; the job of a well-known veteran teacher at the school itself. Klurg, instructor for the Magical Combat class, was dismissed from his position at Sleeping Sands for requiring a student back from medical leave to participate in practice combat scenarios in order to pass his course. The student in question, a young boy, had been injured during the first class of the year and subsequently missed over three weeks of instruction.

"There was no material I could mark the boy on. I was trying to help him," Klurg said in an exclusive interview. "The Director of Knowledge interrupted the class, pulled me aside and fired me."

Other eyewitness accounts report Cassandrhea Tibbins then ended all combat classes and issued marks without seeing first-hand the actual talents of any of the students. Those marks included a top mark for the boy who had missed all of the scheduled classes except the first one.

"He was hurt badly in combat practice on the first day and in the infirmary. We didn't see him again until the day the instructor was fired. I don't understand how he could receive the highest mark in the class," a student of Klurg's course who asked to remain anonymous reported.

"It isn't the only class he was given top marks for and didn't attend. He received top marks in every subject," another student said.

With the earlier threat assessment connected with the acceptance of a young girl, a wanted person in connection with the attack on Pewterclaw during Samhain and several accounts of murder or attempted murder, into the most elite school known to our kind and now the exposure of corruption in the governing body of our entire education system, where does that leave students? Can parents ignore such events and feel safe sending their children to learn in this environment? How long before the entire system spirals and devolves into a mere cesspool of lies?

"That's rather harsh," Sebastian said.

"Harsh," Willow replied. "It's lies."

"Well," Gabriel said, "not all of it."

"Which part, other than Klurg being fired, isn't a lie?" Willow asked.

"She gave you a top mark without seeing your abilities," Seth said. "We all wondered about that ourselves. Klurg was out of line and deserved to be relieved of his job for what he said, but I am not sure your performance on the first day was top-of-the-class combat."

"This year has been very easy for all of us," Kayleb added. "We seemed to breeze through everything except potions. Are we all really that far ahead of other students in every subject?"

"Then there is that girl that almost attended here," Sebastian said. "She seems dangerous. Who knows how many people would have been hurt by her if there hadn't been an uproar."

"Oh, so you know all the facts on her?" Willow asked, standing. "You have already decided that what everyone says must be true. Did you ever think that maybe the paper is lying?"

"I have no idea why you are getting so defensive," Sebastian answered. "All we are saying is that parts of the story are true and other parts are not true."

"That's what I said before. All of the stories written by the junior Quidnunks are part truth and part fabricated tales. In the end, the articles make things out to be much worse than they are. It takes things in a different direction than it should!" Willow yelled. "This story should have been about Klurg having a personal vendetta against me for showing up his son. His being fired was a victory for students who have been bullied. Instead, the facts have been twisted into obscurity."

"I see your point," Seth said. "Unfortunately, there is nothing we can do about it. The story has been printed and read. The damage is already done."

"We could try to find out why it was written like this," Willow said, biting her thumbnail. "If K. Quidnunk is in fact Krissy as we suspect, maybe we can talk to her. At least we might find out why the paper didn't bother to even contact any of us. We are in the middle of this mess."

"That is true," Kayleb said. "For a journalist to write such an article, they should have attempted to contact at least one of us to verify their information."

"Very well, then," Sebastian said. "We will have a word with Krissy after classes. Speaking of which, we should be heading to the wonderful land of auras."

The aura classroom was only a minute walk from the garden. The inside of the room was lit with rose-coloured light bulbs. Attached to the ceiling were several silver disco balls which spun in circles rotating one way and then changing directions, making different patterns on the floor. The room looked like a gymnasium which had been made over for a dance. Bleachers lined the walls for the students to sit on. The floor space was empty except for Miss Kelly and a younger looking man in athletic wear. They were both sitting in the most uncomfortable cross-legged position Willow had ever seen.

"Good afternoon," Miss Kelly said. "For those of you who were in the elemental class last semester, you already know who I am. For the rest of you, I am Miss Kelly, your instructor for this aura class. This handsome young lad beside me is Chee, my teacher's assistant. He will be aiding me throughout this course. As you may be aware from looking at him, Chee is an expert in relaxation and meditation techniques as well as Yoga."

"That looks more painful than relaxing," Willow whispered.

Miss Kelly turned her head in Willow's direction, having heard the whisper. "When your body, soul, and mind are as one, there is no pain experienced in any meditation techniques. I urge those of you with concentration issues to see Chee for some tutoring in physical and metal alignment," she said.

A puff of smoke exploded in front of her. When it cleared, she was standing, her staff beside her. "The art of reading auras is an old tradition. It takes a level of concentration many of you never realized existed. If you think this course will be a walk in the park, think again."

Chee did a backwards flip from his sitting position and landed on his feet beside her. Applause erupted from the students for his agility. He bowed.

"Everything that exists has an aura. Every person... animal... plant... or object exists in harmony with the universe. That means we all vibrate at different frequencies. These frequencies produce a visual energy. So why do we want to be able to read auras?" She paused for a moment. "There are several reasons."

"To tell us the sort of person we are dealing with?" Jessica asked.

Willow hadn't noticed Jessica had been in the room. She leaned sideways closer to Sebastian. "Krissy isn't with her group. Wonder where she might be."

"I don't know, but Klurr is absent from his group as well," Sebastian answered.

Willow scanned the room. Her gaze stopped on Matia. "Do you think something is wrong?" she whispered back.

"Correct! Sebastian, can you give us another example of an instance when one might be glad they can read an aura?" Miss Kelly asked.

"To detect whether or not a person is being truthful," Sebastian answered with confidence.

"Yes! Another?"

"Although still in research," Seth answered, "there is potential that one could detect their own illnesses and correct their auras to heal their own bodies."

"Beautiful answer. Let's try one more... Will?" Miss Kelly said.

"If one can see and feel the vibration of magical auras," Willow said in a quiet voice, "one could potentially reproduce any magical signature."

The room exploded in whispers. Willow looked around at everyone staring at her. "Did I say something wrong?" she whispered to her group.

"Not so much wrong," Sebastian answered. "More weird. Most of us don't see magical auras. In fact, you are the only one I know who claims to be able to."

"Very true, Mr. Sebastian," Miss Kelly said. "Most individuals do not possess the sight of magical auras, or they don't realize they do. Mr. Will, could you give us an example of a magical aura that someone might not interpret as magical?"

Willow searched her memories and found herself thinking about the first time she had seen Annabelle and Lilabeth embrace. It had been the most beautiful light show she had ever seen. True love flowing between them. "Love," she blurted out. "True love has a magical aura that is beautiful."

"Excellent! Yes, love is magical!" Miss Kelly exclaimed.

"Not like she's going to disagree with him anyways. We already know he will be given top marks no matter what he does or says," Jin snorted.

Miss Kelly lifted her staff in the air and slammed it back down on the ground, sending sparks flying upwards. "SILENCE!" she yelled. "I am only going to say this once. Every student I teach earns every mark I give. There are no free rides in my classes. Will is no different. His understanding of magic actually far surpasses that of any other student I have taught at this school. That is what I want to see from my students. Show me you understand the craft and I will mark you accordingly." She paused for a moment. "Whoever wrote that article for the paper is a disgrace. The students who gave interviews are likewise a disgrace. I, along with several other teachers here at Sleeping Sands, have asked for an enquiry into the newspaper's practices. Heed this warning: to anyone involved in the making of a false article or providing false information to a reporter, we will find out and you will be held accountable." Miss Kelly took in a deep breath. "This class is over for today. I suggest anyone wanting to make unrelated comments not bother to attend tomorrow."

"At least we know the teachers are doing something about the article," Willow said. "I hope the enquiry finds all of the other lies that have been printed. Do you think we should show someone what we have already found?" She gathered her books and headed to the door. There was one class left for the day, Dreamwalking.

"No," Seth said. "If anyone found out, it would open up another conspiracy story about the paper being silenced."

The class for dreamwalking was actually being held on the second floor of the same building. Opening the door, Willow giggled at the decor. It was one big room similar to a hall, but filled with evenly-spaced beds, all neatly made.

"Mind if we take spots by the window?" she asked. Without waiting for an answer, she placed her things on one of the beds directly beside a large open window. Leaning her body outside, she inhaled the fresh air provided by a warm breeze. The scent of mixed flowers danced in her senses before fluttering away with the wind.

Looking down, she noticed the side of this building was covered with the same creeping ivy plants as her dormitory. Her hand fell down to lightly caress the leaves she could reach. Closing her eyes, she felt happiness, then she heard the plants singing praises for the groundskeeper, Greenfoot, giving her a new admiration for the bunny-like man.

"Please settle in," a woman's voice said from the front of the room.

"Yes, everyone find a spot," a man's voice said.

Willow moved from the window and sat on her bed. "Is there more than one teacher?" she asked Kayleb, who had taken the spot beside her.

"Not sure," he answered. "I only see one person."

Everyone was anxiously waiting for the teacher to turn around. "There will be no whispering or commenting about freak shows in this class," the woman's voice said. "If I hear any, the culprits will be removed for the rest of the lesson and marks will be deducted from their final scores."

"Are we clear?" the man's voice asked. The teacher turned around. Standing at the front of the room was a woman's body, complete with a woman's head, but with a man's head attached to the front side of her left shoulder. "We are conjoined twins. Each of us has our own personality and standard for this class. Once we enter a dream world, we will become two separate entities complete with our own bodies."

Klurr let out a laugh, “Now they have this thing teaching us. What next? A baby fox teaching hunting skills?”

“Mr. Klurr,” the female voice boomed loudly. “You are relieved from this class until tomorrow and your group will start with a negative five percent. In the future, I suggest you think of your peers before opening your foul mouth.”

Klurr mumbled a few swear words under his breath. He came to a complete stop and exchanged glances with Krissy, who had also rejoined her group, before exiting the building.

“If anyone else wishes to join him, please do so now,” the female instructor continued. “For those of you who wish to learn, I am Moirah Flinch and my brother is Noran Flinch.”

“Please take a look around you,” Noran said. “This is the most popular course we offer at Sleeping Sands. Even with decreased attendance this semester, you can see all of our spots are full. We have no problem having those who disrupt our instructions removed, so that we can give extra attention to those few of you who will excel.”

“Before rushing into the practical side of this course, there are some things we need to discuss,” Moirah said. “Everyone should pick up a medical information sheet from the front of the room on their way out today. We will be using a mild sedative to help us all fall asleep at the same time. If you have an allergy to the medicine we use, please see us before our next class.”

“Right then,” Mr. Flinch said. “Who here has experienced dreamwalking before?”

Willow looked around the room. Absolutely no one was raising their hands. She let out a sigh and lifted her hand in the air slowly. A grumble exploded among the other students.

“Silence!” Ms. Flinch yelled. “I expect by that reaction, you must be the famous Will. I had a feeling you wouldn't be a novice to this form of magic.”

“To be fair,” Willow said, “I was always brought into a dream by someone else or called someone else in. I don't believe I can control anything that happens in dreams, but rather I know how to explore the world I enter. I hope that made some sense."

"It makes all the sense in the realms. There are many different abilities that come with the world of dreamwalking. As you have said, there are those who can control the surroundings, or change the physical reality of a dream. Then there are those who can explore and interpret signs around them. There are other abilities that can be developed in time," Noran said. "Can you share with the others a little about first entering the dream world?"

"My very first experience," Willow answered, "was actually a nightmare. I called out and a friend pulled me out of my dream. Later we found out she is a natural dreamwalker. After that, she brought me into several dreams. At the beginning of each, we appeared in a white hallway. On all sides of the hallway were doors, each one representing either a person we knew who was sleeping or the way to the dream we were meant to enter. There were symbols on the doors to help decipher what was behind them."

"Excellent," Moirah said. "How many times would you say you have had a dreamwalking experience? I ask because you have such a clear understanding of the staging part of the adventure."

"I'm not sure, exactly," Willow answered. "Several."

"Anyone else?" Noran asked. "Anyone at all?"

"I guess we will have to spend a wee bit more time focusing on the basic fundamental rules associated with being in the dream world," Moirah said. "Do we have any questions before we begin today's lecture?"

"How do we know the difference between a regular dream and dreamwalking?" Jessica asked.

"A very good question," Moirah answered. "A regular dream you have at night, be it a prophetic dream or a collection of thoughts that your mind is focused on coming into your subconscious, is a message for you and you alone. A dreamwalking experience involves two or more people meeting in the subconscious realm to explore and answer questions they may have and, in some cases, to simply meet and talk. As we have already said, a planned walking experience starts in a staging room and then moves to a dream world."

"A strong or natural dreamwalker needs to be present for all of such events," Noran added. "You cannot simply decide one day to dreamwalk. You either have the gift or have to learn it before you can lead your own adventures."

"That being said," Moirah continued, "once you have been exposed to the dream realm, you will need to be very careful who you call to join you. There are those who are proficient enough in this craft to enter your dream at the thought of their name."

"Not all of these specialists are friendly," Noran said. "To some, terrorizing the weak is a game. Our minds are fragile things which we must treat with care. It's a sad day when we must realize not everyone who exists plays fair."

"Over the course of this semester," Moirah continued, "we will explore safety and techniques of how not to become trapped in a dream world. You will need to be proficient in theory before you will be allowed to try the techniques firsthand."

The chime sounded, ending the classes for the day. "Please remember to pick up the medical information sheets on your way out. Sweet dreams, all," Noran said.

Chapter Seventeen

"Catch up to me," Sebastian said. "I am going to try to stop Krissy. Hopefully we can get her alone to talk."

Before Willow could say anything, the river elf was already following Krissy out the door. She glanced at the others speechless in awe of the elf's speed.

"We better go after him," Kayleb said. "Who knows what trouble he'll find himself messed up in. I think it's obvious Klurr is involved with bullying that girl in some way."

"You think so?" Willow asked as they made their way through the crowd of students trying to exit the room at the same time.

"I wouldn't be surprised if he was forcing her to write articles as revenge for his father's dismissal," Seth added.

"I don't know," Willow said. "The worst thing a reporter can do is be coerced into writing a false story. I think there is more going on with Krissy than can be easily seen."

There was no sign of Sebastian, Krissy, or Klurr when they finally made their way out of the building. Even worse, there were no clues as to what direction they should go in.

"We can cover more ground if we split up," Gabriel offered. "I'll take Greenfoot's gardens and the stone arena"

"Good idea," Kayleb said. "I can handle the sports field and combat areas. Seth can check in the potions room, hall, and cafeteria."

"I guess that leaves me with the forest area," Willow said.

"I don't think anyone went in there," Kayleb said. "You could just return to the dormitories and see if Sebastian went back there."

Willow flashed her best look of disapproval. "Are you trying to keep me away from danger?" she asked. "I am capable of defending myself."

Kayleb laughed. "Your research in our medical facilities can vouch for that," he said. "We'd like to have you actually make it to the second day this semester."

Willow sighed. She couldn't argue with that logic. Waiting until day three of classes to take risks was probably a good idea. She watched the elves head off in their different directions before heading back to the dormitory, taking a route back that led through the forest.

The warm afternoon breeze caressed the side of her face and tickled the hairs on the back of her neck. As she reached the beginning of the treeline, a whisper of *welcome* whistled gently in her ear. Inhaling deeply, the earthy smell of the forest mixed with pine and sweet wild flowers instantly calmed her. She reached out and touched a tree in front of her, the smooth surface of her palms exploring the grooves and textures of its bark.

"Thank you, my friends," she replied. A path appeared, as if knowing the direction she was heading. Instinctively, she followed it, taking time to admire the various earth tone wild mushrooms that had sprouted in patches mixed in with green moss and fallen branches. This was her world. Nature was her family.

Willow found herself deep at the centre of the woods, listening to the rustling leaves and the lively chatter of nearby animals before she remembered why she was there. This wasn't a fun visit. She was looking for Sebastian. "Are there any other people visiting with you today?" she asked.

Despite how deep she was hidden in the trees, a breeze carrying an answer to her question found its way to her. "There are," the leaves rustled. "Shall we show you the way?"

"Please," she replied.

The creaking noises of trees moving ever so slightly surrounded her. A new path opened up to her right. "Thank you," she said, changing her direction.

The newly-formed trail led almost directly to the opposite side of the woods from which she had started. A branch fell downwards stopping her in her tracks, telling her she had gone far enough. Willow grasped the branch and was lifted high into the tree. From her new vantage point, she could see Klurr and Krissy up ahead. There was no sign of Sebastian anywhere.

"I need to get close enough to hear what they are saying," she whispered.

The branch she was sitting on moved forward and met the branch of a tree closer to the action. Willow laid down on her stomach and squirmed like an inchworm across, continuing from tree to tree until she was positioned directly above Klurr's head. Leaning her upper body down slightly, she eavesdropped in on the conversation below.

"I don't care who is asking questions," Klurr said. "We need another article on the way this place is degrading daily."

"What would you suggest I write?" Krissy asked. "I need to have some base to make a story around."

"How about that freak show running our dreamwalking course, not to mention that old hag, Miss Kelly. They are the ones who should be fired around here!" Klurr yelled.

"That's your opinion. I need a reason. If you can give me some facts, I can do what you want. Find me the gory details and I promise you something spectacular," Krissy said. "I need a good story as badly as you need revenge."

"I can give you students who will admit to witnessing anything," Klurr pleaded. "My family has been disgraced. I can't sleep until I have had my revenge."

"What about that Will kid?" Krissy asked. "Is there any information on him we can use?"

"Don't worry about him," Klurr answered, making a fist and punching it into the palm of his other hand. "I have plans for that piece of worthless space. It will take him a lot longer to recover this time, too. Whoever he has protecting him will be gone soon enough."

"Keep digging," Krissy said. "Bring me something solid, then we will back it up with your witnesses. It has to be believable."

"What about that elf that was following you earlier?" Klurr asked.

"I think I will lead him around some, then let him find me," Krissy said. "I may be able to get more information out of him than he will from me. It could be useful. Lay off of him. We should avoid meeting for a few days as well. I don't want anyone to notice a connection between us."

"Fine," Klurr said. "But if he becomes bothersome, an accident is easy to arrange. Especially one that leads back to poor supervision by teachers."

The branch underneath Willow let out a crack.

"What was that?" Klurr asked, looking around. Before he had a chance to look up, a gust of wind blew in his face. "There must be a storm coming." He spit out a leaf that had landed in his mouth.

Willow closed her eyes. Rain trickled down the sides of her face. The slow rate at which the drops splattered was not enough to saturate, but rather more of a refreshing splash of cool mist on a hot summer day. The sound of rain hitting against the leathery leaves of the surrounding trees echoed loudly, creating the illusion of a strong summer storm.

“We should go,” Krissy said. “I need to get back anyways. That nosy body Jessica is always wondering where I disappear to. I'm starting to run out of believable excuses.”

Willow waited until the two were far out of sight before dropping down off the branch to the ground safely. “I'm so sorry,” she said. “I had no idea the stress my body weight was putting on your limbs.”

Reaching out, she placed her open hands on the tree. A golden warm light flowed from her engulfing the trunk and branch in question. Within moments the crack was healed. The rain stopped.

The woods were different now. Breathing in, she was rewarded with a damp mossy fragrance mixed with the scent of rain still fresh in the air. She inhaled deeply, letting it out as her lips turned upwards forming a content smile. It was different but still beautiful.

“Thank you, my friends,” she said.

A new trail appeared leading to the closest point from the forest to her dormitory. The sun was starting to set as she reached the living quarters. The first star of the evening gleamed and twinkled brightly in the sky. Its white light danced before her as if putting on a production specially made for her. These little things she had taken for granted for too long.

“Beautiful night,” Greenfoot said. “Going out for a stroll in the moonlight?”

“You startled me,” Willow said, her voice shaking. “I was just enjoying the evening. A breath of fresh air sometimes gives me new energy when I feel I am at my lowest point.”

“It's when we have reached our lowest point that we can rejoice at having survived it,” Greenfoot said. He clasped his hands behind his back. “Have a good evening, Mr. Will.”

She watched the Botany teacher walk off then hurried up to her living quarters. All of her roommates were waiting inside.

“Where have you been?” Kayleb asked. “We looked all over.”

“On my route back here,” she said, “I came across Klurr and Krissy. I sort of eavesdropped on their conversation.”

"On your route back?" Kayleb asked. "What route, exactly, did you take?"

Willow slouched into a chair, covering her face with her hands. "Through the forest," she mumbled, peeking through her fingers to gauge a reaction.

"I thought we agreed it was best for you not to look in the forest," Gabriel said, raising one eyebrow.

"Maybe," Willow answered.

"It's done now," Sebastian interrupted. "So what did you find out?"

"I found out that it isn't safe for the four of you to continue looking into this. You should forget it ever happened and leave things alone," Willow said.

"Why would we want to do that?" Sebastian asked.

"If you become a problem, Klurr has a plan to create an in-class *accident*. It is meant to hurt you and he will make it look as if the staff here are responsible. He wants revenge for his father being fired and he will stop at nothing to achieve it." Willow sat back in the chair, resting her neck on its cushioned back.

"I would have thought you would be his target," Seth said.

"I am," Willow answered. "He has special plans to destroy me. Unfortunately, he didn't mention what they are."

"So no one goes anywhere alone anymore," Kayleb said. "We all stay in groups. If we can't all be together, then a group of two and a group of three."

"Are you listening to me?!" Willow yelled. "This is dangerous. It is best if none of you are involved any further."

"I was hoping to follow Krissy, at least until I can find time to talk to her alone," Sebastian said, ignoring the previous comment.

"That isn't a good idea," Willow scoffed. "She knew you were following her. She plans on leading you along for a while and then allowing you to catch her alone. At that point, she plans to extract information from you rather than vice versa."

Kayleb laughed.

"It's not funny," Willow started. "Wait," she said. "Did you just laugh? I thought laughing was a sign of weakness."

Sebastian snorted the water he was drinking out his nose. "In public," he replied, wiping his face dry, "it is in our world. But... with friends, it is a normal reaction even elves have."

"I guess you are growing on us," Kayleb said, smiling.

"Like fungus on a tree," Seth added.

Kayleb and Sebastian broke out in another round of laughter.

"Now I'm a fungus," Willow said. "Great."

"We are quite fond of having you around. We may have to take you with us when the semester ends," Kayleb said.

"Take me with you?" Willow asked. "Outsiders aren't welcome in the elf realm."

"If there is one rule that proves constant time after time," Gabriel answered, "it's that there are always exceptions to any rule."

"Exceptions?" Willow echoed his word as a question.

"Yes," Sebastian answered. "All you have to do is marry a member of one of the royal families. You will be instantly welcomed."

"Royal family," she repeated. "I see, so I just have to find one, fall in love and marry. I'll get right on that. You wouldn't happen to have the royal schedule lying about would you?"

Kayleb laughed. "We are part of the royal family," he said.

Willow did a double take. "You," she stuttered. "All of you? Royal elves?"

"Yes," Sebastian said. "All of us. I believe they call us princes."

"Princes," she echoed. Willow stood up stiff, as if frozen.

"Don't worry," Gabriel said. "In our world, love has no boundaries. Gender is not an issue with our people."

“Gender,” she said. Looking down at her clothing she realized they were referring to her being a boy. Letting out a little squeak, she headed towards her room. “I think I should turn in now.”

Willow flopped on the bed and let out a sigh of relief.

“Did something happen?” Aslo asked.

After filling him in on all the details, Aslo broke out into laughter. He rolled around on her bed in hysterics.

“Brilliant,” she said. “Thanks for that.”

“I'm sorry,” Aslo said, still snickering. “They all think you are a boy. I can't wait until they find out the truth.” He pushed up against her. “In all seriousness, they all have, in essence, declared feelings for you. Genderless feelings, which means they don't care if you are a boy or a girl. They would feel the same either way. It is your spirit they care for. It's an honour. You will have to answer them at some point. I suggest you think long and hard about your reply before you do.”

“Yeah,” Willow said. “I can't think of anything like that at the moment. I have so many loose ends that need to be cleaned up first. My life is a mess. I am a mess. I can't think about my future until I am certain I will have one.”

“So tell them that,” he said. “They will understand. True feelings never fade. On a side note, we also need to worry about Klurr. That has me concerned.”

“Klurr,” Willow said. “He concerns me as well.”

“You do know that you can't win this battle alone,” Aslo said. “You have unusual gifts and a strong spirit, but it's not enough to take on the problems of the world. At some point, you will have to trust others to help. You aren't a superhero. You're a girl. Remember that. It's okay to reach out once in a while.”

“I don't want anyone else to get hurt,” Willow said, her eyes swelling with tears.

“A lot more people are going to be hurt if something doesn't change,” the guardian cat said. “Take help where it is offered. Maybe that is the answer you needed to find in the sand.”

Chapter Eighteen

Sleep refused to make an appearance, having been lost somewhere between thought and curiosity. Willow stood and moved to her closet. Pulling out the pictures of the stained glass windows from her backpack, she laid them on her bed so that they formed one bigger scene. Her eyes scanned over the different images and themes portrayed.

"What am I missing?" she whispered to herself.

Letting out a sigh, she moved to her window and opened it wide, gazing up at the sky. "A stroll in the moonlight," she said, mimicking Greenfoot's sentiments from earlier.

A cool breeze swept by. The moon was full, its rays shining brightly down, casting an opalescent glow on the world below, only interrupted by wisps of clouds passing across its path in the sky. She closed her eyes and took in a deep breath of the crisp evening air. "Moonlight," she said.

"Moonlight!" She rushed back to her bed. "Of course," she said. "Why didn't I see it before?"

That was exactly what she needed. She headed out into the moonlight. Once outside, she stopped to listen to a single cricket under a lilac tree, playing a musical masterpiece, every note resonating beauty in her soul. She applauded the tiny musician before continuing on her way.

Opening the door to the potions classroom, she quietly entered and headed straight for the stained glass windows.

"I'm not sure who you are worried about disturbing at this hour," Gabriel said. "No one else is awake."

"Did you follow me?" Willow asked.

"Yes," Gabriel said. "I believe we made it clear that we were to stay in groups at all times. This would count as one of those times."

"Sorry," she said. "I forgot. Besides, you said yourself no one else is awake."

"So I did," the golden elf admitted. "What is so important that you couldn't wait until morning to come here?"

"Moonlight." Willow smiled as she moved closer to the windows.

"Moonlight?" Gabriel repeated.

"Yes," she said. "I was thinking about it and part of the picture is governed by the sun, but the other is governed by the moon. I figure that moonlight shining through might give a different perspective than sunlight does."

Gabriel moved closer and examined each window. "You're right," he said. "The way the colours shimmer makes their direction reverse. If we put all the windows in order, the magic would appear to be flowing from the bottom to the figure in the middle. How exactly does that help?"

Willow shook her head. "I'm not sure," she said. "But it does show a continuous cycle of some sort. Magic flows down and then back up. We still need the missing bottom pieces."

"So you came all this way to figure out you still don't know what they mean?" Gabriel asked.

"Perhaps I don't," Willow said, smiling. "But I have another piece to the puzzle. If I collect enough, I will be able to figure it out."

The walk back was silent, interrupted only by the call of an owl, its eyes glowing yellow in a hole of a tree. Back at their living quarters, Willow found their roommates were waiting for them.

"Where were you?" Kayleb asked.

"Walking in the moonlight," Gabriel answered.

"I wanted to see the stained glass as it appeared being lit by the moon," Willow said. "I thought it might make a difference."

"Did it?" Seth asked.

"Yes," Willow said, explaining what they had found. "Whatever is at the bottom is the key to unravelling that mystery. It's too bad the pieces are lost, destroyed or hidden by some agency bent on keeping items of power out of the hands of those who could wield them." She scrunched up her face. "I am starting to sound like the terunji conspiracy theorists. I can understand where they come up with all their material."

Sebastian chuckled. "It's a shame they don't know how close they actually are before someone silences them."

"Is there anything else you wish to investigate this evening?" Kayleb asked. "Or can we go to sleep now?"

"I think I am good," Willow said, pursing her lips together. "I still don't like you risking your lives on these things."

"We enjoy this," Seth said. "We haven't had this much fun in... ever."

"Fun?" Willow said. "There is a word that I never thought I'd hear an elf talking about. Did I miss something?"

"It's true," Kayleb said. "Fun isn't a priority in our lives, but we are enjoying trying to solve these mysteries. There is something compelling about seeking out the truth."

"Fine," Willow said. "It's not like you are going to listen to me anyways." She paused for a moment. "There is something I would like to discuss with you all tomorrow, though."

"We look forward to tomorrow," Kayleb said. "Sleep well."

Flopping down on her bed again, Willow called for her guardian friends. Kiera peered directly over her face.

"You know it's creepy when you do that, right?" she asked.

Kiera laughed. "So what new information do you have?"

Willow explained the stained glass discovery. "I am going to tell them I am a girl," she added at the end.

"That's a big decision," Kiera said. "Are you sure you want to reveal that much?"

"I feel guilty not telling them everything," Willow answered, pulling a pillow over her face. "I can just imagine how they will react if they find out, especially if it is from someone else."

"You don't think they will understand why you need to stay hidden?" The black cat asked. "I am not sure you give them enough credit. In the end, this is your choice. Make sure you follow your intuition and not your feelings."

"I know there is a limit to what I can say and what I can't at the moment. I plan to make that clear to them. But if they are in fact expressing feelings towards me, don't they deserve to know I am not a boy?"

"Perhaps it doesn't matter what you are. Perhaps they care about you on a different level," Kiera said. "I would love you no matter what. That is the best love you could ever have. Think about exactly what you want to say while you sleep tonight. Tomorrow brings a new day."

Chapter Nineteen

Willow woke to a banging on her door. Jolting straight up, she rubbed her eyes. Reaching over to the table beside her bed, she grabbed the clock, and let out a tiny squeal. She was already late.

"Will!" Sebastian yelled. "Wake up. We have to go now."

For the first time, Willow was glad she had fallen asleep in her school clothes. She took a quick look in the mirror to make sure her wig was on properly and opened her door just as Sebastian was about to knock again. He pulled back quickly, so as not to hit her in the face.

"Sorry," she said. "Let's go."

"Did you sleep like that?" He asked looking her over from top to bottom. "Your clothes look horrible. Maybe a clean shirt?"

"I thought we had no time?" she asked, grabbing her books and heading out the door. "We are late, aren't we?"

"Yes," he said. "But..."

Willow cut him off. "I'll come back at lunch and change," she said. "Why did you wait around? You didn't have to be late too."

“We are sticking to groups, remember?” Sebastian said. “The others went ahead, so we weren't all late. I figure Finkle will give us a pass today if you tell him we were up late looking at the windows. Maybe throw him a bone. Tell him moonlight makes them look different.”

“Should we give that away?” Willow asked.

“You said yourself, without the bottom pieces, the puzzle can't be solved,” the river elf replied. “It will just wet his appetite and make him believe we are getting somewhere.”

“We have to be careful, too,” she said, hurrying down the pathway to the other side of the campus. “We don't want to make it look like another teacher is showing me favouritism. That would be enough to spark another story in the newspaper.”

“I forgot about that,” Sebastian said. “That could be problematic. We'll have to deal with that when the time comes, I suppose. Whether you tell Finkle or not about last night, I believe he will show you grace today for being late. He has always been nice to you.”

Walking through the empty lecture side of the classroom, Willow could hear the clanging of test tubes and breakers, over top of sounds of bubbling concoctions. The air was mixed with the scents of wild herbs, therapeutic aromatherapy oils and burning gas.

“Sebastian and Will,” Finkle said without looking up from his black book. “How good of you to join us today.”

“Good morning,” Willow muttered.

“Yes,” Finkle said. “It is. Would have been much nicer if I had seen your smiling faces on time. Was there a problem? Perhaps an explosion?”

“No, sir,” Willow answered.

“An incurable sickness, perhaps?

“No, sir,” she answered again, elbowing Sebastian to help.

“I see,” the professor said, pacing back and forth at the front of the room. “An evil spell must have been cast upon you, stopping you from arriving on time and in orderly fashion. Did you sleep in those clothes, boy?"

"No to the spell," she answered. "Yes to the sleeping in these clothes."

"Do you think it's appropriate for you to show up here late and dressed like that?" Finkle asked.

"No, sir," Willow answered.

"What would you do if you were in my position?" Finkle asked. "Any thoughts? Any at all? No answer then?" The professor paused while he tapped his finger against his lips. "Well, you won't be in my class dressed in such a disgusting nature. I expect my students to present themselves with the same care in their appearance as they would put into any potion I would ask them to create. As a result, you are dismissed from the remainder of today's lessons. As for the tardiness, five percent from your group's final mark."

"Am I dismissed as well?" Sebastian asked.

"Do what you will, it makes no difference to me or the outcome of my decision. As with all students you can make up extra marks after classes helping me replenish ingredients. The two of you will see me at the end of the day if you care about the rest of your group," Finkle said, "and dressed properly."

"At least I can go change early," Willow chuckled.

Sebastian flashed a look of disapproval. "I don't think that's the lesson you are meant to learn from this," he said.

"I thought you said he would go easy on me." Willow smiled.

"Apparently," he replied, "I was wrong."

"People change when their backs are up against a corner," Willow said. "I have seen it before. They become frightened and turn the other way. They take the easy road, one that involves very little risk on their part. You can't blame them."

"You're wrong," Sebastian said, grasping her shoulders. "They should follow the right path... do the right thing."

"That's the problem," Willow responded. "How do they know which path is right? I have more information on what's going on than anyone here and I don't even know what's right and what's wrong. I know what I believe is the correct choice, but that doesn't make it right for Klurr, or Krissy, or Greenfoot, or you. Who am I to impose right and wrong on another individual's beliefs?" She fell to her knees and bowed her head towards the ground.

"What is going on?" Sebastian asked, squatting before her.

"I wish I could tell you everything," she answered. "But I can't, at least not yet. Later tonight when we are all together, I will tell you what I can."

Sebastian stood and offered his hand to help her up. She tilted her head upwards to meet his gaze. The sunlight shining bright behind him blocked the view of his head and torso. All that appeared in her line of vision was an outstretched hand.

"Help is offered by outstretched hand," she said under her breath as she took his hand and stood.

"What?" he asked.

"Nothing," she said. "I was just thinking of something I read. We better go. I want to change before next class and still make it on time."

She was already heading towards their living quarters before the elf could say a word. He shook his head and followed her silently.

****

A shower and change of clothes was just what she needed to feel refreshed and ready to tackle new obstacles. She brushed the tangles from her long curly red hair before pinning it up again to hide it under the wig.

"Odd to see you here, at this time," Aslo said.

"Yes, it is," Kiera said. "Did something happen?"

Willow explained to her guardians the events of the morning ending with Sebastian's hand and how it appeared when he offered it to her.

"That seems rather literal," Kiera said. "Don't you think?"

"As opposed to the writing on a boat or a sign of a hotel saying *your destiny*?" Willow asked.

"Point taken," Kiera said. "Much of the Halloween prophecy was very literal. It also had multiple meanings for different people. Have you considered that? The prophecies aren't written solely about you. In fact, last time we thought the prophecy was about you, it was about Clairity and we almost missed it altogether."

"How can it be about them? They aren't involved," Willow said. "They aren't even here. I miss them. Do you think they have turned against me as well? Clairity and Ashlyn, I mean."

"We don't know. We don't have a clue what is going on outside these walls. Until we do, there is little use worrying," Aslo said. "Things will start to make sense again soon. Just keep working on graduating, everything else can wait."

"You make it sound easy." Willow finished polishing her boyish look and opened the door to leave, finding Sebastian leaning against the outside wall of her bedroom.

"Who do you talk to in there?" he asked.

"No one," she started. "Myself." Realizing he was seeing through her lies, she blurted out, "Black cats that sit on my bed."

"Stuffed animals," Sebastian said, laughing. "Interesting, do they talk back?"

"Yes," she said, looking around the room for something to help her escape the conversation.

"You probably shouldn't tell many people about that," he said. "They might think you are a little off, if you know what I mean."

"I do," Willow said. "No one usually believes me about them. I get called nasty names. You won't mention it to anyone, will you?"

Sebastian laughed. "Your secret is safe with me. It's time to head over to illusions class. You are ready, I take it?"

"I am," she answered.

On the way over to their next class, Willow found her mind running through how the forest had created the illusion of a rain storm earlier, using only a few drops of water. It was an example of nature using illusion magic as protection. Maybe there was a delicate balance between nature and magic - a bond between the two that should not be upset. Maybe that was what the stained glass picture was trying to portray.

Sebastian broke her train of thought. "Looks like everyone is lining up for some reason," he said. "Kayleb, what's going on?"

"The door is locked," Kayleb answered. "We can't get in."

"So what do we do?" Sebastian asked.

"Wait for the teacher," Seth said. "She should show up sometime. It's strange for an instructor to be late."

"She should be here," Willow said, pushing through to the door. "It doesn't make any sense to have the door locked. We will all be late." She reached for the door knob. "Ow!" she screamed, her fingers tingling with pins and needles from the shock she received. Shaking her hand, she observed the door closer. "I think it's an illusion."

"Why would there be an illusion of a locked door?" Gabriel asked.

"To see if we could get in, of course," Willow answered. Closing her eyes, she concentrated on the handle being unlocked, then she reached forward and pulled the door open. "I thought so," she said, walking in.

"You almost didn't make it," Drakondia said. "Tell me how you figured out that there was an illusion cast on the door."

"There were several things," Willow replied. "It didn't make sense for the door to be locked and you not to be present for the class."

“If you eliminate what shouldn't happen, you are usually left with truth. That does work sometimes, but not always,” the instructor said. “What else?”

“I saw a dim aura radiating from the door that indicated something wasn't right,” Willow answered.

“Ah yes, auras. We can thank Miss Kelly for that answer, I suppose,” Drakondia snarled. “What else?”

“When I first tried to open the door, I received a strong electric shock,” Willow said. “It left my hand tingly for a few moments.”

“An electric shock,” Drakondia repeated. “How unusual that you should advance to such a level of detection in such a short amount of time.” She ran her long pointed black fingernails over the picture of a spider on her upper chest, as if she were stoking a pet. “There's something not right about you. I felt it when you destroyed my fun house illusion and I feel it now. Tell me, how is it you excel in every subject as well as you do?”

“I'm not sure I understand what you mean. I have no talent in creating illusions at all,” Willow answered.

“No,” Drakondia said. “That's the point. Creating illusions is so much easier that detecting them. You easily handle the harder task without learning what is easy first. How is it you do that? It shouldn't be possible.”

“I don't know,” Willow said, stepping backwards.

The woman's aura darkened like a sky before a thunderstorm. She stood and slammed both of her hands down on her desk. A sinister grin crept over her face, exposing her fang-like teeth. “You don't know?!” she yelled and let out a menacing laugh.

The darkness spread like a poisonous smog itching to take a hold and choke life from its victims. Drakondia's laughter multiplied. It sounded as if there were twenty of her, all starting their hysterics at different times.

Willow covered her ears. Kayleb tugged her arm, pulling her backwards towards the door. The handle was locked again.

“Can you open it?” Sebastian asked.

“I don't know... the laughter, I can't concentrate,” Willow answered. “Can any of you use illusions?”

“What do you have in mind?” Seth asked.

If someone could cast an illusion that her voice was gone,” she said. “I only need a few moments to break the magic on the door.”

“I am not sure any of us are strong enough to fool her,” Gabriel replied. “She is the teacher for a reason.”

“If you join together,” Willow said. “Lend all of your power to one person. You should be able to give me enough time.”

“Is that even possible?” Kayleb asked. “I have never heard anyone lending power in such a way.”

“It is!” Willow yelled over the now-deafening screeches of laughter filling her head. “I have done it. Please try.” All of her energy was focused on keeping the menacing sounds emanating from their teacher from entering her mind and driving her crazy.

Kayleb moved forward, holding one hand in front of him. A beam of magic exploded towards their teacher.

Drakondia laughed. “Do you believe your magic is strong enough to stop me, elf?” she yelled.

Sebastian placed his hand on Kayleb's arm and the flow of magic intensified.

“What are you doing?” Drakondia screeched, her voice resembling nails scratching on a chalkboard.

Seth and Gabriel followed the mountain elf's lead, placing their hands on Kayleb's arm as well. The stream of magic became too bright for Willow to watch. She turned her head towards the door.

“No!” Drakondia screamed.

That was the final noise Willow heard. The laughter subsided, fading away like a mere memory. In the newfound silence, she focused her concentration on the lock, opening the door with ease. The five of them bolted out into the sunlight, gasping for air.

“What was that?” Sebastian asked.

“I don't know, but I think it's time to speak to the Director,” Willow suggested. “It might be out of the question for us to continue attending that class.”

“Maybe,” Seth agreed.

Chapter Twenty

"It's not a good idea for me to meet with you all like this," Cassandrhea said. "Fuelling a raging fire is a bad idea."

"So is being killed by our illusion teacher," Sebastian interrupted. "I'd rather not die at such a young age."

"Killed," the Director said. "Sebastian, dear, you are being rather dramatic, don't you think?"

"It's an accurate account of what we just experienced," Gabriel said.

"Do you all feel this way?" Cassandrhea asked. After acknowledging their nods, she sat down behind her desk. "Did you consider it might be all an illusion?"

"Oh, it was a lot of illusions," Willow said. "She was angry at me."

"Sebastian," the Director said. "Let me see." She outstretched her hand and waited.

The river elf took the Director's hand in his own. They both closed their eyes. The bond they formed began to glow a soft white colour. Suddenly, they opened their eyes, the same glow having replaced their normal green irises, forming a link between them. As quickly as it began, it also ended, both returning to normal.

"Well," Cassandrhea said, "it seems people want to kill you no matter who you are." She sighed as she lifted the receiver from an old-fashioned telephone sitting on her desk. "Send a containment team to the illusions classroom. It appears there is a problem with Drakondia. Run tests and send me results immediately. I will be waiting. If you find anything abnormal with her, keep her detained," she said to whoever was on the opposite end of the line. She returned her attention to the students standing before her. "I couldn't see how you escaped. How did five students survive a teacher's attack?"

"Will told us we could lend our powers to each other," Kayleb explained. "It was a most unusual experience."

"Lend?" The Director twitched her mouth to the side. "How is it you know how to lend magic, when to the rest of the magical world it's an unheard of practice?"

"I did it before," Willow said, "once. A healer was about to give up hope on saving a friend. I gave her a boost of my power to keep trying. Actually, I gave her all my magic and part of my life force as well. I almost died. Someone had to pry me away."

Cassandrhea's gaze went blank. "I know the event you are speaking of. I'm sorry," she said. "How did you know these four could do the same magic?"

"They are closer than they let on," Willow said. "I have known since I first met them that there is a bond between them. A link of some kind." She shifted her weight to her left side. "I do have a question, though. What was that thing you did with Sebastian?"

"It's a memory link," Sebastian said. "Members of the same family can share their experiences that way."

"Same family?" Willow said, smiling. "So you are elf royalty too?"

If disappointment could take a form it would have been Cassandrhea's face at that exact moment. "It seems some elves can't keep secrets," she said. "How much have they told you?"

"Not much," Willow said, her voice quivering.

Cassandrhea glanced at her out of the corner of her eye. "How much have you told them? Do they know everything?"

"No," Willow said. "Not everything." She glanced down at her feet.

A small ring came from the phone. "Hello," Cassandrhea said, picking up the receiver. She was silent for a few moments. "I understand, thank you."

"It seems Drakondia was given an insanity potion. The medical staff is working on her recovery. She will be away for the rest of the semester." The Director placed her hand on her head. "You bunch need to listen to me. This isn't a game," she said sternly. "Will, these four are not to be dragged into your mess. They are not to be involved. At the end of this semester, they are returning to the elf realm and you will not see them again. Do you understand me?"

"Yes, ma'am," Willow answered.

"You four are to finish your studies and keep away from anything out of the ordinary. I put Will in your group to hide his identity, nothing more," the Director scolded. "If things become any worse around here, Will might be leaving us early. I won't have any of you hurt or worse because of my poor judgement."

Willow snapped her head up to meet the gaze of the Director. A frown crossed her face. She could feel her eyes burning. Before a single tear could be shed, she ran out of the room and headed straight to her dormitory.

Flopping down on the bed, she let the tears flow freely, instantly curing the stinging sensation from holding them back. She cried for what felt like days. A paw reached up and smacked her cheek.

"Aren't you cried out yet?" Kiera asked. "You have been at it for far too long. You don't answer your door. You don't answer us. Snap out of it. It's a good thing the weather isn't responding the way it does anywhere else, although I am sure there is a monsoon somewhere."

Willow sat up and looked at her face in the mirror. Her eyes were swollen almost shut, with the little bit that was visible being completely bloodshot. Red cheeks and cracked dry lips finished her look. She sniffled in a pathetic manner.

"Oh dear," Tika said. "This doesn't look good."

"Why is it every time I make a friend, someone snaps their fingers and takes them away?" Willow asked, tears swelling in her eyes again. "Am I really destined to go through life alone?"

"Dear child," Tika said. "We are here for you."

Willow let out a sad laugh among her tears. "Yeah," she said. "When we are alone and no one else can see you. Oh, and I can talk with you sometimes in the correct places. But if I mention you out loud, everyone will think I am crazy and try to kill me." More tears streamed down her cheeks. "I'm sorry," she muttered, throwing the pillow over her face and flopping backwards.

"It's true," Decon said. "At the moment things are difficult, but once we leave here, we can find a home where it won't be strange to have animals living with you. We aren't going to abandon you. Right now, we need you to pull together and make it out of this place."

Willow sat up again. "Maybe it's best if they do make me leave early," she said. Taking a tissue from the box in front of her, she blew her nose.

"Some cold water might bring down the swelling around your eyes," Tika suggested.

"It might take a bit of time," Shelby said. "You have been crying for an extraordinary duration. You may have set a new record."

Willow chuckled, then sniffled. "Why is it, no matter who I am, people want to kill me?" she asked. "Did I do something terrible to deserve this? Did my parents do something wrong?"

"Goodness no, child," Tika said. "People are afraid of those who are different. You, my dear, are different."

"Do you think all this will ever be over?" Willow asked, looking out her window. "Can I ever live normally?"

"We hope so," Kiera answered. "But what is normal?"

Willow laughed. "I don't know, but I am pretty sure it doesn't involve assassins and insane kings," she said.

"You need to drink some water and replenish your fluids," Aslo said. "After that, answer your door and talk to them."

"We are under orders from the Director," Willow said. "She doesn't want me talking to them."

"Maybe you should find out what they want," Kiera said, flicking her tail back and forth. "They have minds of their own."

She drank several glasses of water and fixed her appearance as best as possible before opening the door. All four elves were relaxing in the living section of their dormitory.

"Decided to come out finally, I see," Kayleb said. "It's rather selfish of you dropping all of your responsibilities without thought for those around you."

"I'm sorry," she said. "You don't understand what I am living through."

"No," Gabriel said. "We don't."

"So why don't you explain it to us?" Sebastian added. "Maybe we can help."

"You heard what the Director said," Willow blurted out. "She is right. You don't need to be dragged into something as dangerous as what I am stuck in the middle of."

"Shouldn't that be our decision?" Seth asked.

A banging sounded on their door. Kayleb answered it. "Seems we have been offered to dreamwalk this evening. The instructors want to see at least one member of each group attend and are offering bonus marks. Will you be joining us?"

"I'm not sure I am strong enough to handle that extreme an exercise. I might be more of a hindrance than help," Willow answered.

“Rest up,” the mountain elf replied. “We want you back for all classes tomorrow. Understood?”

Willow agreed and returned to her room.

Chapter Twenty-One

"They went where?" Shelby asked.

"Into a dream," Willow answered. "It is a class on dreamwalking."

"It seems a little odd that it is happening like this. There is no preparation. No discussion of where you will be going. Someone just knocks on the door and says let's do it. That seems strangely reckless for instructors who wanted to take every precaution."

"When you put it that way," she said, "it does seem a little odd, especially after Drakondia was given an insanity potion earlier. Do you think it could be a trap?"

"It's a horrible thing to think," Shelby answered. "Who and why are the questions."

"Klurr," Willow answered. "He said he had a plan for me. Maybe when driving my illusion teacher mad didn't work, he chose another route."

"Do you know where this Klurr is from?" Aslo asked.

"No," Willow answered. "He doesn't make small talk with me much. Our conversations are more, *I'm gonna destroy you,* over and over."

"Describe him," Jawfree said.

"He looks like a bull, with red skin and a ring through his nose," Willow answered.

"That's bad," Shelby said. "Their race is proficient in dreamwalking."

"But there are several of that race in my class and none of them admitted to ever having been into a dream before," Willow said.

"Then I would say this is definitely a trap," Shelby responded.

"He did say he disliked the instructors," Willow mentioned. "If something went wrong this evening, he could blame it all on them. Now I am worried. If they lifted the ban on dreamwalking for tonight's exercise, I should be able to join the dream from a nearby location."

"It's too dangerous," Kiera said. "If this is a trap, it is meant to catch you."

"I know that," she replied. "But I can't just let everyone get hurt in my place. I have to do something. My abilities in the dream world are growing. I have to try. I will take my wand and hopefully be able to at least communicate with all of you in that realm."

"Be careful," Aslo said.

Willow ran at her fastest speed to the building where her classmates were sleeping on the second floor and headed straight for the aura room. Her lungs tightened, gasping for air. Sweat trickled down the sides of her flushed face. Bending over at the waist, she placed her hands on her knees and took in shallow breaths until her breathing returned to normal. Once fully recovered, she headed for the teacher's table in the middle of the room. It was covered with a white fabric tablecloth that flowed perfectly to the floor.

Crawling under, Willow lay down, gripping her wand tight in one hand. Closing her eyes, she concentrated on the rhythm of her breathing. Slowing her heart rate, she relaxed her body to the point at which she felt as if she were floating on a cloud, weightless. She counted backwards from ten. Reaching one, she opened her eyes to a perfectly white room.

Well, I made it here, she thought, checking her appearance.

Yes, you did and as you appeared in the real world as well, Shelby said in her mind.

I can hear you, she thought. *Thank goodness. I was worried about heading in here alone.*

We need to move quickly. Head for the door. I don't want you in here for any more time than necessary, Shelby replied.

The door leading out of the room was wide open. Willow peered cautiously around the corner, expecting to find a trap at any moment. All she found was the usual staging hallway. There were no signs of her classmates.

"Now the hard part," Shelby said, perched on her shoulder.

Willow jerked to a stop. "A little warning would have been nice," she said. "You could have scared me half to death. Shouldn't you stay hidden? Someone could see you."

"I thought I could help you find the right door easier this way," Shelby answered.

"I have a feeling the place we are heading to will be easy to find," Willow said, jolting to a full stop again.

The hallway came to an abrupt end at a door. Seeping through the cracks between the door and its frame, a darker than black mist slid along the floor, creeping slowly in their direction.

"Guess we found it," Shelby said.

"Guess we did," Willow replied. She stood silent, eyes on the scene unfolding before her. The eerie sight sent shivers down her spine, leaving a prickling sensation all over her skin resulting in the formation of tiny goosebumps. Mustering every ounce of courage left in her body, she lunged forward, swinging open the door in one swift motion. Darkness awaited her.

Shelby disappeared back into her picture form on Willow's skin. They were too close now to risk being seen unless absolutely necessary.

She plunged herself into the black. Her eyes adjusted easily to the lack of light, a trait she could thank the Leander for. It wasn't sight, however, that would find the way. A burning sensation ran through her right side. In the far distance, an orange glow appeared. Her feet moved without warning, carrying her swiftly closer to the only clue she had.

A dense smoke crept around her, strangling her lungs of any oxygen they contained. She coughed violently, gasping for air, but her legs continued forward. Sweat raced down her body from the growing heat. From somewhere up ahead, she heard screams of fright. Her legs bolted towards the noise.

The whole dream-scape she had entered was like a page written by the terunji on the appearance of *hell.* She was standing in a barren wasteland - fires bursting out randomly around her. The temperature was close to unbearable. The remains of trees, now charred and blackened, littered the terrain, while rivers of red lava flowed, winding aimlessly through trenches carved out of burnt rock.

At the top of a small hill, she made out the figures of a few of her classmates. As she drew closer, it became evident that she had found Klurr already.

She assessed the scene before making her presence known. Jin had his arm around Jessica's neck and was holding her tightly in place. Klurr was attacking Krissy. Both girls had cuts and bruises. The tears streaming from their eyes evaporated in the heat before reaching the bottom of their faces.

Willow aimed her wand. A blast of white light exploded from its tip, hitting Klurr directly in the side and sending him flying through the air. Jin threw Jessica to the ground, stampeding towards her. A second blast of magic met the force of his speed.

"Thank you," Jessica said, standing. Her eyes met Willow's and she gasped. She nodded and let out a small chuckle of understanding, adding, "again."

Willow reached down and offered her hand to Krissy, helping the girl to her feet. "You need to head back to the hallway and wait," she said.

"Will," Krissy said, her eyes glazed with confusion. "You saved me. How can I thank you?"

Willow sighed. "You have been given a new chance. Retract the false parts of the articles you wrote. I think you will find the truth is more attractive to the public than speculation and lies." She looked around. "You two need to move quickly now, before they return."

"Too late," Klurr said, rage burning in his words. "I brought some of your friends." He held his wand to the temple of Kayleb's head. The rest of his group performed similar actions to the other elves. "You may be able to stop some of us, but I guarantee at least one of your friends will die if you try. Make your move, Will."

A lump formed in her throat. Klurr was right. Her magic couldn't save all of them at once. This was something she couldn't do alone. She thought of Shelby, but risking the appearance of a guardian here was out of the question and even with the bird's help, there was still the chance that they would not be able to rescue all four elves.

Willow called out, in her mind, for Ashlyn with no response. She wasn't sure what her former best friend could do in this situation but there was hope she may have learnt something. She sighed. There was only one person who could help her. She looked directly at Klurr and yelled out, "Lance!"

Klurr laughed. "Who are you calling for? Your father?"

"Me," Lance said from behind Willow. "What in all the realms is going on in here?" he asked.

"We are teaching a lesson here. If you don't want to become a visual aid, I suggest you leave while you can," Klurr snarled.

Lance laughed. The temperature dropped to a chill as the pits of lava froze and the fires burnt blue. "I am the master of this domain," he said, smiling.

Klurr and his friends found themselves inside cages hanging over a pit of nothingness.

"What's the meaning of this?" Klurr yelled. "Do you have any idea who you are messing with?"

Blue flames burned in Lance's eyes, a look of pure pleasure crossing his face. "I think the question is, do you know who you are dealing with?" Lance enquired. "No one has ever reached the bottom of the hole beneath you before their life expired. Would you like to try?" He paused for a moment. "No? Okay, then be a good bull for a bit. I have some business to discuss." The prince glanced over the elves. "We need to talk," he said.

He hadn't looked at her, but Willow knew he was speaking to her. "Could you send the others into the staging room and keep them in stasis so we have some privacy? Circumstances require that I wake first from this dream," she said.

With the movement of one of his hands, her classmates were gone and they were in a familiar sitting room with a fire lit in the stone fireplace. To her surprise, all four elves were also present.

Kayleb took a seat on the couch as if it were an ordinary event. "Lance," he said.

"Kayleb," Lance replied. "How nice to see... all four of you together." He paused for a moment. "Although I must say this is a strange place to run into you." Taking a seat in his usual armchair, the prince crossed his legs. Glancing around the room, his eyes eagerly sized up the situation.

"Thank you for your assistance," Gabriel said, taking a seat beside the mountain elf. "Things were becoming rather intense back there."

"Yes, they were," Lance replied, sipping on a glass of wine that had appeared in his hand. "Would you like some?" he offered, motioning for his guests to help themselves. On the table in front of them appeared a silver carafe filled with the red liquid surrounded by sparkling crystal wine glasses.

"Thank you," Sebastian said, standing with Seth behind the couch. "I think we are fine for the moment."

“Do I detect reservation?” Lance laughed. “Why would I poison you?”

“My apologies,” Sebastian said. “I meant no disrespect. You did, after all, come to our rescue today. We are, of course, most grateful. However, I can't help but wonder why.”

“It seems you are under the impression I came to help the four of you,” Lance said. He swirled the wine in the glass in front of him, inhaling the robust aroma before taking another sip. “I'm afraid you are mistaken. Although the outcome suits both of our needs.”

“Perhaps you could enlighten us as to what exactly is going on here,” Kayleb said. “It appears we are in the dark.”

“As am I,” Lance said. “I was hoping someone might explain a few details to me as well.” He glanced at Willow. “Perhaps we could start with... what are you wearing?”

“I'm disguised,” Willow answered. “I would have thought that obvious.”

Lance laughed. “Like that?” he asked.

“It's not that bad,” she replied. “I rather thought it suited me.” Her face flushed a light pink.

“Right,” Lance said.

“Could we go back to what's going on here?” Sebastian asked. “Do you two know each other?”

Lance darted a cold stare at the mountain elf before returning his attention to the glass of wine in front of him. “Indeed,” he answered.

“I think the question is do all of you know each other?” Willow asked, placing her hands on her hips.

Lance exploded with laughter. Placing his glass on the table, he clapped his hands together. “I'm sorry,” he said. “I can't take you seriously looking like that.”

“Will,” Sebastian said. “We are all royalty and as such have met on numerous occasions.”

“Will?” Lance laughed. “Speaking of William, have you had any news?”

Willow's eyes met his gaze. She stood frozen in her spot like a statue locked in time standing in a garden. She blinked breaking the spell. “I would have thought you would have more information than I do,” she said, emotionless. “He apparently is awake and took a wife.”

Lance almost choked on the wine he was swallowing. “Excuse me,” he said. “He took a wife? Well I didn't see that coming. Someone we know?”

“I have never seen her before. The story goes... he woke up... saw her... married her the next day,” she said. “How is it you don't have this information?”

“Ah, actually I have been looking for you to discuss that,” Lance said. “It seems I am a prisoner in my own world at the moment. I will get to the details of that after you finish the story of where you have been.”

“I told you before I left,” Willow said, “at school.”

“Reports all indicated that you were taken out of the school system. I have been searching for you for months,” Lance said. “Ah, I see. The disguise. It's all starting to make sense now. Someone was hiding you in the school system.”

“Yes, well, your father is trying to kill me,” Willow answered. “There was some concern about assassins posing as students. As it turns out, the disguise really didn't make a difference. Even as *Will,* I am wanted dead.”

“How did you manage that?” Lance asked. “Never mind, I think I can figure it out.” He glanced at her a few times.

“Sorry to disturb the catch-up,” Gabriel said. “Would you mind?” The light elf pointed to what was left of his clothing. It was tattered and torn with black soot marks all over.

“My apologies,” Lance said. “Where are my manners?” His hand flew up in the air. “There, much better.”

“Rather extravagant for the situation,” Kayleb said, referring to the formal black tuxedo he was now dressed in.

“Why are all of you dressed so fancy?” Willow asked. She glanced at Lance and her eyes bulged. “Wait. They don't know,” Willow protested.

“They are going to find out anyways,” Lance said, a glimmer of mischief dancing in his eyes. “Now is as good a time as any.”

There wasn't enough time for Willow to even blink before she was standing before them wearing an elegant black ballroom gown. Her hair was brushed up neatly into a twisted bun with long wispy curls hanging down. “My wand?” she asked.

“Check your wrist,” Lance said.

A small black purse hung gracefully down from her left wrist. She snapped the golden clasp open. The only thing it held was her wand. “Brilliant,” she said.

“Sorry,” Kayleb said. He pointed a finger in Willow's direction, moving it up and down a few times. The elf's mouth opened as if he was about to add something important, but slammed shut again. He filled his lungs to capacity and tried again, only managing a gasp.

Sebastian placed his hand on Kayleb's shoulder. “We may be taken a back a little,” Sebastian said. “Have you always been a girl?”

Lance laughed at the lost stares of the four royal elves. “She has,” he said.

“I really was planning on telling you about that,” Willow said. She hid her hands behind her back, her palms becoming cold and clammy.

Sebastian gulped. “That was the part you were going to tell us? I can't wait to find out the bits you couldn't explain. Is everything we know about you a lie?”

“I doubt that,” Lance said. “She isn't capable of treachery. I am amazed she lasted this long hiding her gender.”

“Excuse us if we don't share your sentiments,” Gabriel said without emotion.

“It's not like that,” Willow pleaded. “I didn't want to hide things from anyone. You have to understand. I had no choice.”

“No choice,” Seth said. “What circumstances could possibly be so bad that you had no choice? What did we do to earn your complete lack of trust?”

“Now, that's brutal,” Lance said. “I am assuming you lads have no clue as to who the young lady standing before you is?”

“How could we?” Kayleb asked. “We have been kept in the dark on everything about her.” She felt the heat of his gaze scorch her face.

“I knew elves didn't concern themselves about the main world much, but there has been such a large fuss about her,” Lance said. “Not even from the descriptions?”

“Why are we playing this game?” Kayleb demanded. “Simply tell us.”

“You're the girl everyone's looking for,” Seth said. “The one we were told was pulled out of the school system. The newspaper articles, they were all about you. All those terrible things you have done...” His words faded off.

“I haven't done anything terrible!” Willow yelled. “How quickly everyone believes the worst. It sickens me.” She walked over and sat on the arm of Lance's chair.

“She is telling you the truth,” Lance said. “She hasn't done any of the things she has been accused of. Trust me. I have been there for most of it. Time is passing us by and I am limited with it, so I am going to move on. You four should try to keep up.” He reached in his pocket. “My father has come up with a new plan for you.”

Willow gulped. “Killing me isn't enough for him?” she asked.

“It's taking too long,” Lance replied. “Although it is the result he hopes for in the end.”

“Reassuring that he hasn't lost sight of his goals,” she said.

"Indeed," Lance said. "He has decided to alienate you from everyone for the time being."

"Of course," Willow said. "The camp... he's behind everything they are saying about me. But how?"

"With this." Lance held up a small vial of liquid. Its golden colour glowed brightly in the radiance of the fire.

Willow took the small test tube in her hand and examined it. "What is it?" she asked.

"It's a memory-altering potion," Lance answered. "Basically, it allows the person administering the potion to rewrite events in the memories of his victim. It creates a new life that the subject truly believes he lived."

"And the camp," she started.

"Was the first test run of the stuff," Lanced said, finishing her sentence. "As well as a small portion of Pewterclaw's population."

"The others," Willow said. "In the other schools?"

"There are plans for them as well," Lance answered. "If they haven't been infected already, they will be before you could reach them."

"Can it be reversed?" Willow asked.

"That's the question," Lance replied. "For every potion that exists, a reversal potion can be made. Unfortunately, my father didn't bother to. He grows more insane by the minute. He is no longer satisfied with revenge against the guardians. Within five years, he hopes to infect every living creature with this potion, forcing them to bow down to his greatness."

"That's mad," Kayleb said.

"Yes, I did say he was insane," Lance answered. "Try to keep up."

"I thought he was as crazy as they come before," Willow said. "Bringing down the fabric of space between the realms is just a drop in the bucket compared to this."

"Oh," Lance said. "He still plans to do that."

"Cornelius must realize there are creatures that the potion will have absolutely no effect on," Willow said.

"He has lost the ability for reasonable thought," Lance explained. "Even his own family isn't safe from his madness."

"What do you mean?" Willow asked, standing.

"I mean he has sealed our access to the openings to other worlds. My siblings and I are virtually prisoners in our own castle. I have little doubt that, at any time, he will use the potion on me and alter my memories as well," Lance said.

"No!" Willow cried.

"It isn't my choice," Lance said. "Willow, you have to make a potion to reverse the effects."

"How am I supposed to do that?!" Willow screamed. "In case you haven't noticed, I am all alone now. You are the only friend I have left."

"Yes, well about that," Lance said. "This is the last time you can contact me until a reversal potion is available."

Willow's eyes stung. She could no longer hold back the pain she was feeling. Tears streaked down her face. "No!" she cried out. "I can't do this alone. I need you." She dove into Lance's lap and buried her head in his chest, letting her emotions run freely. "You can't leave me too," she mumbled between sobs.

Lance embraced her. The room went quiet except for the sounds of her sadness. After she calmed down, he pushed her forward by the shoulders. "Willow," he said softy. "This is what he wants. Don't let him win."

"I don't know what to do," she said, sniffling. A box of tissues appeared on the table beside them making her force a smile. "Thanks," she muttered, as her face reverted to a look of overwhelming sadness.

He reached in his pocket again and pulled out four more vials of the liquid, placing them in the same hand as the other she was still holding. “You have help,” Lance said. “They are sitting right here.”

Willow glanced over at the elves, their appearance blurred by tears. “They will be heading back to the elf realm soon,” she said. “I doubt we will ever meet again after that. This doesn't affect them.”

“She's right,” Sebastian said. “This doesn't affect us. What makes you think we will help someone who lies so easily?”

Lance laughed. “Doesn't affect you?” he snickered. “Have you not been listening to our conversation at all? This affects every living thing in every realm.”

Willow felt a shiver up and down her spine. She stood and took a few steps backwards. The pupils of Lance's eyes had filled with the blue fire he wielded as a weapon.

“This girl is the reason why Cornelius hasn't already taken over everything. Without her, we would already be slaves to his madness,” he continued.

“So she is some special chosen heroine?” Kayleb questioned. “Then she doesn't need help to save the day.”

“No, you fool!” Lance screamed, his face flushing with anger. “She's a girl... just a girl. She also happens to be the last guardian keeper. The others are all dead or in secure captivity.”

“I think we need to relax,” Willow said, looking at Lance. The blue flames had completely engulfed his eyes.

Without warning, the prince stood and grabbed Willow's waist, pulling her into a passionate kiss in one swift motion. The emotions he felt cooled the flush from his face and doused the fire raging within.

“Feel better?” she asked. “Looks like you calmed down some.”

“Yes,” Lance said, smiling. He returned to his seat. “Nothing like kissing a beautiful woman to calm a burning anger,” he mused. “Why such long faces?” he asked, turning his attention back to the elves. “I'll leave that explanation to Willow for later. As I was saying, your realm is not safe from my father's plans. In fact, he has something special planned for you. It's on the list right after the destruction of his arch-nemesis here."

"I don't suppose you are willing to share the plans?" Gabriel asked.

"It won't make much difference if you know," Lance said, his lips curling up ever so slightly, revealing his playful yet devious side. "He is in league with Atlantis."

All four elf princes gasped. "Atlantis," Kayleb said. "You're sure?"

Lance let out a primal laugh. "Yes," he said. "I am quite sure. There is something else you should know. You will need her help to survive. Cornelius sees you as a threat, almost as big a threat as the guardians. He received a great epiphany one day. In other words, he was visited by the serpents in his dreams again and they gave him some important information. Cornelius wasn't willing to share all the details with us, but he did let slip that after both Willow and the elves are destroyed, there will be nothing left to stand in his way."

Willow looked at the five tiny bottles in her hand and decided to place them carefully in the black purse attached to her wrist for safekeeping. "I see how that could work out," Willow said. "If I make it through the rest of the term alive, I promise I will do my best to find a way to reverse the potion."

"I know you will," Lance said. "When you have one, test it well before you find me. I could be dangerous to you."

"I don't believe that," Willow answered. "The first day I saw you, you could have killed me and you watched me run away instead. You even covered up my existence to your brothers."

"Yes, and look where we are now," he joked. "One last dance then... until we meet again?" Lance snapped his fingers and they were standing in the middle of a ballroom dance floor. Music played as if an orchestra was in the room with them. He took her waist and they glided across the dance floor. He led her elegantly through twists and turns. Her body moved fluently with his, as if the two were meant to spend an eternity dancing together in perfect unison.

The elves stood motionless to the side, their eyes glued to the motions of the performance before them.

When the music stopped, Lance bowed and kissed Willow's hand. "It's time for me to go now," he said, walking toward the ballroom door. He stopped before reaching his destination and sighed. "I have to one more time," he said.

He returned to Willow and surprised her with another passionate kiss. "There are still a couple of people you know who have escaped the potion in Pewterclaw if the elves fail you. After I leave, you will wake up first. You will have only a few moments before the others awake." Lance disappeared through the doorway.

Willow reached in the small handbag and grabbed her wand in one hand and the vials in the other, then closed her eyes tightly.

Chapter Twenty-Two

Opening one eye, Willow peered at her surroundings and let out a sigh of relief. She had made it back and her body in the real world had not been discovered. She slithered out from under the table. “Oh no,” she cried. “Could things get any worse?”

She was standing in the middle of the aura room, a wand in one hand and five tiny vials in the other, wearing a beautiful black ballroom dress. She shoved the bottles into the tiny handbag still attached to her wrist and headed to the door.

Upstairs, she could hear the students beginning to stir. Running out into the yard, she headed for the dormitory, looking back over her shoulder to see if she had been spotted. There was no one in the yard, but as her eyes glanced over the second-story windows, she made out several figures: Klurr, Krissy, and the four elves. Picking up her dress, she kicked off the shoes and ran faster, changing her direction towards the forest.

In the distance, Klurr's voice echoed loudly. “It's the redheaded girl! That bounty is mine.”

Looking back again before entering the woods, she saw two figures jump from the second-story window, one she made out as Klurr even from that distance. The other was unknown.

Running through a forest in a gown wasn't as easy as she had thought it would be. The dress caught on branches and bushes, slowing her down. She could hear Klurr's heavy breathing. He was catching up. "I could use some help right now," she said. The trees formed a staircase before her. Willow smiled, climbing to the top.

She sat on the leaves, catching her breath. "Thank you," she said. "That solves one problem anyways. Now I just need to sneak back into my dormitory without anyone seeing me."

She looked to the sky. "Nice night for a stroll in the fog," she said. A low-lying grey mist crept along the forest floor, seeping out into the grass-covered grounds of the campus, slowly swallowing up everything in its path. The buildings were the last to disappear, with only their highest points sticking up above the fog.

"I know you are there, red!" Klurr yelled from below. "I will find you. Mark my words, you will die tonight. There is no escape. You can see as little in this fog as I can, so we are still on equal grounds. You'll have to make a move sometime and when you do, I'll be waiting."

Willow lay flat on the treetops. She realized the bull-boy was right. Perhaps she should have let Lance deal with Klurr and his gang in the dream world when she had the chance. She let out a big breath of air, forcing her cheeks to puff out like a squirrel with its mouth full of nuts.

A strong breeze blew over her body. It wasn't wind she was feeling, but more like an industrial-sized fan had suddenly turned on beside her. She tilted her head out of curiosity. Willow bolted to a stiff upright position, her wand held out in front of her. She gulped down the saliva that had formed in her mouth.

"Why not?" she said, chuckling. "I've seen just about everything else."

She remained motionless, staring at the sandy brown-coloured dragon that was hovering beside her just above the fog. It snorted. Warm air thrust into her face, almost knocking her over. The beast pushed one of its legs forwards to her and bowed its head.

"Are you offering me a ride?" she asked.

The dragon snorted again and pushed its front leg closer. Willow cautiously climbed the leg and mounted its back. Instantly, the beast flew upwards. The wind blew her hair, strands flew loose from the tidy up-do that Lance had chosen for her. She clenched the tiny black purse tightly in her hand, so as not to lose any of its precious cargo. The flight lasted only a minute, before they landed safely on the flat rooftop of her dormitory.

She slid down the leg of the dragon, landing hard on her backside, but laughing the whole time. "How can I thank you?" she asked.

The creature used its face to nudge her towards the door to enter the building and snorted one last time. Willow turned around and ran her hand over the side of the dragon's face while admiring the deep green colour of the beast's eyes, a colour she couldn't help but think she had seen before.

"I guess I do have some friends out there still," she said, disappearing down the stairs.

Surprisingly, she was the first one back to their room. No sooner than she closed the door, it flung open again and Kayleb entered with Gabriel and Seth in tow.

"How?" the mountain elf started.

"You probably won't believe me, but I hitched a ride from a dragon," Willow said, blowing a loose curl from her face.

"A dragon," Seth said. "Where?"

"From the forest to the roof," Willow answered. "Where is Sebastian?"

"Good question," Gabriel said, carrying something from his room. "I'll go look for him. Be back in a second."

"How?" Kayleb asked again. His mouth opened then shut. He shook his head and sat down.

Seth patted him on the back. "It's a good question. I think there is still more we don't know."

The door flung open again, this time Gabriel returned with the missing elf. "Sorry, I got a little sidetracked helping a classmate through the fog. So where are we at then?" Sebastian asked.

"How," Willow responded. "It seems to be the only word Kayleb can remember. Did I miss something?"

The door flung open for a third time. "What in all the realms is going on tonight?!" Cassandrhea yelled, slamming the door behind her. "Why in the world would you dressed like that and running around outside? You know what? It doesn't even matter. Gather your things. You are leaving immediately."

"Wait, you don't understand!" Willow cried. "I didn't have a choice."

"Honestly, I don't care," the Director said, her face flushing red. "I warned you not to involve the elves in whatever schemes you were planning."

"Mother," Sebastian said. "She saved our lives. If she hadn't come after us, we would all be dead at the hands of Klurr by now."

Cassandrhea sat down at the table. "Everyone sit," she said. Willow took a seat as far away from the elf queen as possible. "Explain."

The elves took turns explaining the events of the evening from the knock on the door to waking in the classroom. Willow filled in details of hiding in the aura room.

"That doesn't explain why you are still wearing the clothes," Cassandrhea said.

"Right," Willow said. "I am sure by now you have figured out I have some unusual talents. I can usually perform some harder tasks, but the easier things I am totally useless at. Dreamwalking is no different. While I can't control the surroundings, I can navigate the dream realm and make some of it real."

"How?" Kayleb asked.

"You are starting to worry me," Willow answered. "I don't know how, but it gets stronger with every dream I enter. It started with a scratch, then I brought back a key, then a few other small items... to today... a nice dress," she said, opening the purse. "And vials of a nasty potion I need to find a reversal for." She lifted one up, to let the light shine through it.

"You have got to be kidding," Sebastian said. "That's why he was contacting you. He knew you could bring the potion out of the dream world."

"Why did you think he was looking for me?" Willow asked.

"I don't know, maybe because you two are dating." Sebastian suggested. Every eye in the room glared at the river elf.

"I'm what?" Willow replied, with a question she never intended to be answered. "I'm not dating Lance."

"I don't think any of us believe that," Seth said.

"It's not even possible!" Willow yelled.

"Why are we even discussing this?" Cassandrhea interrupted. "There are more important things for us to be talking about right now."

"Just a moment, Mother," Sebastian said. "What do you mean, impossible?"

"Seriously," Willow said, sighing. "If you all do know Lance, then you must know about his special gift, the necrid flames." She waited for each of them to acknowledge with a nod. "What you may not know is that the flames manifest themselves in Lance's soul. He burns in anguish every minute of every day, but having been born that way, he just assumed it was normal. As with any magic, the fires burn stronger when fuelled by emotion, except with his, they burn on negative emotions. The more anger and hate he feels, the stronger the flames burn inside him. He can come to a point where the fire takes over and he loses control of his actions. On the flip side, positive emotion douses the flames. He maintains a stable balance most of the time."

"How?" Kayleb asked.

"Is Kayleb okay?" Willow asked.

"He'll be fine," Sebastian said. "How does this affect the two of you?"

"Simple," Willow answered. "If the flames extinguish, Lance will die. Love is a deadly emotion for him. I have no doubt he cares about me, but we both know it is impossible. Luckily, he still looks out for me."

"Then when he kissed you earlier," Seth said. "The first time was to calm his anger?"

"Yes," Willow said. "If he hadn't, he could have killed us all."

"And the second time?" Sebastian asked.

"Lance has a rather devious side to him," Willow said. "In all honesty, in some deranged way, I think he was trying to piss you four off."

"It worked, apparently," Cassandrhea said. "Can we return to the more important matters at hand other than Willow's love life?"

"Just one more question," Sebastian said. "Who is William?"

"William was the last portal guard surviving in the main world when we arrived here. He became a good friend," Willow said. "When the bounties were placed on my life, one was also placed on him, but Cornelius wanted him alive. One night, when leaving Pewterclaw, we were attacked by assassins. William was hurt badly. He almost died."

"He's the one you shared your magic with the healer for," Cassandrhea said.

"Yes," Willow answered. "He lived, but barely. A rare poison was used on him. This is a really long story involving albino assassins, Santa Claus, Frostica, yeti, and a whole lot of luck, but to make things short, I ended up with an anti-venom. Lance's brother was also infected with the same poison. The cure woke him immediately. William remained in a coma. He was still in a coma the day I left with the Director."

"So you aren't dating him either?" Sebastian asked.

"Did I mention he married the day after he woke up?!" Willow yelled. She took in a few breaths and calmed her pulse. "No," she said. "We never dated. Although I thought there was a chance one day we might have. He was a good friend."

"Well," Cassandrhea said, "he still could divorce, right?"

"No," Willow answered. "The Pledge is final in our world. It's a magical binding of souls that cannot be undone, except by the death of one of the two partners."

"Bottom line, to make everything crystal clear so we can move along, you are in fact single?" Cassandrhea enquired

"Yes," Willow answered.

"Brilliant," the Director said, clasping her hands together. "Can we continue on, then?"

A loud rapping noise came from the door.

"I should go change," Willow whispered.

"Hurry, child," Cassandrhea said. After watching Willow disappear into her room and close the door, she motioned for Sebastian to see who was knocking.

"Hi," Jessica said. "We wanted to thank Will for saving us earlier. Is he here?"

"He's cleaning up still," Sebastian answered.

"Could we wait?" Krissy asked.

Sebastian sighed and opened the door to let the two girls through. They both froze in their tracks at the sight of the Director sitting at the table.

"Come in, come in," she said. "I was just getting information on what happened tonight. This saves me time tracking you two girls down."

"Of course," Jessica said, taking a seat at the table. "Will saved the two of us. The end of the dream went a bit fuzzy, though. I can only remember there being a standoff of some sort, then waking up."

"Same," Krissy said.

"Will," Jessica said. "I am glad you are okay."

Willow took her seat at the table again, this time disguised as a boy. "I'm fine," she said. "I'm glad you two made it out okay."

"I owe you all an apology," Krissy blurted out, a tear running down her face. "I plan to write a retraction of the articles I have written lately."

"Why did you write them in the first place?" Willow asked.

"I come from an unusual race. Until our eighteenth birthday we are all essentially two different people. At the moment, I exist as Krissy. At other times, I exist as Kevin. We switch back and forth at will. In the first seventeen years we battle ourselves to become the dominant personality. On our eighteenth birthday, based on our accomplishments, either the male or the female persona will become permanent. The other will be lost forever. I thought If I could get the bigger stories... become more famous... do something spectacular... maybe, I might win. I was wrong. This isn't the way."

"The circumstances you are living under are enough to cause anyone to have a lapse in judgement," Willow said, handing the girl a tissue. "Could you not talk to your brother? Maybe there is a way for the two of you to co-exist?"

"It's the way of my people and we accept our fate," Krissy answered. "That doesn't mean I want to stop existing, though." She smiled. "I plan to write a retraction immediately."

"And the story about the redheaded girl?" Seth asked.

"I'll retract everything I wrote that was false," the reporter answered. "I doubt it will make much difference with my brother's and father's stories still out there. Do you know her? Was that her running across the field earlier?"

"That," Cassandrhea said, "was a poorly-timed prank. I have the culprit in hand and will deal with her accordingly."

"Seemed a little strange, for the girl to show up out of the blue and run around an open field in a ballroom dress," Jessica said. "I figured it had to be a joke or something." She glanced at Willow quickly.

"I suggest the two of you return to your rooms now," Cassandrhea said. "There are still people running around in the fog I need to round up."

"I think the fog has cleared up," Willow said. "I looked out the window a few minutes ago and there were only a few patches left."

Gabriel peered out their window. "It's clear," he confirmed.

"Brilliant," Cassandrhea said. "You two hurry back and don't stop to talk to anyone. From what I understand, Klurr and his friends are still lurking out there. Gabriel and Seth, would you mind escorting them?"

After they left, Cassandrhea stood. "I am going to have security pick up Klurr and his friends to hold for questioning. I'll be back to finish our discussion."

Willow moved to the couch. She rolled her neck in circles, stretching all of its muscles before finally slouching back in a relaxing position.

"Are you tired?" Sebastian asked.

"It's amazing how much dreaming can take out of a person," she said, closing her eyes. She felt a familiar form curl up on her lap and begin to purr.

"How?" Kayleb asked.

Willow laughed. "I think we better wait for everyone else to arrive to explain," she said. "Unless Aslo cares to handle the honours now."

"Aslo is the cat's name?" Sebastian asked.

"It is," Aslo replied.

"It talks?" Sebastian raised both his eyebrows and tilted his head from side to side.

"How?" Kayleb asked.

Willow chuckled without opening her eyes. "Of course he talks," she said. "He's a guardian."

Chapter Twenty-Three

Willow felt a tug on her arm. She opened her eyes to see everyone had returned. Aslo was sitting in her lap.

“How long was I asleep?” she asked.

“About an hour,” Sebastian answered. “Everyone's back and curious about your friend.”

“Mmmm,” she groaned, followed by a yawn. “Really, Aslo, couldn't you have filled them in and let me sleep? I would have thought you would be dying to have your voice heard with the amount of time you have been cooped up.” She tilted her head to each side then stretched.

“I thought they might receive me better if you were here to help explain,” Aslo said.

“The cat talked,” Seth said.

“You are elves. There is a guy that looks like a bull trying to kill me. You believe in magic. Please don't tell me you can't accept a talking cat,” Willow said.

“Point taken,” Sebastian said. “So you are a guardian. A normal-looking house cat who talks. Somehow I expected more.”

“This is not my natural form,” Aslo said. “Unfortunately, these accommodations are a little small for my true guardian body.”

“Forgive us. We aren't totally familiar with guardians,” Cassandrhea said. “There is some mention of them in our history, but only a few of our elders remember those days.”

“Are you all cats?” Sebastian asked. “Should I be wondering every time I see one if I should talk to it?”

“No,” Nero appeared, fangs bared. “There are different races of guardians, as you can see.”

Willow lifted her head and looked up. “Be nice, Nero,” she said, chuckling. “How much of a history lesson do you want?”

“Enough to understand,” Gabriel said.

“There were originally six forms of guardians,” Shelby said, appearing on the couch beside Willow's head. “The three that are here remained true to their guardian roles. The other three, spiders, serpents and sea creatures wanted to be worshipped rather than protect. They split from the guardian order.”

“Where are they now?” Cassandrhea asked.

“That's a long story,” Willow said. “Basically they started a war. Eventually, they decided they couldn't win it since the six ancient races were equally matched. They offered rulers of other kingdoms the blood of magical beings, showing them that it gave the drinker strength and power to dominate over others - enter the blood wars.

“Guardians split the races by worlds to protect as many as possible, putting a magical barrier between each. They syphoned off some of their own powers to do so. As a result, they couldn't travel between the worlds - enter the need to enlist people who could act as hosts to carry them.

“They picked individuals to join them in a new realm to work towards keeping the world safe and those who had the gift of being a keeper. A young prince named Cornelius takes the throne after his parents are murdered by a neighbouring kingdom. Just prior to the barriers going up, he drinks the blood of a magical being, thinking it's the only way to protect his world. The guardians come to ask his sister to join them. She agrees. The new king, her brother, offers to go as well. They can't take him because he is already tarnished by the blood he drank. He goes mad and creates a new scenario where his sister is kidnapped and his kingdom unfairly locked away. The serpents hear his madness and visit him in a dream. They offer him greatness if he helps bring down the barriers between the worlds and right the wrong that has been imposed on so many. They find a way to provide him with venom for his wife and himself to drink. It drives him further into madness, but grants him and his family long life and special abilities." Willow stopped for a moment and took a deep breath.

"Impressive summary so far," Aslo said.

Willow laughed. "It's a bit longer. Does anyone want to hear more?"

"Yes," Sebastian said. "It's quite fascinating so far."

"It gets a bit depressing after that," Willow said. She took a deep breath and continued. "A war broke out. It spanned many years. It wasn't going well for the guardians. A call for help came to the world I lived in. I was only a small child at that time. All keepers and guardians left, heading to the main world to join in the fight. For some time, communication was lost. The elder members of what was left of a council in our realm dismantled all portals to the main world in fear of an attack. They removed all references to guardians and what our roles were supposed to be. Unknown to them, two guardians remained in our world. The female was pregnant, a rare thing for their kind.

"They were friends with my parents and promised to take care of me. Knowing I was destined to be a keeper, they joined with me, becoming stuck as images on my skin for sixteen of our years. Their kittens were born as images. At that moment, I became the first keeper who could carry more than two guardians at a time. Our world was attacked by Cornelius' sons. Lance didn't kill me and a handful of us managed to escape to the main world where we met William. I have been following Cornelius' activities since, trying to stop him from bringing down the barriers."

"That's why the bounties are on your head," Cassandrhea said. "He wants you eliminated."

“To be fair,” Willow said, “there is a second bounty placed by someone in Pewterclaw whose identity is unknown. Then of course, there is Klurr.”

“Klurr is in custody,” the Director said. “He won't be doing any more damage for a long time. The Flinch twins are receiving treatment for the potion they were given and should recover without problem. The main question I have is, can anyone connect Will and Willow together?”

“I am pretty sure Jessica knows,” Willow said. “I have had... adventures with her in the past. I also recently learnt she is on the payroll of high-ranking government officials.”

“Jessica?” Cassandrhea said. “How do you come by so much information?”

“With a lot of luck,” Willow answered. “I don't believe she will say anything, though. It's just a feeling I have.”

“Looks like things are under control, for now,” Cassandrhea said. “Hopefully.” She stood. “If nothing else happens...” The Director left her sentence unfinished. Pressing her lips together tightly, she nodded her head. “Get some rest. Who knows what tomorrow will bring,” she said, walking out the door.

All four elves let out a sigh of relief after the door closed behind the woman. “What's your plan now?” Sebastian asked.

Willow stood. Reaching in her pocket, she pulled out four of the containers of the potion. She handed one to each of the elves. “I could use some help,” she said. “I still have my own vial as well. There are a couple of contacts I still have in Pewterclaw who I can try.” She paused for a moment. Her eyes glossed over and she bit her upper lip. “I'm sorry,” she blurted out. “I wanted to tell you, but...” Her words faded and she shook her head.

“But you couldn't,” Kayleb said. “I think we understand that now.”

Sebastian slapped the mountain elf on the back. “Welcome back to the land of the speaking,” he said, laughing. “We thought we'd lost you there.”

"I think most of my questions have been answered now," Kayleb replied. "Except one. If you were a child during the guardian war, how old are you?"

"In ratio to main world years," Willow said, "I age one year for about every ten thousand."

"Well," Kayleb replied, "that solves the ageing problem."

Willow glanced at each of them. "I'm not sure what you four are planning, but I bet the Director won't be happy about it," she said. "We better get some rest."

Chapter Twenty-Four

"Hello, Jade," Hilary said. "What a beautiful day out."

"Hello," the green-eyed girl answered. "May I ask why I am being taken out of school early?" Jade stepped into the back of a large black limousine filled with every comfort possible.

"I would have thought you'd be glad to see me," the Pewterclaw mayor said, patting the perfectly-formed bun on her head.

"I am," Jade said, smiling. "I am just surprised and, I have to admit, quite curious as to why the sudden change of heart on Kasper's part."

"Yes," Hilary said. "Shocking news, really. There has been so much scandal over that redheaded girl you used to know."

"Willow?" Jade asked.

"Whatever her name is," Hilary answered. "No worries. The rest of your camp denounced guardians and have spoken out against her actions. You don't have to pretend to like her anymore."

"They have?" Jade asked.

“Yes,” the mayor answered. “I kept all the newspapers for you. They are stacked neatly on your desk. Her recent activities, however, are somewhat worrisome. The Director of Secrecy decided to take action and search the schools, in case she might be hiding in one plotting some revenge.”

“I'm not really following you,” Jade said. “What sort of revenge and on who?”

“Well, on you, for one,” Hilary said. “Anyone from your camp could be the next target. I, for one, am glad he made the decision. The thought of that wild girl hurting you aches my heart.”

“But why would she hurt me?” Jade asked.

“Why would she hurt anyone? That should be the question,” Hilary answered. “The girl is unstable and now there is proof. There is something I need to tell you, though. The thing that sparked this whole search... well, your father is missing. The authorities have connected the girl to whatever happened to him.” She paused. “They are still looking for him, of course.”

“My father is missing?” Jade asked, looking down at the floor of the car. “When? I mean, how long ago? Are there any clues?”

“Safron is working round the clock, my dear,” Hilary said, pulling Jade into a hug. “He won't rest until everything has been exposed.” The mayor took out a tissue and dabbed tears forming in the corner of her eyes. “We were going to surprise you too,” she said. “We were planning on getting married as soon as the school term was over. We would have been a real family. Don't you worry about a thing, though. I plan to take you in as my own daughter no matter what the outcome.”

“Thank you,” Jade said, still clenched in the woman's arms. “I think I need some time for this all to soak in.”

“Of course,” Hilary said, releasing her. “It's natural. You are probably in shock. No one expects you to work. You can relax in your office and read for a while. I hate to be a pest, but I need to be sure, if you see that girl...”

"I'll turn her in to Constable Black right away," Jade said, interrupting the mayor. "I hope they catch her and send her away somewhere she can never escape from."

"Good," Hilary said. "I am glad we are on the same page. Ah, here we are." The large car stopped. "I'll have someone bring your bags."

The two women walked onto the bridge leading back to the hidden magical city. On the other side, Safron Black was waiting for them with his car.

"Good afternoon, Miss Jade," he said. "It's a pleasure to have you back. I would have preferred better circumstances, though."

"It's good to see you too," Jade answered. "I want to thank you for all the hard work you are doing trying to find my father. I hope you catch that girl soon. If I can do anything to help, anything at all, do ask."

"Of course, young miss," he answered. "I would like nothing more than to bring back your father alive and well." Safron started the car and drove directly to the mayor's office. "Here we are," he said. "You ladies have a safe afternoon."

"Thank you," Jade answered, exiting the car.

The main desk was as busy as usual. One could literally hear the words *hustle and bustle* come to life. Esmerelda's face was hidden by an extra-large bubble she formed from the wad of pink gum she was chewing. The people in line eagerly watched, whispering visions of it exploding and sticking to her large blue beehive hair.

As Jade walked by, she felt the room grow cold with silence. Glancing at the city residents waiting for their turn to report a problem as she passed by, she noticed each look away. Even the office employees refused to meet her glance, sidestepping her to avoid direct contact.

"They don't know what to say right now," Hilary explained as they reached Jade's office door. "It's a delicate situation. They will come around in time."

Jade smiled and nodded. She sat in her chair and ran her fingers against the grain of the desk that had become so familiar to her before leaving for school. On one corner, her eyes caught sight of a stack of newspapers. She licked her lips and reached for them. The pile slid easily across the smooth wood until they sat directly in front of her.

"I'll leave you alone for now," Hilary said. "Here is my diary. You can catch yours up, so you know where to find me at all times." She placed a black agenda on the front portion of Jade's desk. "Return it to my office when you are done."

"Hilary," Jade blurted out. "Thank you for all you have done. I appreciate it."

The mayor smiled and returned to her office. Jade leaned back in her chair and stared at the ceiling for a few minutes before delving into the pile of newspapers and reading every article. A frown crossed her face as she read about her missing father. Another article in the same paper referred to three missing elves of prominent royalty. People were still disappearing.

The entire afternoon flew by and before she knew it, the office was closing for the evening. Jade sighed. She reached for the black book on her desk and quickly copied all of the mayor's notes and appointments over to her own agenda for the next week. Opening the direct access door to the mayor's office, she entered to return the book.

"Jade, darling," Hilary said. "Is everything okay?"

"Yes," she answered. "I was just returning your appointment book. I have this week marked down. I can catch up more in the morning. I thought you might want to go over your schedule for tomorrow."

"How thoughtful of you," the mayor said, taking the agenda from her. "Do you want to talk about anything?"

"Not yet," Jade replied. "I would like to go home and mull over everything. It's hard to accept how deceived we all were by her. But easy to accept that we were all taken."

“I'm glad you see the truth now,” Hilary stated. “You shouldn't be alone, though. She hasn't been caught and might make you her next target. I want to keep you as far away from that girl as possible. Safron will drive you home and leave a few men to keep you safe.”

“You have been so nice to me,” Jade said. “How can I ever repay you?”

“Don't be silly, dear,” Hilary said. “I may not have been able to actually marry your father, but in my eyes you always have been my daughter.”

Safron popped his head in the front door of the office. “Is Jade ready to go?” he asked. “Ah, there you are. I was just in your office looking for you.”

“I am ready,” Jade answered.

“Very good,” the constable said. “Your carriage awaits, my lady.”

Outside, light rain had begun to fall. Jade sat in the back seat of the constable's car staring out at the city's residents scrambling to reach their destination without being hit by the falling water. An image popped into her mind of each of them exploding from a single drop making contact with any part of their bodies. She chuckled under her breath, then coughed to cover it up.

“Not getting sick, are you?” the constable asked, looking in his rear view mirror at her.

“Not at all,” Jade replied. “Just a little tickle.”

“Here we are,” Safron said. “Three of my finest are covering every entrance. No one will get in or out without us knowing about it.”

“I feel much safer knowing that,” Jade replied. “Thank you.”

“We all want to make sure you are safe,” he said, twirling the corner of his moustache. “Get some rest. Tomorrow will bring good news, I am sure.”

"I will," Jade said, stepping out of the car. She looked up and let the cool rain hit her in the face until her eyelashes began to stick together from the wetness.

"You should go in. The damp isn't going to do you any good," Safron yelled from across his car out the passenger window.

Jade waved and ran to the door of her apartment building. Her personal belongings from school were already inside her door when she unlocked it. "Makes me feel like keys are a waste of time," she mumbled to herself.

Throwing her briefcase on the coffee table, she grabbed a towel from the closet and began drying her hair. She filled a copper kettle with water and put it on the burner of her stove to boil while she changed into some warm pyjamas. Settling in with a cup of tea, she curled up in her big chair and reached for a book that was sitting on the side table next to her. She picked it up and instantly felt a jolt of energy from it. It was an energy she knew well. Something about this book contained her father's magic.

Jade's memories drifted back to when she was a little girl.

"It's called hide and seek, Jade. I will hide something and you need to find it," her father said.

"But how do I find it?" Jade asked. Ringlets of blonde hair tied in pink ribbons framed her face. Her perfectly green eyes widened with excitement.

"You feel it," her father answered.

"What will it feel like?" she asked.

He took her small hand and placed it over his heart. "Like this," he said. "Exactly like this."

"I understand," she said. "It will feel like Daddy." Jade counted to ten and then opened her eyes again. "Ready or not, here I come." She raced through the castle, looking under tables and on chairs until she came to a book. Jade stopped and looked curiously at it lying in the middle of a table. She picked it up and smiled. Opening the book, she turned to page six, the same age she was.

Six lines down, words appeared between the lines. "I love you," she read out loud.

"I love you too, Daddy," she yelled. He came out from behind a door and picked her up, twirling her around in circles.

Jade snapped back to reality. A smile that had formed on her face now receded. Her hands caressed the outside of the book. It felt like him. Opening it carefully, she turned to page sixteen, the same number as her age and scanned for a message clouded in illusion. Words formed before her eyes. *Trust Willow. Find her. Help her.* She slammed the book closed, sitting for several minutes looking off in the distance at nothing.

Springing to her feet in one swift motion, she grabbed her briefcase, and headed for the door. *Illusions, don't fail me now,* she thought, disguising herself to make it past the police officers watching her building.

Chapter Twenty-Five

Willow threw open the windows in her room and sat on the ledge, watching fluffy white clouds sail through the sky. In between, warm rays of sunlight kissed the surface of her face. A tiny bluebird perched itself in the ivy beneath her, singing a few high-pitched notes before moving on. At that exact moment, her mind was at peace.

The past few weeks had been uneventful. Classes continued, with the exception of the illusions course. Drakondia was still recovering. Everyone knew she wouldn't be back this semester.

Krissy printed a heartfelt article retracting all of the half-truths and apologizing for her lust for fame, finishing with a promise to report solely on facts in the future. She received praise from the general public for her honesty. Even some of the students who previously left the school had returned.

Willow took in one last breath of fresh air before dressing for the day. It was the weekend. That meant she could laze around Greenfoot's garden, eating apples and reading books. There was a time when doing nothing would have made her feel stir crazy. Now, however, she relished the feeling. It was a chance for her to forget about all that was waiting for her once she left Sleeping Sands.

She looked out the window one more time before heading out of her room. Closing her eyes for a moment, she soaked in the sunshine. *I'll be out there soon*, she thought to herself. She opened her eyes and blinked several times. A completely different scene was unfolding. Students were running about, yelling and crying. She rubbed her eyes and took another look. Willow sighed. "So much for perfect," she said, heading out of her room.

Her roommates had already left for the day. Elves, she had learnt, were generally early risers, at least earlier than her on days off. Their living quarters were quiet and perfectly still. Willow felt a sudden chill overtake her body, the hairs on her arm sticking straight up as if standing at attention. Goosebumps formed up and down her arms. She took in a deep breath, trying to relax. The air was stale as if a thousand years had passed without a door or window opening. She choked on its heaviness in her lungs, coughing to expel as much as possible.

The door flew open. "Hurry!" Cassandrhea yelled, pushing Willow towards her bedroom. "There is no time to wait. Grab your belongings, you have to leave immediately."

"I don't understand," Willow said. "What happened?"

"Kasper is coming," Cassandrhea said. "He is looking for you. A full campus-wide sweep, including physicals. I am afraid he still believes the people from your camp. Something must have happened to make him agitated. Pack what you can. You have five minutes."

Willow grabbed her backpack and suitcase from her room. She threw some extra boy clothes into a bag, as well as her spare wig, before returning to Cassandrhea. "I'm ready," she said.

A doorway was already open and waiting for her. "It leads to Malarchy's apartment. Be careful, you may startle anyone who doesn't know you are dressed like that. Good luck," the Director said, handing her a few gems to use as currency.

Willow headed to the open gateway. Reaching it, she paused for a moment. "Say goodbye to them for me," she said, looking back. Stepping through the threshold, she shed a single tear.

A minute later, Willow found herself standing in Malarchy's apartment. The room was still and dark. “Malarchy!” she yelled out. “It's me, Willow.” There was no answer. Sitting on the couch, she realized she didn't even know if his memory had been altered. At least one-on-one, she could subdue the man.

Looking around, the apartment was spotless as if no one had been living there. Yet all of Malarchy's things remained. The bedroom was in perfect order. She walked by the front door and found several days' worth of mail scattered messily on the floor. Picking up the envelopes and papers, she placed them in a pile on the coffee table.

She sat on the couch again. “I wonder where he could be,” she said.

“From the looks of those letters, he has been gone for two or three days,” Aslo answered. “His appointment book is there, maybe it will have something to hint at where he went.”

A brown, leather-bound appointment book sat neatly on one corner of the coffee table. Willow picked it up and flipped to today's date. She turned the pages backwards to the last entry. “Three days ago, he has marked dinner at seven in the evening and an address,” Willow said. “There is nothing after that.”

“It's a start,” Aslo said. “If he doesn't return, we can check out where he went.”

Willow's stomach rumbled. It was already mid-afternoon and she hadn't eaten anything yet. Rummaging through the kitchen, she found some dried fruits to snack on. The next few hours she found herself pacing, sitting, standing and repeating. She considered leaving the apartment, but without a key to get back in, decided it was better to wait.

“It's getting late,” Aslo said. “Why don't you lie down for a while? We can keep watch for Malarchy's return.”

She rubbed her eyes. Waiting was tiring. Without any fuss, she agreed and lay down on the bed. As soon as she closed her eyes, she drifted off to sleep without waking before the next morning.

Her eyes opened, then closed again. She licked her lips to relieve their dryness and sat up. Swaying slightly from side to side, she toppled over. She forced her eyes open this time and looked around the room.

"Guess it wasn't a dream," she said, placing a bare foot on the cool floor and pulling it back up again. She crawled all over the bed looking for her sock that fell off during the night, eventually hanging upside down to look underneath for where the piece of clothing was hiding. "Ah, there you are," she yelled, stretching her reach and almost falling on her head.

"What are you doing?" Aslo asked, his face meeting hers still hanging over the bed.

"Sock," she answered, holding it up in her hand. She pulled herself back up on the bed. "Any sign of Malarchy?" she asked.

"Nothing," the guardian replied.

Her foot fully clothed, she stepped down and tidied the bed before heading to the living area. A clashing noise came from the front door. Willow rushed over, but found it was only the delivery of the day's newspaper and mail. She picked it up and moved it to the coffee table to join the pile she made the day before.

Sitting for a moment, she reached for the newspaper and opened it, reading out loud the front page headline.

"All schools ordered closed for the year pending investigation." Lowering the paper to her lap, she tossed her head backwards on the back of the couch. "Brilliant," she said. "Why now?" Sitting back up, she read on. Her jaw dropped open as if it were dislocated, swinging back and forth in the wind. How could it be possible she made her way to the front page of the newspaper yet again?

"You'll catch flies if your mouth stays open like that," Kiera said.

"They are closing all the schools. Every student is being searched before they are released," she said. "Can you guess who they are looking for?"

"You, I would imagine," Aslo said. "It would be the reason the Director wanted you to leave in such a hurry."

"Well, yes," Willow replied. A scowl crossed her face that her news hadn't provided the same shock to them as it had to her. She threw down the paper.

"What we need to know is why all of a sudden," Aslo said.

"What I need to know," Jade said, standing in the doorway, "is why you look like a boy?"

"Jade!" Willow yelled. "Are you... you?"

"Yeah," Jade said, elongating the word. "Should I have come in disguise?"

"No, not what I meant," Willow said. "The others from the camp aren't who they used to be. Their memories have been altered."

"So that's what happened," Jade said, sitting down. "Cornelius?"

"Yeah," Willow said. "Using this." She handed Jade the vile of liquid. "It's a potion that allows whoever administers it to change how his victim remembers events."

Jade nodded her head. "You got this from Lance?"

"Yeah," Willow said. "He has probably had his life re-written by his father by now."

"Do we have any allies left?" Jade asked.

"The list becomes shorter by the day," Willow said. "I can't stay here long. There are too many people looking for me now. Even in this disguise, I won't be able to stay hidden for long."

"My father is missing," Jade said. "Hilary is trying to blame you for it."

"We figured he was missing by the stack of mail," Willow answered.

Jade sat staring at the pile on the coffee table. "I think the mayor is behind his disappearance. In fact, I am sure of it."

"Hilary?" Willow asked. "Why?"

"I don't know," Jade answered. "A while back, I overheard some of the office staff say she was always a bride but never married.

The rumours say that she gets engaged and then her fiancés disappear mysteriously before a wedding can happen." A tear burnt its way down Jade's cheek, its salty taste leaving traces on the side of her lips. "When she picked me up today," she continued, "she told me Dad and her were planning to marry when I returned from school."

"Malarchy and Hilary?" Willow said. "That doesn't seem like a very good match."

"It's not," Jade blurted out. "He never would have married her. I think he knew something was wrong and went along with her like I did today."

"The last entry in his daily planner is an address." Willow handed the book to Jade. "It was three days ago about the time he went missing. You wouldn't happen to know whose address that is?"

Jade took the agenda and flipped through the dates. Her eyes glossed over as if they were coated with crystal. She blinked several times. "That's Hilary's home address," she said. "We need to go there now." Jade jumped up from the couch.

Willow grabbed her arm. "Wait!" she yelled. "It would be easier to look around if we knew she wasn't home."

Jade sat back down and pulled out her personal timetable. "I just filled in her appointments in my book today," she said. "Tomorrow she is in meetings from ten in the morning until two. After a long stretch of meetings like that, she usually leaves the office. I'm not sure where she goes, so we will need to be out of there by just after two at the latest."

"That should give me enough time to look around," Willow said. "Can you tell me the easiest route to get there?"

"You aren't going without me," Jade said. "Besides, it's much easier if I show you the way rather than try to explain it."

"Someone might become suspicious if you are missing from the office tomorrow," Willow said. "If you are right there, in the mayor's sight, you have an airtight alibi. You'll be safe. Besides, you can keep tabs on Hilary for me. If her meeting times change, I will need you to keep her busy. Don't take any unnecessary chances."

Jade slammed the book down on the table. "Fine," she said. "If you find anything... anything at all... I want to know about it."

"You will," Willow agreed.

"Willow," Jade said, "I'm glad you are okay. Try to be careful tomorrow."

Chapter Twenty-Six

Willow headed off down the street, swinging her backpack over her shoulder. The map Jade had provided to the mayor's house was crude, but readable. Turning onto Hilary's street, she collided with another pedestrian and fell backwards onto the sidewalk.

"I'm sorry," she said. "I wasn't watching where I was going."

"Will?" a familiar voice said.

Shielding her eyes from the sun with her hand, she peered up to see Jessica and Krissy towering above her.

"What are you doing here?" Jessica asked.

"Walking," she said.

"Walking where?" Jessica asked. "With everything that is going on, I can't just leave you wandering the streets. My butt is on the line here too."

"You of all people must know the latest accusations can't be true." Willow argued. "I was at Sleeping Sands when it took place."

Krissy looked back and forth between the two. "I'm missing something, aren't I?" she asked. "What latest accusations?"

"Will isn't really a boy," Jessica blurted out. "In fact, she is the one everyone is looking for."

Willow's mouth dropped open. "Oh," she said. "Jessica isn't a student. She applies every year in case the Department of Secrecy needs a spy planted in the school. She only attends when necessary. She works for Kasper."

"Wow," Krissy said. "Looks like I missed a real story. I suck at being a reporter." All three girls broke out in laughter.

"If you are doing something," Jessica said, "I am coming too."

"You have no idea how dangerous this is," Willow replied. "Something really bad is happening in Pewterclaw. I am only doing this to find a friend who is missing."

"Malarchy?" Krissy asked.

"Yes," Willow answered. "The last entry in his agenda was at Hilary's house. I am going to see if he left any clues."

"You think she's involved," Jessica said. "I'm right, aren't I?"

"Why do you sound so excited?" Willow asked.

"We have been watching her for some time," Jessica whispered. "If she is involved, I want to help you take her down."

Willow sighed. "Krissy," she said, "you should go somewhere safe."

"Are you kidding?" the young reporter answered. "This is my chance to break a really big story... one that has all the facts this time. I'm sticking to you two like glue."

"Great," Willow said. "I had to run into the two craziest people around on my way to a possible death trap."

"Do you think it will be that exciting?" Krissy asked.

"Let's go," Willow said. "We should probably keep our voices down too. We should be close to her house now."

"We are," Jessica said. "We are standing right in front of it."

Willow smacked herself in the forehead. “So we have been discussing our secret plan in front of the place we are planning on breaking into?”

“Pretty much,” Krissy answered. “This spying thing is fun.”

“There is a back entrance that can't be seen from the road,” Jessica said. “It's the best way in. We can sneak through a hedge round the corner, one at a time.” She led them to a spot where the tall bushes edging the property had a slight gap they could squeeze through.

One at a time, the three girls pushed their bodies through the hedge. The yard was perfectly kept. The grass was uniform height and the same lush green colour as a posh golf course would feature. Bushes were trimmed into fancy designs, each a work of art rivalling the finest statues in any museum. Rose bushes that could have won an award in any contest, were proudly displayed along the edges of the building.

“This way,” Jessica said, leading them to the back door. She checked her watch. “The gardener is due in ten minutes to trim and water. We have to hurry.”

The back entrance way was under an arbour covered in ivy leaves, which also almost completely covered a basement window. The white wooden door boasted a round brass knob. Turning the handle, the door didn't budge. “It's locked,” Willow whispered.

Jessica pushed her aside. Pulling a hair pin from the top of her head, she wiggled it around in the lock until they heard a click. The door opened. The expert lock-picker stood to the side, letting Willow enter first.

The inside was fairly well-lit from the sun shining through the windows. It was a home where everything had a place and was always in it. They followed a trail which spanned through the kitchen, to the dining room and into a beautifully decorated sunken living room. Willow commented under her breath about the white and cream coloured decor that themed the entire house. Continuing on their tour they found the powder room, a music conservatory, and ended in a library.

“We are missing something,” Willow said.

"This house is too perfect to have a crime committed in it," Krissy said, touching an angora wool throw blanket that was lying on the back of a beautiful leather couch, then moving over to read the titles of the books that lined shelves on the walls.

"But there is no way to access the basement," Willow said.

"Basement?" Jessica said. "Maybe there isn't one."

"There was a window outside," Willow said. "I almost missed it too. It is hidden by the garden."

"Maybe there is an outside entrance," Krissy suggested, leaning back against a wall between two book shelves. "Ow," she yelped, hitting her head on a wall sconce and knocking it sideways.

A squeaking noise of gears grinding sounded and one of the bookshelves turned sideways revealing a set of hidden stairs.

"I totally meant to do that," Krissy said.

"I don't suppose we have a flashlight," Willow said. "Guess not."

"Talk about deja vu," Jessica said. "Please don't rip your clothes and try to make a ridiculous torch again."

"Right," Willow agreed. "Skip the torch plan. I can see in dark places anyways." She descended down the stairs. "If you hold on to my shirt, I can lead the way."

"Or," Krissy said, "we could just flip on the lights." She flicked the switch on the inside wall to an *on* position and the staircase lit up.

"If you want to do things the easy way," Willow said.

Jessica chuckled. "Let's move on before someone catches us."

"Ugh," Krissy said, following the two down. "What is that horrible smell?"

"I don't know," Willow answered. "But it gets stronger the further down we go. You may want to keep away from the walls too."

The stairwell looked as if its walls were crying from the moisture dripping down its sides, forming small puddles in every crevice. In between the slabs of grey cement bricks, green and black mold fought each other for a position to exist. A rotting stench of decaying flesh swirled up the stairs towards the open door at the top in a final effort to escape from confinement. At the bottom of the stairs was an unfinished empty room made of grey cement, containing three different closed doors.

“Let's take door number one,” Jessica said, heading for the handle without hesitation. She threw the door open and jumped back. Nothing happened. “That's rather boring,” she said, looking inside.

The room was filled with wrapped-up containers and boxes. Willow opened one that looked like a painting and gasped at its contents. “I need these,” she said. “We have to move them upstairs.”

“How exactly do you plan to remove them?” Jessica asked. “We didn't come here to steal.”

“They are the answer to a puzzle I need to solve,” Willow explained. “It's important to everyone's future. I have no idea how, but I need to move them.”

“We can move them out of the room,” Krissy said. “Between the three of us, there must be some magic we can find to take them with us later.”

Willow and Krissy carried the missing window pieces into the large basement hallway, resting them against a wall until they finished their exploring.

“I wonder what these are,” Jessica said, holding up a vial of yellow liquid.

“Be careful with that!” Willow yelled. “Where did you find it?”

“Right here there are a couple of cases of them,” Jessica answered. “What are they?”

Willow took the vial from her hand. She put a couple of bottles in her pocket. “Stand back,” she said. Her two companions ran out of the room in time to hear a crashing noise.

“Did you destroy them all?” Krissy asked.

"Yes," Willow answered. "They were something far too dangerous to let anyone stockpile a supply of. It was a memory-altering potion. Basically a dose of that and anyone could control what you remember and shape your personality in the future to whatever they want."

"That's why your friends turned against you," Jessica said. "Isn't it? Someone fed them that potion."

"Pretty much," Willow answered. "There is no potion to reverse the effects as of yet. At least we know the good mayor is up to something. I suggest we move on to door number two. You can let Kasper worry about the rest of the artifacts in here."

"We have been trying to figure out how she has been gaining such momentum heading into the elections. Winning the new *Governing Authority* position has been her desire since it was announced," Jessica said. "With a potion like that, she could change the minds of some very influential individuals. That could be enough to make her a very powerful woman."

"Brilliant," Willow said, opening the second door. She immediately wished she hadn't. The smell of damp rot increased a hundred times. "I think we found the source of the smell," she said, turning her face from the door and covering her nose with one arm.

"Do we have to go in there?" Krissy asked, running to a corner to vomit from the stench.

"Yes," Willow answered. "I think we will find most of our answers in there. If you can't handle it, you can stay here."

"Nope," Krissy said, wiping her mouth. "Stomach is empty now anyways."

Willow flicked the light switch on inside the room. "Sure, I try to use a light switch and I get nothing," she said. "I sure wish I had my own little star." Willow paused for a moment, unsure as to why she thought of Iskander and his special ability.

Jessica slammed right into the back of her. "Ow," she yelped. "You could have warned us you were stopping. What is it?"

Suddenly it appeared. A small ball of white light bobbed up and down, dancing around them. It circled them... curved in between them... even jumped over their heads.

"It's glad to see us," Willow said, watching it zip off ahead and then come back. "I think it wants us to follow it."

The little star lit the way through the dark room. The further in they travelled, the more gruesome the scenery. Rats climbed over piles of bones. Some of the critters were stuck in webs attached to an arm or leg bone. The occasional skull made one of the three girls jump and scream. The white ball of light stopped at a cocoon hanging from the ceiling in the shape of a person.

"Help me cut this down," Willow yelled. She pointed her wand at the top threads, while the two girls positioned themselves to catch the husk when it fell. With one quick motion, a blast of light hit the extra-strength webbing and the cocoon fell, toppling over both girls.

"Yuck!" Krissy screamed. The material of the outside of the cocoon was wet and sticky. Her hands and clothes were covered in it.

"We need to open it," Willow said. "I don't know how thick it is. If I use magic, I could hurt whoever is inside."

"You mean there is a person in there?!" Jessica yelled.

"Yes," Willow said. "We need to get them out of there. Does anyone have anything sharp we can use to cut away at this stuff?"

Krissy threw Willow her key ring attached to which was a knife. "Multi-tool... Dad insists I carry it for those times when magic can't help," she said. "Guess I should listen to him more often."

Willow used the knife to cut into the layers of webbing. Once she made a hole big enough, the other two stretched it upwards, so she could safely use magic to make bigger cuts. Finally the cocoon split into two revealing a man. It was Iskander. His skin was pure white and eyes wide open filled with terror.

"What happened to him?" Jessica asked.

"If I had to guess, it looks like a rare form of spider venom," Willow answered. She reached into her backpack and pulled out the wooden box. Opening it, she grabbed the flask of anti-venom for ancient spiders. Filling a syringe, she injected it into Iskander's arm and stood back.

After a minute, he sat up and screamed as he pulled remnants of webs from his face frantically. “Get it off!” he yelled.

“It's okay. It's me, Willow,” she said, trying to calm the man.

“Why are you dressed like a boy?” he asked, eyeing her from side to side.

“Brilliant,” Willow said. “No... thank you for saving me from that big web, Willow... Noooooo... I get... *Why are you dressed like a boy?*” She sighed. “I am in disguise. Too many people are trying to kill me.”

“That makes sense,” he said, taking her hand to steady himself to his feet.

“I think there are others in here,” Willow said. “Can you ask your little star to help us find them?”

Within moments, they were taking down their next cocoon. Cutting it open, they found the remains of the bus driver from Pewterclaw's previous location. Willow screamed at the sight of what was left of his pruned skin and mangled bones. The poor man looked as if someone had taken a straw and sucked every ounce of life out of him. The only thing still intact were his eyes, wide open and still facing in opposite directions.

Willow turned to look ahead. “Guys,” she said, “there are a lot of cocoons in this basement. Some of them are going to be still alive. We need to move fast and find them.”

Iskander's little star moved in front of Willow to light up over twenty of the white shells hanging tightly packed together from the ceiling.

“What time is it?” Willow asked.

“Almost one,” Krissy answered.

“Hilary will be done her meeting in one hour,” Willow said. “We need to make this happen quickly. If we are going to have any hope, we are going to have to take them all down at once. Any survivors might have an extra bruise or two, but I think it's a good trade-off for being freed."

"Let's do it," Iskander said.

Willow aimed her wand at the threads holding the cocoons to the ceiling and with one swift motion used a blast of magic to cut them all. The white husks fell to the ground.

"Stay away from the walls, there are webs all over. We don't want to be caught and helpless," Willow said. "Use whatever you can to open them quickly."

"I'd like to add, watch out for the spider that created all this," Jessica said. "We still haven't seen it yet. It must be lurking around somewhere."

"Actually," Iskander said, "the spider is Hilary."

"I'm sorry," Krissy said. "I thought you said the mayor was a bigass spider who kills people."

"That's what I said. She uses some illusion magic or something to hide her true identity." Iskander began slicing open a cocoon using a weapon he summoned. "I think this one is alive," he said.

Willow rushed over. Inside the cocoon was a beautiful elf. Even in her state, her appearance kept its composure, her radiance glowing. "She's a light elf." Preparing a syringe, she stabbed the elf's arm. "Carry her to the other room. She can recover there, away from all of this. Krissy, can you stay with her?"

"I'd be happy to get out of creepyville," Krissy answered. "We'll be with the stained glass windows if you need us."

"Wait," The elf woman said in a weak voice. "My daughter. Please find my daughter."

Willow took her hand. "You rest for now. We are going to open every single cocoon here."

"Over here!" Jessica yelled. "It's Malarchy."

Willow ran over to Jessica's side and began helping to peel the webbing away from his face. His mouth was frozen wide open, as if he had been about to scream. Willow used the anti-venom then waited for some sign of movement.

Iskander joined them. Kneeling down, he checked Jade's father for signs of life. "There is a pulse, but it is weak. I'll carry him to the other room to recover," the portal guard offered.

Frantically, they continued tearing at the webbing surrounding what were once life forms. They found shells of children, presumably the ones that had been orphaned and disappeared in the city reports Jade had provided. Hope was fading fast to find any other living creatures.

"Here!" Iskander yelled. "Looks like another elf. There is a pulse."

"A mountain elf," Willow said, stabbing her arm with the needle. "Move her with the others, please." She went back to the last few remaining cocoons.

"Only two left. I hope one is that lady elf's daughter," Jessica said, ripping into the cocoon in front of her.

Willow started work on the other until Iskander returned and took over with his summoned weapon. "This one has a glow. I think it might be a light elf," Willow yelled.

"We are too late for the other," Jessica said.

The husk in front of them split open and revealed a girl with beautiful golden curls giving off the same radiance as her mother. Willow gave her the injection. Iskander picked up the frail girl as if she were made from glass and carried her to the others waiting in the room with the stairs.

The child's mother, now fully recovered, rushed to her side. "Thank you for saving us," she said.

"We aren't out of here yet," Willow said.

"Willow," Malarchy said. "Is that you? Why are you dressed like that?"

"Seriously?" Willow complained. "Has no one ever heard of a disguise?" She shook her head. "How are you feeling, Malarchy?" she asked. "Your daughter is frantic with worry."

"Jade's okay?" Malarchy asked.

"She's fine," Hilary said, standing at the bottom of the staircase. She had a tight grasp on one of Jade's arms. Pushing the arm forward, the girl landed on the floor by her father. "Seems I have a few intruders to deal with," the mayor said.

"What are you doing here?" Willow whispered in Jade's ear.

"She left the meeting early," Jade replied. "I couldn't stop her, so I followed her."

"Yes, the dear girl tried to use an illusion on a master illusionist," Hilary said, howling a laugh. "She actually thought she could fool me."

"Are you saying you are an ancient?" Willow asked.

"Not exactly," the mayor said. "But close." The space around Hilary began to shift and distort. Her body began twisting into a different form until her head sat on the body of a giant spider. "My mother was an ancient. She found herself trapped in this world after stumbling through a rip in the barrier between worlds. The spiders of this world are all far too inferior to use as mates. But mother's desire to reproduce couldn't be quenched. She found that the average male of the main world was compatible enough to fertilize her eggs. Of course after, she ate the men. Her children were a new crossbreed. Mother has spent many years creating an army of children to rule this land. We have positioned ourselves all over."

"It will never work!" Jessica cried out.

Hilary laughed. "It already has," she answered. "There are more of us in positions of authority than you can imagine. There is nothing you can do about it."

"But," Willow said, "there is about to be one less." She aimed her wand at Hilary's head.

"You're that girl, aren't you?" Hilary laughed like a mad woman. The high peaks of her voice left the hairs standing up on the backs of their necks. The low parts made a deafening tone that if heard long enough could burst an eardrum. “You do cause a lot of trouble. Everyone wants you dead. So why are you still here?” she asked. “I suppose if you want a job done right, it's best to just go do it.” Fangs extended out of her mouth and she lunged forward.

Willow sent a blast of magic flying through the air and hit Hilary directly in the midsection. The spider flew backwards and up the stairs with Willow in pursuit. Reaching the top of the stairs, she rushed into the library. There was no sign of the mayor anywhere. She walked carefully around the sofa, checking around each corner.

“Above you!” Aslo yelled, appearing on a pillow.

Willow looked up just as Hilary dropped on top of her, pinning her wand arm with two legs. Reaching for her pocket, Willow grabbed Krissy's keys and lunged the pocket knife into the fleshy part of the spider's stomach. The mayor squealed in pain, jumping backwards. Willow's wand was already in action, sending a stream of magic strong enough to knock Hilary through the wall and out the window of the next room.

Willow followed her outside. “This is my world now!” she yelled. All the beautiful ivy, roses, bushes and trees in the garden sent their vines, branches and roots to grab onto Hilary's many limbs holding her steady in one place.

“Your magic isn't strong enough to kill me,” the mayor cried out. “You must realize that by now. Two direct hits and I am not even injured. You might as well give up.”

“I don't plan to use my magic,” Willow said, putting her wand away. “Nature has a way of balancing these things out.” She looked up, smiling at the storm clouds beginning to swirl above them. The wind picked up and rain began to fall.

“It won't make a difference!” Hilary yelled over the gusts of wind. “There are more of us than you can imagine.”

A bolt of lightning flew down from the sky and made a direct hit with the mayor. Hilary's head exploded on contact and her spider-like body went limp.

Willow ran downstairs. "Is everyone alright?"

"We are fine," Jessica said. "I panicked and called for help. This place will be swarming with agents anytime. I'm sorry. I didn't think you could handle the mayor alone."

Willow took in a deep breath and weighed her options. Turning to Malarchy, she handed him the vials of memory-changing potion. "Take these," she said. "Find a way to make a reversing potion. It's the only hope to return those who were brainwashed to their former selves. Whatever you do, don't let the government have them. This potion is too dangerous to ever be used by anyone again. This fight is yours now."

"There is still time," Jade said, crying. "You could run."

"My time is over, there is nowhere left for me to run to," Willow said. "Even if I could make it past the security, every assassin from here to Sleeping Sands is focused on this location by now. I won't make it to the sidewalk."

"We could explain," Krissy said.

"It would take some time for us to clear Willow's name," Malarchy said. "The Directors want to see her taken in, preferably not breathing. They would never even give us the chance to explain."

"Then we'll fight," Iskander said.

"Then they will kill you as well," Willow said. "If I go quietly, you all live on to finish what we started. Everything won't be in vain. You can save the others." She hugged him. "Give a hug to Faramund for me too, after you fix his memories, that is. I will have to leave our furry friends with you as well."

The elf women were huddled in a corner still recovering from the venom that pulsed through their bodies. "May I ask a favour?" Willow asked them. "These stained glass windows, they are the answer to a puzzle that will help your world. There are four prince elves, Kayleb, Gabriel, Seth, and Sebastian. Find them and deliver these to them along with this backpack. Tell them they can find the answer with these."

The golden elf nodded to her daughter. “Deanne, take them through with you,” she said. A portal opened and the girl disappeared into it, levitating the windows wrapped in thick brown paper and taking them with her.

Willow turned to release the guardians to her other friends and bestow the gift of becoming a keeper on them, when she felt a tug on her arm. The female mountain elf grabbed her. Using advanced strength, she threw Willow across the room. She hit the floor, sliding for a fair distance before coming to a stop on a well-polished surface. Her backpack fell in front of her face.

“You can tell them yourself,” the golden elf said. “I am Liandria.”

“And I am Petrella,” the mountain elf added.

Willow heard doors open and the sound of shoes walking on the smooth marble floor.

“Thank goodness,” a familiar voice said. “We were starting to worry.”

“With good reason,” Liandria said. “I am afraid we never would have made it back if it weren't for this boy.”

Willow looked up and smiled. “Hi,” she said.

“Why am I not surprised?” Cassandrhea replied back. She lowered a hand and helped Willow to her feet. “You aren't much for waiting for invites, are you? I have no idea how you managed to involve our race in this mess again, but I suppose that will fall to the elders to decipher now.”

“I had no clue I was going to end up here,” Willow said. “I did the whole death speech thing.”

She looked around. The floor and ceiling were marble with giant pillars carved to look like they were made from swirling material connecting the two. She was standing on the biggest porch she had ever seen.

Over a half wall, luscious green leafy trees grew as far as the eye could see. A multi-coloured parrot landed on a tree branch in front of her. Willow reached out and touched its soft feathers. “Pretty girl,” the bird cawed before flying off.

“Smart bird,” Willow said. “At least it could figure out I am a girl.” She removed the wig she was wearing, shaking out her long curly red hair.

“Looks like your next adventure begins in the elf realm,” Cassandrhea said, putting her arm around Willow's shoulders. “I look forward to seeing where you take us in the future.”

Chapter Twenty-Seven

"What just happened?" Krissy asked, rubbing her eyes perhaps in disbelief, but more likely from the dust particles lingering in the air. "I didn't think elves involved themselves in the everyday lives of outsiders."

"They don't," Malarchy said, a low chuckle hanging off the tone of his voice. "Only our Willow could pull something like this off. I wonder where they took her." An outstretched arm moved towards the place from which the redheaded girl had disappeared. His open hand clenched into a tight fist, grasping nothing but a handful of air before opening again. One eyebrow arched at the result. "And how," he added, abandoning the idea there was a physical answer there that he could touch.

"You don't think they went to their home world?" Jessica asked.

"My dear girl," Malarchy answered. "Let's do away with the pretense you know nothing, shall we?" He paused for a moment. "We both know elves do not invite anyone into their lands. It's one of their most sacred rules. I highly doubt they would break it on a whim, even if Willow did help save their lives."

"I guess we won't know until we see her again," Jade commented. Looking at the long faces of her colleagues, she added, "She'll come back. She's way too stubborn to stay away. Besides, with William and the others still in danger, there is no way she wouldn't resurface somewhere soon."

"FREEZE!" Safron Black yelled. His voice carried down in full force from the top of the staircase. "Nobody moves and nobody gets hurt." Descending a couple of steps, he bent at the waist to have a closer look at whatever perils might be awaiting him. His eyes slanted, the pupils darting back and forth, not wanting to miss even the slightest of details. The upward curls at the ends of his moustache twitched.

"Oh," Kasper Deogole said, pushing by the constable with a huff. "Enough with the cliché police act. Last thing we need is a cheap knockoff murder mystery detective running around and messing things up further." He descended to the main floor. "So," he said, looking at each of the survivors, "anyone care to enlighten us as to what happened? Perhaps explain why there is a very large headless spider carcass on the lawn? Jessica?"

"The spider is, or was, Hilary," Malarchy answered. He was in a better position to handle the Director. They could, after all, be considered on equal footing in Pewterclaw, especially now that Hilary was out of the picture.

"The mayor?" the Director of Secrecy replied. His lips clenched together tightly, making them jut outwards. "I see." He paced back and forth, tapping his finger on the side of his face while staring at the ground. "I may need a bit more information."

Malarchy sighed. "I doubt you will believe it, but Hilary's mother was, or is, an Achaear. Her father was a male from this world. Illusion magic was used to hide her true form. I believe you will find the remains of most of the missing persons through there." His index finger extended towards the partially-opened second door.

"Black," Kasper bellowed. "Take a few men and start removing any remains you find."

“I'd be careful of spider webs,” Krissy warned. “They are quite sticky and disgusting.” She held out her shirt, crinkling up her nose at the unsightly threads that had latched onto her. Her thumb and forefinger pulled a strand away, exposing a tiny spider. She screamed, knocking it to the ground. Mercilessly, she stomped it into the cement flooring. “Sorry,” she cried. “I imagined it had a tiny Hilary head. I might have arachnophobia for life.”

“Yes. Well, point taken,” Safron said, examining the mess that had been made of the clothes of all of the survivors. “We won't take long.”

“Don't count on that,” Jessica said. “There are a lot of bodies and piles of remains.” A scraping noise interrupted the conversation as a few loose pebbles scattered across the floor. The middle door now stood fully opened.

“Somebody tell me why you are all here and what happened. I want an explanation from each of you!” Kasper yelled, his face flushing red. “I want the truth. Leave out nothing. I expect every last detail.”

“You won't like it,” Malarchy said, leaning to allow the wall to support his back. He crossed his legs to find the most comfortable position possible. Under the circumstances, simply not aching was a satisfactory accomplishment. He shifted his weight back and forth several times. “If you are willing to hear us out, we will try to explain as much as we can. Could we perhaps do this outside, where the air is a bit fresher?”

“No,” Kasper huffed. “No one leaves until I know what happened. It involves that girl, doesn't it? Where is she? Are you hiding her here somewhere?”

“Yes... and no,” Jade said, moving away from her father. “We didn't have a lot of time to speak, but from what I gather, a potion was created that can alter memories. It was used on all of our friends at the camp and on some individuals here in Pewterclaw, probably those with some political influence. I knew something was wrong with the statements made by the other members of our camp to the newspaper, but I didn't know why. I also knew something was strange about the mayor. When she retrieved me from school, she informed me that Willow had kidnapped my father. There was a zero percent chance of that being true. So I started snooping. First thing I found was Willow. I asked her to help me find my father. She didn't want me to get in trouble, so she asked me to watch Hilary from the office while she looked around her house. When the mayor left from her meeting early, I followed her and she caught me."

"So we can add breaking and entering to her list of offences now too?" the Director said, showing off his teeth through a lop-sided grin. There was something about the redheaded girl that got under his skin. Perhaps it was his lack of control over her actions. More likely, it was her total lack of responsibility for what went on in her presence. One simply could not run around waving magic in people's faces. It was his job to make sure that didn't happen, and he always did his job well.

"Enough, Kasper," Jessica said. "It's been a long day. I broke in here on an official investigation that Willow was helping me with. I ran into her by chance on the street. During my on-the-spot interrogation of her, she gave me probable cause to search the grounds. So I did. She just happened to come along."

"If she hadn't been here, we would all be spider food," Krissy muttered. "I think she's brilliant."

"And why are you here?" Kasper asked, turning his attention to the young journalist.

"Me?" Krissy squeaked. "I was... following Jessica."

"I see," Kasper said. He turned to Malarchy and motioned for him to take over the rest of the story. There was no use dealing with the girls. Their sense of reality was askew at the moment.

"We were victims," Malarchy explained, patting Iskander on the back. "Hilary had been asking me out for weeks. I noticed something was off about her campaign and thought I would do a bit of undercover work. I pretended to date her and agreed to her marriage proposal. I never actually intended to marry her, of course. She invited me for dinner one night and I found myself being the main course. I think you will find the remains of all of her past romances in that room as well. Seems *Black Widow* was an appropriate nickname for her."

"When Malarchy didn't return, I went to look for him. Hilary caught me off-guard as well. By the time I realized my mistake, it was too late. It was horrible being frozen by her venom. I was helpless, totally unable to move as she cocooned me alive to feed off of my life force slowly," Iskander said.

"It was just the lot of you who were saved?" Kasper asked.

"No, the missing royal elves were here as well," Jessica said.

"Where are they?" Kasper asked.

"I don't know exactly," Jessica answered. "They disappeared sometime between recovering from the effects of the venom and just after Willow had taken care of Hilary."

"So the girl killed the mayor?" the Director pried.

"She killed a monster in self-defence," Malarchy said. His crooked teeth clashed together, letting out a crackling grinding noise. A few moments longer and a call to a dentist might have been required. "A monster that has killed hundreds of innocents to feed on. A monster who would have added all of us to that list and more. She did Pewterclaw another favour."

"Perhaps," Kasper heckled. "But answer me this. Why was it her and not one of you that engaged in battle with the mayor?"

"She has more skill than the lot of us combined," Jade scoffed. "I don't even know how she managed to do it. Her first blast did nothing more than throw Hilary back up the stairs. Not even a scratch. I was positive we were all ending up on the missing bulletin board."

"I agree," Jessica said. "She had to pull off some real fancy magic, or she got very lucky. Either way, we owe her for her ingenuity."

"Okay, so your testimony is," Kasper said, raising an eyebrow. His pupils darted back and forth, watching the faces of his witnesses. "The girl is a heroine again. She had nothing to do with any disappearances. The royal elves are fine and your friends have all been given a memory-altering potion causing them to hate

Willow. Is that correct?" He waited until all five had nodded. "And Hilary was an evil spider, hellbent on what?"

"You mean other than feasting on us?" Malarchy said, his words dripping with sarcasm.

"Obviously," Kasper replied, rolling his eyes.

"We don't know the whole plan," Krissy answered. "There was some talk of there being many others of her kind... all having important high-ranking positions throughout the main world. So I guess world domination comes to mind. Willow might know more."

"That brings us to the next question. Where is the girl?" Kasper asked. "Wait, let me guess. You don't know. Am I right?"

"Pretty much," Jade snickered.

"She disappeared as well. We honestly don't know where she is," Jessica said. "Bring in the lie detectors if you like."

"Lie detectors?" Jade queried.

"A specialized team of investigators who have strength in magics that detects when a person lies," Jessica answered. "They are quite effective in taking statements, but not so great to hang out with."

"That won't be necessary," Kasper said. "I believe the evidence here will either back up your testimonies or discredit you." His body swivelled around quickly to gauge the reaction of each of them. "If any of you are found to be telling untruths, there will be consequences."

Breaking the growing intensity, Safron and a few officers walked through, carrying the remains of several individuals. "Pay no attention to us," the constable said. "We'll pass right by and be out of your hair."

Kasper hit the palm of his hand on his forehead and sighed. "What is in that room?" he asked. The tip of his finger shook as it pointed to the door closest to the staircase.

"Artifacts of some sort," Jessica answered. "There were also cases of the memory potion, but Willow smashed them all. She said they were too dangerous to risk allowing anyone else to have the ability to use them."

"Well," Kasper said, "I am glad she has the ability to decide that for us."

"She is right," Malarchy interrupted. "If that potion has the effect we think it does, no one should be allowed to have that power. I am more interested in the artifacts. Why would the mayor be hiding them down here? They must have some significance to the unfolding events."

"Oddly enough, I agree with you about the potion. However, finding an anti-potion for anyone under its influence is impossible without a sample." Kasper opened the door and walked in, stepping carefully over any wet spots on the floor. A crate creaked open. Dust particles escaped in the air. Packing materials flew to the ground, revealing an ageing vase.

"Just passing through," Safron yelled out, followed by the shuffling noises of shoes heading towards the second room.

"Black, good man," Kasper bellowed without taking attention away from the vase now grasped tightly in his left hand.

The top of the constable's head peered round the door frame, showing just enough to see the curls of his unusual moustache. "Did you need something?"

"Ah, yes," Kasper answered. "Be a mate and send someone to fetch Tereza Scarab and Vern Hemlock. We will need their expertise to unravel this mess."

"Right away," Safron answered. "Mind if I take a few more bodies with me? We are looking at quite a few more cadavers than we anticipated. We may solve every missing person case this City has had in decades."

"Quickly, man," Kasper answered. "We have a time-sensitive situation here. I need a sample of this liquid."

"Is that necessary?" Jade asked. "I know Willow would have a plan to make an anti-potion. She wouldn't leave our friends like they are now."

“Forgive me if I don't rely on the girl who refuses to talk to me directly,” Kasper hissed. Particles of liquid sprayed from his mouth misting onto the floor. “So what about the last door?”

“We never made it past these two,” Jessica answered.

“No one knows what is in there?” Kasper asked. “In all the realms, what is wrong with you people? There could be more live people.” A clicking noise marked each step he took towards the closed door. That, combined with their glossy black finish, gave away that his shoes were fairly new, perhaps even bought earlier that day.

“Wait!” Malarchy yelled. “We don't know what could be back there. I know there could be more victims, but there could be something more dangerous lurking around as well. We should be prepared for the worst.”

“I'll send someone now for the other Directors,” Safron interrupted. With a thud, a child's skull hit the floor, rolling to a full stop as it brushed up on the Director's left shoe. “Sorry 'bout that.”

“Yes, good,” Kasper replied, jumping backwards an inch. “Pick that up. Oh and send a few men down here. We don't know what is behind this door.”

“Should I call in Special Forces?” Safron asked. “Just in case.”

“Good idea,” the Director of Secrecy answered. “We can wait a few minutes for them to arrive. In the meantime, these five citizens have agreed to help remove some of the artifacts.”

“We have?” Krissy moaned.

“And very good of you too,” Kasper said, wrapping his arm around her shoulder to direct her towards the first room. “Be careful to step over the liquid and don't drop anything.” He gave her a slight push on the back, sending her into the dark storage area. “Rest of you too now. Hurry. Hurry. We don't want to leave any clues down here. Oh, Malarchy, a word if I may.”

“Is there something I can help you with, Director?” Malarchy asked.

“Yes,” Kasper answered. “You see, I couldn't help but notice that you have become quite popular not only here in Pewterclaw, but as a diplomat as well.”

“I take that as the highest compliment coming from you,” Malarchy replied. “I can't help but wonder what it is you are actually trying to say.”

“It's simple, really,” Kasper said. “Pewterclaw is now mayor-less. I wondered if perhaps you might consider running for the position. We could use a man like you. My office would fully back your decision if you decided a government life was suitable to your tastes.”

“Ah,” Malarchy said. “Of course, it would also make it easy for you to keep tabs on me, shall we say?”

“You are perceptive,” Kasper replied with a low chuckle. “The arrangement would be beneficial to everyone. Your daughter would remain assistant to the mayor. Both of you would establish a new life in the main world. A good life... one where you could also have a say in matters that might affect your other friends as well.”

“I must admit, you are a persuasive man,” Malarchy replied. “To be honest, I had already decided to apply for the job. Your talents can be put to better use elsewhere.”

“What's the emergency, Kasper? I was enjoying an afternoon on the couch.” Vern Hemlock said, descending the stairs. “And what is that awful smell?”

“Rotting corpses, I would imagine,” Malarchy said.

“Malarchy, pleasure seeing you. Must ask, what on earth are you doing here?” the Director of Dangerous Substances enquired.

“Long story,” Kasper said, shaking Vern's hand. “Best come this way. The liquid on the floor is purported to be a memory-altering potion.”

“Really?” Vern said. “That's very rare... very rare indeed. I'll take a few samples but have to warn you, odds are it's been altered by dirt or dust. Contamination ruins a good potion. We'll give it a try, though. Do we know where it came from?”

“No, unfortunately not,” Kasper answered. “We need an anti-potion, though and quite a lot of it too. Seems there are people running around who have been brainwashed by the late mayor.”

“Good grief,” Vern said. “Hilary's dead?”

“What's this about Hilary being dead?” Tereza Scarab asked, entering the room.

“Yes, yes,” Kasper said. “It's a big scandal. Seems she was a man-eating spider. Long story, will have to fill you in later. For now, Tereza, have your assistants help remove all the artifacts from the room and begin examination upstairs. We have an unknown behind that third door to explore shortly and we may have to evacuate quickly.”

“Well, that won't be a problem,” Tereza said. “Looks like it's just about cleared out. I'll be upstairs if you need me,” she added, carrying a crate from the room.

“I have my samples,” Vern said. “Need me to stick around, in case there's something behind there?” he asked, nodding at the closed door.

“Good idea,” Kasper said.

“The special team is here,” Safron interrupted.

“Good,” Kasper replied. “Send them over. Malarchy, you will want to stay as well, I assume? Black, keep Iskander and the girls topside... move to a safe distance, but have your men keep them around for further questioning.”

The constable called for all men removing bodies to evacuate. After waiting a few moments he said, “All ready, I believe.”

“Have your men open the door!” Kasper yelled. “Let's see what present the mayor left us this time. Prepare for the worst and hope for the best.”

“What exactly would the best be?” Malarchy asked.

Vern laughed. “Anything other than the worst, I would imagine.”

“READY!” the leader of the Special Forces team yelled.

"Ready!" the other members answered.

The door swung open and a cloud of grey mist escaped, blocking any view of what dangers lurked inside. A blast of air filled their senses with the damp earthy smell of rotting wood. "Masks!" the team leader yelled. Immediately, every member of the team's faces were covered with large gas masks, relics from an ancient war.

"Don't be ridiculous," Vern said, pushing them aside. "It's not dangerous... horrible smelling... but not dangerous. Can we shine some light inside? See if we can sneak a peek past the mist?"

A young man hurried from the very back to the foremost position of the team. Holding his arms outstretched, he unleashed a brilliant beam of light out of the palms of his hands. The luminescent ray formed a knife, cutting a slice out of the dense fog hindering their sight. The lit up section revealed a daunting reality.

"My word," Vern said, taking several steps backwards. "I have never seen such a thing before." He removed a handkerchief from his top pocket to wipe the drops of sweat streaming down his face. "We may be in trouble if those are what I think they are."

"They are," Malarchy said, rubbing his chin. His mouth hung open wide enough to accentuate his uneven teeth shaped similar to fangs. "From the looks of them, we don't have much time." He pointed to the white sack closest to them, standing about equal height to the door frame. The beam of light revealed thin black legs pushing up against the sides of the silk cocoon they were encased in. "So what do we do? There could be hundreds of sacks in that room or more. Each one potentially houses an unknown amount of baby spiders. That's enough to wipe out Pewterclaw and the only known antidote to their venom, we don't have."

"Indeed," Kasper replied. "There is no question. They must be destroyed. But how? From what you have all reported, our magic doesn't affect them."

"There is something happening, sir," the young man holding the light said.

Vern took a few more steps backwards towards the stairs. "I imagine you don't really need my help on this one. After all, I handle dangerous substances, not dangerous creepy crawly critters. I'll be upstairs. Yell if you need me."

Paying no attention to the man hurrying away, Kasper peered back inside the room. "I think the light might be agitating them. Their legs appear to be slashing at the cocoon. It won't be long until they break free and we'll lose all containment. Any suggestions?"

Malarchy rubbed the top of his bald head. "Fire," he said. "Burn them. Have a team ready to try electrocuting them if the flames don't work. Tell them to aim for heads."

"Well," Kasper said, "it's the best plan we have." He took in a deep breath, allowing the air to fill his cheeks, making them puff out, before letting it slowly escape. "Black!" he yelled. "Clear the area by another block and have a second team ready with plasma capabilities. If any spiders escape, aim for their heads and shoot immediately." He turned to the Special Forces team leader. "I assume you have fire capabilities."

"Yes, sir," the officer replied. "We have two men on this team capable of creating fire."

"Excellent," Kasper replied. "Clear the area of everyone non-essential."

"I think it may be best if you and I head outside as well," Malarchy said. "There is little we can do to help."

"Right you are," Kasper answered. "You boys make sure you get flames deep inside the room. We need all the cocoons to burn, not just the front ones. Once the sacks are engulfed in fire, hightail it out of here. I expect the rest of the house will burn quickly as well, causing a collapse. We need to keep everything burning as long as we can from outside, otherwise confirmation the targets have been eliminated will be impossible. Good luck."

Malarchy glanced back over his shoulder from the stairs just as the first stream of flames launched through the doorway at Hilary's unprotected babies. A high-pitched shrieking gave him the urgency to quicken his pace twofold.

Several minutes passed. "They are taking a long time," Malarchy said, his eyes locked on the house.

“They have to make sure,” Kasper said. “Lots to burn.”

A paralyzing scream echoed loudly, surrounded by high-pitched shrieks and chatters, etching a nightmarish vision in the minds of anyone within six blocks of the mayor's house. Within moments, Constable Black and his men were fighting to hold crowds of curious townsfolk back from the property limits.

“That didn't sound good,” Vern said. “Are we sure we are far enough away from the danger?”

“Move back, Vern,” Kasper suggested. “Take Tereza and the others with you.”

The Director of Dangerous Substances had barely turned around to leave before an officer emerged from the house dragging one spider on his back and one on his left leg, flames protruding from all angles. The heads of the creatures attached to the screaming man were the same size and appearance as a fully grown adult person. Their bodies, however, were only about a quarter of the size of their mother's.

“Aim for the heads!” Kasper yelled at the second Special Forces team. “Quickly, so we can save the boy!”

Plasma balls launched through the air just as the top spider showed its fangs and bit down, piercing the officer's neck. The colour from his face faded, a mixture of blood and venom pouring down from two visible puncture wounds on his right side just below his hairline. A blank stare crossed his face. His legs gave way, sending him tumbling to the ground, fire engulfing over half the surface of his body. Flames flew up, catching on the top of one of the spider's head causing it to squeal. Legs flailed around as it ran in circles with no apparent direction before it exploded, leaving behind only its arachnid parts.

“Send out another round of plasma!” Kasper yelled. “Don't wait to attack again if this set miss like the first did!”

“She heard you,” Malarchy said. “Looks like she is heading this way. We best turn and run.”

“Good point,” Kasper replied. “Except where to?”

Malarchy scanned the area. They were surrounded by civilians. "I take that back," he said, clenching his eyes tightly closed. The Director copied his movements.

A deafening boom exploded in front of the two men, followed by a splash of a warm liquid against their faces.

Kasper opened one eye and used his hand to remove the sticky substance covering his face. "Well," he said, "that was too close for comfort."

"Agreed," Malarchy said, examining the remains of the attacking creature sitting less than an arm's length away. Turning his head, he coughed. The smell of burnt hair and flesh overwhelmed his senses. He struggled to regain his composure after wiping as much of the exploded remains from his face and clothing. He spit rather than swallowing. "A rain shower right now would be helpful."

Safron allowed a volunteer fireman to move forward from the crowd. He approached the two men and sent a stream of water in their direction rinsing them off from head to toe.

"Thank you," Kasper said. "Being soaking wet is much better than being covered in whatever it was we had all over us."

"So," Malarchy said, heading over to the officer's body lying on the ground motionless, "we know only their non-arachnid parts are susceptible to the elements. I would imagine that would include fire, electricity and extreme cold." He knelt down and checked for a pulse, then closed the man's eyes. "He's alive, but barely. Best we can do for him is to treat the burns. He can feel and see everything, so pain medicine should be a priority."

"What about the venom?" Kasper asked.

"Willow has the antidote with her," Malarchy answered. "I have no way of contacting her. The only other place there might be some is in the camp."

"So," Kasper said, "let's go."

Malarchy laughed. "I think you forget, that is another can of worms. Someone has infiltrated the camp and is using memory-changing potions for which we have no cure. Anyone who goes there risks being affected."

"We need an anti-potion," Kasper said. "But only Willow has a pure sample of the potion to create one from." He tugged the hair on both sides of his head.

"Perhaps," Malarchy said, "you should not have alienated her as you did. Then we would be able to find her."

"Yes, well, can't change the past," Kasper replied. "I am not completely convinced she is as innocent and pure as the lot of you would like me to believe. Of course, I am not one hundred percent sure the memory-altering potion is what you say, either. If I find proof I am wrong, I will of course admit it."

Malarchy reached in his pocket, his fingers reaching out to grab the small vial he had been entrusted with. Once he had it clenched tightly, his fist froze. "Perhaps something will surface," he said. "If you don't need anything else, my daughter has had a very emotional day. I would like to escort her home." He pulled his empty hand from his pocket to wave goodbye.

"Yes, yes," Kasper replied, his back facing Malarchy. Sticking out one hand, he waved it over his head without looking back. "Very well," he said. "I trust I don't have to mention all parties present need to remain in the city for possible further interrogations."

"And yet you did," Malarchy replied. "Jade," he called out. "We'll be going now."

As if waiting for her summons, Jade instantly appeared by his side intertwining her arm around her father's. "Did you give it to him?" she whispered, tilting her head slightly sideways, her eyes glancing up at his stern face.

The corner of Malarchy's lips turned upwards, forming a devious curl on his face. "Why would I do that?" His eyes shifted to the corner to meet hers.

"Where are we headed?" she asked.

"Home," he answered, adding, "for now." He swung his arm around her shoulders and squeezed her gently towards him. "We need to figure out a few things." He tilted his head backwards. "Iskander, old man!" he yelled. "You keeping up?"

"Who you calling an old man?" Iskander replied. "I'm right with you."

"Good," Malarchy replied. "From now on, we three need to stick together. Last thing we need is for one of us to be infected by that potion. So heads up and all alert."

"I have your backs," the portal guard answered. "No need to worry... future mayor."

Malarchy chuckled. "Yes, indeed," he said. "Something else we need to discuss when I am sure there are no extra ears listening."

Chapter Twenty-Eight

"So this is the elf realm," Willow said, shaking her head in disbelief. "I thought it would seem less real somehow."

"Less real?" Cassandrhea questioned. "What did you expect? Surely not a bunch of half-dressed elves running around with bows and arrows, barefoot..." She rolled her eyes.

"No," Willow answered. "Not at all. I just expected..." Her words cut off. She hung her head, as if there was something fascinating about the patterns her foot could make using the rubber tip of her shoe to kick the ground. "I don't know what I expected, exactly, but different. Everything here seems a bit exotic. At the same time, it could easily be a place in the main world."

"You step one hundred yards into this realm and think you have seen all it has to offer?" Cassandrhea asked with a chuckle in her voice. "Trust me. There are wonders here you cannot find in any other place. Although I am not sure how much you will be allowed to witness."

"What do you mean?" Willow frowned. The two lines that formed between her eyebrows were becoming far too defined. If she wasn't careful, they would one day become a permanent feature. “You just said you were looking forward to what direction I would take you in the coming days.”

“I did,” Cassandrhea replied. “But I wasn't talking about places in the elf realm. That decision is up to the royal council to make. Come now and we will find you a room and proper clothes.” She motioned with her hand for Willow to follow her as she opened two carved marble doors. “Ah, Anndee,” she said. “Perfect timing.”

Standing in the threshold of the two doors was the girl she helped save in the main world. A faint scent drifted towards Willow. After catching a whiff, her nostrils flared, stretching to take in as much air as possible. Amazingly, the fragrance embodied the young elf's appearance. If this sweet scent of honeysuckle was a colour, it would have been the same rich golden tones that ran throughout the elf's long curly hair.

“Did the window panes make it here safely?” Willow queried. “I would like to have a better look at them.”

“Window panes?” the young girl asked. She tilted her head just a smidgen sideways. The natural light from the outdoors sought out her face. It cast its warmth on her dainty features before meeting the rich colours of her eyes and reflecting back directly into the gaze of those looking on.

“I am afraid you have Anndee mixed up with her sister Deanne,” Cassandrhea said. “It's an easy mistake to make. They are identical in appearance.”

“Twins?” Willow asked.

“Triplets, actually,” Anndee replied. “We have one other identical sister, Dannee.”

“Of course, that is neither here nor there at the moment,” Cassandrhea said. “Please show Willow to a room and provide her with some... more feminine clothing.” She redirected her attention towards Willow. “We will have to restrict you to the room for now,” she said, using her hand to push the small of Willow's back.

The force propelled her forward through the doors, just barely missing Anndee. She lost her footing, wobbling her way back to a sturdy position over the course of a few steps. "Can I see Sebastian?" she asked.

"No," Cassandrhea answered. The saying might have been *if looks could kill*, but in this case, the tone of the Director's voice held that same contempt. "I don't think you fully realize the situation you are in. We don't usually allow outsiders onto elf lands. Your fate rests in the hands of the royal council."

"My fate?" Willow asked. "As in, you could kick me out?"

"I cannot speak for any decision the council might make," Cassandrhea said. "You, however, will abide by whatever is decided. For now, you should rest and change your clothes. I will attend to setting up your hearing."

"Hearing?" Willow shrieked. "Have I done something wrong?"

Cassandrhea sighed. "Of course you have, you foolish child. You entered our realm without permission. We don't take intruders lightly."

"To be fair, I was thrown through the portal by Petrella," Willow said. "I had no idea what was happening."

"You will have a chance to explain all of that to the council," Cassandrhea said with a familiar scorning tone in her voice. It was one that anyone who had attended Sleeping Sands Academy knew well. "There is no use explaining anything to me. For now, please do as you are told." The doors slammed behind her.

"Well," Willow said, "looks like it's just you and me." The corridor she stood in was frigid, more than just temperature cold. There was a generic, sterile lack of emotion. A tingling ran up and down her spine as if a crisp fall breeze had hit the back of her neck. That was, of course, impossible. The air surrounding her was stale and stationary.

"Obviously," Anndee answered. "Your room is this way. It's important you keep up."

Willow's movements went from a standstill to a brisk walk in an attempt to follow the girl. The clicking of her shoes on the ground became louder with every step. So loud, in fact, she considered stopping for a moment to remove them. There was no possible way she could pull that off. The elf girl she needed to follow was moving far too quickly for her to catch up. If she paused for even a moment, there was a good chance she might be left behind. In this place, that was the last thing she wanted to happen.

As if reading her thoughts, Anndee came to an abrupt stop. She opened a door with one hand, motioning for Willow to enter with the other. Willow's body jerked to a standstill, barely avoiding ramming into the elf girl. If Anndee had not shown her a way into the side room, she never would have seen it.

The walls appeared seamless. There wasn't even a door frame or handle. Willow's head peeked around the corner just enough to see it was, in fact, a large suite she was being ushered into. There was a couch and chair set made from a cream coloured, leather-like material and a marble coffee table with matching end tables. Each was adorned with lamps designed in the realistic shape of beautiful women with flowing robes. Everything was made from a similar white marble with highlights of gold. This was the type of room that could make even the most sophisticated person afraid to touch anything. Even the intricately designed royal blue and gold rug that lay delicately under the whole setting looked as if it had never been walked on.

To the right, a platform elevated an extra-large bed up by one step. Sheer cloth draped down from each of the four posters. It was exactly how she envisioned spending her wedding night one day. Whether or not that happened was in the hands of the royal council. It was yet to be seen if they would agree to let her have a future.

The mattress was perfectly covered by a thick bedspread made of the same colours as the rug. She curbed her urge to run in and throw her body on it, sinking into the fluffiness that only multiple pillows could create. She smirked. It was better to move her attention to something else.

Her gaze drifted to her left. If she felt thirsty, at least there was a bar with a crystal jug of cold water and glasses neatly arranged on top for her to use. Behind that was a fridge and cabinets. Being comfortable enough to explore their contents wasn't likely to happen. A door beside the fridge led to what she assumed was a washroom.

"Hurry up, then," Anndee said. "In you go."

Willow stepped cautiously by the girl. Directly in front of her were two glass doors leading to a balcony. How had she missed them while scanning the room earlier? Her wig flopped down on the table in a messy pile. Of all the beautiful things this room had to offer, it was only the view that interested her.

"I think you will find everything you need here," Anndee said, walking towards the bed. She grasped the bottom of the bed skirt, pulling it up to reveal a set of drawers. "There are clothes in here." Moving to the wall from where they had entered, she tapped twice. The door slid open. "You should choose something appropriate to wear. The royal council can decide to see you at a moment's notice. It would be best not to keep them waiting."

Willow made a mental note of the lack of emotion in her voice and attitude. It was how she had been treated at first by the elves she went to school with. She took in a deep breath, letting it escape slowly.

What did you expect? Aslo asked her in her mind.

"You're the one who saved my sister, aren't you?" Anndee blurted out from the doorway.

"I was one of the people who helped free her," she answered. The young girl knew something about the circumstances that led to Willow coming to the elf realm, but how much?

Anndee stood stiff, as if her body had frozen to the spot. Everything about her was motionless. Even her blue chiffon dress and long golden curls looked more like a portrait than reality. "Then we owe you a great debt," she said as softly as a whisper. Her face turned, providing a profile view of her high cheek bones. A single tear trickled down, falling from her chin like a raindrop. A wet spot appeared just below the collar of her dress. Without any warning, she hurtled forward, grabbing Willow around the waist. "I don't know what would have happened if she had died." Anndee's arms locked in a tight hug. She buried her face in the chest of her hero. There was no need to look at her face to know the elf girl was weeping, an emotion elves rarely showed even their own family.

In a slow motion, Willow moved one of her hands around the girl and patted her back shoulder lightly. Little droplets of moisture formed on her brow. She wasn't hot; in fact, it was the opposite. Her skin was cool and clammy. Her fingers twitched enough for her to notice. It wasn't a voluntary action. She was shaking ever so slightly. The realization that it was usually her crying and someone else consoling her rushed through her mind. How often had she cried on someone else's shoulder? All those people had made her feel better. Now here she was, with someone who needed her to say everything would be alright and she didn't have a clue how to do it.

"I'm not sure I know what you are going through right now," Willow started, "but your sister is fine, so there isn't anything to worry about."

"I know," Anndee said, pulling back a little from their embrace. "It's just... well, we never considered what would happen if one of us died."

Willow sighed. "It would have been hard, but in time you would find the strength to move on with your lives." She wondered if she would be able to take her own advice if the roles were reversed. Of course, she already knew she could. After all, her mother and father were still missing and she had lived her whole life presuming they were dead.

"No," Anndee cried. "It isn't that. My sisters and I were born elf triplets. That means we are each one third of a whole. We are connected as if we are one. For one of us to die, would be like losing one third of my body, mind, and soul. I don't even know if my other sister and I would survive such an event."

"I'm not sure I understand. I have heard that twins and triplets have a special connection... a link mentally," Willow said.

"It's different for elves," Anndee replied, shaking her head. "When an elf gives birth to triplets, the fetus originates as one being, then, for some unknown magical reason, that baby splits into three different individuals. It's an abnormality or birth defect. I knew you were the one who helped my sister, because I could feel what she felt and I could see what she saw. The council was just about to send a search party into the main world when Deanne returned."

"But since you are born separate, you each have separate identities," Willow said. "It doesn't matter if you were once a whole. Now you aren't. Your personalities must have differences."

"Yes," Anndee said, planting herself on the bed. Her legs swung back and forth not able to touch the ground. "We each received different attributes. I am creative; Deanne is smart; and Dannee is athletic. But we need each other to do magic. It resonates through our song. Overall, we are stronger in every way when we are in the same place at the same time."

"I'd like to spend some time with the three of you, if possible." Willow smiled. "When this is all over, I believe we could become good friends."

"I think we'd like that," Anndee said. "But first, you have to get past the council." Her pupils scanned the room, suspicious of the surroundings. Her face tilted towards Willow's ear. Any closer and her lips might have pressed against the bottom lobe. "If things aren't going well, you can ask for a test of character. It's the one thing the council can't deny." The elf's voice was so quiet, the noise of a pin dropping might have been louder.

"A test of character?" Willow whispered back. "What is that?"

"Well," Anndee answered, her voice only a smidgen louder than before, "I don't exactly know, but it is a test. It will be hard and probably dangerous. If you are serious about staying for a while and the council is against it, it could be your way around their decision."

"So if I complete the test, I can stay without permission?" Willow let out a huff. "Has anyone else tried it?"

"Yes," Anndee said, her voice cracking. "But no one has ever returned. The legends say only those who are pure of heart and mind can pass the test."

"Great," Willow said. "I'm not sure I even know what that means."

"I think it's one of those things you need to figure out yourself," Anndee replied, smiling. "The inner struggle is probably part of the test."

"So some part of the test itself knows what I am thinking?" Willow asked, a frown creeping over her face.

"I believe so," Anndee answered. "But I really don't know the particulars. I have only heard the legends. It's up to you, of course... if you want to try it. It seems as if there is something important here that you need to do. This may be the only way you can stay."

"I understand. Thank you." Willow stood. Without thought, she found herself at the double doors. Opening them, she stepped onto the balcony. Her eyes closed, allowing her other senses take over. The crisp breeze picked up her long red hair, massaging each strand with its soft touch. An unfamiliar sweet floral scent tickled her nose as if playfully teasing her to seek out its origins.

"I have to go now," Anndee said, breaking the silence.

"Thank you," Willow started. Turning around, she realized the girl had already left. She was, once again, alone, being treated more like a caged animal than a guest. As beautiful as the suite was, it was, in essence, nothing more than a glorified jail cell.

Leaving the doors open, the wind began airing out the suite. Willow took a seat on the couch, a sigh rolled off her tongue, escaping through her lips. "I suppose you heard all of that," she said out loud.

Of course, Aslo replied to her. *We have a few concerns about this whole mess. There are a few decisions we need to make before any council meeting is called. Since Cassandrhea and the other elves we met know of our existence, it stands to reason that the council will also know we exist. If you do this 'test,' I doubt we will be allowed to accompany you. That makes me nervous.*

We don't know for sure that I will need to take the test... right? Willow examined her fingernails. They were short and jagged from excessive biting. Her teeth clamped down on a small piece of one of her nails that had been left sticking out above the rest. A click sounded and it was gone.

You should be prepared for the worst, Aslo answered. *We already know that the elves don't take kindly to outsiders.*

"Brilliant," Willow said, slouching backwards. "So in other words, I am going to have to take the test. Why are things always so complicated?"

We think you should avoid the test, if at all possible. It's far too dangerous for you to take on alone. It might be safer to go back to the main world, Kiera added.

Willow jumped up and moved to the bed, throwing her bag on it, before plunging down herself. "Well," she said, "let's see what our favourite book has to say." She pulled out *The Portal Prophecies* and laid it in front of her. Her fingers ran across its smooth cover and spine before flipping it open.

Do you have time to find a corresponding prophecy now? Deacon asked.

And then decipher it? Jawfree added.

"Don't know," Willow answered, flipping through the pages. "We won't know unless we try. It couldn't hurt any. Although I have to admit, I was hoping the book would open to the page we needed. Last time, a gust of wind blew the pages..."

Her words cut off. That very well could have been the very answer that she needed. She moved the book to the marble coffee table, laying it open at a random page. Plunking down on the sofa, her legs crossed beneath her. Her eyes shut. Speaking to the wind wasn't something she could do verbally, or even telepathically, for that matter. She not only needed to think what she wanted to relay, she had to feel it as well.

Interesting, Aslo said.

Outside, the wind picked up. The doors rattled, a gust blowing past them into the room. Anything not weighted down flew around as if caught in a mini cyclone. Strands of hair whipped against her face, making her eyes clench tightly closed in order to avoid being blinded by rogue ringlets. Her nose, overwhelmed by the pressure of the wind, struggled to take in air. Parting her lips, she attempted to fill her lungs and was instantly rewarded with a mouthful of red curls. Her lips puckered, trying to spit the locks back out. A few moments later, the wind subsided. A calm came over the room. She breathed deeply, replenishing her body's depleted oxygen supply.

Well? Aslo asked.

"I don't know yet. My eyes are still shut," Willow answered out loud.

We don't have time to waste. Aslo barked. *Now, look at the page and see what it says.*

"Fine," she answered, sighing. Picking up the book, she recited the prophecy from the page it was open at.

Life left behind, a new land dawning

Hidden away the trees form an awning

Secrets reveal beast with pure unite

A sunken world to return to the light

A riddle to solve, the pieces complete

A choice to be made, feels bitter sweet

A heart to be broken, alone in the dark

On a journey, a hero shall embark

Awaken the sleeping to return what was lost

But never forget, all comes with a cost.

Willow pictured Aslo's face in her mind staring at her with the unimpressed expression that only a cat could have.

You are correct, Aslo said. *I am not sure those words help our situation any, or if that is, in fact, the correct prophecy.*

Willow sighed. There were occasions where communicating telepathically wasn't as much of a blessing as it was a curse. "I know," she replied. "But it's the best we have. This is where I am starting. A few of the lines do fit this situation."

Then we will support you, Kiera replied. *Now that we have a prophecy, what do you plan to do with it? It's only worth knowing a prophecy if it is helpful in some way.*

"Yeah," Willow said. "I know. I think it will start to fall in place as we go along, like the others always have. That might not be helpful now, but it's better than nothing. This first line I believe is referring to my arrival in the elf realm."

I suppose it could be taken that way, Aslo said. *But there are some unsettling parts to that prophecy. I want you to avoid rash decisions. No running into situations head-first like a fool this time.*

"Alright," Willow answered, her gaze directed towards the open balcony doors.

The sun was going down behind some trees. As it set on the horizon, it lit up as if it were on fire. Bright hues of red, orange, yellow, and gold danced in the sky, putting on a show before gracefully bowing down at the end of the performance. Almost as quickly as the sun set, the moon took its place in the clear sky. Rays of silver light beamed down throughout the land, casting shadows in the night.

"How beautiful," she whispered.

Chapter Twenty-Eight

Willow's eyes popped open. She bolted to a sitting position. Scanning the room, she let out a sigh. "Right, I almost forgot where I was."

I am surprised you could sleep at all with everything that has been going on, Shelby answered in her mind.

"It's still dark, so I doubt I slept that long," Willow replied to the avian guardian.

Moving to the balcony, she sat down on the cool marble floor, her back against a wall. Pulling her knees close to her chest, she hugged them. They were the perfect height for her chin to rest comfortably on. She sat motionless, staring at the moon as thoughts rushed through her mind. With a gulp, she swallowed back tears, allowing memories to overwhelm her entire being. It was William and his new wife. It was her friends all turning against her. It was Lance no longer able to help her. It was Sebastian, Kayleb, Seth, and Gabriel not being able to see her, even though she was there in their world. It was the thought that if she had to take the test, her guardian friends would not be able to go with her. She sighed. It was having to face that she may have only herself to rely on to fix things and the reality that perhaps not everything could be fixed.

Enough! Aslo bellowed. Even though he was communicating through telepathic means, she felt the word echoing in her mind and her ears ringing from the strength of his tone.

"Sometimes," she said, "it's a real pain having all of you know my every thought."

Moping around like this isn't going to change anything. We have real issues before us to deal with. You need to concentrate on going forward in the here and now! Shelby exclaimed.

"The sun is coming up," Willow muttered under her breath. "A new land dawning..."

Her words cut off as the door to the suite opened, making way for Cassandrhea to stroll in. Glancing over at the woman, she let out a tiny chuckle. Her old headmistress was dressed the same as always, in a high-collar, Victorian style blouse and a skirt that reached the floor. Although she wasn't moving, Willow knew the skirt would flair out as the Director of Knowledge walked, hypnotizing those who watched it for more than a moment. For a split second, she wondered if Cassandrhea had ever actually used this to her advantage.

"Well, don't just sit there!" the Director yelled. "You haven't even dressed yet and the council is forming. Honestly, child, I don't know how you manage to keep surviving when you act like this. Hurry up. Pick out some clothes."

Willow jumped to her feet. How could she have forgotten to change? Now she would be late. She felt all hope of not taking the test of character falling from her reach as she grabbed a white sundress from the closet. Although it was plain, with buttons down the front, it suited her. She examined it hanging loosely bellow her knees in a mirror. With her hair tied back in a ponytail, leaving only a few tufts of curls framing her face, she was almost ready. Slipping on a pair of white flat slipper shoes and adding a light blue cardigan sweater over top were the perfect finishing touches. Her hands disappeared in the pockets. *Big enough for my wand,* she thought. Sliding the wooden stick in its new home, she closed the closet door and smiled. "Ready," she said as her body glided towards Cassandrhea.

"Well, let's move then," the Director said, pointing to the open door.

Willow shivered. The plain white marble walls and floors seemed cooler now, not a natural cool, but a sinister chill that reached straight to her bones. Goosebumps formed on her arms, becoming more defined with every click Cassandrhea's shoes made on the floor. Crossing her arms in front of her, she was glad she wore the fuzzy blue sweater.

Minutes passed. The hallway seemed to extend forever. Looking backwards didn't help the situation. There was no sign of where they had come from, just a hallway. It all looked the same. It felt the same. The never-ending length of nothing took its toll on her senses. It was hopelessness built into structure.

"How far is it?" Willow asked, breaking the deafening silence.

"As far as it is," Cassandrhea answered.

Willow came to an abrupt stop. "What does that even mean?" she asked. "Don't you know where we are going?"

"We don't have time for silly questions," Cassandrhea snapped.

"Don't have time?" Willow screeched, refusing to budge another step. "How can you know how much time we do or do not have if you don't know where we are going?"

"Really, child." Cassandrhea crossed her arms. Her face wrinkled up in disdain. "You have to be difficult. Very well, I will tell you, but grasp what I say. I shall not repeat myself." Her arms dropped to her sides. "This is a hallway of rooms. It begins where we tell it to and leads us to wherever we need to be in the elf realm."

"Like a form of swift travel?" Willow questioned.

"Yes," Cassandrhea answered, motioning for them to start moving again.

“But how does it know where you need to go?” Willow asked, standing firm.

“Do you question how magic can flow through that stick you have hiding in your pocket? Or any other form of magic, for that matter?”

Willow sighed. The fast-paced tapping of one of the Director's feet caught her attention. The two resumed walking again in silence. *Can you still hear me?* she thought to herself, hoping one of her guardian friends would answer.

“I'm not sure this is the best time for us to communicate.” Aslo's voice sounded as if it were amplified twenty times louder than normal.

“I may have forgot to mention, this hallway also projects incoming telepathic messages into a form which can be heard by all.” A smile crept over Cassandrhea's face, her pride beaming, creating an unnatural glow. “If you plan to speak with your guardian friend, it won't be in secret here.”

“We weren't hiding anything,” Willow barked. “It's the only way we can communicate while we are joined together in this form.” Pulling back the sleeve of the blue sweater, she revealed a picture of a black cat on her arm.

“Was that picture always there?” Cassandrhea asked.

“No,” Aslo answered. “I can move anywhere there is skin on her body. I do prefer to be hidden, so more often you will find my portrait on her back.”

“Fascinating.” Cassandrhea said. Silence resumed.

Seconds turned to minutes, minutes to hours. Time became lost in the shuffle. “Ahh!” Willow screamed. “Are we even moving? It seems to me we are walking in the same spot over and over.”

“Technically, we are,” Cassandrhea said. “And we will continue to do so until we arrive at our destination. Look there, up ahead.”

A faint line of light cast shadows that crept towards the two, forming the shapes nightmares were made of. The grey shadow moved forward, mimicking a fog rolling in from a forest. It engulfed the floor and walls, forming trees with hands for branches that swayed and scooped down from all directions causing Willow to duck and cover her head. All around her, hands made of mist developed, pulling at her clothes and hair. She screamed.

"What in the realms are you doing now?" Cassandrhea asked, eyeing the young girl crouched down on the smooth white marble floor.

Willow shook her head, glancing around. The eerie shadows were gone and at the end of the corridor a slightly opened door appeared. There was nothing sinister to be found.

As the door opened further it revealed a lush green field surrounded by woods. Small white flowers grew sporadically throughout the perfectly kept lawn. At the forest edge, the trees grew in a bowed down form, creating a high perched table and matching benches, which were occupied by elves she had never seen before.

Her eyes widened, straining to take in all the sights laid out before her. A family of pink and blue bunnies hopped through, followed by a little man and woman who were no more than six inches tall. They carried a colourful basket of what looked like eggs. Willow opened and closed her eyes several times.

"Where did you think chocolate eggs came from?" Cassandrhea asked, pushing past and heading to the living table.

Willow followed. Moving closer, it became apparent the seated elves were much higher up than they previously appeared. Standing on her tip toes, she stretched her neck as high as it would reach. "Hello," she said. "Are you the royal council?"

A rumble erupted. The trees rustled. Willow made a futile attempt to peek in every direction to locate the source of the noises, but could see no one.

A loud voice bellowed. "You are to speak only when asked to!" A flock of birds hiding in nearby trees took flight, startled by the deep voice.

Willow strained for a look at the face to which the voice belonged. From her vantage point, she could see nothing except for the base of the tree that formed the bench, on which whoever it was sat. She reached out her fingers to touch a part of the tree, without being noticed. *Hello*, she thought. *Could you possibly lower a bit without hurting anyone?* she asked it. *I can't seem to see who I am conversing with.*

I will try, the tree answered to her alone. *But we here of the elf realm are loyal to the elves. Would you have us go against their will, little one? I don't believe you can come to terms with forcing us to make such a decision.*

They can speak to you too? Willow asked.

Not in the same manner as you do, but... yes, the tree answered.

Looking up, Willow could now see the tops of the heads of several of the elves perched above her. *I wish I knew how many are up there*, she thought.

"Are you the girl from the main world who has caused such an uproar lately?" A deep voiced roared down at her.

Willow glanced up and sighed. Even with the tree moving them slightly, she still couldn't see who was speaking. "Could you be a little clearer on which uproar you are referring to?" she asked.

"You know very well that which we speak of, the mess with Cornelius and his children," a female voice spoke.

"To be fair, I think that was caused by them," Willow replied, her hands fidgeting.

"A simple yes or no will suffice. We are more than capable of drawing our own conclusions." This time a stern, steady voice spoke, also female. "Now, were you or were you not involved?"

Willow took in a deep breath and exhaled it again. "I was," she answered.

"And did you, or did you not, cause a situation which put members of the royal elf families at risk?"

Willow exhaled, making a huffing noise. This wasn't a hearing. She was going to be found at fault for everything. It was more than obvious the committee she was standing before already had all the information they needed. "I suppose I was," she answered. "But..."

"But," the female voice yelled from above her. "But what? But you saved them afterwards? Should we thank you for saving our people from a situation you created?"

"No, but..." Willow started. Her sentence was cut off before it started.

"But?" the female elf bellowed. "We are not interested in buts. We are interested in facts and the fact is, if you didn't exist, Cornelius wouldn't have a bounty on your head... he wouldn't have created a potion... and you wouldn't have forced Hilary's hand. Nothing would have happened."

"You can't believe that!" Willow screamed back. "Cornelius would be moving ahead with his sinister plan for world domination with or without me. I just happened to be here to try and stop him."

"Don't be silly, child." The male elf laughed. "For hundreds of years, there has been no problem with Cornelius in the main world. We have had a period of relative peace."

"But the thinning of the space between the worlds... and the influx of beings from other realms entering the main world," Willow said, choking back tears. Crying now wasn't an option. She needed to be strong, even if this council was trying to pin everything bad that happened on her. That was something she was becoming accustomed to, after all. It seemed everyone was quick to blame her.

"Back to the buts," the female voice said again, this time clearly in a mocking manner. "We have been monitoring the situation as it may pertain to our existence. The Directors have all been able to handle every problem that has arisen. That is, until you arrived."

Willow's eyes widened and she took in a quick breath of air. Was there a chance that perhaps she was the problem? Was that what all this meant? Did she create the very situation she was trying to solve?

Don't doubt yourself now, Aslo whispered. *They are playing games with your mind, nothing more. Have faith in yourself and in us.*

"No," Willow said, stamping a foot down. "I think you forget that the guardians are with me and believe in what I have done."

"Ah, yes." The male elf stood and looked over the edge of the tree at her. "The guardians, if that is indeed what they are. A talking cat is not proof to us. Regardless, we must ask these creatures to come forth."

A whoosh sounded as several birds swooped by and then disappeared into the clouds above. Standing in front of Willow were Aslo and Kiera with their children, Jawfree, Deacon, Tika, and Nero. Confused, she looked around before realizing the birds earlier were her avian guardian friends. *I suppose they have a plan*, she thought.

"Are we supposed to believe that one young girl can carry so many guardians?" the female elf said, peering down from her perch.

Aslo took his full form to meet the elves on their eye level. "We don't actually care what you believe or not," he said. "The fact is, we are here."

"So you are the leader of this group?" The male elf asked, slouching back.

Aslo roared a laugh. "We do not have a leader. We simply could not all fit in our full forms in this small area. Of course, if you would like us to try..."

"No," he said. "I think this is fine. If we take you at your word, we have no problem with you or your companions. The girl, however, may pose a threat to that which she claims to protect."

"Don't be ludicrous!" Aslo bellowed loud enough to create a force similar to a gust of wind. "Willow is working with us."

"You may believe that," the female voice said, unaffected by the presence of the guardian before her. "The facts, however, tell a different story."

"You, madam," Aslo said, "don't have all the facts. There are things in your realm which we need to decipher to know what our next step is to be."

"By things you mean, the stain glass windows; the legends surrounding the great trees; and a possible antidote to a certain memory-changing potion? Who knew a creature like you could look surprised?" She laughed. "Did you not think the four princes would report everything to us? So trusting for a being who has lived as long as you have. We know what you would like to do here, but we cannot allow this girl that sort of access to our world."

"I'll take the test," Willow blurted out. "You have a test of character and if I pass, I can stay long enough to finish the things that need to be done."

"How could you know about that?" Cassandrhea asked, her full attention directed at the girl standing beside her.

"Does it matter?" Willow replied. "It's true, right? I can't be denied if I volunteer to take the test."

"Foolish, headstrong girl," Aslo said under his breath. "Didn't I say not to rush into anything? Perhaps for once, you could listen."

"We aren't getting anywhere," Willow said. "The way I see it, the outcome of this meeting was already predetermined and we are simply wasting time going through the motions. This was the only option I had to begin with."

"The girl is correct," the male elf answered. "This is the only option she has, although I have to admit, no one on the council considered she knew about the test."

"Why would we think she would know about the test? Our traditions are not supposed to be known by outsiders," a female elf added. "I don't recall anyone reporting having shared that information with her. Perhaps we should revisit with previous interrogations."

One of the other male elves sighed. "More time wasted. Let the girl take the test and we will be done with this mess. The odds that she can complete it are not worth mentioning. She has, in essence, solved the problem without us doing a thing."

“Very well, then,” the woman's voice said. “Return to the hallway and follow it to where it takes you, young lady.”

Willow could feel every stare directed at her back as she walked towards the open door to the hallway. Stopping at the threshold for a moment, she took in a deep breath and then jumped through without hesitation.

“Wait!” Aslo yelled.

Willow heard the end of the word as the door slammed behind her. “Oh no,” she cried out, sliding to the ground and holding her head in her arms. “How could I forget I was alone?”

Chapter Twenty-Nine

A bright flash went off in Malarchy's face. Squinting, he lifted his hand to act as a shield for his eyes. "What in Pewterclaw is going on?" he screamed.

"Sorry," Krissy answered. "Just needed a photo for my article on our new mayor." She snapped another picture.

"I haven't been elected yet," Malarchy reminded the young journalist. "Remember your promise to keep to the facts from now on."

"I am," Krissy said, smiling. "The article I wrote on Hilary will be coming out in the next issue, along with a complete history of the stories I fabricated from part truths. I added apologies to Willow and anyone else I may have hurt."

"Very good," Malarchy said, returning to the stack of paperwork on his desk. "I hear the next issue will also contain an article by your other half." The pen in his hand glided over a piece of paper with his signature before moving onto the next document.

"Keith, you mean?" Krissy inhaled a large breath of air and exhaled it quickly. Placing her camera on the desk, she took a seat in a chair. "Yes, I believe he is doing a piece on his disapproval of my actions."

"Not an apology for the articles he wrote?" Malarchy asked, his attention steadfast on the work in front of him. "I was sure some of his reporting was also questionable."

"Well," Krissy answered, playing with a paperweight that sat on the corner of the desk, "he hasn't admitted to doing anything wrong as of yet. I have no influence over what he chooses to do. I can only control my own actions."

"I understand," Malarchy replied. "In the end, I hope your newfound honesty is taken into consideration when the choice between who survives, you or your brother, is made."

"Thank you for saying that," the young journalist answered. "I guess I should let you attend to business." She closed the door behind her.

Malarchy waved one hand in the air without looking up from his desk. Only a moment passed before a rapping noise disturbed him. "Come," he yelled. The door made a creaking noise. It needed a little oil. He jotted a note to maintenance. "Did you forget something?"

"Not sure what you mean," Gavin said. "You wanted to see me?"

"Ah, Gavin, yes," Malarchy replied, placing his pen down on the paperwork he had been so invested in. He pushed his chair back from the desk and shifted his weight. "Please have a seat."

"You'll forgive me if I don't get comfortable," Gavin replied. "We have never seen eye-to-eye with the ruling authority."

"By we," Malarchy said, crossing his arms, "you mean the vamprite?"

"Yes, I suppose," Gavin replied. "Although I was referring to my personal clique rather than a statement as to the general race. Either way, it works."

"Let's not dance around the topic," Malarchy said. "I am sure you are aware I am running for the recently opened mayor's position."

"Of course." Gavin's attention appeared firmly focused on the contents of the bookshelf that lined one wall of the office. "There is little reason for an election at all, as you have basically no competition."

"Yes," Malarchy said, raising his eyebrows. "Assuming I win, I would like to offer you a job working for me."

Gavin replaced the book he was holding to its spot on the shelf and turned around. "Job?" he asked. "What sort of job?"

"Research and development," Malarchy said. "Forgive me if don't fill in the details until after you accept my offer."

"Why me?" Gavin finally decided to sit in one of the plush green guest seats. He sank back. Being comfortable was something the vampire was used to. He had no problem displaying that in front of other people.

"To be honest," Malarchy said, "because of Willow. She trusts you and I trust her. I suppose by extension, that means I trust you as well. I need a team of individuals that will be loyal to my cause. Individuals I know are not going to report findings to any Directors."

"Hum," Gavin muttered under his breath. "I see." He crossed his legs. "Where is our famous friend?" he asked.

"Missing," Malarchy said, leaning further back in his chair. He couldn't help but notice there were strong similarities between himself and the vampire sitting before him. The fact that they both were accustomed to the finer things in life was only one. "Hopefully she will reappear soon. Until then, I have some things I need to accomplish to carry on where she left off in this world."

"I get it," Gavin said. "There is something about that girl that compels me to want to help her... worry about her, even. I do not, however, feel the same about you, Mister Future Mayor. Nor do I care about this city."

"I understand that," Malarchy said. "Everything I would ask you to do would be to help the girl. Although it is true by extension you would be aiding the city, perhaps even this world. In the end, maybe a newly-formed government and the vamprite could come to an understanding that would be beneficial to both of our people."

"You have high hopes, Mister Future Mayor. I need an example of what work you would have me doing. You do understand, I can't be completely blind and accept your offer."

"Alright," Malarchy said, standing. He moved to the front of the desk and rested his backside against it. "An officer was infected with a potent spider venom. There is a cure; however, it is only located in two places. One is with Willow. Unfortunately, we can't locate or contact her at the moment. The second is at our old camp with William and Mike."

"So why don't you just go get it?" Gavin asked as he played with his sharp fingernails. "What could you possibly need me for?'

"It isn't that simple," Malarchy answered, ending his sentence with a rather loud sigh. "Cornelius, I am sure you remember him, created a memory-altering potion. It basically allows someone to completely re-write a person's past. He used it to alienate Willow from as many people as he could. The camp was the first place infected. Of course, Hillary also used the potion to win over support."

"Quite the mess," Gavin commented. "Still not seeing where I fit in, though."

"I need an anti-potion made," Malarchy said.

"Well," Gavin chuckled, "you don't ask for much, do you? What makes you think I will help you do that?"

"Willow," Malarchy said, a smile creeping across his lips. "She will be in a bad situation if I can't reverse the memories that have been lost. In fact, if she were to come back now, she would be in life-threatening danger. If that isn't enough motivation, consider that Cornelius still has the potion. He could ultimately turn you and your friends into mindless creatures that believe they were put in this world to serve him."

“An interesting concept, to say the least. But somewhat far-fetched, don't you think?” Gavin asked, smiling. “How far is Cornelius really willing to go?”

“All the way, I am afraid.” Malarchy answered. “Including his own children.”

Gavin's gaze looked up to meet the stare of the man who had been speaking. “Really? Who knew the old man would become that psychotic?” The tone of his voice indicated he didn't actually expect a response.

“Regardless,” Malarchy said. “I think it is important we have a plan of action ready.”

“Tell me again why the Directors aren't working on this themselves?”

Malarchy sighed. “Because they don't have a sample of the original potion to work with.” He took a seat in his chair again.

“And you do?” Gavin asked.

“Yes,” the future mayor replied. “Willow provided me with a small amount. She asked me not to share it with anyone who might have reason to reproduce it, thus leaving me in a predicament. I don't have the ability to do lab work myself and I am restricted, shall we say, as to who I can recruit to work on such a delicate project.”

“And so you contacted me, knowing my past history with Willow and my lack of respect for the current government.”

“To put it bluntly, yes.” Malarchy said. “No one would know about your department except those in it, my daughter Jade, and myself.”

“And once we solve your little problem?” Gavin asked, one eyebrow lifting higher than the other.

“This special division, I would like to continue on. I have seen enough to know that there will always be something threatening our world, whether it's Cornelius or not. There will always be an aspect of the unknown that we need to unravel. Of course, you can give me a detailed breakdown of how you would like to be paid. I have enough connections that I think I can accommodate most reasonable requests."

"And my clique?"

Malarchy grinned. "I didn't expect you would handle this all alone. They will be added to my payroll as well. You can simply provide me with their names."

"Well then, Mister Future Mayor, I think we have an agreement," Gavin said, pausing for a moment. "We accept your offer. I will be in touch after you win the election." The corners of his lips tilted upwards just slightly. "Make sure you do. Vamprite don't deal well with people who enter into fake contracts. We take our word seriously. It isn't a lot to ask that you do the same."

Malarchy cackled. A shadow crossed over his face, creating a highlighting effect on his mouth. His lips parted in a smile, exposing his uneven teeth forming a fang-like pattern that, ironically, the terunji might consider a vampire trait. "Understood," he said. "I look forward to our next meeting."

"As do I," Gavin said.

Malarchy heard the door to his office creak open again, then slam closed. He shook his head and chuckled. Only a vamprite like Gavin could move fast enough to not be noticed leaving a room in such a fashion.

"Are you sure we can trust him?" Jade asked, standing in another doorway which led to her office. "His tactics can be rough around the edges."

"Jade, darling," Malarchy said. "How much did you hear?"

"Just the last part," she answered. "I am not sure I like the idea of making enemies based on the outcome of an election. Can we afford to assume your success?"

"Such faith in your father. I am touched," he answered.

Moving close to his chair, she extended an arm around her father's shoulders and kissed his cheek. "Of course I believe you will win. I just don't like threats against my family."

Malarchy laughed. “That was hardly what I would consider a threat. Think of it more as an expression of caution on behalf of our young friend. He is telling me, in his own way, he doesn't trust me fully. It's nothing more, my dear.”

“I am not sure I fully trust him,” Jade offered, her bottom lip puffing out. “Willow knows him better than I do. But still, I just can't help but wonder, if it came down to a fight, which side he would be on? We could be in real trouble if he turns on us.”

“Have some faith, child,” Malarchy requested, turning his attention back to the stack of papers on his desk. “I have taken this into consideration. I have no intention of being double-crossed by vampires.”

“Perhaps you could fill me in on the plan?” Jade's eyebrows lifted as a playful smile crossed her lips. “Surely you can trust your own daughter.”

“I do and I will, soon,” Malarchy answered. “But for the moment, the less you know, the better. When the time comes and everything is ready, I will personally fill you in on all the important details. Until then, I need you to concentrate on the election. We only have a few weeks left.”

Jade stood motionless, watching her father for several minutes. “Okay then,” she said, clapping her hands together. “I'll make sure you are Pewterclaw's new mayor.”

Chapter Thirty

Willow opened her eyes and rubbed them. She was sitting on the floor of the hallway to nowhere, or everywhere, as the case might have been.

I must have fallen asleep, she thought. Reaching around her neck, she clasped the pink heart-shaped pendant that hung from a gold chain. *Luck, that's something I could use right now.* She took in a big breath of air and let it puff out her cheeks as she slowly exhaled. It was time to start walking. She needed to focus on what she could do on her own and not worry about who she didn't have with her to help.

The hallway seemed to be going nowhere fast. Time passed or didn't pass; she couldn't tell which. Her mind wandered to a movie she had watched with Nathan about a girl who went to another world through a doorway and found nothing. No other life, just an endless void of emptiness. Of course, the girl shot lasers from a gun and eventually was swallowed whole by a giant bug. She stood still for a moment, contemplating the possibility of the same fate awaiting herself. "No," she said out loud. "I am definitely not becoming a giant bug's meal." Gripping her wand tightly, she continued her trek down the hallway.

After what seemed like hours, she stopped again. "Is the test really about how far I can walk?" she yelled. Looking up and spinning around, she waited for an answer. None came. "Brilliant," she said, sighing. "Guess I will just keep walking, then."

She looked down at her feet and noticed a small circular speck of black on the white floor. Using the toe of her shoe, she kicked it. The marble around the circle cracked. Willow jumped backwards, then edged near it again. Each step closer she took, she could hear creaks and cracks coming from under her feet. Before she could bend down to examine the damage, the hallway shook. A series of web-like crevices began to appear. The forming fissures moved towards her in a pattern, which if she hadn't known better, could have been considered merely an artistic design in the marble.

Realizing that whatever was happening beneath her was heading straight for her feet, Willow screamed. There was no choice but to run in the opposite direction, which was exactly what she did. The problem was, she was using all of her energy, but going nowhere. Everything around her appeared as if it were moving in slow motion. Her feet began to drag as if there were weights attached to them. Lifting them became more and more difficult with every step. She looked down. The black circle and cracks were directly under her now. She gasped. How had she not moved at all? She hunched over, her breath labouring. The floor shattered like glass.

She was falling in complete darkness. Her screams made no noise. None of her senses seemed to work. She had no sight, sound, smell, taste, or feeling.

No feeling, she thought. Her memories faded to the numerous times she had fallen down holes and into basements over the past year. Each time, she had felt it. There was a particular way she felt when she fell. The way the air around her would move like the wind. The downward pull of gravity exerting its force on her body. There was none of that here. *I must not actually be falling,* she thought.

"This isn't real!" she yelled without making a sound. "This is an illusion." She heard the word illusion echo before the black around her shattered and she found herself standing on some rocks on the side of a mountain. She glanced up in time to see a door close in the sky.

"Guess I won't be going back that way," she said. Taking one step forward, she felt some rocks give way beneath her foot. Her legs wobbled. Regaining her footing wasn't something she was known for being good at. Still, she struggled her way back to solid ground. "Seems this is the real deal if I fall."

Willow leaned towards the edge and peered over. "And I can't see the bottom, so best I don't take that route down."

The choices were obvious: she couldn't go forwards and a cliff blocked her way to the rear. All that remained was right or left. *Concentrate,* she thought to herself.

Carefully, she moved on the rocks to find a better vantage point from which to assess what the two choices actually held in store for her. In the past, she would have simply chosen one way or the other without proper rhyme or reason. Aslo's words echoed in her mind, warning her not to rush in recklessly. She perched herself on a small ledge and surveyed the landscape.

Her vision panned left. Her eyes widened and her lips curled upwards, twitching slightly, deciding between an expression of delight or awe. If mountains could have an oasis, she was looking at one. It was right there, almost close enough to reach out and touch. A flat platform covered in lush green grass with tiny red flowers, begging her to leap forward and run barefoot throughout. On the far side of it was a densely treed forest.

"Wait," Aslo's voice rang out.

Willow swung around searching for her guardian friend, but he wasn't there. She chuckled to herself. All the years they had been joined, she heard his advice over and over in her mind. He had always been there to look out for her. Now, it seemed it had worn off on her. Even with him nowhere near, she knew what he would say to her if he was. She knew what to do and she could tackle the task before her alone. *This*, she thought. *This is what they have been preparing me for. The day that inevitably would come when they wouldn't be with me.*

Her attention was still consumed by the out-of-place but beautiful meadow. Her eyes slanted. There was something there, something she had missed. But how? It was a pure white, large animal of some sort. Her neck strained outwards as she shifted all her weight to her toes. Some pebbles beneath her gave way, sending her crushing down on her bottom. She grabbed a large boulder beside her and hung on tightly. A waterfall of rocks and pebbles cascaded down, scraping against her before disappearing over the edge of the rocky cliff.

The noise caught the attention of the animal she had been trying to steal a glimpse of. It headed cautiously in her direction. Only the cold grey stone she clung to was preventing her detection. Clenching her eyes closed tightly, she ducked her head and held her breath for as long as she could. After several seconds passed, she was forced to let the air out slowly. Her curiosity spiked. She moved her head into a position from which one eye could see out past the large rock sheltering her.

The animal was closer now. Willow could make out some of its stunning features. It had the body and face of a horse covered in short white hair and adorned with a long white mane and tail. On top of its head sat a single horn that spiralled in a mixture of ivory and gold colours, sparkling at the tip. A rainbow of colours exploded from its horn with the force of fireworks, bits of colours landing just short of where she sat. Everything about it, its sheer perfectness, called out to her to join it... to run to the grassy land where they could play carefree together.

"Wait," Aslo's voice rang out to her again.

She sat down behind the boulder. Placing her thumbnail between her upper and lower front teeth, she sighed. She needed to survey the whole situation before making any decisions. She turned her attention to the right.

Rocks, she thought. *Cold, uninviting, treacherous rocks.* How could there be a choice? She could stumble aimlessly on rocks for who knows how long and perhaps fall to her death. Or she could frolic in a meadow with a majestic animal and see what the forest had to offer her.

A *huh* noise came out with her breath. As she turned her head back towards the warmth of grassy land, her eye caught a movement coming from the side of the mountain she had just been looking at. Her head snapped back to its previous position. Her eyes squinted for better vision. The sun was directly behind where she was looking now, affecting her line of sight. Remaining in one position, she strained to see whatever it was that was hiding. There was no doubt something was there, but what?

A cloud drifted by, blocking the sun's rays for a moment. It was just long enough for Willow to pinpoint an outline. The colour of the creature was only a shade off of the rocks themselves. It was a shape she had seen before, but only once. Her thoughts drifted back to Sleeping Sands. A similar creature had appeared to her at the school. Not just appeared... no, it had saved her when she was in trouble. She remembered the look in his gentle eyes as they had parted on top of the building her sleeping quarters had been located in. *That,* she thought, is *a dragon.*

She sat back down. Her fingers began rubbing circles on her temples. Questions filled her mind. *Why were these two creatures so far apart? Why was a dragon just sitting there in one spot? Which way should she go?*

A warm breeze blew through her hair, passing a faint message into her ear. Lower than a whisper but stronger than a memory. "Perception," it said, "can be more deadly than the greatest of weapons. Seek and rely upon only what you know to be true."

Was this voice a new ally? No, it didn't feel like that somehow. The voice was familiar. She had heard it before, but seldom listened. She covered her face with her hands and thought. Letting out a huff, she smiled. The voice, she realized was her own. Just as Aslo and Kiera and all the other guardians spoke to her in her mind, she too had her own voice she could listen to and that was exactly what she planned to do.

The decision weighed heavy on her mind. She knew nothing of the white unicorn. Where it came from. What its purpose was. If it could help her. The dragon, however, was a different story. She had met one of its kind before. That creature was caring and helpful and, more importantly, she had trusted him. Clearly there was only one choice. She looked back at the meadow. A shadow crept across the green grass, sending shivers up and down her spine. Her eyes locked on the unicorn's for a split second. Goosebumps formed on her arms as every hair stood at attention ready for battle. The beautiful creature was different now. Its cold black eyes revealed a darkness she hadn't noticed before, a darkness that chilled her deep within her bones.

Plotting a course out before she moved, Willow made her way across the rough terrain of the mountainside, hiding her body behind boulders and in shadows along the way. Surprising even herself, she made it to within inches of the dragon without making a major commotion.

The creature opened one eye, revealing a silver coloured pupil at the centre. "What are you doing?" he grumbled in a deep but low voice.

"Not sure," she answered. "I was hoping you might be able to help me fill in a few details I am missing."

The dragon opened its other eye. "Lilybelle," he said. "But it can't be. Whoever you are, hide yourself before you are spotted."

Willow skittered into a position which shielded her body from being seen by the unicorn. "Sorry," she muttered. "Might I enquire what you are doing on the side of this mountain?"

"Hiding, obviously," he answered.

"But why are you hiding?" she asked, leaning backwards on the rocks.

"So I won't be seen, of course." A little puff of smoke escaped from his mouth into the air and disappeared again as he spoke.

"Yes," Willow said. "I understand the fundamentals of what it means to hide, but what I wanted to know is why you feel the need to hide in this particular spot at this specific point in time."

"The unicorn." he replied.

"You are hiding from a horse?" Willow asked, her words sounding out almost in slow motion.

"Not a horse," the dragon said, his voice slightly louder, but still no more than a whisper. "A unicorn... you must know about them."

"Sorry," she said. "Can't say that I do."

The dragon moved his head closer to her body and eyed up and down. "You aren't an elf!" he exclaimed.

"No," Willow answered. "I am not."

"Well, what in the stars are you doing here?" he asked. "And for that matter, how did you come to be on this part of the mountain?"

"That, I am afraid, is a very long story," she answered. "Bottom line is, I am in the middle of a test the elves set up."

"A test?" the dragon asked. "What sort of a test?"

"Don't know," Willow answered.

"What do you have to do?"

"Also don't know." Willow sighed. "I have to complete the test to go back is all I was told, then I found myself here. I was rather hoping you could shed some light on what it is that I might need to accomplish."

"Sorry," the dragon whispered. "But right now I am just trying to survive."

"Trying to survive?" Willow asked, scrunching up her face. "You mean that creature is that deadly? It doesn't look extremely dangerous."

"Well, it is," the dragon said. "In fact, in my present condition it could easily end my life."

"Are you hurt?" Willow asked.

"I am weak," the dragon answered, his large head falling back down on the rocks. "The past few weeks, something odd has been happening where my kind dwell. Our preferred food source has begun to vanish. A once-thriving plant is now on the endangered list. The vegetation which we feed upon is sickly. I am one of the strongest of my kind, so I set out to find a new food source when I became trapped by that evil creature."

"Evil? Isn't that a bit strong of a description?"

"No, child," the dragon chuckled. "The unicorn is one of the most vile creatures in existence. Actually, it is in a way ironic you are here to witness one, since it was an elf woman who banished them many moons ago. An elf woman who you undeniably resemble."

Willow gasped. "I look like her?" she asked. "The Lilybelle you mentioned earlier?"

"Yes," the dragon answered. "She was my friend."

"What happened?" Willow asked, taking a seat as if she were attending one of Diana's story telling sessions.

"She died," the dragon said. "She gave her life to seal away the fifth elf race and the unicorns with them. Her tombstone marks the exact place she sealed the portal. By doing so, she saved us all. Now I am probably one of the only ones to remember her and her sacrifice." A tear fell from the beast's eye as he spoke.

"Promise me," Willow said, "after we escape the side of this mountain, you will tell me the whole story."

"You believe we will escape," the dragon said. "You have faith in something, child. Tell me how are we to achieve this."

"With a little luck," Willow said, touching her locket. "And a bit of magic."

The dragon laughed. "Luck," he said. "Yes, luck I can accept, but magic... no. We cannot use any. Do you see the sleek golden horn on top of that beast's head?"

"Of course," Willow answered. "Earlier it shot out a rainbow of colours that fell to the ground before disappearing."

"A magnificent sight." the dragon said. "However, it is a tool the unicorn uses to find living creatures it cannot see with its own eyes. You see, a unicorn feeds off of magic. It consumes all of its victims' abilities, leaving them helpless, then it devours the remaining life force leaving only a husk behind. Most of its prey don't even figure out what has happened before they die. They are perfect killing machines. Everything about its appearance draws you in... makes you trust it... leaves you vulnerable."

"How terrible," Willow said, a frown covering her face. "So that's why you are stuck here. You can't move or it could attack you."

"I am afraid so," the dragon answered. "At my prime, one unicorn would have been an easy defeat. However, as I am now, that creature could take what is left of my life easily."

"Perhaps I can help and we could escape together," Willow said, pulling out her wand.

"Did you not listen?" the dragon huffed. "You cannot direct magic at it. Its horn will simply collect all you send and absorb it. If anything you will make the unicorn stronger."

"I don't intend to do that," Willow said. "I may be a bit reckless, but I am not completely daft. Can you fly?"

"Yes," the dragon answered. "I may be weak, but I am not totally useless."

"Can you carry my weight as well?"

The dragon looked her up and down and laughed. "I wouldn't even notice the extra cargo. What are you planning?" he asked.

"I am going to make a garden grow around the unicorn. A natural enclosure that will obscure its vision until we can escape," Willow said.

"You can do that?"

"Of course," she answered. "Is there something wrong with that?"

"No," he answered. "It's just the only other I have heard of who used a magic that could create life was Lilybelle. Your similarities are becoming eerie."

"We can figure out that connection once we are safely away from here," Willow said, climbing on the back of her new dragon friend. She took in a breath of air and let it out again. “Ready?” she asked.

“Ready,” he whispered back.

Willow concentrated. A light breeze caressed her skin and vines began to grow in the meadow. They crept around the unicorn and intertwined forming a dome. “Now!” she cried.

The dragon took flight and soared through the air. He looked down and laughed. “Well done, my little friend. I am Zoran.”

“I'm Willow,” she yelled back.

Gliding through the skies felt like a dream. Cool air whipped by her as they soared high in the clouds, leaving her cheeks flushed. Willow opened her mouth and let air fill her lungs to capacity before pushing it out. “Where are we going?” she asked.

“To where the dragons dwell, my little friend,” he answered. “Stay close to me when we get there. We don't usually have visitors.”

“Sounds like a theme in this world,” she answered back.

Zoran laughed. “You are correct. This realm is segregated by race. It has been that way for a very long time. But it wasn't always.” He circled around a few times before forming a diving position and landing in the middle of a crater at the top of the mountain.

Willow let out a gasp. It was a complete society of dragons hidden away from the rest of the realm inside the mountaintop. There were dragons of various colours, sizes and ages, each one staring at them with curiosity.

“This way,” Zoran said. “I will show you around quickly, then tell you the story you wanted to know.”

The odd looking pair strolled through the heart of Zoran's homeland as if it were as natural as the sun rising. Other dragons stopped their activities briefly to stare and on occasion whisper to each other, but none seemed overly concerned with her presence.

“Is everyone sick?” Willow asked.

"Yes," Zoran said. He stopped to help a smaller dragon carry water.

"Your homes are actually individual caves?"

"You are a smart one," the dragon chuckled. "Yes, if you look at the sides of this crater, you can see there are chambers that accommodate us for sleeping and shelter us from weather. There are also those which are prohibited from being used."

"Prohibited?" Willow shrieked. "Why?"

"Because they lead to places."

"Do you know where?" she asked. "How do you know which is which? Are they marked?"

"Just because you find a path that leads somewhere, doesn't mean you should follow it," Zoran barked. "Sometimes it is better to stay put and keep to yourself." The pair stopped at a cave entrance. "This is my home," he said, motioning for her to enter. "When the sun rises, take heed of where it comes up. That is the forbidden wall. Any cavern you find there will lead you to unhappiness. It is best not to wander in that direction."

The inside space was much larger than Willow expected. She was far from an expert on caverns, but she had been in some before. This was much more inviting than any she had seen. It was warm and the floor was covered in a plush moss that cushioned her feet as she walked. She sat down, letting her fingers touch the ground. As she caressed the soft plant in one direction, it puffed out and changed to a darker colour. Moving her fingers back the other way returned the tracks her touch had made to their former condition, as if she had never been there at all. She let out a giggle. Her lips parted in a smile just big enough to reveal her white teeth.

"This is incredible," she squealed.

"I am glad you approve," the dragon huffed, collapsing on the ground and placing his head down. "I am tired," he said. "We must sleep now and tomorrow I will answer your questions as best as I can."

“Of course,” Willow said. She moved to position herself between her new dragon friend's front leg and neck before resting her head against him and closing her eyes. “Sleep well, my friend.”

“Sleep well, Lilybelle,” the dragon said, before drifting into dreams.

Willow's eyes opened. *Lilybelle,* she thought. *I wonder who she was.*

Chapter Thirty-One

Willow's eyes blinked once, then twice, before she jumped in the air. Right in front of her was the face of a child dragon.

It moved closer again, crinkling its nose as it sniffed her. "What are you?" he asked, falling backwards and landing on his butt.

"I'm Willow," she answered, looking around the room for Zoran. No one had ever asked her what she was before. There were so many different races in the realms. She never considered herself to be part of any of them. Her mind raced, overwhelmed by the possibilities. This was a new question to add to the mix. Where did she fit in? Obviously, she wasn't an elf, fairy, dragon, vamprite, kriller, Frostica, or yeti. This was the first time she realized she had no idea where her ancestors came from. She didn't know who she was.

"He isn't here," the young dragon said. "He asked me to watch you while he was gone." His head tilted sideways, as if trying to see a different view of her body. "But he didn't tell me what a Willow was."

"Willow is my name," she said. It was the only thing she could think of on the spot.

"Oh," he answered. "I'm Skilar, nice to meet you. But I still don't know what you are."

"What I am..." Willow said. "Well." She paused. "I suppose you could call me a portal guard." That was more a title than a specific race. Hopefully, it would curb the young dragon's curiosity.

Skilar shrugged his shoulders causing his wings to bunch out a bit and shook his head sideways. "No clue what that is."

"How about witch?" she asked, wondering if all children were this inquisitive. Having a baby was something she hoped the future held in store for her. Of course, she wasn't about to admit that to anyone right now. The timing was most certainly not right for planning a family.

"Nope."

"Empyral?" Her voice went an octave higher as she spoke.

"Um," Skilar answered, "no."

"Okay," she said. "How about we just say, I am a person who practices magic, but not an elf? I don't know how else to explain it."

"So you are a fairy," the young dragon said. "I've never met one before. They aren't allowed to come here. Did Zoran make an exception for you so you could fix the gardens?"

"Fix the gardens?" Willow questioned. "I can try. Can you take me there? I'd like to get started as soon as possible."

"Of course," Skilar said, jumping up and landing with a thud. "I am starving so if you fix it, I can eat. Then I can take food to my family, and they won't all be so tired all the time."

"Are you tired?" Willow asked.

"I get tired fast and have to take naps," he answered. "But the others, they have things to do and can't waste any energy on me. It wasn't like that before. We all had so much fun." Skilar hung his head, intentionally turning his face away from her.

"Sorry," Willow muttered. "Well, let's get moving and see if we can fix the problem. Quicker we do, the sooner you can all play together again."

Skilar swung around, grabbing her in an embrace. He may have been the smallest of the dragons, but his chocolate brown body still towered well over her height. She coughed, the pressure on her chest restricting her air flow.

"You are really strong," Willow said, struggling to force each word from her lips. "My body could break if you don't let go."

Skilar gasped and threw open his arms, releasing her. She fell limp to the ground.

"Ow," she moaned. She lay flat on her back for several minutes, her breath labouring to recover. "Thank you," she managed to say, getting to her feet, her arms still holding her ribs. They were going to be tender for a while.

"Sorry," he said. "I thought you were steady, being a fairy and all."

"Right," she answered. "Well about that, I am not exactly a fairy. I am more... fairy-like."

"That explains why Zoran brought you here then. If you aren't a fairy, then it's okay. You can use your magic to fix the gardens."

"The gardens. Yes," she said. "Can we go there now?"

"You betcha," Skilar said. "Just follow me." He headed out the dwelling entrance.

Outside the sun was rising. Her new young friend was walking straight towards where it was cresting above the mountainside. "Are we allowed to go that way?" she asked, remembering the warning words Zoran had issued the evening before.

Skilar tilted his head back towards her. Lifting his eyebrows he sniffed her again. "Are you afraid?" he asked, his face almost touching hers.

"No," Willow answered, staring at her feet. She kicked at the dirt. "Zoran didn't want me to go near any caves in that direction."

“We won't, silly,” Skilar said, grinning. “The gardens are in front of them. It'll be fine.”

She smirked. The face of a dragon smiling was somehow amusing. It might have been the way the scales on his face made room for dimples, or perhaps the view of all of his teeth. They were much whiter than she had imagined and a tad less sharp. Whatever it was, she would never find a dragon scary again.

The walk took a lot less time than Willow anticipated. Before she knew it, she was standing in the middle of what looked like a graveyard for vegetation. The few plants which remained were mostly brown with brittle leaves that crumbled when touched. She fell to her knees. “What happened here?” she whispered. “You poor things.”

Picking up a handful of soil, she released it into the wind and watched it fall back down. She repeated the process several times before turning her attention back to Skilar. “Don't eat that!” she screamed, rushing over and knocking a half-green leaf from the young dragon's hands.

“Hey,” he hissed. “I'm hungry. That was going to be my breakfast.”

“You can't eat that,” she cried. “It's sick and probably making all of you sick as well. I will do what I can to make them healthy, but something near here is causing this. That is what we have to find and fix to grow on this land again.”

“What do you mean?” Zoran asked.

Willow jumped. “When did you get here?” she asked.

“I have been here working on the problem in our gardens all morning,” he answered. “What do you mean... about finding the cause of the sickness?”

“Exactly what I said.” Willow squatted. Lifting another handful of soil, she let it fall slowly from her hand. The tiny granules cascaded back to where they came from. “The soil is poisoned. The plants that lived here absorbed the poison as if it were a nutrient. This isn't a natural occurrence. Someone did this intentionally. Worst part is, if I wasn't here, no one would know.”

“So,” Zoran said, “the dragons have an enemy. An enemy who is going to great lengths to annihilate our kind without anyone else noticing.”

“It's a complex plan, but the poison has to be coming from somewhere. If we can locate that, maybe we can revert things back to the way they were.” Willow scanned the surrounding area before fixating her eyes on a patch of sickly trees to her left, near the side of the mountain. “What's that?” she asked, pointing.

“It's a natural spring lake. Water comes from the mountain and fills it,” Zoran answered. “Basically, it is our water source.”

“Can we take a look?” she asked. “I hate to think it, but if someone sabotaged the water with poison, it would quickly infect the plant life.”

“Skilar, you go home now,” Zoran said. “Thank you for your help.”

“Aw,” the young dragon answered. “Things were just getting good.”

Willow chuckled. “Have a nap and we can meet up again later,” she said. “There will be lots of time for adventure.”

As Skilar walked away, Zoran extended a leg towards Willow. “Get on,” he said. “It'll be much quicker if I carry you over.”

Willow gasped. “Wow,” she said. “You weren't kidding.” She knew Zoran was correct, but was totally unprepared for exactly how fast the dragon could move when he wanted to.

Zoran let out a deep husky laugh, loud enough to be heard through all of the valley, before landing next to the lake. “Other than the local plant life being dead, this area seems normal to me. I am not sure what you are hoping to find.”

Willow jumped off his back. Reaching out her hand, she touched the dead leaves of trees and reeds as she passed them heading to the water. Again, the dragon had been correct. There didn't appear to be anything wrong with the water. Then again, that wasn't one of her natural magic elements. Sebastian's face popped into her head. His magic was strong with water. Perhaps if he was here, he could tell if the water was contaminated and fix it if it was. She shook her head. There wasn't time for hopeless wishing.

She grabbed a brown reed and pulled it out of the ground to examine it. No sooner than she did, a black and red bubbling goo spurted out from beneath the water where the plant's roots had been. The liquid substance looked like the contents of a burnt pot of stew - thick, black with a few coloured chunky bits. Willow covered her nose and moved backwards. "Whatever that is," she said, "it smells like putrid death. I am willing to bet that is the cause."

"So now what?" Zoran asked.

"Good question," Willow replied. "I can heal the land and make new plants grow, but that mess is beyond my ability. The same thing will happen again. The plants will become infected and die. Even worse, this goo could potentially infect all of this realm's plant life if it continues to spread."

"Got any good news?" Zoran shifted his eyes sideways to look at her without moving his large head.

"Well," Willow muttered, "I do know a couple of elves that may be able to help. Problem is, I need to finish my test to return to ask them to." She sighed. "I still don't have a clue what the test is, or how to complete it."

"I have no advice to give you, other than follow your instincts," the dragon said. "There are some things that each of us must figure out for ourselves."

"Brilliant," Willow said. A strange shaped rock close to the stone wall that surrounded the valley caught her attention. "What's that?" she asked.

"That," Zoran answered, "is where Lilybelle is buried."

Willow hadn't waited for the dragon's answer. She was already walking towards the rock, mesmerized by it. As she came closer, she could make out the shape and carvings. She gasped. It was the same marking she bore on her arm. It was the symbol of a portal guard and it sat on a stone table that resembled the one she had found in the library of her home world. The same table she had used to open her very first portal and escape death. She fell to her knees. What did this mean?

“How long ago did this happen?” she asked.

“Time is not relevant to a dragon,” Zoran answered. “I am afraid we do not gauge it in the same sense you do. We have existed since before most creatures, or rather survived what most did not. We have seen existence end and restart and have seen lives saved from that same fate. I can only tell you, it was a very long time ago that this female elf gave her life to save ours.”

“You said she was similar to me?” Willow's attention didn't shift from the stone carving.

“Yes,” Zoran answered. “The similarities are uncanny. Your appearance, minus the elf traits... certain things you say... your ability to call forth life from the ground. If I didn't know better, I would swear you were her or related to her. Even that locket you wear. I remember the day she died. She said that she was leaving the rest of her luck for us.”

Willow pulled out her locket. “This necklace?” she asked. “Lilybelle had this same necklace? A luck locket? But how? This was given to me as a present by someone far from here.”

“I don't know how, my friend.” Zoran answered. “But I think you have a bigger role to play in the elf world than anyone knows. Perhaps you are meant to finish what Lilybelle couldn't.”

“I think you are right!” Willow exclaimed. She pulled up her sleeve to display the portal guard marking. “It's the same as that carving.”

Zoran's eyes widened at the sight of the picture. “So you are a friend of the great trees?” he asked.

“You know of the trees?” Willow yelled. “Do you know where they are? I need to find them.”

“No,” Zoran answered. “I do not. I met only the one whose fate was sealed on the other side of a portal that once stood here. The others, I only heard tails of. Is this important?”

"Yes," Willow said. "The trees are a big clue as to everything. If I could find them and speak to them, it's possible we could find a solution and fix things in this realm as well as others."

"Well, then," Zoran said, "you will need to visit the fairies. One of these entrances leads to a path to where they dwell. It changes daily. Only the rays of the moon can illuminate which way to go. We will have to wait until night before you can continue on."

"For now," Willow said, "I can heal the ground and grow you some food. If you can harvest several times today, the food could last a week or two while I am gone."

"That would bring some energy levels back up, at least for a little while," Zoran replied.

"I am afraid I can't do much better at the moment," Willow said, brushing the dirt off her knees. "I think you will need healers as well. I am sure you have all ingested the poison."

The dragon sighed. "Your healers cannot help us. A dragon can only be healed by specific sound waves. Unfortunately, those songs are no longer sung."

"Songs?" Willow asked as she picked up a handful of dirt and blew it across the field. "What song? Can I sing it?"

Zoran laughed. "If it were that easy, I would have already asked you to do so. Unfortunately, it requires the range of three voices and an undeniable connection between them. We have not heard such a song since before Lilybelle passed away."

Willow blew another handful of dirt into the wind from a new location and watched the granules fall gently down in different spots. Her head was already pounding from questions. Adding another problem to solve wasn't what she needed. "There must be someone who can. We will just have to find them," she said.

"You are a kind girl," Zoran said. "But this is not your problem. Why do you want to help us? We have done nothing for you."

"You are wrong," Willow answered. "A dragon has helped me before. More importantly, if someone needs help, we should try our best to give it to them. That would make every world a better place. Don't you think?"

"Yes," Zoran chuckled. "I suppose it would." His eyes opened as wide as they could. As he watched, rows of plants appeared and grew ripe before his eyes. "Such a feat not even Lilybelle could have done," he said.

"Hurry up then and eat," Willow said. "Then find some help and harvest this lot so we can grow some more. We only have until the path shows up, then I must move on to complete the test." She sat down and watched her friend devour as much food as he could hold.

Zoran let out a high-pitched growl and other dragons appeared, each one happy to devour the vegetation. Willow recreated plants as necessary to feed them from a small mound on the ground she had made a seat out of, Zoran beside her.

"I wish I could contact my elf friends now," she whined. She closed her eyes and let her mind listen to the musical rhythm of her heart mixed with the sound of her breathing. The two sounds intertwined forming one noise, as if they were meant to be heard together. She understood now what her dragon friend had been saying. These two separate functions combined into one in her mind. They became inseparable to her ears. They were, in essence, one in the larger picture. That is what the dragons needed. But what could make such music?

Willow felt something caress lightly against the side of her face. Opening her eyes, she found a piece of paper and a feather with a sharp tip sitting neatly in her lap. "What is this?" she asked, examining the blank paper. It was simply a plain piece of paper, but at the same time it felt familiar somehow.

"Looks like someone wants you to write a letter," Zoran laughed.

Willow knew he was joking, but his words rang true. "Wait a minute," she said. "I know you."

Zoran glanced over at her and raised an eyebrow. "Are you talking to that paper?" he asked. "It looks rather strange."

"Yes," she said. "And no. I am talking to the paper. But if it is what I think it is, it isn't just paper, if you follow what I mean."

"No," Zoran responded. "I don't."

"When I took the entrance exam to attend Sleeping Sands, a school in the main world for magical individuals," she explained, "I had an argument with my test paper. I came to the conclusion that there was an essence attached to the paper. I never actually pursued who I might have been talking to, but I had my suspicions. If I am correct, things may just be a bit easier than I anticipated."

Willow looked down at the paper. Taking the feather in her hand as a pen, she wrote *Hi*. The writing disappeared and was replaced with. *Glad we found you*. Willow's face lit up at the sight of the words even as they dimmed then disappeared. A new line formed. *Are you okay?*

Thoughts and emotions ravaged through Willow's mind. So many things to say, feelings to express. She took in a deep breath, concentrated everything she had on her unusual pen and paper and started to write:

Yes, I am fine. I am with the dragons, but have to leave very soon. I am afraid I need your help.

The paper responded. *We cannot interfere in the test. I am sorry we weren't there to stop this from happening. Honestly, we were not informed you had come to our realm until after you had already begun this journey.*

I am not asking you to interfere in my test. I will be gone by the time anyone could come. Please hear me out. The dragons' water source is being poisoned. The plant life is already dead. The dragons are ill. This could spread further and take over all of this realm.

The paper responded. *Willow, don't take this the wrong way, but there are no full-blood dragons still living.*

There are. We are in a valley located in the crater of a tall mountain. The water needs to be purified, maybe even needs an antidote. Dragons can only be healed by a specific song. When Zoran explained it to me, I thought of the triplets. Their song, I bet, could save them. I can't stay. I only have a few hours before I have to head to where the fairies dwell.

The paper responded. *You are not making any sense. There are no dragons and no fairies in this realm, Willow. They went extinct many years ago.*

How many things have you seen that you didn't think existed? At least open your mind to the possibility and look for them. Trust me. They exist and need your help.

After a few minutes passed, the paper responded. *We will check all of the mountains for this dragon land and do what we can to help them. Of course, we cannot promise success. You do understand?*

Willow grinned and kissed the paper. As she began to write she noticed it was changing colours from white to a light shade of pink. She laughed. *Are you blushing?* she wrote. Its colour darkened further. *Thank you. This means a lot to me. Oh and when coming up, be careful. Earlier on a plateau with grass, I encountered a unicorn.*

Returning to a normal white, the paper responded. *Wait. What? There are no unicorns in this realm either and haven't been for a very long time.*

There are now, Willow wrote. *I think all of this is connected in some way, I just don't know how yet. Have you made any progress with the bottom stained glass windows I sent you?*

Bottom stained glass windows? the paper wrote back. *We have not seen any. Are you sure you are okay?*

I don't understand, Willow wrote. *I sent them back from Pewterclaw with Deanne for you, just before I was thrown through the portal and ended up here.*

We will look into it.

As the words faded Willow decided to ask one more important question that was weighing heavy on her mind. *The antidote to the mind-altering potion... have you found one?*

Not yet. It is harder than we thought, but we are working on it.

Thank you, Willow wrote. *You have been here for too long. I can see the strain in your writing. It's time to go back. See you when we meet next.*

The paper began to disintegrate in her hands the last words she saw were, *please be careful* before it was all gone.

Willow closed her eyes and let out a sigh. At least now she knew her friends had not abandoned her. They didn't know she was there. Why were the elves trying to keep them apart? Why hadn't they received the bottom half of the windows she had found in Hilary's house?

"Is everything okay?" Zoran asked.

Willow looked up at him. She forgot the dragon was beside her the whole time. "Yes," she answered. "Everything will be fine. I just added a few more questions to the mystery." She smiled. "The friends I told you about are going to look for this place. I do wonder, though, why don't they know you exist?"

A groan came from deep within the belly of the dragon sitting beside her. "We haven't left this mountain in a very long time," he said. "You have to understand... there were circumstances."

"To do with Lilybelle?" Willow asked. Seeing the other dragons finished consuming the plants, she touched the ground and a new batch of green leaves sprouted up from the ground.

"You are far too perceptive, child," Zoran answered.

"Was she the only one who died? There is only one marker." She drew a circle in the dirt by her feet with one finger.

"Yes," Zoran replied. "She died alone, as far as I know. That is something I have never come to terms with. She had many friends spanning many races, but in the end, none of them were willing to put their lives on the line to help her protect us. I suppose that is why no one in this realm trusts any race other than their own." A tear fell down his face and wet the dirt beneath him. "You, Willow, are like her. You are willing to help simply because someone needs help. You remind me of how things should be."

Willow sighed. “I am not sure I can live up to your expectations. I constantly have people helping me. I am more of a messy spill than a pillar of strength.”

Zoran laughed. “In the end, I think you will see you are more like her than you think,” he said. “If it comes down to it, I think I may now have the nerve to stand with you and fight like I should have many years ago.”

Their conversation was interrupted by squeals of delight coming from Skilar as he jumped between the rows of foliage biting leaves as he passed by, all the while laughing with his mouth full. For now, the dragons were happy and well fed. It was up to the elves if these mighty beasts would continue on. Willow grinned. She had at least one friend who would rally behind her if she needed him to and to her, that meant more than the dragon knew.

Chapter Thirty-Two

Willow felt a nudge. She opened her eyes to a close-up of Skilar's face again. She jolted into a sitting position, scooting away from the young dragon. He needed to learn sometimes up close and personal was too close.

"You fell asleep," he said. "It's almost time for the fairy path to light up. You won't have much time once it does. If you go the wrong way, it won't be good."

Willow stood up and stumbled gaining her footing. Taking a moment to fully wake up, she stood in one place, surveying the area around her. The large amount of magic she expended earlier that day was taking its toll on her, both physically and mentally.

"Sorry," she said. "I must have run out of energy and fallen asleep." She looked at the fields, noticing the vegetation was picked clean. Reaching down, she touched the dirt. New plants grew instantly. Willow wobbled a bit before falling over completely.

"Are you alright?" Zoran asked.

"I am," Willow answered. She gawked up at him from an upside-down position on the ground. "I am a bit tired and haven't eaten anything today. I will be okay. My energy levels are just down slightly."

"Can you not make something you can eat?" Zoran asked, sniffing her.

"The food I eat is not naturally occurring in this area. It is dangerous to introduce something new here. It could ruin the ecology and change everything. The plant life here has enough trouble without me adding more to it." Willow used the dragon's leg as a crutch to pull herself back into a standing position. "As soon as I can, I will grow something for myself. How long until the path illuminates?"

"Very soon," Zoran replied. "We should move over there now. After the moon crests above the wall, the paths will light up, but only for a split second. Two will illuminate in different colours. You must choose the one you want to follow."

"Now you tell me there are two?!" Willow screamed.

"Would it have mattered if I told you before?" Zoran asked. "You would still be here in the exact same position anyways."

"It would have been nice to know ahead of time and prepare," she muttered.

"You could prepare a lifetime," the dragon said. "But until you see it, you would not be able to decide."

Willow's eyes glazed over. Her dragon friend was right. Nothing could have prepared for what she was about to see.

In front of the first path, a group of bird-like creatures formed. They swirled in a large circular motion, each leaving a trail of sparkling blue lights behind them, creating a round spherical tube. Leading up to the second entrance, trees covered in pink glowing flowers grew into a connected series of lit archways.

Willow's mind raced back. She had heard of something similar before, but from where? *Of course!* she thought. *The prophecy.*

Life left behind, a new land dawning

Hidden away the trees form an awning

Secrets reveal beast with pure unite

A sunken world to return to the light

A riddle to solve, the pieces complete

A choice to be made feels bitter sweet

A heart to be broken, alone in the dark

On a journey, a hero shall embark

Awaken the sleeping to return what was lost

But never forget all comes with a cost.

"What did you say?" Zoran asked.

"It's nothing," Willow replied. "I just know which way I am going." She kissed his hand goodbye, and Skilar on the cheek, before setting out under the pink flower awning.

At the threshold leading into the cave, she stopped. Taking a deep breath, she closed her eyes and stepped forward. One eye opened, letting her peek at the new surroundings. She let out the air she had been holding. It was an ordinary cave. She sighed. A weight lifted off her shoulders. There was nothing confronting her... yet. She began to walk.

As the light dimmed, her other senses sharpened. Taking in a deep breath of air through her nose, she separated the scents. A damp mossy smell was dominant, mixed with ever so faint whiffs of floral accents hiding in the background.

Her feet became her guide, feeling every inch of the ground beneath them before moving forward. Other than the occasional rock she pushed aside, the floor of the cave seemed solid. Still, she proceeded with caution, making sure of each foothold before advancing.

Willow stopped and tilted her head. Somewhere in front of her, there was a sound. At first, it was too faint to make out. Then she recognized it - the sound of water rushing to a new destination. If she could find it, she could follow the flowing water to an exit.

She quickened her pace, taking only enough time to make sure there was nothing beneath her feet to trip her. The walls narrowed, closing in on her. The noise of fast flowing water heightened, becoming deafening. It was right before her, yet nowhere to be seen. Willow turned sideways, sucking in her gut to fit through the narrowing corridor. The final squeeze was tight, but she managed to push through into a hidden chamber.

Everything remained dark, but she had no doubt she was very close to the source of the noise she sought. A step forward and the ground beneath her gave way. She was falling - no, not falling - sliding. Cool water surrounded her, occasionally splashing up and hitting her in the face. The feeling wasn't unpleasant. In fact, if she could see where she was going, it might have actually been fun. The polished stone slide beneath her mixed with a continuous stream of water, making the ride to wherever she was headed easy.

Up ahead, she could make out a pin prick of a light. Each time she blinked, the light became larger. Her legs kicked, trying to stop or at least slow down the rate at which her body was propelling. Her hands searched the walls for something, anything she could grab onto, but the tubular tunnel was completely smooth. She clenched her eyes tight and gripped her arms around her midsection as she approached the exit. Then, she was actually falling. She could feel air around her, but refused to watch. It would be far worse to see what was coming.

She felt water around her, engulfing her body. It was everywhere. She couldn't see - everything turned dark blue. Her legs kicked and arms floundered, trying to do anything to help her, but ended up only thrashing about uselessly. She needed to breathe - needed oxygen. Her lips parted, letting bubbles escape. Her head pounded loudly with the sound of blood pulsing through, trying to deliver the precious supply of air that was now non-existent. Black and red spots appeared before her eyes, clouding her already distorted vision. She was sinking. Her back hit the sandy bottom. With one last effort, she placed both soles of her feet flat down and pushed up. Her head burst through the surface. She filled her lungs with as much air as she could, while coughing and sputtering out the water that had invaded them.

Glancing around, she surveyed her new location. The water she was standing in didn't even reach her shoulders. What she had thought to be a small lake was actually more of a moat, circling a tiny island, just big enough to accommodate a large tree growing in the middle.

"A tree!" Willow yelled, wading closer.

"Brilliant one we have here," a high-pitched voice said. "Isn't she?"

Willow spun around trying to find the source of the voice, but could see no one. A buzzing noise fluttered by her ear. She spun around again.

Giggles echoed from all directions. "The harder you try, the less you see." This voice was different. It was lower than the last, but still a high-pitched sound.

"Are you the fairies?" Willow asked as another buzzing noise passed her on the opposite side.

"She knows who we are," a third high-pitched voice said. "But why is she here?"

"How did she get here?" a new voice asked.

"The dragons," Willow said, still turning from side to side to try to catch a glimpse of who she was speaking to. "Zoran said I should speak to you. He showed me how to find the path that led here."

"Zoran, you say? We haven't heard that name in a very long time." A small female fairy landed on Willow's nose.

Crossing her eyes, she tried to focus on the small creature. The tiny figure had the appearance of a flower. The stem made up its all-green clothes, namely, leggings, skirt and top. Around her neck sat a ring of tiny pink wings resembling petals. The hair on her head, which on a flower would be the centre part or pistol of a flower, was bright yellow.

"I am Daisi," the flower fairy said, leaning her head forward to examine Willow's face. Her crystallized eyes opened wide as she studied every detail. "You look so much like ..."

"Lilybelle," Willow said.

"It's rude to interrupt." The wings around Daisi's neck began to flutter. The little fairy swooped around the air close to Willow without touching her, just fast enough to avoid being seen. She giggled. "You're not her, though," Daisi said. "You're too slow. What do you think, Elfred?"

A male fairy appeared with a similar appearance, but with yellow wings and red hair. "Hmm," he said, rubbing his chin while he hovered in front of Willow's face. "So who exactly are you?"

"I'm Willow," she answered.

"Well, Willow," Elfred said, "you stink." He flew away holding his nose, returning a moment later with two small leaves. "Here, use this. They should do the trick." He dropped them into Willow's hand.

"But what are they?" Willow asked.

"What are they?" Elfred exclaimed. "What are they, she asks." He sighed. "They are bubble leaves, of course. Go on, rub them in water."

Willow smiled as she rubbed the leaves between her hands. A thick lather formed. "It's like soap!" she exclaimed. She smeared the suds from the leaves over her body and in her hair. While rinsing it off, she watched with delight as bubbles began rising from the water, floating away. Reaching out, she caught one in her hand. It burst. The bubble residue hit her nose, making her giggle.

"Stupid girl!" Elfred yelled. "Don't touch the bubble seeds."

"Bubble seeds?" Willow questioned. Looking down at the palm of her hand, there was a tiny brown spot. "You mean this?"

"Yes, I mean that!" Elfred yelled. He swooped down and picked the seed up from her hand. Making sure not to drop it, he carried it over to where the other bubbles disappeared. "After you use the leaves they create bubble seeds which drift naturally to the optimum site for them to grow. Each plant produces only one leaf.

Once picked, the plant dies. So it's important the seeds make it to be reborn. This is the only place to find bubble plants. You should respect them."

"I'm sorry," Willow said. "I had no idea."

"She had no idea," another fairy scoffed. Her white petals fluttered around, creating just enough breeze to gently blow her pink hair from her face. "She had no idea. Hmm." The tiny woman crossed her arms in front of her chest and turned her face away from Willow. "Where did you think they came from? Perhaps you thought they just popped out of thin air?"

"Well, I didn't think about it," Willow said.

"Didn't think about it?" The fairy flew as close as possible to Willow's face without touching it. "These are rare plants. They don't grow anywhere else. If they were to become extinct, what would you do?"

"Elsa-Mae, perhaps you are being a bit harsh," Daisi said. "It was, after all, just one seed."

"One seed?" Elsa-Mae squealed.

"I would grow more," Willow blurted out.

"Grow more," Elsa-Mae mocked. "Wait, grow more? How in all the realms would you manage to do that without seeds?"

"I just would," Willow answered. "I don't know how. It's just something I can do."

"Like Lilybelle," Elfred said.

"So I have heard," Willow said. "Might I ask about that tree?" She pointed to the tree in the middle of the small island. Wading through the water to the shore, she realized that as her body surfaced, it was dry. She patted her hands all over her clothes. "Why am I not still wet?"

"One is wet when one should be wet," Elsa-Mae said. "One does not need to be wet when one should be dry. I would have thought that to be obvious."

“Yes, well, I suppose it should be,” Willow admitted. “That tree, is it a special tree?”

“It is,” Daisi said. “It once was a lively beautiful tree, but now it sleeps.”

“So it is one of the seven great trees.” Willow said, reaching to touch its bark. “Why did it go to sleep?”

Daisi sighed. “It was the day Lilybelle died. We don't know what happened to the other six, but this one, the tree of love, went into a neverending slumber.”

“The tree of love,” Willow muttered. “Did it have another name?”

“Bettulla,” Elfred answered. “A true goddess of the woods. Once a year, she would shed paper-thin pieces of bark and grant love to all who wrote requests on them. Now she stands here silent, merely a shadow lost in a forest.”

“Is there no way to wake her up?” Willow asked.

“Well, don't you think we would have done it if there was?” Elsa-Mae yelled. “You really are an annoying girl. Why did the dragons send you here, anyways? They generally don't keep contact with anyone, especially us.”

“The elves have sent me on a test of character, except I don't exactly know what it is I am supposed to be doing.” Willow answered. “Zoran thought you might be able to help me answer a few questions I have and find my way.”

“Just like a dragon to leave everything up to the fairies,” Elfred said. “Why should we help you? What are you to us?”

“Well, no one,” Willow said. “I am just someone who needs some help. The dragons need help, too. Someone poisoned their water supply. It is killing all the nearby plant life.”

“Killing plants?!” Daisi yelled. “Why would anyone want to kill plants?”

“We don't know for sure,” Willow answered. “But if someone were to want to kill off everything in a realm, without being detected, wouldn't it make sense to destroy the food source? Of course, none of the inhabitants of this realm seem to acknowledge each other, which makes it much easier to do. The dragons are already sick."

"Sick?" Elsa-Mae asked. "Is it serious?"

"Is that concern I hear in your voice, Elsa-Mae?" Elfred asked. "After all this time, don't tell me you still care what happens to that creature."

"Of course not," Elsa-Mae snapped. "That was decided long ago. It's mere curiosity that you are sensing."

"Is there a story I am missing?" Willow asked, sitting down by the water edge, admiring some flowers. The reflection of the flower on the surface of the lake showed a tall thin plant with a beautiful spiral purple and white flower. The plant itself looked like clear water. As she reached out to touch it, her fingers went straight through.

"It's a backwards flower," Daisi offered. "The flower grows in the reflection. The water that would have been where the reflection is now, is displaced and forms above the waterline. It avoids most danger that way. Quite ingenious for a plant, don't you think?"

Willow nodded. "Quite," she said, smiling. "So is there a story? I would like to hear it. It could, in fact, help sort out a few of the questions I have."

Elsa-Mae sighed. "It isn't a happy story... you won't like it," she said. "I don't see how it could help you on your quest at all."

"I'd still like to listen to it," Willow said. "Besides, I have a feeling you don't get many visitors here to tell your stories to."

"You're right there," Elfred said, sitting down on a reed.

"Alright," Elsa-Mae said. "If you must know, we fairies made a mistake... a mistake that cost the lives of countless creatures. One we still cannot forgive ourselves for."

"What sort of a mistake could be that terrible?" Willow asked.

"Pipe down if you want to hear the story!" Elsa-Mae wailed. "Now, where was I? Oh yes, I remember. An extremely long time ago, before the great trees, we fairies were guardians of the worlds."

"Guardians?" Willow yelled.

Elsa-Mae nodded. "We were granted unbelievable powers to protect all that was. For ages, we did just that with absolutely no problems. We were bored. Nothing ever happened. One day we were frolicking in a meadow, enjoying life, when we met the dragons. They showed us things we had never heard of before and we shared what we knew as well. For weeks, we met every day in the same place. Then, before long, we were staying together, watching the moon come up and wishing on falling stars. It was undeniably true love. The purest form of love there is. We belonged together. There was one problem. Our bodies were hardly compatible. We wanted to be able to hold each other, to kiss, to cuddle. Was that so wrong?" Elsa-Mae broke out into tears.

"It was wrong," Elfred said. "We did the unthinkable and the worlds paid the price for it."

"What did you do?" Willow asked.

"We used our power to change our forms into ones similar to your own... both the dragons and the fairies. We put up a barrier so that no one else could see the act we were committing. For weeks, we stayed hidden. When we finally emerged, the world as we knew it was gone. Sparse pockets of population of some species survived, but very few. The barrier had protected the fairies and dragons from a similar fate. After returning to our true forms, we vowed not to see each other again because of the disaster we had caused."

"You didn't cause it," Willow said.

"We were entrusted with power to keep the worlds safe and we squandered it on our own need for love. If we had done our job... if we had been there as guardians... all those lives wouldn't have been lost!" Elsa-Mae cried.

"Do you even know what happened?" Willow asked.

“Not exactly,” Elfred replied. “But the story doesn't end there. As we returned to our homes and began the rebuild, we discovered something. Every female fairy was with child. Apparently, the dragons were in a similar situation as well.”

“You had children?” Willow asked.

“Yes,” Elfred said. “A new race was born... the elves. With five distinct different types. The ones born of fairies were the river and light elves. The ones born of dragons were mountain and dark elves.”

“You said five, that is only four,” Willow said.

“The fifth was a mixture,” Daisi explained.

“As time passed, the elf race expanded,” Elfred continued. “We kept our distance from the other worlds and we taught our children to do the same. For a long time, we didn't know what was happening on the outside. Then Lilybelle was born. She was a sweet child with extraordinary abilities... so young and pure, yet strong and courageous. The great trees appeared and rallied to her side. At the same time, the fifth group of elves broke free from the rest of this realm. They believed they were better than the rest of existence and wanted to be treated as gods.”

“This sounds familiar,” Willow said.

“They took up residence outside this world, exposing it to things that it was not ready for. They positioned themselves to be perceived as gods. It was Lilybelle who opposed them. She sealed them away and gave her own life to do so. What was it they called their land? Atlantis, that was it.”

“We failed again,” Daisi said. “We let our own flesh and blood stand alone while we hid here like cowards. The dragons did the same. The great trees went to sleep that day and we knew she was gone. This one sits here as an everlasting reminder of the loss we suffered.”

“Now we remain here, serving penance for eternity,” Elfred moaned, bowing before the tree.

"Do you think she'd want that? Lilybelle, I mean," Willow asked. "I heard she wanted to help everyone she could. Don't you think she would want you to do the same? Wouldn't it honour her name if you stopped feeling sorry for yourselves and did something for someone else?"

"What is there for us to do?" Elsa-Mae asked.

"There is another threat. It is very real and affects this realm as much, if not more so, than all the others," Willow said. "A king from another world has made a plan to break down the barriers between the realms and take over as ruler of them all."

"How intriguing," Elfred said. "Seems this plot recycles itself."

"Apparently," Willow replied. "If he thinks me to be in hiding, then he would no longer consider me the number one threat to his plan."

"And who would his number two threat be?" Elsa-Mae asked.

"The elves," Willow responded.

Daisi gasped. "He couldn't enter this realm. It is far too protected."

"King Cornelius and his family have developed a way to weaken the veil that separates the realms. Their overall plan is to break down the barrier completely," Willow responded. "He has the ability to track where and when the conditions are optimal for his forces to punch a hole through the veil and enter a world. There is also reason to believe he has been in contact with Atlantis and is enlisting their help."

"Atlantis," Elfred exclaimed. "That is absurd. Lilybelle sealed them away quite safely. I assure you, Atlantis is not involved."

"Did I mention we found a unicorn on a plateau near the top of the mountain?" Willow asked. "It came from somewhere."

"A unicorn?!" Daisi shrieked. "That's impossible!"

"The elves are helping the dragons. Will you not join with them as well?" Willow pleaded. "Take your chance at redemption and save this realm as well as many others from a terrible fate."

A warm breeze gently kissed the hidden lagoon where they stood, carrying a beautiful sound in a cap full of air as it passed. Suddenly music surrounded them, drifting poetically down from the alps, leaving gentle vibrations as ripples in the water surrounding them. It was one voice... no, two... no, three... three voices intertwining as one.

"The elf triplets," Willow muttered. "They are singing to the dragons to heal them." Shivers ran down her spine as goosebumps formed on her arms. The music was magical - beautiful and eerie at the same time. It resonated deep within her soul, sending a tingling sensation to every nerve ending in her body. She fell to her knees, a smile forming on her lips while tears threatened to streak down her face. With clouds swirling to her emotions, she held them back, not wanting to ruin the moment.

The tones around her became clearer, high notes of ecstasy and low notes of despair. It was undeniably a perfect braiding of every emotion to ever exist.

"How ironic it is elves who sing with such a sense of pure feeling," she chuckled.

A new noise joined the dance, a rustling of leaves. A round of gasps escaped the wide open mouths of the fairies. Branches of the large tree they stood around began to sway, as if stretching after awakening from a long slumber. Its greyish bark slowly lightened as new life sprouted all over. Without wind or storm, Bettulla's trunk twisted and turned, shedding those leaves which had turned brown over the years, showering them down on those below.

Willow held out both hands, moving her body in tune with the music. She let the falling leaves touch her palms before taking their final journey to the ground beneath her. The breathtaking scene left her in complete awe, without the ability to speak.

"Who is going to clean up this mess?" Elfred yelled, ruining the moment. "Our beautiful home has been buried under years of tree waste!"

Willow shook her head. "Are you kidding me?!" she screamed. "Bettulla is waking up. Shouldn't you be happy?"

“Waking up,” Elfred said. “Impossible.” He fluttered up, examining every branch, sprout and leaf the tree had. He moved in close and the tree swayed backwards. Likewise, he glided away from it and the tree bent towards him. The two continued the pattern in time with the music as if dancing.

Willow laughed. “She is playing with you. It's amazing!”

“Playing, you say,” Elfred yelled back. “Are you sure that is what this is?”

“Yes!” Willow exclaimed, running up to the tree and putting her arms around its trunk in a loving embrace. She could feel its warmth... its being... its life. It was as vibrant and colourful as a rainbow after a sun-shower on a hot day.

Taking a few steps backwards, she bowed to Bettulla. The great tree responded by swinging one branch down and into its core, before bending forward in its own rendition of the motion Willow had just performed. The tree of love lived up to its name. The soothing feeling of caring flowed through the air, sprinkling its emotions like a shower of endearment, tenderly washing away any animosity it came in touch with.

“I'm Willow.”

The tree's limbs and leaves drooped and sagged as it spoke one word, “Lilybelle.”

Willow's expression shifted from ecstatic to having the appearance of a shrunken apple head faster than the speed of light. “I am sorry,” she said. “I am not.” She patted her trunk with sympathy, her fingers taking in the tree's inability to grieve for its lost friend. “I know I can't replace her, but I would like to be your friend as well.”

The tree straightened up and nodded. It was too soon to expect any more from her. As Willow knew all too well, only time could heal Bettulla's pain.

“I never thought I would see this moment,” Elfred said, drying tears from his face.

“That's two,” Willow said.

"Two?" Elsa-Mae echoed back at her.

"Yes," Willow replied. "Two of the great trees are now awake. That leaves me five to find."

"I do remember you mentioned you thought they could help, but I don't know how."

"I don't either," Willow said. "But Acacia, the tree of justice, has been my friend since the beginning of my journey and clues about the trees keep popping up. I have to believe they have a role to play in all of this before the dust settles."

"She's still fragile," Elsa-Mae cried out. "Don't go pushing the poor girl before she is ready."

"I won't," Willow answered. "But now I know the same song that heals the dragons can also awaken the trees. The pieces to the puzzle are coming closer together."

"Yes, I suppose that is a small victory," Elfred said, rubbing his chin. "In a way. But it won't help you if you cannot find the other five to wake them."

"Thanks for the reminder," Willow uttered, each word dripping with sarcasm. "I believe I will find all of them somewhere here in this realm, or at least clues as to where else they may be. Each one, I am sure, will be hidden in the same manner as Bettulla was."

"There are many places in which one could hide and remain hidden in a magical realm such as this," Elfred said. "A simple game of hide-and-seek often leads to a missing fairy or two for thousands of centuries."

"Perhaps, if you could," Willow said, "show me the way back to the place where dragons dwell. I need to ask them a few more questions."

"Is it the dragons you seek?" Elsa-Mae asked. "Or the elves?"

Willow closed her eyes. They saw right through her. It wasn't the dragons at all she wanted to speak with. It was the elves she was hoping to see. But even if she left now, she had a feeling they would already be gone by the time she arrived. The fairies had told her as much as they could for now. She needed to try. It was the elves that held the rest of the puzzle pieces she needed.

Chapter Thirty-Three

The path leading back to the dragons' lair wasn't quite as fun as the one that led her to the fairies. It was, in fact, all steep uphill walking, with some areas more like rock climbing than hiking. Still, she continued moving forward, her mind locked on reaching her destination in as little time as possible.

A few loose stones fell beneath her feet. Her body slid. The palms of her hands and knees scraped over the rocky slant as she grasped at anything she could to stop her decent. She stood on a step at the bottom of an incline with cuts and bruises. After several attempts, she sat down with a huff. Taking her necklace in one hand, she closed her eyes and whispered, "I sure could use some luck about now." A few rocks tumbled down, knocking her gently on her ankle from another direction.

Following the steady trail of rolling pebbles led directly to a hidden path which opened into an inner chamber. A drop of water splashed against Willow's cheek. Wiping the drip with one hand, her head tilted upwards. Rain was spitting through an opening in the high ceiling of the cavern. Watching the drizzle, her eyes fixated on the object the sprinkling landed on. A large tree was standing right before her. Its spreading branches were covered with white and pink flowers mixing together to form bowls and light green, lance shaped leaves. A few flower petals showered down on her head as a majestic blackbird swooped down and landed on a branch in front of her.

"Shelby," she exclaimed. "How did you find me?"

"Purely by chance, I assure you. From above, I happened to notice this tree growing underground and flew in to check it out," the avian guardian replied.

"I'm glad to see you," Willow blurted out, her eyes stinging.

"You are a mess, girl," Shelby squawked. "What on earth have you been doing? Never mind, we will have time for that later. You have, I see, found at least one of the great trees."

"Two," Willow said, extending her hand to lightly stroke the dark brown leathery trunk of the tree. "This one is neither awake nor asleep."

"What do you mean?" Shelby asked.

"It's that state when you are first falling asleep or waking up. That point when your mind is sharing being ruled by the conscious and subconscious," Willow said. "She can hear us, but doesn't know if we are real or dream. Can you wake her fully?"

"I'm not sure," Shelby answered. "But I can try."

The black bird ruffled its feathers as it spread its wings. A dark blue aura exploded forth from its centre. Its body quickly became only a silhouette in the background of a miraculous magical display as the aura engulfed the whole of the tree, invading its core.

Rocky debris scattered down into a pile as the tree shifted its position. Shelby flew down landing on Willow's shoulder. Together they watched as branches extended out as far as they could, hitting walls and collapsing more of the cavern in the process. A loud *Ah* sound shook the walls of the cavern.

"I think she is yawning," Willow said, ducking out of the way of a falling rock.

“Brilliant,” Shelby answered. “Perhaps you could ask her to not kill us in the process of regaining consciousness.”

The tree stopped moving and bent forward, swinging its branches behind it to reveal two hollows midway down its trunk. The covering over the two knots opened, exposing giant eyes. The tree blinked several times while tilting slightly from one side to another.

“You are not Lilybelle, and yet you are,” the tree said. “How confusing.”

“I am Willow,” she answered. “And this is Shelby. You have been asleep for a very long time.”

“Have I?” the tree asked. “And Lilybelle, she is gone?”

“Yes, I am afraid so,” Willow answered.

“So why am I awake?” the tree enquired.

“I believe because the threat Lilybelle gave her life trying to stop has returned,” Willow answered.

“Well, there isn't time for catch up, so I will just take a peek myself, if you don't mind,” Shelby said, disappearing onto Willow's skin and appearing as a picture with only half the glory her true self displayed.

The tree closed its eyes and made a motion as if taking in a deep breath. “I only sense one other of my brothers and sisters nearby,” she said.

“Yes,” Willow answered. “Bettulla, the tree of love, has also awakened recently. I only know of one other, Acacia, the tree of justice, who is also awake.”

“I see. In that case, I am Nadia, the tree of hope,” she said. “How did you find me?”

“Sheer luck,” Willow said. “I was having difficulty climbing a steep hill covered in loose rocks just outside this cavern and stumbled upon you by accident. You were already in the waking process.”

“I will emerge and help hunt for my siblings,” Nadia offered. “If you're correct and the threat has returned, I will aid as best as I am able to nullify it. Where is it you are travelling to?”

“To the place where the dragons dwell,” Willow answered. “To the spot that was to seal Atlantis away. They have some means of entering this realm and that is the only place I have to start investigating. It isn't much to go on, but if the fifth elf race has managed to find a way to open a guardian portal, it would explain a lot of things.”

“If they have discovered that,” Nadia said, bending over slightly to match gazes with the girl in front of her, “we are in a lot of trouble. You should hurry and discover what you can.”

“Yes,” Willow said. “Except I still have to get past the climb. I haven't quite figured out how I am going to be able to accomplish that.”

“Silly girl,” Nadia said. “You are no longer alone. I think you will find you have hope, both in your heart and under your feet. Until we meet again, young Willow, I bid you goodbye.”

Backtracking from the hidden room to the path leading to the valley of the dragons took only a few minutes.

Willow sighed. The path looked exactly the same as she had remembered it. “Hope,” she muttered under her breath.

Go on, Shelby said telepathically. *Give it a try. What can you lose when you have both luck and hope on your side?*

Willow smiled. She reached for her locket. “Luck,” she said. “And hope. I do have both of those. Okay, let's do this.”

She began climbing, making footholds as strong as she could before moving up a step. About halfway up the incline, she felt the dirt and pebbles beneath her feet begin to shift. Closing her eyes and biting her bottom lip, she prepared for the worst. One foot slipped backwards, then the other. Her hands felt the beginning of scrapes from rugged stones beneath them. Then her body stopped. Her hands flailed around as if she was trying to fly as her torso bent backwards, her knees balancing her weight. She shifted a few times, wobbling slightly. The backs of her feet were planted firmly against something. Glancing down, she realized it was tree roots that had stopped her slide. The ground rumbled as more roots came up through the stone and formed steps all the way up the incline. Once at the top, she could see the exit into the dragons' lair. Her pace quickened. Perhaps she hadn't missed the elves. After all, she now had hope on her side.

King Cornelius

“How long will this take before it has control of my children?” Cornelius asked.

A short man in a white doctor's coat stuttered as he spoke. “I t-t-t-told you, y-y-y-you need to be c-c-c-careful. T-t-t-take your t-t-t-time when re-wr-wr-wr-writing their m-m-m-memories. Wha-wha-wha-what y-y-y-you say c-c-c-could t-t-t-take hold.”

“Can anyone else here speak properly?” Cornelius yelled. “I don't have the patience to listen to this jabbering fool.”

The king's arm flew out, backhanding his assistant. The frail man staggered backwards, hitting the wall. His body slouched down on the ground. Two guards entered. Bending over, they lifted the unconscious husk of a man and removed him from the room. All voices were silenced. The only noise came from the replacement assistant's knocking knees.

“Your excellence,” his teeth chattered. Drips from a cold sweat ran down his face, draining all remaining colour with them. Lowering his head in a bow, he fell to one knee. “I am Soral. I would be honoured to be of some assistance to my king.”

"Yes, of course," the king answered. "Let's skip the pleasantries. I am here for five doses of the memory replacement drug. I don't need a lecture. I need results. So is it ready for me or not?"

"Most definitely it is!" Soral bit his bottom lip. "But they are such important subjects. We want to take the utmost care before you administer the drug."

Cornelius let out a deep growl from the pit of his belly. "Excuses! All I hear is excuses! I need action. Soral, are you a man of action?"

"I am, your excellency."

"Then give me the potions and let me get on with my plans." Cornelius put one finger under the still-bowed head of his worker and lifted him to a standing position.

"As you wish, my lord," Soral answered.

"Good," the king snorted, lightly slapping Soral's cheek before removing his hand. "We need to be strong now that we are approaching our finest hour."

Soral bowed his head and body while outstretching his hands with a wooden box between them. "These are them, my lord," his voice shook as he spoke. "Simply add to any liquid..."

"I know how a potion works, you snivelling fool!" Cornelius bellowed with the force of a trumpet. "What do you take me for?"

"I meant no disrespect, sire," Soral grovelled. "Please forgive my ignorance."

The king belched. "Out of my way!" he yelled, grabbing the box from Soral's hands. The door slammed shut echoing a clanging noise all the way to the top of the rock staircase. "Guards!" the king screamed, his feet slamming down hard on each step as he ascended to his great hall. "Find my family and have them attend me in our usual meeting room."

The guards scurried off as fast as the orders left the king's lips. Cornelius opened the sliding wood panel doors. Resting his arm on the mantel, his body soaked in the warmth of the fireplace.

"Shall I pour you a drink, sire?" a servant asked from behind him.

"Yes," Cornelius answered without moving. "Pour seven glasses of our finest wine. Today, I celebrate victory."

"As you wish, sire," his servant replied, leaving seven golden goblets filled with red liquid arranged neatly on a serving tray on the table. "Will there be anything else?"

"No," Cornelius replied, his voice cold and stern. "Please leave me. I shall ring if we need anything additional."

The servant bowed to his king's posterior and shut the door behind him. Cornelius' eyes closed. He inhaled deeply, letting the air escape back out. His hand meandered over the surface of the rock mantel, allowing his fingers to linger on a small figure of a snake etched in the stone.

"The time is near, Apopp. Soon, my friend," the king said. His mouth distorted in an evil upwards curl. Swiftly, he turned to the table. The wooden box in his hands cracked as he broke its seal to reveal the tiny bottles inside. In the hearth, the fire crackled as if it were laughing devilishly while observing the liquid from each vial drip into the chalices of wine. Once empty, the king fed the hungry fire the remnants of the small crate and its now empty contents.

The door slid open, revealing the familiar figure of his wife. Without expression, she took her usual seat near the fireplace silently.

"Darling," Cornelius said, picking up the two unaffected drinks. "This is for you. We will save it for the toast."

"Toast," Joseph said, entering the room his hands hidden deep within his pockets. "To what do we deserve such a festivity?" he asked. One missing hand fumbled with a vial of potion, becoming clammy at the sight of the five remaining glasses on the table. He jolted forward slightly at the slap of a hand on his back.

"Careful," Lance said, sneaking up behind him. The rest of their siblings filed in behind, taking up their usual positions in the comfortable room.

“What's this?” Zoe asked.

“Please, my family,” Cornelius said. “Take a glass and have a seat. We have much to celebrate. Things have progressed in our favour.”

Lance exchanged glances with Joseph as he passed him. Taking a golden cup in his hand, he lifted it in the air towards his brother as he passed on the way back. Choosing a firm chair, he sat leaning on its back, waiting for the others to settle in.

“Very good,” Cornelius said, his eyes lighting up. “We have been fortunate in our plans, my dearest family. The girl is missing, presumably in hiding, scared of her future. In the process, she took care of a possible future problem by eliminating Hilary for us. We are now ready for phase two of my plan. So a toast to us.” He lifted his cup in the air.

“To us,” the whole family said, following his motions.

Joseph exchanged a glance with his brother as they drank down the wine. All seven cups set down on the coffee table at the same time.

Lance leaned back and shook his head. Everything was cloudy, a mist moving before his vision and shrouding everything in a slow motion shadow of what was once reality. He tried to speak, but words refused to form on his tongue. They were there, yet missing at the same time; locked inside him somewhere. Muffled sounds shuffled through his mind, all distorted. The people around him were speaking in a jumbled foreign language he had never heard before. Cornelius lifted one of his eyelids and peered in up close as if looking directly into his soul for something to pull out.

“Good,” his father said. “I think we can start.”

Lance heard his words clearly this time. He tried to speak. To ask, start what? No sound came.

“My children,” Cornelius started, “you are to forget most of what has happened in the past. All you need to remember is what I tell you now. You are blessed to be a part of our loving family.”

"Oh, Cornelius," the queen interrupted. "We don't need the pleasantries. You know you only have ten minutes. Just get on with it."

"Why must you butt in?" the king asked. "Our children are going to be the most important rulers ever. Together they will oust every ruler from power and take control of every kingdom in existence. With my plan, they cannot fail. There will be no one who could stand up against them." He raised his fist in the air with authority. "Now, woman, you will let me erase everything that could hold them back and input the will to be invincible."

"This potion can only be used once," the queen answered, slurping her tea. "I suggest you program them correctly. I simply want you to make sure nothing backfires."

"Backfires?" Cornelius screamed. "They need to think on their own for something to backfire. I guarantee you when they first come out of this spell, they will not be strong enough to question my authority."

"Perhaps," his wife answered. "But what about later? Have you asked if this potion can wear off? I wish you had told me today was the day. I would have settled these issues myself with the ones who made the potions."

"There was no need for you to know!" Cornelius yelled. "If the potion becomes weaker, we will deal with that issue at the time. Even then, they would require the ability to have free thought to actually do something on their own. Besides, we are still their parents no matter how much they dislike things we have done." His chubby hands ran roughly over his face, attempting to stop it from turning a deeper shade of crimson. "Now silence with you, while I tell them how we want them to be."

"As you wish," she said, shaking her head. Her tongue pressed against the roof of her mouth, letting out a clicking noise. "Don't say I didn't warn you, though."

The king crossed the room, taking a position in front of his five remaining children. "Now," he started, "my children, you are to understand that you are to work as a cohesive unit. Everything you desire, your brothers and sisters want for you. Everything they desire, you want for them. Your abilities and intelligence will remain as before. You will use every bit of treacherously cunning trickery and wit you have to obtain your goals. Let no one stand in your way. You will follow my specific instructions; however, if any of you are threatened, you can think freely for yourselves as to what to do. Those who oppose us are your enemies."

His feet scuffed the floors as he shuffled his way back to the mantel. "You will discontinue all sleepwalking activities, as they are unsafe to use at this time. All past contacts are to be looked at with a new caution. Anyone could be a possible enemy and treated as such. Do not blindly trust. Above all, remember: kill before being killed is your new motto."

Zoe's head began moving slightly. The index finger on her left hand twitched slightly. As her movements became less robotic, it became undeniable that the stiffness was beginning to leave her body. She was coming free from the potion's effects.

Cornelius sighed. "I guess that is all the time we have," he said. "Now let's celebrate our new victories. I have a job for you to complete for me later this evening."

Lance shook his head. The cloud blocking his vision was retreating. He took a deep breath and let it out again. "I think some of the smoke from the fireplace is getting in," he said, rubbing his eyes. "I almost felt like I was going to pass out there."

Cornelius rang a bell and a servant appeared. "Open the windows and turn on some fans. I expect the chimneys to be cleaned tomorrow. We all seem to be a bit dizzy from the smoke. This is unacceptable with the queen being pregnant."

"Yes, sire," the servant answered, already opening a window.

"Actually," the queen groaned, "I think I will lie down for a while, if you don't mind."

"Of course, darling," Cornelius said. "I will check on you after I send the children to Atlantis." His lips grazed the surface of her skin in the form of a kiss.

"Might I ask the nature of our task?" Joseph asked.

“Yes,” Cornelius said, his lips retracting from a smile to a stern look. “I want you to take a couple of keepers and their guardians to Atlantis.” He threw a hand in the air. “Maybe take one more as insurance as well.”

“Just take them there?” Zoe asked.

“Make sure you hand them over directly to King Cornost. It seems the spots they were using to travel to the elf realm have closed. They need to be able to enter that world to attack, so the guardian portals are the only other option. We need a weak keeper and guardian who can be easily manipulated by thought of the death of one of their own. Then we can force them to open the portal on command.” Cornelius motioned for his servant to bring him another drink. “It is imperative you choose wisely. Whichever keepers you take must not cause a problem for Atlantis. For our plan to work, we need the elves to eliminate each other in battle, leaving us little else to do but claim their lands.”

“A brilliant plan,” Joseph said. “When does Atlantis become accessible?”

“You have two hours,” the king replied before guzzling down his second chalice of wine. His hand extended for a refill. “You best ready yourselves.”

“As you wish, Father,” Lance said, leading the others out of the room to the stairs leading to the lower levels. “Any suggestions as to which prisoners to take?”

“There are a few that come to mind,” Simon answered. “The redhead with the one bird, perhaps?”

“She is too smart,” Lance said.

“What makes you say that?” Zoe asked.

“I'm not sure,” Lance replied. “I have a bad feeling things will go wrong if we take that one. I think we should look at the other choices first.”

“Well,” Joseph said, smiling, “if you say so, I agree. We're a team, so gut feelings are good enough for me. It's better not to take a chance.”

"What if we take the woman from one couple and the man from another?" Ophelia asked. "We can keep their mates here to prevent them from acting up."

"You may have something there, sister." Joseph put his arm around her shoulders and squeezed. "And one child can go with them as an extra insurance policy."

Lance banged on a clear door. "That one right there. The man. He appears to have a wife and close ties to that other man as well." He motioned to a guard to have the men removed from the room they were being held in.

"We could send the two men and keep the woman," Zoe suggested. "Men do have that desire to protect built into them. Shall we test that theory?"

Joseph motioned for the guards to bring the other two and have all three put into an interrogation room. Following them in, he turned a chair around backwards and straddled it. "Hello," he said, a smile covering his face. "I am sure you know, I am Prince Joseph and these are my brothers and sisters. We would like to offer you a job. Your names are?"

"What is it you want?" the younger man asked.

"I can order your files," Joseph said, tapping his fingers on the table in front of him. "But why waste time? Give us your names and we will tell you the deal we are prepared to offer you."

"Aaram Waddington," the older man answered. "What is the deal?"

"The other two?" asked Zoe.

"Lane and Geena," Aaram replied.

"Okay," Joseph said. "We have some friends who need a portal open."

"No," Aaram cut him off.

"You haven't heard our offer yet," Joseph said, waving a finger back and forth in front of the man's face.

"I don't care," Aaram responded without blinking.

“Well,” Joseph said, shrugging his shoulders. “Maybe Lane might disagree. You see, if you two men agree to help, we will let Geena go free.”

“You'll let her go?” Lane asked.

“No, Lane,” Geena cried. “It's a lie. They won't.”

“Oh, we will,” Joseph said. “We simply take you to Atlantis, you open the portal and Geena is a free woman in the main world.”

“We'll do it!” Lane yelled.

“Think about what you are saying,” Aaram complained. “We cannot help them. This goes against everything we have fought for.”

“Our family is out there,” Lane pleaded. “I can feel them, my mother, my son. Let Geena have a chance to see them again. I beg of you.”

“Fine,” Aaram said, hanging his head. “We will agree to help you.”

“Excellent! We leave at once,” Joseph declared, standing. “You have made the right choice.” He motioned for the guards to take Geena back to her cell.

“Oh,” Lance said as the guards were leaving. “We will need the small blonde boy from cell three as well. Not that we don't have faith in your word, but if the two of you, or your guardian friends, do decide to try something, the child will be executed to pay for your insolence. You do understand?”

“Yes,” Aaram said. “We understand. Geena, tell my wife I love her.”

“I love you,” Lane yelled as the door closed.

“Alright, then,” Joseph said. “The entrance to Atlantis awaits.” He opened the door, bowed slightly at the waist while making an ushering motion with one hand.

“Here is the boy,” a guard yelled at them on the stairs.

Lance turned and placed his hand on the child's head, messing his hair slightly. "Hi sport, what's your name?" he asked.

"Jordan," the boy answered.

"Well, Jordan," Lance replied. "You are going on an adventure with these two nice men. They will be taking care of your safety while you are gone. Okay?"

"Okay," Jordan said, pushing past Lance to take Aaram's hand.

"Excellent," Joseph said. "Aaram, you make sure nothing happens to Jordan. He is such a cute little guy. We wouldn't want any harm to come to a single hair on his head."

"We'll keep him safe," Aaram said, his grip tightening on the boy's hand. "Is this the way?" He pointed to a dark corridor in front of them.

"Yes," Joseph said. "Just a bit further. The opening is expected to occur in ten minutes. Lots of time, no need to hurry."

The cold stone pathway led to an alcove filled with guards. Two men in white coats were hanging over a large machine with clipboards in their hands, writing notes with incredible speed.

"How long will it be open?" Zoe asked.

"You will have seven hours. After that, it could destabilize at any time," one man answered. "We were hoping to give you a bit more leeway, but the barrier is stronger around Atlantis than other realms. It's a miracle we are punching through at all. Without help from the other side, we might not be as successful."

"Seven hours will be plenty for what we need to do," Lance said. He took a square stance, placing his hands behind his back while facing where the opening was to appear.

"You are too stiff, brother," Joseph laughed. "Relax, this is a walk in the park."

"If it is that easy, brother," Lance said without moving, "I have to wonder why Father would send all five of us." His hand reached into the inside pocket of his suit jacket, pulling out a pair of sunglasses. Unfolding them, he put them on, then returned to his army-like stance.

Joseph chuckled under his breath. "I see your point." Following his brother's motions he also put on a pair of dark sunglasses.

"I, for one, hope there will be a little conflict," Zoe scoffed as she moved in between her two brothers forming a line. "It's been far too boring lately. Being cooped up doesn't suit me at all. I daresay I deserve better."

"Agreed," Joseph replied. "You deserve to be treated as a queen, my sister."

"Soon," Simon jutted in. "All your dreams and wishes will come true. That's what today is all about. We will step through this portal to a new beginning for all the children of Cornelius." He motioned to a circle of swirling coloured light.

Zoe coughed. Her hand waved back and forth in front of her face, cutting through the dense smoke emanating from the machines operating the portal. "Is it broken?" she asked, choking on the fumes as she spoke.

"Not exactly," one of the workers yelled back at her over the clangs and crashes coming from the equipment he was running. "We knew our systems would have to give everything they had in them to punch this hole. It's up to the other side to finish the opening now. We can only hold things like this until they do. Hopefully soon or we could damage our systems beyond repair."

"It won't affect our return, will it?" Zoe gasped. Drops of liquid fell from somewhere under her sunglasses, presumably from where the smoke had infiltrated and attacked her eyes.

"Not at all," the other worker replied. "Once the portal is open, we can hold its form. Look! Atlantis is responding."

"It's about time," Zoe squawked. The points of her long red nails clicked together letting out an eerie sound similar to teeth chattering.

Aaram squinted. The bright lights from the enlarging circle intensified. "Don't look into the lights!" he screamed, pulling

Jordan's face into his body. A flash of brightness exploded throughout the tunnel. "Is it over?" he asked, his eyes clenched tightly together.

"Quite," Joseph answered.

Aaram's eyes opened slowly. Black and red spots floated in front of his line of sight. He shook his head from side to side. "How long before we can see properly again?"

"Varies," Simon answered, grabbing the man's arm.

"Wait, kid!" Lance yelled. All attention turned to the young boy now standing in front of the circular doorway still forming.

"It's like water!" Jordan laughed as his hand reached out. One finger tapped the surface, sending a ripple of waves in all directions like a raindrop hitting a puddle. His hands clasped together making a clapping sound before reaching out again, this time extending his whole arm into the substance. "It doesn't feel wet." His nose crinkled up as he turned his head slightly to see the people behind him. Before another word could be said, his little body jerked, disappearing with only ripples left behind in the spot where he had once stood. The portal surface returned to motionless glass before their eyes.

"Where did he go?" Aaram demanded.

"Through the mirror," Zoe said. Her hands brushed through her hair, using her reflection to smooth its appearance. "That's better. Shall we go, then?"

"After you," Joseph smiled.

The two sisters led a procession through the gateway. Lane hesitated briefly, sucking in a mouthful of air. He stuck one leg through the opening, following it with a sliding motion of the rest of his body. It was a futile attempt to not let whatever substance the doorway was made of touch him. His head emerged at its destination. His mouth opened, instantly deflating his cheeks. It took a few deep gasps to recover fully. Without warning, his knees wobbled, buckling under his weight and lurching him forward into a group of guards. Like a bowling ball knocking down pins, they fell in a pile. Lane was left standing before them.

Sweat trickled down his face as three guns pointed directly at his forehead. A few coughs escaped from his throat as a large breath of air, as dry and stale as thirty day old bread, scraped his throat and lungs. His contemplation of whether or not the small room they were in had ever been opened before came to an abrupt end with the click of a gun barrel preparing to fire.

Zoe cackled. “I'm surprised you didn't fall flat on your face. Guess they took the fall for you.” Her hand grabbed the barrel of one of the weapons. She slid it away from her prisoner. “We are here to deliver these men to help you, not to watch you execute them.”

“Back down!” a man riding a unicorn yelled from outside the room. “The woman is right, we need them. No one from this party is to be harmed.”

“Woman,” Zoe squealed back. “I am not a mere woman.” Her hand disappeared into one of her pockets and emerged holding a crooked wand crudely wrapped in a green leather-like substance and topped with a bright emerald.

“Settle down now, boy,” the man said, bracing himself as the animal's front two legs left the ground and pounded back down again. Dismounting, his hands ran across the animal's silky white fur. “Good boy.” He reached into his pocket and fumbled for a moment. Looking down at his palm, he smiled and held out three sugar cubes. “You should put that away.”

Zoe lowered her wand to her side as she peered outside the room. Her hand remained tightly clenched around its shaft. “Your advice is noted, but not warranted. We know of your beast's abilities.” Smugness overtook her language as if she were taunting for confrontation.

“Well then, introductions may be in order,” he said. “I am your host, King Cornost of Atlantis.”

“Perhaps,” Zoe answered, “the king of Atlantis has been locked away too long and has forgotten his manners. Am I wrong to expect your full attention for a proper greeting?”

The king laughed. Swinging his body around, his long golden hair flipped behind him, neatly falling down his lower back. Zoe gasped. She hadn't been prepared for the man to be quite so beautiful. Her tongue protruded from her mouth enough to lightly wet her slightly parted lips as they formed an uneven smile. Her index finger instinctively caressed her bottom lip as if she were evening lip gloss across its smooth red surface.

“Please accept my heartfelt apology,” he said, moving inside. “You are Cornelius' children, I take it?” His eyes glanced over each of them before settling on Zoe. “This is far from the ideal way for royalty to meet. Unfortunately, there is little option.” He extended his hand towards the princess. “May I show you to somewhere more comfortable?”

“I am afraid we don't have enough time for a social visit,” Joseph said, taking his sister's hand in his own. “We are here to see what you need is provided to you. After the war is over, perhaps we will have a chance for pleasantries.”

“As you wish,” the king said. “However, it may be easier if I at least knew your names.”

Joseph's sunglasses folded with ease and slipped into the inside pocket of his black jacket. “Of course,” he said. “I am Joseph. My brothers are Lance and Simon... my sisters, Zoe and Ophelia.”

“And the others?”

Simon's hand brushed the shoulders of the two keepers. “Aaram and Lane,” he said. “They each carry two guardians. They have agreed to help.”

“The boy?” the Atlantian king asked.

“Insurance,” Lance answered. “In case our two friends have a change of heart.”

“How very efficient,” Cornost chuckled. “Seems things will be back on track in no time at all. I suppose we should get started. There are three sealed stone portals from here to the elf world. I would like to activate all three. One allows entrance to the mountains... the second enters between the caves and river dwellers... and the third in the glorious forests of the golden elves. Once all three are open, we can begin our attack.”

“Are there none to the main world?” Ophelia asked.

“There are most likely some,” the king answered. “I am not interested in the main world, nor do I have plans to go there at this time. After years of contemplation, we have discovered that the elf realm is what we were meant to rule. We have a debt to repay them for our isolation. Come this way.”

Stepping outside was like jumping into a page of a history book. Beautiful architecture made of white stone with elaborate columns resembled temples built to worship great gods.

Lane lunged forward, his shoe catching on one of the many stones littering the road way winding through the buildings. His hand jutted forward, his fingers grasping at Aaram's shirt to steady himself. His knees wobbled as he stumbled before catching his balance again.

Aaram sighed. “Be more careful, please. I doubt these men will be helpful if you injure yourself. Are you listening to me?”

Lane stood motionless, his jaw wide open and eyes fixated upwards at what should have been a sky. “Where are we?” he asked.

“Underwater, of course,” Cornost answered. “The air pocket around us is flexible, as you can see.” His hand motioned towards a rather large shark swimming full speed at them. It hit the sphere surrounding them, indenting it. The bubble bounced back like an elastic, stunning the shark enough to turn it away. “I suggest you all stay a good distance from the perimeter. They may not be able to penetrate, but being hit by an attempt can leave some nasty bruises.”

“This is incredible,” Ophelia squealed. “It must be amazing to have such a beautiful surrounding all the time.” Her neck tilted backwards, allowing her eyes to follow a school of brightly coloured fish as they swam above them, disappearing behind a coral reef. “Are we floating?”

“I am glad you find our home impressive,” Cornost replied. “It has its own beauty. Having said that, it wears thin when you can never leave... never see a sunrise or sunset... never feel a fresh breeze against your skin. As they say, the grass is always greener on the other side. As for your question, we are in fact floating."

"Wouldn't that give you different views to enjoy... something different all the time?" Zoe asked.

"Theoretically, yes," Cornost said, his attention turning to the oldest sister. "But again, everything has a cost. For instance, see that coral reef over there?" He placed one hand around her shoulder and pointed at a series of mounds that mesmerized her attention with bright colours and intricate designs.

Zoe gasped. Her vision locked on a sea turtle winding its way between the jagged edges of the coral labyrinth. "I've never seen anything quite like it," she answered.

"No, I don't suppose you have," the king whispered in her ear. "Right now, it's a glorious display of marine life at its finest. Tonight, however, this world could slam into it and bounce away. The damage it could cause would be intense. There would be injuries and even some deaths to deal with. After a few times, seeing it loses its luster."

"You can't steer away?" Zoe screamed.

Removing his arm from around the princess, he stood motionless for a moment watching the turtle navigate. "No. We were condemned to this life. Floating aimlessly around the oceans... no purpose... no choice... imprisoned for eternity... forced to drift from place to place and never be found. That is what the elves at the side of the seven great trees decided was to be our fate. That is what we are fighting to be released from. Only the light of the sun rising can remove the membrane that encases our land."

"How terrible," Zoe cried. Her hand caressing his back with the weight of a feather. "What of the other races who dwell in the elf realm? Will they stand beside you or oppose you?"

"They have been dealt with. By now, they are all too weak to engage us in battle. Even without such planning, they most certainly would not be bothered. Lending aid is not in their nature. That is the downfall of their world."

“Your retribution is close at hand,” Lance interrupted. “Shall we move forward, so your people may see the light of a new day as quickly as possible?”

“Yes,” the king replied, a glimmer of excitement dancing in his eyes. “The first two portals are fairly close together, although they exit very far apart. After they are opened, we can move onto the final gateway. It leads deep into the mountains of the elf realm and is located in the middle of our military cemetery. That's where the buried bodies of those who gave their lives trying to fight for our freedom have resided ever since the day we were first entombed alive. The ruins now serve as a reminder of how much we lost to the others of our own race. Shall we see the beasts that are able to open the portals? I have heard much about them. I must admit, my curiosity is piquing.”

Aaram took a deep breath and held out his left arm. The skin rippled beneath a picture of a black cat as it stretched its way to jump from picture to solid form. “This is Saymore,” he said. “He will attempt to open the portals you speak of.”

“Marvellous,” Cornost exclaimed, smacking his hands together. “I have never seen anything quite so extraordinary before. I can't wait to see it in action. This way.” His feet moved with twice the speed they had before, leading the group along the stone path towards two large buildings built like shrines. “Here we are! Everyone up the steps. We added these structures around the stone bases to help keep them safe. Only a handful of my people are allowed inside.”

Saymore's tail twitched back and forth, matching the motion of each of his paws coming down to climb each step higher. His head twisted to the side as he took possession of the top spot. “I will need to change into my true form,” he said. “Please don't be alarmed by the transformation.” His back arched, black fur standing at attention. As his body grew, his front paws slid forward, scraping on the concrete beneath. Skin stretched to its limit over enlarging bones and muscles.

Ophelia jumped backwards, almost falling on the stairs. Lance's arms reached out to catch her before she launched into a full tumble. No words of thank you would form. Her eyes remained fixated on the animal's twisted face as a jaw full of sharp teeth extended out too large to be concealed. The sight became too much. Clenching her eyes closed, she buried her head into the warmth of her brother's chest. She inhaled his musky scent deeply, letting it overtake her senses. "That's disgusting!" she screamed, regaining her full composure.

"It's amazing," Cornost muttered, mesmerized by the end of the transformation. "Such power. Such grace."

A loud crack sounded as Saymore's neck turned from side to side. He let out a sigh. The front part of his body crouched down towards the ground, each muscle in his front legs and shoulders visible. "That's better," he said. "It's been a while since I could stretch like that. Feels good to be me again. You want me to open these two portals. Is that correct?"

"Yes, please," Cornost responded. "That is exactly what I need." His arms raised in the air, palms pointed to the sky. His attention intensely focused on the events before him. One eye squinted, allowing for a half-smile to cross his face. Holding that pose, one might have thought he was a statue if not for the saliva dripping out of his mouth. "For Atlantis!" he bellowed. Cheers rang out from citizens filling the street behind them.

"Where did they come from?" Ophelia asked.

"History is being made, my young friend," Cornost answered, wiping the last of his drool from his chin. "The masses will celebrate tonight as Atlantis rises in the morning! Now to the final location."

Chapter Thirty-Five

"Zoran!" Willow yelled out. She grasped her shoulder and winced. She would need a bandage for the scrape she had just made rushing out past jagged rocks. "Skilar!" The valley lay silent. "Is anyone here?" Her hand caressed a wilting leaf already turning colours from whatever poison was infecting the land. Her body shook. She collapsed to her knees, sharing the pain the plant before her was enduring. Her thoughts exploded. *What sort of monster could do this?*

There are all types of monsters in this world, Shelby responded telepathically. *This is no different from any other. What defines who we are, is what we consider to be the act of a monster versus what we consider just.*

Are we monsters? she asked.

I can't answer that, the guardian bird replied. *You must decide what is right and wrong for yourself. No one else can make that choice. That is what I fight for... freedom.*

How do I know I am making the right choice? What if I make a mistake?

She could hear Shelby chuckle in her mind. *Of course you will make mistakes,* the bird answered. *That's how we know we are alive. All we can do is our best to live by the values we believe in... to respect the right of others to have their own values to live by.*

"Willow?" Zoran's deep voice roared. "You made it back." The ground shook as his large back feet touched down.

She grasped her hair in a bunch, holding onto it until the dragon's wings had completely stopped flapping. "Zoran," she said, lurching forward to hug as much of the beast as she could. "Did the elves come?" Her delicate hands slid over his scales. They were stronger now. Even their colour was different. What had once been a pale grey was closer to that of a shiny black diamond.

"Yes," he replied. "The water source and all of the dragons have been rid of this poison. We owe you a debt of gratitude."

"No," Willow said. A handful of dirt slowly escaped through her fingers. Her lips parted slightly, forcing a stream of air towards the falling grains of earth, catching them midstream. The wind picked up where her breath left off, scattering bits of soil throughout the valley. "You owe me nothing." Her hand reached down, allowing her fingers to run back and forth through the loose ground. The colour of the leafy vegetation surrounding them morphed from sickly to vibrant in seconds. "It won't take me long before everything is back to the way it should be. Then I need to open that portal and find out what is on the other side."

"Open the portal?" Zoran growled. "Lilybelle gave her life sealing it. We cannot open it again."

Willow sighed. "If I am correct, it doesn't matter if this gateway opens. Atlantis already has other ways to enter this realm. That's how a unicorn appeared after so long. That's how your water source was poisoned."

"Atlantis?" Zoran gasped. "But why? How?"

"I believe they are formulating an attack. They chose to eliminate any outside help the elves could potentially have."

Willow's hand released another pile of dry earth. "The only way to find out more is to cross over."

"Your plan is reckless. I cannot allow you to undertake it alone," Zoran asserted.

"She won't be alone," Elsa-Mae said. "I am going with her."

"Elsa-Mae," Willow exclaimed. "What are you doing here?"

"I thought about what you said, and I agree. The fairies made a poor choice allowing Lilybelle to bear the burdens of this world alone. We lost her because of it. I can't change what is done, but I can make a difference as to what is about to happen." Her wings fluttered, holding her in position directly in front of Willow's face. "I need to do this," the fairy said. "Let me help you."

Zoran groaned. "This portal is not big enough for a dragon."

"They would see you coming a mile away," Elsa-Mae barked. "That would ruin the element of surprise, you big oaf."

"Oaf!" Zoran yelled, smoke escaping from his nostrils. "I could barbeque you with my breath." His eyes widened.

Elsa-Mae's hair flew wildly from the dragon's breath. Her body whipped forward directly in front of his snout. She leaned forward, pressing her lips against his facial scales in a kiss before flying away giggling.

Zoran let out a primal laugh. "It's been a while, my fairy princess. I had forgotten how much I enjoyed your company."

"No!" Elsa-Mae replied. "Not forgotten... suppressed. I too am guilty of the same crime."

A mist formed in the corner of Willow's eyes. "You sacrificed your love to punish yourselves, didn't you?" No answer anticipated, she continued. "No one should ever have to put themselves through such a torture. It's time to forgive and move on."

"You don't understand," Elsa-Mae cried.

"No," Willow yelled. "I actually believe I finally do. We are who we are because of the choices we make. Everyone makes mistakes. That is how we learn... how we grow. There is no possible way for one person to be right all the time. Whether it is ourselves questioning our own choices or somebody looking in and criticizing, somehow, somewhere, someone will always think something we did was wrong."

"That's rather profound for a girl your age," Zoran said. "How is it you know so much?"

"A friend of mine helped me see," Willow replied. "It didn't make sense to me at first, but now, it's all coming together. I think inside my heart, I knew it all the time, but it needed to come to the surface... a little nudge to be realized."

A golden butterfly whizzed by her ear. Its wings spread wide, gliding up and down, mimicking the waves of an ocean, before settling on the stone base that would open to Atlantis.

"Guess that's my sign," Willow said. "Don't worry. I will be careful. Let the elves know where I have gone and why."

"Where is it you think you are going?" Sebastian asked.

Willow spun round, finding herself face to face with her friend from school. "Sebastian," she shrieked. "I thought you had gone back already."

"No," he answered. "We are still seeing to a few details here. Seth returned to do some research on a few things. Now perhaps you can tell me where you are going."

"There is good reason," Willow said, taking a step backwards. "There are some answers there we need to find."

"Where?" Sebastian asked, matching her footwork.

"Atlantis," Willow answered.

"Have you gone completely mental?" the elf prince asked. "You simply cannot open the gate to Atlantis and go rushing in. We have no way of knowing what lies on the other side."

"Answers lie on the other side!" Willow screamed. "Answers I need." Her arm intertwined with his. "One way or another, Atlantis is coming. Lance told you that much."

“Probably,” Sebastian answered. “But we don't have to make it easier for them.”

“Well,” Shelby said, appearing before them. “If you are done arguing about opening the portal, perhaps you might take a look and realize it is already open.”

“What?” Willow screamed. “When did that happen?”

“Just now,” Zoran answered. “How would be the question to ask.”

“How indeed,” Shelby said, ruffling her feathers. “There must be a guardian on the other side. But why would they be helping Atlantis?”

“And why now?” Willow asked. “There must have been alternate ways to enter, otherwise the unicorn couldn't have made it across. There was no need to use this portal.”

Shelby sighed. “I would imagine it is because the elf council has our other guardian friends working on strengthening the barrier between these two worlds. Perhaps the reappearance of some of the great trees has had an effect as well. Whatever the case, I think it is safe to say that their previous form of entry is no longer available. We can also make a direct link between Atlantis and Cornelius now. That would be the only way a guardian could be made to open the door like that.”

“All the more reason to go through and find out.” Willow said, heading towards the stone portal.

Sebastian grabbed her arm and pulled her back. “Wait,” he said. “It's too dangerous to go busting in all crazy. It just opened.” He half-smiled at Willow's blank stare. His fingers ran through his sandy coloured hair, brushing it back off his face. “So... it stands to reason that whoever is forcing the guardian to do his bidding is still there... probably with others.” After watching Willow blink a couple times, he let out a huff. “At least wait a bit until they either clear out or come through.”

“It would be advisable,” Shelby interjected into the conversation. “Perhaps a couple of hours. If I am not mistaken, there are other portals from this world to Atlantis. I would like a chance to check them out before we go anywhere."

"Fine," Willow replied, kicking her shoe in the dirt.

"I'll wait here as well," Sebastian said. "Just in case an attack is initiated. We will need as much help as we can find if they come through."

"Agreed," Zoran said. "This time, we will meet them together."

Chapter Thirty-Six

A cork exploded with a loud pop from the champagne bottle Jade was holding. Bubbles ran out of the top and over her dainty fingers. She laughed, pouring what she could into glasses set up on the table before her.

"A toast!" Kasper yelled, raising his glass in the air. "To the new mayor of Pewterclaw, our good friend, Malarchy! They couldn't have elected a more perfect candidate!"

Supporters scurried about, trying to grab a glass of the liquid bubbles to cheer on the election results. The remnants of paper confetti drifted through the air, landing in every possible location they could find. Jessica jumped, her feet leaving the ground a few inches, as a balloon popped with a loud bang in the background, followed by a round of laughter.

"No need to be jumpy," Kasper whispered in her ear. "I think things are going very well. Don't you? After all, this will make it easy for our department to keep an eye on the new mayor. They seem to trust you. I guess I can't blame them. You have always been especially good at gaining the confidence of those around you." He raised the glass flute in his hand, smiling at her silence.

"An excellent party," the Director of New Residents, Fuscia Magnetal, bellowed in a husky voice loud enough for the whole room to hear. She glided through the room in a loud outfit that matched the colour of her name. "There should be more parties like this one. Please make a note of that, new mayor man." Approaching Malarchy, she kissed the air on either side of his face making a sour puckering noise at the same time. "Darling, I know we are going to be the best of friends. Can we schedule a dinner for the near future?"

Malarchy chuckled. "I am afraid I am avoiding dinners out for a while after my experience with Hilary. I hope you do understand... crowded rooms are more my style for the time being."

"Oh, of course," Fuscia sputtered. "That woman did such horrible things. I can't even imagine the number of innocents she murdered. It was that girl who saved you, wasn't it? What was her name again?"

"Willow," Malarchy answered. "And yes."

"Willow," the Director repeated. "And... do we know where she is now? I should like to thank her personally for what she did for Pewterclaw."

"No," the new mayor answered. "She disappeared right after. No one knows where she is at the moment."

Fuscia cracked a fake smile. "Well, let's hope she comes back when we need her to save the world again." Her glass clanked against Malarchy's. "Kasper, darling," she yelled out, her body disappearing into a sea of partygoers.

"Seems you've made some new friends," Jade whispered in her father's ear. Her lips gently pressed against his cheek.

Malarchy laughed. "No, more like I have more people trying to force information from me." His hand patted hers on his arm. "So what is my beautiful daughter up to? Are you enjoying the festivities?"

A flash of light went off before she could answer. Jade blinked a few times regaining her sight. "Hey!" she yelled.

"Sorry," Keith said. "News doesn't wait for anyone. How about a quote for the paper from you two?" The journalist snapped several more pictures in row.

"Please stop. The flash is hard on my eyes," Jade cried. "Why are you here, anyways? I thought Krissy was covering this story."

"You know how it is." A smugness in his voice began to dance before them. "Father felt it was a better idea to send someone to get the hard facts. Since the Hilary incident, it seems my other half may have gone a bit... soft."

"Really," Malarchy said. "I thought reporting the truth was... how did you put it... getting the hard facts. I find it refreshing and anything but soft."

"Ha, ha... ha," Keith spit out. "You will make an amusing mayor. May I quote you?"

"As long as my words are taken in the context in which they are meant, I have no problem with you quoting me," Malarchy answered. "If you change the words or their meaning, however, we shall have a problem." A fire glazed over his eyes as he smiled, revealing his fang-like teeth.

The flash went off again. "What a pose," Keith said, returning an emotionless smile. "If I didn't know better, I might think you were part vamp. I think I have what I need from you for now." His lips puckered, whistling a show tune as he walked away.

"What was that all about?" Jade asked.

"I am not sure," her father answered. "He might just be feeling me out. But I think we best be extra careful around that family for the next little while."

"Even Krissy?"

"Yes, my dear," Malarchy said still watching the reporter pushing his way through the crowd. "She still has to beat her brother to live. That is strong motivation. Whether we want to believe in her or not, we cannot take any chances."

“Any chances with what?” Gavin asked from behind them.

“Gavin!” Malarchy spun around, grasping the vamprite's hand in a firm shake. “Good to see you, my friend.”

“I am not sure the word friend applies,” Gavin retorted. “But we have business to discuss now that you are, in fact, mayor. I trust you haven't forgotten your offer.”

“Not at all. Not at all,” the new mayor replied. “This, however, isn't the best place to conduct a conversation.” His eyes scanned the room for *The Empowered* reporter. A flash went off, blinding him again.

“Just doing my job,” Keith smiled. “Imagine, I was just commenting on your appearance being so similar to one of these beasts and here you are shaking hands and consorting with one. I trust you know how the council feels about their kind...” his voice trailed off and whistling took its place.

“Watch what you say,” Gavin spat at his back. “There are those of my kind who would rip you apart for such comments.”

Kevin laughed. “I trust I can quote you on that?” He disappeared amongst the guests again.

“I can't stand that one,” Gavin said.

“Still,” Malarchy replied, “we have to deal with the press delicately now that I am in the public eye. What I need from you is...”

“I know,” Gavin interrupted. “When and where is all I came to find out.”

“Of course.” Malarchy smiled. “Jade, would you mind taking a stroll with Gavin in the moonlight? The air in here is a bit stuffy. I don't think we need any further confrontations from the newspaper this evening.”

“Of course,” Jade answered, switching from her father's arm to the vamprite's. “Come this way.”

Malarchy took the stage to begin his victory speech. “Good evening.” His voice exploded in the microphone followed by a few loud screeches. "Perhaps someone could adjust this before I begin?" He now had the attention of the whole room, and especially that of Keith Quidnunk. Out of the corner of his eyes, he watched his daughter and new employee exit without being noticed by a soul.

Chapter Thirty-Seven

"So," Jade said, glancing back over her shoulder at the empty space behind them, "you are going to work for us."

"Don't worry," he answered. "I would be able to tell if anyone was tailing us. Are you not afraid to be alone with me?"

"No," Jade said. She shivered. The touch of his fingers through her fine blonde hair was more effective than she cared to admit. "Willow trusted you. I trust Willow. That is something we have in common. She is a friend to both of us."

"But you aren't Willow." Gavin said, circling her like prey.

"I am not," she answered.

Hot breath gently caressed the nape of her neck. Every nerve in her body radiated towards his undeniable presence. Gulping back the saliva pooling in her mouth, she stretched her neck muscles. She wouldn't allow herself to fall for such a blatant vampire trick. Facing him, she struggled to bring her thoughts to words.

"I am Jade. I am not as strong as she is... or as powerful, but I understand what she is trying to do and I support her. If I can help her in any way, I am willing to try. That should count for something."

Gavin smiled, moving his body away from her. "It does."

Jade gasped. With only a split second to make a decision, her hand reached out and grabbed Gavin's shirt, pulling his body in close. A man and woman taking a stroll in the fresh evening air passed by. Her arms clasped around his neck. The strong scent of wild musk filled her nostrils as her head snuggled into his shoulder. She breathed in deeply, his natural aroma tantalizing her senses. Her eyes shut for a split second. Her face flushed. Never before had another person's presence created such an uneasiness deep within her. There had been boys before back in her home world, but they had been more like playthings. Those days were over now. Things were different. She was different. Maybe now...

"I think they are gone," Gavin whispered in her ear, breaking her thoughts. His warm breath grazed her skin with every word.

"Right," she said, scrambling for words. Her grip released. "This way." She pointed down a side alley that was almost invisible.

"Your work?" the vamprite asked. His eyebrows raised. There was literally nothing in the direction the girl was pointing.

"Partly," she answered. "My father helps as well. Together, our illusions are much harder to spot." She hustled him into the small road between two government buildings. A brick door swung open, exposing Iskander.

"Hurry," the portal guard hissed. "There have been patrols out all night down the main street. They pose as couples out for a romantic walk. I only noticed because the same three couples have walked by so many times." The door creaked closed behind them.

"Is this the only entrance?" Gavin asked.

"No," Jade answered. "There is another, but it is more of an emergency exit than a way we want to use to go in and out. There is also a hidden door from the mayor's office that leads here. We think Hilary used it to kidnap people from her office. No one else appears to know it exists. Father is making sure it is armed with the best magics."

"As long as I am not going to end up in some strange death trap," Gavin said, following the portal guard down a thin path.

"Malarchy would not allow his daughter down here if there was any chance of her being hurt," Iskander injected into the conversation. "You are completely safe."

"I hope you don't mind if I make that assessment for myself," the vamprite responded. "Where does this crevice lead?"

"To your laboratory, of course," Jade answered. The tunnel ended at a set of double doors which swung open to reveal a brightly lit large white room. Her aura exploded with bright colours. What they were doing here was cutting-edge. Her emotions fused together into a giant ball of excitement, pride, joy, anticipation, imagination, satisfaction, all dusted with a sprinkling of an uneasiness that left her knees weak.

Gavin's fingers scraped across the top of a cold steel table, the different machines and tools becoming a focus for his attention. His lips curled upwards at the sight of his own reflection on the silver surface. There were so few materials that could retain a vampire's shape-shifting image. The energy vibrations his race gave out were far too fast to be captured in any one form. But this steel was of the purest consistency. "I see you have fully stocked the room," he said. "What is in there?" His index finger raised in the direction of a steel door with a lock on it.

"That," Jade answered. Dangling a large round silver circle with a set of keys attached to it in the air in front him as if it were bait, she continued, "is for dangerous substances. I think it is called a clean room." She giggled. The keys jingled loudly, moving back and forth from his grasp. Teasing him was much more enjoyable than she had imagined it would be.

Gavin wasn't one to play for long. He snatched the keys from her hand. His movements were almost too quick to see before the door was open and he was inside. Jade pressed a button on a remote control and the wall parted revealing the second work space behind some form of glass.

“At least he put on the suit,” Iskander said, laughing.

“It isn't funny,” Jade stomped her foot. “We would have had to quarantine him if he hadn't. Especially since that memory drug is so strong.”

“Relax,” the guard said. “I was only joking. This fella knows where it's at, or your father wouldn't have chosen him for the job.”

Her finger pressed down on a button. “Gavin!” she yelled into an intercom. “There are samples of the memory drug and spider venom in the cold storage. Those are the two things the mayor wants your team to try to formulate an antidote for. The other door leads to the victim that needs serum for a bite. Perhaps you should return and see the rest of the facility before becoming too invested in that one area.”

Gavin made a thumbs-up motion at the window. A few moments later, he re-entered the main laboratory, still buttoning his shirt. “That is an incredible room. Your old man knows what it takes to get results,” he said. “Let's finish up this tour. I'd like to get my team in here as soon as possible. What's left to see?”

“There are a few more small labs that you can assign use to, a storage area stocked with supplies and the living quarters,” Jade answered.

“Living quarters too,” Gavin said, his eyebrows arched. “That's a good idea.” It was true, the less they needed to leave and return, the better the odds no one would suspect what they were doing. His friends would feel more secure as well.

“You have a private office that connects directly to the mayor for information exchanges as well,” Iskander added.

“Well,” Gavin said. Sparks flew as he rubbed his clasped hands together. “Let's start there, shall we? Perhaps there are some instructions awaiting me.”

“As you wish,” Iskander replied, leading the way through a white door leading to a generic corridor.

Gavin read out the words on doors as he walked by them. “Electrical... storage... cleaning supplies... medical room...

bathroom... lab one... lab two... three... four... five... ah, operations office." He turned the doorknob and entered in one motion.

Gavin leaned back and crossed his legs. He could get used to sitting in a fine leather chair. He spun in a circle like a child. "This," he said, "is nice." He opened the drawers in front of him, his fingers running over the contents of each. He chuckled. They had spared no expense, even on stationary that he had little intentions of ever using. Paperclips, staples, and sparkly gel coloured pens weren't things he could be bothered wasting time with.

"You should find everything you need," Jade said. "If there is something missing, you can let me know and I will make sure you get it."

"No," Gavin answered. A sheepish smile crossed his lips. "I think I can manage." A package of pink memo notepads dropped from his hand, landing on the desk and fanning open diagonally before one end hit the floor.

"Is it the colour?" Jade asked.

The vampire's lips parted sightly. His gaze locked onto hers. The world slowed as time flew away between their stares. "No," he said, cutting through the tension as if that one word was a knife.

"I can replace it with something else," Jade said, her attention drawn to his broad chest. It wasn't moving. How long had he been sitting there without taking in any air?

As if reading her mind, Gavin inhaled as deeply as a swimmer who had been underwater for several pool lengths. "I don't believe I will have need for such an item. In fact, I don't know how much need I will have for this size of an office."

"Oh," Jade said, disappointment dripping off her tongue like water from a leaky faucet.

"Did you arrange it?" Gavin asked. Her silence tore at his consciousness. Had she gone to too much trouble to make this office comfortable for him? Voices in his head argued with each other. Why should he care anything for this girl?

Willow, he thought. *She's the prize*. There was something about the redheaded girl that he couldn't quite put his finger on. She was special, different in some way. He felt like he needed her for some reason. No, not just him, everyone needed her. He would gladly share her with others. Still, Jade was a pretty girl. Pretty just wasn't good enough for him anymore. It hadn't been since he met Willow on the witches tour. No one could recreate the feelings he experienced standing next to her. A mixture of peace, excitement, awe and need that had rushed through his veins, left him wanting... yearning more.

"Can we help with anything else?" Iskander positioned himself between the two to break the unnerving connection that had formed.

"No," Gavin replied as if unable to form any other word.

"We'll leave you to your work then," the portal guard said. His hand brushed against Jade's back, nudging her gently towards the door. "You can send a message to Malarchy using that tube." His index finger motioned towards the corner of the room. "Use one of those memo sheets you seem to scoff at to record any questions or requests. Likewise, check the tube daily for replies or further instructions from the mayor."

"I see," Gavin huffed. "My apologies. I hadn't seen that as a possible use. I appreciate the effort that went into all of the preparations for us. Do you know which potion Malarchy would like us to work on first?"

"I believe the man's life comes first," Iskander answered. He squared his body towards the vampire and placed his hands on his hips. There was something off about working with a vampire, but even more so with that question. Morals obviously weren't his strong suit. He might be working with them, but that didn't mean he was trustworthy.

"We'll start as soon as I return with my team. Before we go, what's this for?" Gavin picked up a remote from the top drawer.

Jade reached out, snatching it from his hand. Pushing several buttons, the room slowly changed. The lights dimmed and a panel of wall swung around, revealing a large screen. A few more thumb movements and a news program lit up.

“Again,” the anchorman said, “breaking news is coming to you from the middle of the ocean. A large whirlpool has formed in the Triangle. Could this be an answer to mysteries that have gone unsolved for generations? Experts are referring to this phenomenon as the most prominent occurrence of the century. Normally a vortex of this type is caused by tides. It's formed when opposing currents meet each other. No one, however, seems to have an explanation for the sudden development of this maelstrom. Its appearance has called together the top scientific minds of our time, none of whom seem to be able to agree. We are hearing reports of everything from global warming to alien communication as possible answers. All flights to the area are being cancelled and nearby residents are asked to voluntarily evacuate. It is unclear if the swirling water is increasing in size or remaining the same at this time. Stay tuned to PUG news for further information as it becomes available.” A game show program resumed on the channel.

“What do you think that's about?” Jade asked. With a single thumb movement, the screen disappeared, reverting to the wood panel matching the rest of the wall.

Gavin inhaled abruptly. “Not sure,” he said. “But I have a feeling our mutual friend is involved in some way. Seems the terunji are having fun making up their own explanations again. That is always good for amusement. Regardless, someone from the magic community should check it out.”

“Yeah,” Jade said, still staring at the wall. “I'll talk to my father about it this evening. With all the scientists around, it might be tough to get close to investigate. Perhaps someone with a press pass can help.”

“A press pass?” Gavin repeated.

“Oh,” she answered. “I was just thinking out loud. It isn't important. We best head out. We aren't doing anyone any favours dawdling.” She glanced back at the wall before heading into the hallway to return to the main world, knowing she would be back in her new secret lair soon and Gavin would be by her side.

Chapter Thirty-Eight

It seemed like Shelby was taking forever to return. Willow's hair swung back and forth, lightly slapping against her back. Normally she wouldn't wear it tied back, but today, she needed to focus all of her attention on the task before her.

"You're making me tired just watching you," Zoran said. "Why don't you have a seat? You are going to wear yourself out pacing like that."

"I can't," Willow answered. "I should be doing something. Who knows what is happening to the poor guardian they have captured? Shelby should understand that better than anyone."

"I do," the guardian bird said.

Willow jumped. "Where did you come from?" she asked, her heart pounding. It wasn't often that one of the guardians startled her, but when they did, they usually did a good job of it.

"You need to be more perceptive if you are going through that portal," Shelby answered. "You can't afford to let any of your defences down. You of all people should understand the powers of illusion. Don't let yourself get fooled."

"Did you learn anything?" Sebastian asked, changing the subject. He had seen enough of the redheaded girl to know that arguing was one of her favourite pastimes. Right now, they simply didn't have time. Hopefully new information would be enough to keep her silent.

"Yes," Shelby answered. "The situation is worse than we thought. There are two other portals open. The other guardians are doing everything they can to keep the seal around Atlantis closed. For now, they seem to have it under control. I will need to return to help as well."

"Then it's settled," Willow said. "I will have to go alone. Everyone else should divide between the portals and brace for a fight. We still don't know what the end plan is, but I think we can assume it's not beneficial to anyone living in this realm."

"That's not an option," Sebastian barked. "I'll go with you."

"We need you to convince your people of the danger that is coming," Willow said. "You are the only one they will listen to."

"She's right," Elsa-Mae said. "We each have to rally our kin to the occasion. I can feel the impending war on the voice of the wind. The trees rustle warnings of a hard-fought battle, the outcome of which is not yet set in stone."

Zoran's nose nestled against the small fairy's body. "Perhaps after, we can forgive ourselves for our past shortcomings and live again."

The tiny fairy's hand reached out and caressed the dragon's face. A tear rolled off her face. Willow inhaled the sweet scent of a weeping blue flower that instantly appeared where the fairy's tear touched the ground. Her hand lifted a few petals upwards. *Bells,* she thought. Goosebumps formed on her arms. Even now, with all they had been through, her tears were still falling for Lilybelle. She shivered, unsure of the emotions she was feeling. She wasn't sad as she should have been. It was something else. Grateful, that was what she was feeling. But why?

“Maybe we should forget about anyone going through,” Sebastian suggested. “We could put up a united front and just wait for whatever is going to happen.”

“Except there are answers we need over there,” Willow said. “Not to mention, if there are guardians being used to open these portals, I need to try to help them.”

“You could end up captured,” Sebastian said. “Then you wouldn't be any help to anyone. Please reconsider.”

Willow's lips warmed against the flush of his cheeks. It hadn't been planned. The kiss was over before she realized what she was doing. “I'll be fine,” she whispered in the elf's ear before moving away.

He let out a low chuckle. His fingers traced across the side of his face where her lips had touched him. “You better be,” he replied. “I'll be waiting.”

“There is one thing I must ask of you,” Willow said. “I know you haven't had a chance to decipher the pictures in the stained glass windows.” She paused. “I have a friend in Pewterclaw. His name is Malarchy. If you could find a way to send them to him, he may be able to help decipher it. Also, my backpack that I came here with, he needs the contents.”

“You mean in case you don't return?” Sebastian said, flipping his sandy hair out of his face.

For a moment... just a moment, he reminded her of William. She shook her head not only as a reply, but to clear her thoughts of the Pledge William had taken with a girl he barely knew. “I mean they may need to refer to the prophecies. It isn't fair that it is sitting here not being used when it could help someone elsewhere.”

“I'll do my best,” Sebastian replied. “Time is fleeting and our borders are closed. I may be able to sneak in and out, with some help, but those window panels are quite large and hard to hide.”

“Thank you,” Willow said. She couldn't help but notice how handsome he looked at that exact moment. Was it him she was attracted to or was it the memory of another?

"So," Zoran said, forcing a break in the growing tension, "we split up. Each of us taking one portal. Let's be ready for whatever might come through."

Else-Mae coughed. "Snort your smoke in another direction," she sputtered, flapping her wings to clear the air. "Good luck, Willow. We'll all be waiting for you to return."

"Zoran," Willow said. "I remember you said Lilybelle had a necklace similar to mine that she left with you for luck. I can't help but wonder if she knew the same person who gave me mine. I hope you won't think badly of me, but I have decided to keep the little luck left for myself."

"I wouldn't have it any other way," the dragon replied. "If it was given to you, then you are the one it is meant for. Perhaps if Lilybelle had done the same, she would be here with us today."

Shelby's feathers brushed against her neck. "Don't take any unnecessary chances. Think before you move," the guardian bird said.

Her red hair waved behind her in the breeze. The guardian bird soared upwards. It was a majestic sight she had seen many times, but something about this time was different. Maybe it was the impending doom or fear of the unknown, but she found herself mesmerized by the graceful up and down motion of her friend gliding in the air. Her body froze on the spot, every muscle stiffened. Control returned slowly as the bird disappeared in the distance. It was time.

"Take care," Zoran said, backing away.

She glanced over her shoulder briefly, just long enough for one last look of her friends leaving to fulfill their assigned tasks. Her knees wobbled as one shaky foot thrust forward, followed by the other.

She had never considered herself a particularly courageous person. What she was about to do was going to take every ounce of bravery she could muster. Ever since this journey began back in her home world, she had always had someone with her... a little help here and a little there. It was all too easy to take for granted.

Now she had only herself to rely on. Doubt clouded her mind. Could she actually handle this on her own?

"I can do this," she said. Her pace quickened to the portal. She inhaled deeply then let the air out in one big huff. Stopping to think was a mistake she couldn't afford. With one motion, she disappeared through the gateway.

Chapter Thirty-Nine

"Ow," Willow winced. A pile of rocks just had to be stacked exactly where she stepped through the portal. Blood stained the pebbles beneath her. If only she had thought to bring a few bandages with her, perhaps the palms of her hands and knees wouldn't sting as much right now. At least there wasn't anyone around to see her fall or to take advantage of it.

In this realm it was night. The hairs on her arms stood up to pay respect to a high-pitched howl in the distance. A low-lying fog crept across the dry ground. It surrounded her, inhibiting her vision. Her hands fumbled across the rocky terrain, looking for some form of leverage to pull herself to a standing position. She winced again. Her knee was hurt a little more than she had first thought. A tall rock became her crutch. Her hands ran across it, finding a spot to grasp and push down on. The surface was smooth. Not a natural smoothness, but rather something that had been manufactured with tools. Dry leaves crinkled into dust beneath her hands. The few plants that had once grown as cover over the stone had long since died. If only she could make out the faded words her fingers could feel etched into the rock.

She sighed in relief. The stinging pain diminished as she straightened up. Holding her breath, she moved one foot forward, dragging the other behind in a limp. At least she could put some weight on it. She turned her attention to her surroundings.

"Oh," she whispered. Taking a few steps backwards, her back hit a sharp point. She spun around, ready for a fight. Sparks flew from the tip of her wand. Stone crashed to the ground, crumbling into dust at her feet. A stone statue of a warrior holding the remains of a spear stared back at her. She sighed. A cemetery wasn't where she wanted to be, especially one with broken tombstones and eerie statues. The champion she had just confronted was only one of many scattering the grounds. Presumably, this was the resting place of those who had fought for Atlantis and paid the ultimate price.

Her hands ran over the face of a second sculpture. She admired the work. Whoever made them had talent. From facial features to well-chiselled muscles, they were art. The scantily dressed men had an almost lifelike beauty to them. Of course, that didn't make them any less creepy. Each one held a weapon. Spears, swords, wands, staffs all pointed directly at the portal to the elf world.

"Apparently in death you still protect your people," Willow said. "I'd be in trouble if you were here for more than a scare factor."

A loud bang exploded in the distance. Stems of light appeared on the horizon, appearing to grow up from the ground and reach the stars before exploding into vibrant blooms. An entire garden flashed before her eyes, then withered away within seconds. She had seen fireworks before, but nothing like this. Another design formed in the sky. This time, a dragon soared upwards before spreading its wings and roaring flames scorching the stars. Cheering echoed in the distance. It was a celebration of some sort. At least now she knew which direction to head in.

Willow made her way through the decrepit museum of broken tombstones and monuments towards the celebration. Perhaps she could hide among partygoers and find out something... anything.

Explosions of vibrant colours continued to illuminate her surroundings. It was a welcome distraction, even if it was only for short bouts of time. She was used to having night vision from her guardian counterparts, a trait that would have come in handy in her current location. Stumbling around in the dark wasn't a recipe for success. A flash went off again, bringing light to a large structure directly ahead in her path. It was still too far for her to make out what it was. It was larger than a tombstone or rock warrior. She waited for the next bout of fireworks to move forward a few hundred yards. Everything went dark again. Whatever it was she was heading towards appeared to have some dim lights positioned around it.

Another flash of light and she was almost there. She stood still, waiting for her path to be shown, but the skies remained dark. Whatever celebration had been going on was apparently over now. She sighed. There was no choice but to proceed without any further help.

One leg slid forward, feeling the ground before her and securing a foothold before placing any weight on it. She bit her bottom lip. Another fall and she might not be able to walk at all. "Almost there," she told herself.

She came to a full stop in front of a full-sized dragon. The moonlight reflected against its opalescent scales and beads of pearls that covered the sculpture. Silver claws and eyes jumped out at her. She stood dumbfounded before its majestic beauty. Whoever had crafted such an art had vision of how it would look in the night. It stood on its back two legs; a lantern grasped within one front fist, the light from which shone directly into the beast's gaping mouth. The use of gold for its teeth created an illusion of fire balling in its throat. She moved closer, wanting to soak in the intricate details of the masterpiece before her.

With a jolt, her hands grasped either side of her head. Her teeth clenched together, upper and lower pallets grinding. Falling to a knee, she whimpered. Her leg injury was nothing compared to the bolts of pain radiating through her skull. Her eyes closed.

Willow gasped. What was this madness? The beast standing in front of her... was alive.

Screams of terror surrounded her. She stepped sideways to avoid the path of an elf engulfed in flames running aimlessly in hopes of finding relief. She bent over, heaving the contents of her stomach on the ground. She wasn't sure if it was the shrieks coming from the blackened form as it breathed its last breaths or the smell of seared flesh and hair that had disgusted her. She didn't want to know, either. Despair grabbed a hold of her. Her heart raced. Her body shook. A cold sweat formed on her brow, radiating down through her limbs. She wasn't meant to be here. This was wrong. An evil foreboding forced her legs into motion. She sprinted. Her head turned back for only a second. Instantly, she wished she hadn't looked. She screamed as a ball of fire hurled directly at her from the opalescent beast's mouth. Her hand flew forward and a blast of light escaped from the tip of her wand.

Her chest felt as if it was about to explode. She opened her eyes. A vision... it was just a vision. She bent over, placing her head between her knees, breathing deeply. Her stomach twisted in knots again. The little bits she had consumed before entering this world now added colour to the foot of the white stone warrior standing before her.

Whatever that had been, she never wanted to experience it again. Had she been dreaming? Perhaps she had drifted too far into thought, bringing on another daydream-walking experience. But it couldn't have been. If she was dreamwalking, there would have been other signs. A staging area before entering the dream. Dragons weren't known for such abilities, either. Was she seeing the future? That couldn't be possible either. The beast stood before her, carved in porcelain white.

She examined the monument again. Her eye caught a detail she hadn't seen before: a door in the base that the dragon was standing on.

She strained with all her strength, tugging on the metal ring door handle. Nothing happened. Trying again, she let out a few grunts and perhaps pulled a few muscles. She sighed. She made a mental note that if she lived, she may want to work on her upper body strength. She rubbed her hands together in front of her face. There had to be something nearby that she could use as leverage. A thick root caught her attention. Bending over, her hands caressed it. Whatever this root had belonged to had passed away long ago. It was a longshot, but with enough magic, perhaps she could bring it back enough to help open the door. It was a risk. Her manna could drain considerably. She could already feel her strength faltering. There was no choice, though. She needed to know what was behind the door.

She took a few deep breaths, concentrating on the rhythm of her chest rising and falling. Her heart rate slowed. "Please," she said. "If you can hear me, I need your help."

"I can hear you," the root responded. "My lifelines have been silenced for eternities. I will have to borrow your power to move them. When I have done what I can, I ask that you leave me to the darkness. There is no life worth living in this tomb of wars from the past."

"Can you not leave?" Willow asked. "I could help you relocate."

"I am bound here by magics unknown to all but those of ancient times," the root responded. "There is no salvation for me."

Willow stumbled forward. She leaned on the side of the wall. It was indispensable if she was to stay on her two feet. She hadn't realized how much of an energy drain there would be. Her eyelids felt heavy, as if the weight of the world was pushing down on them.

"A cup of coffee will perk you right up," Zsiga said. "You look like you need to stay on your feet. I just brewed a fresh pot. Would you like some?"

"Zsiga?" Willow said. "How are you here?"

"You know I can blend into the shadows," the guard answered. "I have been here the whole time. Now drink this. You need to stay strong if you are to survive. It's lucky I was here to help. Don't you think?"

Luck, Willow thought. Her hand grasped the heart pendant hanging from a chain around her neck. She pushed her weight back against the wall, forcing herself from a slouched position. A taste of bitter and sweet exploded in her mouth. She gulped back the saliva forming from the sensation. It was a taste of the coffee she had seen made so many times before. Her heart began to race. A second wind of energy filled her core. Stepping forward, she looked for her friend, but she was alone. The root was lifeless again, lying on the ground in front of an open door.

"Thank you, my friend," Willow whispered.

Inside the door were two flaming torches. At least this time, she wouldn't be fumbling around in the dark. She grimaced as her fingers wrapped around the damp rotting piece of wood. She screamed as a many-legged bug crawled onto her hand and up her arm. The torch flew through the air, landing on the ground before extinguishing its light. She sighed. There was only one chance left for light. The edge of her wand pushed a few bugs from the base before she attempted to hold it. She stepped over the piece of wood lying in the path. Bugs scurried away from it, heading back to the damp interior walls to hide in cracks and crevices. She looked away. It was better she didn't know how many more creepy crawly critters were hidden in the wood her hand was firmly planted against.

Her thoughts were interrupted by chatter coming from further within the building. She followed the corridor, coming to a fork. This was familiar. She had been here before. It was almost exactly the same as the dungeon that Mike had been imprisoned in. But she wasn't in the main world. Was this an illusion? How far off was her perception of reality in this world? Maybe she had fallen into a trap and the elves of Atlantis were playing with her mind. There was also the chance that everyone was right and she was actually insane. Of course, in the here and now, none of that mattered. She had to play out whatever game had been started to the end. If this was the same, but different, she reasoned, she would simply do the opposite of what she had done before.

Taking the right passage, her pace quickened. Up ahead, voices became clearer. She could make out two different men, but what they were saying was still distorted. Her breathing quickened to match her racing heartbeat. The walls felt as if they were closing in on her. Heavy footsteps seemed to be right behind her. Was she being chased? She ran. The walls changed like a maze. Scraping one wall, she cut herself. A cut she had experienced in a dream world before. This couldn't be real. Her eyes stung from being clenched tightly. Opening one, she looked forwards and backwards.

She was alone in a straight corridor. Why was she seeing so many things from her past?

She tore a piece of her shirt and wrapped her cut before continuing on. She could feel blood flowing through her veins to her new wound. It wasn't deep, but it was dripping with a good flow. The sooner she found the secret to this lair, the quicker she could leave. It was only a matter of moments before another heavy door came into sight. She reached for her pendant. “Thank you, Meredith. I needed a bit of luck,” she said.

She pulled the handle of the door. It made grinding noises as it pried open. Had it not been for a rock stopping it from completely closing, she might never have gotten it to move. Her body squeezed through a space just big enough for her. On the other side were more torches and cages. The torch in her hand dropped with a thud. No need to chance being bitten by some strange elf bug if she didn't have to. It wasn't that she didn't like bugs so much as she didn't like them crawling on her. They were a necessary part of nature she would never wish ill on. Some things were just better admired from afar.

“Hello,” a man's voice called out.

Willow inched forward, not sure what she would find, or if it would be real for that matter. Remembering Shelby's advice, caution was the first concern. Another familiar sight caught her attention. Cages lined the walls throughout most of this new chamber. The first few were empty. Then she came upon one with two men grasping the bars that jailed them, both peering out at her.

“Who are you?” one man asked.

“I was about to ask you that,” Willow answered. “Why are you locked in there?”

“Perhaps,” a new voice said, “the question we should be asking is how is it there is a keeper in our midst we have never met?”

Two piercing green eyes appeared in the back of the cell. Her gaze locked on them as they moved closer.

Willow gasped. The eyes belonged to a Leander. “You're a guardian!” she exclaimed.

"Indeed," the cat said, still edging closer, its muscles at attention as if stalking prey. "Who are you? Why are you here?"

"I'm Willow," she said. "I came to help you."

"Excuse us if we don't take your word at par," the animal hissed. "There are too many questions we need answers to. Other than the obvious inquiries I have already made, there are some unknown factors that could decide if you are friend or foe. How did you know we were here? Where did you come from? Where are your guardians? What is your involvement with this world? With Cornelius?"

"Although I appreciate your concerns, does it really matter at the moment?" Willow asked. She turned her head, holding her eyes closed tightly. A large crack and flash of bright light led way to the cage door swinging open. "There isn't time for details until we are free from this place. I promise all will be explained when we are safe. Are there guards?"

"We haven't seen any since we have been here. I am Aaram. This is my son, Lane, and the wise one is Saymore."

"What's down there?" Willow asked. "Could there be others?" She nodded in the general direction the room continued in.

"We haven't seen anything past this cell," Aaram replied.

"Take a torch and head back out. Stay out of sight. If you can make your way to the open portal safely, even better," she said.

"There's a boy," Lane exclaimed. "If we leave, they will hurt him."

"A boy?" Willow repeated. "What boy?"

"His name is Jordan," Aaram answered. "His life relies on our compliance."

"We could have easily handled this old cell if we wanted to," Saymore huffed. "Obviously, there was another reason why we remained."

"Jordan? As in Malarchy's son?" Willow asked.

“Well,” Saymore answered. “That at least answers who the boy is, but how do you know Malarchy?” There was something familiar about his twitching tail. It was Aslo! He would make the exact same movements when he was agitated.

“Please don't be upset,” she said. “You can stay here until I check out the rest of the cells, then we can leave together if you like. I have no intention of leaving without Jordan. His family are friends of mine.”

Without waiting for a response, she continued her search. She wasn't sure exactly what she expected to find, but it seemed wasteful not to make sure there wasn't anything else hiding in the dragon's mausoleum. The next few cages were empty. Then she saw something unusual. She came to an abrupt stop.

“Ow!” she yelled. “I thought all of you were waiting back there!”

“You're the one who just stopped,” Saymore hissed. “We have every right to know what's down here as well. I have no intention of letting you out of my sight.”

“Great,” Willow muttered. “You didn't have to follow so closely.”

“Why did we stop?” Lane asked.

“In there,” Willow said. “There is something locked up.” She pointed her wand at the lock.

“Do you think you should do that?” Aaram asked. “Whatever that is, it is locked up for a reason. It could be dangerous.”

“You were locked up for a reason,” Willow said. “Are you dangerous?”

“Yes,” Saymore said, his tail swirling.

Willow sighed. “I came here for answers. I intend to find some.”

“I thought you came here to rescue us,” Saymore scoffed.

“Can't I have more than one purpose?” Willow questioned, entering the cell.

The cage was set up differently than the others. There were shelves, display tables and pedestals. Each housed various items.

In the middle was a glass box protecting a pine cone the size of a small animal. She ran her fingers over the smooth surface of the protective case. “It's too easy,” she said.

“What is?” Lane asked.

“Getting into these boxes,” she answered.

“Don't be silly,” Lane said. “Just lift it. See...” His body shot backwards, hitting the bars of the cell.

“Are you okay?” Willow asked. “I told you it was too easy.”

“He isn't the brightest,” Saymore answered. “But he has a thick skull. He'll be fine. Do you know what all these things are?”

“No,” she said. “But they are hidden here for a reason and protected by magics. That means someone thinks they are of significant importance. Question now is how to eliminate the wards protecting them.” She scratched her head. Looking around, another item caught her attention. A red plush pillow was the resting place of a wand. She held her wand up beside it.

“They are the same,” Aaram said. “That's a rather odd coincidence. Don't you think? I could see similar, but identical?”

“Yes,” Willow answered under her breath. She could hear what the others were saying, but her attention was focused on the thin wooden stick lying comfortably in front of her. She reached out with her free hand.

“Do you think you should do that?” Lane asked.

The wand twitched as her hand came closer. Sparks emanated from it. The wooden stick bounced around as if it were bound inside a small area. A large crackle sounded. Willow blinked. The wand jutted upwards as if levitating and fell back down. Her hand continued forward, past the magic that had held it prisoner, until her fingertips lightly touched the smooth surface of the wood. The barrier was gone. Lifting the wand, she stood holding one in each hand. Her eyes jutted between them; analyzing them; comparing them to each other. They were, in fact, identical. Questions ran through her mind. How? Why?

She turned her attention back to the case containing the pine cone. She directed both wands at the box. Magic channelled through her wand in the same manner as it always had. An equal blast exploded from the tip of each wand. The case shattered into dust.

“Well then,” Saymore said. “That is something you don't see every day.”

“That coming from a talking cat,” Willow mused. “Rather ironic, don't you think?” She smiled. It took both her hands to pick up the large pine cone. “Don't lose this,” she said, placing it in Lane's hands. “What do you think this place is?”

“A museum of trophies,” Saymore answered. He nodded his head in the direction of various weapons and armour in a display case against the back wall. “One good thing, if you want anything else, I believe your double blast took out all the wards in the room.”

Willow walked around in a square. Only one other item stood out to her as important: a sack tied with an old cord almost hidden in a dark corner. Picking it up, she tossed it in the air catching it in the palm of her hand again. Opening the drawstring she peered inside. Fine golden particles glistened up at her as if the bag contained tiny rays of sunshine.

“What is it?” Lane asked.

“Not sure,” Willow said. “I think it may be important, though.”

“There's a set of keys over here,” Aaram said. “Do you think they might be to the cells here? They might come in handy.”

The keys launched through the air. Willow let out a little squeal. Juggling all the items she was already holding, she barely managed to free a hand to catch them. “A little notice next time!” she yelled. The keys jingled in her hand. They were made of some sort of metal she had never seen before, or perhaps a combination of several. There were gold tones and silver tones, as well as some copper, with highlights and lowlights added in. The designs were way too intricate to be used to open something in a decrepit building like this. She attached the ring on her belt; the pouch of golden dust disappeared into her front pocket; and the second wand she tucked neatly away in her back pocket. “We should move on,” she said, taking the lead.

The room ended at another large door. After tugging at the handle for a few minutes, she moved aside and let the two men do the heavy work. She watched them strain for several minutes. Drops of sweat rolled down their red faces. The door didn't budge.

Saymore sighed. “Really,” he said. “Will you two move aside, please?”

Aaram grabbed Willow's hand, pulling her safely away from the door. The guardian cat's eyes began to glow and seconds later, the door blew off its hinges and lay in pieces on the ground.

“You can do that?” Willow asked. She knew that guardians had special abilities, but never had any of her guardian counterparts displayed such power.

“How is it you don't know the abilities of guardians?” Saymore asked. “What kind of a keeper are you?”

“I don't know,” Willow said. “I had no idea guardians could do such direct magic. I have never met one who did.”

“To be fair,” Aaram said, “it is generally against their beliefs to use magic in such a blatantly obvious manner. I think they prefer to work in the background and not be recognized as heroes.”

“But you could change the course of history,” Willow said. “You could make a difference in this fight against Cornelius.”

Saymore sighed. “You understand so little,” he said, entering the next room without hesitation.

Willow followed. “So explain it,” she cried.

Her thoughts were short lived. The feline guardian was paying no attention to her. His tail was motionless and pointed downwards between his two back legs. She followed his line of vision to an albino dragon chained to the floor in the middle of what looked like an underground arena. The beast lifted his head and opened one eye, revealing bright crimson red. He huffed hot air in their direction.

“Have you come with my rations early, elf?” he asked.

“Can you not see us, beast?” Saymore asked. “We are not elves.”

The dragon's head flopped back down. “Look around,” he said. It's dark. My eyesight has dwindled in this lighting over the years.”

“How long have you been here?” Willow asked.

“I do not know how much time has lapsed. Days melt into each other when you do nothing but lie in one spot for eternity.”

“Who are you?” Aaram asked.

“I don't remember,” the dragon answered. It was easy to see the creature was lying. Of course, he had no reason to trust anyone coming into his presence.

“Do you not have a name, beast?” Saymore asked.

The dragon sighed. “I was known as Umaagan when I was free.”

“How is it you came to be locked in here?” Willow asked. “I don't think they brought you in through the door.”

Umaagan snorted a chuckle. “No,” he said. “This structure was built around me... designed specifically to entomb me alive and house me for my end of days.”

“You're the dragon the statute outside is carved after,” Willow said. “But whose side are you on?”

The dragon raised one eyebrow. “Side?” he asked.

“I had a vision,” she said.

Umaagan's large head moved within inches of Willow's. She stood still as the beast strained to see her. A tear streaked down his cheek, evaporating into smoke before reaching the outline of his strong jaw. “Lilybelle,” he said. “Have you come to haunt me, spirit? Do you wish to torture me further?”

“My name is Willow,” she answered. “I only wish to understand what happened here. I have been told of my resemblance to the elf woman. I am, I assure you, not her or a spirit, for that matter.”

“Well, Willow,” Umaagan said, “I am the reason Lilybelle is dead. For that crime, this cell is my penance.”

“But why?” she cried.

“It wasn't intentional, I assure you,” he said. “The battle raged around us. We were losing. I watched my elf army failing. The power of the Atlantian army's magic coupled with their control of the unicorns was destroying us. There was only one card left to play. I had no choice but to shapeshift into dragon form. At least that would even out the odds. I watched my brother fall before he could finish his transformation. He gave his life so I would have a chance to change the direction of our battle. My flames burnt their front lines and the tides began to change. I prepared a massive attack. All of the fire I could muster went into one last blast. At the same time, I was attacked from behind. I don't know what hit me, but it was enough to topple me over. I lost control of my attack. It raged out of control. I had no way to stop it. Pinned to the ground, I watched helplessly as the flames hurled towards my elf friend, engulfing her in a fiery grave. I don't know what happened after that, but somehow she managed to seal the portal before she fell. This world was locked away eternally and surrounded by water. I had no idea she had such power. I have remained exactly in the same spot since that day... still bound by the chains that originally sealed my fate and that of Lilybelle.”

“You said you shapeshifted into dragon form?” Willow said. “What were you before?” Her mind raced. At the school... the dragon that saved her... was that someone she knew?

“An elf, of course,” Umaagan answered. “Do you not know of elf heritage?”

“I do,” she answered. Even though she had just pieced this information together in her mind, the answer was still bewildering her. Why hadn't her friends told her?

“Well, then,” he said, “it shouldn't be too hard to understand that the purest of bloodlines carry the genes of our ancestors; the magics of fairies; or the genes of dragons; or in some rare cases both. Can you not tell which elf line I come from?"

"A mountain elf?" Willow asked.

"Yes," the dragon snorted.

"So why not just transform back into elf form and walk out?" Lane asked.

"If it was that easy, don't you think I would have done that?" he answered. "These chains that bind me also prevent me from changing forms. Fire has no effect in this room. There is no salvation for this old dragon. I have come to terms with my fate."

"Perhaps you have," Willow said. "But that doesn't mean I have." She pointed her wand at one of the shackles locked around the dragon's foot. A thin stream of white light rushed to its target, eager to please its master.

Lane jumped in the air. "Watch it!" he yelled. "Duck!" His body fell flat to the ground, avoiding a direct hit from her magic as it ricocheted off any surface it touched redirecting it in unknown directions. "Make it stop!"

Willow's limbs went stiff. Making magic happen was easy, but she had never thought about retracting her own power. Could that even be done? "How?!" she finally yelled as Aaram dove out of the way of the stream.

"Maybe if you hit it with an equal amount of power," Lane said, looking up from a lying position on the ground. He used his hands to protect his head, not that it would have made much of a difference if he had been hit by the mismanaged magic.

She grabbed the second wand from her back pocket and aimed it. "It's too fast," she cried. "I'll never make a direct hit."

Umaagan chuckled. "Maybe you will free me after all," he said. "A direct hit in my condition could finish me off. It's only a matter of time before your blast hits the largest target in the room."

"Oh no," Willow muttered. "What have I done?" The dragon was right. It wouldn't be long before the angle of the white force found its way to him. It had already come dangerously close. She needed to figure out what to do. Instinct took over. She aimed the tiny wand at the same shackle, firing it without thought.

“What are you doing?” Lane yelled. “Do you have an actual death wish?”

“Just wait,” Willow said, her voice shaking. As the last word faded, sparks flew through the air. The two beams of magic connected midstream, dissipating into a shower of tiny lights, each extinguishing into ash as they fell in a downward spiral. “It worked!”

“Was there doubt?” Aaram asked. “That was a pretty big gamble if there was.”

“True,” Willow answered. “But I figured we wouldn't have been any worse off in the long run. We were pretty much pinned down.”

“We could have crawled to the door!” Lane yelled. “There were options! What about the keys from the other room? Maybe we should have tried them first.”

“I didn't think of that,” Willow said. “Not that it would have done us any good. Those keys are not to this lock.” She held the key ring up beside the cuff. The difference between the two was obvious. “There really wasn't any time for me to decide. It did make sense that a second flow of magic would follow the same path as the first and connect at some point.”

Umaagan let out a hefty roar of laughter. “You are a reckless one, aren't you? I like that. You have spunk. Perhaps in another life, we could have been friends.”

“There is still hope for this life!” Willow yelled. “I haven't given up yet.”

Saymore sighed. “Don't rely on me this time. That is an anti-magic barrier. Even I cannot breach such a strong spell. Whoever created these bindings had help from someone seriously powerful.”

“Then perhaps we need to not use magic,” Willow said, getting on her hands and knees to move in close to the locks.

“Not use magic,” the dragon scoffed. “Do you think you are strong enough to break these chains, when I, a dragon, cannot?”

"No," Willow replied. "No, not at all. I can't even open the heavy doors in this place. But I do have a few talents that are a grey area when it comes to magic."

"Grey area?" Saymore asked.

Dirt cascaded down like a waterfall from Willow's hand. "Yes," she answered without removing her attention from the task before her. "This is the original earth from before the existence of the cemetery, isn't it?"

"I have already answered that," the dragon scoffed.

"Sorry," Willow said. "I was actually thinking out loud." She blew the rest of the dry earth from her hand and watched as the tiny particles hit the ground, transforming from an almost white colour to a rich brown tone. "That's better!"

"Are we redecorating?" Umaagan asked. "While I love your choice of colour for the flooring, I rather think it a waste of time and energy. It won't cheer me up. Although I appreciate the effort."

Willow ignored the sarcastic undertones directed at her. A green sprout pushed its head through the loose top soil that lay in between herself and the dragon.

"House plants, how delightful," Umaagan scowled. "That should make things much homier."

"What are you up to?" Saymore asked, moving in closer. "Did you just," he paused for a moment, "create life?"

Create life, she thought. The words resonated inside her. She never thought of what she did in such literal terms, but the feline guardian was right. The realization shocked her, just for a second. Why should she be surprised? Women did, after all, create life all the time. Giving birth to babies was the same, yet different as well.

"There is someone approaching the building," Umaagan whispered. "Leave now before you don't have the chance again."

"Not yet," Willow answered. The sprout grew into a vine, branching out into four different directions. The leafy bud at the top of each limb scurried into the keyhole of the binding shackles. Silence filled the room with tension. The stems twisted and turned until a loud click sounded. The chains rattled as they fell to the ground. The dragon's body twisted and turned as it shrunk into the naked body of a broken elf.

"You poor creature," Aaram said, placing his shirt over the wrinkles and bruises that covered Umaagan's skin. "Can you stand?"

The elf grasped the shirt and pulled it around his shoulders. "I think I can," he replied, stumbling to his feet. His legs buckled from his weight. "Perhaps not."

"You haven't used your leg muscles in quite some time," Aaram said. "It will be a while before you regain full mobility. Lean on me for some strength."

"Thank you," Umaagan said, pulling himself up against the muscles of Aaram's arm.

"I know this is a touching moment," Saymore said, "but we should move as quickly as possible. There is someone approaching. It would be wise to be gone before they reach us. I don't believe we can outrun them."

"The cat has a point," Umaagan said. "We should try to hurry."

Chapter Forty

"Ah, Malarchy," Kasper Deogole yelled. "I see I just caught you before you left for the day. Brilliant timing on my part." The Director of Secrecy quickened his pace to match that of the newly-appointed mayor.

"What can I do for you, Kasper?" Malarchy asked. "I assume you are not here for a social visit." Holding the door open, he allowed the Director to exit the building first.

"Thank you," Kasper said. "Mind if I walk with you? I get so little time to enjoy the outdoors these days."

"You are already walking with me, Kasper," Malarchy retorted. "I doubt anything I say could make a difference. Shall we take a scenic route through the park?"

"Wonderful idea," the Director replied. "The park is perfect at this time of year. Spring is so invigorating. Don't you think?"

"I highly doubt you are here to discuss the weather," Malarchy said. "Especially while carrying that." He nodded in the direction of a long black umbrella the Director was using as a cane.

“One never knows what is going to happen. Best to be prepared. That's my motto. There is this whole messy thing happening in the Triangle. I think that classifies as weather, now doesn't it?”

“I suppose it does,” Malarchy said, turning his head to look behind them.

“Something wrong?” Kasper asked.

“No,” Malarchy answered. “Not at all. I just like to know my surroundings. I believe that counts as being prepared for whatever might happen.”

“Yes, I suppose it does.” The Director lifted his umbrella and tapped it twice on a park bench. “Shall we?”

“What is this all about, Deogole?” Malarchy asked.

“No need to get testy,” Kasper answered. “I simply want to know your take on the whirlpool that is forming.”

“You mean you want to know if Willow is involved?” Malarchy asked.

A group of birds gathered in front of the park bench the two men were seated on. Each took turns bobbing their heads back and forth while they strut around, occasionally ruffling their feathers over territory. Kasper reached in his pocket. He tossed a few seeds onto the ground. The birds swarmed to the spot.

“It's funny, isn't it?” he said. “They are ready to kill each other over a handful of seeds. They don't even have the intelligence to wonder if the seeds I threw down are safe or not.” He chuckled under his breath. “They trust me without reason. Why? Because someone else did the same thing and it was okay. They assume that because someone was nice in the past, everyone else will be just as nice in the future. I could have wiped out all of the strongest in one sitting. Only the inferior, the ones who aren't strong enough take some by force, would be left.”

“Are we here to talk about the weather, Willow, or the birds?” Malarchy asked.

"You're a smart man," Kasper responded. "I am sure you can make the connection. As for the weather issue, I am sending Miss Kelly, a teacher from Sleeping Sands Academy who specializes in elemental magic, to have a look into the situation. I have to admit, though, it has us stumped. It's definitely a magic of some sort. But where is it coming from?"

"You think that it is originating from wherever Willow is?" Malarchy asked.

"It is a possibility I can't ignore. She disappears, then this. So that leaves the question, what do we do?"

"The Terunji appear to be making their own theories as usual," Malarchy answered. "Why not let them? We could send a team of illusionists to cover it up. The local papers will put a few sensational headlines on the front page for a few days about it stopping as fast as it started and the non-magic world would be oblivious again."

"Yes, yes," Kasper said, throwing another handful of seeds to the birds. "We thought of that. The problem is, the whirlpool is growing. With it becoming larger daily, it's only a matter of time before it overtakes something large. We are talented with magic, but hiding the loss of an entire island might prove difficult."

"I see your point," Malarchy replied. "I am afraid I can't help you, though. I have absolutely no knowledge of Willow's whereabouts or if she is connected to this phenomenon or not. If it's suggestions you are looking for, why not send our own reporters to cover the event? They could move in closer and maybe find some information we can't from here."

"As usual, an excellent idea," Kasper said, standing. "If you do find out anything, you will keep us in the loop I hope."

"Of course," Malarchy said. Remaining sitting, his back stiffened against the bench as he watched Kasper Deogole disappear. "You can come out now," he said. "You have been following us since we left the office. Whatever it is you want, let's get it over with."

A man appeared from behind a tree and planted himself on the bench where the Director had just been sitting. He placed a backpack between them.

“Have we met?” Malarchy asked. It was impossible to tell. The man was wearing a sweatshirt with a hood covering his head. His face remained hidden.

“After hearing that conversation, I think it's better if I remain anonymous for now,” the man said. He pushed a piece of paper under the backpack. “Follow the instructions. Someone thinks it is of great importance that you understand.”

“Is she alright?” Malarchy asked.

The man stood silently, facing in the mayor's direction and nodded yes. His green eyes glistened in the sunlight briefly, then he was gone. There was no doubt from the sight of that one feature, the man had been an elf. An elf that had left a new puzzle to unravel.

The note was simple directions with a memo that another package was waiting for him at the final destination. Unzipping the backpack, Malarchy looked inside. He smiled. He had more than enough clues to work on now. Luckily, it wasn't just the books and papers with scribbled notes. He now had an antidote to the spider venom. His first course of action was going to be to cure that young man.

Chapter Forty-One

It didn't take much to convince the others to help Umaagan to the portal and leave this world. She had only to insist she be the one to save Jordan. After having a chance to contemplate her hasty decision, she regretted not having Saymore stay and help her. Of course, the feline guardian didn't trust her very much. She had never met a guardian she couldn't win over before. She sighed. Perhaps with time they could become friends. Time, however, was something she was short on.

A child's voice screamed out, “Let go of me!” It was a voice she knew. Jordan was close.

Holding her wand in front of her, she rounded the building. No sooner than she had reached the other side, her body hesitated, simply refusing her brain's commands to move. She had told herself she was ready for anything, but this she hadn't anticipated. Standing there, as motionless as she was, was a man she knew far too well. A light breeze caught his dark black-blue hair lifting it from his face. The gaze of perfectly blue eyes pierced through to her heart. She muttered one word.

“Lance.”

The prince turned his head sideways like a lost puppy dog trying to figure out a path home. He returned her stare more out of shock than recognition. Jordan squirmed in his grasp, desperately trying to get away. He never knew what hit him. The root lying limp on the ground used the last of its energy to sweep Lance from his feet. His grip loosened. Willow snatched Jordan into her arms. For a split second, she looked at her prince sitting on the ground. She smiled. “Deja Vu,” she said then ran towards the portal. In the background she heard another man's voice. She recognized it.

“What are you doing down there?” Simon asked his brother.

“I tripped,” Lance answered. “Didn't see this root.”

Simon laughed. “Is there something over there we should investigate?” he asked, noticing his brother's fixed gaze.

“No,” Lance replied. “I think it's time we left this world. I have a feeling we don't want to be around when the gates open and all things evil flow through.”

“Which world are you referring to, brother?”

Lance chuckled. “You know, I'm not sure.”

The two brothers' voices faded as she ran further away. Her heart raced. Lance hadn't known her. Instead of fighting her though, they relived the first time they had met. It was almost exactly the same experience. He had let her escape again. But why? What was her connection to him? Was it love? She sighed. Love at first sight happening twice? Did she love him? Yes, she supposed she did. But what sort of love was it? She didn't have that answer. The questions running wild through her mind would have to wait. Up ahead, she could see the portal. There was no choice but to go through and regroup. There was no way she was going to put Jordan in any further danger. She wouldn't have been able to face Jade again if she had let anything happen to her baby brother when they just got him back. She didn't even slow down to look behind her. Her feet left the ground and planted back down firmly on the other side.

“Welcome back,” Zoran said.

“Thanks,” Willow said, looking around. “I think that's the first good landing I have made coming through a portal at full speed.” Placing Jordan on the ground, she squatted in front of him. “Are you alright?” she asked, brushing his hair with her fingers.

He nodded yes, but the tears swelling in his eyes told another story. His lips quivered slightly. She couldn't help but pull him into a tight hug. He was every bit as adorable as she remembered. A beautiful child caught in the most horrible of circumstances. She could see not only a sadness reflected in his eyes, but also a longing to be reunited with his family.

“We'll get you back to your dad soon,” she said. “You just need to be patient a little longer.”

The words were enough to satisfy the young boy. He threw his arms around her neck and hung on tight. Everything he needed to express came out in that embrace. They sat holding each other for over an hour, during which time, no one even considered breaking their attachment. It would have destroyed the trust forming between the two. When he did pull back, he simply nodded at her then sat on the ground, drawing pictures in the dirt.

“You seem to have won him over easily,” Saymore said.

“He probably recognizes me from our homeland. I imagine it's easier for him to hear things from me than from people he has never seen before.” Willow reached out to touch the feline's fur.

Saymore jumped backwards. “I am not ready to trust you yet, girl,” he said. “Perhaps if you let me meet your guardians?”

“They are reinforcing the barriers between this world and Atlantis in hopes of stopping a breach,” she answered.

“So that's what they were talking about,” Aaram said.

“What who was talking about?” Zoran asked. “I don't mean to butt in, but we are short on time. If there is information about any military movements, we could use the insight.”

“I am afraid I learnt very little,” Willow responded. “At least, very little that I can piece together right away. Every step I take, seems I go three back.”

“We can tell you what we know,” Aaram offered. “Basically, the King of Atlantis found a way to break holes into the barriers between worlds.”

“He must have obtained that from Cornelius,” Willow said.

“Most likely,” Aaram answered. “But it began to fail. I imagine that was about the time your guardians began reinforcing the veil between the two worlds. So they needed another way to invade.”

“That's why Cornelius sent his children. He was providing an alternate way,” Willow said.

“Exactly,” Aaram said. “He promised us the release of my son's wife if we helped and the boy was brought along as extra insurance. It was wrong, I know, but they are ruthless people. Our choices were limited.” He hung his head towards the ground, avoiding direct eye contact.

“No one blames you,” Willow said. “We all would do anything to protect a loved one. It's part of our nature. Now we know we can close the three portals starting with this one.” A bright flash of lightning exploded from the sky, tumbling the portal into a pile of useless rocks.

“I am afraid that won't help,” Saymore said. “They have already positioned enough magic in this world and others to make Atlantis rise. They will come, regardless of your efforts. The only question we have left is where they will appear. With all the reinforcements you speak of, I highly doubt it will be in this world.”

“Then where?” Willow asked.

“I have no idea,” Saymore answered. “Wherever it is, you can bet they will wreak havoc until they find a way to reach their objective.”

“Objective?” Zoran asked.

“Yes,” Saymore said, his tail twitching. “Complete destruction of this realm, of the elves and everything in it. They consider it retribution for the past.”

“This isn't good,” Umaagan said. “Not good at all. They were fierce when we battled them before. But now… now they are ten times as strong and many more in numbers.”

“Stronger?” Willow cried. “Isn't magic failing for them the same as it is for the elves of this world?”

“What did you say?” Umaagan answered with his own question. “If this is true, all could be lost. The magic of elves of this world should never be able to fail. The great trees themselves empowered us. They are our strength.”

Willow's knees bent. She fell to the ground. “Of course,” she said. “The elves weren't just entrusted to take care of the trees. They were working together.” A thin smile crossed her lips. She looked up at the others. The concern on their faces made her uncomfortable. “I'm okay.”

“Are you sure?” Aaram asked. “You have been through a lot today. Perhaps you should rest. I am sure the group of us can take over for you now.”

Willow's attention was lost behind the man talking. On the ground near the pile of rocks that had once been a portal was something she had almost forgotten about. She jumped to her feet. She could hear someone calling her name, but it came through as only a muffled sound. She was on the verge of answers... answers she so desperately needed. She was determined to make the latest piece of the puzzle fit. Maybe, it would make enough of a picture for her to be able to understand.

Kneeling on the ground, she lifted up the large pine cone brought back from Atlantis. “I bet I know what you are,” she said, placing it in a pile of earth. Her hands hovered slightly above the seed. Its husk began to rock gently as if the wind were trying to lift it up and throw it around. Instead, a sprout appeared. The warm musk-like scent of woodsy pine filled her senses. She closed her eyes, letting her soul bath in it. By the time she opened them again, a tree had grown so tall that she couldn't see the top.

“I knew that was a big pine cone,” Saymore said. “But I didn't expect it to grow a tree quite so big, so quickly.”

“Thank you, my friend,” the tree rustled. “I am Lirie, the tree of freedom. I never thought I would escape that place.”

“It was your roots that helped me. Wasn't it?” Willow asked.

“Yes,” the tree answered, its voice merely a whisper on the wind. “The barrier we were creating to lock away Atlantis required one tree on the inside. It was only to be for a moment, while the enchantments went up. We thought our plan was flawless. I would reserve enough energy to retreat and the seal would be final. It didn't quite turn out that way. I was caught. The power the king wielded was more than anyone could have anticipated. I arrived in time to see our forces fail in battle. With Lilybelle gone, sadness overwhelmed me. I cast the spell, but was struck down in the process. They chopped me into pieces, leaving only roots sticking up from the ground. My body and limbs served as a bonfire tribute to their forces. They considered what they had done a victory. Their forces destroyed not only a major foe in Lilybelle, but also one of the great trees. The spell I cast wasn't entirely successful. There would be a way for them to return in the future. The ground was poisoned. What was once a meadow was now the home of the damned, forever to reek of death and despair. What was left of me was rotting in as slow a manner as possible. If it hadn't been for their arrogance, I wouldn't be here at all. He plucked my seed to keep as his own trophy for years to come.”

“The threat has returned,” Willow said, brushing dirt from her knees. She was glad she had found another tree, but still wasn't sure how it helped them. “Do you know how we can defeat them again?”

“We didn't defeat them the first time,” Lirie said. “I do not sense the presence of my siblings. I am but only one.”

“Actually,” Willow said. “There are four of you awake so far. Acacia, Nadia, Bettulla, and yourself. That leaves three left to find. All the magic being thrown around lately probably is messing up your communication. Well, that has happened to me in the past.”

“You could be right,” Lirie replied. “That still means we are three less than we were before and I don't see an army behind you.”

"Are you talking to a tree?" Lane asked. "Trees don't talk. Do they?" Red scratch lines appeared on Lane's face. "Ow," he cried. "What was that for?"

"For being stupid," Saymore answered, licking the underside of his claws clean. "Honestly, here you are talking to a cat and you find it hard to believe that a tree can speak."

"Point taken," Lane said, his hand lightly rubbing the side of his face where the feline guardian's swipe had hit hardest. "It just took me by surprise."

"What we really need to know," Aaram said, "is what the connection is between the three missing trees and the lost elf magic?"

"It would make sense if what you say is true," the tree offered. "Each of the great trees carries its own unique magic. We each fortified the elf powers... enhanced what was already there... but in our own way. The disappearance of any one tree would have had a profound effect on the magics of this realm."

"Well, that sheds a bit of light on things," Saymore said. "But it leaves us with a bigger problem. We are short three trees... have less magic... have a smaller army... and don't know where the battle is going to be fought. The odds are not stacking in our favour."

Willow sighed. She grasped the heart charm hanging around her neck. "I agree," she said. "Luck may not be on our side, especially if we factor in that Atlantis has new friends and Cornelius is just as strong, if not stronger."

"We will need to gather the elves," Umaagan said. "Decisions need to be made."

"Agreed," Saymore answered as if he was the only one being spoken to. "And you, girl. We will need to meet these guardians you claim to be a keeper of. If they are forcing a barrier to hold, we may want to re-evaluate that course of action."

"The elves will know where they were sent to," Willow answered. "Hopefully we can contact them that way. I have no telepathic link when we are separated. I would have thought you to have known that yourself."

"Arguments will not save us," Zoran bellowed. He huffed a few puffs of smoke in the sky. "Now is the time to come together. There is a battle looming in our future. It won't be just any battle, either. It will be a battle that legends will be made from."

Chapter Forty-Two

The last time Jade had entered the hidden lair, it had been to show Gavin around his new workplace. There had just been the three of them, if one counted Iskander, who really just stood around guarding things most of the time. Today was different. The laboratory was abuzz with vampires. Each one was diligently going about his or her own business and all of them were completely ignoring her. In fact, two different vamprites had already bumped right into her as if she didn't exist.

It took her a while to find Gavin. He was wearing a complete set of safety grubs and working behind the glass in the clean room. She tried the intercom without any luck. She tried waving at him, followed by knocking on the glass. No one in either room was giving her even the slightest bit of attention. After trying jumping up and down, as well as stupid faces, she resolved to wait in his office for him to finish working.

Iskander chuckled. “Guess you haven't gotten used to people ignoring you.”

The backpack landed on the desk with a thud. “Just be careful of whatever is wrapped up in that paper. It might be a picture or something,” she scowled. “Why do we have to wait for Gavin to open this stuff anyways? He wasn't around for most of what we all have been through.”

“Because,” Gavin said, strutting in, “your father is worried something might pop out that you can't handle on your own. I would have thought that to be obvious. So what do we have here?” He pulled the zipper on the backpack and spilled out the contents.

“The Portal Prophecies!” Jade squealed. “This is from Willow. But why would she send us the book? She is the one it was meant for.”

“Why indeed,” Malarchy said.

Jade jumped. “Dad!”

“Sorry to frighten,” the mayor said. “I wanted to go through this with all of you.” He picked up the small wooden chest and turned the key already in place. He lifted a vile of red liquid up to the light. “This is the antidote to the spider venom. First and foremost, I would like to have the young man in the other room fixed up. Once he receives a shot, he needs to be taken to the city hospital. He will either recover or not. We can do nothing more for him.”

Gavin pressed the intercom and called a woman to come and take a single syringe to the motionless patient hidden away in the other room.

“I thought the intercom was broken,” Jade said. Her lips puffed out as her arms crossed against her chest.

“Just because I didn't answer you, doesn't mean the system is broken.” Gavin said. “We are at a crucial point in our laboratory work. Not even your funny faces could be allowed to interrupt the possibility of success.”

Jade's face flushed red. The heat reached her eyes, making them water just enough that she felt as if she needed to wipe them dry. “I,” she started. The truth was she had no idea what to say. There was absolutely no reason why she acted as she had. “I'm sorry,” she blurted out. The words flowed from her mouth without consent. Once it started, she couldn't stop. "I wanted to know what all this was. Curiosity got the better of me. Of course, your work is more important." Silence filled the room.

"Well," Malarchy said. The word hung on, as if buying time for him to find another. He hadn't realized just how much his daughter had changed since they arrived in the new world. She was becoming a caring young woman and he was wearing his pride like a man in a well-dressed suit.

Gavin smiled. "Thank you, Jade. I appreciate your understanding." His well-worn snake-skin boots landed on the desk with a thud. Working round the clock to create anti-potions wasn't as easy as it had sounded. Still, the benefits were enough to keep him there. He reached into the top drawer of his desk and pulled out a dark green bottle. His teeth bit down on an old cork, causing it to make a popping noise as it slid out. He spit it on the desk before taking a long swig.

"Is that blood?" Jade asked. The green tint of the bottle made it hard to see exactly what the dark liquid it concealed was.

"It was obtained legally," Gavin said. "It keeps us focused when working long hours." He slouched back in the black executive chair. "So what's in the brown paper? Artwork?"

"We aren't sure," Malarchy said. "Whatever it is, it is from Willow. There is something she wants us to see or figure out."

"No time like the present," the vampire said. "Rip it open and let's see what we have. With an antidote to the venom found, we have enough staff here to work on something new."

Malarchy nodded. The paper ripped easily into shreds. Iskander was one of the strongest men among the guards. His muscles flexed unnecessarily as he turned the different panels of window to face his companions.

"A stained glass window of some sort," Malarchy said.

"It would seem so," Gavin replied. His feet hit the ground with a thump as he jolted forward. He tossed around several papers that lay scattered on his desk from the backpack. "Looks as if Willow was trying to decipher what, if anything, it means. There must have been a reason for her to feel the story this piece depicts is important." He picked up another couple of papers. "They were missing part at the time. I think we have all the panels here though."

"What is it? A tree?" Jade asked.

"Looks that way," Gavin answered. "But there is something about the way they seem to fit together. It's like a puzzle."

"Spend some time on it," Malarchy said. "If Willow thinks it could be important, chances are we will need to understand it. In the meantime, how is our anti-potion going? We'd be in better position if we had the rest of our allies back."

"We are coming close," Gavin answered. "Only way we will know if it works is to test it on someone, though. I'll leave you to figure out how to get me a guinea pig."

"No worries," Iskander said. "We have a few ideas. You just say the word."

"Excellent," Gavin said. "I'll let you know. Now what about these books?" He picked up the original copy of *The Portal Prophecies.* The pages flipped against his thumb, stopping at one with a small crease in its corner. The words trickled off his tongue...

Life left behind, a new land dawning

Hidden away the trees form an awning

Secrets reveal beast with pure unite

A sunken world to return to the light

A riddle to solve, the pieces complete

A choice to be made, feels bitter sweet

A heart to be broken, alone in the dark

On a journey, a hero shall embark

Awaken the sleeping to return what was lost

But never forget, all comes with a cost.

“That must be the prophecy Willow was working off of,” Jade said. Instinctively, her hands grasped the second book with the same title. The pages were all crisp as freshly ironed linen. “She must not have found the other prophecy.”

“Other prophecy?” Gavin asked.

“Yes,” Malarchy answered. “This book was written by a gypsy visionary. Her talent lies in creating a prediction that fits together with another prophecy to make it clearer. Our problem is, and always has been, the prophecies in neither book seem to be in any particular order.”

Flipping through the pages of the first book, Gavin smiled. “You know, I have lived to see a lot of prophecies and predictions in my time. Many written in books just like this. The thing is, every single time there are only two prophecies that matter.”

“What do you mean?” Malarchy asked.

“Simple,” Gavin answered. “Every story has a beginning and an end. This book is no different. The first and last pages are all that matter. In between is the journey we take to get from point A to point B.”

“But the prophecies,” Jade cried. “They have helped us. They have saved our lives.”

“I have to agree with my daughter,” Malarchy inserted. “If it was such a story, wouldn't it read as one? Why are the prophecies not in order?”

“A while ago, there was a new type of book that came on the market. It was one in which the reader could actually help take control of part of the plot,” the vampire answered. “Basically, when you came to a major decision, the book gave you two choices. Pick the first choice and turn the page or pick the second choice and skip to an alternate page. A full story for both choices was recorded in the book, but it read differently depending on the reader's input.”

“So,” Jade said, “you're saying when we solve one prophecy in a certain way, it negates the need for others?”

“Basically, yes,” Gavin answered. “The constants are the beginning and ending.”

“That would mean our destiny is pre-set and we can't change anything,” Jade cried. “I don't believe that, not for a moment.”

“Not exactly,” Gavin replied.

“Can you elaborate?” Malarchy asked.

“We always have a choice,” Gavin said. “Every prophecy in here is giving us a choice... helping us along the way to the end. I think the problem is when we come to an obstacle, there is a hard way and an easy way. The easy way isn't always the best way.”

“You are talking in riddles worse than the books!” Malarchy yelled. “Make some sense!”

“Look at it this way,” the vampire said. “You are walking along and come to a branch in the road. In front of you is an old woman who can see the future. She tells you your path is a hard one and she sees your end if you turn right. What do you do?”

“Go left, obviously,” Malarchy answered.

“And you eventually come to another road end where you must choose. What do you decide? The old woman said she saw you turning right, but not at which crossroads.”

“So,” Jade said, “we go left again.”

“What happens if you keep turning left?” Gavin asked.

“Eventually,” Malarchy said, “you would end up where you started.”

“Exactly!” Gavin exclaimed. “You are back at the beginning in a neverending loop. Now apply that to the book of prophecies.” He flipped open the book to the front. “The first page is the prediction of a child being born. A girl with powers unlike others. One who could save not just her world, but all the worlds in existence.”

“Willow,” Jade muttered.

"Most likely," Gavin said. "Now the final prophecy." His fingers ran through the pages to the back. The book slammed closed. "Unfortunately, it deals with the end of existence."

"And the pages in between?" Jade asked.

"Endless loops of what could happen if," Gavin answered. Paying no attention to anyone else in the room, he jumped up and began rearranging the stained glass window panels. "I think we need to find Willow."

"Shouldn't we be solving the final prophecy?" Jade cried. "It is the end of the realms and all."

"Yes, in good time," Gavin answered. "But if I am right, everything is about to reset again. The loop will start over from the beginning and everything we have all done will be useless."

"What do you mean?" Malarchy asked.

"Look at this arrangement of the window panels. It's a message from the past," Gavin said. "Everything revolves around a woman with red hair. A neverending cycle. I think whoever made this was trying to warn us about the loop."

"The loop?" Jade yelled. "What loop?"

"It's like a reset button," Gavin said.

"We'd go back to where we started," Malarchy muttered.

"Yes," Gavin answered. "Back to the first prophecy."

"You're talking about reincarnation," Malarchy said.

"Yes," the vampire answered. "It must have happened a few times already for there to be clues. I am guessing the terunji documented what they perceived as happening at the time."

"But for that to happen..." Jade's words cut off.

"Willow would have to die," Gavin said. "That's why we need to find her. If we don't, she will be reincarnated and start this whole mess over again. We need to break the loop. We need to face the final prophecy."

"But," Jade said, "if the final prophecy is about the end of the world, doesn't that mean we all would die?"

"No, I don't believe that," Gavin said. He put his arm around her shoulder. "It's still a prediction. We have fate in our hands. Together we can change the outcome. Only difference is, hopefully, it will be the last time we have to."

Chapter Forty-Three

“What are you doing?” Willow asked.

“Eating pancakes,” Sebastian replied, shoving a fork full of food into his mouth. Syrup dripped out the corner of his lips. He swallowed with a gulp. “You want some?”

“No, I don't want some,” she replied. “We are facing a major disaster and you four are shovelling pancakes into your traps.”

“No need to be nasty,” Kayleb said. “Even at war, you still need to eat. Keep your strength up and all that.”

“Exactly,” Sebastian said. “Besides, we have it all covered. I personally delivered the things to your friend in the main world. Seth is ready to test an anti-potion for that nasty memory-altering stuff. Your guardian pals are reinforcing the barrier between this world and the others. We have elves working on dismantling the portals as we speak. You are back and look to be in not too bad condition. So all is fine. Who are they?”

“Not all fine!” Willow screamed. “Not all fine at all.”

"I'm Lane, nice to meet you. Willow rescued us from Atlantis. That portal is pretty much toast."

"Great," Gabriel said. "More outsiders. This should go over well." Grabbing Willow's arm, he pulled her to the side. "You do realize the problem here, don't you?" His voice lowered to almost a whisper.

"Problem?" she asked. "What would you suggest? Perhaps you feel I should have left them prisoners because you don't like visitors to your world?"

"It's not that simple," Seth interrupted. "We have laws that have been in place for many years."

"Then change them," Zoran bellowed. "Too long have we left our children to run the decisions of this world alone. Tell your royal elves, the dragons and fairies are taking their rightful place as head of the family."

"Brilliant," Sebastian said. "We're all set for a party." He wiped a napkin over his mouth before tossing it on the table in front of him. "Shall we call the powers together?"

"Slow down, young drake," Umaagan said. "I might like a taste of those pancakes."

"Really?" Willow asked.

"I was chained up a very long time," Umaagan answered. "They look fluffy, like a cloud with a little sweet nectar topping. Ah." Drool dripped from his chin, hitting the table. "Just a few bites."

"Sure," Sebastian said, handing him a plate and cutlery. "Help yourself there, stranger."

"Stranger?" Umaagan asked. "Do you not know who I am? I should be a hailed hero of this land for the battle in Atlantis."

"Sorry," Sebastian said. "Atlantis isn't a big topic around here. I don't think anyone thought they could make a comeback."

"No one has mentioned the lives that were lost to secure your freedom?" Saymore asked. "Isn't that strange?"

“I guess it is,” Gabriel answered. “I never thought about it. It didn't affect us here and we have little concern about what happened in Atlantis.”

“Didn't affect you?” Umaagan yelled. “Your brothers and sisters gave their lives so that nothing would happen here. Sooner or later, we elves are going to have to realize we are a part of something bigger.” He shoved a whole pancake in his mouth. “Oh, these are fantastic,” he muffled, still chewing.

“Moving speech,” Saymore said. “Perhaps we should discuss this in front of someone who actually has some power.”

“Can I take a few of these with me?” Umaagan asked, filling his hands with food.

“Perhaps a change of clothes might be in order,” Seth said. “Just saying, you may want to shower or something before meeting with the royal council.”

“That may be a good idea,” Saymore said.

“Do we really have time?” Willow asked. It was true, all of them looked as if they had been through a massive battle. Even she had dirt and blood crusted to her hair and body. She was probably in need of some medical attention for her leg as well. She winced and curled over at the thought.

“It could be the only time we do have for a while.” Saymore answered. “Best clean up and tend to our wounds while we can.”

“Are you hurt?” Sebastian asked. His lack of emotion in the question was less than comforting, but at the same time it was more than could be expected from an elf.

“Well, of course she's hurt!” Aaram yelled. “You can see the bruises and cuts on the girl, can't you? While you boys were sitting here not worrying about what was happening outside your little box, she was fighting. Perhaps you'd like to stay here and play with Jordan while the adults save the world.”

The four elves looked down and noticed the young boy clinging to Willow's good leg. Jordan played a few rounds of peek-a-boo before breaking out into laughter.

“Play!” Jordan yelled.

“Little person,” Sebastian said. “Where did he come from?”

“Atlantis, obviously,” Willow answered. “I didn't just conjure him up or anything. He's Malarchy's son. I'd like to get him back to his family as soon as possible. He's been through as much as anyone could ask already.”

“Okay,” Sebastian said. “Showers, fresh clothes, a supply of pancakes, gather the royal council and hide the little guy until we can smuggle him out of here. Anything else?”

“Aslo and Kiera,” Willow said. “They should be at the meeting.”

“Sure, why not?” Sebastian half-laughed.

“Oh, and can we smuggle some of the anti-potion out with Jordan for Malarchy to test for us?” Willow's face lit up with excitement for the first time since returning from her elf-realm journey.

Sebastian shook his head. His signature sly smile formed in the corner of one side of his mouth. "You have no idea what you are asking.”

Chapter Forty-Four

"Well," Cassandrhea said. "Here we are again, and with more outsiders, I see. This should be fun. Do you have any idea how many rules you have broken?"

"Shut up, Mother," Sebastian said, taking a stance beside Willow.

"Nice," the Director said. "I see you have taken on some of the girl's better traits. Don't get too involved in all this. It isn't our fight."

"You're wrong," Sebastian answered with a charming smile. "It's our fight more than anyone else's. We need to own it. Maybe along the way, we might find those magics that have been dwindling from our lives."

"Yeah!" Zoran roared.

Cassandrhea jumped. "How or why is there a dragon here?" she whispered.

“I think the question should be, why hasn't he always been here?” Elsa-Mae said. She fluttered immediately in front of the elf queen's face.

“And a fairy,” she said. “Of course.”

“What is going on here?” A voice bellowed down from the tree table. “What is the meaning of all this? Why is the girl back here?”

Cassandrhea prepared to address the royal council but was interrupted before she had the chance to say a word.

“Well,” Willow said, “I hope you don't mind the short version.” The grass beneath her feet indented from her pacing. “Basically .. you sent me on a test. I met the dragons... and the fairies... hid from a unicorn... found and woke three sleeping great trees... discovered a poison that was destroying this realm as slowly as possible... entered Atlantis through a portal... met and saved Umaagan, Saymore, Lane, and Aaram... confirmed Cornelius is working with Cornost... sent word to you about the other two portals... and returned here with vital information.”

“My, we have been a busy girl, haven't we?” a man's voice said. “What is this vital information?”

“We can't close the two portals,” Saymore said. “Sorry for the interruption, but the girl would have rambled on far too long.”

“If Atlantis is to attack, we must protect our people.”

Saymore's tail flickered behind him. “From what we understand, Atlantis has found a way to rise from the watery grave in which they were entombed alive. They had plans to simply break in through the barrier and wage war. You, however, sent the girl off on what I can only assume was a wild goose chase, which was created so you could utilize her guardian counterparts. While she was gone, you had them strengthen the barrier between the two elf realms. No one anticipated Cornelius would involve himself in such an unimportant battle. However, he did just that. The portals became active. One is already closed. The problem lies here. Atlantis is rising, whether you close those portals or not.”

"With so little knowledge of the situation, you deduced all that? How extraordinary. Of course, you are correct. The test was a farce to keep the girl busy," a female voice said.

"Hello," Willow said, waving her hand in the air. "The girl is standing right here. You can stop talking about me as if I were somewhere else."

"I see no indication of Atlantis rising," the male elf said.

"Of course not," Saymore answered. "Because it will rise in another realm."

"Well then," the female voice answered, "it won't be our problem. We don't need to concern ourselves with what happens elsewhere."

"How can you say that?" Umaagan yelled. "This is our fight. When did elves become so cowardly that we had to make others clean up our messes?"

"I am afraid the council doesn't see it that way," the male voice bellowed down. "Our job is to protect our own."

"Do you think that they won't come for you?" Willow asked. "Once they have destroyed the lives of people who know nothing of your battles, they will find a way here." Words began forming on her lips. Words she hadn't thought of before. Words she somehow knew had to be said. She couldn't stop her verbal assault. "Do you know why your magics are faltering? I do. It's because they were given to you to help you protect the realms. You were never the protectors of the great trees. You were their partners. The elves were meant to work with them. You have lost your purpose."

Gasps echoed amongst the spectators gathered at the forest line behind the tree bench. If not for the grumbles, one unlucky enough to be standing before the royal elf council might not even know they were being watched. Willow wondered how many had been present at her previous appearance.

"The decisions we have made have always been for the well-being of this realm," another council member said. "There are many reasons why we don't involve ourselves in the business of the other realms or allow their involvement in that which is our own. We have no problem admitting one of these reasons is our obvious superiority to other races."

"Superiority?" Willow yelled. "Was that not the very problem with Atlantis? They considered themselves far above all others."

"Yes, my dear," the female voice said. "But there is a difference. King Cornost wanted recognition for his superiority. He wanted to be hailed as a god. They were going to force otherworldly individuals to bow down at their feet and comply. Atlantis had to be sealed away, so as not to interfere with the rights of others to exist. We, however, separate ourselves from other realms and their inhabitants. Do we not have the same right to live as we see fit? We hurt no one."

"That," Aslo said, "is a matter of opinion." The feline guardian strolled up to Willow and rubbed against her. His tail curled around one leg. "If you knowingly allow Atlantis to rise in another place simply so it isn't your problem, I would say you are, in fact, hurting others."

"How long have you been here?" Willow asked.

"Long enough to hear what's going on," Aslo answered.

"Would you have the elf realm destroyed?" the female voice asked.

"No," Aslo responded. "Not at all. The elves are as important as any other race. I am suggesting that by working together, we may be able to come up with another plan."

"We need some time," Willow said. "If we can find the remaining great trees, I think they can help."

"Great trees," Aslo said. "Have you found some?"

"Yes," Willow answered. "Two were here in the elf realm, and a third was trapped in Atlantis."

"What in the realms was a great tree doing in Atlantis?" Aslo asked.

"It was trapped there," Willow said. "The battle was supposed to be a distraction. There was some magic the trees used to banish

Atlantis, but one tree needed to be physically there. It was, of course, supposed to escape. Unfortunately, in the midst of the battle, it didn't work out that way."

"Fascinating," Aslo said. "Then if we find the remaining three trees, perhaps they can fix whatever is broken in the seal. This magic is not something we guardians have knowledge of."

"You are speaking nonsense!" the female elf yelled. "We have seen no proof of any of the great trees being here. Please understand, we cannot leave our fate up to the unknown."

Willow fell to her knees, her hands grasping tight over her ears. For a moment, there was nothing but a loud ringing in her head, no other sounds. She looked up to see Elsa-Mae tapping lightly on her shoulder. The fairy's mouth moved, but no noise reached her ears.

Can you hear me? Aslo asked.

The words resonated in her brain. She knew instantly the sounds were not coming from her ears. *You joined with me. My hearing... what happened?* she thought.

An explosion, Aslo answered. *There isn't any information yet. Medical teams are coming. I expect regaining hearing for everyone affected will take some time.*

Is there anyone not affected? Willow asked.

Guardians are not and fairies, the feline answered.

The triplets, Willow thought, her teeth grinding together. Every inch of her skull throbbed from bells that couldn't be silenced. Who knew that hearing nothing could be so loud? *They may be able to help. When they sing together, it heals dragons.*

So it might work on a large crowd all at once, Aslo interrupted. *You stay put and rest. I'll see if I can find the girls.*

Staying put was exactly what she planned to do. It didn't make any sense to run around amidst the chaos that already existed. Aslo's head nudged her arm. With a nod, he was on his way. She closed her eyes - the pain in her head growing. Light vibrations tingled through her body, becoming stronger like a wave of power. This was a sensation she had never felt before. It was also one she never wanted to feel again. Maybe she was hurt worse than she originally thought. Could this have been some sort of a seizure? There was no sense screaming. Nobody would hear. Gathering all of her strength, she stood. Her legs wobbled. She was falling again. This feeling wasn't coming from her body. The vibrations were coming from the ground.

The grass between her two white sneakers parted. The green blades made way for small cracks forming in the brown dirt beneath. With no time to think, she skittered to the left. She coughed, her chest tightening. She pulled the collar of her t-shirt over her mouth. It wasn't the best filter to breathe through, but it would have to do. Inhaling too much dirt from the clouds spewing out of the crevices could have proved deadly. The tree table and bench the council were sitting at cracked in two down the middle before being swallowed whole by the gaping hole that was forming before her eyes. It was over as fast as it started. Less than a minute was all that was needed to change the landscape forever.

Her bloodshot eyes teared. Tiny drops fell down her face, leaving tracks in the dirt that had settled there. The clouds above threatened rain. She bit back, reeling in her emotions.

She stumbled backwards, landing on her rear. Staying in that position, she scooted away from the newly-formed edge. Most of her senses had been rendered useless by the events of the last few minutes. It would have been easy to fall. If this was Cornost's doing, they were in trouble.

Her head twitched. In the background of the ringing, she could faintly hear something - a symphony of tones melting together. She concentrated on the sound, matching the rhythm of her breathing to the same frequency. If love could be a noise, this was it. As the music grew louder - the painful ringing faded. Other sounds began returning as well; a mother crying for her child; voices pleading for help; the wind howling as if mourning the loss of a friend. The music continued playing. It was one voice. She could see them now. Three girls holding each other's hands in a row. The triplets were all singing, but their voices combined together into one. Deanne flashed a smile in her direction.

Willow understood. They truly were happier together. There was something extraordinary about the sisters. She couldn't put her finger on it, but seeing them together brought back emotions and the feeling she had forgotten something... something important.

"Can you hear me?" Sebastian asked.

Willow didn't move. She could hear him, but her mouth was too dry to make words. He sat beside her. She welcomed his touch as he brushed the dirt from her hair and face. After several minutes, she managed to utter just one word. "What?"

"From what I understand," he said, "a second portal was closed. It caused that explosion. After that, there was some sort of a chain reaction that set off an earthquake. I imagine it all has to do with the pressure that is building up. They must be pushing everything they have to try to make Atlantis rise." He stood and offered her his hand to help her to her feet. "Come. Let's find some water. We have already stopped the third portal from being closed... at least for now."

She nodded. If a doorway closing caused this much damage here, she wondered what it might have done elsewhere. The elves would have no choice but to listen now. Obviously, their world was involved. No matter what they did, they couldn't escape this. Another quake like that would leave their realm in ruins.

Chapter Forty-Five

"Moonlight, shine your divine light. Delve deep beneath the waves and tides to find me the answers that I seek."

The ocean's water crashed upon the cliff below, sending a splash high in the air. The salty water misted down on the top of the rock structure sitting high above the surf. Droplets found each other, combining into larger pools of liquid, each reflecting silver back towards the sky. They continued to join together, twisting and turning, until forming the outline of a woman's body. When her foot hit the ground, it turned a creamy colour. As if paint had been added to her veins, the rest of the woman's body followed suit. Turquoise strands exploded from another splash of water, forming hair, eyebrows and lashes. Green ocean weeds crept up the side of the steep bluff's edge, before winding up the woman's leg, forming a bodysuit similar to that which a surfer might wear.

"Ah, that's better," she said. "You should remember that when the moon rays hit the water's surface, it's no longer in your domain... it's in mine." She circled the old woman. "Honestly, you look like something left after a shark attack. You really should pay more attention to your appearance. Perhaps something a little less hag-ish?"

"I am not here to argue with you over territory or how I look," Miss Kelly said. "But do tell, what brings you to this place?"

"If you are implying I had something to do with this," the woman said, taking a seat on a pile of rocks over-looking the edge, "I'm afraid I am not involved. It's just as much a mystery to me as are the people who come here to plunge into the hundreds of jellyfish that congregate below. They are beautiful, aren't they? And yet so very deadly. It's funny how we perceive things."

"I am not here to ponder the sanity of the inhabitants of this world. I am here to find out what is causing that whirlpool," Miss Kelly snapped.

"Well," the woman answered, "I am here to figure out the same thing. I do have a stake in this world as well."

"Are you sure you aren't involved?" a man's voice asked.

"I had no idea this was a family reunion! Or perhaps an impromptu meeting to discuss our future actions?" the woman asked. "I see you are letting your appearance go as well. What do you call that look? I know. It's a cross between a hippie, a gypsy, and a Tibetan monk? I daresay, I miss the beard. So is there a new name? We have all been known by so many over the years. It is hard to keep up."

"Vincent," he replied.

"Interesting. I think I prefer when you were known as Merlin. We did have some fun. Do you remember how people thought I was the evil Lady of the Lake?"

"You had fun, my dear," Vincent answered. "I believe I have been immortalized in legends as the wizard who was abducted by you."

"Well, how ungrateful." the woman answered. "It worked to transition you into a new era without arousing suspicion as to your age."

"True," Vincent answered.

“And what name would you be going by?” Nick asked.

“Ah, the party grows,” she said. “Nice of the two of you to take the time to join us.” The woman's voice echoed the word *time* against the crashing waves of the ocean.

“We'll be going by Nick and Meredith,” Nick said. “If you don't mind.”

“No,” she answered. “That is your right. I think I will revert to a name I never fully got use out of. Yes. You can call me Pandora. It seems fitting.”

“Are we to assume you have found a box of some sort?” Vincent asked.

“You feeble-minded, moron of a man. Of course not. The box is a metaphor.” Pandora answered. “Honestly, how have you survived all these years?”

“Do elaborate,” Miss Kelly said. Her grey robe caught in the wind and tangled with her flowing white hair. One arm outstretched, holding her staff firm to calm the weather.

“Don't bat your third eye at me, old crone,” Pandora said. “I merely am observing that it may be time for us to take the initiative. The little heroine isn't fairing so well and I have nothing to do with it this time. I haven't had any contact with the brat at all this life. She did spend most of it in a world without any bodies of water, after all. I can't even imagine how such a place could exist.”

“Can you blame her? It must have been a subconscious choice after what happened last time!” Meredith yelled.

“I merely made available a way for her to seal away Atlantis. It was something she knew already but hadn't come into realization of. I did nothing more than any of you have done,” Pandora answered. “How many times has Lady Luck been on her side? That's quite the gift. A heart-shaped pendant, wasn't it? And Vincent, how much detail did you *suggest* to the artist of a certain stained glass window? Then, of course, there is your more recent little gypsy show-and-tell farce. I'd like to know how many predictions were whispered to unsuspecting prophets from the voice of wisdom.”

"That's enough!" Nick yelled.

"Not even close, Santa," Pandora responded just as loudly. "You might be the worst offender yet. How many times have you stopped time in one realm or another to allow the girl to play catch-up? Don't look so surprised. Did you think none of us would notice? The timelines between her death, birth, and ageing don't line up properly from one world to the next. The only logical explanation is Father Time used his abilities to allow her to grow up just enough to fight the good fight again."

"I did," Nick said. "I admit it. But it caused no deaths or pain to anyone. Can you say the same?"

"It isn't my fault she didn't follow instructions," Pandora answered. She sat back down on her rock perch and swirled her hand around as if playing with the jellyfish below. She cleared her throat. "If she would have sat back and let her familiars do her bidding, everything would have turned out different. There was no need for her to go there herself. I can hardly be responsible for the girl's actions."

"But that is why it is important she learn her powers without outside help," Miss Kelly answered. "We can guide her, but we can't give her magic." For a moment, the tone of the elemental magic teacher's voice bordered on compassion before returning to its normal stern sound. "None of that matters now. Please enlighten us as to the metaphor you referred to earlier. What actions are you planning on taking?"

"I am not scheming anything," Pandora answered. "But we need to seriously consider allowing me to unleash my familiars on this world."

"You can't be serious," Meredith said.

"Of course I can," the ocean witch said. "Look at us. We first came here as a strong coven of thirteen. We were young and looking for a place in the universe to call our home. We agreed to take root here. I don't even know how many of us are left, but without a full coven we are bound to these forms. We all know what happens when we die. We have seen the girl reincarnate many times. But she is different. She seems to radiate to us. Kristophe is proof of what can happen to the rest of us. The thought of him living out there somewhere with all that power and not even an inkling that he has it makes me shiver. Being reborn without any memories of who I am frightens me more than death."

"Without our original thirteen members, we cannot return to our otherworldly forms," Nick said. "We all have to accept that we have longevity now, but are not immortal."

"But that's my point," Pandora pleaded. "We can take things into our own hands. We can lead our own destiny. I can open the box and unleash all that these people consider evil to rid the world of all that truly corrupts it. I can leave hope in the box for us." She grabbed Vincent's hands in her own. "Let's unleash the Four Horsemen... let's set forth the proverbial apocalypse... let's walk hand-in-hand into Armageddon." Her hand rested on Nick's shoulder. "We can start again."

"No," Nick answered. "Not only do the inhabitants of this world have a right to live, I am not sure we have the power to stop them now."

"Don't be silly," Pandora said.

"He's right," Vincent offered. "These people grow more intelligent every day. Those who have the gift of magic are far more proficient than we may care to acknowledge. Even if we gathered all of those of us remaining, it is possible we would lose."

"Nonsense," Pandora laughed. "Let's find out." Her sea green eyes changed to a burning fire orange colour.

"Silence!" Miss Kelly bellowed. Her staff rose in the air and a bolt of lightning came down.

"Oh no you don't, old hag," Pandora said. The ocean swelled. The tip of a wave reached up to meet the fork of light came down. A loud crash sounded. Ice the size of footballs showered down around them.

"Look out!" Vincent yelled, throwing up a canopy shield over the five. He reached down and picked up a piece of the ice. "I have never seen weather that could create this." His face was blank and cold.

“Look what you have done!” Miss Kelly roared. Her staff came down on the ground with a boom. The earth beneath them cracked. The lines grew larger as the cliff that supported them shook violently, attempting to unattached from the rest of the world.

“What I have done?!” Pandora screamed. “Your bloody staff is ripping apart the ground!”

“I had no part in that. Whatever it was, we should be glad it stopped almost as quickly as it started.” Miss Kelly said. “Wait. Look! What is that under the water?”

“That's not possible,” Pandora said. Her dainty fingers lightly covered her lips.

“What is it?” Vincent asked.

“Atlantis.” she replied. “They must have botched the spell in another way. This is bad for your little heroine. She has her hands full with Cornelius at the moment. No way she can handle Cornost at the same time.”

“She is resourceful,” Nick said. “I won't count her out of the equation yet.”

“Yes, but I may have aggravated the self-proclaimed King of Atlantis a little over the years.” Pandora said.

“What do you mean?” Miss Kelly asked.

Pandora sighed. She stepped over one of the larger cracks to join the other four. “I was a little bored. None of you ever visit anymore. We never have any fun. I may have played a few games of pinball under the sea.”

“You used an entire nation as a ball to bang around for pleasure?” Meredith screamed.

“You make it sound so horrible,” Pandora replied. “They were the bad guys, after all.”

“When one gets stung by a bee, one may consider it to be an enemy. That does not make it wise to attack the hive with a stick,” Vincent said.

“Back to your Confucius days, I see,” Pandora scoffed.

"Wise words should be taken to heart," Vincent answered. "Your name choice may be on the button, though. If Atlantis is freed, it could bring a different meaning to opening Pandora's Box. Except this time, the contents may come looking for you."

"Well," Pandora said, huffing. "If we had taken care of them in the first place, we wouldn't have this problem."

"We all vowed when we came here and chose this place as our home, we would not interfere with the right of others to exist," Miss Kelly said. "After all, we are the aliens to all of these realms."

"I know," Pandora answered. She stomped her foot on the ground, then jumped back in case the motion caused another crack to form. It didn't. A frowned formed on her sea-kissed lips. "But things changed. We should have learnt that lesson the first time our tree-hugger ended up as kindling, hand-in-hand with that lovesick puppy of a boy. It's impossible for everyone to exist together. Whether it's greed, or lust, or power, someone will always challenge for that which another has. You may not like it, but we have no choice but to take a side."

"You may be right," Miss Kelly conceded. "But for now, let's give Willow a chance. She may yet surprise us. We can call an official meeting if things turn south."

"I trust I don't have to remind you all that if this world is destroyed, we will be as well," Pandora said. "One cannot reincarnate into a world that does not exist."

"We are well aware of the consequences," Nick answered. "None of us want it to get to that point. We are quite happy with our lives, such as they are. Perhaps when this over, you should consider taking up a hobby of some sort... other than pinball or toying with fishermen."

"You do know how to hit where it hurts," Pandora answered, a ring of sass returning to her words. "Very well, I will wait. But in the meantime, what do we do about that?" She pointed to the whirlpool. "It's messing up the Triangle. It's my absolute favourite place to play. I hate to see it like this."

"There are forces at work here that we have no sight into," Miss Kelly answered. "Without knowing what magic is involved, I am afraid it is too dangerous for us to interfere at this time. It's up to Willow to decide if Atlantis rises or not. Our roles in this mess, if any, will come after Cornost reappears. The non-magical have made up their own explanations. We need not worry about them for now. People are being evacuated to safety. The magical are drawing their own conclusions as well. I am due to report back to them with findings."

"What will you tell them?" Meredith asked.

"Needless to say, mentioning Atlantis rising would be like opening Pandora's Box," Miss Kelly said, a sly smile creeping over her lips.

"Did you just tell a joke?" Vincent asked. He burst out into laughter. Tears rolled down his face and he grasped his sides. He gasped for air, trying to find further words, but was rewarded with only another bout of hysterics.

"Very funny," Pandora said.

Miss Kelly took in a deep breath of the sea air and let it out with a huff. "Yes, it was," she said. "It's always good to keep a little bit of humour handy in critical situations." She paused, facing out towards the large swirling pool of water as if she could see. "They will need to know there are dark times afoot. Preparations should be made for a battle. It may not be today, or even next week, but when Cornost comes, it will be with rage. If Willow falls this time, they will need to be ready."

Chapter Forty-Six

"Welcome back," Malarchy said without looking up from his paperwork.

"How do you always know when I am here?" Krissy asked.

The mayor smiled. "How was your trip?" he asked, completely ignoring the girl's question.

"It's not like it was a vacation or anything," Krissy whined. She skipped through the doorway, taking a seat in a chair. Speaking to the young reporter lately had become an invitation into whatever one happened to be doing at the time.

"I know," Malarchy said. "I was more curious as to what you found out, if anything."

"That's not very friendly," Krissy said. She picked up the paperweight from the desk and examined it thoroughly. There wasn't much else to keep her distracted in there. The mayor's office was, to put it plainly, boring, especially for a young reporter. "I didn't have very much time, really. I think the Directors dropped the ball. Once the illusion magic went up, I had to leave. There was no need for a reporter to be sniffing around after that. It would be too suspicious." She dropped the paperweight, shifting her weight to cross her legs.

"And?" Malarchy said.

Krissy pouted her lips. "And what?" she asked.

Malarchy dropped his pen on the desk and rubbed his temple. A pinkish flush raised over his cheeks. Taking a deep breath, he nodded his head ten times. "Did you find out anything?" he asked, articulating each word perfectly.

"Well," the young journalist said, "it was the usual conspiracy theories that you hear, especially near the Triangle. A lot of reports of alien activity. No one there seemed to have any conclusive information. So on the good side, there wasn't a lot of panic to deal with. There were a few locals talking about prophecies of the coming of a great evil. I did get as many details about that as I could, but I think they are the same rehash of stories told in any place where a disaster is happening. Most beliefs will point to the end of times when something horrible occurs."

"Yes, yes," Malarchy said. "I myself have been reading up on them. So there wasn't anything useful, then?"

"I didn't say that," Krissy said. A smile crossed her lips, causing dimples to appear. "I did manage to take these." A stack of pictures drifted down, landing face-up on top of the pile of papers the mayor was busy signing.

The last picture didn't have a chance to settle before it found its way into Malarchy's hand. "What am I looking at?" he asked.

"Not sure," Krissy answered. "It looks like in the middle of the whirlpool, there is a giant hamster ball. I suppose it's more like a terrarium. If you look at the blown-up ones, you can almost make out some contrast in colours, suggesting a landscape of some sort."

"Can we measure how far from the surface it is?" Malarchy asked.

“Nope,” the journalist pulled out a steno pad and pencil. “The storm is too violent to get close enough to measure something like that.”

“How did you come about these pictures, then?”

“Sorry,” she answered. “Restricted information, that is. I have my sources. You are the first to see them, if that counts for anything.”

“Yes,” Malarchy answered. “It definitely does. I appreciate your loyalty. I assume there is no way to tell where the hamster ball is coming from?”

“Not a chance,” Krissy answered. “But not from this world. If I were to make a guess, I would say it appears to be stuck in between two realms.”

“Your theory sounds interesting,” the mayor said. He slouched back in his chair and clasped his fingers together behind his bald head. “Explain.”

“It isn't advanced science or anything,” Krissy said. She sat forward and put her arms on the desk. “It's as if it were stuck in a wind tunnel. If the two realms each have a slight opening and air is being sucked in from both sides, the pressure could be enough to push an object back and forth with the flow.”

“So whatever it is, we can expect it is trying to appear either here or there,” Malarchy said. “Interesting. But we don't know which place it is actually trying to reach.”

“No,” Krissy said. “But I bet wherever the other realm is, you'll find Willow there.”

“Indeed,” Malarchy said. “You'll leave that part out of your official report and the paper, I trust? I don't think Willow needs any more publicity.”

“Of course,” Krissy answered. “Besides Jessica is handling the official report. I am just typing up the article for the paper.” She headed for the door.

“Before you go,” Malarchy said, “I do have one other job you might have some interest in. Of course, it may be a tad bit dangerous and would require your complete secrecy for the time being."

"Really?" she said, spinning around in a half circle. "Sounds like fun. Do tell."

"I may have a concoction to counter the memory potion affecting the rest of my people," Malarchy said.

"That's wonderful!" Krissy squealed.

"Oh, yes," Malarchy said. "It is. If it works. We need to test it. There is no way we can storm the camp not knowing if it will be effective."

"I suppose that could be bad."

"Yes," the mayor said. "Very bad. But if we had someone from a local newspaper who wanted to set up another set of interviews with one or two infected people... well, you can see the possibilities I am sure. It would be beneficial to everyone."

"Especially," Krissy said, "if the reporter had exclusive rights to the story after everyone was cured. It could be the article of the century."

"I could see you receiving at least an award from the mayor's office for your work," Malarchy said. "That might go a long way towards the decision between you and your brother. When is the birthday? Is it coming up soon?"

"Too soon for comfort," Krissy said. "I'll do it. I'll go to the office now and leave some clues. Someone will send out the requests. Is there a particular place you had in mind for the meeting?"

"Somewhere with drinks," Malarchy said. "Let me know ahead of time. I'll set it up so the potion will be served in the beverages."

"You are a sly man," Krissy said. "Remind me not to get on your bad side."

A faint knock on the office door interrupted their discussion. Standing on the other side was the same hooded figure who had met the mayor in the park.

"We meet again," Malarchy said. "Another delivery?"

"You could say that. Except it's too big to bring here."

"Sebastian?" Krissy said, her nose crinkled up. "Why are you being so weird?"

The elf sighed. "Krissy, how are you?"

"Good," she answered. "But what's with the outfit?"

"I'm trying to be inconspicuous," Sebastian answered.

"Well, it's not working," she replied. "Are you trying to be a spy? That's exciting. I bet it has something to do with Willow."

"Shush," he whispered. "If you have a place we can meet, please write down instructions to it. I will meet you there."

"No need," Malarchy said, scribbling a note on a scrap piece of paper and throwing it down a hidden chute. "We have places we can go." He grabbed his coat and pushed past the two teens through the doorway. "Come along. I have a feeling this is going to be a very long night. We might as well get started."

"Where are we going?" Krissy asked.

"Just keep up," Malarchy said. "It isn't far."

"We need to take a walk through the park," Sebastian demanded.

"It's out of the way," Malarchy answered. "Is it imperative?"

"More than you know," the elf answered.

Sebastian pushed ahead of the other two. He stayed several steps in front of them, almost as if he was embarrassed to be associated with them.

The elf's pace quickened as they came close to the centre of the park. Malarchy could hear his breath labouring. Perhaps a desk job had a few disadvantages. His heartbeat raced. He could feel the blood rushing through his veins pounding in his temples. Krissy had moved ahead of him now. His stride slowed in an attempt to regain his composure. He didn't relish the thought of the two youngsters mocking his physical condition. He stopped for a moment. His own concern about appearances had hindered his awareness of his surroundings.

He took a few deep breaths. His nostrils flared. There was something familiar about the park today. Something was there with them. There was no breeze. The birds were silent. The trees stood motionless, watching him. A dense fog rolled in. It came from every direction. He was completely hidden, even from his companions.

"Willow," Malarchy said. "You're here, aren't you?"

"It isn't safe," she whispered. "We need a place where we can lay low. There is something very important I need to give you."

"You can't give it to me here?" Malarchy asked. "The fog has surrounded us. I can assure you I cannot see a thing."

"It won't fool the Directors for long," Willow answered. "There is too much at stake for everything to be disclosed here. You have to trust me that what I have with me is something you wouldn't ever want to risk."

"Alright," Malarchy said. Using a stick, he drew a crude map in the ground, marking an X in the middle. "You'll meet Jade there. She'll lead you to us in a safe location. Give me about an hour to make the preparations. So you know, she will be using her talents."

"Fine," Willow whispered.

Grass sprouted over the map that had been etched in front of the mayor. The fog lifted. There was no sign of Willow. He sighed. At least he had time to fully regain his composure before taking the short stroll to the park bench where Sebastian and Krissy were waiting for him.

"Are you okay?" Krissy asked. "You were huffing pretty extreme and then disappeared in the mist. I was worried you had a coronary or something."

"I'm not that out of shape," the mayor answered. It was a lie. He made a mental note to order some exercise equipment for his office if he survived this ordeal. "We have much to do. This way." He took the lead again, but at a manageable pace. They needed to make sure no one followed them. Whatever it was that Willow had found, he knew it had to be extremely precious.

Chapter Forty-Seven

There was only one thing Jade hated more than waiting, and that was not knowing what she was waiting for. She shivered. The wind tonight had a bit of bite to it. The street lights flickered before going out. The blonde hairs on her arms stood at attention, as if foretelling a coming catastrophe. It was only now, as she stood alone in the darkness, she noticed a red tint lingering around her - a blood moon.

This was the first of its kind she had seen. It was memorizing, reminding her how many things in life could be beautiful and deadly at the same time. Her thoughts turned to Gavin. That was nothing unusual for her lately. In fact, several times a day she caught herself drifting off in her thoughts about the vampire. But tonight it was different. A blood moon was thought to affect the vamprite in unpredictable ways.

She tapped her foot on the ground. This was taking far too long. If she stayed in this spot much longer, she could be discovered. There were anti-illusion specialists that worked for the government, after all. What was her father thinking? She wasn't nearly strong enough to fool them. Her breath formed a small cloud as it hit the cold air. She smiled. Her mouth opened again, allowing the misted air to escape in the pattern of a circle. This was the distraction she needed. Time passed quickly as she attempted several different patterns. Few of them actually looked like anything in particular, but each made her a little giddier than the last.

"Having fun?" Gavin asked.

Jade jumped. "What are you doing here?" she asked in a low voice. "You shouldn't be out here."

He lined her arm in his. "You were gone a little too long. I wanted to make sure you were okay," he said.

The warmth of his body radiated towards her. It amazed her how aware she was of her spatial sense when he was near. She forced a smile, hoping he wasn't reading her thoughts.

"You don't seem too upset to see me," Gavin said, flashing her a smile that brought colour to her cheeks.

Determined to say something witty, she opened her mouth but a cheesy giggle blurted out. When did she become such a pathetic lovesick little girl?

"Are you okay?" he asked, brushing a few strands of hair from her face.

"Yeah. I'm just a little worried. She should have been here by now," Jade said. She looked away from him, hoping to hide the heat rushing to her face again.

"Jade," Willow whispered.

"Where are you?" she answered.

"Shush," Willow answered. "Just walk in the direction you want us to go. Don't look around or anything. I'll be following you."

Gavin took Jade's hand and pulled her towards the alley entrance to their secret lair. Jade followed as if she were a rag doll being carried around by a child. What had come over her? She took one more look up at the sky. Maybe the blood moon was affecting her more than it was Gavin.

The heavy door closed behind them. "Just keep walking," Willow said. "Don't look back until we reach the others."

It wasn't hard to comply. Everyone was gathered in the first room they came to. "So," Jade said, turning around, "what is all the secrecy about?" Her eyes glossed over. She fell to her knees. This was so much more than she could have ever imagined. Tears streaked down her cheek. "Jordan!" she screamed.

"Jade!" Jordan yelled. He jutted out from behind Willow, running straight for his sister's arms.

"How?" Malarchy asked, falling to his knees beside his two children. His arms embraced them. There would be time for answers to all his questions after a short reunion.

A few minutes passed. Aaram moved forward. "Malarchy," he said. "It's been a while. I don't want to interrupt, but we do have a few things to discuss."

"Aaram? Lane? How is this possible?" he asked. The whites of his eyes turned a shade of red darker than the moon outside.

"It's a long story," Aaram said. "We can get to the details later. In the end, all that matters is that this young lady saved us." He put an arm around Willow's shoulder and squeezed her tight.

"Geena?" Malarchy asked.

"We don't know," Lane answered. "Cornelius's sons agreed to release her if we helped them, but..." His words faded off.

"Hopefully we can reunite you with Diana and Nathan soon," Malarchy said, hugging the men.

"They're alive?" Aaram cried. "Where are they?"

"It's complicated," Malarchy replied. "They were given a memory-altering potion. Gavin and his team has been working round the clock to make an antidote. We are actually making the preparations to test it."

"Perfect timing!" Willow smiled and hugged the vampire. "It's good to see you." She handed him a bottle of purple liquid.

"Always good to see you," he said with his usual charismatic charm. His lips pecked her on the cheek. "What do we have here?" He held the vial up to allow light to shine through the liquid it contained.

"My friends created that. It may work if yours fails," Sebastian said, positioning himself between Willow and the vampire. Without the hood covering his face, there was no chance of misinterpreting the glare he was sending.

Gavin laughed.

"Still as popular as always, I see." Malarchy said, pushing between the two boys to break the tension that was building. "Perhaps we can direct our attention to the giant hamster ball trying to pop out of the ocean."

Sebastian switched his attention to Malarchy. He uttered only one word, "Atlantis."

Gavin laughed again. "The lost city that was rumoured to have sunken into the sea. People have been searching for that place for ages. What does that artifact have to do with all this?"

Sebastian chuckled. "Apparently, some people buy into terunji stories," he groaned. "Atlantis was a rogue elf kingdom that was banished a long time ago. We had no idea where they were locked away, until recently."

"So everyone pays the price for elf problems," Gavin said, squaring his shoulders towards the elf prince. "Typical elvish thinking."

"Enough," Malarchy bellowed. "If we start with political disagreements between ourselves, we are doomed. I don't care what your race or beliefs are. Everyone in this room is working as an equal. It doesn't matter how it started or who started it. We have come together to figure out a way to stop it with as little loss of life as possible. Understood?"

"Understood," Gavin said. "I can agree to a truce... for now."

Sebastian flipped his sandy coloured hair back, revealing the intense green of his eyes. "For now," he said, flashing a coy smile.

"Fine," Malarchy said, throwing his arms in the air. "You two hardheaded morons are welcome to kill each other once the world is safe again. Who knows, maybe we can find a few more meatheads to join you before the day is over."

Willow didn't have to look at the man to know the intense disapproval he was flashing in her direction. There wasn't much she could do about it. It puzzled her just as much as anyone else why young males seemed drawn to her. If it was any consolation, she never actually ended up with any of them. Mike was proof of that. He was happily in a relationship now. He was a special friend to her and always would be, but nothing more.

Her thoughts shifted to William and his new wife. A chill ran down her spine. She closed her eyes to picture him, but the vision that came in clear was not of the guard she had thought she was in love with. It was of her dark prince, Lance. He had saved her life more times than she cared to think about. Even now, under the power of the memory-altering potion, he had let her escape. She turned her attention to Gavin and Sebastian. Both had been strong for her, even with their own agendas. Then there were the other three elf princes.

It was confusing. Love, even the very word, made her anxious. It was something she hadn't known for most of her life. Since leaving her home world, she had come to realize there were many types of love. What she hadn't figured out was how to know which was which. One thing she did know, there had to be a difference between loving someone and being in love with them.

"Are you listening?" Jade said. "Willow?" She tapped her on the shoulder. "Are you with us?"

"Sorry," Willow said, pink creeping into her cheeks. "I was just thinking. What were we talking about?"

"Stopping Atlantis..." Malarchy said.

"Right," Willow whispered. "The great trees are going to try to keep them contained."

"Trees?" Gavin said. "Think I am missing something."

"Me too," Krissy said.

“I know about Acacia, the tree of justice,” Malarchy said. “But you said trees.”

“Yes, I found three more. One with the fairies, one with the dragons and one in Atlantis. They will do what they can, but we would need to find the final three for them to do more than hold them in stasis for a while.”

“Dragons and fairies?” Jade said, her eyebrows arched high, crinkling her forehead.

“They are many creatures that reside in other realms,” Sebastian said. “Dragons and fairies just happen to be native to the elf realm. Of course, we don't normally share such information.”

“Of course,” Gavin said. “I'm sure that the knowledge of your pets is a matter of national security.”

“They aren't pets!” Willow yelled. “They are sentient beings, the same as you and I. In fact, most dragons are nicer than many individuals I have met in this realm.”

“Sorry,” Gavin muttered.

Sebastian flashed a smile that could have rivalled the vampire's own charismatic abilities. “It's how Atlantis is rising, that is the problem. I don't think we can rely on finding the other trees in time. They could be anywhere and in any realm. The odds are against us.”

“I agree,” Malarchy said. “Do we know anything?”

“We know they are working with Cornelius,” Willow said. “Lance was there.”

“Lance?” Jade said. “But I thought he...”

“His father didn't spare anyone to the memory potion,” Willow said, cutting off her friend's words. “He didn't know me at all.”

“Did he attack you?” Jade asked.

“No,” Willow said. “He let me escape. It was exactly like the first time we met... as if history was replaying itself.”

"Well, maybe now would be a good time to bring up the window panels," Gavin said.

"Did you figure them out?" Willow asked.

"It's a rather touchy subject," Jade said. "Now might not be the time."

"No," Malarchy said. "She needs to know. If we are to stop the cycle, it has to be now."

"Cycle?" Sebastian asked. "What cycle?"

"Reincarnation," Gavin answered.

"Whose?" Willow asked.

"Yours," Malarchy answered.

"Mine?" Willow asked. "I don't understand."

"We think the picture depicts you in a birth-to-death cycle," Gavin said. "Always fighting the same fight over and over again."

"If we are right," Malarchy said, "you will come to a choice. On one hand, it will appear that everything you hold dear will be guaranteed to be safe, but you will die. To you it may seem like the sacrifice is the only choice to make, but it will only be a temporary solution, like putting a bandage on a wound that needs stitches. On the other, it will seem like insurmountable odds of anything surviving."

Willow gazed into space. Things were starting to make sense now.

"That's absurd!" Krissy cried.

"No," Willow said. "Atlantis is an example."

"What do you mean?" Sebastian asked. "You had nothing to do with Atlantis. That was long ago."

"But what if I did?" Willow asked. She found a chair and sat down. The thoughts swirling in her mind were making her knees weak. "Think about it. Cornost is virtually the same as Cornelius.

Atlantis was sealed away with magic. It was a temporary fix and now the bandage we put on it is coming loose."

"But..." Sebastian started.

"I'm getting to that," Willow said as if she knew his thoughts. "There was an elf girl named Lilybelle."

"Yes," Aaram said. "Several times we heard about your resemblances."

"Not just resemblance," Willow said. "I've been told we were close to identical, including the same heart pendant that Meredith gave me. Lilybelle fought and died in that battle. Her death marked the disappearance of the great trees."

"I think you are forgetting the timelines for death and birth don't correspond," Malarchy added.

"True," Willow said. "But if Meredith was somehow involved..."

"Nick could have been too." Iskander finished her sentence.

"Exactly," Willow said.

"Okay," Gavin said. "You are losing me again. Who are Nick and Meredith? What do they have to do with all this?"

"They are portal guards," Iskander said. "Better known as Mr. And Mrs. Claus."

"As in Santa Claus!" Krissy screamed. "They are real?"

"Better question," Sebastian said. "How can they affect when Willow was born?"

"Everyone from our world has at least one unique gift," Malarchy said. "Dreamwalking, illusion, stealth, strength, speed are all common examples. Some have less common gifts. Like Meredith possesses the gift of luck, and Nick can disrupt time."

"You're talking about Lady Luck and Father Time," Krissy said. "They are famous fictional characters. I think every realm has heard of them."

“Indeed.” Sebastian said. “They have been mentioned in bedtime stories for generations. Is it possible these people are the inspiration for those stories?”

“I don't know,” Malarchy said. “That would suggest that they might be older than the portal guards. How is that possible?”

“I think a visit to see them may be in order,” Willow said. “But no matter what, we still have to deal with Atlantis first.”

“Agreed,” Aslo said, making an appearance. “This time we need to make sure to take care of the problem properly.”

“Aslo,” Malarchy said. “Good of you to grace us with your presence. I don't suppose there is any information you can share with us that may shed light on the situation?”

“I can't help,” Aslo said. “At least not yet. There are certain things that Willow must figure out for herself. There are some blanks even I don't know.”

“Perhaps you won't,” Saymore said. “But I feel no pressure not to speak.”

“You will not interfere,” Shelby cawed.

“Shelby,” Saymore said. “How did you find your way into this mess? Last time I saw you, well, you were broken beyond self-healing.”

“Willow saved my life,” Shelby said. “She healed me.”

Saymore's tailed flickered back and forth. “Interesting. Why?”

“Why?” Willow screamed. “Why wouldn't I have? Shelby deserves the same right to live and exist as anyone else.”

Saymore chuckled. “That, in itself, is a fascinating concept.”

“You have had your fun,” Nero said.

“You are here too?” Saymore asked. “Goodness, how many of us are there here?”

“There are a few of us,” Kiera said. “I believe you know everyone except...”

"Our children," Aslo finished her sentence.

"Children," Saymore said. "That isn't possible."

"It is," Aslo said. "Things aren't always as simple as they seem. Please let them figure this out."

"I don't know what you critters know," Gavin said. "But if it can help us, you need to spill it. We are running out of time."

"Sometimes," Malarchy said. "Knowledge can do more damage than good. They have their reasons for not disclosing whatever it is they know. I trust them enough to leave it like that. Perhaps we can concentrate on what we do know about Atlantis. Is there anything else we might be missing?"

"The unicorns," Willow said, her face blank and colourless.

"Unicorns," Krissy repeated. "The most innocent, pure, beautiful animals ever considered to exist? I collect figurines of them. They are supposed to be gentle beasts."

"Try demon-like, evil, magic-stealing, deceptive killers," Willow said. "I almost ended up one's dinner. Most magic is useless against them."

"I never would have guessed," Gavin said. "Not that I have met one in-person, but they always are described as stunningly beautiful, much like the ladies in this room."

"That's the point," Willow replied, ignoring his obvious attempt to be charming. "They appear approachable. By the time their prey figures out they are deadly, it's too late. The worst is their horns. Any magic directed at them, they can collect and then use it against the caster."

"That would be a problem," Iskander said.

"Imagine several of them with an abundance of power built up," Willow said. "If they were positioned properly, could they raise Atlantis?"

"There isn't enough information to know the answer to that," Gavin said. "It might be possible. But it would take a long time to make the calculations, find the positioning, have the right amount of power stored up. That doesn't even take into consideration the type of magic needed or the precision in timing."

"We know unicorns have been sighted in the elf realm," Sebastian said. "But what about near ground zero in this world?"

"I didn't see one when I was there," Krissy said. "I also wasn't looking for one. With all the illusions and wards being used to hide the situation from the terunji, I doubt anyone would be able to find one if it was there."

"Let's secure as much as we can," Malarchy said. "If your trees can hold them for now, it'll buy us some time."

"I'm going to head over to the newspaper office and leave some notes for my family," Krissy said.

"Notes?" Willow asked.

"Yeah," Krissy replied. "I am going to make it so tempting, one of them will call a couple of your friends here to interview them. I'll even make a scribble about meeting at the Magic Coffee Bean Cafe. Once the bait has been taken, you can swoop in and try out your stuff. Don't worry. I am going to lead them in the wrong direction."

"Pretty smart," Gavin said. "That way you don't endanger yourself."

"I don't think I need to say this," Malarchy said. "But Willow, you need to stay well-hidden. You are not going to take part in the testing. I don't want you anywhere near anyone from the camp until after they are back to themselves."

"You mean if they ever are back to themselves," Willow said.

"They will be," Jade said.

"I have a place where we can hang out," Sebastian said. "We can take care of Jordan for you as well. I am sure you will be busy."

Willow didn't like the thought of not being included in the action. It wasn't the first time she had been sidelined for her own good, but that didn't make it any easier. There wasn't any choice but to agree. At least spending time with Jordan would be fun.

“I think I'll take a stroll by the cafe and check out the area for possible surveillance spots,” Gavin said. “I would like to be as prepared as possible for whatever may happen.”

“Good idea,” Malarchy said. “Why don't you take Jade along?”

“Sure,” Gavin said. He held out his hand to her. “Shall we?”

Jade took his hand. This was going to be an interesting evening.

Chapter Forty-Eight

Slipping out into the cool evening air, Jade shivered. She had forgotten how chilly it was. She had also forgotten about the blood moon. “Are you okay being out?” she asked.

“Are you?” Gavin responded.

“I meant because...”

“Of the moon,” Gavin finished her thoughts. “I'm a vampire, not a werewolf. The moon has no effect on me.”

“Even though it's a blood moon?” Jade asked.

Gavin laughed. “It's just a name. It's based on the colour, not actually on blood. You do know that most of the legends about my people are made up, right?”

“Of course,” Jade said. It wasn't really a lie. She did know the terunji made up many stories about vampires. What she didn't know was which, if any, were real. She was far too intelligent not to realize that even the terunji tales had some tiny part to them that was based on reality.

They slipped out of the illusions put in place to hide the secret entrance. The walkway remained dark. Whatever had happened to the street lights earlier hadn't yet been fixed. Gavin slipped his hand into hers and squeezed. She welcomed the warmth of his hand.

“You're cold,” he said. “Don't you have a coat?”

“I didn't bring one,” she answered. “I didn't think it would get this chilly.”

“Here,” he said, placing his jacket over her shoulders. “Best I can do at the moment.”

He flashed her a smile that she thought he had only reserved for Willow. She felt heat rising in her face again.

Gavin chuckled. “If there wasn't a blood moon tonight,” he said, “I would have thought you were blushing.”

“Right,” Jade answered. “The moon.” His musky scent from the jacket filled her senses. She inhaled deeply. This man captivated her. He was in her mind, under her skin and in her heart. For the first time in her life, she didn't know what to say or how to act.

“Look,” Gavin said, pointing to a group of musicians who had set up in one corner of the park. “How about a dance?”

She had no time to answer before she was in his arms. He twirled her around in time to the music as if she weighed nothing. Her body responded to every move he made. She wasn't even sure how long they were there. Time meant nothing. Only the two of them mattered. Their bodies melted into one. This was a feeling greater than anything she had ever experienced before. She never wanted it to stop.

“Are you enjoying yourself?” the vampire asked.

“Yes,” she replied. “It's been a long time since I have danced like this. It reminds me of my home. We would have dances in the courtyard under the light of the stars. The smell of the flowers from the neighbouring garden would drift down on us like perfume on a beautiful woman.”

“That sounds wonderful.” Gavin whispered in her ear. “But I am glad you are here with me now. You move so gracefully.”

“Thank you,” she said. “You are the one who has the hard part. You lead. I just follow.”

“You'd be amazed how many toes I have had squished by ladies who can't follow my lead,” he replied. “It's rare to find a partner who I can move this fluidly with.”

“Willow,” she said. It just popped out of her mouth. She was glad it had. She needed to know if he was serious about her friend or not. Was he just flirting with her for something to do? Maybe he wasn't flirting with her at all.

He stopped moving and pulled away from her slightly. “Are you jealous?” he asked.

She hadn't expected that. “No,” she stuttered. Her heartbeat quickened. Heat rushed to her cheeks as her face flushed red again. Her mouth went dry.

Gavin smiled. “I think you're lying,” he whispered in her ear, nipping it slightly with his teeth.

She pushed backwards from him. “We should check out the cafe,” she suggested.

“As you wish,” Gavin said. “I thought you were enjoying our dance.”

“I was. Thank you,” she replied. “I just...”

“Willow is my friend,” Gavin said. “I feel a need for her to be around. I haven't quite figured out what it is, but I am not the only one. The elf is the same and others, I imagine. I can tell you, it isn't the same feeling I have when we are together.” He pulled her back into his arms. “I know you feel it too.”

“I do,” Jade whispered. “But...”

“Shush,” Gavin said. “We can take all the time you need. I am in no rush. Explore your feelings. When you are ready, I'll be waiting. Okay?”

“Okay,” she answered. That was what she needed to hear. She took his hand. It would be easy to let him lead her anywhere.

"The cafe isn't far," he said, changing the subject. "I can't remember there being very many places to just hang around and watch people. We may have to take shifts drinking coffee on the patio for a couple of days."

Jade laughed. "I hope not. I'm not a big fan."

"Neither am I, actually," Gavin admitted. "You become accustomed to drinking it. Sugar helps a lot. Unfortunately, a cafe rarely will allow you to sit and drink water for hours at a time."

"I see your point," she answered.

They passed several couples along the way. This time, however, they actually looked as if they were a couple too. That was going to make it easier for them to do spy work around town. They were fluent now. It was as if they had gone to a new level, one she had never reached with anyone else before.

"Yup," Gavin said. "Looks like I was right."

Jade had been so lost in her own thoughts, she hadn't even realized that they had arrived at their destination. "This isn't a busy street," she said.

"No," he answered. "I think that's why Krissy picked it. The fewer witnesses, the better. I think I can get someone working as a waiter without any problem."

"We'd look odd just standing around staring at the place," Jade said. "It would be way too suspicious."

"Like we look now?" he whispered in her ear.

"Exactly," she said, noticing patrons of the cafe starting to stare. "Maybe we should order a coffee on the patio? It might warm me up some."

"Whatever the lady wishes for," Gavin said.

"A heater," Jade said. She was glad to see the patio was surrounded by heaters turned on high. Even choosing a table as close as possible to one, the chill still remained. She sat back, pulling Gavin's jacket around her. It would take a bit before she was toasty warm.

“Comfy?” Gavin asked, placing two coffees on the table.

“Mmmm,” Jade said, inhaling the steaming cup of java. “It smells good. This might not be all bad after all.”

“I talked to the owner,” the vampire said. “He said I could start work tomorrow. Things are looking up.”

“Start work,” Jade asked. “I thought you were sending someone else?”

“Why delegate what I can do myself?” Gavin answered. “This way, I know the right amount of the potion has been given and I can observe what happens at the same time. You can see for yourself. There isn't anywhere to set up surveillance.”

“How can I help?” Jade asked.

“You can't,” he answered. “Anyone from your camp could recognize you. It would put the whole plan in jeopardy. I'll have a few mates in and out for coffee for back up. Maybe the elf can get involved too. Everyone else will have to be hands-off.”

She gulped back a mouthful of hot coffee. He was right, of course. Chances were, the only memories affected by the potion were those connected to Willow. There was a good chance that someone from the camp would know who she was. That would not only ruin their chances of testing the anti-potion but could potentially put her in danger too. Whoever was behind the drugging of the camp most likely didn't know they had missed a few of Willow's friends in the city. She could become a target.

“You're right,” she answered. “It's just hard to be left on the sidelines looking in. I'd like to help them too. I feel useless not doing more.”

“I understand,” Gavin replied. “You're doing more than you give yourself credit for. Everything that is happening is because you and your father made it happen. Your friends are lucky you care so much about them.”

“Thanks,” Jade said. She placed the mug down on the table. There was no more steam escaping up from the creamy brown liquid. The thought of drinking an iced coffee didn't appeal to her.

Perhaps in a few weeks, when the evenings were warmer, a cold drink would be more appetizing.

"Are you done?" Gavin asked.

"Yes," she answered. "I think so. Thank you."

"Well, then," he said, "I'll walk you home before reporting back to the boss."

Chapter Forty-Nine

Gavin cleared the dirty dishes from one of the tables. It was his third day employed as a waiter in the cafe without having seen any sign of a reporter or any members of the camp. An entire evening had been spent memorizing different faces from pictures to make sure he wouldn't miss them. There was, of course, the off chance that whoever set up the meeting didn't follow Krissy's scribbles and chose another cafe to meet at. He looked around. That wasn't likely. This was the perfect location to hold such an interview. It was in the open and yet, with so few patrons, it was also very private.

Today's weather was the perfect contrast to the other night's. The afternoon sun was beating down on the patio in full force. Heaters had been replaced with umbrellas. Ice cubes were in high demand among the few customers they had. Pots of hot coffee went to waste.

Gavin loosened the collar around his neck. He wasn't used to wearing anything that covered that area of his body. As if the white, high-collared, long-sleeved shirt wasn't enough, a black bowtie made it even worse. The less he had to do, the more time he had to think about how uncomfortable he felt. Today was particularly slow. He was about ready to rip the tie off when he heard a cough.

"Ahem."

"Good afternoon," Gavin said. He hadn't noticed a new customer arrive. "Table for one?"

"No," the young man answered. "I need something bigger. I'm expecting a few acquaintances to meet me here. Something out of the way of any traffic flow would be preferable."

"This way," Gavin said. Anyone could see that there wasn't any traffic flow, since there weren't any customers at the moment. Not wanting to argue the fact, he led the man to a table for six in the opposite corner of the patio. "I think you'll find that you won't be disturbed here. You also have a view of everything in the area."

"Perfect," the man replied.

"Can I get you a drink while you wait?" Gavin asked.

"An iced witches brew with a shot of confidence should do," he answered. "Lemon on the side and light on the ice. Might as well get the most of what I pay for."

"Right away," Gavin answered. He was all for being frugal when money was tight, but how much could this guy possibly expect to save having the lemon served off the glass? Still, the customer was always right. He prepared the drink as ordered. By the time he returned, there were new people sitting at the table. He recognized them from the pictures. This was it. This was the moment he had been waiting for.

"Your drink, sir," Gavin said, placing the cup in front of the man he assumed to be the reporter. "What can I get you?" he asked the others. The first man he recognized as Mike. That could be a problem. They had briefly met in the dungeon before Halloween. Beside him was his girlfriend Sissy, who was also Cornelius's disowned daughter. The other man was Faramund, a portal guard and close friend of Iskander.

"Might as well have the same," Mike said without looking up. "I'll have it with a shot of romance." He removed his hat, revealing his short red hair, and placed it on his lap.

"Sounds good," Sissy smiled. "Make mine the same."

"Make it three," Faramund added. "But I prefer a shot of strength."

"Very good," Gavin answered. That was one obstacle out of the way. If they hadn't all ordered drinks, there might have been a problem. He emptied a tiny vial of liquid into each glass. He trusted his own work more than that of an elf he had never met before, so he was testing it first. The problem still existed that if potion didn't do its job, there wouldn't be a chance to try the second batch. He filled the rest of the drinks the same as he prepared for the reporter, adding the requested special shots at the end.

By the time he returned to the table, the interview was well underway. The young man stopped speaking to allow the drinks to be placed. Gavin had heard enough to know that the line of questioning was good enough to solicit a response if the potion worked.

"Here you are," Gavin said, placing the glasses down on the table. "It's a hot one, so drink up. Refills are on the house."

"Wonderful," the reporter said, guzzling down the rest of his drink before holding out the glass so another one could be brought.

"Very good, sir," Gavin said. "I'll be right back." That hadn't been the person he had hoped would down a drink. Still, maybe the others would follow by example.

By the time he returned with the reporter's beverage, the other three had finished their drinks. "Refill?" he asked. They all accepted his offer.

The only thing to do now was wait. He wasn't sure how much time to give it before he declared the first attempt a failure. His hand slid into his pocket and removed the second vial of liquid just far enough so he was the only one who could see it. He shoved it back in again. This round was too soon. He would have to hope that the interview took some time and that the heat from the sun kept the group thirsty. He knew the reporter would have no trouble taking at least one more free brew, if not more.

“Can I get anyone anything else?” Gavin asked.

“Why not?” the reporter answered as if on cue. “Might as well splurge.”

“I'll be right back,” the vampire answered. He wasn't sure how the reporter thought he was splurging, considering the drink was free.

“What do you mean?” Faramund yelled.

The guard was standing at the table with his fists clenched. That could be a sign that the potion was working, or it could simply be that Faramund realized the reporter was a bit of a jerk. Either way, Gavin needed to move as close as possible to find out.

“I don't know what you are so upset about,” the reporter said. “You are on record as saying the girl is a fraud.”

“I don't know what is going on here,” Mike said. “None of that is true. At least, I don't think it is.”

Gavin pretended to trip, the contents of his tray sent flying.

“You idiot!” the reporter yelled. “Look at this mess. It's all over me.”

“I am so sorry, sir,” Gavin said. “There is a bathroom right over to the left of the bar.”

“Unbelievable,” the man said. “We'll return to this after I clean up.”

Gavin wiped the table while watching the man scurry off like a rat who had found a piece of cheese. “Are you Willow's friends or enemies?” he asked.

“Do you know what's going on?” Mike asked. “Have we met before?”

“That depends,” Gavin said. “Friends or enemies?”

“Friends, I think,” Mike said. “Although it appears we have been enemies for a short time. We want to know what's going on. Nothing makes sense.”

“This is from Malarchy,” Gavin said, handing him a folded piece of paper. “Follow the instructions if you want to know. Oh, and stay away from anyone from your camp that may have followed you here or you could end up back the way you were.”

Gavin tossed his apron on the bar. “Hey, boss!” he yelled. “I quit. Don't worry about the pay. Not worth my time to pick it up.” Walking out, he ripped off the tiny black bowtie and tossed it into a garbage bin. The top three buttons of his shirt popped off simultaneously. His neck cracked. He had done his part, now to let the others know.

Chapter Fifty

Ditch the reporter. Follow the main path into the park.

Stay left at the fork. Look for a friendly face.

"That's all it says?" Sissy asked. Wandering around a park this size, not knowing who they were looking for, wasn't her idea of fun.

"I've read it to you three times now," Mike said. His nostrils flared as they always did when his blood pressure began rising. He was generally a happy guy, but when he became frustrated, his temper would rear its head. "You know as much as I do. There's a bench. Why don't you guys sit down and I'll take a quick look through the rest of the park?"

"Fine by me," Sissy said. "I was getting tired anyways." She plopped down on the bench, scaring away a few birds that had settled on the ground behind it.

"I'll be right back," Mike said. "Keep alert. We don't know what's going on. Even worse, we don't know who our enemies are."

“That's the worst part. Isn't it?” Iskander said. “How much do you know?”

“My friend,” Faramund said. “It is good to see you.” The two men embraced.

“It is also good to see you,” Iskander replied. “If you are, in fact, you.”

“We aren't sure we know what that means,” Mike said. “We are a little hazy over the events of the past while. It's as if we have been living two distinctly different versions of life.”

“But,” Iskander said, “which version is it you are living now?”

“It is hard to differentiate between the two,” Mike said. “They both seem so real and yet they can't both be real.”

“I can say one thing,” Faramund said. “I was, am, and always will be a portal guard. The fact that I no longer have the marking on my arm tells me the life I have been living is a lie.”

“Yes,” Iskander said, revealing his mark. “There aren't many of us with the mark left. Only those who resided outside the camp. That should tell you something.”

“Why is that?” Mike asked.

“The guardians are the reason behind the mark,” Iskander said. “When you sided against Willow, you sided against them as well. A choice had to be made. If you were an enemy, they couldn't continue giving you special powers.”

“That makes sense,” Mike replied.

“So what now?” Sissy asked.

“That,” Iskander answered, “is up to the mayor.”

“Hilary?” Mike asked.

“You haven't heard?” Iskander asked. “Hilary is dead. Malarchy is the mayor of Pewterclaw now.”

“Hilary is dead?” Sissy cried. “Lara will be so upset. We need to tell her right away. The poor girl, Hilary was her favourite aunt.”

"Hold on there," Iskander said. "This Lara, who is she?"

"She's William's wife," Sissy said. "You've met her. Don't you remember?"

"I have never met the woman," Iskander said. "And if she is related to Hilary, we have a problem. Hilary was working with Cornelius. She was a giant spider."

"What?" Mike said, laughing. "That's the most ridiculous thing I have ever heard."

"It's true," Iskander said. "She almost ate me. Willow saved us. There is a good chance this Lara is the one who stole your memories if she was, in fact, related to the old mayor." The guard pulled a phone out of his pocket. "Did you hear all that?" he asked.

"Yes," Malarchy said through the device. "Make sure the others can hear me too."

"They can," the guard answered.

"I thought the girl Lara had no family. At least I believe that's what the paper said." Malarchy offered.

"She doesn't," Mike said. "That's right. We found her in a town that had been destroyed. She was alone and had no one. That's why we brought her to the camp. She became one of us."

"So," Malarchy said, "how could Hilary be her aunt?"

"I don't know," Mike said. "It doesn't make any sense. But I know that she is related to Hilary. We even had lunch with them."

"But it can't be both ways," Malarchy said.

"No, it can't," Mike answered. He sat on the bench beside Sissy and put his arm around her. This was overwhelming his mind. He could only imagine what it was doing to hers.

"There is a saying," Malarchy said. "That which doesn't make sense..."

"Can't be true," Mike said, finishing his statement. "Why didn't you tell us sooner? If it was all a lie, why didn't you help us?"

Malarchy sighed. "We wanted to," he answered. "Without an anti-potion, there was no way you would believe us. You didn't remember your real life. It was stolen from you. You have no idea how many people have been working on this cure. As it is, it appears it only partly works."

"What do you mean?" Faramund asked.

"You now remember the life you once had, but you also remember the life that was made up for you. We had hoped that bringing back your memories would mean that you realized which ones were real," Malarchy said. "It seems that you must choose for yourself which life you want to continue living from this point on."

"I have told you my choice," Faramund said, folding his arms across his chest. "I am and always will be a portal guard. Mark or no mark, it is my destiny."

A tear trickled down Sissy's face. "We've been so happy. All of us," she said. "There has been no fighting, no deaths, and no danger. How can that be wrong?"

"If it was real," Mike answered. He took a deep breath. "I don't want to live a lie. We need to know the truth."

"If you continue down this path," Malarchy said, "you will find the truth. That I promise you. But you will shatter one reality forever."

"What do you plan on doing?" Sissy asked.

"With your help," Malarchy replied, "we want to introduce the memory-restoring potion to everyone else at the camp. That would also mean exposing the person behind all this at the same time. I know this is a lot to take in all at once, but we need your help."

"Is there anyone else who could back up your story?" Mike asked.

"Indeed," Malarchy answered. "Jade is here. Then there is Gavin, a vamprite. Most of the others I don't believe you have met. Of course, there is Willow and the guardians."

"She is here?" Mike asked.

"More or less," Malarchy answered. "I don't want to throw her into the mix while you feel animosity towards her. You do understand."

"Yes," Mike said. "I feel relief she is alright and the urge to destroy her at the same time. I can't differentiate which feeling is real. I mean, how do we know you didn't just plant the reality you wanted into our heads?"

"I suppose you don't," Malarchy said. "But you do know us. Your memories of myself, Jade, and Iskander should be intact. That should throw some clues as to your life prior to today. We have a safehouse where you can stay tonight and think things over. Tomorrow we can see how you feel. It is possible that your real memories will come in clearer with time."

"That sounds like a good idea," Mike said.

"Iskander will show you the way and stay with you this evening," Malarchy said. "We'll meet tomorrow morning."

"Fine," Mike said. Something nagged at the back of his mind. Sissy had been right. These past few months, they had all been happy. Was that really an illusion? If it was, did it matter? He wasn't sure that shattering a life of happiness for one of constant fighting was the best choice. If Lara was behind it all, he couldn't think of calling her a monster for clouding their vision to give them a better life. In this case, right and wrong seemed to overlap each other, perhaps they even switched places. In one life they fought to be happy. In another they had no need to fight, they were already happy. Maybe, for Sissy and himself, there needed to be a third choice.

Chapter Fifty-One

"Esmerelda," Kasper said, extending his arms to embrace her. "You look ravishing, as always." His lips brushed the side of her face. "Please come in and have a seat."

The clerk made a deep nasal sound barely resembling a laugh. "Director," she said. "You do know how to treat a lady." Her hands alternated smoothing the sides of her blue beehive hairdo.

"Yes," Cassandrhea said. "He's a regular Casanova. Perhaps we could keep the flirting for after the meeting."

"Please ignore my colleagues," Kasper said, offering the woman a cup of tea. "They can be rather abrupt in these types of situations. I trust you have something to report."

"Well," she said, pulling a stick of gum from inside her tall hair. "I have been watching the mayor just like you asked." She placed the unwrapped gum in her mouth. After chewing it a few times, she continued. "He hasn't had much happen. He had a delivery from an elf company. I don't know what that's about. Elves are quite sneaky things." She turned to Cassandrhea. "No offence to you."

“None taken,” the Director of Knowledge replied. “Please continue.”

“That young reporter girl comes around a lot,” Esmeralda said. A large bubble formed from the gum. Before it exploded on its own, she inhaled it back into her mouth, making a loud popping noise.

“It's not unheard of for a reporter to snoop around the mayor,” Jessica said.

“I agree,” Esmeralda replied. “But it is strange she has an open invitation to see him anytime. Most mayors avoid reporters like the plague.”

“That is interesting,” Kasper said. “Anything else?”

“Well, there is one more,” the clerk said. “There is a vampire named Gavin that has come in a couple times. Again, the boss left instructions for him to pass. I thought it might be something weird at first, but then I saw him walking with Jade. So I think there might be some not-so-discreet activities going on there, if you know what I mean. The mayor is probably trying keep things low-key, what with the big elections coming up.”

“Yes,” Kasper said. “The poor man. I couldn't imagine having a daughter who took up with a vamprite. It would be the end of me. I can see why he would want to keep that hush-hush.”

“That's all I can say. Other than that, he does his daily duties quite well,” Esmerelda said. “Things have never run as smoothly as they do now.”

“Thank you, my dear,” Kasper said. “Perhaps you can wait around in the lobby. I may need to interrogate you further in private.”

“Of course,” she replied, her fingers sliding down the front of his crisp white shirt.

“Oh please,” Cassandrhea said. “This is making me sick. Was I called here to discuss something important or witness your affair?”

Kasper waited for the door to close. “My sincerest apology,” he said. “There are those in my employment who require a certain touch.”

"It's your touch we don't want to hear about," Miss Kelly added. "If you don't mind, can we return to the topic we were brought here to discuss? The maelstrom is indeed caused by some form of magic. What type it is, I have no idea. In my opinion, something is trying to rise from within the ocean. Whatever it is, it appears to be contained at the moment. In the past few hours, another force has surfaced putting the storm into a holding pattern. The whirlpool is virtually gone; however, the cause still exists."

"That agrees with the data I have as well," Jessica said, tossing photos on Kasper's desk. "Krissy made a copy of these for me. They show something beneath the surface. It's a sphere of some sort. It could be a civilization."

"Is it dangerous?" Kasper asked.

"In every way," Miss Kelly said, "I think it's safe to say it is."

"Your conclusions are based off of what?" Kasper asked.

"If we take into account the severe devastation that would occur simply from this mass breaking through and rising, well, we can wipe out all islands in that area as the best scenario," Jessica said. "It's unprecedented, so we can't even begin to measure how far the effects would be felt."

"What comes after that could be far worse," Miss Kelly said. "I sense hostility, rage, and extreme power. We will be in for a fight."

"Can we destroy it before that happens?" Kasper asked.

"No," Miss Kelly answered. "It is neither here nor there. Stuck between two places, but not in either at the moment."

"Do we know where there is?" Kasper asked, sitting on the edge of his desk. His eyes remained fixed on the photos in his hands. "Maybe from the other side we can do something?"

"There is no way to know," Miss Kelly said.

"I think it is unlikely that anything could be done from there anyways," Cassandrhea said. "If you can't from one side, it would be the same for the other."

"Yes," Miss Kelly said. "I agree. There is no way to deal with whatever it is until it rises. If it rises. Our best plan of action is to start preparations for an attack."

"Are we sure that there will be an attack?" Kasper asked. "This is a significant decision. I don't want to create a panic by alerting people to what might not even happen."

"It might not," Cassandrhea said. "But it will happen somewhere. I am willing to bet once they attack one realm, they won't stop. Maybe not a magical wide alert, but we should consider increasing forces in the area for now. I don't think anyone will consider that unreasonable."

"Fools!" Miss Kelly yelled. "What I see as possible warrants more than an increase in men at the site. You need to take this seriously."

"Right now, things are under control," Kasper replied. "You said so yourself. If things change, we can act. What we need to do is find a solution before a war starts." He circled round his desk and slouched back in his high-back leather chair. "Do we have any news of the girl?"

"You mean Willow?" Jessica asked.

"Yes, I mean Willow," Kasper snapped. "What other girl is there that I would be asking about?"

"I have no information on the child," Miss Kelly said. "Her activities are well masked or she is outside this realm."

"Is the girl really that important?" Cassandrhea asked. "She is only one person, after all."

"One person with an aptitude for trouble," Kasper answered. "She seems to be near everything that happens. I have a feeling if we find her, we'll find answers and perhaps solutions as well."

"She is not the cause," Miss Kelly said. "Although she may be trying to solve the same problems as us. Trust me, Kasper. The girl is not the enemy."

"I am not convinced that is entirely true," he replied. "I will, however, keep your advice in mind. We should double our efforts to bring her in."

"You are stubborn," Cassandrhea said. "Your relentless pursuit of this girl will be your downfall. I agree with Miss Kelly. She isn't plotting against anyone. There is no evil intent. She may be naive and delusional, and her actions may take a strange route, but what she does, she believes is the best for everyone."

"That's the problem!" Kasper yelled, snapping his fingers and pointing. "She doesn't have the right to decide what is best for everyone. How is a young girl qualified to make such choices? That's what makes her dangerous. That's why I must find and stop her."

"She's not the problem, Kasper," Miss Kelly said. "She may, however, be the solution. There are forces stronger than you at work in the universe. Every now and then, they pick a hero."

"And you think Willow was chosen to save the world?" Jessica asked.

"I am blind," Miss Kelly said. "Yet I see more than most people could ever imagine. That is what I see for the girl. I suggest strongly we do not interfere in whatever role she plays."

"And I suppose you both agree?" Kasper asked.

"I don't know everything about her," Cassandrhea said. "But I will say there is something different about her magic. It is extraordinary, to say the least. Whether she is a chosen one or not, I cannot say. I can, however, say if she isn't given proper guidance, she could be dangerous to both herself and others. After this current problem is solved, we may want to have more control over her activities."

"You can't be serious!" Jessica cried. "You want to use her to solve all our problems then lock her up like a criminal because she did?"

"Now, Jessica," Kasper said. "I know you don't understand, but it is a question of keeping people safe. We have to do what is best for the greater good."

“The greater good,” Miss Kelly said, chuckling.

“I don't see what's so funny,” Kasper said.

“No, you wouldn't,” Miss Kelly answered.

Chapter Fifty-Two

"Good morning," Malarchy said. "I trust you slept well."

"Yes," Mike answered. "Thank you." That was a lie. Both he and Sissy had been up restless most the night, wrestling with the demons known as lies.

"Good to see you again," Gavin said.

"You were our waiter," Sissy said. "Is that how we were slipped the poison?"

"Poison?" Gavin said. "You mean antidote."

"I'm not sure I do," Sissy said. "I am having a hard time believing you. Just because you tell me which reality is in fact real, doesn't make it true. When it comes down to it, we have to believe someone... all of you, or the rest of our friends at the camp. The fact of the matter is, that redheaded brat made our lives miserable. Lara is right. With her gone, we have been happy and peaceful."

"Sissy," Mike said.

“I'm saying what I know you are thinking,” Sissy said. “She is nothing but a burden we can do without. What has she ever done for us?”

“She saved Mike's life in that dungeon, for one,” Gavin said.

“No,” Sissy said. “Lara did that.”

“No,” Malarchy said. “That was Willow. She also helped your brother Lance to save you.”

“You're twisting things!” Sissy cried. “Lara saved me. That's when I met Mike and we fell in love.”

“I want you to think reasonably,” Malarchy said. “It's impossible for Lara to have done those things. They happened before you met her.”

“You're trying to turn me against Lara!” Sissy screamed. “That's what this is all about. She has been the best friend to all of us. She has saved us countless times. She nursed William back to health. How can you say such horrible things about her?”

“So you don't remember Willow doing those things?” Gavin asked.

“I remember it both ways,” Mike said. “You can't blame us for being skeptical. I admit there are questions raised about certain memories. But it isn't enough to make us turn against a friend.”

“An interesting dilemma,” Faramund said. “Considering I remember Willow as being our loyal friend as well.”

Mike darted a glance in his direction. “Yes, I suppose that's true. The memories don't overlap. If you think of one, that's what you remember. If you think of the other reality, it's what seems real.”

“See what I mean?” Malarchy said.

“Yes,” Gavin answered. “The antidote wasn't as effective as I had hoped. We still have the elf version we could try.”

“Could you give it to them?” Malarchy asked.

“I'd rather not,” Gavin answered. “I'd like to give them time to see if the potion has any further effects. It's better not to mess up their psyche any more than it already is at the moment. But if we could find a new test subject, we could see if the elves are as smart as they claim to be.”

“There's another potion?” Mike asked.

“Yes,” Malarchy said. “Willow didn't leave anything to chance. Lance gave her samples of the potion before he himself was drugged by his father. She split it into two. One she gave to me to find a solution. I in turn recruited Gavin. The other she gave to her elf friends. They came up with a different potion.”

“We didn't know if either would work,” Gavin said. “I trusted my work more than the elf's. Seems that thinking may have been flawed.”

“So we are your test subjects?” Sissy said. “Like rats in a lab.”

“We had to test it somehow,” Gavin said. “You three were the ones the reporter contacted. You were never in danger.”

“We aren't going to get anywhere arguing,” Malarchy bellowed. “I take it you two have decided not to help us for the time being?”

“We can't,” Mike said. “Sissy and I are not getting involved.”

“That doesn't mean we will sit by and watch you steal happiness from our friends, either!” Sissy cried.

“Again,” Malarchy said. “Which set of friends are you worried about? Or have you resigned your thinking to align with Lara? Don't answer. It doesn't matter. I have no choice but to confine you here until after this is all over.”

“Did you ever think maybe you have it backwards?” Sissy asked. “Maybe Willow brainwashed you with some concoction?”

Malarchy laughed. “No,” he said. “Iskander will remain here with you. Please don't try anything silly. I am mayor of this city now and have the entire police force on my side. I'll need your wand to keep safe.”

Mike nodded to his girlfriend. "It's okay," he said. "Regardless of what happens, they won't hurt us."

Sissy placed the stick in the mayor's hand. It had been a long time since she had been confined without the use of her wand. Her thoughts drifted back to the cold cell she had been locked in at the mercy of the Frostica. There had been Nick in another cell. Across from him were the two dogs, Jawfree and Deacon. She could see images float through her mind. The taste of peppermint. The sadness of realizing her father wasn't coming. The joy of seeing Lance's face. He placed her wand back in her hand. Mike was with him and William. Lara was there too. No wait, the face was changing. It was Willow. But it couldn't have been. Was it? Lara didn't meet William until he woke up from the coma. But she was there.

The room spun. Her head felt heavy. Sissy's knees buckled. Then darkness.

"Sissy!" Mike yelled. "This is too much for her to handle. Don't you understand? We don't want to be a part of any of it."

"That's your choice," Malarchy replied. "We know this is difficult for you. All we ask is you stay put for a few days. After that, I will set you up with a home and job away from here if that's what you want. You two can live out your time together."

"Agreed," Mike said. "We won't try to leave. You hold up your side to the bargain."

"Faramund," Malarchy said. "We will need your help."

Chapter Fifty-Three

"Why have you brought me here?" Zsiga asked. "What is it you need to show me that couldn't wait?"

"Patience, my friend," Faramund said. Tricking a friend wasn't something that the guard relished the thought of, but Malarchy had been right. He was the easiest way to bring someone from the camp to the city without anyone noticing. He could teleport in and out within mere seconds. Zsiga happened to be on duty at the time. "You'll be happy once you see clearly."

The park was empty except for a few lovebirds stealing kisses in the moonlight. Faramund stopped at a park bench and motioned for his friend to have a seat.

"Zsiga," Malarchy said, joining them. "It's so good to see you again."

"Malarchy," the guard said. "I haven't thought about you in a long time. Why is that?"

“Who knows?” the mayor said. “But we are here now, old friend. I wanted to celebrate. Gavin, if you wouldn't mind... a drink for my friends.”

Gavin had used some colourful language when he learnt he'd have to put on a waiter's outfit. When he ripped the last one off, he had told himself never again. Yet here he was, holding a silver tray and serving drinks. Even worse, one had the elf potion in it. If it was better than the one he made, he'd never hear the end of it. He handed a glass to each of them, making sure Zsiga's had the anti-potion in it.

“Thank you,” Zsiga said.

“Bottoms up,” Malarchy said.

The three men downed their drinks in one gulp.

“What exactly are we celebrating?” Zsiga asked.

“Your freedom,” Malarchy said. “We hope.”

The reaction this time was different from before. Zsiga began swaying as if he were drunk. He tried to walk, but his legs refused to support his weight. He fell face-first onto the ground.

“Well, that's new,” Gavin said.

“Brilliant,” Malarchy said. “We didn't kill him, did we?”

“No,” Faramund muttered, squatting beside his friend. “I think he's asleep.”

“Okay,” Gavin said. “Well, he can't stay here. We need to move him somehow. He's a pretty big boy. I think someone might notice us carrying him out of the park.”

“There aren't many ways to move a sleeping man who won't wake,” Faramund said. “If you have another suggestion, please share.”

“I'll put enough illusion on you that you won't be noticeable to the naked eye,” Malarchy said. “We need to move him somewhere and restrain him until we know if this batch of potion worked or not. Might as well take him to the lab.”

Malarchy took the lead. If there was anyone in their path, he could easily stop them to chat. It wasn't something he wanted to do particularly, but as mayor he had to make some public appearances. He decided this counted as just that. There were only two instances where he found himself being used as a distraction. The first was an elderly lady walking her silver fish named Gold. A magic barrier had been created around it to keep water in place. It used its fins to move the liquid forward. When Malarchy mentioned what a good pet she had, it bared a mouthful of razor-sharp teeth at him. Needless to say, that conversation ended abruptly.

The second was a young couple who were overjoyed at meeting the man they had voted for. Their overabundance of excitement wore thin on his nerves quickly. He held out as long as he could, discussing their ideas on how to make Pewterclaw a better place to raise a family. He excused himself diplomatically. When they finally reached Gavin's office, he slouched back on the couch, releasing all of the air in his lungs. He felt as if he had been holding his breath since they left the park. He loosened the tie around his neck.

"My sentiments exactly," Gavin said, ripping off his bowtie. "I hate these things. Whoever invented them was sadistic." He grabbed the unlabelled green bottle from his drawer. The cork made a popping noise as he removed it with his teeth. A red blotch appeared on a white sheet of paper lying on the desk where the cork landed. He gulped back the contents.

Malarchy laughed. "Indeed," he said. "How's our guy doing?"

"Sleeping like a baby," Faramund answered.

"Tie him to a chair," the mayor said.

"Is that necessary?" Faramund asked.

"Yes," Malarchy answered. "If it didn't work, we need to give him Gavin's potion. Don't forget who we are dealing with. This is, after all, a man who can disappear before your eyes and blend into the shadows to never be found again."

"Wow," Gavin said. "That's an impressive talent."

"Did it work?" Jade asked, her breath labouring.

"Did you run here?" Gavin asked.

"I did," Jade answered. "I saw you, well Dad. I figured you had to be bringing him back here." She plopped on the couch beside her father. "You look terrible. Was there a fight?"

"Not exactly," Malarchy answered. "I was cornered by a yuppie couple with a hundred and one ideas on how to make the world better for the child they may or may not decide to want."

"Nasty," Jade said, laughing.

"I barely made it out," Malarchy said, smiling.

"So do we know if it worked?" Jade asked.

"He passed out," Gavin answered. "We won't know until he wakes up."

"Why don't you fetch Willow?" Malarchy said.

"You think that's a good idea after how Mike and Sissy reacted?" Jade asked.

"I think," Malarchy said, struggling to a proper sitting position, "that his reaction to her is the fastest way to find out what we are dealing with."

"Can't argue with that," Gavin said, taking another swig from his bottle.

"Fine," Jade said. "I'll be back soon. I don't want to watch you drink that stuff anyways. Yuck. It's horrid."

Gavin waved the bottle in the air. "It's all legal," he said. "No laws broken."

"That doesn't make it any less disgusting," Jade said, walking out the door.

Chapter Fifty-Four

Spending the last few days with Jordan had been an experience Willow hadn't expected to enjoy as much as she did. Making plants grow was one thing, but bringing a life into the world as a mother would be something completely different. She decided right then that having a child was something she wanted to do. Of course, she would need to figure out her love life first.

Jade opened the office door to usher her in. “I hope this goes well,” she said.

“I do too,” Willow answered, eyeing the sleeping man.

“Willow,” Faramund said. “I'm sorry.”

“It's not your fault,” Willow said. It was difficult to watch the man tearing up. She knew that this was hard on him. He must have been worried about the others... about Sarah. Still, she decided it was best to keep her distance at the moment. She positioned herself on the opposite side of the room. Sebastian found his way in between them.

"Name's Sebastian," he said. "You're Faramund. I've heard all about you." He offered his hand to shake.

Faramund accepted his offer. "I haven't heard a thing about you, other than there were elves mixed up in all this."

"Yeah," Sebastian said. "We're the ones that were there for Willow when the lot of you deserted her."

"I don't know who you are, elf," Zsiga said, his muscles flexing. "But none of us would ever desert Willow, and I don't appreciate you saying I would. Why don't you come over here and untie me?"

"Hold on now," Malarchy said. "Stay back." It would be easier to see what the guard knew if Willow wasn't seen just yet. "Zsiga, can you tell me where Willow is right now?"

"At school," Zsiga said.

"When did she leave?" Malarchy asked.

"Just a couple days ago," Zsiga said. "Why are you asking me this? And why am I tied up?"

"Because," Willow said, moving into his line of vision, "sometime during the school year, the camp was infiltrated and all of you turned against me. I haven't been at Sleeping Sands Academy for a while now."

"What are you talking about?" Zsiga asked. "This is madness."

"No, my friend," Faramund said. "Our memories were stolen and replaced. I carry both with me. I am happy you don't have to deal with the same pain of not knowing what is real and not."

"Untie him," Malarchy said.

"Are you sure that's safe?" Sebastian asked.

"It is your friend's creation that we used to cure him," Gavin said. "You do trust your friend who made the anti-potion, don't you?"

"Nice," Sebastian said.

Gavin flashed a smile. He had won that round, but his potion appeared to be inferior. There would be payback and he knew it. "So now we know the elf potion is better, how do we distribute it to everyone else at the camp?"

"There is more to worry about than just that," Malarchy said. "If what Mike and Sissy said is true, this Lara is related to Hilary."

"Related to Hilary?" Willow screamed. "That would make her a..."

"Spider," Jade interrupted. "She must have some illusion magic in play at the camp. It would be stronger than we can break through."

"But," Malarchy said, "a trained group of Special Forces may be able to help out."

"You aren't suggesting bringing in Kasper," Jade said. "You know how he feels about Willow. He'd try to capture her."

"That's why Willow would stay hidden," Malarchy said. "I can't think of a better way to bring down another spider queen and gain access to the rest of the camp."

"I can help," Willow pleaded. "I am the one who took care of Hilary, after all. I want to be a part of this."

"There are others who can channel electricity," Malarchy replied. "It is too dangerous for you to be anywhere near the camp until we have control of it again. Even then, I would imagine we will need to relocate it."

"I'll keep her safe," Sebastian said. "You take care of the others."

"What about Mike and Sissy?" Faramund asked.

"When this is over, we will give them the chance to take the other potion and reverse the remaining effects," Malarchy answered. "But in the end, the choice will be theirs. You will have the choice to erase the false memories as well."

"So," Gavin asked, "how do we get this party started?"

"We don't," Malarchy replied. "You are going to stay here and take care of my daughter and son. Or have you forgotten you don't have the best relationship with Kasper either? I want to keep you far away from this mess. Faramund, Zsiga, and myself will meet with the Director and set things into motion."

"How are you going to explain having an antidote?" Willow asked.

"I'm not," Malarchy answered. "I'm going to convince him to sedate everyone before taking on Lara. We'll give them all a shot while they are still under without Kasper having to know a thing."

"Won't he notice that everyone is waking up with their memories back?" Jade asked. "I mean, he isn't stupid."

"That's the beauty of the plan," Malarchy said. "We can blame their condition on Lara's illusion abilities. I just have to make him believe she was powerful enough to mess with all of their heads. That way we can say the potion must never have actually existed."

"I have to hand it to you, old man," Gavin said. "You really are sly. You sure you're on the right side?"

"I had my fill of making the wrong choices in my life," Malarchy answered. "It cost me my wife. It almost cost me my children. I plan to spend the rest of the time I have left doing the best I can to be a good citizen and making a place where my family can be safe."

Chapter Fifty-Five

"Malarchy," Kasper said. "What a surprise. What brings you here today?"

"I have some important information for you," Malarchy answered. "This is time sensitive. We have to act fast before she finds out we are on to her."

"Her?" Kasper said, raising an eyebrow.

"Lara," Malarchy answered.

"What is this about?" the Director asked, a tone of disappointment leaking through in his words. "Why do I care about Lara?"

"Because she is related to Hilary," Malarchy answered.

"I'm listening," Kasper said, leaning back in his chair.

"We were wrong," Malarchy said. "We thought the camp had been given a memory potion. It was Lara all along. She is a spider like Hilary. Her illusion magic is what has entranced the camp."

"The camp isn't giving me any problems," Kasper replied. "Tell me why I care if they are under some spell or not."

"You mean other than the fact that it's your job," Malarchy said.

Kasper chuckled. "Yes," he said. "Other than that."

"If Lara has the power to hold that many people in her power, imagine the damage she could do if she left the camp," Malarchy said. "Let's say a visit to your office?"

"An interesting thought," Kasper said.

"If your team could capture such a creature and extract information about other relatives," Malarchy said. "Not to mention extracting venom from her for research."

"How do you know all this?" Kasper asked.

"Faramund and Zsiga came to Pewterclaw to do an interview," Malarchy answered. "They stayed a little too long. It seems her illusions wear off if her victim is away from her for an extended."

"Interesting," Kasper said. "Let's not beat around the bush. What is it you need from me?"

"A team of anti-illusionists to take back the camp," Malarchy said. "A sleeping gas to put out the camp. We can secure them until their memories return. Your team takes care of spider lady."

"Credit?" Kasper asked.

"Your office takes it all," Malarchy said. "I'll give you a glowing review for figuring out the issue and taking down the bad guy, or spider in this case. My people will only be there to take charge of the care of camp members. We'll handle clean-up and medical."

"So," Kasper said, "my team are in and out and hailed the heroes. We also have exclusive rights to the arachnid."

"Yes," Malarchy said. "I have no interest in anything other than my people."

"Deal," Kasper said. "When do you want to do this?"

"How fast can you put it together?" Malarchy asked.

“An hour fast enough?” Kasper asked. “How do we get in and out?”

“Faramund will teleport us,” Malarchy answered. “We'll take them by surprise. Gas the whole camp. I doubt it will effect Lara, but everyone else should be passed out cold. Your guys can play with the spider and mine will secure our friends until the illusions wear off.”

“At the bridge in an hour, then?” Kasper asked.

“We'll be there,” Malarchy said.

Chapter Fifty-Six

"Make sure you secure the masks, gentlemen," Kasper said. "The gas will be effective for the first twenty minutes after it is released. A team of five will move in and release the sedatives into the air at predetermined places. We wait five minutes before storming. Most of the camp should already be asleep, so we don't expect much in the way of resistance. Keep as many innocents out of the picture as possible. Once the girl Lara appears as a spider, use all force to take her. We want her alive if possible, but if it comes down to it, Miss Kelly is joining us to channel electricity strong enough to end the fight. Any questions?"

"No sir!" the men chanted.

"Good," Kasper said. "Take your positions."

Five men took evasive manoeuvres entering the camp. Within seconds, a blast of smoke rose up and engulfed the area.

"Masks on, men!" Kasper yelled. "Use your helmet lighting to see. Countdown to deployment in four minutes."

While they waited, they listened to a few muffled screams and cries for help. Then silence. The gas began to lift. First the outlines of buildings came into view, then a few scattered bodies lying motionless. The plan was going as predicted.

"Ten seconds!" Kasper yelled. His hand came down. He pointed his finger like a gun and then motioned a shot. The rest of the men ran towards the camp. The search for Lara was underway. She didn't disappoint.

"What do we have here?" Lara said, standing in the middle of the camp. "Men trying to be big and strong?"

"Stand down!" Kasper yelled. "Surrender yourself and no one needs to be hurt."

Lara stuck her hands out as if she were waiting to be handcuffed and taken away. "Come get me," she offered.

"Careful, Kasper," Malarchy said. "This could be a trap." After seeing how Hilary reacted, there was no way this girl was going to be taken that easily.

"Team A, bring her in," Kasper yelled.

A group of men separated from the others, making their move with weapons aimed directly at the woman. The leader broke formation to place handcuffs on her wrists. That was a fatal mistake. Lara changed before their eyes into a gigantic spider a similar size to that which Hilary had been. With one swipe, the man sliced in half. Webs flung through the air, capturing the rest of the team. It took mere seconds for her to wrap them fully with her silk and inject them with deadly venom.

Lara laughed. Her head still that of the woman who had stood there a few moments ago, but her body transformed into a hairy arachnid's. "You fools are no match for me. Your pathetic weapons can't hurt me."

"Fire at will," Kasper ordered. "Make sure not to hit our men. They could still be alive."

Flames and lasers blasted at the creature. She stood her ground. Her laughter ceased. A cloud of smoke surrounded where she was standing. Kasper raised his arm for a cease-fire.

"May I?" Miss Kelly asked.

"Please," Kasper answered.

A swirling blast of air cleared the smoke rising from the target area. The men cheered. There was no sign of the spider. An eerie laughter broke through the cheers. Lara jumped down from a building into the middle of another group of soldiers, wrapping them up tightly in her webs.

"Did you think it would be that easy?" she asked. "Illusions are my specialty You may be able to break less powerful spells, but you are no match for mine." She disappeared.

"Where did she go?" Kasper yelled. "Track her. Use all force necessary. Dead or alive, bring her down. Someone get in there and help those men."

Malarchy motioned to Zsiga to aid with removing people from cocoons. His special talents would allow him to move undetected even by the spider queen. "We're on it," he replied to the Director. "You concentrate your efforts on Lara."

"Gladly," Kasper said.

Screams came from deep within the camp. "Sir," a soldier said. "She has taken out another two teams. As soon as we think we have her located, she appears somewhere else. She's too fast for us. At this rate, we'll be wiped out in less than ten minutes."

"Miss Kelly, if you wouldn't mind, fry that hairy beast before she eats anyone else," Kasper said. "Call back the troops. Special Forces will have to take care of this one. Pity. I would have liked to study her alive."

Surviving soldiers scurried back from the camp. They were no more than small bugs for Lara to trap in one of her webs of illusion. Miss Kelly walked passed them alone. Her staff struck the ground with every other step, creating sparks.

"I thought she was blind," Malarchy said.

"Yes," Kasper said. "She is quite legally blind. It's her third eye you can't hide from. Best part, she can't be affected by illusions because she can't see."

"And once she finds Lara?" Malarchy asked.

The whole camp lit up like a light bulb. The men squinted, turning their heads. The light show went on for several minutes, then the men all had to cover their ears. High-pitched shrieks filled the sound waves. Someone or something was injured. Another bout of bright lights and the screams fell silent.

"Wait," Kasper whispered. "There!"

Miss Kelly's figure appeared out of the smoke. She leaned heavily on her staff, limping back to where the men had positioned themselves. There were no more sparks coming from her movements. She looked older somehow. The battle had taken its toll on her. Even her staff lacked luster, appearing grey and aged.

"I'm fine," she said. "Don't look at me like I am done for. A little battle like that can't keep me down. She was only one spider, after all." She collapsed on the ground at Kasper's feet.

Faramund knelt beside her. "She's alive," he said. "I think she is suffering from exhaustion. Best hope there isn't a second spider lurking around."

Malarchy and Kasper both glared at the guard. They hadn't anticipated that possibility. If there was another enemy like that lurking nearby, they could be in serious trouble.

"Search the grounds!" Kasper yelled. "Use extreme caution. Malarchy, the camp is yours. We'll take care of the carcass. Oh, would you mind giving Miss Kelly a place to rest? I don't want to leave the poor old girl lying here in the open."

"Let's start moving people to the medical building first," Malarchy said. Being out of sight was a must for the rest of their plan to work.

The medical building had been empty. Zsiga had already filled half the beds with men who had been injected with spider venom.

"Over there," Zsiga said. "Looks like a few syringes of anti-venom. We are going to need every drop." Even though each of them had brought their own supply of the powerful cure, it wasn't enough for the number of injured. With extras they might just make it.

"I'll handle the venom patients," Malarchy ordered. "The rest of you start with the camp. We have limited time. Pick an empty barracks. Each person must be restrained until they have their memories restored. Quick and discreet."

He handed his supply of the memory potion cure to Iskander. Time was of the essence. Not just for his own people, but for the soldiers lying motionless. He knew what they were feeling. They could see everything. They could feel everything. They were trying to scream for help, but their mouths couldn't form any words. Stuck inside themselves, every minute would set them back mentally. It was like living in their own personal horror movie. He had been there. He wasn't going to let them suffer any more than they already had. Some, he knew, would already be scarred for life. They would never recover. He picked up a syringe and injected the anti-venom into the arm of the first man.

"How are they?" Kasper asked.

"Probably horrible," Malarchy answered. "They have all been poisoned with venom. Luckily, we found a supply here of the antidote. We hope there is enough for all of them."

Kasper picked up a syringe. "So this is the cure," he said.

Malarchy glanced at him. "Yes," he said. "You can play with whatever is left. We need to help the victims first."

"If we could duplicate it," Kasper said, "we'd have a supply for future need."

"The men come first, Kasper," Malarchy said, injecting another soldier with the precious cure. "They don't have time to wait for you to develop more, if you even can. This is, after all, an ancient mixture that was hidden away for years."

"How did the girl come to have it in her possession?" Kasper asked.

"I believe it was a gift," Malarchy answered. "I have no other details. She has more friends than you know."

"I see," Kasper answered, placing the syringe back on the table.

"Malarchy!" Iskander yelled. "We have a problem."

"What is it, man?" Kasper said. "Spit it out."

"Half the members of the camp," he said, his breathing laboured, "are missing."

"Missing," Malarchy said. "What do you mean?"

"I mean they aren't here," Iskander answered.

"Maybe they went out for the evening," Kasper said. "Or moved on."

"Or," Malarchy said, "became spider food. We need to search for a den."

"A den?" Kasper said.

"Remember the rooms under Hilary's house?" Malarchy said. "One for storage, one for feeding, and one for breeding. Lara must have a place like that near here."

Kasper gasped. "If she was capable of breeding as many children as Hilary was..." His words faded off. "I'll get more men. We'll comb the area."

"Quickly," Malarchy added. "If we could. There might be a few camp members in cocoons still alive. Iskander, I need you to stay with the surviving camp members. They'll be confused when they wake up and don't remember any of this. Do we have a list of those missing?"

"Yes," Iskander replied. "It's not good."

"No matter who is on the list, it won't be good," Malarchy said. "Let's see it."

The guard was right. This list wasn't good. Willow and Jade would take the news hard. There was no getting around sugarcoating the truth. Odds were, anyone whose name was listed was already gone. Now the question was, who would break the news to them?

Chapter Fifty-Seven

"Missing?!" Jade yelled. "What do you mean, they are missing?"

"I know this is upsetting," Malarchy replied, "but you need to calm down. We don't know where they are right now."

"Doesn't that mean..." Krissy stopped mid-sentence. Tact wasn't one of her finer qualities. In fact, she tended to blurt things out as they came to her. That was a reporter's curse. This time she bit her tongue, but not fast enough. She could feel the weight of the girls' stares directed at her. "We should send more people to help look?"

"Yes," Malarchy said. "We are going to send as many people as we can."

"The elves can help," Sebastian offered. "Some of us, at least. I know a few who would like to know how things are faring in this realm."

"That would be helpful," Malarchy replied. "Thank you."

Sebastian nodded. “I'll be back,” he said.

“I suppose Kasper is still there?” Gavin said.

“He is,” Malarchy said. “His men are doing most of the searching at the moment. The rest of our camp is still recovering. Many of them are broken mentally and physically. It will take some time to piece their lives back together. Aaram and Lane will be joining us to help in that regard.”

“I suppose help from a guy like me wouldn't be allowed,” Gavin blurted out. He shoved his hands in his pockets while rocking back and forth between his toes and heals, waiting for an answer.

“In this case,” Malarchy replied, “we'll take whatever help we can. I'd welcome you. We need to all work together.”

“I'll grab my things,” the vampire said. “And a few friends.” That hadn't been the response he had imagined, but it was the one he wanted to hear.

“Thank you,” Malarchy said.

“Don't forget me,” Krissy said. “I'm going too.”

“I wouldn't have expected any less,” Malarchy said, a smile creeping over his face. Since arriving in this world, they truly had made some exceptional friends. These were the bonds that would move forward in their lives. These were the people who could make a difference.

“I can help too!” Jade yelled.

“I want you to stay here,” Malarchy said. “With your brother and Willow.”

Jade grabbed the paper from her father's hands. The words written on the page blurred before her. Tears swelled in her eyes. She covered her mouth with one hand to muffle her whimpers. The names were written like a list being checked off. She fell to her knees.

“You need to be strong,” Malarchy said. “We're going now. Keep the hope. We are going to do everything in our power to find them.”

Silence filled the room. It was just the two girls now. Willow crossed her legs. She hadn't moved from the same spot on the floor since the meeting had begun. Her lack of emotion was disturbing. Jade plopped down behind her. She threw her arms around her neck and squeezed tight.

“Are you okay?” Jade asked. It was all she could think of.

“No,” Willow said. “I am anything but okay.” Her eyes glossed over, filled with a million tears that couldn't ever escape.

“Do you want to know?” Jade asked.

“No,” Willow answered again. “I don't. At least, not yet. I still have other things to do. Atlantis... Cornelius... Cornost. This isn't over yet. There's a battle coming. I can feel it. If I haven't even won a battle without sacrificing myself, how can I fight more than one at the same time?”

“With help from your friends,” Jade answered. “We are here for you. I am here for you.”

“I know,” Willow replied. Her hand touched Jade's. “How can I ask more of anyone? You've all been through so much already.”

“You aren't asking,” Jade answered. “We're in this together. This is our world too. If it blows up, it won't be good for me, you know.”

Willow smiled. “I guess it would put a damper on things. Can we just sit here a while?”

“Sure,” Jade answered. “We have nowhere to be tonight.”

The paper in Jade's hand fell to the ground, landing face-up. Willow never once looked at the list. Tonight, nothing mattered except she had a friend to ease the burden. Tonight was just for her. Tomorrow she could begin fighting once again.

The Missing

Neil

Mary

Richard

Sabrina

Camile

Pete

Jessie

Dezi

Victoria

Ashlyn

Clairity

Nathan

Chapter Fifty-Eight

There were those moments in life that were meant to be spent with family and friends. Then, there were those which were meant... no, not just meant, but rather required to be spent alone. This was one of those times.

Memories of days past filled Willow's mind - visions of everything good that happened in all the years she lived. Pictures flashed, one on top of the other. Her subconscious became the frame for a rotating photo album of the moments that etched a permanent place in her psyche. The sequence settled on Jade's brilliant green eyes. It was said a person's soul was reflected in their eyes. The once cold and calculating impression found in Jade's had long since vanished, now holding a warmth and radiance. No one, not even the two of them, guessed they would become best of friends.

She let out the breath of air she was holding. Being friends with anyone never seemed to turn out well for the other person. The last thing she wanted was for someone else she cared for to end up hurt or worse.

A gusty breeze slammed the door shut behind her. Her teeth chattered - a side effect of shivering. The icy chill that had plagued the morning air for the past several days wasn't ready to give up its reign over the area just yet. Perhaps it was her mood that was causing the fluctuations in the weather. She hadn't considered it before now, but it was a possibility. When she first learnt about her weather-changing abilities, controlling them was anything but easy. It took a while for her to master not making it rain when she cried. These were more subtle weather anomalies, quite possibly attached to her deeper-rooted emotions.

She shook her head. There was no time to play psychiatrist inside her own mind. Whatever the cause, she was sure it would end when both Cornelius and Cornost were defeated - nothing else mattered until that goal was accomplished. Now, if she could only figure out how to do that.

As if hugging herself, she grabbed her sides. Goosebumps lined her arms under the wool sweater she had chosen to wear. The latest blast of cold air ripped through her carefully layered clothing with ease, as if scoffing at her attempt to neutralize Jack Frost's powers. She blew on her clasped hands, wishing she had remembered to wear gloves.

A large bird circled the skies, letting out a few warrior shrieks as it searched for prey. The moon was still in full view, even though the sun was slowly coming up over the horizon. A few early-morning risers, with coffee cups in hand, staggered down the sidewalks - still partly in dreams they weren't ready to let go of.

She smiled at the thought of coffee. It wasn't just a warm drink to her. It was a symbol of some of the happiest moments in her life. Zsiga's face appeared in a puddle in front of her.

"A cup of coffee will perk you right up," Zsiga's silhouette said. "You look like you need to stay on your feet. I just brewed a fresh pot. Would you like some?"

Hot coffee would have been perfect, but illusions were only illusions. Willow waved her hand through the image and it dissipated in rings of ripples. Her fingers rubbed together, chasing off the remnants of wetness. The guard hadn't actually been with her in Atlantis and he wasn't here now. She needed to focus and pay attention to her surroundings more. Everything was at stake, and not just for her.

There was no denying Pewterclaw was a beautiful place to live. Small boutique shops and cafes lined boardwalk-style sidewalks, helping residents and visitors whittle away the hours of the day. The large central park posted warnings around its perimeter to be mindful not to become lost in its vast space. It was, in every way, the perfect place for a young couple to start a family. However, it was also the one place Willow doubted she could ever call a home. Even after all was said and done - even if she was somehow victorious, there would always be those who blamed her. She knew that far too well. Kasper Deogole, the Director of Secrecy, was at the top of that list. The only reason she could walk around as freely as she was right now was because he was busy dealing with the situation in the camp.

Whatever it was that happened there, Willow couldn't afford to get mixed up in it... at least not yet. She would have to trust that other people could handle those problems. Leaving this morning without knowing whose names were written on the missing list was difficult, but necessary. There would be time to mourn the loss of some friends and celebrate the survival of others later. Of course, if she failed her task, there might not be any survivors.

You need to stop being so harsh on yourself, Kiera's thoughts rang out in Willow's mind. *Have faith in yourself.*

They had been with her for as long as she could remember and yet sometimes, she still forgot they could hear everything she was thinking. A half-chuckle escaped with her breath. If there was one thing she could count on, it was Aslo and Kiera remaining by her side to the very end. Loyalty... another form of love. She drew a blank as to where the felines' allegiance came from. What had she done to deserve their unyielding devotion?

There is no time to waste. I need to be harsh on myself because that is what the situation calls for. I would have my hands full with Cornelius alone. I'm not sure I can take on Cornost as well. I don't even know where to begin. Willow slid down the base of a young tree to the ground, pulling her knees into her chest to form a chin rest. The sides of her lips curled in the same angle as her vision stared... down.

"You look lost," a familiar voice said.

"Professor, what are you doing here?" Willow asked. She hadn't thought about her Alchemy and Potions teacher from Sleeping Sands since being forced to leave in such a hurry.

"Well," Finkle said, "I would have thought that to be obvious. Once they shut down the school, where else would I go?" Loud cracking noises emanated from his back and knees as he lowered himself to a sitting position beside her. He winced, wrinkling up his face.

Willow's hand brushed across the grass. Her fingertips danced, responding to the different sensations they felt. It was soft, prickly, thick and thin. So many different feelings, much like her own emotions. It relaxed her - made her think clearly. "Did you always know who I was?" she asked, realizing her old teacher only knew her as a boy.

"No," Finkle answered. "Not at all. I had my suspicions when the redheaded girl appeared that one night. It wasn't until they removed the stained glass windows that I knew for sure. I should have seen it sooner. The whole thing had Cassandrhea's signature all over it. She's a sly one."

"I'm sorry," Willow answered. "I know how much you loved the windows. If it's any consolation, I don't think they led anywhere - at least nowhere you would want to go."

"No worries, child," he responded. "No worries at all. I do think you are right, though. Those windows weren't what I was looking for... nor did they even lead in the right direction. But never mind that. I believe you have something you need to find."

"How do you know that?" Willow asked. He shouldn't have known anything about her search for the missing great trees. In fact, only the elves actually knew about the trees.

"I have my ways," Finkle answered. "How I know isn't important. What is important is that I may be able to direct you to where you need to be."

A cool breeze found its way to Willow's face. She lost count of the number of times the familiar goosebumps had formed on her arms that morning. The tiny hairs at the base of each stood up, as if silently screaming a message of caution. The guardians fell silent. This was her decision to make - to trust this man, whom she never fully trusted before, or follow her instincts and run far away from there. The problem was, if she ran, where would she go? Finkle knew something. She had exhausted all her other resources and no one else appeared to have any information. She took in a large breath of air and exhaled it slowly.

"Do you know exactly where I need to go?" she asked, tilting her head to meet his gaze.

"I believe I do," he answered. A glimmer of danger danced in his eyes as one side of his mouth curled upwards. No other words followed.

"And you will tell me?" Willow asked. The idea of having to pry the information from her former teacher wasn't one that she relished. Every inch of her already knew he was up to something. The question was what.

"Of course," he answered. "Actually, I already have." He paused for a moment, relishing in her confusion. "Remember when I told you there were other organizations... ones that don't necessarily see eye-to-eye with our hidden magical world?"

"Yes," Willow answered. "Well... one. Are there more?"

"Well, of course there are more than just one," Finkle said, an edgy tone lingering in his voice. The part-smile his face previously donned vanished, leaving behind a stern scowl. "As long as there are people, they will form organizations for just about everything. But that is neither here nor there. I am actually referring to the one we discussed during the school year."

"The one that collects magical things to keep them from being used?" Willow asked.

"Yes," Finkle answered. "Aren't you looking for a few magical things?" He attempted a couple of winks, which looked more like the wind blew dust in his eye.

Willow jumped to her feet. “Do you think that's where they are?” she asked.

“I think... if I didn't have anywhere else to look, it would be a good place to start,” he replied, using the base of the tree as leverage to regain a standing position. His bones cracked louder than when he sat down. For a moment, his body remained crooked. He let out a yelp as his back snapped into a vertical position.

“Didn't you say they don't like us?” Willow asked, ignoring the man's muttering of complaints about his growing list of aches and pains. “From what I gathered from our previous conversation, I doubt they will let me wander in and use magic.”

“It's true their purpose is to keep magical artifacts from the hands of those who can use them,” Finkle said, brushing the dirt he could reach off his backside. “However, I believe this is a special case... shall we say. I am sure they are well aware of the events of late and are monitoring the same situation everyone else is. They don't want the world to end any more than you or I.”

“I see your point,” Willow said. There was still something not quite right about this conversation. It was as if the voice of a guardian was nagging at her, but they were silent. “I don't know how to find them.” she admitted, rubbing the crease between her eyebrows with two fingers, as if she hoped that would make it go away.

“But I do,” Finkle stated.

“And you'll take me there?” Willow asked.

“I can tell you the way, but I cannot accompany you,” he answered. “It's a trip you alone must make.”

“What's the catch?” she blurted out. She had learnt enough about the man from his desire to solve the puzzle during the school year to know there was something in the equation for him.

“Catch?” Finkle asked. Clouds moving across the sky blocked the sun's rays, casting a shadow across his face, at the same moment a crooked smile resurfaced. “You always were very bright... much more advanced than the others in your class. There is something I want you to do for me. I need some information about a certain magical object that I have been studying for years. I don't believe The Organization has it, but I do think they know where it is. All I need is for you to try to find out. It's nothing illegal."

"And what is this object?" Willow asked, one eyebrow arching higher than the other.

"A pearl," Finkle answered. "It's called the Pearl of Diplomacy."

"Why do you want to know where it is?" A tingling sensation ran up her spine, leaving a lump in her throat.

"My dear child," Finkle started, "finding this item could verify my life's work once and for all. It would validate everything I have struggled to prove over the years. My body is ageing. I don't have a lot of years left to finish."

"What does it do?" she asked. If The Organization truly collected magical items that they didn't want to fall into the wrong hands, she knew the pearl must have a specific use.

"No one knows for sure," Finkle answered. "It's a key of some sort... to another time or place, perhaps. My peers have scoffed at me for years about its existence. I need to know for sure and my trails have run cold. It isn't anything sinister, I assure you. I help you and you help me."

"You want to make a bargain?" Willow asked. "You do realize that if the world ends, you will too."

"Oh yes," Finkle said, winking. "My natural time is almost up anyways. I don't mind going a bit early. These aches and pains are becoming tiresome. The choice is yours. Of course, I will need your word you will honour our deal."

Choice, she thought. What choice was there? He was her only lead. She extended her hand to meet his, sealing their agreement. At that moment, she wondered who exactly she had made a bargain with.

Chapter Fifty-Nine

"Will someone please tell me what is going on?!" William screamed. Sitting in the command centre, while people he didn't know ran about the camp, wasn't something he was used to. Since he first entered this world, the duties of being the one in charge rested firmly on his shoulders. Now, for some reason, leadership was in the hands of a stranger.

"Relax," Malarchy said in his usual collected demeanour. "You've just regained your memories. We don't want to overwhelm anyone until we are sure the serum has taken full effect."

"What serum?" William bellowed back. "And who are all these people?"

"I am going out there," Diana announced. A few short steps was all it took before Faramund directed her back towards her seat at the table.

"We can't let you do that," Malarchy said. "It's for your own safety. Please try to relax."

“My own safety?” Diana said as a question, although she really hadn't expected anyone to answer. “Where is my grandson? Why isn't he in here with us?”

“I know this is hard for all of you, but you have to trust us,” Malarchy replied. One of his fingers tapped on a few loose papers strewn on the table.

“Where is my grandson?!” Diana yelled.

“We don't know!” Malarchy hollered back, his fingers now rubbing his temple, preparing for the worst. “Everything possible is being done to find those who are missing.”

“Missing?!” William yelled, slamming his chair against the side of the table. “Are you telling me that anyone not in this room is missing?”

“Yes,” Malarchy answered. The skin between his brows creased under the weight of William's stare. The veil of illusion fell. His face dropped into his hands - the names on the list a burden too great for him to bear any longer. Even the strongest of characters had a breaking point. This... at that exact moment... was his. Everyone in the room heard the crack that broke his resolve, bleeding into tears.

“So why aren't we out there helping to find them?” William shouted at the top of his voice, red taking over his normally white face. A part of him regretted pushing the man further into the depths of depression, knowing ailments of the mind were not as easy as those that were physical to recover from. There were no bandages that could cover what was only felt.

“Because you are still recovering,” Malarchy answered, his usual calm nature diminished by the sudden wave of sadness. “You would do little good out there without knowledge of the events that have led up to now.”

“What about Willow?” William asked, staring at the table. “Don't we owe it to her to at least try to find her? Didn't she save your life too?”

“Willow is fine,” Malarchy replied, wiping his reddened eyes with a handkerchief. “She is with Jade in Pewterclaw.”

"She isn't safe there. Assassins attacked us on the bridge." The table vibrated from the weight of the palms of his hands pounding down.

"Is that the last thing you remember?" Malarchy asked as if the sadness was now no more than a mere a memory.

"What do you mean?" William replied.

"How did you defeat the assassins? How did you return to the camp?" The mayor's eyes squinted in anticipation.

William sat down again. The answers to those questions eluded him. His face fell into his hands. The rhythm of his breath held an uneasy shakiness - a sound few had heard before. Diana's constant sobbing became deafeningly loud in his thoughts. The weight of her sadness pressed down on his shoulders like a falling boulder on a coyote in an old cartoon he once watched. "Please," he begged. "Tell us what happened."

"Are you sure you are ready?" Malarchy asked. "The things I am going to say will not be easy to hear. If anyone would rather stay in the dark, now is the time to speak up."

"He's right," Zsiga interrupted. Steam rose up from a freshly-poured cup of coffee sliding across the table. The mug stopped directly under William's nose. "It isn't easy to hear. I have already been filled in." He forced a smile, hoping to install confidence or even courage in his friends. "The coffee is fresh, so help yourselves. I am going to see if I can be of use in the search."

"Thank you," William muttered, staring at the cream still swirling as the dark brown liquid assimilated it. "Malarchy, can you start at the beginning?"

"Of course," the mayor answered. "The beginning for you is before that of the others. The reason you cannot remember anything after the attack on the bridge is because you were seriously injured in the fight. I'm not going to go into details, someone can fill you in later. The bottom line is, you were infected with a rare and deadly venom that nearly cost you your life and resulted in a coma. By the time you woke, the other events in the camp were already well underway. There was no possible chance you could have avoided that which was next to occur."

Malarchy's voice remained steady in his usual flat and unemotional tone. Signs of the moment of weakness experienced earlier were all but forgotten. He recounted the events that brought them to where they now sat, ending the tale with a loud sigh. Details of Lara and Hilary having a spider side were purposefully left out of the conversation, as well as why the others were missing. That was a horror even he wasn't sure could be calmly explained to them. Everyone had fears, reverting to a babbling fool was his. How did one tell someone they sat by and let loved ones be taken away and possibly eaten without lifting a finger to save them?

"You are leaving something out," William said, breaking the silence. He didn't need Clairity's abilities to sense the mayor's sigh was based more on apprehension than anything else.

"Yes," Malarchy admitted. His lips pressed tightly against each other as if trying to hold words from escaping. "I don't know how to say the rest."

"Is it that bad?" Sarah asked, speaking for the first time since the meeting began. Her voice quivered slightly, getting stuck on the words her mouth so desperately wanted to form. She placed her hand on her shoulder - trying to massage away the tension that filled her mind.

"It is," Faramund answered. His hand gently caressed hers.

"Yes," Malarchy added. "Worse than anyone could imagine." A rough sound escaped from his throat where a lump formed. He coughed before speaking again. "William, you publicly announced your relationship with Lara... a relationship that included the Pledge." He paused for a moment. "Both Hilary and Lara used their illusion magic to hide their true identities. They were, in fact, both part Achaear."

"Spiders?" Sarah screamed.

A dull expression covered William's face. His eyes stared off into a place no one else could see. "You are telling me that I married a spider... of my own free will?" The calmness in his voice caused the opposite reaction in everyone else.

"Not actually married," Malarchy explained, taking a seat at the table. "The whole relationship was an intricately woven illusion. She created a world in which you all lived. Your memories were replaced with what she wanted you all to see. There was nothing any of you could have done. Her powers of illusion were beyond reason. That, coupled with the memory-altering potion Cornelius dreamed up... well, let's just say the camp was at her mercy. Unfortunately, mercy I don't believe was part of her vocabulary."

"The others," William said, interrupting the mayor.

Malarchy sighed. "We don't know," he answered after weighing his options.

"The others," William repeated, slightly louder. His knuckles turned white under the pressure of the fists they formed.

"Her race feeds off of the life essences of other beings. I'm sure you realize she needed to feed at some point. We believe the others were taken somewhere for that purpose."

"They're dead?!" Diana shrieked.

"Not necessarily," Malarchy answered. "Iskander and I were cocooned for some time by Hilary. Willow found and saved us from an untimely fate. The same could be true for most of our friends. We have to be optimistic."

"Well, now we know," William muttered. "Let's go help look." He turned his head to meet Malarchy's gaze head on.

A shiver ran up and down the mayor's spine. There was something dead in William's stare - something unnerving. He doubted the information that was left would help. "There's more," he said, gulping back saliva. He wasn't used to his composure being affected by anything. Today was proving to be one of the most difficult days of his life, comparable only to the day his wife Nebulah was murdered.

"More?" Sarah asked. "What more could there be?"

"We don't know if there are possible egg sacks in the same location. Hilary had numerous younglings hatching when we found them. There is little any of us can do to fight them. We need to leave it to the specialists."

“Egg sacks,” William said. “Are you telling me I mated with a spider and my children are threatening to eat the rest of the camp?”

Malarchy sighed. “I never thought of it in those terms, but you are correct. I went through the same thing with Hilary while I was cocooned. You are lucky you don't remember the whole process. It is, and always will be, vividly etched in my mind.”

William let out a hefty laugh. “But I wasn't cocooned or forced... was I? I wilfully engaged in...” His words faded. Terror filled his eyes - a look seen in far too many men who crossed paths with these creatures. His skin transformed into the grey-green colour of a person suffocating. There was barely enough time to grab the garbage pail before vomit projected from his mouth.

“I'm sorry,” Malarchy said. “I know this is hard to hear. You need to take some time. We don't know the exact details and probably never will. You may not have been involved. She may have used other cocooned men to father her offspring.”

“Time!” Diana exclaimed. “Does my grandson have time?”

“Even if you go out there,” Iskander said, “even if you find the spot... if there are others already hatched, you will be no match for them. Only two people we know have been able to destroy them. Willow and Miss Kelly, an elemental master and instructor from Sleeping Sands.”

“Why isn't Willow here?” Diana snapped. “This is all her fault. If she wasn't born, we'd all be fine right now. That girl is a menace.”

“Those are Lara's words,” Faramund said, his arms folding across his chest. He squared his stance to her. “Perhaps the antidote hasn't taken full effect yet.”

“Those are my words!” Diana cried, her face distorting from hate. “I can remember feeling them when she left for school... before Lara. Everyone she meets ends up hurt. She could at least have the decency to clean up her mess.”

“She didn't send Lara here, Hilary did,” Malarchy interrupted.

“If Hilary did, it was only to isolate Willow,” Diana exclaimed. “Don't tell me you don't see the connection. People are getting hurt because of that girl.”

“Emotions are running a bit high at the moment. Let's not forget the reason we are here at all is because of Willow,” Malarchy said, a tinge of red creeping into his face.

The door swung open. “We've located a cave,” Aaram huffed, running in with Lane following. He stopped abruptly, his eyes meeting his wife's. “Diana, my love.”

“How is this possible?” she cried, rushing into his arms. “I have dreamt of the day when we would be together again.”

“Aaram and Lane were rescued from Atlantis,” Malarchy said. “Rescued, I might add, by Willow, the girl you were just blaming for this situation.”

“Blaming?” Lane said. “That poor girl has gone through so much to help everyone. How could you believe her to be responsible for this?”

“I'm sorry,” Diana said. “Of course, you are right. I'm just stressed from the worry. I don't know what I'd do if Nathan didn't make it.” A shaky smile formed on her face for a split second.

Malarchy wasn't sure if it was worry or hate that caused the trembling. Regardless, he knew there was more hidden beneath that smile. He thought back to his earlier break in reality. Diana was close to a meltdown of her own. The question was, how long would it be until they heard the final crack? He winced at the thought, knowing depression wasn't the only mental problem that a person can end up with if pushed the wrong way when already under duress.

“The camp has been cleared as well,” Aaram said, breaking the mayor's train of thoughts - a welcome distraction.

“Wonderful news,” Malarchy said, a slight upward curl forming at the corner of his lips. The clapping noise of his two hands meeting each other gained the attention of most of the room. “Iskander and Faramund will escort each of you to your quarters. I must ask you to remain there until we have definite answers.”

Faramund gestured for William to accompany him. The guard remained silent until they approached the door to his cabin. “You haven't been in here since before that night in Pewterclaw,” he said. “When you woke up in the hospital, Lara had already decked out another cabin. You moved in there with her. I am not sure why. Everything in your room will be exactly as you remember it.” He bowed.

William closed his eyes. The door handle felt cool and smooth, easily turning under the pressure of his grasp. Familiar scents mixed with dust and stale air filled his senses. He inhaled deeply. A faint Willow smell, sent memories and emotions surging through his body. How could he have turned his back on her like that? How could he ever face her again? Then a new feeling took over - a rage boiled the blood flowing through his veins. How could she have believed he would do that to her? Why hadn't she come to save him?

His fingers left a trail in dust that gathered, stopping at his chain necklace. The memory of gifting it to Willow to wear pulsed through his psyche. He continued the trail in a circle around where it sat abandoned on his desk. Had she abandoned him in the same manner as his chain? He pushed the thoughts from his mind. He needed a distraction from all of this before he drove himself insane in the same manner many of the camp had already. He scanned his bookshelf for something to read, his hand coming to rest on a book he already started. Pulling it out from the shelf, it fell open to a page that contained a piece of paper.

William,

If you are reading this, I couldn't be happier. I wish I had been there to see your eyes open again for the first time. School is about to start and I am most likely at Sleeping Sands. You know they said no contact in or out for the whole school year.

Problem is, I am having a hard time leaving. There was so much on that list we were going to talk about. So much I wanted to say and never made the time to say it. I keep thinking there must be something else I can do.

I guess what I want to say is I need you. Nothing feels right without you here. I look around and I think of you. I miss you more than I can express in words.

I love you.

Tears swelled in the corners of his eyes. It was his turn to feel exactly the same as she had when she wrote this letter.

Chapter Sixty

Professor Finkle left her alone, heading off to make the required arrangements for Willow to travel to The Organization's headquarters. She still wasn't sure she understood. Her old teacher already tried several times to explain that The Organization was actually the name of the organization - a rather silly name to use and awfully confusing. But then, who was she to judge, considering she came from a world without a name and a town that was called The Town? Her efforts to control a giggle failed miserably. The silliness going through her mind multiplied. At least it was a distraction from wandering the streets aimlessly for the next few hours.

A familiar laugh come from the patio of a cafe she walked by. Curiosity took control. She turned her head just enough that, even from under the hood of her sweatshirt, her gaze met two beautiful, deep-blue eyes. She gasped. Snapping her head back into a forward position, her pace quickened. *Maybe he didn't notice me*, she thought, disappearing down the first alley she came to.

“You!” Lance yelled, heading towards her.

Willow panicked. In the rush to leave the street, she hadn't noticed the alleyway she chose was a dead end. She was trapped. There was no choice but to face him. Her fingers fiddled around in a pocket, grasping a hold of one of the syringes she brought with her in case this moment arose.

His hand grabbed her shoulder tightly. “Who are you?” he asked, squeezing harder.

“Ow!” she cried. “That hurts.” She met the gaze she had come to know so well one more time, expecting to find anger and hate. A smile formed on her lips. The blue flames in his eyes danced with curiosity and nothing more.

“I'll ask again,” he said. “Who are you?”

“Willow,” she answered.

“Well, Willow, I'm...”

“Lance,” she said, cutting him off. “Prince Lance.”

“It appears I am at a disadvantage, as you appear to know me, but I don't have a clue who you are,” Lance said, a playful tone resonating in his words.

“You can let go now,” Willow said. If fear ever existed, it was gone. The familiar lilt of the prince's voice told her he was more amused with the situation than a threat.

“You are avoiding my question,” Lance stated. His hand dropped from her shoulder to hold her free hand. “I have no intentions of releasing you completely until I have some answers... answers I feel as if I should already know.”

“You do already know. You have just forgotten,” Willow said. “Or rather, your memories were overwritten by a potion.”

Lance laughed. “I doubt it would be possible to do such a thing to me. But if it were, please, do tell, who would have the audacity to do it?”

“Your father,” Willow blurted out.

Lance's expression mutated from curious to stern in less than a second. "My father," he said. "What sort of a farce are you trying to pull, girl?"

"I'm not pulling anything," Willow answered. She held out a couple of syringes and offered them to him. "You knew he planned to use the memory-altering potion on you and your brothers and sisters. You gave me samples in the hopes I would be able to find an antidote. In fact, you said I should inject you without explanation if we met and you didn't know me... in case you were given a new memory that might be violent towards me."

"Why would my father do such a thing? We are a close family."

"I don't know how close you are with your father. We never actually discussed those feelings before. I can tell you he wanted to control you better. His plan is domination of all the realms. He needs your abilities to achieve that goal. The problem is, in doing so, he could rip apart existence as we know it," Willow replied.

Lance's grip released. His hands both tightly held against his head. His eyes clenched tightly together. He winced, dropping to one knee.

"Don't try to fight it!" Willow shrieked. "You'll end up hurting yourself." She crouched down to a squat, putting her arms around him.

"Why should I believe you?" he asked without breaking her embrace.

"You don't have to," she whispered in his ear. "Take these." She placed ten syringes in his hand and pushed it away from her before standing. "Investigate for yourself. Just don't let your parents know you suspect anything. Keep those in case you decide to use them." Seeing her opportunity, she ran down the alley to the street.

"Wait!" Lance yelled, but she was already gone. He blinked, staring at the syringes lying in the palm of his hand. Could this strange girl be telling the truth? A voice inside told him to believe her every word. His head pounded. Shoving the syringes into his pocket, he made his way back to the cafe.

Chapter Sixty-One

"Brother," Joseph said, slapping him on the back. "We've been looking for you. Where did you run off to?"

"I thought I saw someone I knew," Lance replied. "Is it time to head back already?"

"It is," Zoe squealed, linking her arm in his. "You look a little off. Are you okay?"

"Fine," Lance answered, flashing a pearly white, toothy grin. If there was one thing his family was always good at, it was charm. He could put on a fake smile and make anyone, even his sister, believe he was happy.

"Good," Zoe said, not giving her previous questions another thought. "The portal is already opened. We were to be back early for dinner." She released his arm, taking the lead.

The gateway back to their home world was only a few alleys away. Lance stepped through, his pace showing no hesitation. "I'm going to wash up before greeting Mother and Father," he said. "I'll meet you back at the dining room." He watched his siblings disappear from the corridor before changing his direction. There were answers he needed and they couldn't wait.

***

The smooth metal doors of the main lab swung open with a single push - the force strong enough to cause a bang against the wall.

Small bits of glass clashed together, combining with the vibrations of a silver tray settling on the stone floor - resulting in an almost musical sound.

“S-s-s-sir,” a man in a white lab coat stuttered.

Lance paused for a moment. Thoughts of his own parents directing a weapon of control at him swirled in his mind, overtaking any reason he had left. He lunged forward at the scientist, pinning him to a wall by his neck with one hand. “Did my Father have you make a memory-altering potion?” he demanded.

“S-s-s-sir,” the man repeated.

Lance's hand squeezed tighter around the scientist's throat. “Did my Father have you make a memory-altering potion?” he asked again.

“Ye-ye-ye-s,” the man sputtered, his face turning a reddish-purple colour. Bubbles of saliva escaped from the corners of his mouth, trickling down like foam.

“Did he use it on me?” Lance asked, keeping his grasp firm. His nostrils flared every time he exhaled in the unusual deep breathing pattern his anger adopted.

“Ye-ye-ye-s,” the man spit out.

Lance huffed. “Is there an anti-potion?”

“I-I-I can't br-r-reathe,” the scientist muttered.

Lance released his grip on the man, keeping him pinned against the wall. “Is there an antidote?” he asked calmly.

“Y-y-y-our fath-e-e-er di-di-didn't want one,” the man replied. “Even if he d-d-did, I d-d-don't think it w-w-would help.”

Lance growled. "Why's that? And try not to stutter. It's beginning to annoy me."

"Y-y-ou were g-g-g-iven two d-d-oses," the man replied.

Lance laughed - the blue flames dancing wildly in his eyes. His rage exploded like a detonated bomb, the necrid flames exerting their control. As if on instinct, his hand tightened around the man's neck, refusing to release until every ounce of life finished draining from the man's body. He let go, admiring his work as the scientist's body fell to the ground, slumping over in a pile. He picked the dead man up over his shoulder like luggage to carry to the main hall.

"Lance," Cornelius called out. "What in the realms are you doing?"

Lance turned his attention to his father, the blue flames still swirling. "I ran into this fool on my way to my room. His stuttering annoyed me, so I took care of it." The body made a thud as it hit the floor.

"I see," Cornelius replied, oblivious to his son's condition. "I thought I already killed him for that. Oh well, guess he's dead now. Good job." He patted Lance on the back. "It's almost time for dinner."

"Yes," Lance said. "Under the circumstances, it might be best if I washed up first."

"Of course," the king agreed. "That would be a good choice. Don't worry about this mess. The guards can clean it up. See you in a bit." Cornelius disappeared into the living area of the castle.

He had no memories of the walk to his room or undressing. Lance found himself sitting on his bed, fresh out of the shower, only managing to half-dress - the rest of his clothes beside him, neatly laid out in a pile. Every piece was exactly the same as the outfit he wore earlier, which now resided in a garbage container. Being a prince in this world meant never wearing anything more than once before throwing it away.

He chuckled. That mentality summed up every aspect of his life in one word, disposable: his clothes were; the staff was; the guards were; and he was. The jacket hanging out one side of the trash caught his attention. Curiosity demanded investigation. He found the syringes still safely hidden in the inside pocket. Treating them as if they were the most precious cargo in existence, he placed all ten on top of his dresser.

"Who am I?" he asked the image staring back at him in the mirror. There was no answer. He took in a deep breath and released it again, stabbing himself in the arm with one syringe. Looking directly into his own eyes, he asked one more time, "Who am I?" His reflection remained silent. His eyes clenched tight.

Two fists pounded down on the dresser, the force shaking the mirror until it turned crooked on the wall. The thought of being lost forever - a mere puppet to the will of someone else, made him feel sick. He was meant to rule. His brothers and sisters were meant to rule. They weren't meant to take orders from anyone. That included his father.

Lance opened the top drawer and brushed the syringes in, pausing at the last one. His hand gripped around it like a pen. Stumbling backwards, the backs of his legs hit the edge of the bed. He tumbled to a sitting position, still staring at the contents of his hand. If he was given two doses of the memory-altering potion, then perhaps two doses of the antidote would change him back.

The sharp tip of the needle plunged into his skin, diving into the largest visible vein. A rush of heat flowed through his body. His vision glazed over, beginning to blur, then darkness fell upon him.

Chapter Sixty-Two

Willow spent hours walking around Pewterclaw, waiting for her old potions teacher. Waiting made her anxious. Nothing to do translated into time to worry. Worry was an opportunity for her mind to make up new things to worry about - things that probably hadn't deserved the attention. There was already something in the air that made her nervous. The temperatures were fluctuating far too much. Rather than blaming herself, she settled on the believing the weather anomalies to be a side effect of Atlantis trying to rise.

The trees are struggling, Aslo said telepathically. *Something is draining their magic.*

Draining? Willow thought.

Yes, Aslo replied. *It's as if someone or something is tapping into their manna and syphoning some off. At this rate, they won't be able to hold the effects of the rising in check for long.*

Any ideas what is causing it? Willow asked.

None, Aslo answered. *There doesn't appear to be any reason for their power loss. Unless, of course, unicorns have found their way into the mainland.*

Is that really possible? Willow asked. *Could they be here without anyone noticing?*

What do you think? Aslo responded.

I think we need a plan to deal with some unicorns on top of everything else, she answered. *That won't be an easy task.*

I agree. If they can, in fact, release stored magic from their horns in a single beam, Aslo theorized, *and they were positioned correctly, the blasts could help Atlantis make a clean break. It would be something similar to what Neil did when Cornelius invaded our world. He stretched the fabric of space enough for them to punch a hole the right size for their army to pass through. Atlantis would only need a few moments to enter this world.*

In theory then, if we take out the unicorns, we damage their plans, Willow said.

In theory, yes, Aslo responded. *I am sure they have back-up plans as well, though.*

"Willow," Finkle said, grabbing her arm. "This way." He ushered her down an alley to a door leading into the Department of Secrecy.

"Have you gone mad? I can't go in there!" Willow shrieked. "Who knows what Kasper Deogole will do to me if he catches me?"

"Then be quiet," Finkle demanded. "Kasper isn't around. Neither is anyone else, for that matter. Everyone is busy cleaning up the mess at your camp. Even guards are on a skeleton crew rotation. We just have to be as silent as possible."

"Why do we have to go in here at all?" Willow whispered.

"Because, my dear," Finkle answered. "They have the only working teleportation portal between magical cities that I know of."

"They have what?" Willow asked, her nose crinkling up.

"A doorway that leads from one city to another," Finkle explained. "Not to mention, one that takes us to within walking distance of The Organization."

"Somehow, this sounds a little too easy," Willow uttered. "There must be a catch."

"Yes," Finkle agreed. "A rather large one. If we aren't caught on this side, we still have to find our way out on the other."

Willow's footsteps matched the professor's exactly, using only the tips of her toes. She planted each step meticulously, as if avoiding stepping on a landmine. Other than a single walking patrol, which was easy to hide from, there weren't any problems making it to the portal.

"Professor," Willow said, staring at a circular platform lit up by sparkles, "what about the guards on the other side? Are they all helping at the camp too?"

"A good question, my child." Finkle replied. "One I am afraid I don't have an answer to." He grabbed her arm, pushing her onto the platform. "No time like the present to explore the possibilities."

Stars flashed in her eyes, reminding her of a laser show she once saw Nathan watching. This one, however, was interactive. Her body tilted from side to side, then upside down, without moving a muscle. The motion came to an abrupt stop. She lunged forward, gagging from the sensation.

"Ah," Finkle said. "We made it."

"Was there ever any doubt?" Willow asked, still gasping for air, colour slowly returning to her face.

"Well," Finkle said, "it hadn't actually been tested yet. But seems to work just fine, if you ask me. Shall we move before we are found?"

Both of Willow's eyebrows lifted, forcing wrinkles to appear on her forehead. The realization she had just been a guinea pig for one of Deogole's projects astounded her. Her imagination shuffled scenes, showing how pleased the Director would have been, if she somehow ended up mangled during teleportation. The feel of

Finkle's grasp on her arm, tugging her along behind him like a rag doll, snapped her back to reality.

"Hurry now," he ordered. "We want to get out of town as quickly as possible. Especially before someone recognizes you. Did I mention Klurg and Klurr are prominent residents here?"

"No, Professor," she answered. "I believe you left that part out."

"Oh well," he said, picking up the pace to a jog. "They are. Best save our breath for running. You may want to keep your wand out... just in case."

Running was exactly what they did. Still, by the time they reached the second intersection, they were being pursued. The sound of Finkle's breathing deepened with every moment that passed. They rounded a corner, passing through the city gates. Seconds later, the professor pulled her off the road, into a forest.

"I believe you can help us disappear." Finkle said, his hand waving in a circle, motioning for her to speed things up. He glanced over his shoulder towards the road.

Willow knew what he meant. The trees bowed to her request, forming stairs with their branches. She climbed to the top, the professor following. Her breath laboured from the run, but not as heavily as the professor's. He collapsed into a heap with one hand held over his chest - his face a solid crimson colour, droplets of sweat beading down the sides.

"Phew," he said. "I'm too old for this."

"Are you alright, Professor?" Willow asked. Her pulse and breathing already returning to normal. Her old teacher, however, still appeared to be in all sorts of pain.

"I will be," Finkle answered. "Getting old isn't much fun. Look over the edge to the left. Do you see the town?"

"Yes," Willow replied. There wasn't much to look at other than a stone fountain where all the lane-ways met in the middle. "Is that where The Organization is?"

"Goodness no," Finkle said, holding his side. "That's where I'll be waiting for you."

"You really aren't coming with me?" Willow asked.

"No, my dear," he said. "They might not let you in if you aren't alone."

"So where is this place?" Willow asked, a frown creasing her face. This trip was becoming a bad idea faster than she cared to admit. Luckily, Aslo was there to remind her.

Finkle extended his finger. "Do you see those mountains?"

"Yes," Willow replied. They were hard to miss, considering the white covered peaks took up most of the view from where they sat perched above the trees.

"Head to the base and look for a cobblestone trail that winds upwards. Follow it. The Organization will find you," Finkle explained.

"That's it?" Willow asked. "Just follow the road and hope someone grabs me?"

"Yes," Finkle said, gulping back some form of liquid stored in a silver flask. "No one knows where their actual base of operations is. This is the only known way to contact them. Even this is hush-hush in most circles. It took a fair bit of detective work to get this far."

"Great," Willow mumbled just loud enough to be heard. At least part of the journey would be across the tree tops.

Below, the sounds of men frantically searching the forest drifted up to her ears. Willow sat motionless, staring off into space - waiting for the commotion to settle enough for the professor to climb back down.

It wasn't the trip ahead she was thinking of, nor was it her own safety. For the first time since hearing about the camp, it was the people she once called friends that consumed her thoughts. Were they okay? Who was on the list of the missing? What if they were all dead?

There was a selfish side to her feelings. She was about to be alone again. The help of friends was a luxury greatly missed. She shook her head. There was nothing she could do to help them and vice versa. There was no choice but to accept that there were some things she needed to rely on someone else to take care of. Similarly, there were some things she needed to rely on herself to be able to accomplish. Malarchy would do everything he could to save anyone in the camp. Her task was written in stone - cobblestone. She needed to find the remaining trees and deal with Cornost and Atlantis.

The colour drained from her face. Cornelius was still out there too. The king's silence wouldn't last forever - the calm before the storm. It wouldn't be long before he tossed his presence into the mix. No amount of planning would help.

The guardians remained silent. There wasn't anything for them to say that hadn't already been said. Only time would tell how these events would play out.

Willow suddenly wished *The Portal Prophecies* was with her. How could she forget to bring it, or at least read the final prophecy? Maybe there was something that could have helped her.

She lay flat on her back, her gaze fixated on the sky. The stars twinkled above, each cluster holding its own story. She had no idea what they were saying, but there was some message encrypted in their beauty. Her hand extended above her, one finger tracing the outline of pictures in the sky. There were patterns: the portal guard mark; a snake; a heart with an arrow pierced through it; a book opened at the middle, light flowing out; and a tree. She smiled, wondering if everyone saw the same patterns, or if they differed depending on the person gazing at them.

Finkle remained silent. The noises of men underneath ceased. It was time to take the next step in her journey.

Chapter Sixty-Three

Normally, Malarchy was a sound sleeper. Tonight, however, a booming voice outside his quarters made rest impossible. "Deogole!" he yelled.

"Malarchy, good man," Kasper replied. "What are you doing roaming about? I thought you were sleeping."

"I was," Malarchy muttered, rolling his eyes. He yawned.

"What was that?" Kasper asked. "Never mind. I'm glad you are here. We are removing cocoons from the cave."

Malarchy's face expressed sheer terror - the sort expected from a heroine in a poorly made B-movie horror flick. "Removing? Why aren't you opening them? People could still be alive."

"Yes," Kasper retorted. "I am aware of the urgency. We have to move them, I am afraid, and quickly. We found two connected rooms. One holds the cocoons presumably housing your camp mates, or rather what's left of them. The other is filled with egg sacks on the verge of hatching. So you see, moving the cocoons is the only choice. You'll find them all in the medical centre. Miss Kelly and Special Forces are attending to the other issue as we speak."

"Thank you," Malarchy said. "I'll head over there now."

"Yes - yes," Kasper said. "Oh, one more thing... after this mess is taken care of, we should discuss your future. I'm afraid your choice of help in this matter is somewhat questionable."

"Really?" Malarchy said, arching one eyebrow. "How's that?"

"I'm just concerned what fraternizing with vampires could do to your career," Kasper answered, shoving his hands in his pockets. His body teetered back and forth, alternating between putting pressure on the heels of his feet and the toes. "I don't need to tell you how important appearances are in our line of work."

"Perhaps it's time for a change, then," Malarchy retorted. "If you don't mind, I'd like to attend to the casualties."

"Of course. Of course," Kasper said, walking away, waving one hand over his head.

Malarchy shook his head. There were more important things to think about than starting a revolution in the magical community to accept all individuals, even vampires. There would be time to play politician, but not while there were people... friends, who could still be alive, suffocating under the weight of cocoons. Finding survivors was priority number one on his *to-do* list.

The lights flickered like bug zappers being invaded by multiple winged insects. Malarchy ransacked every drawer - the final one containing a sole flashlight. A lonely man stared back at him from the surface of a silver tray. He covered up the reflection with anti-venom shots and various other sharp medical instruments. If anyone was still alive, they would need to be treated immediately.

The images in the depths of his mind unleashed to his consciousness, reminding him of the horror he felt, frozen by the venom as his life force slowly drained away. He couldn't move or speak, but felt every last thing. Aware through the whole process, he could do little other than scream within the confines of his own mind for help. It almost shattered him. Then again, after the episode earlier, maybe it had. Minds have always been such fragile things. His heart wept for the survivors yet to be found. Most of these victims were still in their youth. Even if they clung to life, the distinct possibility remained that they could be mentally damaged beyond repair.

"Do you need some help?" Gavin asked.

Malarchy spun around. How ironic the one person here in the middle of the night offering to help was a vampire. This man proved more reliable than many he encountered since being forced to flee his home world. After this crisis ended, he would find a way to show people that vampires weren't as bad as they were made out to be.

"Yes," he answered. "Seems I am on my own here. I need to open all the cocoons and inject any survivors with the anti-venom. If you would like to start cutting into the husks, I'd be grateful. I don't need to remind you about time being of the essence."

Gavin had already begun opening the first cocoon before Malarchy finished speaking. The sticky substance surrounding the bodies of the victims attached itself to anything it came in contact with. Plunging one hand into webbing only proved to trap it, just as the smaller version trapped flies. He grabbed a knife from the sterile table. Hacking and slicing the cocoon created high-pitched vibrations most ears could never hear. "Do we know what this stuff is?" he asked.

"No," Malarchy admitted. "We should take a sample back to the lab for a closer look. We might find something we can use against these creatures."

"You mean there are more?" Gavin asked, still slashing at the first husk.

"I am sure there are." Malarchy added a second knife to the fibre-battle the vampire was losing. "If I am right, there are many more." His hand plunged inside the cuts, wiggling and twisting in every direction until finally, the first cocoon opened. He sighed. They were too late for this one. He barely recognized the doctor, Richard, from the remains that were left. "Nothing we can do here," he said.

The second cocoon proved consistent with the first. The doctor's assistant and spouse, Mary, would now be known as victim number two. Gavin's clothes became his personal towel - anything attached to his hands now displayed as a fashion statement. His neck stretched from side to side, relieving built up pressure with a series of popping noises.

“We knew they wouldn't all make it. Keep the faith, old man... someone must have survived.”

“Yes.” Malarchy agreed. He hadn't known the couple well, but for others in the camp, it was a different story. “William will take the loss of these two to heart. I am concerned with him blaming himself for all of this.” He stood, staring at the remains of the nurse whose help, in the past, was instrumental in saving lives. Perhaps, out of respect a part of him felt the need to mourn for her.

“This one has life signs!” Gavin exclaimed.

Thoughts went on the back burner. The second-born Shinning brother, Dezi, lay motionless in the open cocoon. His glazed-over eyes stared back, begging Malarchy to release him from fear's grasp. A needle plunged into the young man's arm, injecting him with the anti-venom before moving his body to a clean bed. The next two casings proved the same level of success. Dezi's triplet brothers, Jessie and Pete, were both still alive.

“These three don't seem to have any negative physical effects at all... except for the venom,” Gavin pointed out.

“Yes,” Malarchy agreed. “They are preserved well. Perhaps she didn't have a chance to feed on them yet. I gave them sedatives to allow them to sleep while we finish our work. They don't need any extra trauma on top of what they've already been through. I'm not sure how long it will take before they regain a normal conscious state. I suppose that is up to the strength of their individual psyches.”

“Good plan,” Gavin said. “We can dump the dead bodies before they come to. We have another one here.”

Malarchy glanced inside. He knew the boy it held. “Neil, the one who could bend reality... a most unusual talent. I hope he found it in his heart to forgive Jade before he passed.” The mayor blinked away any signs of emotion that might have existed before moving to another cocoon. He made short work of the thick webbing. Another syringe found its way into his grip, the tip diving in. “Ashlyn,” he explained. “She seems intact, for the most part.”

Gavin hadn't looked over, nor had he said a word. The contents of a cart clattered to the ground. As if in a trance, he slowly backed away from the cocoon he was working on, his eyes never left the spot in which it lay.

“Gavin, is there something wrong?” Colour drained from Malarchy's face as he approached the spot where the white encasement lay. “How could this happen?” he asked, backing up to stand beside the vampire. “Would you be so kind as to find Micca for me? He is the only medical staff we have left. I think we are going to need his help.”

Chapter Sixty-Four

The cobblestone path wasn't what could be described as hidden. It actually stuck out, being made of bright copper and red colours. Willow had assumed there would have been a certain level of difficulty, maybe even a few traps or riddles that needed to be answered before she could pass. What she found was actually a bit of a letdown. There was nothing to do but climb. Of course, the new surroundings kept her mind occupied, with scenery almost reminiscent of the elf realm's dragon valley. Lush vegetation grew in patches in an otherwise grey rocky terrain.

A shiny rock caught her attention, glittering a sheer black. Thin sheets flaked off in her grip, each one tinted and translucent, reminding her of the lenses in a pair of sunglasses. She peeked through to test her theory, gasping at how the world surrounding her instantly turned into a black and white portrait - an example of one of nature's tricks, a magic in its own right.

She always admired living things, but never took enough time to really appreciate the non-organic items that made up the realms in which she lived. The corners of her lips cured upwards, smiling at the rock before shoving it in her pocket - a silent promise made. If she survived this ordeal, it would be the first addition in a rock collection. She chuckled. Without realizing it, she had chosen her first hobby.

Her head whipped left, trying to catch a glimpse of whatever was making rustling noises in the few bushes running parallel to the path. Curiosity always won her attention over vigilance. She pushed Aslo's voice issuing words of caution to the back of her mind. That word, *caution*, held little meaning, at least until her tasks were completed. Being out of time created the need to take some risks. Her hand swatted at branches. Whatever was hiding beneath them couldn't have gone far. She reached in deeper, hoping to make a visual path to the ground. The bush revealed no secrets.

She yelped, feeling a sharp prick on her finger as it came in contact with a thorn. She examined her hand, watching a drop of red blood trickle down the length of her finger to her palm, leaving a wet trail from where it came. She squinted, her focus hazed. There was something churning in the pit of her stomach - a sick feeling - one she knew from experience meant something was wrong. This altered awareness was one she experienced far too often of late. Her heart raced, every so often skipping a beat. The plant was a trap. Was it poison or a drug? Panic set in. *Aslo, Kiera*, she thought. *Run. You need to get away.* She felt her legs buckle beneath her as she crashed to the ground, unaware if her warning reached the guardians in time. The world swirled in circles before going completely black. Silence.

Chapter Sixty-Five

Willow was still a bit dizzy when her eyes opened. She squinted, trying to focus on details in the unfamiliar yet pleasant room. A large bed covered in fine silk sheets cushioned her body's aches and pains in the right places. There was no doubt she picked up a few new bruises when she fell. Her gaze rested on one of the beautiful paintings, framed in gold, that adorned the walls. She blinked a couple of times - positive the young girl in it moved. Whatever was on that thorn, it was strong. Continuing her surveillance of the room, she noticed it was filled with fine works of art. One round table sat in a corner, a golden pitcher with pink roses resting directly in the centre of its surface. She sat up.

"Good morning," a woman said, sitting in a chair beside her.

Had she been there the whole time? "Good morning," Willow muttered, still not sure how she missed the woman when she first opened her eyes.

"So you are the famous Willow," she said. "I am Lucinda."

"Where am I?" Willow asked. "Why have you brought me here?"

"Where do you think you are?" Lucinda snapped back. "You were the one looking for us."

"Is this The Organization?" Willow asked.

"Officially, I can neither confirm nor deny that," Lucinda answered. "But unofficially, I can show you around. Should you find what you are looking for along the way, all the better." The woman smiled without opening her mouth.

Willow returned the gesture with a forced smile of her own. "Thank you," she said. There was something oddly familiar about the way she felt in the presence of this woman. An uneasiness balled in her throat. Her hands wrapped around her waist. Queasy was the word of the day.

The hallways were decorated in much the same manner as the room had been. Some of the finest art in existence lined the walls, with the occasional table thrown in here or there, acting as a pedestal to a sculpture or piece of pottery. From their appearances, they were all rare. She winced at the thought of a clumsy accident breaking one. That could prove too expensive for her nonexistent wallet. A large arched doorway framed in a decorative floral moulding marked the end of the corridor.

Do you hear that? Aslo asked.

Willow's time had wasted away taking in so much of the ornamental surroundings. Visual overload left little room for the processing of her other senses. A clicking noise in the background had gone unnoticed. Realizing the mistake, she paused to listen. Whatever the cause, Lucinda seemed to be the point of origin, more specifically from the underside her dress.

Her vision rested on the woman's outfit. How could she have not noticed it before? It was an old-fashioned dress, much like the ones William showed her at Halloween. This particular ensemble was a crimson-red colour with black lace trim and a large, puffy butt. She coughed back a giggle, amused by the sight of the woman's extended rump.

“Are you alright?” Lucinda asked.

“Yes, fine,” Willow answered. “Just a tickle in my throat.”

She wasn't sure what the noise was, but she was positive that this woman, if she was from The Organization, was not born of this world.

“I think you might find what you are looking for in here,” Lucinda said, gesturing towards the open arch. She moved to one side of the corridor, allowing easy access past.

Willow shuffled by, forcing her best smile. She gasped at the sights that awaited her. She knew some of the exotic plants were from this world and others from places she had never visited before. Even having never seen most of them before, she still somehow knew each and every one. Reaching out, she let her fingers run across the rubber surface of one giant leaf.

“How did you manage to collect all of these?” she asked.

“The Organization has its ways,” Lucinda answered, still standing outside the doorway. “We keep them safe for a reason. I am not able to disclose anything further.”

The base for the entire room was made out of a system of roots that led to two large trees intertwined with one another. Both looked as if they were petrified fossils of a time long past. Her palms felt the base of each tree. Closing her eyes, she concentrated, first on the rhythm of her heartbeat and then the sound of her breathing. The two intertwined into one steady pattern. Before long, she could feel the same wave-like sensations in both trees. The tempo quickened, strengthening. Her whole body pulsed up and down in time to an almost musical beat. Her eyes opened to the realization that she was in fact moving. The root beneath her was responding to the motions in its own way. The two trees woke from their long slumber.

“Hello, I am Willow,” she said.

“Hello, little one,” the tree on her left said.

“We are the trees of knowledge and power,” the right tree said. “Bound to each other throughout eternity. For with knowledge comes power and with power comes knowledge. The two are inseparable... as are we."

"You say your name is Willow," the left tree said. "Yet you look like another."

"Yes," Willow answered. "Lilybelle - I know the story." The thought of explaining to them Gavin's theory of reincarnation crossed her mind, but with Lucinda and whoever else was listening in lurking about, she decided it could wait for a better opportunity. "Which one of you is knowledge and which is power?"

The tree to her right swung down directly in front of her in one swift motion - its branches coming within an inch of her face. "It doesn't matter which is which, child. We are as we are. You may call us Sapientiza. One name is all we need."

"But you are two of the great trees?" Willow asked. If they were two, she need only find one more, but if they were collectively only one, then she still needed to find two.

"We are two," The right tree said, swinging back into place.

"And we are one," The left tree said.

"Glad we cleared that up," Willow muttered. "Can you help the others?"

"Yes," the right tree said.

"We can feel their struggle," the left tree said. "We don't know who you are, little one. We aren't as easy to fool as our brothers and sisters."

"But we will help them," the right tree said. "If you are who you seem to be, you have another tree left to call forth from slumber."

"Why do you not call forth the tree of life?" the right tree questioned.

"Do you know where I can find it?" Willow asked, her head whipping back and forth between the tops of the two trees, not knowing which, if either, to face.

"Find it?" The left tree said. "You should know how to find it and awaken it from its slumber. Perhaps you are not the one we thought you to be. If you are not, hope is lost. If you are, you need to do what you are meant to do."

"Why riddles?!" Willow screamed. "Can't there be a straight answer? I don't want to read between lines or look for the possibilities."

"Sometimes things are only meant to be understood by those who can understand what is being said," the right tree explained.

"We leave you here, Willow. We caution you to be swift. The six of us will not last with our power being drained," the left tree said.

A sprinkling of gold dust shimmered over the trees as they disappeared before her eyes. Willow felt the ground beneath her shift. She screamed, racing for the door. As the trees vanished, so did the roots she stood on. She lunged at the doorway, hearing the rest of the contents of the room crash to a lower level behind her. Looking over her shoulder, all that remained was a gaping hole.

"Well, that was interesting," Lucinda said, standing over Willow. "Are you okay?"

Even with pain surging through every inch of her body, Willow couldn't help wondering if the woman always carried a parasol. The sheer beauty of the shade umbrella demanded attention - yet, somehow this was her first time seeing it. There was more to Lucinda than she let on. An omen, perhaps that the woman hid parts of herself in plain sight.

"I'm okay," she muttered, wincing a little at a pain in her side. "Are there any other trees here?" she asked.

"I'm afraid not," Lucinda answered.

Willow's eyes never left the woman's parasol. The reds and blacks swirled around as she twirled it above her head. Her vision fixated on black spots, appearing more and more like tiny eyes, staring back at her. They were seeing inside her - seeing her for what she really was. She gasped for air, wanting to look away, but unable to do so. She was trapped, mesmerized by an umbrella of all things.

Cassandrhea's skirt, she thought. The two items were the same, both controlling the people who watched them twirl. She had fallen prey to the same technique she had scoffed at only months ago. There was nothing she could do now. The room, the woman - everything around her, was gone. All that remained were tiny eyes spinning in circles, watching her.

The acidic taste of bile filled her mouth. Vomit balled in her throat, wanting to be released. Memories of where she was and what she was dong faded. Then came the realization, she didn't know who she was.

There were muffled voices in the background, but the words made no sense. Nothing mattered but the eyes. That was her world. She would never look away.

Chapter Sixty-Six

William opened his eyes, allowing them to adjust to the light before attempting to move. He scratched his head, acknowledging that at some point the evening before, sleep overtook him. He released his grip on the letter Willow wrote, smoothing out the crinkles as best he could before folding it neatly and returning it to the book he found it in. His fingers lingered on the spine of the novel for a second as if memorizing every detail - not wanting to forget anything about it or its spot on the shelf - a new addition on the growing list they needed to talk about. That talk was going to happen - he would make sure. Right now, there were other priorities needing his full attention.

Something was happening outside. The scurrying of men was what had broken his slumber in the first place. If recovery from this ordeal was ever to be possible, he needed to know exactly what was going on. He needed to be back in charge again. This was his camp. The protection of his people fell on his shoulders.

He ran his hands through his hair, pushing it off his face. The wrinkles in his clothes made it obvious that he hadn't changed, but that would wait. If there was news about the missing, he wanted to hear it as quickly as possible.

No one paid much attention to him on the walk to the command centre. He veered left, dodging a couple of Deogole's men who were too busy to notice they were on a collision course with him. He mused at the irony of the situation. Most his life had been spent trying to be invisible - to make the camp invisible. Now that it was a reality, he hated it.

The nutty scent of fresh brewing coffee warmed his insides, welcoming him before the door fully opened. He inhaled deeply, savouring the moment. This sensation was familiar. He chuckled at the thought of coffee being the key to keeping his sanity. How many people had said that over the years, but for an entirely different reason?

The vacant seat at the table caught his attention. It had represented the seat of authority for so long. Now, all he saw was a wooden chair, empty and uninviting - if it represented nothing else, at least it still was his.

He settled in at the perfect moment. Zsiga placed a steaming mug in front of him. He smiled, nodding a *thank you* he knew his friend would understand. Normally, that message would have sounded telepathically, but his mind was awkwardly silent. He hadn't noticed before now. Pulling the sleeve of his shirt up confirmed the one thing he lived for was missing - the portal guard mark was gone. The empty spot where it once appeared would now serve as a constant reminder of his failure. He failed himself. He failed his people. He failed Willow.

“It's okay,” Zsiga said. “I know what you meant.”

“It's not okay,” William muttered. “This could never be okay. Thank you for the coffee, my friend.”

“It's not forever,” Faramund said. “They had to do it. Willow wasn't safe around us.”

“The fact that any of us would have purposefully hurt Willow doesn't help the matter any,” William argued. “No magic, no matter how strong, should ever have been able to make us do that.”

“Yes. I agree.” Miss Kelly spoke. No one noticed her sitting in a chair in one corner of the room - her silence proved a worthy mask.

“I don't believe we have officially met,” William said, turning his attention to the blind woman and her staff.

“Observant, aren't you,” the old woman cackled. “I am simply resting from a long night of magic. Pay no attention to me.”

“I believe,” Faramund said, “we weren't paying attention to you, until you added yourself to the conversation.”

Miss Kelly laughed loud enough to hide the sound of the door opening.

“Did I miss a good joke?” Malarchy asked. “I could use the distraction right now.”

“Has anything been found?” William asked. He wasn't sure if he wanted an answer. The old woman said she expended a lot of magic during the night; that was enough information for him to already know they found something.

“Yes,” Malarchy confirmed. “The caves proved to be her stomping grounds.” He always considered tact to be one of his greatest abilities, besides illusions, of course. In this case, there was no way he could explain what happened tactfully.

When he began helping Pewterclaw after Halloween, there were people to inform about the loss of their loved ones. He handled that without a second thought. This was different. Telling people he knew - people who were his friends, that someone they cared about was gone, was a much harder task, compared to if they had been strangers.

“Please tell us,” Sarah pleaded.

“Yes, of course,” Malarchy replied. “They found cocoons in the front area of the cave. For safety, they removed them intact to our medical facility.” He paused, his eyes locked on nothing. Breathing through his nose, he sniffled.

“We need to know,” William said. “You don't have to gloss over the details.”

Malarchy took in a deep breath and released it slowly. “There are survivors. Jessie, Dezi, Pete, Clairity, Ashlyn, and Nathan will all make a full physical recovery.”

Sarah let out a shriek. Her eyes swelled with tears before she burst into a full sob. Whimpers and cries filled the room - the first noise to come from those who had sat silent for most of the morning. Aaram and Lane embraced each other in relief, the news of Nathan's survival as much of a blessing as their own rescue from Atlantis.

“The others?” William asked, his voice quivering.

Malarchy closed his eyes and placed his hands in a praying position in front of his face, resting the tips of his fingers on his nose. He wasn't religious the way most of this world was. In fact, he wasn't sure what he believed in, if anything. The hand gesture somehow seemed a natural response to the situation.

“They are all still in an unresponsive state. We expect they will each wake up on their own, in their own time. The only other survivor is Victoria. There are, however, complications with her health. We aren't sure how to help her at the moment.”

Words failed to form. William wanted to know more about the young girl, but his mind shuffled through images of those who hadn't survived. Putting aside his grief for his friends wasn't an easy task. Finally, he cleared his throat. “What complications?” he asked.

“You won't remember this, William, but back when you were attacked by the assassins, Victoria tried to heal you,” Malarchy explained. “Her abilities weren't strong enough to make a difference. Given her age, it is understandable. Willow did something none of us had seen before. She put her strength into Victoria's magic, boosting it enough to give you a fighting chance. She also almost paid for that with her life. It turns out what she actually did was transfer some of her own life force to you to keep you alive.”

“Thanks for making me feel worse about that situation,” William said, his lips pressing together tightly. “What does that have to do with Victoria's condition?”

“I think Micca is better to explain that to you,” Malarchy replied.

Micca took in a deep breath. He was a potion maker by trade, not a full healer, yet he was nominated to take over the role of doctor. He never minded helping Richard and Mary, but his confidence was failing at the thought of being the sole remaining member of the medical team. “I think Victoria learnt something from Willow that day. I also think Lara figured out what the girl was capable of. From what we have been told, the cocoons were all arranged in a circular fashion, with Victoria in the middle. Those who were found on the outside ring were deceased. Those closest to the centre were still alive and in excellent condition... compared to others we have found recently.”

“For the amount of time that Lara was here, there should have been many more bodies,” Malarchy added. “Hilary's lair was riddled with piles of bones and remains.”

“So you're saying Victoria kept them alive?” Sarah asked.

“That's the theory,” Micca answered. “She must have been healing them the whole time. I'm sure Lara was happy with the situation. The fewer deceased, the longer it would take for people to notice. She had an almost completely renewable food source.”

“So what's wrong with her?” William asked.

“Similar to what Willow did, when the healing required was greater than her ability, she began infusing it with her own life force in small amounts. She must have realized the danger from seeing the outcome of Willow's large influx back before school and chose to trickle it out slowly, hoping it would replenish itself. Those closest to her received the strongest healing. They survived. The power syphoned down to the outer ring. Although she may have prolonged the lives of those on the outside for a while, it wasn't enough in the end.” Micca inhaled deeply. “The result of all of this is Victoria unnaturally aged.”

“Aged?” William said. “How much did she age?”

“Her body is the equivalent of a woman of this world nearing one hundred,” Micca replied. “Her bones are fragile and her internal organs could, quite possibly, begin to fail at any time. I doubt she will ever regain consciousness. There is nothing I can do for her.”

“There must be something we can do!” Sarah screamed.

"I have known many magical beings in my lifetime, some with great powers," Miss Kelly said. Leaning on her staff, she pulled herself up to a crooked, albeit standing position. "I have seen one who can stop time, but never have I seen one that can erase the effects of time. That is not something anyone should have the ability to do."

"We can't just give up!" Sarah yelled. "We have to try to do something."

"I am not suggesting you give up," Miss Kelly said. "In fact, quite the opposite. You know of the one who can stop her from further ageing."

"Nick," William said.

"That should buy you some time," Miss Kelly said.

"Buy us some time to do what?" Sarah asked. "You just said you have never known anyone who could perform such magic."

"Someone, no," Miss Kelly said. "Of course, there are legends. I'm sure you know by now that there is some truth behind every story you hear. Just because I do not approve of it being a possibility does not mean it isn't one."

"Yes," William said. "We are well aware of the terunji changing the truth to suit an explanation they can accept."

"I'm sure you have heard about the Fountain of Youth," Miss Kelly said.

"And you know where it is?" Malarchy asked.

Miss Kelly chuckled. "I have no idea," she replied. "But I do know a professor from Sleeping Sands who has spent his lifetime searching for it. If anyone has a direction for you to go in, it is him. I cannot validate if it is real or not, you understand. All I can offer is hope."

"Which professor?" Malarchy asked.

"Finkle," Miss Kelly answered. "Professor Finkle. He taught potions, I believe. Find him and you may find a starting point to help your young friend. I am needed elsewhere. It has been a pleasure meeting you all." She paused at the door. "I'd consider changing location of your camp if I were you. Far too many people know where you are now. It won't be safe for you or anyone who may want to return." She peered back at the group and winked.

"I am afraid there isn't enough life left in her to wait for such an adventure," Micca said. "Unless we could somehow stop her from ageing any further."

"Faramund," William said, "would you mind fetching Nick for us?"

The question didn't need to be asked. Faramund was already at the door, preparing to teleport to the north to find the one man who could stop time. As the guard left, Aaram returned. Everyone was so focused on the discussion at hand, no one noticed that, at one point, he disappeared.

"Is something wrong?" Malarchy asked.

"Yes," Aaram said. "I went to tell Diana the good news about Nathan." He paused to catch his breath. "She's gone."

William stood. "Gone?" he asked. "Are you sure?"

"I was up most the night helping with the removal of the cocoons. The last time I saw her, she was going to lie down to try to rest. Stress nearly caused her to collapse. I kissed her good night. This morning, however, the bed doesn't look as if it was used."

"Maybe she tidied it up before leaving," Malarchy offered. "Diana was always very neat. I can't remember one time seeing a single hair on her head fall out of place."

"I've looked all over the camp," Aaram argued. "There is no sign of her anywhere."

"That makes no sense," William said. "Where would she go? I'm sure she is around somewhere, anxious about hearing news."

"But," Sarah started, "if she was anxious for news, wouldn't she be here with us?"

Sarah had a point. This was one more problem to throw into the fire. William thought back to the day everyone in camp was made a portal guard - everyone except Diana. They assumed the reason was because she was related to Cornelius. Willow even went so far as to suggest she may need to not have the marking to get close to her brother in the future - to help those who were captured. Now, he wondered if there might have been another reason.

He shook his head. He couldn't worry about *what ifs* at the moment - not when there were enough real problems sitting right under his nose. If Diana was missing, they would have to find her and deal with whatever was going on with her later. “Aaram, Lane, and Sarah,” he said, not wanting to let on to his train of thoughts. “The three of you can continue the search for Diana.”

“Kasper's men will be clearing out soon. They are taking samples of everything right now,” Malarchy said. “It will be easier to find her once they are gone. Micca and I will wait for Nick. We'll move everyone else out of the medical facility. Of course, if we stop time for the building, we won't be able to move her with the camp.”

“Although that's true,” Micca said, “no one will be able to enter the building either. She will be completely safe.”

“I hate the thought of leaving her alone like that,” William said. “I'll start looking into other places to set up camp. Perhaps Nick can give us some ideas of how to bring her with us.” His eyes surveyed the room. For the first time, he noticed someone was missing. “Where's Mike?” he asked. “He wasn't on any of the lists.”

“Mike,” Malarchy answered. “He and Sissy have asked to be set up away from all this. I am finding him a job and a home.”

“He's leaving us?” William asked.

“Yes, it appears so,” Malarchy answered. “Wanting a real life is something I'm sure you have considered as well.”

William didn't answer. The truth was, he had thought about it. If things turned out well, it was something he wanted to add to the list.

Chapter Sixty-Seven

Willow shook the haze from her head, wondering where she was. The buildings and roads appeared similar to the town she was supposed to meet the professor in, but there were no people. Everything was silent. The fountain in the middle of the intersecting streets caught her eye. She reached out and let her hand pass through the liquid. She rubbed her fingers together, noting the lack of wetness that should have been present. The water that normally fell freely had halted mid-stream - suspended in air, as if time itself stopped.

"Time," she said, understanding its significance.

"Yes, my dear," Nick interrupted.

"Why are you here?" Willow asked, embracing the man around the waist as far as her arms could reach. As surprised as she was to see him, she was relieved as well. "Is this real?"

"With a little luck, it is," Meredith interrupted.

Willow's smile widened as far as it possibly could. She rushed into the open arms of the woman. Whether this was real or not, she was happy to see them.

"Can we get over the mushy stuff?" Pandora asked. "We are here because you are in trouble and this time, we can't afford to stay out of it. This time, our existences are on the line as well."

"Calm down, Pandora," Victor said. "Let's not scare her."

"She should be scared!" Pandora yelled. "Maybe that will jog that absent-minded memory of hers. It's time for her to find herself."

"Enough," Miss Kelly said, appearing out of a shadow. "You have overstepped your boundaries, Pandora. We agreed Willow would be given a chance to figure things out on her own. Why have you gathered us here? Explain yourself."

"Explain myself!" Pandora shrieked. "While all of you are playing dress-up in this world, I am the one who has been watching our little muffin. Do you know where she is right now?"

"Enlighten us, Pandora," Nick said. "Let's not beat around the bush."

"She is being held in a trance by the leader of The Organization," Pandora said, crossing her arms over her chest. "A trance I doubt they plan on letting her out of. It's time this little girl woke up. If she can't handle things, we need to step in."

"Perhaps," Victor said, "Pandora has a point."

"Finally!" Pandora exclaimed. "Thank you. Let me unleash my powers."

"We have already been through this," Miss Kelly said. She rested her staff against the side of the fountain, taking a seat on the stone ledge beside it. "We have to put our faith in Willow."

"Excuse me," Willow interrupted. "Could someone tell me what's going on?"

Pandora threw her arms in the air. "She's clueless," she scoffed. "Completely clueless. Do you know why she is here? She is looking for the trees."

Victor took a seat beside Miss Kelly. He rubbed his temple. "Pandora has another good point. If she hasn't figured out about the trees yet..."

"What about the trees?" Willow interrupted. "Do you know where I can find the last one?" Her eyes scanned the faces of the people who gathered there for answers, but were met only with disappointment.

"They are yours to call."

"Pandora!" Miss Kelly yelled.

"It's too late to tiptoe around the issues!" Pandora hollered back. "She needs to know."

"Yes!" Willow shrieked. "Please! If it can help me find the last tree, I need to know. I understand that there are some things I need to figure out on my own, but I think this might be the exception to the rule."

"You don't need to find the last tree!" Pandora yelled. The silence of her peers was enough to let her know she could continue, at least for the moment. "They are your familiars."

"Familiars?" Willow said. "A witch's helper?"

"Not exactly," Meredith answered.

"They are nothing more than a mass of your own magic, my dear," Pandora said. "You created them to do your bidding. You command them. They aren't real."

"That's not true!" Willow shrieked, tears pooling in her eyes. How could that be true? Acacia was her friend.

"Please," Pandora said. "They are no different from those guardian pets you tote around."

"What?!" Willow screamed.

"Pandora!" Miss Kelly yelled. "That's enough."

"What do you mean the same as the guardians?" Willow asked. "I want to know." The calm of her voice sent chills through those who heard it. "I need to know."

“Very well,” Miss Kelly reluctantly agreed. “We can all create familiars. Basically, they are a manifestation of our magic in a physical form. These forms are then able to carry out our instructions. A familiar has only the power its master knows at the exact moment it was created. In a past life, you created the trees as a gesture of love and kindness for the world we came to call home... each one imbued with its own unique purpose.”

“That's why they have different names,” Meredith added. “The tree of love... the tree of hope. They each helped you keep the balance.”

“Then came the wars,” Victor added. “The trees fought valiantly by your side.”

“For some reason,” Nick continued, “the trees remained, slumbering each time you were reincarnated. We aren't sure why. When you found them, they would awaken. When they did, it seemed they retained the power that you originally had when you created them. They were, in essence, more powerful than you, since you couldn't remember your full abilities.”

“Then came Atlantis,” Pandora huffed. “It was a mess.”

“Only because you interfered,” Miss Kelly scoffed.

“Interfered?” Willow asked.

“I gave you knowledge of the spell to be rid of Atlantis,” Pandora said.

“That was you?!” Willow cried out.

“Yes,” Nick said. “You didn't know how to use that kind of power yet. That is why we have always watched, but chose not to interfere with the timelines you were living. You needed to figure out your abilities on your own, or they would undoubtedly fail when you tried to use them.”

“You chose to live this life from the beginning,” Meredith said. “You didn't have to. You loved it here. You loved the people, the animals, the plants... everything. You wanted to keep it safe... to protect it. In essence you gave your life, time and time again, in hopes of preserving all that you loved.”

"You came close with Lilybelle," Pandora said. "It was the only time I can recall you having a chance to win. I thought you could handle it. I was wrong. It restarted the reincarnation cycle again. But something was different this time. Before you passed, you must have realized the danger you were leaving behind. You created new familiars with the instructions to protect the world and keep its inhabitants safe."

"The guardians," Willow said.

"Yes," Victor replied. "Along with them, one tree remained awake. We don't know why. They have remained ever since."

Willow used her hand to cover her mouth. This wasn't true. It couldn't be true. "But they are real." Tears streaked down the sides of her cheeks, the taste of salt hitting her mouth.

"No, my dear," Miss Kelly said. "I am afraid they aren't. They have no feelings. They have no free thought."

"So you see," Pandora said, "you can call that last tree to you. It will have to answer. It is programmed to do only what you want."

Willow's eyebrows pushed together, creating two creases in the skin between them, the pressure forcing the sides of her lips to curl downwards. "If that is true, how did the guardians split? I mean, I created all six types. How is it I am battling two of them? They should be forced to do my will."

"That," Victor said, "is a good question. One we haven't been able to answer. We believe without your direction, they lost sight of their purpose."

"Perhaps they twisted the instructions you gave," Pandora added. "Regardless, you should be able to take control of them again."

"But," Willow started. She paused, choosing her words carefully. "If the guardians aren't real, how did they have children?"

"What?" Victor asked.

"I have been wondering about that myself," Miss Kelly said.

"You knew?" Pandora asked.

"Of course I knew," Miss Kelly snapped. "How didn't you know?" She peeked over her shoulder, anticipating the arrival of another.

"That's a good question," Lance said, stepping through the same shadow as Miss Kelly had earlier. "One I'd like to hear the answer to."

"Lance," Willow exclaimed.

"Well," Pandora said, "the puppy has found his master. Have you regained your memory?"

"Watch yourself, witch," Lance advised. "I have indeed regained my memories and with them, the full extent of my power." A blue flame raged in his eyes, dancing as if his wicked smile was a ball it was attending.

"Perhaps you would like to share how you managed this?" Pandora asked, not backing down.

"It was the antidote to the memory-altering potion," Lance explained. "The first dose didn't work, so I decided to try a second. Of course, I almost died. If it weren't for the necrid flames and my predisposition to death, I wouldn't be here right now."

"But you remember everything," Victor said. "How extraordinary."

"Indeed," Lance agreed. "I wouldn't suggest anyone else try more than one dose, though." His gaze direct towards Willow. "You may want to mention that to your friends when you see them again."

"I don't understand," Willow said.

"Good grief!" Pandora exclaimed. "Haven't you figured it out yet? We are all known by names, many different names. Look at Nick. Throughout the years, terunji have called him Santa Claus, Father Time, and Old Man Winter, to name a few. Lance and yourself are no different. It isn't a difficult concept to grasp. You love each other, but can never be partnered or married. Your abilities are exact opposite. Think of the things you can do. Who are you?"

"Pandora!" Meredith scorned. "She isn't ready."

"Am I?" Willow started. She paused for a moment. This was far too much to process. It wasn't possible. She was just a young girl. How could she be...

"Mother Nature," Lance said, finishing her thoughts. "Of course, you have other names as well, but that is the most common. In a word, you are life personified."

"If I am Life, then you are..." her voice faded.

"Death," Lance said. His voice never faltered as he spoke the word. He was calm and collected, as if nothing could affect his emotions. "Of course, I have other names, the Grim Reaper being one. I am sure you are aware life and death cannot exist without each other. They need each other. They love each other. But in the end, they must remain separate. There can be no union between the two. That is our story. That is our fate."

"And yet you continue to follow her life after life, death after death," Pandora smirked. "I think you like to punish yourself."

"There are so many forms of love," Willow cried. "There must be one we can express for each other."

"I have searched many lifetimes without finding one," Lance replied. "If there was a way, I would know. But that isn't what we are here to discuss. Where were we? Oh yes... the guardians."

"I don't care what anyone says," Willow blurted out. "They are alive. They have shown the ability for individual thought. They have made their own choices. I cannot control them. They can reproduce."

"Yes," Miss Kelly said. "I think I am starting to see."

"Says the blind woman," Pandora scoffed.

"Your gift is life," Miss Kelly continued, ignoring the other woman's comment. "You were dying. If you passed the gift of life on to your familiars, using the last of your life force, it is possible you created a new species."

"That, I could believe," Lance said. "I can verify they each have a unique life force."

“It would be the same for the trees,” Miss Kelly said. “I do, however, believe you will need to look inside yourself to find the last tree. The tree of life, by its name alone, suggests that it remains close to your heart.”

“Without the final tree,” Pandora said, “everything is lost. It's time to admit that and take action. We can let loose our power and let this world start again while we still can.”

“I am afraid the time for that is gone,” Miss Kelly admitted. “We no longer have the power needed to do anything close to what you suggest. I came here from fighting one offspring of an Achaear - its blood mixed with one from this world. It took every ounce of power I possess to destroy it. I am afraid we are now simply participants in the battle for survival. We must follow Willow.”

“We already know she has her hands full with Cornost and Atlantis. The outcome doesn't look good. Not to mention the fact that we have no knowledge of Cornelius' plans.” Pandora argued.

“He plans a mass attack using the memory-altering potion in the next two days. I believe he will target one city at a time, using the water source.” Lance offered. There was an absence in his voice - something missing.

Willow slid down the base of the stone wall surrounding the fountain, ignoring the feeling of sharp stone scratching her back. “I don't even know if I can escape where I am right now,” she complained. “How can I fight two enemies? Both are well-guarded in other realms, I have no way of even reaching them.”

Lance watched her. The sight of the girl who made him feel so alive, crouching down in a ball, not knowing what to do, made his heart weep. Blue flames exploded inside him. “I'll take care of Cornelius,” he offered.

“What?!” Willow screamed. “How?”

“If you do this and the girl fails,” Victor said, ignoring Willow's questions. “There will be no return. There will be no reincarnation.”

“If she fails,” Lance answered, his usual sly smile returning to grace his face, “all of our fates will be the same. I think you forget, I am Death. I do not fear myself.”

"True," Victor agreed. "I wish you luck, my friend."

"Wait," Willow said. "What are you talking about?" She latched onto Lance's hand before he could leave. "What are you planning to do?"

He placed his free hand on hers. Leaning in, his lips gently caressed her cheek. "Let me help you," he whispered. "You worry about getting free from wherever you are and Cornost. I can handle Cornelius. Don't worry about me. I have a plan."

The moment her grip loosened, he was gone. A sick feeling grew in the pit of her stomach. A part her wondered if she would see her prince again or if that moment marked their final goodbye. Her heart ached. Tears streamed down her face.

"Ahem. If you are done with this very touching moment," Pandora interrupted. "Perhaps we could get back to the issues at hand. You do still need to break free from a trance."

"I can pause time," Nick said.

"Long enough for a distraction?" Victor said. He winked a glimmer of hope. "You will have a few moments to escape the hold your captor has on you. Make the most of them."

"What should I do?" Willow asked.

"I would have thought that to be obvious," Victor answered. "Run."

Chapter Sixty-Eight

Willow blinked, finding reality. The spell was broken. Time wasn't on her side. She pushed the urge to contemplate recent events out of her mind. Real or not, there was one thing she knew to be true - she needed to run. That was exactly what she did. The door to the room was open. She scowled at the thought her captors considered her incapable of breaking free from their hold.

Her breath laboured. Shooting pains scaled up and down her already aching legs. Everything looked familiar. There seemed to be no end, the same scenery recurring over and over again. One word came to mind - lost. She wasn't in the building anymore, but rather in some sort of a park. The branch of a bush bent forward, accidentally knocked by the force of her perpetually moving legs. She stopped, an apology rolling off her tongue. Silence followed.

This isn't real, she thought. No familiar chatter offering guidance came. Her guardians, if they could hear her, weren't answering. She flopped on the park bench.

I've seen this before, she thought, retracing every detail since her arrival at The Organization, beginning with the moment she first woke up. Her eyes darted from side to side. A film of memories played for an audience of one. All the sights and sounds of every step - every word, replayed.

“I remember!” she shrieked, jumping up.

Surveying her surroundings, her senses formed an alliance, working together to search for something... anything to help her break free. All she found was laughter. It echoed in the space around her with no indication of where the noise originated.

“Lucinda,” she called out.

“Try as you might,” the voice said, “no one has ever escaped one of my paintings.”

Those words confirmed her worst suspicions. She was a living piece of art. If the painting ever found itself in a museum, she wondered how many people would come, point at her, and comment on how lifelike she seemed. The Organization was in many ways a museum, albeit a personal collection. Painting after painting lined the walls of every room. Did each one contain someone or something The Organization locked away? She smacked her forehead, realizing the clues that she paid no attention to. She hadn't just imagined the girl moving in the first picture she saw. There was no denying, others were trapped here - each a prisoner of a psychotic collector's living, self-created world of demented art.

“At least you found what you were looking for,” Lucinda said. A mad cackling faded off in the distance.

Willow sighed. She hadn't found what she was looking for. One tree was still missing. People were relying on her. Lance was taking on his own father to help. There was a fine line between panic and fear. She was standing on one side or the other, but didn't know which, searching for a way out.

Her gaze returned to the same spot over and over and a large tree that seemed somehow unique - a different quality went into its creation. The artist captured a sadness, perhaps even a loneliness in the droop of its branches and leaves. Mesmerized by its beauty, she found herself standing in front of it. Her hands trembled, inching closer to the bark that covered its trunk. The tree responded to her touch with a warmth. Happiness filled her core. She threw her arms around it, knowing she found the final tree... the tree of life.

"I am happy to see you as well," it whispered. "But sad at the same time that you are now a prisoner with me."

Willow released her grip. "I see your point," she said. "There must be a way to escape. Besides, if magic can put us in, it makes sense that magic can also take us out." Two identical wands slid from the confines of her back pocket. Directing their tips away from each other, she concentrated her power. Her eyes clenched tight, the possibility of backfire frightening her. Silence followed. An eyelid opened, examining its surroundings.

"Nothing happened," the tree whispered.

"So I see." The corners of her mouth arched downwards. The two wands were already gone from sight, returning to their safe home in her left back pocket. The tips of her fingers squeezed inside the other, wiggling around to grasp any contents they could find - searching for something, anything that could help. Their reward was an old gum wrapper that looked as if it had been washed a few times and some lint. Her front pockets were a different story. Turning them inside out, their contents spilled out onto the ground, including some rather odd items from her trip to Atlantis. An old key ring made an immediate return to its temporary home - no doors or locks meant keys had little use, but losing them was a bad idea. One never knew when a key or two might come in handy. The black shiny rock joined the keys.

She twitched at the dim glow coming from the last item - a pouch of some sort of golden-coloured dust. The contents of the small drawstring bag tempted her. She remained still, her gaze locked on the granules, as if waiting for them to speak some profound message.

"Why not," she mumbled. As soon as magic became a part of her life, residue trails left by auras became visible, all in different colours for different forms. Most people, even the most magically adept, never saw enchantments the way she did. Gold was the predominant colour of her own magic. Maybe there was some connection between her own power and the contents of the bag. It was a far reach admittedly, but it was better than not trying at all.

Her hand plunged in, as much as could fit, which amounted to her fingertips. The dust glistened in her palm for a moment before launching in the air. It levitated to the highest point visible, then slowly scattered down across the park. She wobbled. The ground beneath her began to tilt and crack upon the touch of the golden particles on its surface.

Willow grabbed the tiny bag, her arms stretched, finding each other wrapped around the base of the tree. Her memories faded back to the elf realm - the last time she experienced the earth beneath her shake.

A series of cracking noises caused her to tighten her hug, holding on for support as the quakes became stronger. A crevice appeared, dividing the park into two. Growing in size, it headed straight for her. Luck had been on her side when she barely avoided falling into the one in the elf world. This time, however, it looked as if that fate would not be duplicated. She screamed, reinforcing her grasp around the tree for a second time. Her eyes closed tight enough they might as well have not existed.

"You can look now," the tree mused.

Taking the tree's advice, she peeked, finding herself in the middle of a room similar to the one which the other two trees had been in. Her foot kicked one-half of the picture that had imprisoned her. It fell into two completely separate pieces. Nothing else in the room seemed affected. Beside her, a table displaying a strange box caught her eye. She recognized a similar style stained glass as had made up the windows Professor Finkle was obsessed with when she attended Sleeping Sands. Its picture, however, was a mermaid holding a giant pearl.

"You should go," the tree whispered. "Leave this place as quickly as you can."

Nothing could have made Willow argue with that logic. She grabbed the box off the table on the way to the doorway a few branches pointed towards. One last glance over her shoulder showed the tree of life disappearing in the same manner the other two had before, leaving behind only an afterthought of regret for not asking its name. That thought came and went. There were other things she needed to concentrate on, finding a way out of the building making the top of the list.

Hallways turned into more hallways, a never-ending maze meant to confuse and frustrate. Her wand found its way back into her fist. This had to be another illusion. She pointed at a wall, sending sparks flying. Plaster and wood crumbled into dust, making enough room for her to step through. A layer of white soot covered her hair and clothes. The door was in her sights. She jolted forward, echoes of pursuers chasing her warned of the lack of time. If the door was locked, they would be upon her. Another blast escaped her wand. The doors fell. She didn't wait to make sure it was safe, but vaulted over the rubble without breaking pace.

The sun had begun its descent. That was the only gauge of the length of her absence. It had been at least a full day, maybe longer. A rock beneath her foot gave way, sending her stumbling forward. There was nothing to grab to catch herself. She fell. The world spun around in circles. Every bump of the mountainside bruised her body wherever it touched. She came to a rolling stop at the bottom, wincing at the pain.

Keep running, Aslo demanded. *You have to get up.*

It was good advice, but he wasn't the one in pain. Drawing on every ounce of courage left, she pulled herself up. The rest of the trip would be fuelled by pure adrenaline and willpower - there was no magic about that. Her feet moved faster than they ever had before, driving her to the forest. Glancing back from the final steps of the climb to the treetops, provided a glimpse of the first signs of the members of The Organization. She collapsed. Being somewhere she couldn't be reached relaxed her. The trees would keep her safe.

She took in a deep breath, anticipating the calm scents of the forest to whisk her mind away to a better place, but instead she was rewarded with lungs filled with smoke - choking out the air. The forest burnt - an effort to coax her out of hiding, no doubt. But how had they known where she was? The painful cries of the woodland dying pushed all other thoughts out of her mind. She needed to help them. Clouds swirled and rain began to fall. It wasn't enough to put out the already raging blaze. Willow turned her arms upwards, summoning a torrential rain that continued to fall until every last flame was doused, leaving only puffs of smoke floating upwards. To her dismay, they formed a message.

We let you escape this time. Go now and save the world. Do not seek us out again.

Had they let her go? Who were these people? And how powerful? One thing was for sure, she had no intentions of going anywhere near that place again if she didn't have to.

Chapter Sixty-Nine

William tapped his fingers on the table. The notebook in front of him was already overfilled with doodles. He pushed it away and slouched back, greeted by the glares of two girls. “Hello,” he said. “Can I help you?” They somehow seemed familiar, but not familiar, at the same time. He dismissed the feeling as a residual effect of the memory-altering poison and its cure.

“I'm Krissy, a reporter for *The Empowered* newspaper.”

William threw his pencil in the air. “Of course you are,” he said. “Is there anything else joining in this circus? Some clowns, perhaps?”

“I don't know about clowns, but would you settle for a vampire?” Gavin asked, taking a seat at the table.

Sarah screamed. Her small-framed body hid behind Faramund, shaking.

“A vampire,” William repeated. “What would a vampire be doing here?” He scratched behind one ear with the eraser end of another pencil.

“Helping in the search for your friends and the cleanup, I might add,” Sebastian said.

“And you are?” William asked.

“An elf,” Krissy whispered.

“Elves,” William said. “I see.”

“Yes,” Malarchy interrupted. “A lot has happened in the time you were entranced. I apologize, Sarah, I forgot that your family was killed by some rogue vampires. Gavin, I assure you, is not a threat... to you or anyone else at the camp. Krissy is also on our side, as are the elves.”

“I'm sorry for your loss,” Gavin said.

“Please, fill us in on some details,” William remarked. “How did we come to have so many unusual friends?”

“Willow, of course,” Gavin answered.

“And what exactly are each of you to Willow?” William asked.

“We were there for her when you weren't,” Gabrielle said, stealing a spot at the quickly filling table. “While you were married to someone else.”

William's hands smashed down on the table. The legs of his chairs squealed as they scraped across the floor. The coffee in his cup splashed from side to side. A few drops escaped, hitting the table surface. “That was all an illusion. It was never real. I had no control over it!” he yelled. “I will ask one more time... what are you to Willow?” His face flushed red.

“I think we should all relax,” Malarchy said, placing a hand on William's shoulder. “Have a seat and we will explain.”

“Are all of you in love with her?” The room fell to silence for a moment.

“I believe I am,” Sebastian said.

“The answer to that isn't as easy as you might think,” Gavin theorized, drawing attention away from the elf. “When I am near Willow, I have a feeling of euphoria. I am happy... free... alive.

There is something in her that brings that out. I don't know what it is. I need her. I would do anything to help her succeed. It is love in a way, but I am not in love with her. There is such a fine line between the two. I admit even I, at one point, was oblivious to the truth. Now that I have found someone who I truly have feelings for, I see the difference."

"Fascinating," Malarchy mumbled. "That sounds exactly like what happened with Mike."

"An interesting notion," Seth said. "It would explain why we all feel so deeply attached to her at the same time."

"This is crazy!" William hollered. "If you are trying to tell me I don't feel the way I know I do, it won't work."

"I can only refer to my own feelings," Gavin explained. "You all must search inside yourselves for the answer separately."

"If I might," Krissy interrupted, "could I have a quote for the paper?"

William's head slowly turned towards the reporter. "Are you serious? What could I possibly say to you that I would want put into print?"

Her voice lowered to just barely audible. "I thought if you had a message for Willow, we could disguise it in an article. She is probably out there alone again. Hearing from you might make her at least a little happier."

William sat down. His head fell into his open hands. "Of course," he said. "Thank you for giving me the opportunity."

"Before you two become too involved," Malarchy said, "I'd like to discuss a few things. First, Faramund found Nick. He put a time stop on the building Victoria is in. She will have to remain there until we find a way to reverse her unnatural ageing. Second, Diana has yet to be found. I'm not sure what to make of the situation, but for now I want you to consider her to be dangerous, just in case. Aaram and Lane are looking for her. Everyone in this room is our new team for now."

"What about the others who are recovering?" William asked.

"They are doing just that," Malarchy responded. "They will not be ready to help us for some time. Even if they fully physically recover, I don't anticipate a mental recovery until well after whatever we are up against is dealt with."

"Where do we start?" William asked.

"We know the attacks will come on two fronts," Malarchy explained. "I suggest we split into two groups. The elves have more information on Cornost and Atlantis. I suggest the four of you start there. Perhaps Jessica and Krissy can assist you from this world. Everyone else will concentrate on Cornelius. We don't know where or when his attacks will come, but we know they will be soon."

"What about Deogole?" Jessica asked.

"Tell him what you like," Malarchy scoffed. "Maybe you can even get him off his rear to help out with a potential battle. I would ask you leave out the information about the camp moving. The less he knows about that, the better."

"How long before his men clear out?" William asked.

"The last of them will be leaving today," Malarchy answered. "You should concentrate on setting up camp somewhere new as soon as possible."

"You read my mind," William said, his eyes scanning the new faces in front of him. "There are far too many people who have access to this one."

Gavin laughed. "You have more to worry about than the lot of misfits sitting before you," he snorted. "You are also not in a position to take offers for help for granted."

William nodded. "You're right," he said. "I am sorry. If nobody else needs me, I'll be researching a new location." He turned to Krissy. "Come along if you want that quote. If anything happens, I'd appreciate being filled in with the details." The door slammed behind him, leaving Krissy scrambling to gather her things and follow.

"Is he always that stubborn?" Gavin asked.

Malarchy snickered. “Worse sometimes, but he's a good leader. I'd trust him with my life.”

“Good,” Gavin replied. “Because it looks like you might have to.”

Chapter Seventy

It took a few hours before she made her way to the centre of the town Finkle was to meet her in. It seemed so much closer looking down from the treetops. Her legs rejoiced at the thought of rest, almost forcing her into a sitting position on the stone base of the fountain. It was the same fountain from her dream - if it was a dream. Reality and illusion seemed to be doing their very best to confuse each other lately.

She winced at a sharp pain. The strange box tucked under her arm jabbed one corner into her side - a reminder of its existence. It was lucky she hadn't squeezed it any tighter. Having stained glass shatter, sending shards ripping into her flesh, wasn't on the top of her *to-do* list for the day. There wasn't time to properly examine it earlier. Here, now, she saw how stunning the art work really was, both beautiful and odd at the same time. The images changed when her view of the box altered. Actually, the mermaid transformed. Her hair colour alternated from one to another, as did the colour of her eyes. Willow jumped to a standing position, eyeing the strange treasure she recovered from The Organization. Had it winked?

“Didn't mean to scare you,” Finkle said.

“It's fine,” Willow lied, having no intentions of telling her former teacher that it wasn't him that startled her, but rather the female figure on the box. The mermaid's hand now pointed to a lock positioned in between the rocks she was perched on. That was new. A faint scent of sea salt drifted by. Illusions - reality - perhaps nothing was as it seemed. Maybe that was the truth. Reality itself was the illusion she chose to accept.

“Well,” Finkle said, “this is interesting.” He picked up the box. “No latches or hinges. I wonder how it opens.”

“What?” she asked, lost in her own thoughts. The box crashed against the ground. “What are you doing?!” she screamed.

“Trying to open it, of course,” The professor answered, picking it up again. “Doesn't look like that's the way, does it?”

“That's definitely not the way.” Her hands reached out, grabbing one end of the box. Finkle's grip tightened, rather than releasing. “Let go!” she yelled.

“This isn't the time to argue,” Finkle replied. “You retrieved this for me as part of our deal. Remember? This is now my property.”

“You only wanted information.” The box moved back and forth between the two like a rope in a game of tug-of-war.

“Yes,” Finkle said. “This is so much better. Thank you. I'll be taking it now and heading on my way. I have much to do.”

“You're going to leave me here?!” Willow shrieked. “How am I supposed to get back?”

“I'm not sure,” the man replied, smiling. “You can't go the way you came. I guess you'll have to find another way.” A low chuckle escaped from somewhere deep within his throat.

“Fine.” Willow let go of the box and was instantly rewarded with a splashing of cold water. As hard as she tried, she couldn't stop herself from giggling at the sight of her teacher stumbling backwards, losing his balance and landing on his backside in the fountain. His legs dangled over the side of the stone ledge, as water doused his head.

“You've had your fun,” Finkle said. “But in the end, I win.” He held up his prize triumphantly, grinning like a child whose mother said *yes* in a store.

“Professor,” Willow called out. “I know how to open it.” It wasn't a lie. It also most certainly wasn't the truth. It was somewhere in between and hopefully enough to convince Finkle he still needed her. Whether she liked it or not, the professor was her only way back to Pewterclaw.

“How?” A shadow fell over his face, adding to his desperation. Willow saw the same look once before, when the professor believed she solved the puzzle of the stained glass windows in his classroom. He moved too quickly to avoid. The box fell between them. “Tell me!” he screamed.

There would be marks on her shoulders where the man grabbed a hold of her. Her head ached from being whipped back and forth. There are somethings a person never needed to know the feeling of - being a rag doll in a dog's mouth was one of them.

“Not until we are both safely back,” she cried. “If you want to know the secret I have found about that box, you will need to keep me around. That means I need to stay in one piece, too.”

Finkle laughed. “Well played,” he admitted, loosening his grip. “Well played, indeed.” He picked up the box. Enough drips from his wet clothing made their way down to his socks and shoes to fully saturate them. Even shaking himself off a bit didn't stop the sloshing noise that accompanied every step. “Come on, then,” he said. “We best get going.”

Willow followed, keeping a few paces behind him. Even if he was acting as if nothing had happened, she now knew exactly what this man was capable of. Whatever was in that box was worth more to him than the greatest riches to a greedy king - a king, like Cornelius. Her mind shifted gears. Had that meeting been real? Was Lance really going to face his father to help her?

Chapter Seventy-One

“Was it wise to let her go so easily?”

“Do you think I made a mistake?” Lucinda asked.

“She could be a problem for us later.”

“You are still sore she got the better of you at that silly school,” Lucinda mused. “No, my dear Drakondia, this was my plan all the time. I anticipated every move. I knew she would escape. Trust me, she received the message loud and clear to stay away from meddling in our affairs.” Her hand reached out just enough for her fingertips to gently glide over the surface of the other woman's jaundice-tinted arm.

“Of course,” Drakondia said. “I should have realized.” She didn't move from her seat on the floor near Lucinda's feet. The gentle caress on her arm was more than enough reward to keep her satisfied. Her free hand reached up to the tattoo on her chest, mimicking Lucinda's movements. Her fingers glided over the three-dimensional picture of the large hairy spider. “What news of mother?”

Lucinda sighed. “Things haven't been going well,” she answered. “We need strong men for her to mate with. The latest offspring were worth no more than a meagre food source at best. They would not have survived. Reports mentioned that both Hilary and Lara managed to produce offspring using men from that camp... men who managed to survive the process. If we do not find her suitable suitors soon, we may have to pay them a visit.”

“Poor Mother,” Drakondia moaned. “She must be devastated.”

“Come!” Lucinda yelled in answer to a loud knock on the parlour doors.

“Visitors,” the young woman appearing from behind the panels announced. She tugged on the bottom of her jacket to straighten the butler-like outfit before speaking.

“Men?” Lucinda asked.

“Yes. They appear to be looking for the young girl who was here earlier.”

“Are they strong?” Drakondia stood up. Her slick black eyes bulged with anticipation.

“They appear to be.”

Drakondia howled a laugh. “Perfect,” she said. The remains of her sinister smile revealed teeth formed like fangs, a small forked-tongue darting in and out between them.

“Send them in,” Lucinda ordered. “We don't want to keep Mother waiting.”

The woman disappeared for only a moment before returning, two men in tow. “May I present Lucinda, the Lady of the Manor.”

“Drakondia,” Klurg said. “What brings you here?”

“Klurg,” she answered. “And your boy too.” Her eyes enlarged as she rubbed her hand on the back of the beast-like man's shoulder, circling him as if he were prey. “How nice of you to join us.”

Klurg smiled at her, his eyes ogling her low-cut shirt that moved with her every step. “We were looking for that redheaded girl. The bounty is still available. If we manage to find her, perhaps we could celebrate together later." A large, purple tongue escaped his mouth, slathering his lips in saliva.

"No need to look any further," Lucinda lied. "She is under lock and key. We were just trying to figure out what to do with her. Now we can simply give her to you and be done with the mess. How wonderful! I think this calls for a celebration. Don't you?"

"Yes." Klurg agreed. "I've been meaning to train this young pup of mine in the finer arts of women. You ladies could show us both a thing or two, I am sure."

"Oh," Lucinda said, "you have no idea what you are in for."

King Cornelius

Lance stared at the table before him. His porcelain cup of what was once steaming hot coffee had long since gone cold.

“Is something bothering you?” his father asked.

Lance's gaze moved from the white tablecloth to his father's face. The same blank stare of two dead eyes remained - his mask removed. “Fine,” he replied, adding more cream to his cup, seemingly unaware of the overflow it caused.

“Yes. Well,” the king said, still watching his son, “I have some good news.”

“Excellent.” Joseph patted his brother on the back. “Don't keep us in suspense.”

“Your Aunt Diana has found her way home.” The king gestured behind him.

Without any body motion, Lance's gaze followed his father's movements until coming in contact with the tall slender woman.

"Lance," she said, taking a seat at the table.

"No need to worry, my sister. I have already told you. That part of my son's life is over."

"Yes," Diana said. "You told me. But I was the one who met with him while he was running around behind your back, head over heels in love with Willow. The thought of my poor nephew being taken by that hussy makes me ill."

"Am I missing something?" Lance asked, his glare still fixated on the woman.

"I think we all are," Joseph said.

The king sighed. "You once were in league with the girl yourself. Yet here you are, willing to admit your mistakes. I am willing to trust you... afford my son the same courtesy."

"I was blind to how dangerous she was," Diana snapped. "For that, I am sorry. I see now that it is in the best interest of myself and my family that you are successful. I pledge my loyalty to you. All I ask is that no member of my family is hurt."

"Of course," the king said. "Your family is our family, after all."

"Diana!" Grace yelled.

"I apologize, my dear," Cornelius said. "Don't just stand there. Come in. You are most welcome at our table."

"What is this about?" Grace asked. Standing in the doorway with light shining behind her, revealed a thin and fragile body. The embrace that followed between the two women lacked strength and in some ways emotion.

"You are family," Cornelius insisted. "We had no idea. I must apologize for your treatment. We will make it up to you."

"What does he mean, Diana?" Grace asked, pushing her mother-in-law to arm's length.

"Cornelius is my brother," she explained.

Grace gasped. “Your brother!” she shrieked. “Your brother is the one who did this to us?” She stumbled over her own feet, trying to move backwards. Tears swelled in her eyes.

“Shush,” Diana said. “It isn't his fault. You will see the truth. He isn't to blame for any of this. In fact, we are the ones who were wrong.”

“He tortured us!” Grace screamed. “You have no idea what we have endured all these years.”

“He didn't know who you were,” Diana argued, retreating to her seat at the table. A fresh cup of coffee sat waiting for her return with swirls of cream freshly added. The cup clanged as a spoonful of sugar made contact, joining in the circular dance. “That isn't his fault. Now Cornelius knows everything about us.” The spoon clanged once again hitting the saucer.

“Have you gone mad?!” Grace yelled.

Diana's voice raised. “No!” she shouted. The stern look of a mother scolding her child replaced her usual pleasant appearance. “My eyes have been opened to the truth. I was hoping I could shed the light for you as well.”

“It is of no consequence,” Cornelius interrupted, tired of hearing the women argue. “She will see in the end.” He nodded to the guard standing in the doorway. “Give her a room. I want her to be as comfortable as possible.” He paused for a moment before adding, “But keep it locked for now.”

“How exactly did you find us?” Lance asked his aunt as if Grace had never been in the room.

“The same way you contacted Willow, of course,” Diana answered. “I called to your father in my dreams. He answered me.”

“I thought we all agreed to no dreamwalking,” Simon commented.

“Yes,” Cornelius agreed. “We did. This was a special case.”

“If you don't need me for anything,” Lance said, “I'd like to go work off some extra energy.”

"Good idea," Zoe said. "You seem a bit tense. Shall we join you?"

"As you wish, my sister," Lance replied. "You are always welcome by my side."

Lance kept his silence while descending the stone staircase two steps at a time. Only Joseph was able to keep up to his pace and even then only enough to see him disappear into the main laboratory - the metal door still swinging back and forth. He, in turn, paused just long enough for his siblings to follow.

The day was over. Workers had returned to their rooms. Lance slouched over a stainless steel table, his head resting on his arms.

"Are you alright, brother?" Joseph asked.

Lance laughed. Not a regular funny laugh - this was a deep, from the stomach, howl that sounded more like it came from a wounded animal. The noise stopped abruptly. His hand slammed down on the table, leaving the remaining syringes behind.

"What are those?" Ophelia asked.

"They are a cure," Lance answered. "A cure to the memory-altering potion our father hand-fed us. He spewed his lies into our heads and made them real."

"And I suppose if we use these, we will remember everything?" Joseph said, examining one needle and its contents.

Lance laughed again. "I'm afraid it isn't that easy for us," he said. "Our father gave us two doses to make sure we obeyed his every word. Unfortunately, that means one antidote isn't strong enough. I took two to regain my memories. If not for the necrid flames, I would be dead right now."

"So," Joseph uttered, "the rest of us cannot take a double dose."

"Correct," Lance said.

"If this is all true," Zoe grumbled, "why do I believe you? Shouldn't I be siding with Father?"

"I'm not sure," Lance replied. "It may be the way our new memories were worded."

"Well," Joseph said, "I, for one, always thought that the five of us should be in charge of things. Father is family, but we are the ones who are meant to rule. Together we are stronger than anyone else, including him."

"And the four of you shall," Lance said.

"Four?" Simon questioned. "What exactly is the plan?"

Lance knocked over a box. Small bottles of potion spilled out, clanging together as some shattered. "We need to destroy the potion," he said. "It is too powerful to leave lying around."

Joseph patted his brother's back. "This is it? I'll take care of that. What else?"

"Someone should find the woman Grace and help her escape. The rest of us need to release the prisoners. The four of you can lead them to the main world. I'll remain here and take care of Mom and Pop."

"Take care of them?" Ophelia asked.

"He plans to set the necrid flames loose," Joseph explained. "You are going to sacrifice yourself for us. That is an admirable death."

Zoe gasped. "There must be another way."

"There isn't," Lance insisted. "I need to make sure he cannot escape. The rest of you will then be free to live your lives as you see fit."

"And Diana?" Joseph asked.

"Collateral damage," he answered. "She picked the wrong time to switch her loyalties. There is an opening to the main world for another hour. We will have to move quickly."

"Very well," Joseph said. "Zoe, find the woman and leave with her. Move as far away from the opening as possible. I'll find you."

"But," Zoe started.

“Go!” Joseph ordered. “Now!” He took in a deep breath. “I'll handle the destruction of the potions. Simon and Ophelia can help you evacuate whoever it is you want to save. We'll meet up at the gate.” His fingers fumbled over the syringes still lying on the table. “Can I take these? Someone in the main world may need them.”

“Yes,” Lance answered, without looking at his brother. He was already halfway out the door, heading for the lower levels and one prisoner in particular

Ophelia glanced over her shoulder. A series of crashes followed by breaking glass escaped with every swing of the metal door. This was really happening. Returning her focus in front of her, she was already falling behind. Both her brothers' legs were much longer than her own. She wasn't by any means the shortest of the five. That honour was reserved for Zoe. By the time she reached them again, several holding cells were already opened.

“Ophelia,” Simon exclaimed, “take this group up to the portal and go through with them. Make sure you find a safe place.” He grabbed a guard and snapped his neck. “The guards aren't our friends now. Don't be afraid to use force.” He followed Lance until all of the rooms emptied - all except one.

“It's your turn,” Lance said. “Make sure they all find their way. I'll be following.”

“Are you sure, Lance?” Simon asked.

“It's too late to turn back,” Lance replied. “Go now.” Lance watched the corridor empty. He turned the handle of the last remaining door and stepped inside. “Raven.”

“It's been a while,” the woman answered. “I was starting to think you forgot about me.”

“I'm here to help you escape,” Lance said.

“Why?” Raven asked, standing to face the prince.

“Let's just say that your daughter is quite the young lady,” Lance replied. “You need to move quickly. We have a small window of opportunity.” He led the way through the corridors to where the opening to the main world waited.

“Nephew,” Diana grunted, “I am disappointed to see you challenging your own family like this. I wondered if she managed to smuggle some of her little antidote to you.” She cackled unnaturally as the workers dove out of the way of the broad blade she swung wildly about. They scrambled to their feet, racing through the open portal. “What are you looking for?” she asked. “Oh, your brothers and sisters? They made it through before I arrived. We'll find them again after your father takes care of you.”

“Go,” Raven ordered.

“If you do this, you will be trapped here,” Lance said. “You will die here. You need to be with Willow.”

“There is nothing stronger than the love between mother and child. That bond is unbreakable. Not even death itself can sever it,” Raven answered. “If this will help her be safe, I will gladly give what is left of my life. Now go,” she demanded. “Lasel, go find Shelby. Watch over her for me.”

Lance looked back over his shoulder for only a moment, but long enough to see the guardian escape and Diana slice her blade into the side of Willow's mother. The portal was closing. There would be no escape for anyone else.

Chapter Seventy-Three

Relief. That one word summed up everything Willow felt stepping foot in Pewterclaw again - an odd feeling for her. Lately, the thought of someone recognizing her sent shivers of terror marching up and down her spine. Whether it was a law-abiding citizen or an assassin, it always meant trouble.

She leered back at the man following her, shuffling his feet, while still hugging the strange box. Whispered words failed to reach her ears - words meant only for the mermaid whose image graced the surface of the locked container.

Since arriving back in the city, she took the lead. There was little chance of Finkle disappearing. He needed her to open that precious box. She grimaced, wondering how he was going to react when he found out she hadn't actually known how to open it, but rather just where the lock was. Regardless, there was no way she was going to spend a night alone with her former teacher.

She turned up the alley leading to the secret laboratory. Jade, already waiting at the door, waived them inside with urgency.

"Hurry," Jade said. "Where have you been? I've been worried sick. Who is that?"

"That," Willow answered, "is Professor Finkle, my alchemy and potions teacher from Sleeping Sands." She exaggerated a wink a few times, hoping that her friend would understand a message of caution.

"Oh," Jade said. "I'll show you both to rooms for the night."

"Is it safe here?" Finkle asked.

"Very," Jade confirmed. "You can both get some rest."

After showing the professor to a room and locking him in, Jade added a few illusions, making sure he stayed put until morning.

"Thank you," Willow said. "I know you have a lot of questions, but can they wait until morning. It's been an exhausting day and I could use some sleep."

"Do you want to know?" Jade asked.

Willow let the breath out of her lungs making a huff noise. "Yes," she answered. "And no. It's not that I don't care... I do. I am just not sure I can handle the news."

"I understand," Jade said.

"How is he doing?" Willow yelled at her back.

"As good as anyone could in his position," Jade said. "He woke up to the news he was married to a giant spider; he was contained to quarters while they searched for her nest and killed the offspring he could have technically fathered; he was told he stood by while his *wife* ate his friends; and was forced to accept he turned his back on you." Jade paused for a moment. "You did know they weren't actually married. It was all an illusion. He never had any real feelings for Lara."

"I know," Willow said. "That doesn't mean he has feelings for me. Maybe I built up something in my mind that wasn't really there. It wouldn't be the first time."

Jade embraced her friend. "I think you are wrong. Dad says he's been beating himself up over what he did to you. He even gave Gavin and the elves a hard time. Get some sleep. We can talk tomorrow."

Chapter Seventy-Four

The world around her was familiar yet somehow distorted. It was a few minutes before she realized where she had seen the same surroundings before - in the visions Shelby shared with her. Willow was given a glimpse of the place where the avian guardian was taken to and tortured. This place she was in was Lance's home. She circled around, unable to believe she was standing in Cornelius' palace.

"Willow," Lance called.

She opened her mouth, but no words formed. Was this real? Was she dreaming? The guardians were silent, but that didn't mean much. It seemed they did little talking lately. She wasn't sure if that was on purpose or not. She swallowed back the saliva pooling in her mouth. "You're hurt," she managed to say.

Lance smiled. His body slid down the wall that he was relying on to hold him up. "This is just a dream," he said.

She took a seat on the floor beside him. “If this is a dream, make yourself look a little better,” she demanded, tears pooling in the corners of her eyes.

“I can't,” he answered. “I came here to say goodbye.” He coughed. “I wanted you to know, Cornelius is gone. Your mother sacrificed herself to help me. She gave up everything to save you.”

“I'll get help,” Willow cried. Tears freely fell down her cheeks as she watched her prince.

He reached for her hand. “It's too late for me, Willow,” he said. “Diana was here too. She joined with her brother in the end. What you tell the others is up to you.” His head tilted towards hers. His eyes were gone - all that remained were blue flames. “Thank you,” he whispered. “For being here with me at the end. William is a good man. He'll take care of you. Don't give up on him.”

She screamed for him to stay, but it was too late. His image faded away before her eyes. Her hand fell to the ground as his dissipated. The surroundings began to vanish. She found herself sitting in the middle of a white room. He was gone. Her prince was dead.

Her eyes stung, blurring her vision. Tears fell faster with no end in sight. He sacrificed himself to save her. She felt more alone now than she ever had before.

She yelled out, “Why?!”

No one answered.

Chapter Seventy-Five

"Good morning Willow," Jade said. Her smile quickly vanished. "What's wrong?" she asked

She knew those puffy, red eyes would give away how much she cried through the night, but hoped she could contain her sadness. Now that seemed impossible. Tears already started their free fall, streaking lines down the sides of her face.

"I wish she would tell us as well," Aslo said, appearing on the table. "We haven't been able to hear any of her thoughts all night."

"Lance is dead," she sobbed. "He sacrificed himself to take out his father so I only had to deal with Cornost and Atlantis."

"He must have cared for you very much," Jade said. She knew there were times when words were useless - especially, trying to ease pain. That was a lesson she learned from her own mother's death. Only time could heal some wounds.

"My mother stayed to help him," Willow blubbered. "I'll never meet her."

"I'm sorry," Shelby said.

"I know what you are thinking," Willow declared. "I don't know about your partner. Lance only mentioned my mother and Diana being there to the end. I believe they evacuated everyone else."

"Diana was there?" Malarchy asked, appearing in the entrance. "That explains why we couldn't find her. I was hoping she was here. Nathan will be waking up soon." He kissed his daughter on the cheek before taking a seat. "Why was she there?"

Willow sniffled a few times, needing to collect her thoughts before speaking. Lance's words stung in her mind. Nathan had been through so much already. He didn't need to know his grandmother turned on them, paying for that decision with her life.

"She helped them," she mumbled. "It was like I thought, back when the portal guard sign first didn't appear on her arm. She convinced her brother she was ready to join him, then stabbed him in the back to help the others escape." Lying was never something she enjoyed doing. Normally, she wasn't very good at it. She knew now the real reason why the symbol never appeared. Somewhere, hidden within Diana, lived the tiniest bit of doubt. That doubt grew until it consumed her. She knew, but no one else needed to.

"She was a good woman," Malarchy said. "Knowing how she died should console her family in some ways."

Malarchy was a smart man who usually knew everything. From the tone he used, Willow figured he already discovered the truth, but was willing to overlook it, the same as she had - for the sake of those left behind.

"I hope so," Willow replied.

"I'll send a few search teams out to look for lost people," Malarchy said.

"I'm on it," Gavin interrupted.

"I'll go with you," Iskander offered. "At least I can recognize our people."

"If you don't mind," Shelby added, "I'd like to help as well."

Willow nodded, donning her best fake smile. Her gut feelings told her that they wanted to leave because they were uncomfortable being around her in this emotional state. She couldn't blame them. If she could escape from herself right now, she would have.

"Willow," Jade said. "Are you okay?"

How could she answer that? She wasn't okay. She barely heard the words her friend uttered. Her world lay in ruin - shattered. The table steadied a dizziness that sneaked up on her, overwhelming her senses. Her forehead became cold and clammy, not quite to the point of perspiring.

"I think I should lie down," she muttered. "A few extra hours of sleep may help." She left without waiting for anyone to answer. Before she was out range, she faintly heard Malarchy mention he needed to attend to creating Mike and Sissy's new lives.

The room was still messy from the night before. She tidied the blankets a bit before taking a seat in the neatest spot - complete with pillow to hug. Her body flopped backwards, the pillow covering her face. It was her shield from the cruelty that was her reality.

"Ahh!" she screamed, not out of fear but rather from frustration. The pillow fell to her now outstretched legs. She sighed. Sleep wasn't an option. She reached for the pillow again, but it wasn't there. She sat up straight.

"Okay," she said. "Where am I now?"

"Somewhere between here and there," Deanne answered.

The child-like laughter of the three girls echoed all around her. It came from everywhere and nowhere. *More reality or illusion,* she thought. It felt real, but how could it be? She was sitting in the middle of what appeared to be a storm cloud. Grey mist swirled around hues of pinks and purples. The occasional flash of light went off in the distance.

"Close," Anndee said.

"Can you hear me?" Willow asked.

"Yes," Dannee answered. "In this place, words do not need to be spoken to be understood."

"Why am I here?"

The three girls appeared before her, linked by their hands. "We are sad for the loss of our brother," they said in unison.

Willow rubbed her eyes. "Are you saying you three are part of the same group he was?"

The girls giggled. "We are one of them," they answered. "As are you."

"We didn't want to interfere in your journey," Deanne said.

"Are you not elves?"

"No," Dannee replied, followed by more giggling.

"We have been known by many names, as have our brothers and sisters," Anndee explained. "Some people like to refer to us as The Fates. We rather like that name."

"The elf homeland is our favourite place," Deanne added. "We settled there. They provide us with an identity - when necessary."

"So they know?"

"Not everything," Dannee said. "But enough. We do not interfere in the lives of other species as much as we once did."

"But we do still listen to what they ask," Anndee added. "We smile on those who are deserving and lend them favour."

"I see," Willow lied. "You want to help me?"

"We do," the girls said, synchronized.

"We like the life we have now," Deanne admitted. "But a battle must be fought somewhere."

"The unicorns drain the power of the trees," Dannee warned. "They will not survive more than two days if you do not take action."

"We can't find them," Willow confessed.

“The unicorns use magic to absorb magic,” Anndee explained. “If someone could see magical auras, they could be easily found.”

“There are so many unusual things you have not experienced in the main world,” Deanne said. “There are vessels that fly through the sky giving its passengers a clear view of the ground below.”

Willow smiled. “Of course.” She read about flying machines capable of transporting people with Nathan.

“When the unicorns are gone, the trees can seal the opening that is forming on this side,” Dannee said. “That would force Atlantis to rise in the elf world.”

“We can weaken the barrier in that one spot just enough to let them through.” Deanne continued. “That would minimize the initial damage.”

“Then we all could stand together for the final battle,” Anndee finished.

“The elves will let us join in?” Willow asked.

“Yes,” Dannee said. “We have already discussed the plans. Those available from the thirteen and your friends will be permitted into the elf realm to help.”

“The main world will be safe,” Deanne added. “And there would be no threat of outside interference helping Atlantis.”

“Gather your friends quickly,” Dannee advised. “The time draws near.”

“How will we find our way to you?” Willow asked.

“Find your way to where?” Aslo asked.

Willow grasped the pillow on her legs and pulled it back over her face. She was back in the room again. Magic was starting to mess with her mind. “I think I need to talk to the others,” she said. “We have a plan.”

“Did I miss something?” Aslo asked.

“Most definitely,” she answered, already halfway through the door.

“Oh,” Krissy said, coming to a full stop. The two girls almost smacked right into each other. “I'm sorry,” she mumbled.

“Are you okay?” Willow asked, not actually needing an answer. The young reporter's usual bubbly personality at some point transformed into seriousness, hiding sadness behind it. “Oh,” she said. “It's today.” With everything that was going on around them, Krissy's dilemma was shoved to the back. Now her birthday was here and a choice was going to be made.

“How did you know?” Krissy asked.

“Let's talk,” Willow said, returning to her room.

Chapter Seventy-Six

William shook his head, not willing or able to believe his eyes. He tried rubbing them, without success. Everywhere he looked, people were hugging and crying. The camp was buzzing again.

Shelby landed on his shoulder. “They were released,” the guardian bird explained.

“Released,” William said. “Don't tell me Cornelius has had a change of heart.”

“No,” Shelby replied. “Cornelius is dead. Lance evened the odds for Willow.”

“And Lance, is he here too?” William asked.

“No,” Shelby said. “He sacrificed himself.”

William shook his head. “Does she know?”

“Yes,” Shelby answered. “She knows. There were two others lost as well. Willow's mother and Diana.”

“Diana was there?” William asked.

“There will be some talk,” Shelby said. “She was a good woman who tried to help. At some point, people should know she gave her life for them.”

“Yeah,” William muttered, barely hearing the bird's words. Lance made the ultimate sacrifice for Willow. How could he compete with that? He thought about the message he sent in the newspaper article with Krissy. Somehow it seemed pale in comparison. If she read that now, he'd probably lose her forever.

“Any instructions?” Faramund asked.

“Yes,” William said. His heart ached, but for now he needed to ignore the pain. These people needed someone to help them - someone to lead them. “Have Zsiga work on arranging meals for our new guests. Iskander can make the sleeping arrangements. You should let Malarchy know they are here, if he doesn't already know. Let's keep recent events to ourselves for the moment so as not to cause any panic.” he scratched his head. “When that is all done, let's make a late night vigil. We can deal with grieving for those lost together.”

“Where will we hold it?” Faramund asked.

“In the training fields. It's the only place big enough for everyone. There are candles in the supply room. Take as many as needed. It will mean less to move in the long run.”

“Lasel and I will help with preparations where we can,” Shelby offered.

“Your mate survived,” William said. “I am glad.”

“Yes,” the guardian bird said. “But we are dealing with the loss of our keeper. These emotions are strong. We understand what others must be feeling.”

“We will need Micca to make a schedule for visiting those still recovering,” William continued. “I doubt it is good for the patients for a large crowd to all be in there at once. He can use his discretion to stagger visits.”

“Is there anything else?” the guard asked.

"Yes," William answered. "Normally, I would ask Mike to handle it, but since he isn't with us anymore, we will need someone to pick up supplies. Ask around... see if anyone volunteers. With this size of a camp, what we have stockpiled won't last long."

Chapter Seventy-Seven

"Do you know when?" Willow asked.

"No," Krissy answered. "Just sometime today."

It was hard not to notice the tears forming in the journalist's eyes. Willow had lived through more than her fair share of troubled times, filled with the strain of trying to hold back sadness, to know the signs. "I'm sure things will work out in your favour," she said.

"That's what I am afraid of," Krissy responded. "I know I complain about Keith a lot, but the truth is, I don't want him to disappear. It's as if I have this huge struggle going on inside me. I don't want to go and I don't want him to go. Either way, I won't be happy. Even though we share an existence, he is still very much my brother."

"I'm sorry," Willow said. "I'd never thought of it like that." A full speech formed in her mind - one she felt was quite brilliant. There wasn't any time to share it, though.

Krissy fell off the bed, her body convulsing as if having a seizure. The only other time Willow had seen such a sight was when the three Shinning boys were poisoned by a love potion. She knelt by the girl's body, using her hands to try to steady the shaking.

"Krissy," Willow called.

Willow's world began spinning. *Oh no,* she thought. *Not again.* She was falling. Reality swirled around her, masked in illusion. At least for once, she wasn't feeling sick. Perhaps she had become accustomed to these out-of-body and into-mind experiences. She closed her eyes knowing there was nothing she could do but wait for the ride to end.

"Willow," Krissy whispered.

Willow opened one eye to examine her surroundings. She let out the breath she held. "Why does this keep happening to me?" she asked. "At least it didn't take long. So where are we? Is this the meeting for your birthday?"

"I assume you are the girl we have been hearing so much about as of late?"

Willow glanced up at a man and woman sitting behind a large wooden desk. Her neck wouldn't be able to stay in that position for long without becoming stiff and sore. Memories of the elf realm filled her thoughts. Did people actually feel more powerful by physically looking down on those standing at a lower altitude?

She sighed, answering, "Yes." There is one thing she knew was fact - lately, when someone asked about *that girl* they were referring to her. There was no reason to ask for clarification - it only led to frustration and anger.

"I suppose it is useless for us to ask how you arrived here, at a private meeting of our world," the woman said.

Willow moved back a few steps, providing her with a better view of the two judges. Their facial features were hidden by large wigs, reminiscent of the ones used by judges during the era of the witch trials in the main world. Although they were sitting, she could tell they were both wearing black gowns made to hide their normal attire.

"I have no idea," Willow replied, shrugging her shoulders. "Krissy looked like she was having a seizure. I tried to help her and here I am."

"I see," the woman said. "Albeit that doesn't make any sense, I believe you."

"Thank you," Willow uttered. What else could she say? None of the last few days made any sense to her, so how could she expect anyone else to make sense of it. At least someone here believed her. That was more than she could say about any other realm she visited.

"Please sit," The man requested, although it came out as more of an order. "Krissy Quidnunk and Keith Quidnunk, we are here today as you celebrate your eighteenth birthday to examine the lives you have etched out for yourselves and the right of passage into adulthood of our race. You will both have a chance to present your cases to us for consideration. Krissy Quidnunk, you may rise and begin."

Krissy stood, but no words formed. Her hands trembled. The colour drained from her face, quickly being replaced with a greyish-tone.

"If I may," Willow said. "I think that Krissy is having an inner conflict about how she feels going into this hearing."

"Apparently," the woman said, "we don't have a choice but to hear you."

Willow ignored the comments and continued. "I submit that survival is the strongest natural instinct for all individuals."

"Young lady," the man said. "If we are to listen to your story, please do away with the cliché lawyer act. In your own words would be fine."

"Yes, your worship-fullness," she said, instantly regretting the word choice. Even Krissy groaned. "As I was saying, basic survival instincts require Krissy to want to survive. There is, however, something else that every living thing shares. Something more powerful than any of us can imagine. Do you know what that is?" She paused.

“Please end the anticipation,” the woman said, rolling her eyes.

“It's love,” she answered. “I don't pretend to be an expert. In fact, I am still learning so much more about it every day. But I have discovered that there are far too many forms of love to identify in one lifetime. It's where magic resonates within us. It's more powerful than reason. It is the best part of us.”

“What is it you are trying to get at?” the woman questioned.

“If you would, just bear with me for one moment,” Willow said. “I think you will understand. Love is an undeniable force. There is the love for a friend, the love for a mate, the love of food, a mother's love for her child and there is a love between a brother and a sister.”

Keith look over at Krissy briefly, then returned his gaze to his shoes, his own reflection staring back in the spit shine that covered their black surface. His thoughts, whatever they were, remained privileged information, shared only between himself and his image. Willow found herself wondering if this was the first time the two siblings had physically seen each other.

“Even if Krissy and Keith share the same person, they are still, in essence, brother and sister,” Willow continued. “Krissy's feelings of love for her brother are conflicted with her need for survival. She doesn't want to put one before the other.” She took in a large breath of air. “Is there no way they can both continue on?”

“Is this how you feel, Krissy?” the woman asked.

Krissy nodded her head, still unable to form any cohesive words. She was on the brink of a breakdown at the worst possible time.

“And Keith,” the man said, “are we to understand you feel the same as Krissy?”

The silence was deafening. Every second that passed felt like an eternity. Willow shifted the weight between her legs.

Keith looked up. He blinked over top of a blank stare several times. “Yes,” he muttered, his voice cracking on the word. He cleared his throat. “Yes,” he repeated in a stronger, more affirmative voice.

“Well, then,” the woman said, removing a thin pair of glasses from her face. “As you know, on the eighteenth birthday of every individual in our world, a decision has to be made as to who enters adulthood. You are each told you are being tested. From that time forward, we see the young engage in competition between themselves as to which persona will survive.”

“The test, however, isn't a physical test to pass,” the man explained. “We never tell our young to engage each other. The actual test is one from within... to see how you can coexist... how you can deal with each other and by extension, how you will interact with the rest of society.”

“You have both demonstrated what is necessary to contribute to our adult society in a positive way,” the woman stated. “We are happy to welcome you both.”

“Excuse me,” Willow said. “For clarification, do they both pass? Does that mean they continue on exactly as things have been?”

“Yes,” the woman replied. “They both pass. As for how they continue on, that is up to the two of them to decide. I am sure they can come to an agreement. I believe they owe a great deal of debt to you as well. Your understanding of the universe is extraordinary for a girl of your age.”

“I'm sure we don't have to mention this,” the man said. “But this is a privileged hearing. The information that has been shared here is not to be repeated. Our people are bound to that promise with their lives. We impose the same strict rules on you as well.”

“I understand,” Willow agreed.

“This meeting is adjourned,” the woman said. “You are free to go.”

“Great,” Willow said. “How exactly do I do that?” She heard laughter fading in the background and a new voice becoming clearer - closer.

“Willow! Krissy!” Jade yelled.

Her first sight were two cold and beautiful green eyes. "Jade," she said, using her elbows to prop herself up on the ground. Her limbs felt stiff and sore. Krissy matched her movements.

"What happened?" Jade asked. "You both looked like you were having some sort of a fit."

"Nothing," Willow said, remembering the warning that was issued. "We need to gather everyone together. We have a plan."

Chapter Seventy-Eight

The usual faces filled Gavin's office. The vampire made himself comfortable, reclining in his cushioned leather chair enough to allow his feet to plant themselves on the desk. The cork from a dark green wine bottle was clenched in his jaw, the end hanging out one side his mouth. He spit it into an empty pencil holder sitting amongst the clutter he called *boring paperwork.* His hands raised in the air, one still tightly gripping the bottle. "He scores!" he yelled, followed by a noise mimicking a crowd going wild.

"Thank you for sharing your skill," Malarchy said, pushing past the girls standing in the doorway watching. "What is so important as to disrupt me during office hours?" he asked.

"We have a plan," Willow said.

"This plan appeared out of thin air since this morning?" Malarchy asked, with the usual level of sarcasm in his tone.

"Sort of," Willow admitted. She was tired of explaining the unexplained. It was much easier to agree and move on than waste precious time with details.

“So,” Gavin said, “don't keep us in suspense.”

“As you know, all the trees have been found,” Willow started.

“Wait,” Jade said, “they have?”

“Oh. Well, they have,” Willow said. “They are still ineffective because their magic is being syphoned off by the unicorns.”

“The unicorns again,” Gavin mocked. “Evil unicorns.”

“Yes, Gavin,” Willow said. “Evil unicorns. Can we move on?”

“By all means,” the vampire agreed, taking a swig of the thick liquid contained in his bottle.

“If the unicorns are destroyed, the trees can close the rift on this side, forcing Atlantis back towards the elf realm.” Willow continued.

“But we have looked for the unicorns and found nothing,” Jessica said. “If they are there, the magic around them must be advanced to keep them hidden.”

“I don't know about the magics hiding them, but I do know that the magic they are stealing leaves a trail. An aura only some individuals can see.”

“And let me guess... you can see that trail,” Gavin said, pointing at her and winking at the same time.

“Yes,” Willow answered. “If I can look down from above, I can pinpoint the locations of the unicorns.”

“I get it,” Krissy said. “If you fly over in a plane or a helicopter, you can find them. Then we just have to destroy them.”

“Sounds easy enough,” Jessica said. “What's the catch?”

“The unicorns are dangerous,” Willow replied. “We can't use magic against them. They can suck it up and throw it back.”

“That means we need to use conventional weapons,” Jessica proposed.

“Yes,” Willow agreed. “But keep in mind, unicorns can use magical attacks on whoever attacks them.”

“Let's test your theory,” Malarchy said. “Jessica, can you and Krissy arrange a flight over the area for Willow?”

“Right away,” Jessica answered.

“For now, let's keep Kasper out of the mix,” Malarchy instructed. “We don't need to add any more into the cauldron. It already has enough leaks.”

“Understood,” Jessica agreed.

“The rest of us will gather the troops,” Malarchy said.

“You will need to ask Nick to call his allies as well,” Willow added

Malarchy's eyebrow arched upwards. “Are these people we have met?” he asked.

“Some, perhaps,” Willow said. “They seem to pop up here and there.”

Krissy fumbled with a copy of the newspaper, sitting on the desk. “Willow,” she said. “I almost forgot this. I think you should read the interview.”

Willow took the paper, containing an interview with William. Krissy asked him for a quote representing how he felt about the events which recently transpired. His answers weren't headlining the front page, but that didn't matter, they were technically tailored for only one reader.

The edges of the newspaper trembled in her grip. For a brief moment she disappeared - not hearing, seeing, or acknowledging anything around her - other than the words, speaking to her in his voice - a voice she longed to hear - William's voice.

I cannot express how sorry I am for the lies that were spread while my peers and I were under the effects of an unusually strong illusion spell. It was strong enough to reproduce the traditional marriage ceremony of my people. I can assure you that it was not true. At this time, my friends are recovering from the residue effects of the magic we were subjected to. There were some casualties. It will take some time for all of us to come to terms with the loss. I myself am struggling with my part in the fake world I was forced to be a part of.

Willow always was and remains an important part of each of our lives. Although I don't know exactly where she is, I can hope this message reaches her. I stand with her. I believe in her. She will always have a home with us. I don't blame her if she can't find it in herself to forgive me, but if there is any possibility, I'd like the chance to put it on the list.

"Willow!" Jade screamed, managing to push a chair under her friend before her bottom hit the ground.

Willow wasn't answering, her fingertips were busy tracing over the final words. William was willing to talk about what happened - willing to work through it. She felt a tear forming in the corner of her eye. Not a tear of sadness, but a tear that represented all that was happy in the world. A wave of guilt flowed through her body. How could she have doubted him? She should have known it wasn't real. She should have trusted him.

"Thank you," she whispered. The two girls had made an impact in each other's lives that day that neither could ever forget nor begin to repay.

"Well," Gavin interrupted. "We should start moving. We now have a plan, after all. One question, what happens when Atlantis pops up in the elf realm?"

Willow's lips parted, allowing air to enter and saturate her lungs, pushing it out again with force. "We make our stand there," she stated. "That's where this ends. Speaking of which, can we look at the final prophecy?"

"I'd like to," Gavin said, "but the book disappeared."

"When did that happen?" Jade asked.

"Not sure," Gavin answered. "It was sitting on the corner of my desk. It isn't there anymore."

"It couldn't have gone far," Jade said. "We'll look around and bring it to the meeting when we find it."

"If we find it," Malarchy added.

Something in his tone made Willow believe the mayor didn't think they would find it. Had someone taken it? What good would it do to steal such a book? Was there someone in their midst who wanted her to fail? Had the book wanted her to fail? There were too many questions. She knew far too well she wasn't about to find any answers sitting around.

Chapter Seventy-Nine

It felt like an eternity had passed since Willow last visited the camp. The hustle and bustle surrounding her was new. People were everywhere. Some faces she couldn't put a name to and some she knew well. Those faces - the faces of people she grew up with, were the ones that affected her the most, each one smiling at the sight of her. She knew they meant well, but also knew the smiles were manufactured, coming across as little more than poorly-executed illusions of happiness. She understood why. They, like herself, all knew firsthand what it meant to be Cornelius' victim.

"Are you okay?" Faramund asked. The green gas of his teleporting skills dissipated around them. "I can stay by your side if you need me."

"Thank you," Willow answered, her mind preoccupied.

"I see you made it," Zsiga said, sneaking up on them. His arms embraced her in a friendly hug. "We've missed you."

Willow imagined the smile she was offering the guard was no better than the ones members of the camp offered her. She expected someone else to be there for her arrival. Hiding the disappointment proved impossible. “Yes,” she mumbled. “It's good to be back.”

“He's in his quarters,” the guard said. “In case you want to talk in private before the meeting with everyone else. There is still some time.”

“Thank you,” Willow answered. It would be awkward to see William for the first time in front of an audience. The news he was alone was welcomed. At the same time, she found herself fidgeting and stalling all the way to his door.

She formed a fist and raise it to knock, pausing in midair, unable to force her knuckles to make contact with the wood. Before solving her dilemma, the door opened. She stood there, fist raised.

“Were you going to knock?” William asked.

Willow blinked twice, lowering her hand. “You opened the door as I was about to,” she lied.

“Right,” he said. “Should I close the door again so you can finish?”

“Very funny,” Willow answered, offering a meek smile. “Can I come in?”

“That's a silly question,” he said, retreating inside, leaving the door open.

Willow followed, shutting the door behind her. Everything was exactly as she remembered. William helped complete her mind's reconstruction of the room by sitting in the chair at his desk and leaning back. The main difference was the awkwardness that lingered in the air between them. It choked out the pleasant pictures painted by memories and replaced them with the cold reality that things had changed. She fumbled for words, needing to say something – anything.

“You look good. The room looks the same,” she said, instantly regretted the spew of small talk she was throwing up. This wasn't someone she was meeting for the first time.

"It is," William said, raising his eyebrows. Spinning the chair, he focused his attention on the paperwork strewn across his desk. "Did you come here to see my decor?"

"No," Willow answered. A hot flush filled her cheeks. She wasn't sure if it was from sadness, embarrassment, or anger. "I'm sorry I took up so much of your time," she muttered.

William's hand slammed the door shut before she fully opened it. "I'm sorry," he whispered. "Please stay."

"I don't know what to say," Willow explained. "I feel like we are strangers."

He grabbed her shoulders, turning her body to face his. "We've both been through a lot," he said. "But that's all that has changed."

Her arms flung around his neck, her body pulling close to his in a tight embrace. His scent filled her senses. "You've been cutting wood," she said.

He let out a low chuckle before letting his arms surround her waist, tightening the hug. "I made sure to only cut the trees which were already dead," he replied.

She smiled. Maybe things weren't as different as she thought. "I read the interview," she blurted out, pulling back from him enough to see his face. Her hands ran over the two-day stubble of a beard that replaced his normally smooth skin. "Did you give up shaving?"

He laughed. The twinkle in his eye confirming he was genuinely happy at that moment. He rubbed the sides of his face. "I think I like it," he said. "What do you think?"

"I reserve my judgement for a later date," she joked, taking a seat on the edge of the bed again.

He rolled the chair over to her. His hands held hers. "We have a lot to talk about," he said. "But first, are you alright? I heard about Lance."

She wasn't prepared for him to mention that name. The smile that had just formed, vanished. "I haven't had time to fully contemplate his passing," she answered. "It's going to take some time."

"Of course," William agreed. "You loved him."

The words stung. "Yes, I did love him," she replied. As his grasp on her hands faltered, she replaced it with her own on his. "He was an important part of my life, but I wasn't in love with him. It took me a while to understand the difference. There are so many forms of love. It was confusing for me at first to feel any of them."

"That clears up a good portion of the list," he said.

Willow's fingers brushed back strands of sandy coloured hair that fell over his eyes. "So what's left on it?"

"Is now the time?" he asked. "There are more pressing affairs waiting."

"When you were unconscious, I swore to myself that when we met again, we wouldn't put our talk off," she explained. "There were things I wanted to say... things I should have said. I thought I might not ever have the chance again."

He brushed the loose strands of her curly, red hair behind her ears, his hand gently caressing the side of her face. "What was so important that it would give you such regret?"

She couldn't find the courage to look him directly in the eyes. This moment was more frightening than anything she faced before. She wet her lips. All the times she steadied her breathing and heart rate in the past meant nothing now. Control was a word without meaning. "I," she started, hesitating. "I am in love with you." She said it. It was a small accomplishment. Compared to the silence between them now, it seemed easy.

"Then we will make it work," he finally answered. "It's probably a good thing you can't hear my thoughts right now."

Her eyes moved to meet his and were greeted by a goofy smile. She rested her head against his chest, wanting the moment to never end. Her hand brushed over his forearm, leaving the mark of a portal guard behind.

Chapter Eighty

"I hate to break up this touching reunion," Tika said.

Willow's face turned fifty shades of red. She forgot the guardians were there, hearing everything that was going on. She smiled. Of course, William was unaffected by their heartfelt discussion being overheard. In fact, it was almost the complete opposite - his full attention now devoted to the two guardians, hugging and petting them. It was obvious how much he missed them and that they felt the same.

"We are here too," Shelby admitted, appearing from a dark corner of the room. "We didn't want to disturb you two. Willow, this is Lasel."

"I'm glad you found each other," Willow said. "I actually wanted to speak with all of you before the official meeting."

"What is it?" Aslo asked, appearing on the bed.

"Each of you need to make your own choices as to whether you want to continue on or carve out a new place for yourselves in this world."

"Willow," Aslo said. "We are bound..." His words were interrupted.

"No," she stated. "I know everything. I know how you came into being. You may have started as my familiars, but something changed. I was known as Lilybelle back then. I wanted to create a force to protect the world while I couldn't. It was my dying wish."

"Yes," Aslo agreed. "That is how it happened."

"But," Willow continued, "that isn't how it ends. I don't know if it is because of my rare gift to create life, or if it is because I transferred some of my remaining life force to you, but you are alive. That is why only three of the six guardian races remained loyal. That is why you can reproduce. You each have the freedom of choice. Any hold I may have had over you, I release. You are free."

Willow smiled. This was a sight she never expected to see. Sitting in front of her in neat rows were all of her guardian friends, blank stares on their faces, eyes blinking."

"You're serious?!" Tika exclaimed.

"Well, of course I am serious," Willow replied with a chuckle in her voice. "Why wouldn't I be?"

"Thank you," Aslo said. "I cannot speak for the others, but my place is with you. Kiera and I have always thought of you as a part of our family." A liquid wet the fur in the corner of his eyes. One by one, the others agreed with the feline guardian.

"I want each of you to consider your role in the final battle. It won't be pleasant. You can let us know when you are ready. At least wait until after the meeting to make your final choice." Willow's hand brushed the fur on the side of Aslo's face.

"Agreed," Jawfree replied.

"There are guardians in the camp that are not present. Please share this information with them."

Tika and Nero returned to their place as William's guardians, their images on his upper arms somehow completing him. Aslo let out a playful roar before taking his place with Kiera and their children on Willow's back. The remainder of the guardians were already on their way to share the news with peers.

“I guess it's time for me to find out who we lost,” Willow uttered, biting her lip.

“You don't know?” William asked.

“No,” Willow replied. “I didn't think I had the strength at the time to handle the news.”

“And now?” William asked.

“I know it won't be easy,” she answered. “But with your help, I think I can make it through.”

“Alright,” he said. “Get comfy and I will tell you everything.”

Chapter Eighty-One

The command centre was packed to capacity, waiting for them. The talk with William took a little longer than anticipated. Willow clung to his arm, knowing vision could be blurry at best with puffy, red eyes. She always knew there were casualties - even prepared for the inevitable. But in the end, she wasn't ready for the realization of just how many of her friends were gone. They would never speak again; never laugh again.

She waited for William to make his way to the table first. It was almost painful to feel the intense stares focused directly on them. She searched for a word in her mind to describe what she was feeling. Only one came - vulnerable. The spotlight wasn't her comfort zone. This, however, was worse. It wasn't just being up front and centre. These people wanted to know how their future, if there was going to be one, would unfold.

At least William was there. This was the sort of situation where he was at his finest. She tightened her grip on his arm. There was a certain amount of pride that came with understanding he was a natural born leader. That pride, however, she knew came at a price. It also meant he may not ever settle down.

The sight of their usual seats unoccupied sent shivers down her back. A sense of foreboding trouble filled her thoughts. William claimed his spot at the head of the table without hesitation. Willow reluctantly took the empty chair to his left. Steam from the coffee already before them swirled into patterns above their cups. It was as if the hot liquid waited for exactly that moment to send out signals. Her eyes fixated on the miniature clouds, trying to identify any message they might hold. A spider; a snake; a unicorn: they were all relevant and yet too vague to actually be some form of communication.

“Willow,” Zsiga said. “Did you want some?”

“Sorry,” she replied.

“Sugar for your coffee,” the guard said. “Did you want any?”

“Yes,” she replied, “thank you.” In that small moment, the pictures all disappeared. Had she actually seen something? It was more likely all in her imagination. Of course, there was the possibility she was going crazy. There was a fine line between psychic and psycho. Her sudden outburst of laughter drew attention from most of the room. The weight of their stares silenced her instantly. “Sorry,” she muttered, her head hanging down.

“If we can get started now,” William said.

There was no need for Willow to look to know who he was directing that statement at. Her hands clasped together on the table. She instantly regretted the decision, realizing she wouldn't be able to fidget with them in full view of everyone.

“We have a plan,” William continued.

Pictures fell down on the table, each one an aerial view of the Atlantis site - a letter X marked on it. Jessica stood, smiling at the visual display she created. “These pictures show the exact location of unicorns.”

“Unicorns again?” Gavin said.

"Yes," Jessica answered. Before she could continue, the door flew open.

"Hello," Nick said, walking in. "Hope we haven't missed much."

"We?" William asked, one eyebrow arched.

"Yes," Nick replied, turning his head to glance over his shoulder. "I've brought a few friends."

Willow squinted, then rubbed her eyes. For a moment, she thought she was in another strange dream-like vision. There, standing behind Nick were all of the others who she met at the fountain - the ones who helped her escape The Organization. Questions swirled in her mind. There was so much she wanted to know - that she needed to know. "You're real," was all she managed to say.

"Yes," Pandora said. "Quite real." She sighed, placing one hand on her hip. "I voted not to come. Apparently, that didn't count for much."

"Nick," William said. His eyes fixated on the new guests. "Am I missing something?"

A jolly laugh rolled off the man's lips. "Yes, my friend," he said. "But that will have to wait for a more convenient time. I suggest we move swiftly."

Willow wasn't interested in pleasantries. Her neck stretched upwards, tilting to the side. It was the best view around Nick.

"They aren't here," Miss Kelly said. "But they are the reason we are. If The Fates feel it is their duty to shine in your favour, we cannot ignore their wishes."

"If you ask me," Pandora said, "those three are simply sticking their noses in where they don't belong. Next time, they should make sure before they shoot Cupid's arrow."

"Did you say Cupid's arrow?" Sarah asked.

"Yes," Pandora answered. "They don't always agree and it makes a mess."

"A mess," Sarah said, raising an eyebrow.

"Where do you think love triangles come from?" Pandora asked.

"We aren't here to discuss trivial events," Victor interrupted. "Shall we get back to the topic at hand? We are wasting the gift Lance gave us."

"Alright!" William yelled. "I want to know who you people are and why you are here."

Willow placed her hand on his arm. "It's okay," she said. "They are friends. I can fill you in with the details later."

"Fine," William reluctantly accepted, the red flush in his face indicating it was anything but fine. "We need to get rid of the unicorns. Once they have been eliminated, the trees will seal this side of the portal, forcing Atlantis back to the elf realm."

"So what are we waiting for?" Aaram asked.

"It's not that easy," William answered. "We won't be able to use magic to defeat them. Their horns can absorb magic and store it to use as a weapon. We believe they are building their power at the moment to release back at the barrier to this world. That theoretically would punch a hole big enough for Atlantis to surface."

"So how do we defeat them?" Miss Kelly asked.

"I think I should take some of this to Kasper," Jessica offered. "His men are trained in non-magical combat. It would also allow more of us to go to prepare in the elf realm."

"How do we get into the elf realm?" Malarchy asked. "Last I heard, they don't like strangers."

"The Fates have taken care of that," Willow said. "We will be welcomed. The elf realm will be where we make our final stand."

Chapter Eighty-Two

Jessica waited patiently in Kasper's office for the Director of Secrecy to arrive. She jumped at the sound of the creaking door. Her hand covered her mouth, trying to prevent breath from escaping. "You startled me," she exclaimed. "I wasn't expecting you."

"Easy," Malarchy said. "You need to stay calm. Has he been called?" He took a seat in front of the desk.

Miss Kelly strolled in behind him - silent. She leaned against the wall, both her hands grasping the staff that never left her side. To those that hadn't known her, it was a walking aid for an old, blind woman. Of course, those who knew her well realized she could see better than most people without the use of eyes.

"Yes," Jessica said. She pushed down on her knee to steady its shaking - failing miserably. She needed a distraction. Finding a new hangnail to chew off was like hitting a jackpot. The skin around her thumbnail ripped in her teeth, leaving a pink line mixed with a spot of blood behind. She moved on to the next nail.

Being nervous wasn't something she was used to. In all the years she worked for Kasper Deogole, not once could she remember feeling this unsure about a simple meeting. Perhaps her uneasiness stemmed from the guilt of playing double agent.

"Well," Kasper said. A file folder slammed down on his desk. "To what do I owe the pleasure of this unusual gathering of the minds?"

"I see I'm in time to join the party," Cassandrhea said, walking in. The door slammed behind her. "It's a tight squeeze in here today. You really should find a bigger office, Kasper."

"Did we come here to see how many people we could fit in my office? Perhaps we could make a game of it?" the Director of Secrecy mocked.

"No," Jessica said. The pictures flew from her hand landing on the file folder in the middle of the Director's desk. "This is what we came here to discuss."

"X marks the spot," Kasper exclaimed. One hand shoved into his pocket, the other held a picture tight in its grip. "Are these treasure locations?" He threw the photograph down. A finger from his free hand pressed to his nose. "I know. These are secret pirate stashes. How many paces should I take?" He cackled, amusing only himself.

"No," Jessica repeated. After putting up with his condescending nature for years, she decided enough was enough. "These are the locations to unicorns."

"Unicorns," Kasper mimicked her word. He rounded the desk stopping right in front of her and leaned forward. "What am I supposed to do with unicorns?"

"Evil unicorns," Malarchy interrupted. "We need you to destroy them."

Kasper's attention shifted. "I never pegged you for the type to play into madness," he said. "A mayor needs to keep a cool head. First frolicking with vampires and now riding unicorns. It won't be good for business... your business that is."

"It isn't madness!" Miss Kelly shouted.

"Said the blind woman," Kasper mocked. "Except I'm not a deaf man. Tell me. Have you seen them with your own eyes?"

"Enough, Kasper!" Cassandrhea yelled. "Unicorns are very real and very dangerous. They are hard to track as well. We are lucky to have this information. If they are destroyed, so is the threat to this world."

"So why come to me? Why not go hunt down these elusive beasts and save the world? That is what the bunch of you do, right?"

"They can collect and store magic energy," Malarchy explained. "They can wipe out a magic attack faster than we could put it into effect."

"How do you know they are there?" Kasper asked, taking a more serious tone. "Don't expect me to run into this blind. I want the whole story."

"Magic leaves a trail... an aura," Miss Kelly explained. "That aura is visible to certain individuals. The unicorns are drawing power from a force set up to close the rift."

"Should I bother asking who the person is who can see magic trails?" Kasper questioned, pausing for an answer. "So I can assume from your silence the redheaded girl is in on this plan? Is she the force that is closing the rift?"

"No," Malarchy answered. "Trees are."

"Trees," Kasper said, smiling. "This keeps getting better. Trees are going to save the world. I had the bunch of you pegged as environmentalists, but this is going a bit far."

"Yes, Kasper, trees," Cassandrhea said. "Seven magical trees."

"Perhaps if I may explain," Miss Kelly offered. "The trees were originally created as familiars."

"The girl's familiars?" Kasper asked.

Miss Kelly simply nodded. She shifted her weight forward to rest it on the staff planted firmly between her feet.

“And where is she now?” Kasper added. “Wait! Let me guess. You don't know.” The Director let out a huff. He examined another picture on his way back around his desk. The well-worn chair squeaked as he sat down. Several people suggested he replace it with a new one. It took him years to adjust it perfectly to his body. To start again now would be counterproductive. “What's in it for me?”

“I would have thought that to be obvious,” Jessica said, her teeth grinding together. “You would save this realm.”

“Save this realm, yes,” Kasper said. “But whatever is trying to rise has to go somewhere. What is it you aren't telling me?”

“It will rise in the elf realm,” Cassandrhea acknowledged. “There is no need for you to worry about that. The elves will handle whatever comes. You handle your world and we'll handle ours.”

“Deal,” Kasper said. “You make sure you keep up your end of the bargain. If we find a threat coming from your realm, we will take action. When this is all over, I will need to sit down with each of you and discuss your roles in all of this.”

“Understood,” Malarchy agreed.

“Jessica,” Kasper said, “you and Malarchy will stay here with me. Cassandrhea, I assume you have more pressing matters to attend to. Miss Kelly, disappear to wherever it is you disappear to. No time to waste. We have unicorns to slay.”

Chapter Eighty-Three

Willow realized how much she missed the elf realm the moment she stepped through the portal. “Pretty girl,” a colourful, low-flying bird cawed.

“Thank you,” she answered with a curtsy.

“Enough with the flattery,” Elfred groaned. “Follow me. I'll take you to where we are preparing for the attack.” The small fairy's wings fluttered furiously, propelling him out of sight.

“Wait!” she yelled. “We don't move at super-fairy speed.”

A loud noise echoed from above. It was part growl, part laugh and part what sounded like a *hello*. The breeze picked up. Dust and leaves scattered through the air. Willow grabbed her hair in one hand, having been whipped by her own strands enough in the past to know it was best to keep them in one place when a dragon was landing.

“Zoran!” she yelled, her words barely audible over the sound of large flapping wings.

"Willow, my friend," the dragon answered. "Hop on, and your friends too. I'll give you a lift to where you need to be."

"Thank you," she said, climbing up scales like stairs. She motioned for the others to follow. Riding a dragon wasn't for everyone. A few of her friends were more than a little hesitant at the proposition. Zoran peered over his shoulder, snorting a blast of hot smoke to indicate his disapproval at the length of time they were taking.

"Are you sure about this?" Gavin asked.

"Don't tell me a vampire is afraid of a dragon," Willow teased.

"Falling," Gavin said. "I'm not too fond of falling. Don't these things come with seat belts?"

"Just hang on," Zoran said. "We're going to go fast."

The dragon wasn't kidding. The first group arrived at the makeshift camp within seconds. Tents stood in a row, each one with a name plastered on it stating its purpose. Everything had its place and was in it. No less could be expected of the elves. They wasted little time making preparations. All the details were attended to.

"This place is amazing," Krissy said, snapping a picture, albeit no one saw a camera. Two elves pulled her aside. The young journalist may have been allowed into this realm, but from the looks on the elves' faces, they weren't yet ready to share secrets with the outside world via newspaper articles. Of course, the search of Krissy's personal effects failed to find any device capable of taking pictures. "Sorry," she offered, shrugging her shoulders.

"Willow!" Sebastian yelled. He waived his hand high above his head, motioning for her to join him, before turning his attention back to piles of burlap bags stacked to form a wall.

"What are these for?" Willow asked.

"We need some cover," Sebastian answered. "We don't know what type of weapons Atlantis has developed. This should take at least some of the danger out of the equation."

Willow chuckled. It was hard not to. The elf prince stood posture perfect, both hands planted firmly on his hips. His head bobbed up and down, with the silliest grin plastered on his face, acknowledging his own accomplishments. Luckily, his moment of self-adoration meant he hadn't heard her.

"Well," Pandora grunted from behind them, "what do we have here?"

Sebastian heard that. "It's my idea," he boasted.

"I see," Pandora mused. "Interesting idea, but don't you think it's a tad too close to the water?"

Sebastian and Willow exchanged glances before looking back at the woman, both blinking over blank stares.

"Well," Pandora continued, "seems like the two of you need a bit of a science lesson. Since time is running short, I'll make this quick. Right now, Atlantis is sealed in a bubble, which technically is neither here nor there. That means it isn't actually occupying space in this realm. When it rises, the bubble will pop. At that point, it will once again take up part of the elf world."

Pandora's lips pressed together. Her eyes widened as she waited. The expressions of her two new students weren't changing. The blinking continued. "Oh, for goodness sakes!" she yelled, her arms flailing as she spoke. "Aren't you two listening? When Atlantis rises, it will become a mass of land again... in the middle of that body of water. The water that is there now will be displaced. It has to go somewhere."

Willow and Sebastian exchanged glances again. At first there was an awkward silence. "That means," Willow started.

"The water is going to flood this area," Sebastian finished.

Pandora snapped her fingers. "Now we are on the same page." She turned towards the water and gloated.

"Fall back!" Sebastian bellowed. "Fall back to the second staging area. Quickly, there is no time to lose. Make sure everyone is evacuated from this area."

It took only a matter of minutes before Willow was watching the last of her friends disappear on the back of Zoran, with William still yelling something at her she couldn't quite make out. She assumed it was a few obscenities about her staying behind.

Victor's arms lifted straight out to his sides. The sleeves of the white, robe-like top he was wearing hung down to the middle of his thighs. A pattern of black spots appeared on the crisp white linen. He almost resembled a moth. Ascending into the sky, he disappeared from sight.

The giggles of three girls floated on the airwaves. The triplets appeared buzzing around in circles above them. Small white wings fluttered on the backs of their white dresses. The similarity to Cupid or any angelic figure more apparent than before. Had they struck her with a love arrow? That was a question she most definitely wanted an answer to.

"We'll be waiting for you," Deanne cooed.

The three girls disappeared, joining with a white cloud. Now only Pandora, Sebastian, and Willow remained. The weather shifted. Pandora turned her head to Willow, her eyebrows waggled inquisitively. Willow shook her head, answering the silent question. Something else was affecting the weather.

"Here we go," Pandora declared. "Brace yourselves. Atlantis is rising."

It was as if the small island heard her call. Water began to gurgle. White bubbles formed around a large circular shape. The top of the dome-like prison appeared in the centre of the water. The glistening sun hit the encasing, glaring brightly enough to momentarily blind. Willow used her hands to shade her eyes, wanting to see everything that happened. That, she soon found, wouldn't be possible.

Her wand, her only shield against pending doom, had already found its way into her trembling hand. The water was coming. Nothing could have prepared her for that moment. A wave, taller than the trees, headed their way. Her feet dug into the ground - hands outstretched, gripping tightly the tiny piece of wood on which her fate rested.

Sebastian stood by her side, frozen. The wave closed in, towering over them. A blast of metallic colours escaped from the tip of her wand, making contact with the water. She gasped. All of her magic... every ounce... could only control a small area of what was speeding straight for them. Even Sebastian's extensive knowledge of water magic wasn't going to be enough. Cue cards shuffled in her mind, flashing images of her life before her eyes.

"Stand back, you two," Pandora commanded, her hands outstretched before her. A crystal blue glow surrounded her, before flowing out from her hands, stopping the wave mid-fall. "You two need to retreat," she insisted. The blue magic was no longer simply encasing her body, she was becoming the same liquid she was stopping from crushing them.

Willow gasped. She was so preoccupied by Pandora's transformation, she completely missed another one going on right beside her. She turned to yell to her elf friend to run, but found a sandy coloured dragon instead.

"I know you," she whispered. "You are the dragon who saved me at Sleeping Sands. Sebastian, is that you?" The palm of her hand caressed the scales on his face.

"Can we do the reminiscing another time?!" Pandora yelled. "You two need to leave now."

"What about you?" Willow asked, looking down from her perch on Sebastian's back.

"Don't worry about me," Pandora said. "There is a reason they call me Goddess of the Sea. I'll hold it off as long as I can."

Willow thought she saw a majestic smile form on the woman's completely liquid face. They were soaring above the trees when a crash sounded. The wave spilled down onto the ground below them, stopping just shy of the second camp. Sebastian made several passes over top the rushing water. There was no sign of Pandora.

Chapter Eighty-Four

Willow did a double-take, wondering if she stepped onto the set filming a scene from a poorly made disaster movie. The elves, dragons and fairies stood lined up, waiting for destruction and mayhem to come to them. How long would it take before Cornost's army emerged from the watery prison now the locks had been pried open?

Sebastian landed in the back of the less organized, makeshift camp. Elves ran about trying to set things up. Willow slid down one of the dragon's front legs straight into William's arms. The air in her lungs pushed out as he tightened them around her.

"I thought I'd lost you again," he whispered softly in her ear, tickling her lobes with his breath.

The dragon snorted. A puff of smoke surrounded them. Willow choked. Gasping for air, she burst out into a fit of coughs. Tears streamlined down her reddened face, spouting from bloodshot eyes. Before she could recover enough to say even one word, he was gone. As sad as it made her feel, she couldn't help but think somehow the triplets had a hand in the emotions that were at play between herself and the elves. There would be time for those questions later - now, there was a battle to prepare for.

“He'll be okay,” Willow said. “I'll talk to Sebastian later.”

“Sebastian?” William asked, his eyebrows arched. “That dragon was Sebastian?”

“Long story,” Willow muttered. “If you find General Umaagan, he'll be happy to explain.” The general was overjoyed to have anyone listen to any of his stories. No one could blame him. After being locked up alone in an Atlantis jail for all those years, being able to talk at all was a treat for him. She turned her attention to the front line, but found someone else standing in her path.

“Pandora?” Victor asked.

Willow shook her head. “She stayed to hold the water back so we could escape. There was no sign of her afterwards.”

The man nodded. His head hung down, keeping his silence and masking emotions as he walked away.

“We cannot feel her energy pattern,” Dannee noted. The three girls floated down as if they were leaves falling from a tree. Their naked feet barely touched the ground before they formed a chained circle around Willow. All three girls began skipping in sequence.

“Did you use one of your love arrows on me?” Willow asked.

The skipping stopped. “Who told you about that?” Deanne demanded.

“That's our secret,” Anndee said. The lines forming between her eyes coupled with the downward curl of her small lips looked unnatural - in some ways eerie.

“There seems to be some movement!” an elf yelled from the front of the defensive line. “Something is happening.”

“Looks like we'll have to save that talk for later,” Dannee snickered.

The three girls maintained their grip on each other. Their bodies began to rise, legs outstretched behind them. Swirling in a circle they chanted. “One is three and three is one. This is our will, so let it be done." The same phrase repeated over and over, each time a little faster, matching the speed at which they twirled.

Willow gasped. The three girls disappeared into a cloud of white fluff above her. A bright light appeared. If it were night, it could have been a star, except it was coming closer. Willow rubbed her eyes, thinking the smoke might still be affecting them. Taking another look, the figure of a woman appeared in the middle of the light. "What just happened?"

"I'm not sure," Zsiga answered.

That was the highest Willow ever jumped in her life. The guard caught her on the way back down. She needed to start being more aware of her surroundings when something odd happened. One hand rested on her chest, feeling it beating twice as fast as normal.

"Sorry," Zsiga said, placing her back down on the ground. "That tends to happen a lot." Sometimes he forgot how well he blended into shadows.

"No," Willow said. "I was preoccupied."

"I can see why," the guard replied.

"Who are you?" Willow asked, turning her attention back to the woman.

"We are a combination of ourselves" was the answer, spoken in three distinct voices intertwined into one. They were not those of girls, but rather those of grown women. "We allow our inner children to explore this world. It is through the eyes of a child that one can discover and ultimately learn the most. This situation, however, calls for a more mature touch." The woman's feet never touched the ground. She floated forward to take a place between Miss Kelly and Victor.

"They scare me," Zsiga said.

Willow chuckled. "Me too."

"**We have arrived**," a man's voice boomed with a force loud enough to make ripples in the water that swished over the newly formed shoreline. Cheers followed.

Their positions made it impossible to see how many troops Cornost held behind him or what sort of attack was to follow.

"**Perhaps there is an amicable way for this to end. I will discuss my terms with Lilybelle,**" Cornost bellowed. "**Send forth the girl and lives may be spared today.**"

Willow took one step forward. A tug on her arm pulled her backwards into a stumble. "Whoa there," William said, catching her. "Where do you think you are going?"

"To talk to Cornost, of course," Willow answered.

"Oh no, you're not," William ordered. "That is one very big trap you'd be walking into."

"I agree," Miss Kelly said. "It's unlikely he wants a chat over a cup of tea after being locked away for so long. I am sure he blames you."

"I sense no honesty in the man's words," Victor added.

"I still have to try," Willow said.

"Well, you aren't going alone," William demanded. "You can't even swim."

"No," Aslo said, appearing in his full glorious form.

"We will go with her," Kiera added.

"We will protect her and bring her back," Aslo promised. "You all must prepare. There is no doubt that a battle will begin shortly after we reach Atlantis."

"That's insane!" William yelled.

"It allows us to take out the first wave of the attack. Cornost doesn't know how many of us there are." Aslo replied. "Willow is our Trojan horse - so to speak."

"Her magic isn't going to be of any help out there," William argued.

"This has been decided," Aslo roared.

"But," William started. A hand on his shoulder stopped him. Miss Kelly simply nodded. Defeated, his hand fell to his side.

***

The walk to the shoreline wasn't particularly long. Being sandwiched between the two feline guardians provided reassurance, allowing her to maintain composure. A group of birds soared upwards above her. She smiled. The avian guardians would be another secret weapon no one would expect. The closer she moved to the water's edge, the shakier her knees became. William was right; she never learned the finer art of swimming. Growing up in a realm that lacked bodies of water meant there was no need. Her face crinkled up, realizing for the first time how odd that was.

The swooshing sounds of waves rolling in from the rising of the land mass, serenaded her approach. Water trickled over her toes. Goosebumps formed on both legs, before branching out to her arms - products of both fear and the chill of cold liquid on her bare feet.

"How?" was the only word she could manage. She reached for her back pocket, freezing mid-movement to Aslo's shaking head. He had a plan.

The two guardians moved forward and together let out a roar louder than Cornost's words. On pure instinct, Willow's hands reached to cover her ears - a useless exercise. She was far too close to the noise for it to make a difference. She fell to one knee, ears ringing from the sound, eyes glued forward. The water rippled against both sides of an invisible bridge making its way across the water's surface to Atlantis, resembling a shark's fin rushing towards prey.

"Are you okay?" Aslo asked.

She simply waved in response, already testing her footing on the clear pathway before her. For the first few steps, her knees knocked. Her feet, unsure of their hold, slid awkwardly. Falling down wasn't an option, considering she would more than likely go flying off one side or the other - drowning before the fight even started. She needed to pull herself together quickly.

Aslo nudged her back to the middle of the bridge. If only she could hover like the joined triplets had. She stopped for a moment, inhaled deeply, then placed one foot forward as steady as if she were on solid ground. The only thing that mattered was where the next step would land. Time passed by like a soft breeze. She now stood a mere hundred feet away from the king and his vast forces.

"Well," Cornost said, "I see you brought your pets. How nice of you to allow us to see the hand you have to play."

"This is a meeting to discuss a way to avoid a war, is it not?" It didn't take a genius to see the situation wasn't in their favour. The king sat high upon the largest of the unicorns gathered. Behind him, hundreds more awaited instructions. The first wave of attackers Cornost assembled were meant to do major damage. The elves may have prepared, but they couldn't have anticipated the size of Atlantis' forces.

"Yes, of course," Cornost said, a laugh hinged on his words as they formed. "You and your friends surrender and I rule. That's the only way no one gets hurt." The elf's chuckle turned into a wild noise that one might imagine pure evil to have - if pure evil could laugh.

"We won't surrender," Willow insisted.

"Then taking your life shall be the example we set for your friends," Cornost replied. "Look around you, girl. You can't win. You can't use magic. You are all alone. I could crush you with one blow and not even break a sweat."

"But," Willow answered, "I'm not alone."

Cornost howled another laugh. "Two guardians against an entire army? They may be immortal, but there are ways to handle that problem. Cornelius taught me that. I'm sure he'd pay a pretty price for them too."

"I'm afraid Cornelius is dead," Willow said, masking her emotions.

"You resourceful little minx," Cornost cackled, the smile never leaving his lips. "I admit, I didn't see that one coming. Oh well, it saves me the trouble after dealing with the lot of you. I suppose I will have to find a use for your friends somehow."

"Like you did with the opalescent dragon and the great tree?" Willow asked. Keeping him talking seemed like a good plan, or rather the only plan she had.

"So you are Lilybelle," Cornost stated, his eyebrows raising.

"I am Willow," she answered.

"Then how do you know about such things?" the king demanded.

"Because," she answered, "I am the one who helped them escape."

The king's face flushed red. The sound of teeth grinding sent a shiver up her spine. She wobbled slightly as Cornost's mount reared - its two front legs crashing back down. The sheer force sent a wave hurling towards the shore. Instinctively, her feet moved backwards, putting some extra distance between herself and danger. The guardians remained firmly planted in their spots in front of her.

"Do you think that will make a difference?!" Cornost screamed. "Your two pets will be taken care of so quickly, you won't get anywhere even close to solid ground."

"That may be true," Aslo snarled.

"But then again," Tika said, appearing on the bridge, Nero by her side, "they aren't the only guardians that have come to play."

The word *run* echoed in her mind. She didn't need to be told twice. Looking over her shoulder briefly, she saw the king's sceptre come down. The mounted army rushed forward. All of her furry guardian friends now formed a wall between danger and herself. Shelby led the avian guardians on an attack, swooping down, knocking several unicorns off the magic bridge.

Her breath laboured, but she continued her sprint. She was only a little over halfway when the first unicorns broke through the guardian barrier. Their sheer numbers were too overwhelming to contain. The steady trotting noise behind her amplified. Other than the occasional splash, it was all she could hear. The avian guardians were her sole protectors now. She wondered how long that could last.

Her hand slid round to her back pocket, grasping her wand. It might be useless, but it was the only weapon available. Her legs ached. The shore was close, but not close enough. She mused at the irony of her mouth being completely dry when she was surrounded by nothing but water. Her thoughts faded quickly - the hooves were too close for her to have a chance to outrun them now. She needed to make a stand - at least she would go out fighting. She turned to face her oncoming attackers, wand ready.

The water on either side of her bubbled, as if boiling. Something else was rising. The unicorns stopped, refusing their rider's commands to go forward. Someone whispered, *Run.* Before she could turn, Willow caught a glimpse of the water taking the shape of a large woman.

"Hello, boys," Pandora said, her watery form towering over the bridge. "You didn't think a little water could kill the Goddess of the Sea, now did you?" She laughed.

Willow cringed, knowing a few nightmares were going to be born from today's events. Pandora's new body, if one could call it that, was one of them. A giant, completely formed out of water and cackling - picture perfect as if described in the pages of a good book.

Willow's feet touched the ground. Water crashed down on the bridge, taking everyone on it to the depths of the sea. Soaking wet, she scooted backwards, away from the grumbling waves. Her back banged up against something solid. Scrambling to her feet, she climbed up Sebastian's leg to safety on his back. He soared high above the trees, offering an aerial view of the end of Pandora's onslaught, knowing it wouldn't last long. All power had its limits. Willow's eyes searched for signs of the guardians, but found none. The knowledge they were immortal wasn't enough. She feared them lost.

"Don't worry," Shelby said, flying beside them. The avian guardians took flanking positions, acting as if they were escorting the dragon to the line of defence. "They are fine. We just have to wait for them to wash up on shore."

Sebastian changed direction, heading back to the elves. They won the first fight, but the war was far from over.

Chapter Eighty-Five

Nothing would have thrilled Willow more than to slide down Sebastian's front leg into William's arms again. Remembering Sebastian's reaction earlier, she decided to take it slow. The triplets invaded her thoughts. She was sure they were behind how the elf princes felt about her, but couldn't prove it yet. Until she could, it was better to avoid hurting feelings unnecessarily. As it turned out, she didn't have to worry at all. William was in control on the front lines. It wasn't all that surprising. She always knew he was born to lead.

“Brace yourselves!” William yelled. “They could arrive at any moment.”

“We ready?” Willow asked.

“As ready as we can be,” he answered. “What are we up against?”

“Aslo and the guardians took out a large number of unicorn riders with Pandora's help,” Willow said. “We are still outnumbered.”

“The guardians?” he asked.

Willow shook her head. "Only the avian guardians returned. Pandora's waves dragged the others under with Cornost's men. I don't know how long it will take them to recover. I think we can guarantee we won't have their help for the rest of the battle."

"There are still a few of us in the camp," Saymore said, his tail flicking back and forth. "We decided to come to your aid."

"Thank you," Willow replied.

"Don't mention it," Saymore said, walking away.

Willow chuckled. He was the strangest guardian she ever met. That, in itself, further confirmed they were individuals and not just furry balls of magic. For better or worse, each had its own personality.

"Incoming! Airborne!" Shelby yelled down.

"Dragons prepare!" William ordered.

Willow watched several male elves transform before her into dragons. Those who had not mounted the backs of the beasts, preparing to take the battle to the sky.

"Keep the fight away from the camp!" William yelled his final order as they took flight.

Gavin gasped. "By sea, air, and land," he muttered.

"What did you say?" William asked.

"Nothing," Gavin answered. "It was just something I read."

"It was the prophecy, wasn't it?" Willow exclaimed.

The vampire sighed. "If you must know, it was."

"You could share information," William pointed out. "You know the book is missing and none of us can seem to remember that particular passage."

"Yeah," Gavin said. His hand rubbed the back of his neck. His lips pressed tightly together, as if never planning on uttering another word.

"Well?" William hollered.

"I thought it would make things worse if you knew," Gavin answered. "I don't remember it word-for-word. After the part about the attack coming by sea, air, and land, it went on to say something about the use of each of the elementals."

Fire was already blazing through the trees scattered along the shore. "That's two," Willow said.

"Two what?!" William yelled.

"Two of the elementals represented," Miss Kelly explained. "Water was the first attack. This one is fire." She pointed to the raging flames spreading through the woodland. "We can expect two more attacks. One will include the use of the ground we stand on. The other will be made of the very air we breathe. What form they take remains to be seen."

"Great," William said. "How do we fight that?"

"Skilar!" Willow yelled. "What are you doing here?"

"I've come to help, of course," The young dragon replied. "My family is all fighting, so I want to too." He didn't wait for a reply.

"Wait!" Willow screamed. "Shelby, can you lift me?"

"I should be able to handle your weight," Shelby answered.

"We need to stop him." Willow said, already mounted on the bird's back. "How fast can you fly?"

"Not as fast as a dragon, but I will do my best."

The ride was much bumpier than she was used to. She grabbed a hold of a few feathers to steady herself. Rather than helping the situation, they simply came loose. Her body slid sideways.

"What are you doing?!" Shelby yelled, trying to compensate for the shift in weight. "You'll fall if you keep that up. Not to mention, it hurts!"

"I'm not trying to!" Willow bellowed back. "This is awkward."

"It's not exactly easy for me, either," Shelby replied.

"What are you two doing?"

"Zoran!" Willow yelled. "I have an idea. Shelby, fly over top of Zoran and stay almost touching his back." She pretended not to hear any questions about why. As she figured, the guardian bird gave up and did as she requested. "Now join with me."

"Are you crazy?" Shelby asked.

"Trust me," Willow replied. She held her breath as she fell, landing on Zoran's back. Her hands grasped a scale and held on tight.

"You okay?" Zoran asked.

"Yeah, great," she answered. "We need to stop Skilar."

"Skilar?" Zoran roared. "What is he doing here?"

"He said he wanted to help fight," Willow replied. "I tried to stop him, but he wouldn't listen. There." She pointed. "Straight ahead."

"I see him! Hold on tight!"

Willow felt her stomach rise into her throat, then fall back down again. The colour drained from her face. She gulped back saliva pooling in her mouth, hoping to stop nausea from running its course. It didn't work. She held her breath.

"No!" she screamed. They were too late. Skilar's body was falling to the ground. "Shelby, catch him."

Shelby appeared beside them, but Skilar was almost to the ground. Willow clenched her eyes tight, not wanting to watch.

"It's okay," Zoran said. "Umaagan caught him. Let's hope he isn't too badly hurt from the blow he took."

One hand covered her chest, holding back the pounding of her heart. It was true. Beneath them, Umaagan was landing in dragon form with Miss Kelly and Skilar on his back.

"Take us down," she said. Willow rushed to the young dragon's side, tears falling freely from her eyes. "We have to help him," she cried.

Miss Kelly shook her head. “He is beyond what my magic can do,” she answered. “Death will come swiftly.”

Willow looked past Miss Kelly. “Deanne, Anndee, Dannee, please sing.”

“We would have to separate,” the woman said. “We would not be able to join back together again in time to help with a battle. The only way we can use our magics properly is if we remain together.”

“I don't care!” Willow cried. “You can save him.”

“Is this one dragon's life worth that much?”

“Every life is worth that much,” Willow answered.

The woman nodded. Her eyes became distant; glazed over as if lost deep in thought. “Yes,” she agreed. Instantly the three girls appeared in the same spot, their hands connected.

The beauty of their song reached the ears of all who would listen. Skilar's wounds began to heal. It wasn't just Skilar, though. Zoran and the other dragons, on both sides, were healing as well. The fighting stopped. The beasts landed all around them, some turning back into elves to bow at the triplet's feet.

“Awkward,” Willow said, looking away from the naked elves.

Zoran laughed. “It's beautiful, if you ask me.”

“Well,” Victor said, sneaking up behind them. “Isn't this a sight? With two battles down, that means we have two left.”

“Umaagan,” Miss Kelly called. “Would you please lead the dragons and elves back to the camp? Take the triplets with you, too.”

“It would be my pleasure,” Umaagan replied. “What, may I enquire, is your plan?”

“To find a way to stop the next attacks,” Miss Kelly answered. Her staff hit the ground, sparks flying on contact. “We need a barrier between us and the camp.”

Willow glanced over her shoulder at the line of retreating soldiers. As soon as the dragons were out of sight, she called for rain to douse the flames. What was left of full forests were merely charred remains. She subdued the instinct to revitalize the trees. Her energy was needed elsewhere.

"Trees!" she exclaimed. "That's it. We need the trees. Acacia, can you hear me?"

"I can," the great tree said. "I told you when you needed me, I would come. My brothers and sisters have joined me."

"Thank you," Willow said. "If you could form a barrier between here and the camp, I would be ever so grateful."

"That we can do," Acacia answered.

"What now?" Willow asked.

"We fight," Miss Kelly answered.

"Are we forgetting that they still have unicorns?" Victor asked.

"Leave that to us," Elsa-Mae said.

It was a sight to see. A lineup of fairies, each flapping their petal-like wings and carrying a small bag. Quicker than a blink, they were a similar height to everyone else.

"How?" Willow asked.

"This is our normal size," Elfred explained.

Willow cocked her head. Apparently, their bodies grew but their voices remained the same. It made for an odd combination.

"We prefer to stay smaller," Elsa-Mae added. "We are much more adorable that way."

"Ahem." Elfred cleared his throat. "We, by pure accident, found out a long time ago that when we held something in small version and grew bigger, the item did too." He lifted the sack. It was indeed much larger.

"And what does that bag carry?" Willow asked.

"Why, fairy dust, of course," Elfred answered. "Brilliant, isn't it?"

“That depends,” Willow replied. “What do you plan to do with it?”

“Glitter bomb,” Elsa-Mae said, breaking out into laughter.

“I don't think she understands,” Elfred said.

“You don't understand?” Elsa-Mae scoffed. “It's simple, of course. Fairy dust is a special type of magic. It can only be used by those who don't want to use it for the wrong reasons.”

“Except us fairies, of course, we can use it for anything,” Elfred added.

“Excuse the interruption,” Elsa-Mae continued. “We plan to drop it on the remaining unicorns. They will suck it in better than an anteater dining on an ant hill. When they try to attack, all that will spew from their horns is glitter.”

“It'll be a few hundred years before this stuff clears out,” Elfred added.

“Now might be a good time,” Miss Kelly said. “Looks like there is some movement over there.”

“Operation Glitter Bomb away!” Elfred exclaimed, leading the small group of fairies.

“What's that?” Victor asked, pointing to some bubbles forming near the shoreline.

“I think we know what that is,” Miss Kelly answered. Victor nodded.

Willow's head alternated between the two. She, apparently, was the only one who hadn't known what was going on. As the bubbles took shape, it became clear. Willow smiled. “Pandora,” she said.

Her watery form gave way to a solid appearance. The water behind her parted, allowing a trail of guardians to follow her onto the ground safely.

“You're all okay,” Willow cried.

“Did you expect any less?” Aslo asked, shaking the wetness out of his fur.

Willow wiped her face. “Thanks for the shower,” she moaned.

Also snorted. The battle and trip back took its toll on the group. Exhaustion grabbed a hold on them - a grip that only rest could loosen.

The ground shook. There was no time for a partial retreat. Something was coming from Atlantis. “Is the land moving?” Willow asked.

“Earth magic,” Miss Kelly said. “Whoever is in control is making a bridge to cross on.”

Pandora pushed free from leaning on Victor. “What is that?!” she yelled.

Soil and rocks pulled together in a whirlwind. Each speck of dirt found a place, moulding together into one large body. When the wind settled, a giant rock creature was left behind. Its mouth opened, releasing a hair-curling roar. Within moments, more than a dozen monsters stood before them.

“Why don't they move?” Willow asked.

“They are shielding their master,” Miss Kelly answered. She slammed her staff down on the ground. “Chee.” Her teaching assistant appeared at her side.

“He's a familiar?” Willow asked.

“Yes,” Miss Kelly smiled. “A quite talented one, in fact. It's too bad you used so much energy, Pandora. Now would be a good time to unleash your familiars.”

“Ha,” Pandora snorted. “Stand aside, old woman.” She pulled out a golden box.

“I thought the box was a metaphor,” Victor said.

“Well,” Pandora answered, “I lied.” She opened the box, allowing a bright light and mist to escape. “Come forth, my pets. Destroy my enemies.” The mist took the shape of four hooded men on horses. Each ghostly figure held a blade similar in appearance to a scythe. "Go now. Ride like the wind."

"They didn't have any faces," Willow said, goosebumps already reforming over her entire body. "Why don't they have any faces?"

"What face would you give to a plague?" Pandora asked. "They are pure pandemonium and destruction." She nodded, impressed with herself.

"And the box," Victor asked.

"After our little meeting, I thought about it," Pandora said. "It made complete sense. It takes less energy to unleash them this way."

"Really?" Victor asked.

"Yes," Pandora answered. "Oh, this is the best part."

The horsemen raced forward at their targets, scythes in the air. One by one, their sharp blades cut through the creatures, sending piles of dirt and rock toppling to the ground. When all that was left was rubble, they returned, disappearing back into the box from which they came. Pandora shut the lid and locked it. The box disappeared. She fell to her knees.

"You should head back to the camp and rest," Willow suggested.

"Yes. I agree," Miss Kelly added. "Victor, take Pandora back, and the guardians as well."

Victor watched the fairies fly over top of them. Elfred extended a thumb in an upright position. "That would leave only the two of you," he said.

"Yes," Miss Kelly answered. "You can count." She chuckled. "Go now." She motioned towards a gap that formed in the trees to allow passage. "And Victor, if we fail, you are the last line of defence."

He nodded.

If Willow had turned around to watch them leave, she would have missed the show. Glitter rained down all around them. "I guess the fairy dust worked," she said.

"Looks like it did," Miss Kelly answered. "Cornost doesn't look very happy." Her staff pointed forward towards the King of Atlantis dismounting his unicorn, the red colouring of his face almost glowing.

"What's he doing?" Willow asked.

"It looks as if," Miss Kelly answered, "he's sucking in air. If this is an air attack, you best brace yourself. We'll need to counter it with as much force as possible."

Willow nodded. The clouds swirled at her command. Weather was something she had no problem controlling - that included the wind.

Cornost's jaw dropped open. The noise that escaped was like no other Willow had heard before, mixing pain, sorrow, anger, and hate into one. The sound reached them first - a mere distraction to what was coming next. What was left of the forest uprooted and was hurtling towards them.

"Now!" Miss Kelly yelled.

Willow unleashed the power of nature to fight against the invisible force on a direct collision course with them. Winds howled in every direction. Even with both of them using all the air magic they had combined, it wasn't enough. Willow felt her feet slip backwards. Vines surged out of the ground, coiling around her feet and legs as they grew and anchoring her in place. She glanced back at the great trees. There was little they could do to defend against this type of attack. Leaves and branches whipped recklessly about. She winced, wondering how much damage was being done to the makeshift camp. They had underestimated Cornost and were paying the price. Chee disappeared. Miss Kelly's power had begun to fade. They were losing the battle.

Cornost's laugh became louder. He walked through the battling gale-force winds without hindrance. "Well, what do we have here?" he asked. "That's a nice touch you have with the vines. I have to admit, you have been a formidable opponent." He threw his head backwards, his throat spitting out primal grunts. “And who might you be?”

Miss Kelly didn't answer.

“I know what you're thinking,” he sang. “But not a single strike of lightning can make it to the ground in this high of a wind.” A wicked smile faded from his face. His eyes went blank. He fell to his knees.

Something hit him. At first, Willow wondered if she missed a lightning bolt. An arrow whizzed by her, striking Cornost directly in the heart - followed by yet another.

The winds were silenced. Willow eyed the man kneeling on the ground. The vines recede back from whence they came. She groaned at the unwrapping, knowing more bruises were in her future.

“What's he doing?” Miss Kelly asked.

The proud king crawled in front of her. He took her hand in his. “You are the most beautiful woman I have ever met,” he declared. “My love for you is eternal.”

“What's the meaning of this?!” Miss Kelly yelled.

The laughter of three girls exploded. “A gift from Karma,” Deanne said.

“You told our secret,” Anndee complained.

“You shouldn't have done that,” Dannee added.

“With all three arrows in the heart at once, he might never stop loving you. We should seal it with a combo arrow,” Deanne smirked.

Before Miss Kelly could utter a word, three arrows intertwined as one pierced the man's heart. He bowed down, kissing her bare feet.

“Get off,” Miss Kelly scolded, heading towards the camp. “Don't follow me. This is ridiculous! Someone detain this man.”

Willow's laughter was shortlived. There was, in fact, extensive wind damage. The injured lay waiting for medical attention. Her pace steadily increased: a walk; a jog; a full run.

Her arms wrapped around William's neck. “Was anyone lost?” she whispered.

“No,” he answered back. “But there are a lot of injured. This realm will be healing for a very long time. Are you okay?”

“Yeah,” she replied. “You?”

“Fine. We should help.”

Willow nodded.

Chapter Eighty-Six

“Let the celebration begin!” Cassandrhea proclaimed.

“Not words I ever expected to hear her say,” Willow chuckled. “I didn't know elves celebrated.”

“We do,” Sebastian said, grabbing her waist and twirling her into a dance. Spinning in time to a band, they circled a large bonfire. Her back bumped into another couple. Gabrielle took her hand, exchanging partners. The next dance belonged to Kayleb, followed by Seth. William watched from the sidelines, his eyes never leaving her.

Music has a way of brightening moods, bringing out the best in everyone. As much as she enjoyed the fast-paced tunes, there was a certain sense of relief when the band members announced they were taking a break. Her legs ached in places she hadn't known could ache. Using as much magic as was needed earlier left her sluggish. Combining the two meant tonight, dancing was more of a chore than fun.

“I think it's time we get a few things straight,” William demanded. He squared his shoulders to the four elves, asserting his male ego.

“Calm down,” Gavin interrupted. “We've done enough fighting for one day.”

“No,” Willow said. “He's right. We need to straighten things out. The triplets need to answer a few questions.”

“You don't have a sense of humour,” Anndee pouted. “It was all innocent.”

“What was all innocent?” Sebastian asked.

“I want to know everything you did,” Willow said, wagging her finger at the girls. “From the very beginning.”

“Alright,” Deanne agreed, rolling her eyes. “We were only trying to help.”

“Love isn't something to mess around with!” Willow yelled.

“You have it all wrong,” Dannee interrupted. “One arrow from one of us only lasts long enough for the first kiss. If you aren't meant to be together, the spell ends when the lips touch.”

“Or if the one who was hit meets true love,” Deanne added, “that breaks the spell instantly. We are all for soulmates connecting. Love is a beautiful thing.” A few sparkles floated down to the ground, forming the image of a hovering rose.

Willow blew air over the palm of her hand, directing it towards the fake flower. The sparkles scattered, breaking the illusion. “So who did you hit?” Willow asked.

“The mean guy was first,” Dannee stated. “The one that put that stuff over your mouth. He was so nasty to you. We wanted him to be a little nicer.”

“Mike,” William exclaimed. “That explains why his feelings for you disappeared when he met Sissy. At least I know you never kissed him.”

Willow shot him a disapproving glare. “No. I never kissed him. Who was next?”

“The vampire,” Anndee offered. “We worried about him hurting you on the Halloween tour. We couldn't follow you, so we thought this was the next best thing.”

“What?” Gavin asked. The tone of surprise in his voice wavered, giving way to a low chuckle. “I admit it. I felt it. I guess I found the right girl, though.” He grinned, flashing pure white teeth. “At least things are finally beginning to make some sense.” His head shook. Even as a vampire, the past few months held some strange things that he never contemplated the possibility of happening before.

“Who else?” Willow asked, crossing her arms over her chest.

“You have to understand,” Deanne pleaded. “You were distraught and all alone. They were being so mean to you. You needed a friend.”

“Did you hit me with one of your arrows?” Sebastian asked.

“We did,” Dannee said. “We hit all four of you, actually.”

Sebastian threw his hands in the air. They fell down, making a smacking sound as they hit his legs. “Great!” he yelled. “Undo it.”

“We can't,” Anndee replied. “Once shot, it remains in effect until either you two kiss or you find true love.”

“Then we have no choice but to kiss,” Sebastian exclaimed.

“Slow down,” William said, moving to position himself between the elves and Willow.

“Was there anyone else?” Willow asked.

“We wanted to help,” Dannee said. “He has followed you through so many lives.”

“You didn't,” Willow cried.

“There is no doubting there is love between you,” Anndee added.

“Yes,” Willow said. “But not that type of love. Do you have any idea how much he struggled with his feelings because of this? Wait, you said the spell ends with a kiss. How many times did you shoot him?"

"How many times did you kiss him?!" William yelled, turning his back to the elves.

"When the first kiss failed, we decided to try again," Deanne answered, ignoring William. "We made a few attempts. We were sure you two were meant to be together."

"Perhaps we were meant to be together," Willow said. "But not in a romantic way. That's what confused him to the very end. He had these feelings that weren't right. Everyone has been telling the truth all along. There are some things that we need to find out for ourselves. How Lance and I fit together is one of those things."

"And me?" William asked. "Did you shoot me with one of your love arrows too?"

"There is one way to find out," Deanne mused. "If we say no, would you believe us? If we say yes, would you doubt your own feelings? Kiss her and be sure. "

"You better get it over with," William mumbled. "There's a lineup waiting for a kiss." He rubbed the back of his neck as he strolled away.

Willow felt her heart snap in two. She didn't want to kiss anyone else. William was the only one for her. She knew that now. All she could do was watch him leave. "Will any kiss do?" she asked. "Are there rules?"

"It has to be on the lips and both must participate," Dannee answered. "But those are the only rules."

"So it could be a peck... like two friends greeting?" Willow questioned.

"Yes," Anndee replied. "As long as the lips touch."

"That makes things less complicated," Willow said. She approached Sebastian and puckered her lips like a fish.

"You have to be kidding." The elf laughed.

“Do you want to be free of the love triplets' spell or not?” Willow puckered her lips again, making a few kissing sounds.

Sebastian laughed. “Fine,” he said. His lips formed a similar pattern. He leaned in and pressed them against hers. The two made a smacking noise. He backed away, nodding. “Yup,” he said. “Feeling is gone.” The other three elf princes followed suit.

Willow wiped her lips. It wasn't that she despised the elves, but rather she felt guilty. Every time she came close to making things work with William, something stole it away from her. She needed to find him. She needed to know once and for all if he was in love with her or not. She thought back to her declaration of love. He hadn't answered back with his own proclamation, but rather made a statement that they would make things work. Maybe the triplets were the ones behind his feelings.

Her legs moved without command, running in the same direction as William - aimlessly. There was no trail or clues to follow. Pure instinct led her. Exhaustion consumed her. A familiar burning sensation rushed up and down her legs. The events of the day began to have a greater effect on her body as every minute passed. She headed to the shade of her trees, touching Nadia's trunk. “I could use some hope right now. I appear to be all out of luck.”

“There is only one tree that can help with love,” Nadia said. “Bettulla is the tree you should visit.”

Willow forced a smile. “Thank you, my friend,” she whispered. Her head hung down. The stroll over to the tree of love felt like an eternity to her body. Aches and pains extended to every muscle.

“I wondered if you'd find me,” William said.

His expressions were too hard to read. That was nothing new. In one hand he held a piece of bark and in the other a pen. He always did his best thinking while he doodled.

“What are you writing?” she asked, choking on her tears.

“This?” He replied. He turned the bark towards her. All that was visible was his name written on it. “The tree of love. Write the names of a couple on her bark and she will grant you a lasting love. But I don't know what is real."

"If you don't know, then I guess it isn't," Willow muttered.

"It isn't that simple," William said. "Magic has a hand in this. You doubted me. Allow me the same privilege."

He was right. "I don't want you to kiss me for the first time only because you think it may break some spell."

She doubted him when she read in the papers he had accepted Lara's pledge. The Pledge - that was the answer. "I pledge myself to you," she blurted out without thought. She held her breath. She had really done it this time.

William moved closer to her. His gaze met hers. He nodded. "I accept your pledge for eternity." His hands took hers. Two golden hoops encircled them. After rotating around them completely twice they disappeared, forming golden bands on their ring fingers. "I should never have doubted you," he whispered.

"Nor I you," she answered back.

"None of that matters now. No magic can bring together a couple that isn't meant to be." He leaned forward, kissing her lightly on the lips.

"Feel any different?" she asked.

"Yeah," he smirked. "A whole lot happier."

He threw the bark in the air, chuckling at Willow's gasp. Her name was written on it after all. The palm of his hand merely hid it from her view. A breeze caught it, lifting the love request back to the tree from where it came. The two embraced, watching the request absorb back into Bettulla. A heart appeared midway up the trunk with their two names etched in it - a constant reminder of true love that could never be erased.

"Thank you," Willow whispered.

William took her hand. "I think it's time to go home. We still have some things to clear up there. I'd like to be able to say it's over."

“I'll have to come back to help the elves rebuild,” Willow said.

“Let's make sure the triplets are on vacation when you do,” William replied, laughing.

“There you two are!” Cassandrhea exclaimed.

“Looking forward to getting rid of us?” William asked.

“Well,” the Director answered, “it's nothing personal, but yes.”

“We'll gather our crew together and head home, then,” he said, bowing before her.

“The portal is already opened,” she replied, pointing towards a door of swirling colours. “No rush, of course.” She patted the neat bun formed at the back of her head. “I took the liberty of rounding up your friends, though.”

Willow snorted, trying to hold back laughter. The guardians took no time to join with the couple. The extra drowsiness of their exhaustion added to her own. She leaned in, towards William, using him as a personal pillar of strength, while he directed the others to pass through the portal. They were the last two remaining.

“Are you okay?” he asked.

“Yeah,” she answered, standing under her own power. “I could use some sleep.”

“You can pass out as soon as we get back,” he promised.

“You go first,” she said. She watched William pass through the doorway. “I wanted to say goodbye,” Willow said.

“I'd like to say I'll miss you,” Cassandrhea replied. “We probably won't meet again.”

“I can come back to help,” Willow offered.

“We can handle it,” the Director stated. “The fairies and dragons are helping after all.”

“There she is,” Sebastian said. “We were worried we missed you. Just because we aren't in love with you anymore doesn't mean we don't consider you a good friend.”

“You aren't trying to leave without saying goodbye,” Zoran said. “Are you?”

“Of course not,” Willow answered. She hugged the beast's leg. “And Skilar,” she cried, rushing over to the young dragon, throwing her arms around his neck. The four elf princes were next: Kayleb, Gabrielle, Seth, and Sebastian. One by one, she embraced each of them, not knowing if they would ever meet again. A piece of her heart tore a little. Now she understood why the elves stayed so distant from everyone. Saying goodbye was hard.

“Don't forget about us?” Elfred said.

“I could never forget about any of you,” she said, sniffling. She blew the fairies a kiss. “I will miss each and every one of you.”

“Now,” Zoran said. “You sound like you aren't ever coming back. We expect you to visit.”

She exchanged glances with Cassandrhea. “Of course. I plan to visit every chance I can,” she lied. “Provided I am allowed to.”

“Why in the realms wouldn't you be allowed to?” Cassandrhea asked. “You best hurry. Your friends are waiting on the other side.”

Willow waved goodbye, stepping through the doorway without glancing back - her new life waiting on the other side.

Chapter Eighty-Seven

To her surprise, none of her friends were waiting on the other side. None of the ones that returned from the elf realm, that is.

"I was starting to worry," Jade said, throwing her arms around Willow's neck.

"Where is everyone?" Willow asked.

"Right after the others returned, Jessie, Dezi, and Pete woke up," Jade answered. "They needed to be restrained... they were so freaked out. It took every guy in the place to bring them under control."

"Do they know?"

"About Victoria," Jade said, her head shaking. "No. I bet it would be a million times worse if they did. They need to cope with what happened to themselves before handling news like that. We don't know what they went through at Lara's mercy. I worry about the effects it still has on my father. It's as if he disappears into another zone sometimes. I can tell by the horrific expression frozen on his face, he's thinking about Hilary."

"I can't see them waiting too long before asking for her," Willow said.

"I know," Jade agreed, kicking at the grass with the toe of her shoe. "I don't think anyone will get much sleep tonight."

Willow sighed. She was ready to collapse on the spot.

"Did you want to try to help?"

"No," Willow answered, yawning. "I am too tired to be of any help. I'd end up messing something up or getting in the way."

"You feel like talking?" Jade asked, one side of her upper lip raised higher than the other.

Willow smiled. "Sure." Lying was becoming a bad habit she needed to break. How could she say no to the enthusiasm itching to burst out of her friend? "Do you mind if we lie down, though?"

"Yeah, no problem," Jade squealed, pulling her friend's arm.

Being dragged along was better than walking. Willow couldn't help but smile at Jade's zeal for life. Besides, girl talk was something she desperately needed more of in her life. There had been no one to share the experience of her first kiss with; no one to cry to when William wouldn't wake; no one at Sleeping Sands. There was something important in her life again - something she wanted to share.

The two girls flopped on the bottom bunk of one of the beds in the building Jade slept in. Albeit that particular room held multiple beds, they were the only two occupying it that evening. Willow scooted back against the wall. As much as she wanted to rest her head on the fluffy white pillow, she pulled it to her chest instead, locking it in a tight hug, her chin resting on the part that stuck out.

"Is it true?" Jade asked, bouncing on the mattress.

"What?"

"That there was some love spell being used on the elves?" Jade asked. Her eyes widened, leaving no doubt she was offering her full attention.

"Oh," Willow answered. "Yeah. It seems a young matchmaker went a bit crazy. It wasn't only the elves, either."

"Really," Jade said. "Tell me everything."

Willow was pretty sure her friend heard most of it already. "The effects of the arrow's spell only wear off after a kiss or if the person shot finds their true love. That's why I was so popular. It wasn't really me at all."

"So how many guys were affected?"

"Mike, the four elves, and Lance," Willow answered. "Oh, and Gavin."

"Gavin?" Jade's voice lifted a few octaves higher. She bit down on her thumbnail, not breaking it, but rather softly grazing it with her teeth.

"Yeah," Willow said. "I didn't even know. He said he knew, but figured he found a true love that broke the spell. It's mysterious. I wonder who it is."

The room fell silent. Willow glanced up from her pillow. Staring off into no-man's-land while smiling wasn't something Jade ever did. She waved one hand in front of her friend's face. "Anybody home? Jade. Are you... daydreaming?"

"Sorry," Jade mumbled. "What?"

"It's you," Willow squealed. "You're the girl he's in love with, aren't you?"

Jade shook her head. "I don't know," she said. "Maybe." Red crept into her cheeks as she spoke. Her teeth chomped on her bottom lip.

"It's totally you," Willow exclaimed. "And you like him too. I can tell."

Jade grabbed a pillow and held it over her face. Not even the fluffy white disguise could hide her beaming smile. She squealed. "I do," she finally admitted. "I really like him. I've never felt like this before. I thought I did, but it wasn't even close. I have to admit, I was a little nervous that he had feelings for you." She buried her face again, letting out another squeal.

Willow threw her arms around her friend's neck in a tight embrace. "You don't have to worry about me anyways," she said.

"What do you mean?" Jade asked.

Willow held up her hand, proudly displaying the gold band on her ring finger.

"The Pledge?" Jade asked. "William? You didn't."

"I did," Willow replied. "I don't know what came over me. I just blurted it out."

"I wish I had your confidence," Jade admitted. "I can't believe you found your lifemate. I'm so happy for you."

Willow opened her mouth, but a squeal came out instead of words. She nodded. The two girls lay back on the bed facing each other. Chatter continued for hours. They laughed. They cried. They shared their deepest secrets.

She wondered how soon it would be before her other friends took the Pledge as well. They were all over the age to choose a lifemate. It wouldn't be long before they all had families of their own. Willow's eyelids grew heavy. Giving up the fight, they shut. Somewhere between reality and the world of dreams, she realized how much she loved Jade. Not a romantic love, but rather she loved her as a best friend. She wanted to see her happy. Love was complicated, but she decided it was worth figuring out.

Chapter Eighty-Eight

Willow yawned, stepping through the doorway of the command centre. The invigorating aroma of fresh brewed coffee perked up her heavy eyelids. “Mmm,” she muttered, eagerly warming her hands on either side of the mug Zsiga offered. “Thank you.” She paused for a moment to watch the stream rise. There were no hidden pictures or messages in the vapours today. Her lips curled upwards as they pressed against the side of the white mug, allowing a small amount of the mellow liquid to pass through. It was perfect.

William's pen scratched furiously on the pad of paper in front of him. With barely any room left on the page, it was obvious he had been there a while. He rubbed his eyes, making the dark circles under them more noticeable.

“Good morning,” Malarchy said.

“Morning,” she muttered back, not wanting the cup to travel too far from her taste buds. Watching Jade's head rest on Gavin's shoulder made her lips curve up a little further. This wasn't the same group she was accustomed to sitting around the table. So many faces were missing, replaced by new friends. Things had changed. That was something no magic could stop. Change was a part of life she would have to accept. She alternated glances between everyone gathered there. Each one had a story to tell - written between the lines forming on their faces. Emotions, experiences, worries, fears - they were all there.

"Professor," she said. "Why are you here?"

"We've asked Professor Finkle here to help the Shinnings," William answered without looking up from his scribblings.

Gavin reached into a backpack between his legs. *The Portal Prophecies* book slid across the table. "I figure I should return this," Gavin said. "I honestly thought that not having it was the best route to travel."

Willow's hand traced over the words on the front cover. A smile formed over her face. This book held so many answers - answers that led her to adventures few could ever imagine possible. Although she was happy everything turned out the way it had and the conflicts were over, a part of her was sad the book had run its course and had no further stories to share.

"Better late than never," she said, opening it to the very end of the book. "Gavin," she said, her eyebrows pushing in towards each other, "I thought you said there was a whole prophecy at the end."

"There is," Gavin replied.

Willow held up the book. "All it says is the title, *The Final Prophecy*," she argued. The book landed with a thud, flipping to another page. Her fingers traced the words as they faded before her eyes. "The prophecies are disappearing." No matter which page she turned to, the results were the same.

"I think," Pandora said, "that means your part in this book's life is done. The prophecies are no longer written for you. Balance is, for now, restored to the realms."

"Balance?" Willow questioned.

"Yes," Pandora said. "The balance between right and wrong has been re-established."

"So it's really over?"

Pandora laughed. "For now, perhaps," she grunted. "It takes very little to tip the scales one way or the other."

Willow stared at the front cover. Her fingers lightly traced the words in the book's title as they too disappeared. A strange feeling swelled in the pit of her stomach. *The Portal Prophecies* had been such an important part of her life, losing it left an emptiness.

William moved her hand from the book. He winked at her with a smile. This was her first view of his whole face since sitting down. His bloodshot eyes were proof he hadn't yet slept.

The book slid across the table to Malarchy. "You best keep this for research. Who knows, maybe one day new prophecies will show up," William advised.

Malarchy nodded. The book disappeared from the table into a black leather case. A breeze flowed in from the door.

"Here they are! All cleaned up," Iskander said, leading the Shinning boys to the table. "Hopefully too tired to cause any more problems."

"Good, then let's begin," William said. "Professor, the box, please."

"Yes. Of course," Finkle babbled. His hands lingered on the fancy box for a few minutes before sliding it into the middle of the table.

"Are you sure you boys want to take on this task alone?" William asked. "It won't be long before we have the camp cleaned up and moved. Then we will have the extra manpower to send along with you to help."

"We'd like to get started as soon as possible," Jessie said. "The sooner we leave, the sooner we come back to help Victoria."

"I believe Willow knows more about opening the box than I do," the professor declared. He dabbed his forehead with a small, white handkerchief that quickly returned to his jacket pocket.

"It isn't a big secret," Willow said. "It's plain as day. There is a lock between the rocks." She pointed to the spot on the stained glass picture.

Jessie pulled the box into his view. His fingers traced over the image. "There isn't anything there," he said, pushing his eyebrows together, forming a crease between them.

"What?" Willow asked. "I can see it."

"Apparently," Finkle said, "you are the only one who can see it. Is this another special gift that you have been hiding from us?"

"Can you describe the key hole?" William asked.

"It's older looking," Willow answered. "It almost reminds me of some of the keys we saw in the Frostica world." She paused, pointing her finger up in front of her lips. "I wonder..." She dug into her pocket, pulling out the key ring from Atlantis. The keys rattled as they hit the table. Willow cocked her head to one side. "That's odd," she said. "I can't see the lock anymore."

"But I can," Jessie responded, standing over the box, key ring in hand.

"How extraordinary," Finkle added. "You must need to be in possession of the key to see the lock. Why don't I take those?" he said more as a statement than a question.

"I think Jessie best keep them for the moment," Malarchy offered. "Go ahead. Open it up."

The keys jingled. Jessie's large hands fumbled through them, looking for a match to the small lock. On the fourth try, a click sounded. The box opened. "I'm not sure what all of this is," the oldest Shinning brother said. He lifted out papers and maps. "I don't even know what language these are written in."

"May I?" Sarah asked. Her hands outstretched to catch a notebook already sliding across the table. One finger pushed reading glasses further up her nose by their bridge, before returning her attention to the laptop and keyboard in front of her. She worked with ease, never noticing, or at least not paying attention to, the stares locked on her, hopeful for answers. "It isn't written in any language I can find."

"I knew it," Finkle blurted out.

"Knew what?" Malarchy asked.

"I'll share information," Finkle said. "But I want in. I am going with you boys on your quest. I have a right to. This has, after all, been my life's work. We wouldn't even have the box if it weren't for me."

Willow darted a glance that could maim.

"With some help," the professor added. "Do we have a deal?"

"Yeah," Jessie said before anyone else could object. "We have a deal. Now what information do you have?"

Willow sighed. Her own experiences making deals with Finkle proved the man less than trustworthy. The Shinning boys didn't have a clue what they were getting into.

"We are looking for the Pearl of Diplomacy," Finkle offered. "From the pictures on the box and the text, I believe it is connected to mermaids."

"Actual mermaids," Sarah said, removing her glasses and placing the end of one arm in her mouth. Her teeth crunched down on the handle.

"You find that hard to believe?" Finkle asked.

"No," Sarah answered, her fingers typing. "There are many reports throughout history of mermaids. I have a few listed right here."

"That one was me," Pandora said, pointing to the screen over Sarah's shoulder. "And that one. I think most of these are probably me."

Sarah's gaze shifted to face Pandora. "You lure innocent men to their deaths?" she asked, her eyebrows arching.

“It sounds terrible when you say it like that,” Pandora replied. “I can tell you, as Goddess of the Sea, I have no information about your elusive mermaids.”

“Why exactly are you here?” William asked, the eraser end of his pencil tapping the table and bouncing back into his hand repeatedly.

“Be nice,” Pandora said. “I did help with the Atlantis problem, didn't I? Besides, I have a certain skill set that could help these boys.”

“If you don't lure them to their deaths,” Sarah muttered.

“I heard that,” Pandora scoffed. “I haven't done that in ages.”

“Let me make some copies of the papers we found,” William said. “It won't hurt to have more than one group working on them.”

“Pandora is right,” Willow said. “If you are in fact looking for mermaids, she will be useful. She can also keep an eye on Professor Finkle.”

“I resent that,” Finkle said.

“You deserve it,” Willow scoffed.

William slid papers into the middle of the table, keeping one set for himself. “Help yourselves. There's enough for anyone who wants a set.” The original documents returned to their resting place in the box. “I think you three boys should have an extra set each. You may come across the need to barter with the other ones. That brings us to the problem of where to start.”

“I believe Krissy handed me a partial answer,” Malarchy offered. “While she was reporting in the Triangle, she came across some myths about mermaids and a secret society that protects them.”

“You think this secret society is where we should start?” Dezi asked.

“Yes,” Malarchy answered.

“Except isn't it a problem if they are in fact a secret organization?” Pandora asked.

“My dear lady,” Finkle said, “no organization can be truly secret. There is always some trail that leads to the front door.”

“As much as I hate to agree with Professor Finkle,” Malarchy said, “he is correct. While I was with Kasper on the unicorn mission, I ran into an odd bunch. They were asking questions about strange fish sightings. They gave me their business card. Apparently, they run under the name Merliance.”

“I've searched that term and can't find any information on a business with that name,” Sarah said.

“We couldn't find anything in the city journals, either,” Jade added.

“So contacting them is where we start,” Pete said.

“I would exercise caution,” Finkle warned. “Very few secret societies like to be found. We don't want to become a potential threat to their existence.”

“Funny,” Willow said. “You never gave me that warning about The Organization.”

“There aren't many options,” Jessie replied, ignoring Willow's qualms with the professor. “Let's hope that box gives us a ticket in. I think it's time for us to head out. There isn't much else we are going to learn around this table.”

“Stay close to the water,” Pandora said. “I'll be watching.”

“Well then,” Finkle said, teetering his weight between the toes and heals of his feet. He shoved his fingers in his mustard coloured vest pocket and pulled out a watch. “Shall we?”

Willow watched the door close behind the group. “We're all going different ways,” she said.

William threw his arm around her shoulder and squeezed. “One day,” he said, “we'll be back together again. You'll see. Things will work out.”

She managed a meek smile. As much as starting her new life with William meant, she was still sad to see the people she knew all her life leaving.

“I have a question,” Sarah said, interrupting.

“We will answer it to the best of our abilities,” Faramund said, taking her hand.

Red crept into Sarah's cheeks. There was a connection between her and the guard that grew stronger daily. Now it was to the point of being undeniable - they were ready to become a couple. It was only a matter of one of them working up the nerve.

“I have noticed there aren't any babies...” Her words trailed off.

William smirked. “Are you interested in having one?” he teased. He received a punch in the arm for the remark. “Ow,” he said, holding his arm, a smile covering his face.

“I'll answer you,” Malarchy offered, shooting William a glare of disapproval. “As you know, we have been granted longevity. This means the rate at which a woman can have a child also takes longer. In a way, every child that is born is a gift to our people. Once a child is born, he or she is given the same extended life we have.”

“So a mother doesn't carry the child for extended time?”

“No,” Malarchy answered. “The baby develops at the same rate it would in this world and is born in approximately the same time frame. It is only after birth that ageing slows.”

Sarah nodded at no one in particular. “If I were to have a child,” she started.

“As long as you have been given the gift of extended life, your child, once born, will also be given the same,” Malarchy answered.

Sarah's lips curled upwards, her thumbnail locked between her teeth. Willow wondered if the triplets had visited the camp unannounced. Sarah's glazed-over eyes stared into nowhere, revealing her secret that love was on her mind.

“Do we know how long the others will be in recovery?” Malarchy asked, breaking the sappiness threatening to engulf him.

“No,” William answered. “It could be days, weeks, or months. Micca seems to think each patient will take their own time through the process. We'll keep a team on alert.”

“Then I suppose that's it,” Malarchy said, his hands slapping down on the table. “We'll be heading back to Pewterclaw. Let us know if there is anything you need. Make the camp move quickly. I don't know how long it will be before Kasper comes looking for Willow.”

“It's already planned,” William replied. “We'll send you the details once we are safely established. Faramund can find you.”

Malarchy nodded. “Jade... Gavin,” he called on his way to the door. The two men left Jade to say her goodbyes.

“Make sure you visit,” Willow said, tears streaking down her face.

“I will,” Jade replied. The two girls embraced before going their separate ways.

Chapter Eighty-Nine

One Year Later ...

As much as William liked the rugged man look, he figured it was time to make his wife happy. A whiff of the lemon-scented shaving cream covering his beard attacked his sinuses. He sneezed, foam flying everywhere. The tin made a fizzing noise emptying its contents into his hand to reapply in the spots that had flown off. The first stroke of the straight edge against his neck meant there was no turning back. “Goodbye, beard,” he said, rinsing the blade in a bowl of water. The second pass of the razor was underway.

The door flung open. “William!” Faramund yelled before tripping.

“Ow,” William winced, the blade cutting into his flesh. He reached for a paper towel and held it over the flowing blood. “What in the realms are you doing?” he asked.

“It's time,” Faramund said, still face down, lying on the ground.

“It's time?!” William yelled. Dropping the paper from his grip, his long legs took only one stride to hurdle over the guard and only two more to reach the open door. The quickest route led through the training yard, which also happened to be busy today. He ducked under swords and sidestepped spells, not stopping to notice the looks he was getting. “Sorry!” he yelled, almost running into Gavin.

The vampire wiped his mouth of the shaving cream that blew off William's face as he passed. He laughed, exposing the white points of his teeth.

William stopped at the door to the medical centre, bending over to catch his breath. His heart raced. Not since the day he took Willow as his lifemate had he felt it beat that hard.

“Are you alright?” Malarchy asked, patting him on the back.

“It's time,” was all he managed to say.

“You would have been better off waiting for me,” Faramund said, the last of his teleportation gas dissipating

“Thanks for telling me now,” William replied, his breath still laboured.

“You sure you want to go in there like that?” Faramund asked.

A blank stare met the guards gaze. “Why wouldn't I want to go in?” He asked. “I should be by Willow's side.”

“I think what Faramund means is, you may want to put on some pants,” Malarchy said, chuckling.

William looked down, realizing all he was wearing was underwear. He laughed. “I suppose I was going to forget something.”

“I took the liberty of bringing you some,” Faramund offered.

“You may want to wipe off the rest of that shaving cream and put a bandage over that cut,” Zsiga said, tossing him a towel. “The sight of you could frighten anyone.”

“Thanks,” William said.

A cry came from inside the medical facility. William looked at the door. The colour drained from his face. He inhaled deeply.

"You better get in there," Malarchy said, giving him a push on the back strong enough to send him through the doorway. "And remember to breathe."

"William," Micca said. "Go right in."

William nodded an acknowledgement as he passed by. Rounding the curtain, he had the first sight of his wife, holding their new child.

"You're late," Willow said.

"I'm sorry," he replied. "I ran as fast as I could."

Willow laughed. "I hope this isn't a new fashion statement."

William felt his uneven facial hair and smiled. "Maybe," he said, sitting beside her on the bed. "Do you like it?"

"Absolutely not," Willow replied. "By the way, this is your new son."

"He's beautiful," William said. "He's going to need a name."

Willow looked into the blazing-blue eyes of the baby in her arms. "He already has one," she said. "It's Lance."

He nodded. It was William's turn to understand. There was one type of love that even death couldn't stop - the bond between mother and child. Lance had found his place in the puzzle that was their life, filling in the last missing piece.

GLOSSARY

These terms may be found throughout *The Portal Prophecies*. Not all terms may appear in every volume. Additional terms may be added to future volumes as needed.

Acacia - An ancient tree with consciousness. Acacia is thought to be one of the first creatures in existence. Its physical appearance is depicted as a type of willow tree.

Achaear - An ancient spider race. Once guardians, the Achaear preferred a life dedicated to their own race rather than the protection of others.

Albino Assassin - A race of beings white in appearance with deadly black wings which power their shadow and teleportation magics. Their knowledge of combat exceeds that of all other known races.

Allaren - Avian Guardian who takes the form of a black bird to bond with another being.

Ancients - Those in existence before the mass population of the worlds. They are thought to be some of the oldest living beings. There are different aged Ancients, ranging from supreme beings to guardians.

Apopp - One of the most prominent Xiuhcoatle (Serpent Race). He controls all contact from his race with other worlds.

Aquanor - An ancient sea creature race. Once guardians, the Aquanor preferred a life dedicated to their own race rather than the protection of others.

Blood Wars - Wars created by men in order to expand their kingdoms. The blood wars were started by certain ancient races to gain advantage over guardians. Men became obsessed with obtaining and drinking the blood of magical creatures to gain temporary abilities that aided them in battle. The wars ended in the creation of the portals.

Council - A group of mentors, originally appointed to train new abilities in those who were aiding the guardians. After a prophecy was made about the end of the guardian home world, the power of the Council was taken over by men and quickly corrupted.

Coven - A group of witches who practice magic together. There are usually thirteen members.

Cycle - 1 cycle is 10,000 years in main world time.

Displaced - The essence of a living being which was removed from its body before physical death occurred.

Dreamwalker - An individual with the power to enter and control dreams. They can also call people into their own dreams.

Empowered, The - The underground newspaper for empyral and the magical.

Empyral - Beings living in the main world, but having come from other worlds. They are generally happy to take residence in the main world and do not pose a threat to society.

Faeries - A magical race. Their eyes are a shimmering white and silver. The females have wings. Not much is known about actual faeries. They rarely interact with other races and it is much more common to find one of their many cousin races.

Frostica - Ice faeries. Their bodies appear humanoid, but their faces are more animal like. They are about two feet tall. Their bite is deadly.

Glaquool - An advanced bodiless race, made up of different gases, who crave experience and knowledge. They discovered they could hide in objects, which on touch, allowed them to displace the essence of the being and take its place.

Green-eyed Recluse Collegiate - A school specializing in illusion magic.

Guardians - Combination of ancient races who protect the rights of all beings to exist and grow in which ever direction they choose. If faced with a choice, they will always choose to protect the greater good.

Gypsy - Term used to describe a group of witches who travel around constantly, hiding from a powerful necromancer.

Hannulate - Peaceful and fun loving creatures who live in magical realms. A direct cousin to faeries. They were once one of the most beautiful races to exist. During the blood wars, they were forced to adapt to survive, by developing sharp teeth and razor claws that could extend at will.

Keeper - Individuals who can host guardians to allow them to pass through portals. It was believed a keeper could only carry two guardians of the same race at a time.

Kriller - A race of the most intelligent creatures to live. The speed at which their brain works causes changes in the formation of their facial features. They communicate with each other telepathically and then work together to complete necessary tasks.

Leander - Feline Guardians who take the form of a black cat to bond with another being.

Light - A person able to read energies and can lend energy to another person to enhance their natural abilities.

Main World - The modern day world. It is the largest realm and connects all of the worlds by portals.

Medium - A witch who specializes in contacting the deceased.

Necrid Flames - A blue flame that engulfs and destroys all living material.

Necromancer - A witch who specializes in death magic.

Olcsanka - A wolf/bear guardian who takes the form of a wolf to bond with another being.

Portal - A doorway to another world that can only be opened by guardians. Once open any creature can use it if it remains active. Guardians can only pass through a portal when bonded to a keeper.

Portal Guard - Those chosen to protect, who travel through portals and ensure the safety of all realms.

Portal Prophecies, The - A book of prophecies made by Iris and Raven prior to the wars and recorded by Diana. There is also a book written by a gypsy named Estonia by the same name.

Portal Stones - The four corner stones required to open any portal.

Samhain - The witches' new year, when the divide between the realms is thinnest, allowing supernatural activity or contact.

Sleeping Sands - The most prestigious of the schools for the Empyral.

Terra former - A person with a rare ability to manipulate weather and soil to sustain life. They can also grow plant life on command. There are few documented people with this ability. The extent of their abilities is not known.

Terunji - People living in the main world who are completely oblivious to the magic around them.

Transmutton - Yeti.

Underground, The - A hidden city. Its inhabitants are all magical, whether from the main world or other realms.

Vamprite - A race of shape shifters led by a young prince, Drake. During the blood wars they learnt that drinking human blood could keep their people young, strong, and beautiful. The main world knows them as vampires.

Wand - A wooden rod used to channel any form of magic and turn it into any form of physical magic the user needs.

Wisps - Bodiless beings who keep their form generally in the shape of a sphere composed of raw energy, or light. Considered a possible explanation for ghosts.

Winks - The smallest of the Faery family. A scale for them would be from the size of a fruit fly to that of a house fly. They all have wings and, unfortunately, a mischievous nature. Although they mean no harm, their pranks and jokes often lead to destruction. Considered a possible explanation for poltergeists.

Witches - A name given to any humanoid with unusual amounts of magical powers. There is some difference between main world witches and those from other worlds. There are different types of witches, practising different types of magic.

Wizard - A witch who practices alchemy and potions. They have a more scientific approach to magic. Wizards can still channel magic through a wand.

Xiuhcoatle - An ancient serpent race, once guardians.

Yeti - Abominable Snowmen.

Author's Message

I hope you enjoyed reading *The Portal Prophecies* as much as I did writing it. While it's sad to see Willow, William and Lance go, I have a few new projects coming up that may be of interest.

ABOUT THE AUTHOR

C.A. King is the recipient of several awards, including: The Hamilton Spectator Readers' Choice Award for 2017 Best Author; The Brant News Readers' Choice Award for 2017 Best Author; Readers' Favorite award in the short story/novella category; the 2017 SIBA Award for Best New Adult; the 2017 SIBA Award for Best Novella; 2018 Readers' Favorite International Book Awards: Gold Medal in the Fiction - Supernatural genre; and 2018 Readers' Favorite International Book Awards: Bronze Medal in the Fiction - New Adult genre

Currently residing in Brantford, Ontario Canada, she lives with her two sons. She began her writing career after the tragic loss of her parents and husband. Redirecting her emotions through writing became therapeutic in her battle with depression and in 2014 she decided to publish some of her works.

Keep in touch with the author online on most social media platforms

Other Titles from C.A. King

The Portal Prophecies

These great titles in C.A. King's The Portal Prophecies series are available now at most online book retailers:

A Keeper's Destiny

A Halloween's Curse

Frost Bitten

Sleeping Sands

Deadly Perceptions

Finding Balance

Volume I (Books 1-3)

Volume II (Books 4-6)

The prophecies are the key to their survival. Can they solve them in time?

Shattering the Effects of Time

Join the Shinning brothers, Jessie, Dezi and Pete as they set out on a quest to save their younger sister. No magic known to them or their friends has ever been able to reverse the grip of time. A few legends, however, exist mentioning ancient items that may hold the key to do exactly that.

This brand new series will take you on a search for the Fountain of Youth and Mermaids; a quest for the Holy Grail; a trip to visit Daryl the mountain guru, in the hunt for the Cinamani Stone; on a search for Ambrosia, the food of the Gods; and other adventures.

Surviving the Sins: Answering the Call

The prophecies are being rewritten. This time someone is using the seven deadly sins: Lust; Gluttony; Greed; Sloth; Wrath; Envy; and Pride, to unlock an ancient evil. The book falls into Jade's hands to answer destiny's call. Can she survive the sins?

Surviving the Sins: Pride

No one is safe when a witch's pride is at stake.

Prudance is back in Pewterclaw, and she isn't about to give up her prestigious status without a fight - especially not because of vampires. As an eighth-generation witch, she plans to do whatever it takes to stop the proposed new legislation from becoming law, including waking the dead for help.

Humility isn't in her vocabulary. With an ego spinning out of control and ancestral power at her fingertips, Prudance weaves a plot to keep Jade and Gavin separated. Will it be enough to satisfy the spirits she summoned?

When her pride costs more than she bargained for, someone has to pay the tab - but who will it be?

Surviving the Sins: Lust

What Mother doesn't know won't hurt her.

Lucinda has spent her entire existence running The Organization and looking after Mother's needs without complaint. That's about to change. A burning desire had manifested inside her - one she could no longer deny... Lust.

When Constable Safron Black shows up unexpected with news of an imprisoned God, Lucinda unravels. With power fuelling her passion, she'll do anything to make Morynx her mate.

****

Jade and her friends find themselves at a standstill. They have already failed to stop Pride from completing its task and they haven't located any victims for the other six sins. A strange fire in the municipal office puts them hot on the trail of what could be answers. Will they be in time to stop the dial from moving and further opening the way for Morynx?

When Leaves Fall: A Different Point of View Story

Ralph wakes up to what others only experience in a nightmare. Chained to a shed, he has no idea where he is, or who his captor is. His memories a blurred at best. As the days press on he finds himself experiencing a roller coaster of feelings. Hunger, thirst and pain become his only companions. Flashbacks of a happier time are all he has to keep him going. As his situation deteriorates, he finds himself doubting the very things he wants most - a family.

When Leaves Fall is a dramatic-thriller with a twist. Keep the tissue box close for the ending.

Tomoiya's Story

A Vampire Tale. She had a secret but she wasn't the only one who had something to hide.

Book I ~ Escape to Darkness

Book II ~ Collecting Tears

Book III~ Coming Soon

Peach Coloured Daisies: A Cursed by the Gods Story

He couldn't die. An ancient curse meant she always did. This time, that was going to change - one way or another.

When Daisy's grandmother, her last living relative, passes away, she doesn't know where to turn. Things go from bad to worse when a local psychic tells her about a curse. Alone and confused, she ends up in front of her college professor's office, ready to cry her heart out in his arms.

Matt Demi might be the son of a God, but he's living the life of a cursed man. He's had to watch the woman he loves die on her twenty-first birthday countless times. Nothing he does seems to be able to affect the outcome. When she shows up at his office scared out of her wits by a psychic's prediction, he vows this time will be different.

With only three days, Matt will need to embrace a side of him he swore off long ago to save her, but will he lose himself in the process?

Flower Shields: A Four Horsemen Novel

Meet the four horsemen: Michael, Gabrielle, Uriel and Raphael. For centuries their job has been to guard the gates of hell, making sure they never open. Without the keys, there was never any real threat. That's about to change. There are rumours on the horizon that demon followers unearthed scrolls that explain exactly how to find the lost keys. This new battle is a race to see which side locates them first.

Michael couldn't care less about the love story behind how and why the world was created. In fact, nothing matters to him other than keeping the gates to hell closed. If one of the lost keys ever fell into the wrong hands, all humanity would be doomed. He's not going to let that happen - at any cost.

****

Tara's life is nothing short of a disaster. She's managed to flunk out of college with about the same amount of dignity as every relationship she's been in. The only constant in her life has been her love for flowers. When she's attacked at work, a stranger comes to her aid. Michael might be good-looking, but he's also arrogant, bossy and crazy. He's also her only chance to figure out who attacked her and why. Should she follow her heart and trust him - or listen to her head and run?

Drawing Strength From Words: A Four Horsemen Novel

Meet the four horsemen: Michael, Gabrielle, Uriel and Raphael.

For centuries their sole purpose has been guarding the sealed gates to hell. Without keys, there was never any real threat. That was about to change...

For Gabrielle, protecting mankind was merely a job for which she received little credit. The vast insecurities of men altered history itself, portraying her as a masculine brute. Taking a back seat to her brothers seemed the right thing to do, but left a bitter taste in her mouth and an impenetrable barricade shielding her heart.

****

Ryder bounced around the system from the moment both his parents were killed. Between that and run-ins with the law for crimes he never committed, it seemed the whole world was conspiring against him. Never growing attached to anyone was rule number one: a rule he'd never broken until a white-haired vixen, with blocks of ice on her shoulders, walked right into his life. Melting through those frosty layers became all that mattered, even if that meant sacrificing himself in the process.

Miracles Not Included

A heartfelt romantic story about: life; love; loss; and learning to love again. If only life came with instructions and a warning label ~ Miracles Not Included.

****

Chris was born to be a writer. Even the smallest of details couldn't pass without notice, often becoming part of a plot for her next novel. The one thing she never saw coming was her husband's sudden illness.

Jason loved his wife from the moment they met. Nothing could ever change that - nothing except the death sentence he'd been handed - a terminal cancer diagnosis.

His story was ending: Hers was starting a new chapter and more than one miracle was needed to turn the page.

Twisted Tales of a Dead End Street

A paranormal mystery laced with comedic undertones: Twisted Tales of a Dead End Street.

Nine neighbours were invited to the mysterious dinner party at 9 Nine Street. Their host, the owner of the mansion, had more planned for the evening than just roast beef.

When the secret of their quiet street was revealed, everything changed, blurring the lines between the tangible and the paranormal.

Was the number nine the difference between life and death? Would any of them survive long enough to uncover the truth? They would each soon find out this wasn't a simple case of who-done-it so much as one of what was being done and by whom.

Shot Through The Heart: A Faerie Tale

A tale of two worlds - one filled with magic; the other void of it. But what happened to those trapped between the two? Adelia was about to find out...

Magic and structure were the foundations of her existence. Temptation controlled the ability to destroy everything she knew. The world of men held a powerful allure over her heart, waking that which had long been dormant. It enticed her, snagging her in a web of emotions.

A decision had to be made. Was feeling love for the first time worth sacrificing magic and immortality?

Do Not Open Until Halloween

When eighteen year old Caitlin agreed to babysit her eccentric Aunt's two cats and house, she had no idea that Justin was finally going to ask her for a date the same weekend. Torn between family and crush, she chose to take her best friends' suggestion to heart, arranging a small Friday night gathering. Little did she know a fairy was about to crash the party with trouble hot on her wings.

Caitlin will have to dig deep to find even a smidgen of belief in magic or there won't be any hope of saving her new friend from being hunted.

In this young adult fantasy, award-winning author, C.A. King, explores the answer to one of the questions readers have always wanted to ask...

Where do fairies come from?

www.ingramcontent.com/pod-product-compliance
Lightning Source LLC
Chambersburg PA
CBHW030824310726
48980CB00006B/619/J
9781988301488